THE TIME IN BETWEEN

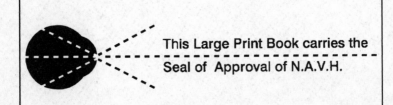

This Large Print Book carries the
Seal of Approval of N.A.V.H.

THE TIME IN BETWEEN

MARÍA DUEÑAS

THORNDIKE PRESS
A part of Gale, Cengage Learning

GALE
CENGAGE Learning·

Detroit • New York • San Francisco • New Haven, Conn • Waterville, Maine • London

LIBRARY OF CONGRESS CATALOGING-IN-PUBLICATION DATA

Dueñas, María, 1964–
  [Tiempo entro costuras. English]
  The time in between / by María Dueñas ; translated by Daniel Hahn.
    p. cm. — (Thorndike Press large print basic)
  ISBN-13: 978-1-4104-4627-5 (hardcover)
  ISBN-10: 1-4104-4627-1 (hardcover)
  1. Large type books. I. Hahn, Daniel. II. Title.
PQ6704.U35T5413 2012
863'.7—dc23   2011045530

Published in 2012 by arrangement with Atria Books, a division of Simon & Schuster, Inc.

Printed in the United States of America
1 2 3 4 5 6 7 16 15 14 13 12

To my mother, Ana Vinuesa

To the Vinuesa Lope and
Alvarez Moreno families,
for their old days in Tetouan
and the memories they treasured thereafter

To all former residents of the
Spanish Protectorate of Morocco,
and to the Moroccans who lived with them

PART ONE

The Fountain of Cybele in Madrid

CHAPTER ONE

A typewriter shattered my destiny. The culprit was a Hispano-Olivetti, and for weeks, a store window kept it from me. Looking back now, from the vantage point of the years gone by, it's hard to believe a simple mechanical object could have the power to divert the course of an entire life in just four short days, to pulverize the intricate plans on which it was built. And yet that is how it was, and there was nothing I could have done to stop it.

It wasn't really that I was treasuring any great plans in those days. My ambitions remained close to home, almost domestic, consistent with the coordinates of the place and time in which I happened to live, plans for a future that could be within my grasp if I reached out my fingertips. At that time my world revolved slowly around a few presences that seemed to me firm and eternal. My mother had always been the most solid of them all. She was a dressmaker, working in a shop with a distinguished clientele. She was experienced and had good judgment, but she was never any more than a salaried seamstress, a working woman like so many others who for ten hours a day sacrificed her nails and pupils cutting and sewing, checking and adjusting garments destined for bodies that were not her own and gazes that would rarely be

11

aimed at her. I knew little about my father in those days. Nothing, to be exact. He had never been around, nor did his absence affect me. I never felt much curiosity about him until my mother, when I was eight or nine, ventured to offer me a few crumbs of information. That he had another family, that it was impossible for him to live with us. I swallowed up those details with the same haste and scant appetite with which I polished off the last spoonfuls of the Lenten broth before me: the life of that alien being interested me considerably less than racing down to play in the square.

I had been born in the summer of 1911, the same year that the dancer Pastora Imperio married El Gallo, when the Mexican singer Jorge Negrete came into the world. When the star of that age they called the Belle Époque was fading. In the distance the drums of what would be the first great war were beginning to be heard, while in Madrid cafés people read *El Debate* and *El Heraldo,* and on the stage La Chelito fired men's passions as she moved her hips brazenly to the tempo of popular songs. During those summer months King Alfonso XIII managed to arrange that, between one lover and the next, his fifth legitimate child, a daughter, was conceived. Meanwhile, at the helm of the government was Canalejas the liberal, who couldn't predict that just a year later an eccentric anarchist would put an end to his life, firing three bullets to his head while he was browsing in the San Martín bookshop.

I grew up in reasonably happy surroundings, with more constraints than excesses but nonetheless with no great deprivations or frustrations. I was raised in a narrow street in a fusty old neighborhood in Madrid, right beside the Plaza

12

de la Paja, just a couple of steps from the Palacio Real. A stone's throw from the ceaseless hubbub of the heart of the city, a world of clothes hung out to dry, the smell of bleach, the voices of neighboring women, and cats lying out in the sun. I attended a makeshift school on the mezzanine of a nearby building: on its benches, meant to be used by two people, we kids arranged ourselves in fours, with no sense of order, pushing and shoving, shouting our renditions of "The Pirate's Song" or our times tables. It was there I learned to read and write, to master the four functions of basic arithmetic as well as the names of the rivers crisscrossing the yellowed map that hung from the wall. At the age of twelve I completed my schooling and became an apprentice in the workshop where my mother worked. My logical fate.

The business of Doña Manuela Godina — the owner — had for years produced fine garments, very skillfully cut and sewn, highly regarded all over Madrid. Day dresses, cocktail dresses, coats, and cloaks that would later be shown off by distinguished ladies as they walked along La Castellana, around the Hippodrome, and the Puerta de Hierro polo club, as they took their tea at Sakuska or entered the ostentatious churches. Some time passed, however, before I began to find my way into the secrets of sewing. At first I was the whole workshop's girl: the one who took the charcoal from the braziers and swept the cuttings from the floor, who heated the irons in the fire and ran breathless to buy thread and buttons from the Plaza de Pontejos. The one who was in charge of getting the just-finished garments, wrapped in big brown linen bags, to the exclusive residences: my favorite job, the greatest joy of my budding

13

career. That was how I came to know the porters and chauffeurs from the best buildings, the maids, housekeepers, and butlers of the wealthiest families. I watched — unseen — the most refined of ladies, daughters, and husbands. And like a mute witness I made my way into their bourgeois houses, into aristocratic mansions and the sumptuous apartments of charming old buildings. Sometimes I wouldn't get past the servants' area, and someone from the household would accept delivery of the dress; at other times, I was directed to go to the dressing room, so I would make my way down corridors and catch glimpses of drawing rooms, where my eyes would feast on the carpets, chandeliers, velvet curtains, and grand pianos that sometimes were being played and sometimes not, thinking all the while how strange it would be to live in such a universe.

My days shifted effortlessly between these two worlds, and I became less and less aware of the incongruity that existed between them. I would walk down those broad roads rutted with carriage tracks and lined with large imposing doorways just as naturally as I would pass through the crazy network of winding streets that formed my neighborhood, streets filled with puddles, rubbish, the cries of vendors, and the sharp barks of hungry dogs. Where everyone always went in a hurry, and at the cry of *"Agua va!"* you had better take cover to avoid being splattered with urine. Craftsmen, minor businessmen, employees, and newspaper vendors lately arrived in the capital filled the rental houses and gave my neighborhood its villagey feel. Many of them only left its bounds when obliged to; my mother and I, on the other hand, did so early each morning, to get over to Calle

14

Zurbano and quickly buckle down to our day-to-day tasks in Doña Manuela's workshop.

After my first two years as an apprentice, the two of them decided that the time had come for me to learn how to sew. At fourteen, I started with the simplest things: fasteners, overcasting, loose tacking. Then came buttonholes, backstitches, and hems. We worked seated on little rush chairs, hunched over wooden boards supported on our knees, where we placed the fabric we were sewing. Doña Manuela dealt with the customers, cutting, checking, and correcting. My mother took the measurements and dealt with all the rest: she did the most delicate needlework and assigned the remainder of the jobs, supervising their execution and imposing rhythm and discipline on a small battalion consisting of half a dozen older dressmakers, four or five young women, and a number of chatterbox apprentice girls, always keener on laughing and gossiping than on doing their work. Some of them ended up good seamstresses, and the ones who couldn't sew well ended up doing the less desirable tasks. When one girl left, another would replace her in that noisy room, so incongruous compared to the serene opulence of the shop's façade and the sobriety of its luminous front room to which only the customers had access. The two of them — Doña Manuela and my mother — were the only ones who could enjoy its saffron-colored drapery, its mahogany furniture, its luminous oak floor, which we younger girls were responsible for waxing with cotton rags. Only they, from time to time, would receive the rays of sunlight that came in through the four high balcony windows facing the street. The rest of us remained always in the rear guard:

15

in the gynaeceum, freezing in winter and hellish in summer. That was our workshop, that grey space around the back whose only openings were two little windows onto an interior courtyard, where the hours passed like breaths of air between the humming of ballads and the noise of scissors.

I learned fast. I had agile fingers that adapted quickly to the shape of the needles and the touch of the fabrics. To measurements, draping, and volumes. Neck, bust, outside leg. Under bust, full back, cuff. At sixteen I learned to tell fabrics apart, at seventeen to appreciate their qualities and calibrate their possibilities. Crêpe de chine, silk muslin, georgette, Chantilly lace. Months passed as if turning on a Ferris wheel: autumns spent making coats in fine fabrics and between-season dresses, springs sewing flighty dresses destined for long, faraway Cantabrian holidays, the beaches at La Concha or El Sardinero. I turned eighteen, nineteen. Bit by bit I was initiated into handling the cutting work and tailoring the more delicate components. I learned to attach collars and lapels, to predict how things would end up. I liked my work, actually enjoyed it. Doña Manuela and my mother sometimes asked me for my opinion; they began to trust me. "The girl has a fine hand and a fine eye, Dolores," Doña Manuela used to say. "She's good, and she'll get better if she stays on track. Better than you, you needn't worry about that." And my mother would just carry on with what she was doing, as if she hadn't heard a thing. I didn't look up from my working board either. But secretly I watched her out the corner of my eye, and in her mouth — studded with pins — saw the tiniest trace of a smile.

The years went by, life went by. Fashion

changed, too, and at its command the activities of the workshop adjusted. After the war in Europe straight lines had arrived, corsets had been cast aside, and legs began to be shown without so much as the slightest blush. When the Roaring Twenties came to an end, however, the waistlines of dresses returned to their natural place, skirts got longer, and modesty once again imposed itself on sleeves, necklines, and desires. Then we launched ourselves into a new decade and there were more changes. All of them together, unforeseen, almost one on top of another. I turned twenty, the Republic arrived in Spain, and I met Ignacio. It was one September Sunday in Parque de la Bombilla, at a riotous dance that was crammed full with workshop girls, bad students, and soldiers on leave. He asked me to dance, he made me laugh. Two weeks later we began to sketch out plans to marry.

Who was Ignacio, and what was he to me? The man of my life, that's what I thought then. The calm lad who I sensed would be a good father to my children. I had already reached the age when girls like me — girls with no professional expectations — had few options other than marriage. The example of my mother, who had raised me alone and in order to do so had worked from sunrise to sunset, had never seemed to me a very appealing fate. In Ignacio I found someone with whom to pass the rest of my adult life without having to wake up every morning to the taste of loneliness. I was not stirred to the heights of passion, but rather an intense affection and the certainty that my days by his side would pass without sorrows or stridency, sweetly gentle as a pillow.

Ignacio Montes, I thought, would come to be

the owner of that arm of mine that he would take on a thousand and one walks, the nearby presence that would offer me security and shelter forever. Two years older than I, thin, genial, as straightforward as he was tender. He was tall, with a skinny build, good manners, and a heart whose capacity to love me seemed to multiply with the hours. The son of a Castilian widow who kept her well-counted money under the mattress, he lived intermittently in insignificant boardinghouses and was an eager applicant for bureaucratic jobs as well as a perpetual candidate for any ministry that might offer him a salary for life — War, Governance, the Treasury. The dream of nearly three thousand pesetas a year, two hundred and forty-one a month — a salary that is set forever, never to be changed, dedicating the rest of his days to the tame world of departmental offices and secretarial offices, of blotters, untrimmed paper, seals, and inkwells. It was on this that we based our plans for the future: on the back of a perfectly calm civil service that, one round of exams after another, refused stubbornly to include my Ignacio on its list of names. And he persisted, undiscouraged. In February he tried out for Justice and in June for Agriculture, and then it started all over again.

In the meantime, unable to allow himself costly diversions, and yet utterly devoted to making me happy, Ignacio feted me with the humble possibilities that his extremely meager pocket would allow: a cardboard box filled with silkworms and mulberry leaves, cones of roasted chestnuts, and promises of eternal love on the grass under the viaduct. Together we listened to the band from the pavilion in the Parque del Oeste and rowed

18

boats in El Retiro on Sunday mornings when the weather was pleasant. There wasn't a fair with swings and barrel organ that we didn't turn up at, nor any *chotis* that we didn't dance with watchlike precision. How many evenings we spent in the Vistillas gardens, how many movies we saw in cheap local cinemas. Drinking a Valencian *horchata* was a luxury to us, taking a taxi a dream. Ignacio's tenderness, while not overly bold, was nevertheless boundless. I was his sky and his stars, the most beautiful, the best. My skin, my face, my eyes. My hands, my mouth, my voice. Everything that was me made up the unsurpassable for him, the source of his happiness. And I listened to him, told him he was being silly, and let him love me.

Life in the workshop in those days, however, followed a different rhythm. Things were becoming difficult, uncertain. The Second Republic had instilled a sense of apprehension in the comfortable prosperity surrounding our customers. Madrid was turbulent and frantic, the political tension permeating every street corner. The good families extended their northern summer holidays indefinitely, seeking to remain on the fringes of the unsettled, rebellious capital where the *Mundo Obrero* was declaimed loudly in the squares while the shirtless proletariat from the outskirts made their way, without retreat, into the Puerta del Sol. Big private motorcars began to be seen less and less on the streets, opulent parties dwindled. Old ladies in mourning prayed novenas for Azaña to fall soon, and the noise of bullets became routine at the hour when the gas street lamps were lit. The anarchists set fire to churches, the Falangists brandished pistols like bullies. With increasing frequency the aristocrats and *hautes bourgeoises*

19

covered their furniture up with sheets, dismissed the staff, bolted the shutters, and set out hastily for foreign parts, taking jewels galore, fears, and banknotes across the borders, yearning for the exiled king and an obliging Spain, which would still be some time in coming.

Fewer and fewer ladies visited Doña Manuela's workshop, fewer orders came in, and there was less and less to do. Drip by painful drip, first the apprentice girls and then the rest of the seamstresses were dismissed, till all that were left were the owner, my mother, and me. And when we finished the last dress for the Marchioness of Entrelagos and spent the next six days listening to the radio, twiddling our thumbs, without a single soul appearing at the door, Doña Manuela announced, sighing, that she had no choice but to shut up shop.

Amid the turbulence of those days in which the political fighting made theater audiences quake and governments lasted three paternosters, we barely had the chance to cry over what we'd lost. Three weeks after the advent of our enforced inactivity, Ignacio appeared with a bouquet of violets and the news that he had at last passed his civil service exam. The plans for our little wedding stifled any feelings of uncertainty, and on a little table we planned the event. Although the new breezes that swept in with the Republic carried on them the fashion for civil weddings, my mother — whose soul housed simultaneously, and with no contradiction, her condition as single mother, an iron Catholic spirit, and a nostalgic loyalty to the deposed monarchy — encouraged us to celebrate a religious wedding in the neighboring church of San Andrés. Ignacio and I agreed; how could we not, without toppling that hierarchy of order in which he submitted to all my desires and I deferred to my mother's without argument. Nor did I have any good reason to refuse: the dreams I had about celebrating that marriage were modest ones, and it made no difference to me whether it was at an altar with a priest and cassock or in a large room presided over by a Republican tricolor flag.

So we prepared to set the date with the same parish priest who twenty-four years earlier, on June eighth, as dictated by the calendar of saints' days, had given me the name Sira. Sabiniana, Victorina, Gaudencia, Heraclia, and Fortunata had been other possibilities that went with the saints of the day.

"Sira, Father, just put Sira — it's short, at least." That was my mother's decision, in her single motherhood. And so I was Sira.

We would celebrate the marriage with family and a few friends. With my grandfather, who had neither his legs nor his wits, mutilated in body and spirit during the war of the Philippines, a permanent mute presence in his rocking chair next to our dining room balcony windows. With Ignacio's mother and sisters who'd come in from the village. With our next-door socialist neighbors Engracia and Norberto and their three sons, as dear to us as if the same blood flowed right across the landing. With Doña Manuela, who took up the threads again to give me the gift of her final piece of work, in the form of a bridal dress. We would treat our guests to sugar-plum pastries, sweet Málagan wine and vermouth. Perhaps we would be able to hire a musician from the neighborhood to come up and play a paso doble, and

21

some street photographer would take a dry-plate picture for us, which would adorn our home, something we did not yet have and for now would be my mother's.

It was then, amid this jumble of plans and preparations, that it occurred to Ignacio to prepare me to take the test to make me a civil servant like him. His brand-new post in administration had opened his eyes to a new world: that of the administration of the Republic, an area where there existed professional destinies for women that lay beyond the stove, the wash house, and drudgery; through which the female sex could beat a path, elbow to elbow with men, in the same conditions and with their sights set on the same dreams. The first women were already sitting as deputies in the parliament; the equality of the sexes in public life was proclaimed. There had been recognition of our legal status, our right to work, and universal suffrage. All the same, I would have infinitely preferred to return to sewing, but it took Ignacio just three evenings to convince me. The old world of fabrics and backstitches had been toppled and a new universe was opening its doors to us: we had to adapt to it. Ignacio himself could take charge of my preparation; he had all the study topics and more than enough experience in the art of putting himself forward and failing countless times without ever giving in to despair. As for me, I would do my share to help the little platoon that we two would make up with my mother, my grandfather, and the progeny to come. And so I agreed. Once we were all set, there was only one thing we lacked: a typewriter on which I could learn to type in preparation for the unavoidable typing test. Ignacio had spent months practicing on other people's machines, passing through a *via dolorosa* of sad academies smelling of grease, ink, and concentrated sweat. He didn't want me to have to go through the same unpleasantness, hence his determination that we should obtain our own equipment. In the weeks that followed we launched ourselves on our search, as though it would turn our lives totally around.

We studied all the options and did endless calculations. I didn't understand about detailed performance features, but it seemed to me that something small and light would be most suitable for us. Ignacio was indifferent to the size, but he did take extraordinary care over prices, installment payments, and terms. We located all the sellers in Madrid, spent hours standing at their window displays, and learned to pronounce exotic names that evoked distant geographies and movie stars: Remington, Royal, Underwood. We could just as easily have chosen one brand as another; we could just as well have ended up buying from an American establishment as a German one, but our choice settled finally on the Italian Hispano-Olivetti on Calle de Pi y Margall. How could we have known that with that simple act, with the mere fact of having taken two or three steps and crossed a threshold, we were signing the death sentence on our time together and irreparably twisting apart the strands of our future.

CHAPTER TWO

"I'm not going to marry Ignacio, Mother."

She was trying to thread a needle and my words made her freeze, the thread held between her fingers.

"What are you saying, girl?" she whispered. Her voice seemed to emerge broken from her throat, laden with confusion and disbelief.

"That I'm leaving him, Mother. That I've fallen in love with another man."

She scolded me with the bluntest reproaches she could bring herself to utter, cried out to heaven, begging God to intercede, appealing to the whole calendar of saints, summoning dozens of arguments to persuade me to retract my intentions. When it became clear that none of it was doing any good, she sat down in the rocking chair next to my grandfather's, covered her face, and began to cry.

I bore the moment with a feigned fortitude, trying to hide the nerves that lay behind the bluntness of my words. I was afraid of my mother's reaction: Ignacio had come to be the son she'd never had, the presence that filled the masculine gap in our little family. They talked to each other, they understood each other, they got along. My mother made the stews he liked, shined his shoes, and turned his jackets inside out when the attrition of time had begun to rob them of their luster. He, in turn, complimented her when he saw her in her finery for Sunday Mass, brought her egg-yolk sweets, and — half in jest and half seriously — sometimes told her that she was more beautiful than I.

I was aware that my daring would bring down all that comfortable domesticity. I knew that it would topple the scaffolding of more lives than just my own, but there was nothing I could do to stop it. My decision was firm as a post: there would be no wedding and no civil service exams; I wouldn't learn to type on the little table and never would I share children, bed, or joys with Ignacio. I was going to leave him, and the strength of a gale would not be enough to curtail my resolve.

The Hispano-Olivetti storefront had two large display windows that showed their products off to passersby with proud splendor. Between the two of them was a glass door, with a bar of burnished bronze crossing it diagonally. Ignacio pushed it and we went in. The tinkling of a little bell announced our arrival, but no one came out to meet us right away. We stopped there, inhibited for a couple of minutes, looking at everything displayed with such reverence, not daring even to brush against the pieces of polished wood furniture where those typewriting marvels rested, one of which we were about to select as the one most suited to our plans. At the back of the spacious room devoted to the displays, there was apparently an office. From it came men's voices. We didn't have to wait much longer. The voices

25

knew that there were customers, and one of them — housed in a rotund body, darkly dressed — approached us. As soon as the affable clerk greeted us, asking what we were interested in, Ignacio began to talk, describing what he wanted, requesting information and advice. Mustering all his professionalism, the clerk proceeded to enumerate the features of each machine on display in rigorous detail, with such monotonous technical precision that after twenty minutes I was ready to fall asleep from boredom. Ignacio, meanwhile, absorbed the information through all his senses, indifferent to me and to anything other than gauging what was being offered to him. I decided to move away from them, totally uninterested. Whatever Ignacio chose would be a good choice. I couldn't care less about keys, carriage return levers, or margin bells.

So I dedicated myself to walking through the other parts of the display in search of something with which to appease my boredom. I stared at the big advertising posters on the walls proclaiming the store's products with colored illustrations and words in languages I did not understand. Then I approached the windows and watched pedestrians hurrying past along the street. After a while I returned unwillingly to the back of the store.

A big cupboard with mirrored doors ran along part of one wall. I considered my reflection in it, noticing that a couple of strands had come loose from the bun in my hair. After attending to that I took advantage of the opportunity to pinch my cheeks and give my bored face a little color. Then I examined my attire at leisure. I had made myself get into my best dress; after all, this purchase was supposed to be a special occasion for us. I smoothed out my stockings, upward from my ankles; slowly and deliberately I adjusted the dress on my hips, at the waistline and collar. I retouched my hair again and looked at myself from the front and the side, calmly observing the copy of myself that the mirror glass returned to me. I struck poses, made a couple of dance steps, and laughed. When I tired of the sight, I continued wandering around the room, killing time as I ran my hand slowly over the surfaces, snaking languidly around the pieces of furniture. I barely paid any attention to what had really brought us there; to me there was nothing to distinguish between those machines apart from their size. There were big, solid ones, yet there were small ones, too; some seemed light, others heavy, but to my eyes they were no more than a mass of dark unwieldy contraptions unable to generate the slightest charm. I positioned myself reluctantly in front of one of them, brought my index finger toward the keys, and pretended to press the letters closest to me. The *s,* the *i,* the *r,* the *a.* "Si-ra," I repeated in a whisper.

"Lovely name."

The man's voice came from just behind me, so close that I could almost feel his breath on my skin. A shudder ran up my spine and I turned around, startled.

"Ramiro Arribas," he said, holding out his hand. It took me a moment to react, perhaps because I wasn't used to anyone greeting me so formally, perhaps because I had not yet managed to absorb the impact this unexpected presence had on me.

Who was this man, where had he come from? He clarified it himself, his eyes still fixed on mine.

"I am the manager of the establishment. I'm

27

sorry not to have attended to you earlier; I was trying to place a call."

And watching you through the blinds that separate the office from the showroom, he should have added. He didn't say it, but he let it be guessed at. I intuited it from the depths of his gaze, the sonority of his voice, from the fact that he had approached me rather than Ignacio and the length of time he held my hand. I knew that he had been watching me, considering my erratic wanderings around his establishment. He had seen me arranging myself in front of the mirrored cupboard: readjusting my hair, conforming the lines of the dress to my shape, and fixing my stockings by running my hands up my legs. Perched in the shelter of his office, he had absorbed the outlines of my body and the slow cadence of each of my movements. He had appraised me, calibrated the shapes of my silhouette and the lines of my face. He had studied me with the sure eye of someone who knows exactly what he likes and is used to getting what he wants with the immediacy that his desires dictate. And he resolved to show this to me. I had never seen this before in any other man; I had never believed myself capable of awaking such a desire in anyone. But just as animals scent food or danger, with the same primal instinct I knew that Ramiro Arribas, like a wolf, had decided to come for me.

"Is that your husband?" he said, gesturing toward Ignacio.

"My fiancé," I managed to answer.

Perhaps it was only my imagination, but I thought I sensed the trace of a satisfied smile at the corners of his lips.

"Perfect. Please, come with me."

He made way for me, and as he did, he positioned his hand gently at my waist as though it had been waiting to be there its whole life. He greeted Ignacio pleasantly, dispatched the salesclerk to the office, and took up the reins of the matter with the ease of someone who gives a clap and makes pigeons take flight. He was like a conjuror combed with brilliantine, the features of his face marked with angular lines, a broad smile, a powerful neck, and a bearing so imposing, so manly and decisive, that beside him my poor Ignacio looked like he was a century away from reaching manhood.

He learned that the typewriter we were planning to buy would be for teaching me to type, and he praised the idea as though it were a matter of great genius. Ignacio saw him as a competent professional who offered technical details and beneficial payment options. For me he was something more: a tremor, a magnet, a certainty.

We took a while longer to finalize the negotiations. Over the course of that time the signals coming from Ramiro Arribas didn't stop for a single second. An unexpected, glancing touch, a joke, a smile; double entendres and looks that pierced the depths of my being. Ignacio, self-absorbed and unaware of what was happening before his very eyes, finally decided on the portable Lettera 35, a machine with round white keys on which the letters of the alphabet were set with such elegance that they seemed to be carved with a chisel.

"Superb decision," the manager concluded, praising Ignacio's good sense. As though he had been the master of his own free will and hadn't been manipulated with the great salesman's wiles to buy that particular model. "The best choice for slender fingers like those of your fiancée. Do please allow me, miss, to see them."

I quickly sought Ignacio's gaze to gain his consent, but I didn't find it: he had gone back to focusing on the typewriter. I held my hand out shyly. Faced with my fiancé's innocent passivity, Ramiro Arribas stroked my hand slowly and shamelessly, finger to finger, with a sensuality that gave me goose bumps and made my legs shake like leaves in a summer breeze. He only let go when Ignacio looked away from the Lettera 35 and asked for instructions on completing the purchase. They agreed that we'd leave a deposit of 50 percent that afternoon and make the balance of the payment the following day.

"When can we take it away?" Ignacio asked.

Ramiro Arribas consulted his watch.

"The boy from the warehouse is doing a few errands and won't be coming back this afternoon. I fear it won't be possible to get your model till tomorrow."

"And this one? We can't keep this one?" Ignacio insisted, keen to close the negotiations as soon as possible. Once the model had been chosen, everything else seemed to him to be bothersome procedures that he wanted to eliminate swiftly.

"Please, don't even suggest such a thing. I can't allow Miss Sira to use a typewriter that other customers have been fiddling with. Tomorrow morning, first thing, I'll have a new one ready, with its own case and packaging. If you let me have your address," he said, looking at me, "I'll take charge personally of getting one to your house before noon."

"We'll come and collect it ourselves," I interrupted. I could sense that the man was capable of anything, and a wave of terror made me shudder to think that he might show up before my mother, asking for me.

"I can't come over till the evening, I have to work," said Ignacio. As he spoke, an invisible rope seemed to tie itself slowly around his neck, ready to hang him. Ramiro barely had to take the trouble to pull at it just a little.

"And what about you, miss?"

"I don't work," I said, avoiding his gaze.

"You could arrange to make the payment, then?" he suggested casually.

I couldn't find the words to say no, and Ignacio didn't even sense how that simple-seeming proposal was looming over us. Ramiro Arribas accompanied us to the door and bid us farewell warmly, as though we were the best customers in the shop's history. With his left hand he vigorously patted my fiancé's back, with his right he shook mine once again. And he had words for us both.

"You've made a superb choice in coming to Casa Hispano-Olivetti, Ignacio, believe me. I assure you, you won't forget this day for a long time. And you, Sira, please come back at about eleven o'clock. I'll be waiting for you."

I spent the night tossing and turning in bed, unable to sleep. It was madness, and I still had time to get out of it. All I had to do was to decide not to go back to the shop. I could stay home with my mother, help her to beat the mattresses and scrub the floor with linseed oil, chat with the women who lived next door on the square, then make my way toward the Cebada market for a quarter pound of chickpeas or a piece of cod. I could wait

31

for Ignacio to return home from the ministry and make excuses for my failure to fulfill my task with any simple lie: that my head hurt, that I thought it was going to rain. I could lie down awhile after lunch, feigning some general malaise. And then Ignacio would go alone, he would complete the payment to the manager, pick up the typewriter, and it would all be over. We would never hear of Ramiro Arribas again, he'd never again cross our path. Bit by bit his name would sink into oblivion and we'd move ahead with our little everyday lives. As though he'd never caressed my hands, desire just there below the surface; as though he'd never consumed me with his eyes from behind the blinds. It was that easy, that simple. And I knew it.

I knew it, but I pretended not to know. The next day I waited for my mother to go out on her errands. I didn't want her to see me getting myself ready: she would have suspected I was up to something strange if she'd seen me all done up so early in the morning. As soon as I'd heard the door close behind her, I began hastily to get myself together. I filled a basin to wash myself, I sprinkled myself with lavender water, heated the curling tongs on the stove, ironed my only silk blouse, and removed my stockings from the line where they'd spent the night drying in the night dew. They were the same ones from the previous day: I had no others. I forced myself to calm down and put them on carefully, so that I wouldn't cause a run. And each of those mechanical movements, repeated a thousand times in the past, for the first time had a defined recipient, an objective and a goal: Ramiro Arribas. It was for him that I was dressing and perfuming myself, for him to see me,

32

for him to smell me, for him to touch me lightly once again and once again lose himself in my eyes. It was for him that I decided to leave my hair loose, falling lustrous halfway down my back. For him I tightened my waist, squeezing the belt hard over my skirt till I could scarcely breathe. For him: all just for him.

I made my way along the streets with determination, prompting eager glances and impudent compliments. I forced myself not to think: I avoided calculating the significance of my actions and didn't want to stop and guess whether that trajectory was taking me to the threshold of paradise or directly to the slaughterhouse. I went down the Costanilla de San Andrés, crossed the Plaza de los Carros, and down Cava Baja headed for the Plaza Mayor. In twenty minutes I was at the Puerta del Sol; in less than half an hour I reached my destination.

Ramiro was waiting for me. He quickly sensed my silhouette at the door and broke off the conversation he was holding with another employee and headed toward me, collecting his hat and a raincoat on his way. When he was standing there beside me I wanted to tell him I had the money in my pocket, that Ignacio sent his regards, that I would perhaps start learning to type that very afternoon. He didn't let me. He didn't even greet me. He only smiled, holding a cigarette in his mouth, gently grazed his hand over the small of my back, and said, "Let's go." And with him I went.

The chosen place could not have been more innocent: he took me to the Café Suizo. Having confirmed with relief that our surroundings were safe, I believed that I might still be able to effect

33

my salvation. I even thought — as he looked for a table and invited me to sit down — that perhaps this meeting had no more duplicity to it than the simple display of attentiveness to a client. I even began to suspect that all that brazen flirtation might have been nothing more than an excess of fantasy on my part. But that was not how it was. In spite of the irreproachable surroundings, our second meeting brought me back to the edge of the abyss.

"I haven't been able to stop thinking about you for a single minute since you left yesterday," he whispered in my ear the moment we had settled.

I felt unable to reply. The words couldn't reach my lips: like sugar in water, they dissolved in some uncertain place in my brain. He took my hand again and caressed it just as he had done the previous afternoon, without taking his eyes off it.

"You have calluses on your hands — tell me, what have these fingers been doing before they came to me?"

His voice still sounded close and sensual, quite apart from the noises that surrounded us: the clink of the glass and crockery against the marble of the tabletops, the buzz of morning conversations, and the voices of waiters placing orders at the counter.

"Sewing," I whispered, not lifting my eyes from my lap.

"So you're a seamstress?"

"I was. Not anymore." I lifted my gaze, finally. "There hasn't been much work lately," I added.

"Which is why you want to learn to use a typewriter."

He spoke with complicity, familiarly, as though he knew me: as though his soul and mine had been waiting for each other since the beginning of time.

"My fiancé thought about enrolling me to take some examinations so that I could become a civil servant like him," I said with a touch of shame.

The arrival of the refreshments halted our conversation. For me, a cup of hot chocolate. For Ramiro, coffee, black as night. I took advantage of the pause to look at him while he exchanged a few phrases with the waiter. He was wearing a different suit than on the previous day, another impeccable shirt. He had elegant manners, and at the same time, within that refinement that was so alien to the men who surrounded me, he oozed masculinity from every pore of his body: as he smoked, as he adjusted the knot of his tie, as he took his wallet from his pocket or brought the cup to his lips.

"And why would a woman like you want to spend her life in a ministry, if that's not too forward a question?" he asked after taking his first sip of coffee.

I shrugged. "So we can have a better life, I guess."

Again he came slowly closer to me, again his hot voice was in my ear: "Do you really want to start living better, Sira?"

I took refuge in a sip of chocolate to avoid answering.

"You've got a smudge; let me wipe it," he said.

And then he brought his hand to my face and opened it over the contour of my jaw, adjusting it to my bones as though this were the mold from which I had once been formed. Then he put his thumb in the place where the smudge supposedly was, close to where my lips met. He caressed me

35

smoothly, slowly. I let him do it: a mixture of terror and pleasure prevented me from moving.

"You've got some here, too," he murmured, his voice hoarse, moving his finger.

Its destination was one end of my lower lip. He repeated the caress. More slowly, more tenderly. A shiver ran up my spine; my fingers gripped the velvet of the seat.

"And here, too," he said again. Then he caressed my whole mouth, millimeter by millimeter, from one end to the other, rhythmically, slowly, more slowly. I was about to sink into a well of something soft that I could not define. I didn't care if the whole thing was a lie and there was no trace of chocolate on my lips. I didn't care that at the next table three venerable old men suspended their chatter to contemplate the scene, burning with desire, furiously wishing they were thirty years younger.

Then a noisy group of students trooped into the café, and their racket and laughter destroyed the magic of the moment like someone bursting a soap bubble. And right away, as though awaking from a dream, I became aware of several things at once: that the ground hadn't melted but was still solid beneath my feet, that the finger of a man I didn't know was about to go into my mouth, that an eager hand was crawling along my left thigh, and that I was a heartbeat away from throwing myself headfirst off a precipice. My clarity of thought now recovered, I jumped to my feet. Rushing to take up my bag, I knocked over a glass of water that the waiter had brought with my chocolate.

"Here's the money for the typewriter. At the end of the afternoon my fiancé will come by to

36

collect it," I said, leaving the bundle of notes on the marble.

He held me by the wrist.

"Don't go, Sira; don't be angry with me."

I tugged myself free. I didn't look at him or say good-bye; I just turned and with forced dignity began to make my way to the door. It was only then that I noticed I'd spilled the water on myself and that my left foot was soaked.

He didn't follow me; he probably sensed it wouldn't do him any good. He just stayed sitting there, and as I moved away he launched his final dart at my back.

"Come back another day. You know where to find me now."

I pretended not to hear him. I picked up my pace through the crowd of students and blended into the hubbub of the street.

Eight times I went to bed hoping that when morning came things would be different, and the eight mornings that followed I awoke with the same obsession in my head: Ramiro Arribas. His memory assaulted me at every turn, and I couldn't keep him from my thoughts for a single minute: making the bed, blowing my nose, as I peeled an orange or went down the stairs one by one with his face engraved on my retina.

Meanwhile, Ignacio and my mother worked away at the plans for the wedding, but they were incapable of making me share their enthusiasm. Nothing pleased me, nothing could raise the slightest interest in me. It must be nerves, they thought. I struggled, meanwhile, to get Ramiro out of my head, not to recall his voice in my ear, his finger caressing my mouth, his hand running

37

up my thigh, and the last words he fixed in my eardrums when I turned my back on him in the café, convinced that by walking away I'd be putting an end to the madness. *Come back another day, Sira. Come back.*

I fought with all my strength to resist. I fought, and I lost. There was nothing I could do to impose the least rationality on the uncontrolled attraction that man had made me feel. However much I looked around me, I was unable to find the resources, the strength, anything to cling to in order to stop myself from being dragged away. Neither the husband-to-be whom I planned to marry in less than a month, nor the upright mother who had struggled so hard to bring me up to be a decent, responsible woman. I wasn't even stopped by the uncertainty of barely knowing who that stranger was and what destiny had in store for me at his side.

Nine days after my first visit to the Casa Hispano-Olivetti, I returned. Like the previous times, I was once again greeted by the tinkling of the bell over the door. No fat salesman came to greet me, no shop boy, no other employee. Only Ramiro.

I approached, trying to make my steps sound firm; I had my words ready. I wasn't able to say them. He didn't let me. As soon as he had me within his reach he put his hand to the back of my neck and planted on my mouth a kiss so intense, so carnal and prolonged that my body was startled by it, ready to melt and be transformed into a puddle of honey.

Ramiro Arribas was thirty-four years old, had a past filled with comings and goings and a capacity for seduction so powerful that not even a concrete

38

wall could have contained it. First came attraction, doubt, and anxiety. Then passion, and the abyss. I drank in the air he breathed and I walked beside him, floating six inches above the cobblestones. The rivers could burst their banks, the buildings could crumble, and the streets could be wiped off the maps; the heavens could meet the earth and the whole universe could collapse at my feet, and I could bear it if Ramiro were there.

Ignacio and my mother began to suspect that something unusual was happening to me, something more than the simple tension brought about by the imminent marriage. They were not, however, able to figure out the reason for my excitement, nor did they find any cause to justify the excessive secrecy with which I moved at all hours, my erratic departures, and the hysterical laughter I occasionally found myself unable to contain. I managed to maintain the equilibrium of that double life for just a few days, just enough to see how the scales tipped with every passing minute, how Ignacio's side fell and Ramiro's rose. In less than a week I knew that I had to cut myself off from everything and launch myself into the void. The moment had come for me to take a scythe to my past. To level it to the ground.

Ignacio arrived at our house in the evening.

"Wait for me in the square," I whispered, opening the door just a few inches.

My mother had learned about my decision at lunchtime; I couldn't let him go on any longer without knowing. I went down five minutes later, my lips painted, my new bag in one hand and the Lettera 35 in the other. He was waiting for me on the usual bench, on that bit of cold stone where we'd spent so many hours planning a common

39

future that would never come.

"You're going off with someone else, aren't you?" he asked when I sat down beside him. He didn't look at me; he just kept his eyes fixed on the ground, on the dusty earth that the tip of his shoe was busy turning up.

I just nodded. A round, wordless yes. Who is it? he asked. I told him. Around us the usual noises continued: children, dogs, and bicycle bells; the tolling of San Andrés calling to last Mass, the wheels of the carts over the cobbles, the tired mules heading for the end of the day. Ignacio took a while to speak again. He must have sensed such determination, such certainty in my decision that he didn't even let me see his confusion. He didn't make a scene, nor did he demand explanations. He only spoke one more sentence, slowly, as though allowing it to slip out.

"He will never love you as much as I do."

And then he stood up, took up the typewriter, and began to walk with it toward the void. I watched his back moving away, walking beneath the murky light of the street lamps, perhaps suppressing an urge to dash the machine against the ground.

I kept my eyes fixed on him, watched as he left the square until his body faded into the distance, until I could no longer make him out in the autumn evening. And I would have liked to remain there crying at his absence, regretting that farewell that was so brief and so sad, blaming myself for having put an end to our hopeful plan for the future. But I couldn't. I didn't shed a single tear, didn't rain down a single reproach upon myself. Just a minute after his presence had faded, I, too, got up from the bench and walked away. I left behind my neighborhood, my people, my little world forever. My whole past remained there as I set out on a new stage of my life, a life that seemed luminous and whose immediate present could imagine no greater glory than that of Ramiro's two arms giving me shelter.

Chapter Three

With him I learned a new kind of life. I learned to be independent of my mother, to live with a man, and to keep a maid. To try to please him every moment and to have no other aim but to make him happy. And I also got to know another Madrid: the Madrid of sophisticated fashionable places; of shows, restaurants, and nightlife. Cocktails at Negresco, the Granja del Henar, Bakanik. Film premieres at the Real Cinema with organ accompaniment, Mary Pickford on the screen, Ramiro putting bonbons in my mouth, and me lightly grazing the tips of his fingers with my lips, almost melting with love. Carmen Amaya at the Teatro Fontalba, Raquel Meller at the Maravillas. Flamenco at Villa Rosa, the Palacio del Hielo cabaret. A lively, effervescent Madrid, through which Ramiro and I flitted as though there were no yesterday and no tomorrow. As though we had to consume the whole world every instant in case the future were never to arrive.

What was it about Ramiro, what did he do to me that turned my life upside down in just a couple of weeks? Even today, so many years later, I can put together a catalog with my eyes closed of everything about him that seduced me, and I'm convinced that if I'd been born a hundred times, a hundred times over I'd have fallen in love with him as I did then. Ramiro Arribas, irresistible, worldly, handsome as the devil. With his brown hair combed back, his stunning bearing of pure manliness, radiating optimism and confidence twenty-four hours a day, seven days a week. Witty and sensual, indifferent to the political asperity of the times, as though he were not quite of this world. A friend to everyone without taking anyone seriously, the constructor of grand plans, always knowing just the right word, just the right gesture for each moment. Now the manager of an Italian typewriter company, yesterday a German car rep, the day before yesterday what difference did it make, and next month God alone knew.

What did Ramiro see in me, why did he become infatuated with a humble dressmaker about to marry an unambitious civil servant? True love for the first time in his life, he swore to me a thousand times. There had been other women before, of course. How many, I asked? Some, but none like you. And then he would kiss me and I thought I was dancing on the edge of a faint. Nor would it be hard for me today to assemble another list of his impressions of me: I remember them all. The explosive blend of an almost childish naïveté with the bearing of a goddess, he said. A diamond in the rough, he said. Sometimes he treated me like a little girl and then the ten years that separated us seemed centuries. He would anticipate my whims, fill my capacity for surprise with the most unexpectedly inspired ideas. He'd buy me stockings at the Lyon silk shop, creams and perfumes, ice creams in exotic flavors; custard apple, mango, and coconut. He would instruct me — teaching me to use my cutlery properly, to drive his Morris, to decipher restaurant menus, how to inhale when smoking. He would talk to me about figures from the past and artists he'd once met; he'd recollect old friends and anticipate the splendid opportunities that might be awaiting us in any remote corner of the globe. He'd draw maps of the world, and he made me grow. Sometimes, however, that little girl disappeared and I'd rise up as a woman fully formed, and he wasn't at all bothered by my lack of knowledge and experience: he desired me, he revered me just as I was and clung to me as though my body were the only mooring in the turbulent oscillations of his existence.

I installed myself with him from the start in his masculine apartment beside the Plaza de las Salesas. I brought hardly anything with me, as though my life were beginning anew, as though I were someone else and had been born again. My reckless heart and a few clothes were the only possessions I brought to his home. From time to time I'd go back and visit my mother; in those days she used to take on sewing work at home, but there was so little of it that she had barely enough to survive. She didn't approve of Ramiro, disliking the way he behaved with me. She accused him of having dragged me away impulsively, of having used his age and position to trick me, to force me to give up all my existing bonds. She didn't like that I was living with him unmarried, that I'd left Ignacio, and that I was no longer the way I'd always been. However hard I tried, I was never able to convince her that Ramiro hadn't been the one pressuring me to act like this, that it was simply unbounded love that had brought me to him. Our discussions got harsher every day: we exchanged terrible reproaches and clawed at each other's entrails. To each challenge from her I would reply with some bit of insolence, to each reproach with an even fiercer contempt. It was unusual for a meeting not to end with tears, shouts, and slamming doors, and so my visits became increasingly short and infrequent. And my mother and I more distant every day.

Until one day there was an approach on her part. She only did it in the role of an intermediary, certainly, but that gesture of hers — as we might have predicted — brought about a new turn in our separate paths. She showed up at Ramiro's house in the middle of the morning. He was already out and I was still asleep. We had been out the previous night, first seeing Margarita Xirgu at the Teatro de la Comedia, then afterward going out to Le Cock bar. It must have been nearly four in the morning when we went to bed, and I was so exhausted that I didn't even have the strength to wipe off the makeup that I'd recently begun using. Half asleep I heard Ramiro leaving at around ten; half asleep I heard the arrival of Prudencia, the maid who kept our domestic disarray in some order. Half asleep I heard her go out for the milk and bread and half asleep I heard a short while later that there was someone at the door. I thought that Prudencia had come back, having left her key behind, which she had done before. I got up, flustered, and in a foul mood approached the insistent knocking at the door, shouting, I'm coming! I didn't even bother to put anything on: Prudencia's stupidity didn't deserve the effort. Sleepily I opened the door to find not Prudencia, but my mother. I didn't know what to say. Nor did she. She just looked me up and down, her attention caught successively by my disheveled hair, the black mascara tracks running under my eyes, the remains of carmine around my mouth, and the indecent nightdress that allowed more naked flesh to be seen than her sense of decency would allow. I couldn't bear her gaze, I couldn't face her. Perhaps because I was still too bewildered by my late night, perhaps because the serene severity of her attitude disconcerted me.

"Come in, don't stand there in the doorway," I said, trying to hide the fluster that her unexpected arrival had caused.

"No, I don't want to come in, I'm in a rush. I just came by to give you a message."

The situation was so tense and outlandish that I would never have believed it if I wasn't living through it that morning. My mother and I, who had shared so much and were so alike in so many ways, seemed to have been transformed into two strangers distrustful of each other, like stray dogs sizing each other up warily from a distance.

She remained standing at the door, serious, erect, her hair in a tight bun in which the first grey strands could be seen. Tall and dignified, her angular eyebrows framing the reproach in her stare. Somehow elegant in spite of the simplicity of her attire. When at last she stopped examining me carefully, she spoke. However — and in spite of what I had feared — her words were not intended to criticize me.

"I've come to bring you a message. A request that isn't mine. You can accept it or not, you'll see. But I think you should say yes. You think about it; better late than never."

She would not cross the threshold, and her visit lasted only one more minute: as long as it took to give me an address and a meeting time that same afternoon before turning her back without the slightest formality of a good-bye. It seemed strange to me that she hadn't communicated anything more, but I didn't have too long to wait for what I feared to be said: just as long as it took her to start going down the stairs.

"And wash that face, comb your hair, and put something on, you look like a whore."

I shared my astonishment with Ramiro at lunchtime. I couldn't make any sense of it, I didn't know what could be behind such an unexpected request. I was suspicious and begged him to go with me. Where? To meet my father. Why? Because that was what he'd requested. What for? Even with ten years of wondering I still wouldn't have been able to guess at even the vaguest reason.

We had settled that I should meet my mother in the midafternoon at the address she mentioned: Hermosilla 19. A very good street, a very good building; much like the ones that in another time I had visited carrying newly sewn clothes. I was painstaking in composing my appearance for the encounter: I had chosen a blue woollen dress, a matching coat, and a small hat with three feathers tipped gracefully over my left ear. It had all been paid for by Ramiro, naturally: they were the first pieces of clothing to touch my body that hadn't been sewn by my mother or myself. I was wearing high-heeled shoes and my hair fell loosely down my back; I barely wore any makeup. This afternoon I didn't want any criticism. I looked at myself in the mirror before going out. A full-length one. The image of Ramiro was reflected behind me, smiling, admiring me with his hands in his pockets.

"You're amazing. He's going to be impressed."

I tried to smile gratefully at the comment, but I just couldn't. I was pretty, it's true; pretty and special looking, someone quite different from whom I'd been just a few months earlier. Pretty, special looking, and scared as a mouse, scared to death, regretting that I'd accepted that unusual request.

From my mother's expression when we arrived, I deduced that she was displeased to see Ramiro at my side. Seeing our intention to go in together, she stopped us without a thought.

"This is family business; if you don't mind, you'll remain here."

And without waiting for a response, she turned and crossed through the imposing black iron and glass door. I wanted to have him beside me, I needed his support and his strength, but I didn't dare face her down. I merely whispered to Ramiro that it would be best if he left and I followed her inside.

"We've come to see Señor Alvarado. He's expecting us," she announced to the doorman. He nodded and without a word he turned to accompany us to the elevator.

"Thank you, there's no need."

We went through the wide door and began to climb the stairs, my mother ahead of me, stepping firmly, without even touching the polished wood of the banister, in a suit I didn't recognize. Me behind her, fearful, clinging to the handrail as though to a life vest on a stormy night. The two of us silent as tombs. Thoughts gathered in my head as we went up the steps one by one. First landing. Why did my mother move around so familiarly in that unknown place? Mezzanine. What would the man we were coming to see be like, why this sudden insistence on meeting me after so many years? Main floor. The rest of my thoughts remained crowded together in the limbo of my mind. I didn't have time for them; we'd arrived. A large door to the right, my mother's finger on the bell pressing firmly, without any sign of intimidation. The door opened at once, a shriveled old maid in a black uniform and spotless white cap.

"Good afternoon, Servanda. We've come to see the master of the house. I imagine he's in the library."

Servanda's mouth was left half open, the greeting hanging from it, as though she had been visited by a couple of ghosts. When she managed to react and it seemed she was at last going to be able to say something, a faceless voice could be heard over hers. A man's voice, hoarse, strong, from the back.

"Let them come through."

The maid stepped to one side, still caught in a nervous fluster. She didn't need to show us the way: my mother seemed to know it all too well. We walked down a broad corridor, passing large rooms, their walls covered with hangings, tapestries, and family portraits. Arriving at a double door, open on the left-hand side, my mother turned toward it. We then noticed a large man waiting for us in the middle of the room. And the powerful voice again.

"Come in."

A large desk covered in paper, a large bookcase filled with books, a large man looking at me, first my eyes, then down, then back up again. Discovering me. He swallowed, I swallowed. He took a few steps toward us, put his hand on my arm, and

49

squeezed, not too hard, as though wanting to be sure that I really existed. He smiled slightly, as though with an aftertaste of melancholy.

"You're just like your mother was twenty-five years ago."

He kept his gaze fixed on mine as he held on to me for a second, two, three, ten. Then, still without letting me go, he looked away and fixed his gaze on my mother. The weak, bitter smile returned to his face.

"How long it's been, Dolores."

She didn't answer, nor did she avoid his eyes. Then he released his hand from my arm and held it out toward her; he didn't seem to be after a greeting, just a contact, a glancing touch, as though hoping that her fingers would come out to meet his. But she remained immobile, not answering the invitation, until he seemed to awake from the enchantment, cleared his throat, and, in a tone that was as courteous as it was determinedly neutral, offered us a seat.

Instead of heading for the big work table where the papers were gathered, he invited us toward another corner of the library. My mother settled into one armchair, and he sat opposite. And me alone on a sofa, in the middle, between the two of them. Tense, uncomfortable, all three of us. He busied himself lighting a cigar. She remained sitting erect, her knees together and her back straight. Meanwhile, I scratched with my index finger at the wine-colored damask upholstery of the sofa, my attention focused on the task, as though I were trying to make a hole in the warp of the fabric and escape through it like a little lizard. The atmosphere filled with smoke, and the throat clearing returned as though in anticipation

50

of some intervention, but before this could be spilled into the air my mother spoke. She was addressing me, though her eyes remained on him. Her voice forced me at last to lift my gaze to the two of them.

"Well, Sira, so this is your father, you meet him at last. His name is Gonzalo Alvarado, he's an engineer, the owner of a foundry, and he has lived in this house forever. He used to be the son and now he's the master of the house, that's how it goes. A long time ago I used to come here to sew for his mother. We met then, and well, anyway, you were born three years later. Don't think it was some cheap soap opera in which the unscrupulous young master tricks the poor little dressmaker or anything of the sort. When our relationship began, I was twenty-two years old, he was twenty-four: we both knew perfectly well who we were, where we were, and what we were up against. There was no deception on his part, nor any more than the appropriate illusions on mine. It was a relationship that ended because it couldn't go anywhere, because it never should have begun. I was the one who decided to end it, it wasn't him deciding to abandon you and me. And it has always been me who has insisted that you should have no contact. Your father tried not to lose us, insistently at first; then, bit by bit, he began to get used to the situation. He married and had other children, two boys. For a long time I heard nothing of him, until the day before yesterday when I received a message from him. He didn't tell me why he wanted to meet you at this point; that we will learn now."

As she talked, he watched her attentively, with serious appreciation. When she fell silent, he

51

waited a few moments before speaking. He seemed to be thinking, measuring his words so that they might express precisely what he wanted to say. I made the most of those moments to observe him, and the first thing that occurred to me was that I never would have been able to imagine a father like this for myself. I was dark, my mother was dark, and in the very rare imaginary evocations I'd had of my progenitor, I'd always painted him like us, just another man, with a tanned complexion, dark hair and slim build. Also, I had always associated the image of a father with the appearance of those around me: our neighbor Norberto, the fathers of my friends, the men who filled the taverns and the streets of my neighborhood. Normal fathers of normal people: postal workers, salespeople, clerks, café waiters, or at most owners of a tobacconist's, a grocer's, or a vegetable stand in the Cebada market. The gentlemen I saw in my comings and goings along Madrid streets delivering orders from Doña Manuela's workshop were to me like beings from another world, another species who in no way fit the mold I had mentally cast as paternal. And yet before me was just such a specimen. A man who was still good looking despite his somewhat excessive corpulence, with hair already greying that in its day must have been fair, and honey-colored eyes now a little red, dressed in dark grey, the owner of a grand home and patriarch of an absent family. A father unlike all the other fathers, who finally began to speak, addressing my mother and me alternately, sometimes both of us at once, sometimes neither.

"Well now, let's see, this isn't easy," he said by way of beginning.

A deep breath, a drag on the cigar, smoke out. Eyes raised to meet mine at last. Then right to my mother's. Then to mine again. And then he spoke again, and barely paused, for such a long and intense time that when I finally noticed we were almost in darkness, our bodies had been transformed into shadows, and the only light we had was the weak, distant reflection from a green tulip lamp on the desk.

"I've found you because I'm afraid that one of these days they're going to kill me. Or I'll end up killing someone and they'll put me in prison, which would be like a death in life, it comes to the same thing. The political situation is about to explode, and when that happens only God knows what will become of all of us."

I looked at my mother out of the corner of my eye, seeking some reaction, but her face didn't betray the slightest sign of concern: as though instead of the warnings of an imminent death she'd heard someone announcing the time or predicting a cloudy day. He, meanwhile, went on voicing his premonitions and exuding streams of bitterness.

"And since I know that my days are numbered, I've set about doing an inventory of my life, and what have I found that I own among my belongings? Yes, money. Properties, too. And a company with two hundred employees for which I've worked myself to the bone for three decades, and where when they don't organize a strike they humiliate me and spit in my face. And a wife who when she saw that someone had set fire to a couple of churches went with her mother and sisters to pray rosaries at San Juan de Luz. And two sons I don't understand, a couple of wastrels who've turned fanatic and spend their days shooting people from the rooftops and worshipping the revered son of Primo de Rivera, who has brainwashed all the young gentlemen of Madrid with his romantic nonsense about reaffirming the national spirit. If I could, I would take them all into the foundry and get them working twelve hours a day to see if the national spirit might be restored in them by blows of the hammer and anvil.

"The world has changed so much, Dolores, don't you see? The workers are no longer satisfied with going to the festival of San Cayetano and to the Carabanchel bulls, as the words of the *zarzuela* would have it. Now they're trading their donkeys for bicycles, they're joining unions, and the first time things go bad for them they threaten the boss with a bullet between the eyes. Probably they're not wrong; living a life filled with deprivation and working from sunrise to sunset from your earliest years isn't to anybody's taste. But what's needed here is much more than this. Raising a fist, hating those they have above them, and singing *The Internationale* won't fix much; countries don't change to the rhythm of an anthem. They naturally have more than enough reasons for rebelling, as there have been centuries of starvation here and a lot of injustice, too, but this won't be fixed by biting the hand that feeds them. For that, to modernize this country, we'd need brave employers and qualified workers, a solid education system, and serious government leaders who remain in their posts long enough to get something done. But everything here is a disaster, everyone looks after himself, and no one bothers to work seriously to put an end to such madness. The

54

politicians on both sides spend their days lost in their diatribes and fancy speeches in the parliament. The king is doing just fine where he is: he should have left long ago. The socialists, anarchists, and communists fight for their own interests just as they should, except that they ought to do it with good sense and order, without grudges or explosive tempers. The wealthy and the monarchists, meanwhile, flee like cowards abroad. And between one lot and the other, we'll finally see the military take over, and then we're going to be sorry. Or we'll get ourselves into a civil war, unite against one another, take up arms, and end up killing one another, killing our brothers."

He spoke emphatically, without pausing. Until suddenly he seemed to come back down to reality and understand that both my mother and I, in spite of having kept our composure, were utterly disconcerted, not knowing where he was going with the discouraging predictions he was making or what we had to do with that crude vomiting up of words.

"Sorry to be telling you all this in such an impulsive way, but I've been thinking about it for a long time and I've now reached the moment to act. This country is falling apart. It's a madness, it's senseless, and as for me, as I've told you, one of these days they're going to kill me. The ways of the world are changing, and it's not easy to adjust to them. I've spent more than thirty years working like a beast, losing sleep for my business and trying to do my duty. But either the times aren't on my side or I'm very wrong about something because in the end it's all turned its back on me, and life seems to be suddenly spitting its vengeance at me. My sons have left me, my wife has abandoned me, and the day-to-day life in my company has turned into a hell. I've been left alone, I have no one's support, and I'm convinced the situation can only get worse. Which is why I am preparing myself, putting my affairs in order, my papers, my accounts, arranging my final wishes, and trying to leave everything organized in case one day I don't come back. And just as in my business, I'm also trying to put some order in my memories and my feelings, some of which I still have, though not many. The blacker everything around me becomes, the more I rummage among my feelings and retrieve the memory of the good things life has given me. And now that my days are running out, I've recognized one of the few things that was really worthwhile. Do you know what that was, Dolores? You. You and this daughter of ours who's the spitting image of you in the years we were together. That was why I wanted to see you."

Gonzalo Alvarado, this father of mine who at last had a face and a name, was speaking more calmly now. Halfway through his speech he began to look more like the man he must have been on any other day: sure of himself, forceful in his gestures and his words, used to giving orders and to being right. It had been hard for him to start; it couldn't be pleasant to face a lost love and an unknown daughter after a quarter century of absence. But he had now regained his composure, the owner and master of the situation. Firm in his speech, sincere and raw as only someone with nothing left to lose can be.

"You know something, Sira? I really loved your mother; I loved her very much, very much indeed. If only everything had been different, so that I

56

could have kept her with me forever. But regrettably that's not the way it was."

He looked away from me and turned back to her. Toward her big hazel-colored eyes tired from sewing. Toward her beautiful maturity with neither cosmetics nor embellishments.

"I didn't fight for you much, Dolores, did I? I was unable to confront my family, and I wasn't worthy of you. Then, as you know, I adjusted to the life that was expected of me, I got used to another woman and another family."

My mother listened in silence, apparently impassive. I couldn't have said whether she was hiding her emotions or whether those words didn't provoke either cold or heat in her at all. She remained, quite simply, stern in her posture, her thoughts inscrutable, sitting upright in the beautifully tailored suit I'd never seen her in before, doubtless made from the fabric remnants of some woman with more material and more luck in life than she.

Rather than stopping in the face of her impassivity, my father kept on talking. "I don't know whether you'll believe me or not, but the truth is that now I find myself coming toward the end, my heart grieves that I've let so many years go past without taking care of you both, and without even having gotten to know you, Sira. I should have insisted more, I shouldn't have given up trying to keep you close, but things were the way they were. And Dolores, you were too dignified, you wouldn't allow me to devote only the leftover scraps of my life to you. If it couldn't be everything, then it would be nothing. Your mother is very tough, girl, very tough and very firm. And I, I was probably

57

weak and a fool, but, well, this isn't the time for regrets."

He remained silent a few seconds, thinking, not looking at us. Then he breathed in slowly through his nose, breathed out again hard, and shifted position, leaning forward in his armchair as though wanting to be more direct, as though he had decided to approach head-on what he seemed to have to tell us. He seemed finally ready to extract himself from the bitter nostalgia that kept him flying over the past, ready now to focus himself on the earthly demands of the present.

"I don't want to occupy you any longer with my melancholy thoughts, forgive me. Let's get to the point. I've called you here to transmit my last wishes. I ask you both to understand me and not misinterpret them. My intention is not to compensate you for the years I haven't given you, or to demonstrate my remorse with gifts, still much less to try to buy your good regard at this point. All I want is to leave the ends nicely tied up, which rightfully I think should be put in order for when my time comes."

For the first time since we'd settled down, he rose from his armchair and made his way toward the desk. I followed him with my gaze, observing the broad back, the fine cut of his jacket, the agile step despite his corpulence. Then I looked at the portrait hanging on the back wall toward which he was headed, large and impossible not to notice. It was an oil in a gilt frame of an elegant woman dressed in the fashion of the beginning of the century, neither beautiful nor the contrary, with a tiara on her short wavy hair and a severe expression on her face. When he turned around he gestured toward it with a movement of his chin.

"My mother, the grande dame Carlota, your grandmother. You remember her, Dolores? She passed away seven years ago; if she'd done it twenty-five years ago, you, Sira, would probably have been born in this house. Anyway, we'll let the dead rest in peace."

He was talking without looking at us now, busy with whatever he was doing behind the desk. He opened drawers, took out objects, riffled through papers, and returned to us with his hands full. As he approached he didn't take his eyes off my mother.

"You're still beautiful, Dolores," he observed as he sat down. He was no longer tense, his initial discomfort only a memory. "I'm sorry, I haven't offered you anything, will you drink something? I'll call Servanda . . ." He made as though to get up again, but my mother interrupted him.

"We don't want anything, Gonzalo, thank you. Let's finish this, please."

"Do you remember Servanda, Dolores? The way she used to spy on us, the way she'd follow us and then go telling tales to my mother?" Suddenly he gave a laugh, hoarse, quick, bitter. "Remember when she caught us locked in the ironing room? And now look, how ironic after all these years: my mother rotting in the cemetery, and me here with Servanda, the only person who takes care of me, what a pathetic fate. I should have dismissed her when my mother died, but where could the poor woman have gone then, old and deaf and with no family. And besides, she probably had no choice but to do what my mother told her to do: it wasn't the time to be losing her job just like that, even though Doña Carlota had an unbearable nature and would drive her servants down a road of misery."

He remained seated on the edge of his armchair, without leaning back, his large hands resting on the heap of things he had brought over from his desk. Papers, packages, cases. From the inside pocket of his jacket he now took out some metal-framed glasses and positioned them on his face.

"Well then, to practical matters, one thing at a time."

First he took up a package that was really two large envelopes, bulky and held together at the middle by an elastic band.

"This is for you, Sira, to open up a new path in your life. It isn't a third of my capital as by rights should be yours as one of my three descendants, but it's all I can give you at the moment in cash. I've barely been able to sell anything, things are going badly for every sort of transaction right now. And I'm not in a position to leave you property, either: you're not legally recognized as a daughter of mine and the inheritance taxes would swallow you up, not to mention that you'd be embroiled in endless lawsuits with my other children. But here you've got almost a hundred and fifty thousand pesetas. You seem smart like your mother; I'm sure you'll be able to invest them well. With this money I also want you to take care of her, to make sure she doesn't lack for anything and to support her if one day she needs it. The truth is, I would have preferred to split the money in two, half for each of you, but as I know Dolores would never accept it, I'll leave you in charge of everything."

He held the packet out; before taking it I looked over at my mother, disconcerted, not knowing what to do. With a nod — quick and concise — she conveyed her consent. Only then did I hold out my hands.

"Thank you very much," I mumbled to my father.

He prefaced his reply with a mirthless smile. "No reason to thank me, daughter, no reason at all. Well then, let's get on."

He took up and opened a small box lined in blue velvet. Then he took another, this time maroon colored, smaller, and did the same. And so on successively till there were five. He left them open on the table. The jewels inside didn't shine brightly, there wasn't much light, but that didn't mean we couldn't guess how valuable they were.

"This was my mother's. There's more, but María Luisa, my wife, has taken them away with her on her pious exile. She has, however, left the most valuable ones, probably because they're the least discreet. They're for you, Sira. It would be safest if you never wear them: as you can see, they're a little showy. But you can sell them or pawn them if you're ever in need and you'll get a considerable sum for them."

I didn't know how to reply; my mother did.

"Absolutely not, Gonzalo. All that belongs to your wife."

"Not at all," he interrupted her. "All this, my dear Dolores, is not my wife's property: all this is mine and my wish is that it should pass from me to my daughter."

"That cannot be, Gonzalo, it cannot be."

"It certainly can be."

"It can't."

"It can."

The discussion ended there. Silence on my

61

mother's part, the battle lost. He closed the boxes one by one. Then he piled them in an orderly pyramid, the largest at the bottom, the smallest at the top. He moved the heap over toward me, sliding it along the waxed surface of the table, and when I had them in front of me, he turned his attention to a few sheets of paper. He unfolded them and showed them to me.

"These are some certificates for the jewels, with descriptions and appraisals and all that sort of thing. And there is also a notarized document affirming that they belong to me and that I am passing them on to you of my own free will. It'll be useful to you should you ever need to prove that they're yours; I hope you'll never have to prove anything to anyone, but just in case."

He folded up the pieces of paper, put them in a file, deftly tied a red ribbon around it, and placed that in front of me, too. Then he took up an envelope and drew from it a couple of leaves of yellowed paper, with stamps, signatures, and other formalities.

"And now one further thing, almost the last thing. How can I explain this to you?" A pause, an intake of breath, then a slow exhalation before he continued. "This document has been drawn up by me and my lawyer, and it has been notarized. What it says, in brief, is that I am your father and you are my daughter. What use will it be to you? Perhaps none, because if one day you try to make a claim to my inheritance, you'll find that I've bequeathed it while I'm alive to your half brothers, meaning that you will never be able to obtain any more from this family than you will take with you when you leave this house today. But to me it is valuable: it's a public recognition of something I should have done many years ago. I state here what it is that connects you and me, and now you can do whatever you please with it: show it to half the world or tear it in a thousand pieces and throw it in the fire; that is up to you alone."

He folded the document, put it away, and handed me the envelope, then took up another from the table, the final one. The previous one had been large, of good-quality paper, with elegant handwriting and a notary's letterhead. This second one was small, brownish, common looking, with an appearance of having been passed through a thousand hands before reaching ours.

"This is the last one," he said, not raising his head.

He opened it, removed its contents, and examined it briefly. Then, without a word, passing over me this time, he gave it to my mother. Then he got up and went over to one of the balcony windows. He remained there in silence, his back to us, his hands in his trouser pockets, contemplating the evening — or nothing, I don't know. What my mother had received was a small pile of photographs. Old, brown, and of poor quality, taken by a street photographer for next to nothing some spring morning more than two decades ago. A young couple, attractive, smiling. Complicit and close, caught in the fragile net of a love as great as it was inconvenient, unaware that after their years apart, when they were once again confronted with each other and with that testimony of yesterday, he would turn toward a balcony so as not to look at her face and she would clench her jaw so as not to cry in front of him.

My mother ran through the photographs one by

one. Then she handed them over to me, without looking up. I considered them slowly and returned them to their envelope. He came back over to us, sat down, and took up the conversation again.

"With that we're done with all the material issues. Now comes the advice. It's not, daughter, that at this point I'm trying to leave you with some moral legacy; I'm not someone who inspires confidence or who preaches by example, but if you'd allow me a few more minutes after so many years, I'm sure that's not too much to ask, right?"

I nodded.

"Well, my advice is as follows: leave here as soon as possible. Both of you, go far away, the farther from Madrid you can go the better. Out of Spain, if possible. Not into Europe, as the situation there doesn't look too good either. Go off to America; if that's too far, to Africa. To Morocco; go to the Protectorate, that's a good place to live. A quiet place where nothing at all has happened since the end of the war with the Moors. Start a new life far from this crazy country, because when you least expect it something enormous is going to explode and no one here will be left alive."

I couldn't contain myself.

"And what about you, sir, why aren't you going?"

He smiled bitterly. Then he held his big hand out to mine and gripped it hard. It was hot. He spoke without letting go.

"Because I no longer need a future, my daughter. I've already burned all my bridges. And please, don't call me sir. I've completed my cycle, a bit prematurely no doubt, but I no longer have the desire nor the strength to fight for a new life. When you undertake a change like that you have to do it with dreams and hopes, with illusions. To go without them is merely to run away, and I have no intention of escaping anywhere; I'd rather stay here and confront whatever is coming. But you, Sira, you're young, you must start a family, raise them well. And Spain is becoming a bad place. So that is what I recommend, as a father and a friend: leave. Take your mother with you, so she can watch her grandchildren growing up. And look after her as I wasn't able to do, promise me that."

He kept his gaze locked on mine until I nodded. I don't know in what way he expected me to look after my mother, but I didn't dare do anything but agree.

"Well, with that I think we're finished," he announced.

Then he got up, and we did the same.

"Take your things," he said. I obeyed. Everything fit in my handbag apart from the largest of the cases and the envelopes of money.

"And now let me embrace you for the first and undoubtedly the last time. I doubt very much that we'll see each other again."

He wrapped my thin body in his big build and squeezed me hard; then he took my face in his large hands and kissed my forehead.

"You're just as lovely as your mother. I wish you good luck in your life, my daughter. May God bless you."

I wanted to say something in reply, but I couldn't. The sounds remained trapped in my throat, the tears welled up in my eyes, and all I could do was turn around and go out into the hallway in search of the front door, stumbling, my sight cloudy and a stab of black sorrow wrenching my guts.

I waited for my mother on the staircase landing. The door had been left half open, and I watched as she came out observed by the sinister figure of Servanda lurking in the corridor. Her cheeks were ablaze and her eyes glassy, emotion finally perspiring on her face. I wasn't there to witness what my parents did and said to each other in those five short minutes, but I've always believed that they, too, embraced and said good-bye to each other forever.

We went down the steps just as we had come up: my mother ahead, me behind. In silence. With the jewels, the documents, and the photographs in my handbag, the hundred and fifty thousand pesetas wedged under my arm, and the noise of my heels hammering on the staircase marble. Arriving at the mezzanine, I couldn't contain myself: I grabbed her by the arm and forced her to stop and turn around. My face was right in front of hers, my voice was just a terrified whisper.

"Are they really going to kill him, Mother?"

"How should I know, daughter, how should I know . . ."

Chapter Four

We went out into the street and began our return journey without exchanging another word. She picked up the pace and I struggled to keep up with her, fighting the discomfort of my new high heels. After a few minutes, still stunned, I found the courage to speak.

"So what do I do with all this now, Mother?"

She didn't stop to answer me. "Keep it somewhere safe," was her only response.

"All of it? And you won't keep anything?"

"No, it's all yours; you are the heir, and besides, you're already a grown woman and I can't interfere with what you do with the things that your father has decided to give you."

"Are you sure, Mother?"

"I'm sure, daughter, I'm sure. Maybe just give me a photograph, any of them, I want only one memento. The rest is all for you, but in God's name I beg you, Sira, by God and holy Mary, listen to me well, girl."

She stopped at last and looked me in the eye under the dim light of a street lamp. Beside us passersby walked in a thousand directions, oblivious to our agitation.

"Be careful, Sira. Be careful and be responsible," she said in a low voice, forming her words quickly.

"Don't do anything crazy. You've got a lot now, a lot; so much more than you could ever have dreamed of having, so for God's sake, my child, be cautious; be cautious and sensible."

We kept on walking in silence until we parted. She returned to the emptiness of her house without me, to the mute company of my grandfather, who had never known who his granddaughter's father was because my mother, stubborn and proud, had always refused to give him a name. And I returned to Ramiro. He was waiting for me at home, smoking in the half light as he listened to the radio in the living room, anxious to know how it had gone for me and ready to go out for dinner.

I described the visit to him in detail: what I'd seen there, what I'd heard from my father, how I'd felt, and what he had advised me. I also showed him what I'd brought from that house to which I would probably never return.

"This is worth a lot of money, girl," he whispered as he looked at the jewels.

"And there's more," I said, holding the envelope of notes out to him.

In reply, he allowed himself just a whistle.

"What are we going to do with all this now, Ramiro?" I asked with a knot of concern.

"You mean what are you going to do, my love: all this is just yours. If you want me to, I can take charge of determining how best to keep it. It might perhaps be a good idea to deposit it all in the safe at my office."

"Why don't we take it to a bank?" I asked.

"I don't think that would be good, the way things are going at the moment."

The fall of the New York Stock Exchange a few

years earlier, the political instability, and a mountain of other things that didn't interest me in the slightest were the explanations with which he backed up his proposal. I barely paid attention: any decision he made would seem right to me. I only wanted to find a safe place as quickly as possible for that fortune already burning my fingers.

He returned from work the following day laden with bits of paper and leaflets.

"I haven't stopped turning your situation around and around in my head, and I think I've found the solution. Best would be for you to set up some sort of commercial enterprise," he said as soon as he came through the door.

I hadn't been out of the house since getting up. I'd spent the whole morning tense and nervous, remembering the previous afternoon, still shaken by the knowledge that I had a father with an actual name, a fortune, and feelings. This unexpected proposition only increased my agitation.

"Why would I want a company?" I asked in alarm.

"Because that way your money would be safer. And for another reason, too."

He spoke to me then about the problems in his company, about the tensions with his Italian bosses and the uncertainty of foreign businesses in turbulent Spain. And about ideas, too. He talked to me about those ideas, unfolding a list of projects the likes of which I'd never imagined. All innovative, brilliant, destined to bring outside inventions to the country and open up a path to modernity. Importing English mechanical harvesters to the fields of Castile, North American vacuum cleaners that promised to leave urban homes as clean as a whistle, and a Berlin-style cabaret for which he already had a site in mind on Calle Valverde. Among them all, however, one project emerged more brightly than any other: Pitman Academies.

"I've been mulling over it for months, ever since we received a leaflet at work through some old clients, but in my position as manager it didn't seem appropriate for me to approach them personally. If we set up a firm in your name, it would all be much simpler," he explained. "Pitman Academies are running in Argentina at full throttle: they have more than twenty branches, thousands of students who they are preparing for posts in business, banking, and administration. They're taught typing, shorthand, and accounting using revolutionary methods, and after eleven months they come out with a certificate under their arm, ready to devour the world. And the company just keeps growing, opening new sites, hiring staff, and generating income. We could do the same, set up Pitman Academies on this side of the pond. And if we propose the idea to the Argentineans, saying that we have a legitimate firm backed up with enough capital, we'll stand a much better chance than if we approach them as private individuals."

I didn't have any way to judge whether it was a sensible project or a harebrained scheme, but Ramiro spoke with such certainty, with such mastery and knowledge, that I didn't for a moment doubt that it was a brilliant idea. He went on and on about the details, continuing to amaze me.

"What's more, I think it's worth bearing in mind your father's suggestion to leave Spain. He's right: everything is too tense here, any day now something powerful could blow up, and this isn't a good time to undertake a new enterprise. That's why I think we have to follow his advice and go to Africa. If everything works out, once the situation has calmed down, we can hop back to the Peninsula and expand right across Spain. Give me a little time to make contact in your name with the owners of Pitman in Buenos Aires and convince them about our plan to open a large branch in Morocco, either in Tangiers or the Protectorate, we'll see. A month at most and we'll have our reply. And as soon as we have it, *arrivederci* Hispano-Olivetti: we'll be off and get this thing running."

"But why would the Arabs want to learn how to type?"

Ramiro's first reaction was a resonant laugh. Then he enlightened me.

"The things you say, my love. Our academy is aimed at the European population living in Morocco: Tangiers is an international city, a free port with citizens coming from all across Europe. There are lots of foreign firms, diplomatic missions, banks, and financial companies of all kinds; the employment possibilities are immense, and everywhere they need qualified staff who know typing, shorthand, and accounting. In Tetouan the situation is different but equally full of possibilities: the population is less international because the city is the capital of the Spanish Protectorate, but it's full of civil servants and people who aspire to be civil servants, and all of them, as you well know, my love, need the preparation that a Pitman Academy can offer them."

"What if the Argentineans won't agree?"

"I doubt that very much. I have friends in Bue-

71

nos Aires with excellent contacts. We'll manage, you'll see. They'll let us have their method and know-how, and they'll send representatives over to teach the employees."

"And what will you do?"

"Me on my own, nothing. But us, a great deal. We'll run the firm. You and me, together."

I prefaced my reply with a nervous laugh. The picture that Ramiro was proposing could not have been less plausible: the poor unemployed dressmaker who just a few months earlier had contemplated learning to type because she didn't have so much as a plot to die in was about to transform herself as if by magic into the owner of a business with fascinating prospects.

"You want me to run a company? I don't have the slightest idea about anything, Ramiro."

"What do you mean? How is it that I have to tell you just how much you're worth? The only problem is that you've never had the chance to show it: you've wasted your youth shut away in a burrow sewing clothes for other women and with no chance to devote yourself to anything better. Your moment, your great moment, is yet to come."

"And what will the Hispano-Olivetti people say when they find out you're leaving?"

He smiled slyly and kissed the tip of my nose.

"Hispano-Olivetti, my love, can go screw themselves."

Pitman Academies or a castle floating in the air, it was all the same to me if the idea came from Ramiro's mouth; if he spelled out his plans with feverish enthusiasm as he held my hands and his eyes tumbled into the depths of mine, if he repeated to me how much I was worth and how well everything would go if we gambled on a future together. With Pitman Academies or the cauldrons of hell: whatever he proposed was my law.

The following day he brought home the informational leaflet that had captured his imagination. Paragraph after paragraph described the history of the company: established in 1919, set up by three partners, Allúa, Schmiegelon, and Jan, based on the system of shorthand conceived by the Englishman Isaac Pitman. An infallible method, rigorous teachers, absolute responsibility, personalized treatment, a magnificent future after obtaining the certificate. The photographs of young people smiling, already seeming to savor their brilliant professional prospects, confirming the veracity of the promises. The pamphlet radiated an air of triumphalism that could have shaken even the most cynical: "Long and steep is the path of life. Not all reach the wished-for end, where success and fortune await them. Many are left by the wayside: those who are inconstant, weak-natured, who are negligent, ignorant, who trust only in luck, forgetting that the most resonant and exemplary triumphs were forged through the power of study, perseverance, and will. Each man can choose his own destiny: Make yours!"

That afternoon I went to see my mother. She brewed a pot of coffee and as we drank it, with the blind, mute presence of my grandfather beside us, I made her privy to our plans and suggested that once Ramiro and I had settled in Africa perhaps she could join us. As I'd expected, she didn't like the idea one bit, nor did she agree to go with us.

"There's no reason you have to obey your father

73

or believe everything he's told you. The fact that he's got problems with his business doesn't mean anything is going to happen to us. The more I think about it, the more I think he was exaggerating."

"If he's so frightened, Mother, it's for a reason; he's not going to go and make things up . . ."

"He's afraid because he's used to giving orders without anyone answering back, and now it upsets him that the workers — for the first time — are beginning to raise their voices and demand their rights. The truth is, I can't stop wondering whether accepting this fortune, and above all the jewels, wasn't a crazy thing to do."

Crazy or not, the fact was that from then on, the money, the jewels, and our plans became part of our day-to-day lives, quietly not brashly, but ever present in our thoughts and conversations. As we had planned, Ramiro took charge of the arrangements to create the company, and I restricted myself to signing the pieces of paper he put in front of me. Besides that, my life went on as usual: busy, fun, and filled to the brim with love and foolish naïveté.

The meeting with Gonzalo Alvarado had allowed my mother and me to smooth over the rougher parts of our relationship, but our paths continued irremediably along different courses. She supported herself stretching out to the utmost the final remnants that had come from Doña Manuela's workshop, occasionally sewing for some neighbor, remaining inactive most of the time. My world, in contrast, was already something quite different: a world that would have no place for patterns or linings, in which almost nothing remained of the young dressmaker I had once been.

The move to Morocco was still a few months away. During that time, Ramiro and I went out and came home; we laughed, smoked, made love like lunatics, and danced the carioca till dawn. Around us the political scene remained explosive, and the strikes, the labor disputes, and the violence on the streets continued as usual. In February the left-wing Popular Front coalition won the elections; the Falangists reacted by becoming more aggressive. Words were replaced by pistols and fists in political debates; the tension was heightened. Yet what did all that matter to us, if we were already just a couple of steps away from a new phase in our lives?

CHAPTER FIVE

We left Madrid at the end of March 1936. I went out one morning to buy some stockings and when I returned I found the house in turmoil and Ramiro surrounded by suitcases and trunks.

"We're leaving. This afternoon."

"Did Pitman Academies answer?" I asked, my stomach in knots. He replied without looking at me, pulling out trousers and shirts from the wardrobe.

"Not directly, but I've learned that they're considering our proposal very seriously. So I think this is the time to start spreading our wings."

"And your job?"

"I quit. Today. I'd had more than enough of them, they knew it was only a matter of days before I'd go. So it's good-bye, Hispano-Olivetti, we won't be meeting again anytime soon. There's another world waiting for us, my love; fortune favors the brave, so start getting things together, because we're off."

I didn't reply, and my silence forced him to interrupt his frantic activity. He looked up at me, smiling briefly at my confusion. Then he came over, grabbed me by the waist, and with a kiss tore all my fears up by the roots and gave me a transfusion of energy that could have flown me directly to Morocco.

Our haste allowed me only a few minutes to say good-bye to my mother; little more than a quick hug practically at the door and a don't-worry-I'll-write. I was glad there was no time to prolong the good-bye — it would have been too painful. I didn't even look back as I trotted down the stairs; in spite of her fortitude I knew she was about to burst into tears and that wasn't the moment for sentimentality. In my state of utter unawareness, I felt that our separation wouldn't last long, as though Africa were just a few blocks away and our trip wouldn't be for more than a few weeks.

We disembarked in Tangiers on a windy afternoon in early spring. After leaving a harsh grey Madrid, we arrived in this strange, dazzling city, filled with color and contrast, where the dark faces of the Arabs with their djellabas and turbans mingled with those of European settlers and others fleeing their past, in transit to a thousand other destinations, their suitcases filled with uncertain dreams. Tangiers, with its sea, its twelve international flags, and its striking vegetation of palms and eucalyptus, with Moorish alleyways and new avenues driven by impressive motorcars with CD license plates: *corps diplomatique.* Tangiers, where minarets and the scent of spices lived comfortably side by side with consulates, banks, frivolous foreign women in convertible cars, and the aroma of Virginia tobacco and duty-free Parisian perfumes. The terraces of the harbor's bathing resorts greeted us with awnings fluttering in the sea air, Cape Malabata and the Spanish coastline visible in the distance. The Europeans, dressed up in light-colored lightweight clothing, protected by sunglasses and soft hats, sat with their legs crossed indolently, sipping their aperitifs as they perused the international press. Some were devoted to business, others to administration, and many of them to a life that was idle and deceptively carefree: the prelude to something uncertain that had yet to arrive and that not even the most audacious were able to foresee.

While awaiting concrete news from the owners of Pitman Academies, we were lodged at the Hotel Continental, overlooking the port and just beside the old town. Ramiro cabled the Argentine firm to inform them of our change of address, and I took charge of making daily inquiries to the hotel management concerning the letter that would mark the beginning of our future. Once we had received our reply, we'd decide whether to remain in Tangiers or install ourselves in the Protectorate. In the meantime, while the communication took its time crossing the Atlantic, we began to move about the city among other expats like ourselves, part of that mass of beings with varied pasts and unpredictable futures who were dedicated body and soul to the exhausting chores of chatting, drinking, dancing, watching shows at the Teatro Cervantes, and gambling their futures on a hand of cards, unable to ascertain whether life had a sparkling destiny in store for them or a sinister end in some dark alleyway.

We began to be like them and entered a time that was anything but tranquil. There were vast hours of love in our bedroom in the Continental while the white curtains fluttered with sea breezes; furious passion beneath the monotonous sound of the fan blades mingling with the labored rhythm of our breaths; and the salty taste of sweat on our skin and the rumpled sheets overflowing the bed, spilling onto the floor. We went out constantly, enjoying the streets night and day. At first, not knowing anyone, we went around alone, just the two of us. On days when the east wind wasn't blowing too hard, we'd go to the beach by the Diplomatic Forest; in the afternoons we'd walk along the recently constructed Boulevard Pasteur, or watch American movies at the Florida Kursaal or the Capitol, or we'd sit at some café in the Small Souq, the pulsing center of the city, where Arabs and Europeans intermingled congenially.

Our isolation, however, lasted only a few weeks: Tangiers was small, Ramiro sociable in the extreme, and in those days everyone seemed to have a great urgency to interact with one another. Soon we started greeting faces, learning names, and joining up with groups when we walked into places. We'd have lunch and dinner at the Bretagne, Roma Park, or the Brasserie de la Plage, and at night we'd go to the Bar Russo, or Chatham, or the Detroit on the Place de France. Or to the Central with its group of Hungarian dancers, or to watch the M'Sallah music-hall shows in their great glazed pavilion, filled to bursting with the French, the English, Spaniards, Jews of various nationalities, Moroccans, Germans, and Russians who danced, drank, and discussed politics, either local or international, in a jumble of languages against the backdrop of a spectacular orchestra. Sometimes we'd end up at the Café Hafa by the sea, sitting under the awnings till dawn, on mats laid over the ground, with people reclining as they smoked hashish and drank tea. Rich Arabs, Europeans of uncertain fortune who at some time in the past might perhaps have been rich, too, or perhaps not. It was unusual for us to go to bed before dawn in those bewildering days, between our anticipation of news from Argentina and the idleness imposed by its delay. We'd frequent the new European quarter of the city and wander through the Moorish one, living with the combined presence of exiles and locals, with waxy-complexioned ladies wearing sun hats and pearls as they walked their poodles and dark-skinned barbers working in the open air with their ancient tools. With the street vendors of creams and ointments, the diplomatic corps in their impeccable attire, the herds of goats, and the fleeting, almost faceless silhouettes of the Muslim women in their haiks and caftans.

News came daily from Madrid. Sometimes we'd read articles in the local Spanish-language newspapers, *Democracia, El Diario de África,* or the republican *El Porvenir;* other times we'd just hear them from the mouths of the newspaper vendors in the Small Souq shouting their headlines in a jumble of languages: *La Vedetta di Tangeri* in Italian, *Le Journal de Tanger* in French. Occasionally I'd receive letters from my mother — brief, simple, distant letters. That was how I learned that my grandfather had died, silent and peaceful in his rocking chair, and between the lines I gathered how hard it was becoming, day by day, for her just to survive.

It was a time of discoveries, too. I learned a few phrases in Arabic, but nothing very useful. My ears got used to the sound of other languages — French, English — and to other accents in my own language, such as Haketia, that dialect of the Moroccan Sephardic Jews with its roots in old Spanish that also incorporated words from Arabic and Hebrew. I discovered that there are substances

80

you can smoke or inject or snort that will jumble your senses, that there are people capable of gambling away their mother at a baccarat table, and that there are passions of the flesh that allow for far more combinations than just those of a man and a woman horizontally on a mattress. I learned, too, that there are things that happen in the world that my dim education had never touched upon: I found out that years earlier there had been a great war in Europe, that Germany was being ruled by someone called Hitler who was admired by some and feared by others, and that someone who one day occupied a given place with a feeling of permanence could the following day vanish in order to save his skin, to avoid being beaten to death or ending up in a place worse than his darkest nightmare.

And I discovered to my utmost dismay that at any moment and with no apparent cause, everything we believe to be stable can be upset, derailed, twisted from its course. Unlike what I had learned about people's political leanings, about European affairs and the history of the countries of the people who surrounded us, this wasn't a piece of knowledge I acquired because anybody taught me, but because I happened to experience it myself. I don't recall the exact moment, and what happened wasn't absolutely concrete, but at some indeterminate point things between Ramiro and me began to change.

At first it was nothing more than a difference in our routines. Our involvement with other people grew, and he started to have a more focused interest in going to this or that place; we no longer wandered aimlessly, unhurried through the streets, no longer let ourselves be carried away by inertia as we had in the early days. I preferred our former state, alone, with no one but each other and the remote world around us. But I understood that Ramiro, with his larger-than-life personality, had begun to be liked by people all over the place. And since whatever he did seemed to me to be well done, I put up unquestioningly with the endless hours we spent surrounded by strangers, despite the fact that most times I barely understood what they were talking about, sometimes because they were speaking in languages that were not my own, sometimes because they were discussing places and subjects as yet unknown to me: concessions, Nazism, Poland, Bolsheviks, visas, extraditions. Ramiro could get by reasonably well in French and Italian, he had a bit of broken English and knew a few expressions in German. He had worked for international companies and developed contacts with foreigners, and what he wasn't able to manage with exact words he filled in with gestures, roundabout expressions, and inferences. I transformed into his shadow, into a presence that was almost always mute, indifferent to anything but feeling him beside me and being an appendage of his, an always obliging extension of his person.

There was a while, a time that lasted the duration of the spring, more or less, when we managed to combine the two sides and find a balance. We retained our periods of intimacy, our hours just to ourselves. We kept alive the flame of the Madrid days and at the same time opened ourselves up to new friends and joined in the comings and goings of local life. At a certain moment, however, the balance began to shift. Slowly, ever so gradually, but irreversibly. Public hours began to filter into the space of our private moments. Familiar faces stopped being just sources of conversation and anecdotes and began to emerge as people with a past, with plans for the future and the capacity to interfere. Their personalities emerged from anonymity and began to take shape more roundly, to become interesting, attractive. I still remember some of their names; I can still recollect their faces, even though they are now long dead, and their distant origins, which at the time I was unable to locate on a map. Ivan, the elegant, silent Russian, slender as a reed, with a fleeting glance and a handkerchief always poking out of his jacket pocket like an out-of-season silk flower. That Polish baron whose name now escapes me, who boasted of his supposed fortune to the four winds and had only a walking stick with a silver handle and two shirts with collars that had gradually frayed over the passing years. Isaac Springer, the Austrian Jew with his gold cigarette case. The Croatian couple, the Jovovics, both of them so beautiful, so alike and so ambiguous that at times they passed for lovers and at others for siblings. The sweaty Italian who always watched me with cloudy eyes; Mario he was called, or perhaps Mauricio, I no longer know. And Ramiro began to get more intimate with them, to make himself a part of their desires and concerns, an active part of their plans. And I watched as, day by day, he very smoothly became closer to them and farther from me.

It seemed the news from the Pitman Academies would never arrive, and to my surprise the delay didn't seem to be causing Ramiro the slightest concern. We spent less and less time alone in our room at the Continental. There were fewer and fewer whispers, fewer references to all the things that till that moment had captivated him about me. He barely mentioned what used to drive him wild and what he had never tired of naming — my glowing skin, my goddess hips, my silky hair. He no longer complimented the charm of my smile, the freshness of my youth. He almost never laughed at what he used to call my blessed innocence, and I could tell that increasingly I was provoking in him less and less interest, less complicity, less tenderness. It was then, in the middle of those sad days when uncertainty filled me with mental anguish, that I began to feel unwell. Not only in my spirit, but in body, too. I felt bad, then terrible, worse. Perhaps my stomach hadn't become completely used to the new foods that were so different from my mother's stews and the simple dishes of the restaurants in Madrid. Perhaps that heavy, humid heat of early summer had something to do with my growing fragility. Daylight made me too uncomfortable, the smells of the street disgusted me and made me want to vomit. I struggled to summon the strength to get out of bed, the retching reappearing at the least expected moments, and I was overwhelmed by sleepiness at all hours. On some occasions — the minority — Ramiro seemed to be concerned: he'd sit down beside me, put his hand on my forehead, and speak sweetly to me. On other occasions — the majority — he would be distracted, lost to me. He paid me no heed, drifted away from me.

I stopped accompanying him on his nighttime outings: I barely had the energy and spirit to stay on my feet. I started to spend time on my own in the hotel, long, thick, stifling hours; hours of sticky haze, without a breath of air, lifeless. I imagined that he was dedicating himself to the same things he had been doing lately and in the same company: drinks, billiards, conversation and more conversation; stories and maps sketched on any scrap of paper on the white marble of the café tables. I thought he was doing the same things he'd done with me, but without me, and I could not guess that he had moved on to a new phase, that there was more; that he had gone beyond the borders of mere social life among friends to enter a new territory that was not at all unfamiliar to him. Yes, there were more plans. And also hands of cards, fierce poker games, parties till dawn. Betting, boasting, shady transactions, and exorbitant plans. Lies, toasts to the sun, and the emergence of a side of his personality that for months had remained hidden. Ramiro Arribas, the man of a thousand faces, had up till that moment shown me only one of them. It wouldn't be long before I'd see the rest.

Every night he would come home later, and the worse for wear. His shirttails half untucked over his trouser waistband, his tie knot almost down to his chest, overexcited, smelling of tobacco and whiskey, stammering excuses in a thick voice if he found me awake. Sometimes he didn't even touch me, falling into bed like a dead weight and instantly asleep, snoring so loudly that it was impossible for me to reconcile myself to sleep in the few remaining hours before the morning truly began. Other times he would embrace me awkwardly, slobbering his breath on my neck, then move away the clothes that were getting in his way and empty himself into me. And I let him do it without reproach, with no understanding at all of what was happening to us, unable to give that

85

indifference a name.

There were some nights he didn't arrive at all. Those were the worst: spending the small hours awake watching the yellow lights of the docks reflected on the black water of the bay, dawns spent wiping away tears and the bitter suspicion that it might perhaps have been a mistake, a massive mistake from which there was no longer any going back.

The end wasn't long in coming. Ready to confirm once and for all the cause of my malaise but without wanting to worry Ramiro, I set off early one morning to the doctor's office on Calle Estatuto. Doctor Bevilacqua, General Practice, Disorders and Illnesses, read the golden plaque on his door. He listened to me, examined me, asked questions. And there was no need for a test or for any other procedure to confirm what I already suspected, and what Ramiro — as I later discovered — had suspected, too. I returned to the hotel in a jumble of bewildered feelings. Hope, anxiety, joy, dread. I expected to find him still in bed, to kiss him awake and tell him the news. But I never got the chance to tell him that we were going to have a child because when I arrived he wasn't there. All I found was the room turned upside down, the closet doors wide open, the drawers pulled from their runners, and the suitcases scattered on the floor.

We've been robbed, was the first thing I thought.

I was struggling to breathe and had to sit down on the bed. I closed my eyes and took a deep breath, another, a third. When I opened my eyes again, I ran them over the room. Just one thought repeated itself in my mind: Ramiro, where is Ramiro? And then my eyes lighted on an envelope on the little nightstand, leaning on the base of the lamp, with my name in capital letters in the vigorous strokes of that handwriting I could have recognized from the far end of the world.

Sira, my love:
Before you read on, I want you to know that I adore you, and that your memory will live on in me until the end of time. When you read these lines I already will no longer be near you, I will have set out on a new course, and though I wish it with all my soul, I fear that it is impossible for you and the baby that I sense you are expecting to have a place in it right now.

I would like to ask your forgiveness for the way I've treated you lately, for my lack of devotion to you; I trust you will understand that the uncertainty created by lack of news from Pitman Academies has led me to seek out other ways to undertake the move toward my future. A number of proposals were studied, and just one of them selected; it's an adventure as fascinating as it is promising, but it demands my dedication body and soul, and so there is no way of contemplating your presence in it at this time.

I have no doubt that the project I am embarking on today will be a total success, but for now, in its initial stages, it requires a considerable investment that exceeds my own financial capacities, which is why I have taken the liberty of borrowing your father's money and jewels to meet the initial costs. I hope one day to be able to return to you everything that I am today taking as a loan, so that in years to come you can pass it on to your descendants just as your father did to you. I also trust that the memory of your mother in her self-denial and fortitude will be an inspiration to you in the coming phases of your life.

Good-bye, my love. Yours always,

Ramiro

P.S. I would advise you to leave Tangiers as soon as possible; it is not a good place for a woman on her own, still less so one in your present condition. I fear there may be some people interested in finding me, and who failing to find me might seek you out. When you leave the hotel, try to do so discreetly and with little luggage: although I will seek to do it by all means possible, the urgency of my departure means I do not know if I will have the opportunity to settle the bill for the last months and I would never forgive myself if it should trouble you in any way.

I don't remember what I thought. I retain intact the image of the scene in my memory — the bedroom turned upside down, the empty closet, the blinding light coming in at the open window, me on the unmade bed, holding the letter in one hand, clinging to the recently confirmed pregnancy with the other while thick drops of sweat slipped down my forehead. But the thoughts that went through my mind at that moment left no trace, because I have never been able to recall them. What I am sure of is that I got on with the task at hand like a machine that had just been activated, with movements full of haste but with no capacity for reflection or the expression of feeling. In spite of the contents of the letter and in spite of the distance, Ramiro was still determining the rhythm of my actions, and all that was left for me to do was, simply, to obey. I opened a suitcase and with both hands filled it with the first things I could grab hold of, without stopping to think about what would be necessary to take and what could be left behind. A number of dresses, some spare change on the nightstand, a hairbrush, a few blouses and a couple of old magazines, a handful of underwear, mismatched shoes, two jackets without their skirts and three skirts without their jackets, loose pieces of paper that had been left on the desk, some jars from the bathroom, a towel. When that chaos of clothes and objects reached the suitcase's limit, I closed it, and, with a slam of the door, I left.

In the midday chaos, with customers coming in and out of the dining room and the noise of the waiters, all the people weaving back and forth and the voices in languages I didn't understand, almost nobody seemed to notice my departure. Only Hamid, the little bellhop who looked like just a boy though he no longer was one, approached solicitously to help me carry my suitcase. I refused him wordlessly and went out. I began to walk at a pace that was neither firm nor unsteady, without the slightest idea of where I was headed and not worrying about it. I remember having gone up the slope of the Rue de Portugal; I still have a few scattered images of the Grand Souq: a mass of kiosks, animals, voices, and djellabas. I wandered aimlessly and occasionally had to move aside to stand against a wall when I heard a motorcar horn behind me or the cries of *Balak, balak* from some Moroccan hastily transporting his merchandise. In my confused ramblings I passed at some point by the English cemetery, the Catholic church, Rue Siaghine, Paseo de la Marina Española, and the Great Mosque. I walked for a time that was endless and imprecise, without noticing any tiredness or any sensation, moved by an alien force that propelled my legs as though they belonged to a body not my own. I could have gone on walking much longer: hours, nights, maybe weeks, years and years until the end of time. But I did not, because on the Cuesta de la Playa, as I passed like a ghost in front of the Escuelas Españolas, a taxi stopped beside me.

"Need me to take you anywhere, mademoiselle?" asked the driver in a mixture of Spanish and French.

I think I nodded. The suitcase must have made him assume I meant to travel.

"To the port, or the station, or will you be taking a bus?"

"Yes."

"Yes what?"

"Yes."

"Yes the bus?"

I nodded again: it was all the same to me, bus or train, a boat or the bottom of an abyss. Ramiro had left me and I had nowhere to go, so any place was as bad as any other. Or worse.

CHAPTER SIX

A gentle voice tried to wake me, and with a massive effort I managed to half open my eyes. Beside me I could make out two figures — blurry at first, then clearer. One of them was that of a man whose face, though vague, turned out to be faintly familiar. The other silhouette belonged to a nun in an impeccable white headdress. I tried to get my bearings and could only see high ceilings above me, beds alongside, the smell of medicine and sunlight coming in through the windows in torrents. Then I realized I was in a hospital. The first words I murmured are still in my memory.

"I want to go back home."

"And where is your home, my child?"

"In Madrid."

It seemed to me that the figures exchanged a quick glance. The nun took my hand and squeezed it gently.

"I think right now that won't be possible."

"Why not?" I asked.

It was the man who answered: "Traffic in the Strait has been stopped. They've declared a state of war."

I couldn't understand what that meant, because no sooner did the words enter my ears than I fell back down into a well of weakness and infinite sleepiness from which it took me days to rouse myself. When I did, I remained hospitalized for some time. Those weeks I spent immobilized in the Tetouan Hospital Civil served to put my feelings into something like order and to allow me to weigh up the extent of what the recent months had entailed. But that was at the end, in the final days. In the early days, in those mornings and afternoons, in the small hours, at the times when others had visitors but I never did, when they brought me food I was unable to taste, all I did was cry. I didn't think, didn't consider, didn't even remember. I just cried.

When those days were over, when my eyes dried because I no longer had any capacity for crying, memories began to return to my bed like a precisely ordered procession. I could almost see them harassing me, lining up to come in through the door at the end of that big, light-filled hospital ward. Memories that were alive and autonomous, big and small, that approached, single file, suddenly scaling the mattress and invading my body through an ear, or under my fingernails, or through the pores of my skin, until they entered my brain and battered at it without the slightest pity, with images and moments that my will had wanted never again to recall. And then, when the tribe of memories was still arriving but their presence was becoming less noisy, something else began to invade me with a dreadful coldness, like a rash: the necessity to analyze everything, to find a cause and a reason for everything that had happened in my life during the past eight months. That phase was the worst: the most aggressive, the most tormenting. The one that hurt most. And though I cannot calculate how long it lasted, I do know with absolute certainty that what managed to put an end to it was an unexpected arrival.

Up till then, all the days had passed among women giving birth, the Sisters of Charity, and white-painted metal beds. From time to time a doctor in a smock would appear, and at certain hours of the day the families of the other residents would arrive, speaking in murmurs, cuddling the newborn babies and between sighs consoling those who — like me — had been left along the way. I was in a city where I did not know a soul: no one had ever been to see me, nor did I expect anyone to. I wasn't even completely clear what I was doing among that alien population: I only managed to retrieve a muddled recollection of the circumstances of my arrival. A swamp of thick uncertainty occupied the place in my memory that should have held the logical reasons that had brought me here. Over the course of those days my only companions were memories mixed with the murkiness of my thoughts, the discreet presence of the nuns, and the desire — half longing, half fearful — to return to Madrid as soon as possible.

My solitude was broken one morning quite unexpectedly. Preceded by the white, rounded figure of Sister Virtudes, there appeared the face of that man who so many days earlier had spoken a few blurry words to me about a war.

"I've brought you a visitor, my child," announced the nun. I thought I could make out a slight trace of concern in her singsong tone. When the new arrival identified himself, I understood why.

"Commissioner Claudio Vázquez, ma'am," said the stranger by way of greeting. "Or is it 'miss'?"

He had a tanned face in which two dark, shrewd eyes shone. His hair was almost white, his bearing supple, and he wore a light-colored summer suit. In my weakened state I wasn't able to tell whether he was an older man with the bearing of a younger man or a younger man prematurely grey. In any case, it mattered little at that moment: the more urgent thing for me was to find out what it was he wanted from me. Sister Virtudes gestured him toward a chair along a nearby wall; swiftly he drew it closer to the right side of my bed and sat down, placing his hat at his feet. With a smile as kind as it was firm he gestured to the sister that he'd rather she leave.

The light was coming in in torrents through the broad windows of the hospital pavilion. Beyond them, the wind was lightly rustling the garden's palm and eucalyptus trees beneath a dazzling blue sky, testimony to a magnificent summer day for anyone who didn't have to spend it lying in a hospital bed in the company of a police commissioner. With their impeccable white sheets stretched taut, the two beds on either side of me, like almost all the others, were unoccupied. When the sister left, disguising her vexation at not being able to witness the meeting, the commissioner and I were left in the pavilion with only the company of two or three distant bedridden patients and a young nun silently scrubbing the floor at the far end. I was scarcely sitting up, with the sheet covering me up to my chest, allowing only two increasingly weakened bare arms, my bony shoulders, and my head to emerge. My hair was pulled back into a dark plait to one side of my face, which was thin and ashen, drained by my collapse.

"The sister told me you're already somewhat recovered, so we've got to talk, all right?"

I assented with just a nod of the head, unable even to guess what that man wanted with me; as far as I knew, being torn apart and confused were not against the law. Then the commissioner drew a small notebook from the inside pocket of his jacket and consulted some notes. He must have been going over them recently because he didn't have to riffle through pages to find them; he simply directed his gaze to the page in front of him and there they were.

"Well then, I'll begin by asking you some questions; just answer with a simple yes or no. You are Sira Quiroga Martín, born in Madrid on June eighth, 1911, correct?"

His tone was courteous, which didn't mean it was not direct and inquisitive. A certain deference to my condition lessened the professional tone of the meeting, but it didn't hide it completely. I corroborated the accuracy of my personal details with a nod.

"And you arrived in Tetouan this past July fifteenth, coming from Tangiers."

I nodded again.

"In Tangiers you were lodged from March twenty-third at the Hotel Continental."

Another nod.

"In the company of" — he consulted his notebook — "Ramiro Arribas Querol, native of Vitoria, born October twenty-third, 1901."

I nodded again, this time lowering my gaze. It was the first time I had heard his name after all that time had passed. Commissioner Vázquez didn't seem to notice that I was beginning to lose my composure, or perhaps if he did, he didn't want me to notice it; in any case he proceeded with his interrogation, ignoring my reaction.

"And at the Hotel Continental you left an outstanding bill of three thousand seven hundred and eighty-nine French francs."

I didn't reply. I just turned my head to one side to avoid catching his eye.

"Look at me," he said.

I ignored him.

"Look at me," he repeated. His tone remained neutral: it was no more insistent the second time than the previous time, neither friendlier nor more demanding. It was, quite simply, the same. He waited patiently for a few moments until I obeyed him and looked at him. But I didn't reply. He reformulated his question without losing his temper.

"Are you aware that at the Hotel Continental you left an outstanding bill of three thousand seven hundred and eighty-nine francs?"

"I think so," I replied finally in a whisper. And again I drew my eyes away from his and turned my head back to one side. And I started to cry.

"Look at me," he insisted a third time.

He waited awhile, until he realized that this time I no longer had the intention, or the strength, or the courage to face him. Then I heard him get up from his chair, walk around the foot of the bed, and approach on the other side. He sat down on the neighboring bed, on which my eyes were set, his body destroying the smoothness of the sheets, and fixed his eyes on mine.

"I'm trying to help you, ma'am. Or miss, it's all the same to me," he explained firmly. "You've gotten yourself into a tremendous bit of trouble, although I realize it's not your own fault. I think I know how it all happened, but I need you to confirm my suspicions. If you don't help me, I won't be able to help you, you understand?"

With some effort I managed to say yes.

"Well then, stop crying and let's get down to it."

I dried my tears with the turndown of the sheet. The commissioner gave me a brief minute. No sooner had he sensed that my crying had abated than he was conscientiously back at his task.

"Ready?"

"Ready," I murmured.

"Look, you've been accused by the management of the Hotel Continental of having left a pretty sizable bill unpaid, but that's not all. The matter, regrettably, is much more complicated. We've learned that there is also a charge against you from the Casa Hispano-Olivetti for fraud to the value of twenty-four thousand eight hundred and ninety pesetas."

"But I, but . . ."

He gestured for me to stop talking. He had more to say.

"There is another charge against you for stealing jewelry from a private residence in Madrid."

The impact of what I'd heard destroyed any capacity I had to think or answer coherently. The commissioner, aware of my confusion, tried to calm me.

"I know, I know. Calm down, don't trouble yourself. I've read all the papers you were carrying in your suitcase and from them I've been able more or less to reconstruct what happened. I've found the note you were left by your husband, or your fiancé, or lover, or whatever this Arribas was, and also a certificate confirming these jewels were given to you, and a document setting out that the previous owner of these jewels really is your father."

I didn't remember having brought those papers with me; I didn't know what had become of them since Ramiro had put them away, but if they were among my things it had to be because I had taken them from the hotel room myself without being aware of doing so at the moment of my departure. I sighed with some relief to learn that in them might perhaps be found the key to my redemption.

"Talk to him, please, talk to my father," I begged. "He's in Madrid, his name is Gonzalo Alvarado, he lives on Calle Hermosilla, number nineteen."

"There's no way we can track him down. Communication with Madrid is terrible. The capital is in turmoil, a lot of people are displaced: detained, fled, or leaving, or hidden, or dead. Besides, things for you are even more complicated because the charge came from Alvarado's own son, Enrique, I think that's his name, your half brother, right? Yes, Enrique Alvarado," he confirmed after checking his notes. "It seems a servant informed him a few months back that you had been in the house and had left quite changed, carrying some parcels: they suppose that the jewels were in them, they believe that Alvarado senior might have been the victim of blackmail or submitted to some kind of extortion. In short, a pretty ugly business, even if these documents do appear to exonerate you."

Then he drew from one of the outer pockets of his jacket the papers that my father had given me when we had met months earlier.

"Luckily for you, Arribas didn't take them with him along with the jewels and the money, perhaps because they might have been compromising for him. He ought to have destroyed them in order to protect himself, but in his rush to disappear he didn't. You should be grateful to him, because right now that's the only thing that's going to save you from prison," he observed ironically. Then immediately afterward he closed his eyes briefly, as though trying to draw his last words back in. "Forgive me, I didn't mean to offend you; I imagine that in your state you have no intention of being grateful to a man who's treated you as he has."

I didn't reply to his apology, just weakly formulated another question.

"Where is he now?"

"Arribas? We don't know for sure. Perhaps in Brazil, could be Buenos Aires. Maybe in Montevideo. He boarded a transatlantic ship under the Argentine flag, but he could have disembarked at a number of ports. It seems he was accompanied by three other individuals: a Russian, a Pole, and an Italian."

"And you aren't going to go after him? You aren't going to do anything to follow his trail and arrest him?"

"I'm afraid not. We don't have much on him, just an unpaid bill that he shares with you. Unless you want to press charges for the jewels and the money he took from you, though to tell you the truth I don't think it would be worth it. It's true that it was all yours, but the source is pretty unreliable and you're being accused of theft as well. Anyway, I think it unlikely that we'll hear of his whereabouts again. They're usually pretty smart, these con men, they know the ways of the world and how to disappear and reinvent themselves four days later at any spot on the globe in the most unexpected manner."

"But we were going to start up a new life, we were going to open a business, we were just waiting for confirmation," I babbled.

"You're referring to the thing with the typewriters?" he asked, taking another envelope out of his pocket. "You wouldn't have been able to do it — you didn't have the authorization. The owners of the academies in Argentina didn't have the least interest in expanding their business to the other side of the Atlantic, and they made this clear in April." He saw the confusion in my face. "Arribas never told you that, did he?"

I recalled my daily visits to the reception desk, hopeful, longing to receive that letter that I believed would change our lives. Ramiro had already had it for months without ever letting me know. My resolve to defend him was dissipating, turning to smoke. I clung with what little strength I had to my last remaining trace of hope.

"But he loved me . . ."

The commissioner smiled with a touch of bitterness mixed with something like compassion.

"That's what all his kind say. Look, miss, don't fool yourself: men like Arribas only love themselves. They can be affectionate and seem generous; they're usually charming, but at the moment of truth the only thing that interests them is their own hide, and at the first sign of things getting a little tricky they're out the door like a shot. They'll step on anyone they need to so as not to be caught in a lie. This time the person hurt worst has been you; bad luck, without a doubt. I don't question that he thought highly of you, but one fine day a better project came along and you became a

100

burden he was no longer interested in dragging along. That's why he left you. Don't try and think about it any more. You're not at fault for anything, but there isn't a lot we can do to alter what is irreversible."

I didn't want to plunge further into those thoughts about the sincerity of Ramiro's love; it was too painful for me. I preferred to return to practical matters.

"And the thing with Hispano-Olivetti? What am I supposed to have to do with that?"

He breathed in and breathed out hard, as though readying himself to broach something that didn't appeal to him.

"That business is even more tangled. Right now, there's no cast-iron proof to exculpate you, though personally I would surmise that it's another scam into which you've been drawn by your husband, or your fiancé, or whatever this Arribas is. The official version of the facts is that you are the owner of a business that has received a number of typewriters that were never paid for."

"He thought of setting up a business in my name, but I didn't realize . . . I didn't know . . . I didn't . . . ."

"That's what I believe, that you had no idea about all the things he was using you to front. Let me tell you what I think really happened. Correct me if I'm wrong: your father gave you some money and some jewels, correct?"

I nodded.

"And then Arribas offered to register a company in your name, and to put all the money and jewels away in the safe of the company where he worked, correct?"

I nodded again.

"Well, he didn't do it. Or rather, he did do it, but not as a simple deposit in your name. With that money he made a purchase from his own company, pretending that it was an order from the import-export firm he told you about, Quiroga Typewriters, for which you appeared as owner. He paid punctually with your money, and Hispano-Olivetti suspected absolutely nothing: just one more order, a large one, well negotiated, and that was that. As for Arribas, he then resold the machines, I don't know to whom or how. Thus far everything was quite correct as far as Hispano-Olivetti's accounting was concerned, and satisfactory for Arribas who, without having a single cent of his own money, had done a terrific deal in his favor. Well, a few weeks later he arranged another large order in your name, which was again fulfilled in a timely manner. The full cost of this order wasn't met at the time; only a first installment came in, but since you were known to have good credit no one was suspicious: they imagined that the rest of the sum would be met according to the terms agreed. The problem is that the payment was never made: Arribas once again sold the merchandise, again took the profits and got out, with you and with all your capital practically intact, as well as a good slice he had managed to get with the resale and the purchase he never paid for. A coup, yes indeed, although someone should have suspected something because as I understand it your departure from Madrid was rather abrupt, was it not?"

Like a flash I remembered arriving at our home on the Plaza de las Salesas that March morning, Ramiro's nervous rush in taking the clothes from the wardrobe and filling suitcases, the urgency he instilled in me to do the same without wasting a second. With these images in my mind, I confirmed the commissioner's assumption. He went on.

"And so to cap it all Arribas didn't just take your money, but he had also used it to get greater profit for himself. A very smart guy, no doubt about it."

Tears came to my eyes again.

"Stop that. Keep your tears to yourself, please: there's no point crying over spilt milk. But unfortunately, these things have really happened at the least convenient and most complicated time."

I swallowed, tried to control myself, and managed to resume the conversation one more time. "Because of what you were saying the other day about the war?"

"We still don't know how all this is going to end, but right now the situation is extremely complicated. Half of Spain is in the hands of the rebels, and the other half remains loyal to the government. The situation is unstable and no reliable news is getting out; in short, an utter disaster."

"And here? How are things here?"

"Moderately calm at the moment; in the weeks just past, everything was in much greater turmoil. This is where it all started, didn't you know? It was here that the insurrection arose; it was from here, from Morocco, that General Franco appeared and the troop movements began. There were bombardments in the first few days; the Republic's air force attacked the High Commission in response to the uprising, but through bad luck they missed their target and one of the Fokkers caused quite a few civilian injuries, the death of several Moorish children, and the destruction of a mosque, which was considered by the Muslims to have been an attack on them, and they automatically took the side of the rebels. At the same time, there were also countless arrests and shooting of defenders of the Republic who were against the insurrection: the European prison filled almost to bursting, and they set up a sort of detention camp in El Mogote. Finally with the fall of the Sania Ramel Aerodrome here, very close to this hospital, the government's bastions in the Protectorate were all done for, meaning that now the whole of the north of Africa is controlled by rebel soldiers and the situation is more or less calm. Now the worst of it is happening on the Peninsula."

Then he rubbed his eyes with his left thumb and index finger; after that he moved his palm slowly upward, over his eyebrows, his forehead, and the roots of his hair, over the crown of his head and down the back of his neck until it reached his collar. He spoke low, as though to himself. "Let's just see if this damned business comes to an end once and for all . . ."

I pulled him out of his contemplation: I couldn't contain my uncertainty a second longer. "But am I going to be able to leave or not?"

My untimely question forced him back to reality. Decisive.

"No. Absolutely not. You won't be able to go anywhere, least of all to Madrid. At the moment the government of the Republic is there: the people are supporting it and getting ready to resist for as long as they possibly can."

"But I've got to go back," I insisted weakly.

"That's where my mother is, my home . . ."

He struggled to keep his impatience in check. My insistence was troubling him more and more, though he tried not to contradict me, bearing in mind my delicate state. In other circumstances he might have treated me with much less leniency.

"Look, I don't know which side you're on, if you're with the government or in favor of the insurrection." His voice had recovered all its strength after the brief moment of decline; most likely tiredness and the tension of these turbulent days had momentarily taken their toll. "To be honest, after everything I've had to witness in these past weeks, your position doesn't trouble me all that much; in fact, I'd just rather not know about it. All I do is go on with my work, trying to keep political issues on the sidelines; there are too many people worrying about them already, unfortunately. But ironically, luck — for once, though it's hard to believe — has come down on your side. Here in Tetouan, the heart of the uprising, you'll be absolutely safe because no one but me will take an interest in your business with the law, and believe me, it's pretty murky business. Enough to keep you — under normal conditions — in prison for quite some time."

I tried to protest, alarmed and filled with panic. He didn't let me — he halted my objections with a raised hand and went on talking.

"I imagine that in Madrid by now they've stopped most police proceedings along with any legal cases that aren't political or on a significant scale: with all they've been through, I don't imagine anyone has any interest in coming to Morocco in pursuit of an alleged typewriter company swindler and thief of her father's estate, accused by her own brother. A few weeks ago these would have been reasonably serious matters, but nowadays they're trivial compared to what's happening in the capital."

"And so?" I asked, unsure.

"And so what you're going to do is stay right where you are, not make the slightest attempt to leave Tetouan, and do everything you can to avoid causing the least bit of trouble. My assignment is to oversee the supervision and security of the Protectorate zone, and I don't think you're a great threat to that. But just in case, I don't want you out of my sight. So you'll stay here awhile and steer clear of any kind of trouble. And you are not to consider this a piece of advice or a suggestion; it's got the full force of an order. It's a rather unusual kind of detention: I'm not putting you in jail or restricting you to house arrest, so you will enjoy relative freedom. But you are absolutely forbidden from leaving the city without my prior consent, is that clear?"

"Until when?" I said, without affirming what he had asked. The idea of remaining alone for an indefinite period in that unfamiliar city seemed the worst possible option.

"Until the situation calms down in Spain and we see how things are resolved. Then I'll decide what to do with you; right now I have neither the time nor the means to deal with your affairs. For the immediate future, you'll only have one problem to face: the debt to the hotel in Tangiers."

"But I have no way of paying that much . . . ," I explained, again on the verge of tears.

"I know: I've searched your luggage from top to bottom, and apart from a jumble of clothes and a few papers, I've been able to confirm that you don't have anything else with you. But for now you're the only person we've got whom we can hold responsible, and in this matter you're just as implicated as Arribas. Which means that in his absence, you will be the one who'll have to meet the demands. And I'm afraid I won't be able to get you out of this, because Tangiers knows I've got you here, absolutely under control."

"But he took my money . . . ," I insisted, my voice breaking with tears again.

"I know that, too, and stop that damned crying once and for all, would you please? In his note Arribas makes it all clear: in his own words the scoundrel expresses quite openly that he means to leave you high and dry and without a cent, taking all your belongings with him. And dragging a pregnancy with you that you ended up losing no sooner than you set foot in Tetouan, stepping off the bus."

The confusion in my face, mixed with my tears, pain, and frustration, forced him to frame a question.

"You don't remember? I was the one waiting for you there. We'd got a tip-off from the police in Tangiers alerting us to your arrival. It seems some bellhop in the hotel made a comment to the manager about your hasty departure; he thought you looked strange and raised the alarm. They then discovered that you had left the room with no intention of returning. Since the sum you owed was considerable, they alerted the police, tracked down the taxi driver who had taken you to the La Valenciana bus stop, and discovered that you were headed here. In normal circumstances I would have sent one of my men to fetch you, but with things being so tempestuous lately I now prefer to supervise everything personally to avoid unpleasant surprises, so I decided to find you myself. No sooner had you gotten off the bus than you fainted in my arms; I brought you here myself."

A few blurry recollections were starting to take shape in my memory. The stifling heat of that bus, which everyone just called La Valenciana. The shouting inside, the baskets with live chickens, the sweat and smells coming off the bodies and the bundles that the passengers, Moors and Spaniards, were carrying with them. The feeling of a thick moisture between my thighs. And once we'd arrived in Tetouan, the extreme weakness as I got off, the shock when I realized that a hot substance was running down my legs, a thick, black trickle that I was leaving behind me. No sooner had I touched the tarmac of the new city than a man's voice was emerging from a face half obscured under a hat brim. "Sira Quiroga? Police. Come with me, please." At that moment I was assailed by an infinite weakness, my mind clouding over and my legs no longer able to support me, and I lost consciousness. Now, weeks later, I was once again looking at that face, still uncertain whether it belonged to my executioner or my savior.

"Sister Virtudes has been in charge of passing information on to me about your progress. I've been trying for days to speak to you, but until now they denied me access. They told me you have pernicious anemia, as well as a number of other things. But, well, it seems you're doing better now, which is why they've allowed me to see you and are going to discharge you in the next few days."

"And where will I go?" My anxiety was as overwhelming as my fear. I felt unable to confront

108

an unknown reality all by myself. I'd never done anything without help, I'd always had someone walking ahead to show me the way: my mother, Ignacio, Ramiro. I felt useless, unfit to face life and its challenges alone, unable to survive without a hand leading me firmly, without a head making decisions for me, without a nearby presence in whom to trust, and on whom to depend.

"On that matter," he said, "I've been looking for a place — don't think it's easy, the way things are now. In any case, I want to learn more of your story. So if you feel strong enough I'd like to come back and see you again tomorrow, in case there may be some detail that will help us to resolve the problems that were dumped on you by your husband, your fiancé . . ."

"Or whatever that son of a bitch was," I completed with an ironic grimace as weak as it was bitter.

"Were you married?" he asked.

I shook my head.

"That's better for you," he concluded decisively. Then he consulted his watch. "Well, I don't want to tire you out any further," he said, getting up, "I think that's enough for today. I'll come back tomorrow, I don't know what time; when I have a moment free. We're up to our eyeballs right now."

I watched him as he made his way toward the hospital exit, walking with the agile, determined step of someone who isn't in the habit of wasting time. Sooner or later, when I was fully recovered, I'd have to find out whether that man really did believe in my innocence or just wanted to be rid of the heavy burden that had fallen on him, as though from the sky, at the most inconvenient time. I couldn't think about that then: I was exhausted and afraid, and the only thing I wanted was a deep sleep, and to forget about everything.

Commissioner Vázquez returned the following evening, at seven, maybe eight, when the heat was no longer so intense and the light more filtered. No sooner did I see him come through the door at the far end of the pavilion than I lifted my weight on my elbows and with great effort, almost dragging myself, sat up. When he reached me, he sat down on the same chair as the day before. I didn't even greet him. I just cleared my throat, readied my voice, and began to tell him everything he wished to hear.

CHAPTER SEVEN

That second meeting with Don Claudio took place on a Friday in late August. The following Monday he returned to collect me. He had found lodgings for me and wished to accompany me there. In other circumstances, such apparently chivalrous behavior might have been interpreted differently, but at that time, neither he nor I doubted that his interest in me was strictly professional, that I was simply an object worth having in his safekeeping in order to avoid serious complications.

I was dressed when he arrived, perched on the edge of the already made bed in mismatched clothes that were now too big for me, my hair in an untidy bun. The suitcase at my feet was filled with the miserable remains of my calamity, and my bony fingers were clasped on my lap as I struggled unsuccessfully to gather my strength. When I saw him arrive I tried to get up, but he indicated with a gesture that I should remain seated.

Positioning himself on the edge of the bed opposite mine, he merely said, "Wait. We have to talk."

He regarded me for a few seconds with those dark eyes capable of drilling through a wall. By now I realized that he was neither a grey-haired young man nor a youthful old man: he was a man somewhere between forty and fifty, schooled in manners and skilled in his police work, well built, with a soul somewhat battered from dealing with scum of every kind. A man, I thought, with whom I ought not to have any sort of problem.

"Look, this isn't standard procedure. Due to current circumstances, I'm making an exception for you, but I want you to be absolutely clear about the real situation. Although I personally believe that you're just the unsuspecting victim of a con man, the whole matter has to be settled by a judge, not me. But things being the way they are in these confused times, I fear a lawsuit is out of the question. And nothing will be gained by keeping you locked up in a cell till God knows when. So, just as I told you the other day, I'm going to allow you your freedom, but — pay attention — under supervision and with limited movement. And to remove any temptation I'm not going to return your passport to you. Also, you remain free on the condition that while you recover, you'll find a decent way to earn a living and save enough to pay off your debt to the Continental. I asked them to give you one year to settle the outstanding bill and they accepted. So now you can start finding a way to scrape up this money, from under a rock if need be, but honestly and without getting into any trouble, is that clear?"

"Yes, sir," I murmured.

"And don't fail me; don't try any tricks with me, and don't force me to come down hard on you, because if you cross me I'll set the machinery in motion, and you'll be shipped off to Spain at the earliest opportunity and get seven years in the

Quiñones women's prison before you know what hit you, understand?"

At such a grave threat I was unable to say anything coherent; I just nodded. Then he got up; a couple of seconds later I did the same. He moved quickly and nimbly; I had to make a tremendous effort just to keep up with him.

"So let's be off," he concluded. "Leave that, I'll take the suitcase, you can't even lift your own shadow. I've got the car at the door; say good-bye to the nuns, thank them for looking after you so well, and let's go."

We made our way through Tetouan in his car, and for the first time I was able to appreciate the city that would for an undetermined time become my own. The hospital was on the outskirts; bit by bit as we progressed farther in, the volume of people grew. At nearly midday, the streets were full. Although there were hardly any motorcars around, the commissioner was constantly having to sound his horn to open up a passageway between the bodies moving unhurriedly in a thousand directions. There were men in light-colored linen suits and panama hats, boys in shorts running races, Spanish women with their shopping baskets laden with vegetables, Muslim men in turbans and striped djellabas, Arab women covered in voluminous garments that allowed only their eyes and feet to be seen. There were uniformed soldiers and girls in flowery summer dresses, barefoot local children playing amid the chickens. And the constant din of voices, stray words and phrases in Arabic and Spanish, interminable greetings to the commissioner each time someone recognized his car. It was hard to imagine that in this very setting only weeks earlier there had emerged a movement that was now being considered a civil war.

We didn't initiate any conversation over the course of the drive; our journey wasn't supposed to be a pleasure trip, but a precise step in a procedure for moving me from one place to another. From time to time, however, when the commissioner sensed that something that appeared before our eyes might seem strange or new to me, he gestured to it with his jaw and, his eyes always fixed straight ahead, spoke some concise words to name it. "Riffians," I remember him saying one such time as he indicated a group of Berber women dressed in striped full skirts and big straw hats with colored pom-poms. The ten or fifteen brief minutes of our journey were enough for me to absorb some of the shapes, smells, and names that I would become familiar with during that new phase of my life. The High Commission, the prickly pears, the caliph's palace, the water carriers on their donkeys, the Moorish quarter, the Dersa and the Ghorgiz, the *bakalitos,* the mint.

We got out of the car at the Plaza de España; a couple of Moorish boys rushed over to carry my luggage and the commissioner allowed one of them to do so. Then we went into La Luneta, located next to the Jewish quarter, next to the medina. La Luneta, my first street in Tetouan: narrow, noisy, irregular, and rowdy, full of people, taverns, cafés, and chaotic bazaars where you could buy anything and everything. We reached a large door, went in, and ascended a staircase. The commissioner rang a bell on the first landing.

"Good morning, Candelaria. I'm here with the delivery you were expecting," my companion said to the plump woman in red who had just opened the door, gesturing toward me with a brief movement of his head.

"But what kind of delivery is this, Commissioner?" she replied, placing her hands on her hips and giving a powerful guffaw. Then immediately she stepped aside and let us pass. Her place was sunny, gleaming in its modesty, and of somewhat questionable aesthetics. While she had a seemingly natural flippancy, beneath it you sensed that this visit from the police was making her extremely uneasy.

"A special delivery," he explained, putting the suitcase down in the little foyer beneath a calendar with the image of the Sacred Heart. "You'll have to put this young lady up for a while, and for the time being, without charging her anything; you'll be able to settle accounts with her once she starts to earn her living."

"But my place is filled to the brim, by Christ on the cross! And I get sent at least half a dozen bodies a day that I have to turn away!"

She was lying, of course. This olive-skinned woman was lying, and he knew it.

"I don't want to hear about all your problems, Candelaria; I've told you you're going to have to put her up somehow."

"Since the uprising people haven't stopped turning up in search of lodging, Don Claudio! I've even got mattresses on the floor!"

"That's enough of your tales. The traffic in the Strait has been interrupted for weeks and these days not even seagulls are making the crossing. Like it or not, you'll have to do what I ask; look at it as payment for all the things you owe me. And what's more, you don't just have to give her lodging, you have to help her. She doesn't know anyone in Tetouan, and she's got a pretty ugly story behind her, so make some space for her because this is where she's going to be staying from now on, is that clear?"

"Like water, sir," she replied, without the slightest enthusiasm. "Clear as water."

"So I leave her in your safekeeping. If there's any problem, you know where to find me. I'm not too pleased that this is where she'll be staying; she's already been corrupted, she's not going to learn a lot of good from you, but anyway . . ."

"You don't distrust me now, do you, Don Claudio?"

The commissioner didn't allow himself to be fooled by the woman's playful tone.

"I always distrust everybody, Candelaria; that's what they pay me for."

"And if you think I'm so bad, why in heaven's name are you bringing this jewel to me, my dear commissioner?"

"Because as I've already told you, the way things are, I don't have anywhere else to take her — don't think I'm doing it because I want to. In any case, I'm leaving you responsible for her. Start dreaming up some way for her to make a living: I don't think she'll be able to return to Spain for quite some time, and she has to make some money because she's got a bit of business to settle around here. Let's see if you can't get her hired as a saleswoman in some shop, or in a hairdresser's; somewhere decent, mind you. And be so kind as to stop calling me your dear commissioner — I've told you a hundred times."

She observed me then, paying attention for the first time. Top to bottom, quickly and without curiosity, as though she were simply assessing the

116

amount of weight that had just been dumped on her. Then she returned her gaze to my companion and with mocking resignation accepted the assignment.

"You can be sure that Candelaria will take care of it, Don Claudio. I don't know where I'll put her, but you can rest assured knowing that she'll be in heavenly bliss here with me."

The celestial promises of the landlady apparently didn't sound at all convincing to the policeman, as he still needed to tighten the screws a little more to conclude the negotiations. With modulated voice and index finger raised vertically to the level of his nose, he offered a final piece of advice that didn't allow for any banter in response.

"Just watch out, Candelaria, watch out, be very careful — things are unsettled at the moment and I don't want any more problems than are strictly necessary. So don't think of getting her mixed up in any of your trouble. I don't trust a hair on your head, or hers, so I'll make sure you're watched closely. And if I hear of any strange goings-on I'll bring you before the commission, and not even a Sursum Corda will get you out of there again, clear?"

We both murmured a heartfelt "Yes, sir."

"So the thing is, she's to get better, and then, when she can, start work."

He looked me in the eye, then seemed to hesitate a moment, debating whether to give me a handshake in farewell. Ultimately he chose not to and concluded the meeting with a recommendation and a prediction condensed into four concise words: "Be careful. We'll talk." Then he left, trotting nimbly down the stairs while adjusting his hat, his open hand holding it by the crown. We

117

watched him in silence from the doorway until he had disappeared from view and were about to go back into the house when we heard his footsteps finish their descent and his voice thunder in the stairwell.

"I'll take you both to jail, and once you're there not even the Holy Child of the Remedio will get you out!"

"And screw you, too, you bastard," was the first thing Candelaria said after shutting the door with a shove from her voluminous rear. Then she gave me a reluctant smile, trying to calm my confusion. "A devil of a man, he drives me raving mad; I don't know how he does it, but he doesn't miss a thing, and he's constantly on my back."

Then she sighed so deeply that her bulky bosom filled and emptied as though she had a couple of balloons inside her percale dress.

"Go on, my angel, in you go, I'll be putting you in one of the rooms in the back. This damned uprising! It's turned us all upside down and filled the street with arguments and the barracks with blood! Let's see if all this ruckus ends soon and we can get back to normal life. I'm going out now, I have a few little matters to deal with; you stay here and get settled, and then, when I'm back at lunchtime, you can tell me all about it, nice and slowly."

And with some shouting in Arabic she demanded the presence of a young Moorish girl, just fifteen years old, who came in from the kitchen, drying her hands on a cloth. The two of them started to clear up some bits of junk and change sheets in the tiny, airless room that would be transformed into my bedroom. And there I settled, without the slightest idea of how long my stay would last or what course my future would take.

Candelaria Ballesteros, better known in Tetouan as Candelaria the Matutera — the Smuggler — was forty-seven years old. She passed herself off as a widow, but even she didn't know whether her husband had in fact died on one of his many visits to Spain or whether the letter she'd received seven years earlier from Málaga announcing his demise from pneumonia was no more than the tall tale of a shameless scoundrel to extricate himself from his marriage and make sure no one came looking for him. Fleeing the miseries of the day laborers in the olive groves in the Andalusian countryside, the couple had installed themselves in the Protectorate in 1926, after the Rif War. After that, the two of them had devoted their efforts to various enterprises, whose meager returns he had conveniently invested in partying, brothels, and large glasses of Fundador brandy. They hadn't had children, and when her Francisco vanished, leaving her alone without the contacts in Spain to continue dealing contraband, Candelaria decided to rent an apartment and establish a small boardinghouse. This did not, however, stop her from doing her best to buy, sell, rebuy, resell, sell on credit, exchange, and trade whatever she could lay her hands on. Coins, cigarette cases, stamps, fountain pens, socks, watches, lighters — all of them of shady origin, all with uncertain destinations.

In her house on La Luneta, between the Moorish medina and the newer Spanish *ensanche,* she indiscriminately lodged anyone who showed up at her door asking for a bed, usually people of little means and even fewer hopes. She treated them

119

like anyone else she met: she tried to strike a bargain. I'll buy from you, sell you, sort it out for you; you owe me, I owe you, you sort that out for me. But carefully — always with a certain caution — because Candelaria the Matutera, with her tough bearing, her stormy dealings, and that self-confidence seemingly capable of knocking over the very meanest sort, was no fool, and she knew that when it came to Commissioner Vázquez, she'd better not mess around too much. Perhaps a joke here, a sarcastic comment there, but without letting him get anything over her, never overstepping what was legally acceptable because, as she put it herself, "if he catches me up to something, he'll whisk me off to the police station, and then God only knows."

The sweet little Moorish girl helped me to settle in. Together we unpacked my few belongings and hung them on wire hangers in the closet that was really no more than a wooden crate with a little leftover bit of fabric hung over the front. That piece of furniture, a bare bulb, and an old bed with a coarse stuffed mattress made up all the fittings in the room. An out-of-date calendar with a picture of a nightingale on it, courtesy of El Siglo barbershop, brought the only touch of color to the whitewashed walls marked by the leftovers of a sea of leaks. In one corner, on a trunk, a number of household odds and ends had accumulated: a straw basket, a battered washbowl, two or three chipped chamber pots, and a couple of rusty wire cages. The room was austere, verging on poverty, but it was clean. As she helped me to organize that mess of rumpled clothes that made up the entirety of my belongings, the girl with the jet-black eyes kept repeating in a gentle voice, "Siñorita, you no worry; Jamila wash, Jamila iron Siñorita clothes."

I did not have much strength, and the little extra I'd used to move the suitcase and empty out its contents brought on a sudden wave of dizziness. I sat down at the foot of the bed, closed my eyes, and covered my face with my hands, resting my elbows on my knees. My balance came back in a couple of minutes, then I returned to the present and found that young Jamila was still beside me, watching with concern. I looked around. It was still there, that poor dark mouse hole of a room, with my rumpled clothes on the hangers and my suitcase disemboweled on the floor. Despite the chasm of uncertainty I felt opening before me, I realized with a sense of relief that, however badly things were going, at least I already had my own little hole in which to take shelter.

Candelaria returned an hour later. The others arrived at more or less the same time, the wretched catalog of guests to whom the household offered room and board. The parish was made up of a hair products representative, an employee of the Telegraph and Mail Department, a retired schoolmaster, a couple of sisters advanced in years and shriveled as salted fish, and a rotund widow with her son, whom she called her little "Paquito" in spite of his deep voice and the thick down that he sported on his upper lip. They all greeted me politely when the hostess introduced me and then settled in silence around the table, each in their assigned place: Candelaria at the head, the others spread along the two sides. The women and Paquito on one side, the men opposite. "You at the other end," she commanded. She began to serve the stew, speaking without respite about how much the price of meat had gone up and how well the melons were doing that year. She wasn't aiming her comments at anyone in particular and yet seemed to have a great desire not to yield in her chatter, however trivial the subject and slight the attention of her fellow diners. Without a word, everyone set to their lunch, bringing the cutlery from their plates rhythmically to their mouths. No other sound could be heard than the voice of the hostess, the noise of the spoons against the crockery, and the sounds of chewing and swallowing. A moment of inattention on Candelaria's part eventually allowed me to figure out the reason for her incessant chatter: at her first pause, calling for Jamila from the kitchen, one of the sisters took advantage to drive in her wedge.

"They say Badajoz has fallen." The words of the younger of the two older sisters didn't seem to be directed at anyone in particular either — to the water jug, perhaps, or the salt shaker, or the cruets or the picture of the Last Supper that presided, slightly askew, on the wall. Her tone was meant to seem indifferent, too, as though she were commenting on the temperature that day or the taste of the peas. I learned right away, however, that her comment was as innocent as a recently sharpened blade.

"What a shame; so many good lads who've given their lives to defend the legitimate government of the Republic; so many young, energetic lives wasted, with all that pleasure they could have given to a woman as appealing as you, Sagrario."

The acid-charged reply had come courtesy of the traveling salesman and was met with a laugh from the rest of the men. As soon as Doña Herminia noticed that her little Paquito had also found the salesman's comment funny, she gave the lad a good thwack that left the back of his neck red. Supposedly helping the boy out, the old schoolteacher intervened at this point with his sensible voice. Without lifting his head from his plate, he pronounced, "Don't laugh, Paquito, they say that laughing shrivels the brain."

The moment he'd finished the sentence the child's mother weighed in.

"That's why the army rose up, to put an end to all that laughing, all that joy, and all the licentiousness that's driving Spain to ruin . . ."

Then it was as though hunting season had opened. The three men on one side and the three women on the other raised their voices almost as one, a chicken coop in which no one was listening to anyone and everyone started yelling, letting insults and outrages fly from their mouths. Vicious commie, sanctimonious old cow, son of Lucifer, bitter old hag, atheist, degenerate, and dozens of other epithets shot through the air in a crossfire of angry shouts. The only people who remained silent were Paquito and myself: me because I was new there and had no knowledge or opinion about the outcome of the fighting, and Paquito probably out of fear of another blow. At that moment his mother was accusing the schoolmaster of being a foul Freemason and Satan worshipper, her mouth filled with half-chewed potatoes and a thread of oil running down her chin. At the other end of the table, meanwhile, Candelaria was being transformed, second by second: rage increased her bulk, and her face, which just a moment before had been so agreeable, began to redden until, unable to contain herself any longer, she gave the table a thump with her fist, so hard that the wine jumped from the glasses, the plates clattered, and the stew splashed onto the tablecloth. Like a thunderclap, her voice rose above the other half dozen voices.

"If you talk about this damned war in this blessed house one more time, I'll throw you all into the street and toss your suitcases off the balcony!"

Reluctantly, and exchanging murderous glances, they all furled sails and concentrated on finishing their first course, struggling to contain their fury. The mackerel of the second course was devoured in near silence; the watermelon for dessert threatened danger because of its crimson color, but the tension never exploded. Lunch ended without any further incident; for that, I would only need to wait till dinner. It would all come back then, the ironic comments as a starter, and the double entendres, then the poison-tipped darts and the exchange of blasphemies and people crossing themselves, and finally the untrammeled insults and flying crusts of bread aimed at the eyes of the person opposite. And as a coda, we again heard Candelaria's warning of the imminent eviction of all the guests if they persisted in reenacting the two sides of the conflict. I learned then that it was normal for this ritual to play out at the three daily meals at the boardinghouse, day in and day out. Never once, however, did our hostess cut a single one of the guests loose, despite the fact that they all kept their war nerves on the alert, their tongues sharp, ready to assail the opposing side mercilessly. Those days of scant trade were no time for the Matutera to voluntarily give up what each of those poor homeless devils was paying for room, board, and the right to a weekly bath. So, in spite of all her threats, there were few days that didn't see one side of the table hurling opprobrium at the other, as well as olive pits, political slogans, banana skins, and at the most heated moments an occasional gob of spit and more than one fork. The essence of life itself on the scale of a domestic battle.

CHAPTER EIGHT

And so my stay at the La Luneta boardinghouse began in this way, surrounded by these people about whom I never learned much more than their given names and — very superficially — the reasons they were lodging there. The schoolmaster and the civil servant, both elderly bachelors, were longtime residents; the sisters had traveled from Soria to Morocco in mid-July to bury a relative and saw the Strait closed to marine traffic before they were able to return home; something similar had happened to the hair products salesman, kept in the Protectorate against his will as a result of the insurgency. The mother and son had other reasons that were less clear, though everyone assumed they had come in search of an elusive husband and father who one fine morning had gone out to buy tobacco on Toledo's Plaza de Zocodover and decided never to return home. In time, amid the almost daily skirmishes at the boardinghouse, along with the actual war advancing relentlessly throughout the summer and followed minutely from afar by that gathering of displaced, irate, frightened creatures, I began to get used to this boardinghouse and its underworld. I became closer as well to the owner of the business, which, considering the nature of the clien-

126

tele, I assumed could not bring her very much income.

I didn't go out much in those days: I had nowhere to go, nor anyone to see. I was usually alone, or with Jamila, or with Candelaria when she was around, which was infrequently. Sometimes, when she wasn't bustling off to do her wheeling and dealing, she would insist on taking me out with her, for us to find some work for me. "Otherwise you'll end up with a face like old parchment, girl, if you don't give yourself so much as a flicker of sunlight," she would say. Sometimes I felt unable to accept the invitation, not feeling strong enough, but other times I'd agree, and then she'd take me here and there, through the fiendish maze of streets of the Moorish quarter and the modern, gridlike roads of the Spanish *ensanche* with its beautiful houses and well-turned-out residents. In every establishment whose owner she knew, she would ask if they could find a position for me, if they knew of anyone who had a job for this girl who was so dedicated and ready to work day and night, as I was supposed to be. But those were difficult times, and even though the sounds of gunfire were still far away, everyone seemed discouraged by the uncertain outcome of the fighting, worried about their people back home, about the whereabouts of this one or that one, the advancing of the troops at the front, who had lived and who had died, and what was still to come. In such circumstances almost nobody was interested in expanding a business or hiring new staff. And even though we usually concluded those outings with a glass of mint tea and a tray of savory morsels in some seedy café on the Plaza de España, every frustrated attempt was for me one

127

more shovelful of anxiety dumped onto the pile, and for Candelaria — though she never said as much — a new gnawing worry.

My health improved at the same rate as my spirits, a snail's pace. I was still all skin and bones, and the pallid tone of my complexion contrasted with the faces around me tanned by the summer sun. My emotions were still taut, my soul weary; I still felt as torn apart by Ramiro's abandonment as I had on that first day. I was still pining for the child whose existence I had only been aware of for a few hours, and I was once again consumed with worry over what had become of my mother in Madrid. Still frightened by the charges against me and by Don Claudio's warnings, terrorized at the thought of being unable to make restitution and the possibility of ending up in prison, I had panic as my constant companion.

One of the effects of being crazily, obsessively in love is that it dulls your senses, your capacity for perception, till you no longer notice what is happening around you. It causes you to focus your attention so much on a single person that it isolates you from the rest of the universe, imprisons you inside a shell, and keeps you at a distance from other realities, even those right in front of you. When everything was thrown to the wind, I realized that those eight months I'd spent alongside Ramiro had been so intense that I'd barely had close contact with anyone else. Only then did I become aware of the scale of my loneliness. In Tangiers I hadn't bothered to form relationships with anyone: I wasn't interested in anyone but Ramiro and things to do with him. In Tetouan, however, he was no longer there, and with him had gone my grip on things and my points of reference. So I had to learn to live alone, to think of myself, and to struggle to make the weight of his absence gradually less devastating. As the Pitman Academies leaflet had said, long and steep is the path of life.

August came to an end, and September arrived with its shorter evenings and cooler mornings. The days passed slowly over the bustle of La Luneta. People went in and out of the shops, cafés, and bazaars, crossed streets, paused outside shop windows, and chatted to acquaintances on street corners. As I observed from my vantage point the changing light and all that unstoppable energy, I realized that I, too, urgently needed to get myself moving, to begin some sort of productive activity in order to stop living off Candelaria's charity and to start gathering the money to pay off my debt. I hadn't yet figured out how to do this, however, and to compensate for my inactivity and my non-existent contribution to the economy of the household, I forced myself at least to participate in some of the domestic chores and not be just a lazy lump of furniture. I peeled potatoes, set the table, hung the clothes out to dry on the rooftop terrace. I helped Jamila do the dusting and clean the windows, I learned a few Arabic words from her and allowed her to lavish her endless smiles upon me. I watered the flowers, shook out the pillows, and anticipated little necessities that sooner or later someone would have to deal with. As the temperature changed, the boardinghouse in turn began to ready itself for the arrival of autumn and I helped with that. We stripped the beds in all the rooms — we changed sheets, took off the summer bedcovers, and brought the winter blankets down from the attic. I noticed then that a lot of the linens needed mending, so I took a big basket of bed linen out to the balcony and sat down to mend tears, strengthen hems, and tidy up frayed edges.

And that day something unexpected happened. I never could have imagined that the feeling of a needle between my fingers would be so pleasing. Those rough bedspreads and coarse linen sheets had nothing in common with the silks and muslins of Doña Manuela's workshop, and the mending of their imperfections was a world away from the delicate backstitching that I had dedicated myself to in order to assemble clothes for the fine ladies of Madrid. Nor did Candelaria's modest dining room resemble Doña Manuela's workshop, nor did the presence of the Moorish girl and the incessant comings and goings of the rest of the quarrelsome guests correspond with the figures of my old working companions and the refinement of our customers. But the rhythm of my wrist was just the same, and the needle was once again moving quickly before my eyes as my fingers toiled away to get the stitches just right, just as they had done for years, day after day, in another place and for other ends. The satisfaction of sewing again was so pleasing that for a couple of hours I was taken back to happier times and managed temporarily to dissolve the leaden weight of my own miseries. It was like being back home.

Evening fell and there was barely any light left by the time Candelaria returned from one of her incessant outings. She found me surrounded by piles of recently mended clothes, with the last towel in my hands.

"Girl, don't tell me you know how to sew."

For the first time in a long while, I smiled, and

my reply was an almost triumphant yes. And then the boardinghouse owner, relieved at having finally found some use for the burden that my presence had become, took me to her bedroom and proceeded to dump out the entire contents of her closet onto the bed.

"You can lower the hem of this dress and turn out the collar of this coat. This shirt has seams that need fixing, and the skirt needs to be let out a little at the waist since I've put on a bit of weight lately and there's no way I can get into it."

And so on, until there was a huge mountain of old clothes I could barely carry. It took me just one morning to fix the imperfections in her worn-out wardrobe. Satisfied with my efficiency, and resolved to gauge the full potential of my productivity, Candelaria came home that afternoon with a piece of cheviot wool for a three-quarter coat.

"English wool, the very best. We used to bring it over from Gibraltar before all this fuss started; now it's extremely difficult to get hold of. Do you dare?"

"Get me a good pair of scissors, two yards of lining, half a dozen tortoiseshell buttons, and a spool of brown thread. I'll take your measurements right now and tomorrow morning it'll be ready for you."

With those frugal means and the dining table as my center of operations, by dinnertime I had the commission ready for trying on. It was all complete before breakfast. No sooner had she opened her eyes, still sticky with sleep, and her hair held in a net, than Candelaria had arranged the coat over her nightdress and incredulously considered the effect in the mirror. The shoulders sat impeccably on her frame, and the lapels opened out to

131

the sides in perfect symmetry, masking the excessive size of her bosom. The fit was graceful with a generous waist and a skillful cut so that it disguised the bulk of her marelike hips. The broad, elegant cuffs put the finishing touch on my work and her arms. The result couldn't have been more satisfactory. She looked at herself, facing forward and in profile, from the back and three-quarters on. Once, again; now buttoned, now open, collar up, collar down. Her talkativeness contained for the moment, she focused on making a precise evaluation of the product. Again from the front, again from the side. And at last, the verdict.

"Well, I'll be damned! Why didn't you ever tell me you had hands like that, my angel?"

Two new skirts, three blouses, a shirtdress, a couple of suits, an overcoat, and a winter smock soon took their places on her hangers as she bargained for new pieces of fabric on the street, paying as little as she could.

"Chinese silk, just feel that, touch it," she chattered excitedly as she opened her parcel and laid before my eyes a couple of yards of flame-colored fabric. "The Indian from the lower bazaar got two American lighters out of me for this — damn him to hell and back — it's just as well I had a couple of them left from last year, because the bastard only wants silver hassani coins now; everyone's saying they're going to withdraw the Republican money and replace it with Nationalist banknotes — girl, such madness . . ."

On another outing she brought back a half roll of gabardine — "the good stuff, honey, the good stuff." A pearly satin remnant arrived the following day, accompanied by the corresponding account of how she'd gotten hold of it, and none-too-honorable references to the mother of the Jew from whom she'd acquired it. A leftover piece of caramel-colored flannel, a bit of alpaca, seven yards of patterned satin, and so on, until between dealing and swapping we had reached almost a dozen fabrics, which I cut and sewed and she tried on and praised. Until one day, when her clever ways of getting hold of the material were exhausted, or she thought her new wardrobe was at last well stocked, or she had decided the time had come to focus her attention on other tasks.

"With all the things you've made for me, your debt to me up to today is settled," she announced. And without even giving me time to savor my relief, she went on: "Now we're going to talk about the future. You've got a lot of talent, girl, and that shouldn't be wasted, specially not at this moment when you're just a little bit lacking in the cash to get yourself out of the mess you're in. You've seen how complicated it is to find you a position, so it seems to me that the best thing for you to do is to concentrate on sewing for the people in Tetouan. But the way things are, I'm afraid you'll find it hard to get people to open their doors to you. You'll have to have your own place, set up your own workshop, and even then it's not going to be easy for you to get customers. We've really got to think it through."

Candelaria the Matutera knew every living creature in Tetouan, but to be quite sure of the state of the sewing business and focus on finding just the right location, it was necessary to go out quite a few times, catch up with the odd contact here and there, and do a thorough study of the situation. A couple of days after the birth of the idea we had a one hundred percent reliable picture

133

of the lay of the land. I learned then that there were two or three well-established prestigious designers who were frequented by the wives and daughters of the military commanders, a few respected doctors, and the businessmen who were still solvent. One level down, you'd find four or five decent dressmakers for street wear and Sunday coats for the women of the more well-to-do families of the administrative staff. And finally there were several handfuls of insignificant seamstresses who made their rounds from house to house, cutting percale smocks, altering hand-me-downs, taking up hems, and darning socks. The landscape was hardly ideal: there was considerable competition, but somehow I'd have to work things out and manage to find a niche for myself. And even though, according to Candelaria, none of those sewing professionals was by any means dazzling, and most of them were made up of a cast of characters who were domestic, almost family, that wasn't any reason to underestimate them: when they worked well, dressmakers could earn their clients' loyalties for life.

The idea of going back to being active again raised conflicting feelings in me. On the one hand it managed to create a little flutter of hopefulness that I hadn't felt for an eternity. Being able to earn money to support myself and settle my debts by doing something I liked and I knew I was good at was the best thing that could have happened to me just then. At the same time, anxiety and uncertainty plagued my soul. To open my own business, humble though it might be, required initial capital, contacts, and a whole lot more luck than life had been offering me lately. It wouldn't be easy to carve out a space for myself as just one more dressmaker; to overcome loyalties and win customers I'd have to come up with something out of the ordinary, to set me apart.

While Candelaria and I struggled to find a path for me to follow, a number of her friends and acquaintances began coming to the boardinghouse to place a few orders with me: just this blouse, girl, if you wouldn't mind; just a few overcoats for the kiddies before the cold sets in. On the whole they were humble women, with spending power to match. They would arrive with many children and a few scraps of fabric, and they'd sit down to talk to Candelaria while I sewed. They sighed over the war and cried about the luck of their people in Spain, drying their tears with the end of the handkerchief they kept bundled up in their sleeve. They complained about the poverty of the times and wondered anxiously what they would do to help their offspring to get on in life if the conflict continued or an enemy bullet killed their husband. They paid little and late, or sometimes not at all, as best they could. And yet, in spite of the constraints of the clientele and the modest nature of their commissions, the mere fact of being back at my sewing managed to mitigate the harshness of my distress and open up a tiny chink through which a slim ray of light began to filter.

CHAPTER NINE

At the end of the month it began to rain, one afternoon, then the next, and the next. In three days the sun barely came out; there was thunder, lightning, and mad winds that scattered leaves onto the wet ground. I kept working on the garments that the neighborhood women commissioned from me: clothes with neither grace nor class, creations in coarse fabrics whose function was to protect bodies from the inclemencies of the weather with little attention to aesthetics. Until one afternoon, when I had just finished a jacket for a neighbor's grandson and was about to start on a pleated skirt ordered by the janitor's daughter, Candelaria came in, enveloped in one of her excitable moods.

"I've got it, girl, it's all set, it's all arranged!"

She'd come in from the street wearing her new woolen jacket tied tightly at the waist, a shawl over her head, and her old shoes with the twisted heels covered in mud. She continued to chatter rapidly as she removed her outer clothes, recounting the details of her great discovery. Her powerful bust rose and fell rhythmically with her labored breathing as she spelled out her news while peeling off layers like an onion.

"I've just come from the hairdresser's where my

dear friend Remedios works. I had a few bits and pieces of business to sort out with her, and while Reme was doing a permanent wave on a *gabacha* —"

"A what?" I interrupted.

"A *gabacha*. A frog. A Frenchy," she clarified hurriedly before going on. "The truth is, that's how it looked to me, that she was a *gabacha*. I then discovered that she wasn't French, she was a German I hadn't met before, because all the others, the consul's wife, and the wives of Gumpert and Bernhardt, and Langenheim's, too, who isn't German but Italian, those ones I do know all too well, as we've had some small dealings. Anyway, as I was saying, as Reme was combing away, she asked me where I got such a splendid jacket. And I, of course, told her that I'd had it made for me by a friend, and then the *gabacha*, who, as I said, turned out not to be a *gabacha* at all but a German, looked at me and did a double take. Then she got into the conversation, and with that accent of hers that sounds like she's about to sink her teeth into your neck, well, she told me she needs someone to sew for her, and if I know any high-quality dressmaker's establishment, really high end, because she hasn't been long in Tetouan and she'll be staying awhile, and basically that she needs someone. So I said to her —"

"That she should come here for me to sew for her," I concluded.

"What are you saying, girl? I can't have a dame like that here. These women go around with generals' wives and colonels' wives, and they're used to other kinds of things and other kinds of places, you have no idea how stylish this German woman was, and the kind of money she must have."

"So?"

"So, I don't know what crazy things were happening in my head, but I told her straight out that I'd heard that there's going to be a haute couture house opening."

I swallowed hard.

"And I'm supposed to run it?"

"Well, of course, my angel, who else?"

I tried to swallow again but this time couldn't manage it. My throat had suddenly gone dry as sandpaper.

"How am I supposed to set up a haute couture house, Candelaria?" I asked, fearful.

Her first response was to laugh. Her second, five words enunciated with such self-confidence that it left no room for the least doubt on my part.

"With me, honey, with me."

I survived dinner with a battalion of nerves dancing through my guts. Before dinner Candelaria hadn't been able to clarify anything more for me because no sooner had she made her announcement than the sisters arrived in the dining room with a triumphant commentary on the liberation of Alcázar de Toledo. Soon the rest of the guests joined us, one group overflowing with satisfaction and the other brooding in disgust. Then Jamila began to lay the table and Candelaria had no choice but to head for the kitchen to set about organizing dinner: sautéed cauliflower and one-egg omelet; everything economical, everything nice and soft so that the guests couldn't re-create a battle at the front by hurling cutlet bones furiously at one another's heads.

The well-seasoned dinner came to an end with

its customary strains, and each of the residents retired promptly from the dining room. The women and Paquito headed for the sisters' room to listen to Queipo de Llano's nightly harangue on Radio Seville. The men left for the Unión Mercantil to have their final coffee of the day and chat with one another about the progress of the war. Jamila cleared the table and I was about to help her with the dishes when Candelaria, with a solemn expression on her dark face, pointed me toward the corridor.

"Go to your room and wait for me, I'll be right there."

It didn't take her two minutes to join me, which she spent speedily putting on her nightdress and housecoat, checking from the balcony that the three men were well on their way up Callejón de Intendencia and making sure that the women were conveniently enthralled by the crazy radiophonic torrent of words from the rebel general. "Good evening, gentlemen! Be of good cheer!" I was waiting for her with the lights out, barely settled on the edge of my bed, troubled and nervous. It was a relief hearing her arrive.

"We've got to talk, girl. You and I have to have a very serious talk," she said in a low voice as she sat down beside me. "So let's see — are you all ready to set up a workshop? Are you ready to be the best dressmaker in Tetouan, to sew clothes no one has ever sewn before?"

"I'm ready to, of course I am, Candelaria, but —"

"I'm not interested in any 'buts.' Now you listen closely and don't interrupt. After the meeting with the German woman at my friend the hairdresser's, I've been asking around and it turns out that lately

139

we've started to have people here in Tetouan we never had before. Like you, or the scrawny sisters, or Paquito and his fat mother, or Matías the hair products man. With the uprising you all ended up here, trapped like rats, unable to cross the Strait to return to your homes. Well, other people have had more or less the same thing happen to them, but instead of being a herd of starvelings like the lot of you, whom fortune has dropped on me, they're people of means, do you understand what I'm telling you, girl? There's a very famous actress who came over with her company and had to stay. There's a handful of foreign ladies, especially Germans, whose husbands — according to what people are saying — helped Franco get his troops across the Peninsula. And others like that: not many, true, but enough to give you work for quite a while if you can get them as clients. They don't have loyalty to any other dressmakers because they're not from here. And what's more — and this is most important of all — they've got good money. They're foreign and this war doesn't mean anything to them, so they feel like partying and they're not going to spend however long this mess lasts dressing themselves in rags and torturing themselves over who's won what battle, you understand me, my angel?"

"Of course, I do, Candelaria, but —"

"Sssshhhh! I've told you I don't want to hear any 'buts' till I've finished talking. Now let's see: what you need now, right now, right away, without delay, is a high-class place where you can offer your customers the best of the best. I swear on my mother's grave I've never seen anyone sew like you in my life, so you've got to get to work immediately. And yes, I know you haven't got a bean, but that's what Candelaria is for."

"But you don't have any money either; you spend all day complaining that you don't have enough to feed us."

"You're right, I'm broke. It's been very hard to get hold of merchandise lately at the borders. They've posted soldiers armed up to the teeth, and it's not humanly possible to get past them to Tangiers to find goods unless you have fifty thousand safe-conducts, which no one is going to give me. And getting to Gibraltar is even harder, with the Strait closed to traffic and the low-flying warplanes ready to bomb anything that moves. But I've got a way for us to get the rooms we need to set up the business; something that — for the first time in my whole damned life — has come to me without my seeking it out and for which I haven't even had to leave my house. Come over here and I'll show you."

Then she went over to the corner of the room where all the useless odds and ends were heaped.

"First just pop down the corridor and check if the sisters have still got their radio on," she commanded in a whisper.

By the time I returned with confirmation that that was indeed the case, she had moved away the cages, the basket, the chamber pots, and the basins. All that was left in front of her was the trunk.

"Lock the door, turn on the light, and come over here," she demanded imperiously without raising her voice any more than she had to.

The bare bulb on the ceiling quickly filled the room with a dim glow. When I appeared at her side she had just lifted the lid. At the bottom of the trunk was a piece of rumpled, filthy blanket.

141

She lifted it out carefully, almost delicately.

"Take a good look in there."

What I saw rendered me speechless, nearly life-less. A pile of dark pistols, ten, twelve, perhaps fifteen or twenty of them were scattered at the bottom in disarray, their barrels pointed every which way, like a platoon of sleeping assassins.

"Did you see them?" she whispered. "I'll close it back up. Give me the material to put on top, and turn the light out again."

Candelaria's voice, though quiet, was just as it always was; I never knew how mine sounded because the impact of what I'd just seen prevented me from formulating a single word for quite some time. We returned to the bed and she resumed her whispering.

"Some say this business with the uprising took people by surprise, but that's a dirty lie. Absolutely everybody knew there was some powerful stuff brewing. Everyone was preparing for quite some time, and not only in the barracks and at the Ll-ano Amarillo. They say that even in the Spanish Casino there was an arsenal hidden behind the bar; it's anyone's guess whether that's true or not. In the first weeks of July, I had a customs agent lodged in this room awaiting his posting, or at least that's what he said. Things smelled a bit fishy to me, why should I lie to you, because if you ask me that man wasn't a customs agent or anything even close. But, well, since I never ask questions because I don't like people getting involved in my dealings either, I made up his room, put a hot meal on the table for him, and that was that. After July eighteenth I never saw him again. Whether he joined the uprising, or he ran off through the Moorish villages to the French zone, or they took him off to Monte Hacho and had him shot the next morning, I haven't the faintest idea. And I didn't ask, either. The thing was, after four or five days, they sent this little lieutenant over to me to collect his belongings. Without a word I handed over what little there was in the wardrobe, made the sign of the cross, considered the matter closed. But when Jamila was cleaning the room for the next guest and sweeping under the bed I suddenly heard her scream as if she'd seen the devil himself holding his pitchfork, or whatever the Muslims take for the devil. Right there, in the corner, she'd run the broom into this pile of guns."

"So then you kept them?" I asked in a whisper.

"What else was I going to do? Was I supposed to go out searching for the lieutenant at headquarters with everything that was going on?"

"You could have handed them over to the commissioner."

"To Don Claudio? You're crazy, girl!"

This time it was me who with a loud "sssshhhh" quieted her down.

"Why would I give the pistols to Don Claudio? As it is, he's got me on a leash, you want him to lock me up for life? I kept them because they were in my house, and what's more, the customs agent still owed me for two weeks, so the guns were more or less payment. They're worth a lot of money, girl, even more now, the way things are, so those pistols are mine and I can do whatever I please with them."

"And you're planning to sell them? That could be very dangerous."

"Well, for crying out loud, *of course* it's dangerous, but we need the cash to set up your business."

"Candelaria, don't tell me you're going to get yourself mixed up in all this trouble just for me . . ."

"No, child, no," she interrupted. "Let's see if I can explain. I'm not getting mixed up in any trouble on my own, we're doing it together. I'll be responsible for finding someone who wants to buy the merchandise and with whatever I can get for it we'll set up your workshop and split the profits fifty-fifty."

"Why don't you sell them yourself and get what you can for them without setting up a business for me?"

"Because that's bread for today and hunger tomorrow, and I'm more interested in something that'll give me a return in the long run. If I sell the goods and in two or three months everything I get for them goes straight into the cooking pot, what will I live on if the war goes on?"

"What if they catch you trying to sell the pistols?"

"Then I'll tell Don Claudio it's something we're both in together, and we'll end up going wherever he sends us."

"To prison?"

"Or the civilian cemetery, depending on where the bastard decides."

Although she had made this last grim prediction with a teasing wink, my feeling of panic was increasing by the second. Commissioner Vázquez's steely stare and his severe warnings remained fresh in my memory. Stay away from any trouble, don't mess around with me, behave respectably. His words had created a whole chain of undesirable associations: police station, women's prison, robbery, fraud, debt, charge, trial. And now, as if

144

that were not enough, arms dealing.

"Don't get yourself mixed up in this trouble, Candelaria, it's too dangerous," I begged her, scared to death.

"Then what will we do?" she asked in a rushed whisper. "Live on air? Eat snot? You arrived without a cent, and I no longer have any means myself. As for the other guests, the only ones who pay me are the mother, the schoolteacher, and the telegraph man, and we'll see just how long they manage to stretch out the little they have. The other three wretches and you have showed up with just the clothes on your backs, but I can't throw you out on the street. Them out of charity and you because the last thing I need would be to have Don Claudio coming after me for explanations. So you tell me how I'm going to manage."

"I can keep sewing for the same women; I'll work more, I'll stay awake all night if I have to. We'll split what I earn between the two of us . . ."

"And how much is that? How much do you think you can earn making tatty old clothes for the neighbors? A few coins here and there? Have you already forgotten how much you owe in Tangiers? Are you planning to live in this lousy little room for the rest of your life?" The words tumbled out of her mouth in a flustered, hissing torrent. "Look, honey, with those hands of yours you've got an enormous treasure, and it's a terrible sin not to make the most of it as God wants you to. I know life has given you some harsh blows, that your fiancé behaved very badly toward you, that you're in a city where you don't want to be, far from your country and your family, but this is what there is, what's happened has happened and time never goes backward. You've got

145

to press ahead, Sira. You've got to be brave, take risks, fight for yourself. With the misadventures you've been through, no nice young gentleman is about to come knocking on your door to set you up in an apartment. What's more, after your experience, I don't think you're going to want to depend on a man for quite some time, either. You're very young, and at your age you can still hope to make a new life for yourself. Something better than letting your best years shrivel away sewing hems and sighing over what you've lost."

"But this thing with the guns, Candelaria, selling the guns . . . ," I murmured fearfully.

"That's what there is, child; that's what we've got, and I swear to you on my mother's grave that I mean to get as much as I can from them. You think I wouldn't prefer that it was something cleaner, that instead of pistols they'd left me a cargo of Swiss watches or silk stockings? Of course I would. But it just so happens that the only things we've got are weapons, and it just so happens that we're at war, and it just so happens that there are people who might be interested in buying them."

"But what if they catch you?" I asked again uneasily.

"And there she goes again! Well, if they pick me up, we pray to Christ of Medinaceli that Don Claudio has a little pity in him, we swallow a spell in the clink, and that's all there is to it. I should remind you that you only have eleven months left to pay your debt, and at the rate you're going you won't be able to cover it in twenty years sewing for the women on the streets. So however honorable you may want to be, the way you're insisting on going about things, not even a guardian angel will be able to keep you out of prison. Or from

146

ending up spreading your legs in some run-of-the-mill brothel giving soldiers just back from the front a little release."

"I don't know, Candelaria, I don't know. It scares me so much . . ."

"You know, I get the shits, too, thinking of death, even though you may think I'm made of stone. Doing my usual little deals isn't the same thing as trying to put a dozen and a half revolvers on the market during wartime. But we have no other way out, child."

"How would you do it?"

"Don't you worry about that, I'll track down my contacts. I don't think it'll take more than a few days to shift the merchandise. And then we'll find a place in the best part of Tetouan, we'll set everything up, and you'll get started."

"What do you mean, 'you'll get started'? What about you? Aren't you going to be in the workshop with me?"

She laughed silently and shook her head.

"No, child, no I won't. I'll be in charge of getting you the money to pay the first few months' rent and buy what you need. Then, when everything's ready, you'll get to work and I'll stay here, in my house, waiting for the end of the month when we divide up the profits. What's more, it's better if people don't associate you with me: I've hardly got the best reputation, and I don't belong to the same class as the ladies we need as customers. So I'll take charge of providing the initial money, and you provide the hands. Then we share. That's what's called an investment."

A slight scent of Pitman Academies and Ramiro's plans suddenly invaded the darkness in the room, and I was about to travel back to an

147

earlier phase in my life that I had no wish to relive. I banished the feeling with invisible slaps and returned to reality in search of more clarification.

"What if I don't earn anything? If I can't get the customers?"

"Well, then we're in a mess. But don't be too pessimistic. There's no need to go expecting the worst: we've got to be positive and just face up to the matter. No one is going to come along and sort out your life or mine what with all the miseries we have behind us, so we either struggle for ourselves or we won't be left with any choice but to fight hunger off with our fists."

"But I gave the commissioner my word that I wouldn't get into any trouble."

Candelaria had to struggle not to laugh.

"And my Francisco promised me — in front of the village priest — that he'd respect me till the end of his days, and the son of a bitch beat me more than a rug, damn him. It's hard to believe, girl, just how innocent you still are after all the blows luck has given you lately. Think about yourself, Sira, think about yourself and forget everything else, because in these bad times, it's a case of eat or be eaten. What's more, things aren't really as serious as all that: we're not going to shoot anyone, we're just going to move some merchandise we have left over, and as they say, if it's a gift from God, then Saint Peter should bless it. If everything works out well, Don Claudio will see your business all set up, nice and clean and shiny, and if he ever asks you where you got the cash, you tell him I lent it to you out of my savings, and if he doesn't believe you or he doesn't like the idea, he should have left you in the hospital in the care of the Sisters of Charity

148

instead of bringing you to my place. He's always tied up with a heap of problems and never wants any trouble, so if we give him everything without making any noise, he won't bother with investigations. I'm telling you, I know him well; we've been butting heads for years now. You don't have to worry about him."

Despite her bravado and her peculiar philosophy of life, I knew that Candelaria was right. The more times we went around and around the subject, however much we turned it upside down and inside out, looked at it front and back, this pitiful plan was quite simply a reasonable solution to remedy the miseries of two poor women, alone and rootless, who in rough times were dragging heavy pasts behind them. Propriety and honor were lovely concepts, but they didn't give you food to eat, or pay your debts, or take away your cold on winter nights. Moral principles and irreproachable behavior were for another kind of creature, not for an unhappy pair with battered souls.

Candelaria interpreted my silence as a proof of assent. "Well then? I start moving the goods tomorrow?"

I felt myself dancing blindly on the edge of a precipice. In the distance, the radio waves were still broadcasting General Queipo's incendiary speech from Seville between bits of interference. I sighed deeply. My voice sounded, at last, low and sure. Or almost.

"Let's do it."

My partner-to-be, satisfied, smiled and gave me a tender pinch on the cheek. Then the wily old survivor got ready to leave, rearranging her housecoat and hoisting her large frame up over the shabby old cloth slippers that had probably

been with her for half her lifetime. Candelaria the
Matutera, the opportunist, quarrelsome, shameless, and charming, was already at the door on
her way out to the hallway when, still speaking in
a half whisper, I threw out my last question. In reality, it hardly had anything to do with what we'd
been talking about that night, but I felt a certain
curiosity to know what her reply would be.

"Candelaria, whose side are you on in this war?"

She turned, surprised, but didn't hesitate a
second before replying in a potent whisper.

"Me? I'm a diehard supporter of whichever side
wins, my angel."

CHAPTER TEN

The days following that encounter with the pistols were terrible. Candelaria bustled about incessantly from her room to mine, from the dining room out to the street, from the street to the kitchen, always in a hurry, focused, muttering a muddled litany of grunts and growls whose meaning no one could decipher. I didn't interfere in her comings and goings, nor did I ask how the negotiations were doing; I knew that when everything was ready she'd be sure to fill me in.

A week passed, until — at last — she had something to announce. She returned home after nine o'clock that night, when we were already sitting before our empty plates, awaiting her arrival. Dinner went ahead as usual, lively and confrontational. When it was over, as the guests scattered around the boardinghouse to get on with their final activities of the day, we began to clear the table together. As we were carrying away the dirty dishes and cutlery, she spilled out to me drop by drop the remainder of her plans. "Tonight the matter will all be set, honey; the deed will be done. Tomorrow morning we'll start to get your thing moving; I can't wait to be over with this damned mess, angel, once and for all."

No sooner had we finished the chores than each

of us shut herself in her room without exchanging another word. The rest of the troop, meanwhile, were finishing their nighttime routines: eucalyptus gargles, the radio, hair curlers in front of the mirror, going over to the café. Trying to feign normality I threw a good-night out into the air before going to bed. I remained awake awhile, until bit by bit all the activity died down. The last thing I heard was Candelaria leaving her room and then — barely making a sound — closing the front door.

I fell asleep a few minutes after she'd gone out. For the first time in days I didn't toss and turn for hours, nor was I visited by the dark portents of the previous nights — prison, police station, arrests, death. It was as though my nerves had finally decided to give me a respite on learning that the grim business was nearly over. I submerged myself in sleep, curled up with the sweet premonition that the following morning we'd begin to plan our future without the dark shadow of the pistols over our heads.

But my rest didn't last long. I don't know what time it was — two, three perhaps — when a hand grabbed my shoulder and shook me vigorously.

"Wake up, girl, wake up."

I partly sat up, disoriented, still asleep.

"What's going on, Candelaria? What are you doing here? You're back already?" I managed to say with some difficulty.

"A disaster, child, a huge catastrophe," the Matutera replied in a whisper.

She was standing alongside my bed, and through the fog of my sleepiness her voluminous figure seemed rounder than ever. She was wearing an overcoat I didn't recognize, big and broad, done

152

up to the neck. She began to unbutton it quickly as she gave flustered explanations.

"The army has been watching all the roads into Tetouan and the men who were coming from Larache to collect the merchandise didn't dare come this far. I waited till nearly three in the morning without anyone showing up, and eventually they sent me some Berber kid to tell me that the access routes were much more heavily guarded than they'd thought, that they were afraid they wouldn't be able to get out alive if they were to come into town."

"Where were you supposed to meet them?" I asked, forcing myself to put everything she had been saying into place.

"In the lower Suica, around the back of a coal yard."

I didn't know the place she was referring to but didn't try to clarify it any further. In my still sleepy head our failure was already being sketched in thick dark strokes: good-bye to the business, good-bye to the dressmaker's studio. Welcome back to the uneasiness of not knowing what would become of me.

"So it's all over then," I said, rubbing my eyes to remove the last vestiges of sleep.

"Nothing of the sort, honey," Candelaria stopped me, finishing taking off her coat. "We may have been forced to change our plans, but by all that's holy I swear to you those pistols will be flying out of this house tonight. So get moving, girl, get up, there's no time to lose."

It took me a moment to understand what she was saying to me; my attention was focused on another matter: the image of Candelaria undoing the large shapeless dress she was wearing under

153

the coat, a sort of loose smock of coarse wool that barely allowed you to make out the generous shape of her body. I watched in amazement as she undressed, not understanding the meaning of what she was doing and unable to work out the reason for that hurried stripping at the foot of my bed. Until, having removed her skirt, she began to extract objects hidden among her dense flesh. And then I understood. She had four pistols carried in her garters, six in her belt, two in the straps of her brassiere, and another pair under her armpits. The remaining five were in her handbag, tied into a piece of cloth. Nineteen in total. Nineteen butts with their nineteen barrels ready to leave the warmth of that robust body to be transported to a destination that at that very moment I began to suspect.

"And what do you want me to do?" I asked, terrified.

"Take these weapons to the train station, hand them over before six in the morning, and bring back the nine and a half thousand pesetas that were agreed on for the merchandise. You know where the station is, don't you? Across the Ceuta road, at the foot of the Ghorgiz. There the men can collect it without having to enter Tetouan. They'll be coming down from the mountain and they'll head right over to collect it before dawn, without having to set foot in the city."

Shock cut my sleepiness off at the root and suddenly I was awake as an owl.

"But why do I have to be the one to take them?"

"Because when I was coming back from the Suica, making a detour to figure out the best way to arrange things for the train station, that son of a bitch Palomares was coming out of the El An-

154

daluz bar as it was closing. He stopped me at the gate of the Intendencia Barracks and told me that tonight he just might decide to come by the boardinghouse to carry out a search."

"Who's Palomares?"

"The nastiest piece of work of all the cops in Spanish Morocco."

"One of Don Claudio's?"

"He works under his command, yes. When he's with him he sucks up to him, but when he's off on his own, all his nastiness comes out. He's terrorized half of Tetouan with threats of locking them up for life."

"Why did he stop you tonight?"

"Because he felt like it, because that's the kind of pig he is, and he likes lashing out and frightening people, especially women; he's been doing it for years, and these days even more."

"But did he suspect anything about the pistols?"

"No, child, no; fortunately he didn't ask me to open my handbag nor did he dare touch me. He just said to me in that horrible voice of his, Where are you going so late, Matutera, you're not mixed up in one of your shady little deals, you crooked old bitch, and I replied, I've just been visiting a dear friend of mine, Don Alfredo, who's in a bad way with kidney stones. I don't trust you, Matutera, you're such a slut, a crook, the brute said right back to me, and I bit my tongue to stop myself from answering back, although I was about to shit all over his ancestors. But I just kept walking with my handbag tightly under my arm, trusting to Holy Mary that the pistols wouldn't shift around on my body, and then I heard his filthy voice behind me saying, Just the same I'm going to come by your boardinghouse and give the place a good search, you old tart, just to see what I might find."

"You really think he's going to come?"

"He might, he might not," she replied, shrugging. "If he manages to find himself a poor whore who'll turn a trick for him and give him a bit of relief, then he'll forget all about me. But if he can't get it up tonight, I wouldn't be surprised if he knocked on the door, threw the guests into the hallway, and turned my house upside down without batting an eye. It wouldn't be the first time."

"So you can't leave the boardinghouse all night, just in case," I whispered slowly.

"That's right, my angel," she said.

"And the pistols have got to disappear immediately so that Palomares doesn't find them here," I added.

"Exactly."

"And we have to hand over the guns today because the buyers are waiting for them and won't risk their lives coming into Tetouan to get them."

"You couldn't have put it more clearly, my princess."

We remained silent for a few seconds, looking each other tensely in the eye. We must have looked pitiful, her standing half naked with rolls of flesh spilling out of her bra and girdle, me sitting cross-legged under the sheets in my nightdress, with my hair disheveled and my heart clenched. Not to mention the scattered black pistols.

Finally Candelaria spoke, her firm words emphasizing her certainty. "You've got to deal with it yourself, Sira. We have no other way out of this."

"I can't do it, I can't . . . ," I stammered.

"You've got to do it, honey," she repeated darkly.

156

"If you don't, we're lost."

"But you're forgetting everything else they have over me, Candelaria — the hotel debt, the accusations against me by the company and by my half brother. If they catch me doing this, I'll be finished."

"You'll be finished if Palomares turns up tonight and finds us with all this in the house," she replied, gazing back to the guns.

"But Candelaria, listen . . . ," I insisted.

"No, you listen to me now, girl, and listen well," she said imperiously. She spoke with a powerful hiss, her eyes open like saucers. Crouched down beside the bed till she was at my level, she proceeded to grab me by the arms and made me look right at her. "I've tried everything, I've thrown everything I've got into this, and things didn't work out," she said. "Luck can be a bitch like that: sometimes she lets you win, and other times she spits in your face and makes you lose. And tonight she said to me, No way, Matutera. I haven't got any ammunition left, Sira, the game's up for me. But not for you. You're the only person now who can stop us from going under, the only one who can take out the merchandise and bring back the money. If it weren't necessary I wouldn't be asking you, God knows. But we have no choice, child: you've got to get going. You're in this just like I am; this one's both of ours, and we've got a lot riding on it. Our future is disappearing, girl, our whole future. If we don't get this money, we won't make it through. Now everything is in your hands. You must do it, for you and for me, Sira. For both of us."

I wanted to keep refusing; I knew I had powerful reasons to say no, no way, absolutely not. But

157

at the same time I knew Candelaria was right. I had agreed to be a part of that dark game, no one had forced me. We'd formed a team, each of us with a role to play. Candelaria's was first to negotiate; mine, to work afterward. But we were both aware that sometimes the boundaries of things are elastic and imprecise, that they can shift, become blurred or diluted like ink in water. She'd done her part of the deal, and she'd tried. Luck had turned her back on her and she hadn't managed to succeed, but that didn't mean that all the possibilities had been exhausted. It was only fair that now I should take the risk.

I took a few seconds to speak; first I had to clear out of my head some images that threatened to leap at my jugular: the commissioner, his prison, the unknown face of this Palomares.

"Have you thought about how I'd do it?" I asked finally in a whisper.

Candelaria breathed out noisily in relief, recovering her lost spirits.

"The easiest thing in the world, my precious. Wait just a second, and I'll tell you how."

She left the room still half naked and returned in less than a minute, her arms filled with what seemed to be a huge piece of white linen.

"You're going to dress like a little Moorish girl, with a haik," she said, closing the door behind her. "You could fit the whole universe in one of these."

That was certainly true. Every day I saw Arab women wrapped up inside these broad shapeless clothes, which resembled large cloaks and covered their heads, their arms, their whole bodies, front and back. Underneath this garment, one could certainly hide anything one wanted. A piece of fabric usually covered their mouth and nose, and the top part came down over their eyebrows. Only their eyes, their ankles, and their feet remained in view. I couldn't have thought of a better way to go through the streets hiding a small arsenal of pistols.

"But first there's something else we have to do, honey; let's get to work."

I obeyed without a word, allowing her to direct the situation. Without a thought she pulled the top sheet off my bed and brought it to her mouth. With a fierce bite she tore off the top hem and then began to rip the material, tearing a strip a couple of hand spans wide.

"Do the same thing with the bottom sheet," she commanded. Between teeth and tearing it took us only a few minutes to reduce the sheets off my bed to a couple of dozen long strips of cotton. "And now, what we're going to do is tie these strips around your body to hold the pistols. Raise your arms, I'm doing the first one."

And so, without my even taking off my nightdress, the nineteen revolvers were attached around me, bandaged firmly with the strips of bedsheet. Each strip was for one pistol: first Candelaria would wrap the weapon in a folded-over piece of the fabric, then she'd put it against my body and go around me two or three times with the band. And finally she'd tie the ends tight.

"You're all skin and bones, girl, you don't have any meat left on you where I can tie the next one," she said, having completely covered me front and back.

"My thighs," I suggested.

And so she did, until — spread out under my chest and over my ribs, kidneys, shoulder blades,

159

sides, arms, hips, and thighs — all of the cargo had finally been accommodated. I was like a mummy, covered in white bandages that made all my movements difficult, but that I'd have to learn to move around in right away.

"Put these on, they're Jamila's," she said, placing at my feet some worn brownish-colored leather slippers. "And now the haik," she added, holding up the large white linen cloak. "That's it, wrap yourself up right to the head, and let me see how that looks on you."

She looked at me with a half smile.

"Perfect, just another little Moorish girl. Before leaving, don't forget, you've also got to arrange the veil over your face so it covers your mouth and nose. Come on, then, let's go out, I've got to explain quickly to you where you're going."

I started to walk with difficulty, finding it hard to move my body at a normal pace. The pistols were heavy as lead and forced me to keep my legs apart and my arms away from my sides. We went out into the corridor, Candelaria walking ahead and me moving clumsily behind her; a big white bulk that bumped into the walls, the furniture, and the door jambs. Without noticing I knocked into a shelf, throwing its contents onto the floor: a plate from Talavera, an unlit oil lamp, and a sepia-colored portrait of some relative of Candelaria's. The glass and porcelain shattered as soon as they hit the floor tiles, and the noise made the mattress springs creak in the four adjacent rooms as the sleeping guests were disturbed.

"What's happened?" shouted the fat mother from her bed.

"Nothing, I just dropped a glass of water.

Everyone back to sleep," replied Candelaria with finality.

I tried to reach down to pick up the mess, but I couldn't bend my body.

"Leave it, girl, leave it, I'll sort it out later," she said, moving some bits of glass aside with her foot.

And then, unexpectedly, a door opened just ten feet away from us. We were met by the curler-covered head of Fernanda, one of the aged sisters. Before she had the chance to ask us what had happened and what a Moorish woman in a haik was doing knocking over the furniture in the corridor at that hour of the morning, Candelaria launched a dart at her that rendered her mute and unable to react.

"If you don't get back to bed this instant, when I wake up tomorrow I'll tell Sagrario you've been seeing the assistant from the dispensary on Fridays in the *cornisa*."

Fear that her pious sister should learn of her amours was more powerful than her curiosity, and without a word Fernanda slipped like an eel back into her bedroom.

"Onward, honey, it's getting late," the Matutera said in a commanding whisper. "Better if no one sees you coming out of this house; you never know if Palomares is around, and then we'd be screwed from the start. So we'll go out the back."

We went out onto the little patio behind the building and were greeted by the black night, as well as a twisted vine, a pile of junk, and the telegraph man's old bicycle. We remained hidden in a corner and began speaking in low voices.

"Now what do I do?" I murmured.

She seemed to have everything well thought out and spoke firmly.

161

"You go up onto this bench and climb over the wall, but you've got to do it very carefully. If not, you're going to get the haik tangled between your legs and find yourself face-first on the ground."

I looked at the wall, which was about six feet high, and the smaller adjacent one I'd have to scale to get to the top and be able to jump down to the other side. Preferring not to wonder whether I'd be capable of doing it encumbered by the weight of the pistols and wrapped in all that cloth, I simply asked for further instructions. "And from there?"

"When you've jumped, you'll be in the yard behind Don Leandro's grocery store; from there, if you climb onto the boxes and barrels he's got scattered about, you can easily get into the next yard, which is behind the pastry shop of Menahen the Jew. There, at the back, you'll find a little wooden door that'll let you out into a side alley, which is where the sacks of flour come in for the bakery. Once you're outside, forget who you are. Cover yourself up well, hunch yourself over, and get walking toward the Jewish neighborhood, and from there, you go into the Moorish quarter. But take care, girl: don't rush, and stay close to the wall, dragging your feet a little as though you were an old woman, so that no one will see you walking too nicely and some undesirable won't try something. There are a lot of young Spanish lads who can get captivated by the charms of the Muslim women."

"And then?"

"When you get to the Moorish quarter, walk around the streets a few times just to be sure that no one's watching or following you. If you meet anyone, change your route cleverly or get as far away from them as you can. After a bit, come back out of Puerta de la Luneta and head down to the park — you know where I mean, right?"

"I think so," I said, struggling to map the route in my mind.

"Once you're there you'll find yourself opposite the station: cross the Ceuta road and go in wherever you find it open, slowly and well concealed. Most likely there won't be anyone there but a couple of half-asleep soldiers who won't pay you the slightest attention. You'll probably find some Moroccans waiting for the train to Ceuta; the Christians won't start arriving till later."

"What time does the train go?"

"Half past seven. But the Moors, as you know, have quite a different rhythm to their schedules, so nobody will find it strange that you're wandering around there at six in the morning."

"And should I board the train, too, or what do I do?"

Candelaria took a few seconds to reply, and I guessed that her plan hadn't been plotted out much further.

"No, in theory you don't need to take the train. When you reach the station, sit down for a little bit on the bench under the timetable board, let them see you there, and that way they'll know that it's you who's got the merchandise."

"Who is it that has to see me?"

"Don't worry about that: whoever has to see you will see you. After twenty minutes, get up off the bench, go to the café, and find some way for the man working behind the counter to tell you where you are to leave the pistols."

"That's it?" I asked in alarm. "And if the café man isn't there, or if he ignores me, or if I can't

163

speak to him, what do I do?"

"Sssssshhhh. Don't raise your voice, they'll hear us. Don't you worry, somehow you'll find out what you have to do," she said impatiently, unable to imbue her words with the reassurance that was evidently needed. Then she decided to level with me. "Look, child, everything's gone so bad tonight that they couldn't tell me more than that: the pistols have to be at the station at six in the morning; the person carrying them has to sit for twenty minutes under the timetable board; and the café man is the one who will tell you how to make the delivery. More than that I don't know, my child, and I'm really sorry about that. But don't worry, precious, you'll see how once you're there everything will work itself out."

I wanted to say I doubted it very much, but her worried face warned me not to. For the first time since I'd known her, the Matutera's resolve and her tenacity in finding ingenious solutions to the muddiest situations seemed to have hit rock bottom. But I knew that if she'd been in a position to act herself, she wouldn't have been afraid: she'd have managed to get to the station and do what was required using whatever wiles she had at hand. The problem was that this time Candelaria was tied hand and foot, immobilized in her house by the threat of a police search that might or might not happen that night. And I knew that if I wasn't able to respond and take a firm grip on the reins, it would all be over for us. So I summoned up some strength from nowhere and armed myself with courage.

"You're right, Candelaria: I'll find a way, don't worry about it. But first, tell me one thing."

"Whatever you want, child, but move fast, it's

less than two hours to go till six," she added, trying to disguise her relief at seeing me ready to keep fighting.

"Where will the guns end up? Who are these men from Larache?"

"You don't care about that, girl. What matters is that they arrive when and where they're supposed to; that you leave the merchandise where you're told to and collect the money they have to give you: nine thousand five hundred pesetas, remember that, and count the notes one by one. Then you return in a flash. I'll be waiting here holding my breath . . ."

"We're taking a huge risk, Candelaria," I insisted. "At least let me know who it is we're dealing with."

She sighed deeply and her chest, barely half covered by the smock she'd thrown over herself at the last minute, rose and fell again as though under the influence of a pump.

"They're Masons," she whispered in my ear, as though afraid of pronouncing a curse. "They were supposed to arrive tonight in a van from Larache, most likely they're already hiding out near Buselmal Springs or in some vegetable garden on the Río Martín plain. They come through the villages, they don't dare travel on the main roads. They'll probably pick the guns up wherever you leave them and won't even get on the train. I'd say they'll probably return to their city directly from the station, going back through the villages again and avoiding Tetouan completely; that is, if they aren't caught first, God forbid. But anyway, that's just a guess, because the truth is I haven't a goddamn clue what these men are up to."

She sighed deeply, looking out into the emptiness, and then went on in a low voice.

"What I do know, child, because everyone else knows it, too, is that those involved in the uprising have violently taken their anger out on anyone who has anything to do with Freemasonry. Some of them were shot in the head during their own meetings; the lucky ones fled as fast as they could to Tangiers or the French zone. Others were taken to El Mogote and someday they'll be shot and never heard from again. And probably there are a few hiding in cellars, lofts, and storerooms, afraid that one day someone will betray them and they will be beaten out of their sanctuaries with rifle butts. That's why I couldn't find anyone at first who would dare buy the merchandise. After asking around I managed to get hold of the contact in Larache, and that's how I know that's where the pistols will end up."

Then she looked me in the eyes, serious and dark like I'd never seen her before.

"Things are ugly, child, very ugly," she said through clenched teeth. "There's no pity here, no consideration, and anyone who's worth anything gets taken away before you can say amen. Many poor wretches have already died, decent people who never killed a fly. Be very careful, honey; you're not going to be the next one."

Again I drew a crumb of good cheer out of nowhere, so that the two of us might convince ourselves of something even I didn't believe.

"Don't worry, Candelaria; you'll see, we'll get out of this somehow."

And without another word, I made my way to the bench and began climbing with that sinister cargo strapped to my skin. I left the Matutera behind me, watching from beneath as she made the sign of the cross amid whispers and vines: In the name of the Father, the Son and the Holy Spirit, may the Virgin of Miracles go with you, my angel. The last thing I heard was a noisy kiss she gave to her fingers at the end of the ritual. One second later I disappeared behind the garden wall and fell like a bundle into the grocer's yard.

Chapter Eleven

I reached the way out of baker Menahen's in less than five minutes. In the process I caught myself several times on nails and splinters that were impossible to see in the darkness. I grazed my wrist, tripped on the haik, slipped, and nearly lost my balance as I climbed up a huge pile of boxes stored in a disordered heap against a wall. Once I'd reached the door, the first thing I did was to arrange the haik so that all that could be seen of my face were my eyes. Then I slid the rusty bolt, took a deep breath, and stepped outside.

There was no one in the alley, not a shadow or a sound. My only company was the moon, moving freely between the clouds. I started walking slowly, sticking close to the left side, and before long I'd arrived at La Luneta. Before turning onto the street I paused at the corner to determine the lay of the land. Yellowish lights hung from the cables over the road to serve as street lamps. Looking left and right, I was able to recognize some of the establishments — now asleep — in which chaotic life went on during the day: the Hotel Victoria, Zurita Pharmacy, Levante Bar where they would often sing flamenco, Galindo the tobacconist's, and a salt depository; the Teatro Nacional, the Indian bazaars, four or five taverns whose names I didn't know, La Perla Jeweler's, which belonged to the Cohen brothers, and La Espiga de Oro, where we'd go every morning to buy our bread. All of them silent, closed, peaceful as the dead.

Once on La Luneta, I struggled to adapt my pace to the weight of my cargo. After a short stretch, I directed myself toward the *mellah,* the Jewish quarter. The linear pattern of its extremely narrow streets comforted me, for its precise grid made it impossible to lose one's bearings. Then I entered the medina, and at first everything went well as I passed by familiar places: the Bread Souq, the Meat Souq. I didn't meet anyone, not a soul, not even a dog or a blind tramp begging for alms. All I could hear was the muffled sound of my own slippers dragging along the paving stones and the murmur of some fountain or other lost in the distance. I noticed that the pistols seemed less and less heavy, that my body was getting used to its new dimensions. From time to time I patted myself down just to confirm that everything was still in place: first the sides, then the arms, then the hips. I was still tense and couldn't quite manage to relax, but at least I was walking with reasonable calm down the dark, winding streets between the whitewashed walls and the wooden doors studded with thick-headed nails.

To banish the worry from my head, I made myself imagine what those Arab houses were like on the inside. I'd heard they were beautiful and cool, with patios, fountains, and galleries of mosaics and tiles; with carved wooden ceilings and sunlight caressing the flat roofs. There was no way you could tell all that from the street, where all you could see were their whitewashed walls. I kept

169

musing in this way, until after a while, when I thought I'd walked enough and was a hundred percent sure that I hadn't raised the slightest suspicion, I decided to head toward Puerta de la Luneta. And it was then, precisely at that moment, that I noticed — at the end of the alley I was walking down — a couple of figures approaching. Two soldiers, officers in breeches, with sashes at their waists and the red caps of the Spanish regulars; four legs walking resolutely, their boots sounding on the cobbles as they talked in quiet, nervous voices. I held my breath as a thousand grim images torpedoed my mind like explosions battering a wall. Suddenly I feared that just as I passed them all the pistols would come loose from their ties and scatter noisily onto the ground; I imagined that it might occur to one of them to pull my hood back and expose my face, that they would make me speak, that they'd discover I was a Spanish compatriot of theirs dealing guns illegally and not some local woman on her way to nowhere in particular.

The men passed alongside me; I stuck as closely as I could to the wall, but the alley was so narrow that we almost brushed against one another. They didn't pay me the least bit of attention, however, ignoring my presence as though I were invisible and continuing their conversation as they proceeded hastily on their way. They were talking about detachments and munitions, about things I didn't understand or want to understand. Two hundred, two fifty at the most, one of them said as they passed. No, absolutely not, I'm telling you that's not right, replied the other vehemently. I didn't see their faces, I didn't dare look up, but as soon as their voices faded into the distance I picked up my pace and finally felt I could breathe again.

Just a few seconds later, however, I realized I shouldn't have declared victory quite so soon: looking up, I discovered that I didn't know where I was. In order to keep my bearings I would have had to take a right turn three or four corners earlier, but the unexpected appearance of the soldiers had thrown me so much that I hadn't. At the thought that I was lost, a shiver ran over my skin. I'd crossed the streets of the medina many times but still didn't know its secrets and mysteries. Without sunlight to guide me and in the absence of the usual activity and sounds, I hadn't the faintest idea where I was.

I decided to turn back and retrace my steps but was unable to do so. When I thought that I was about to walk into a little square I knew, I found an archway instead; when I expected a passageway, I came across a mosque or a flight of stairs. I proceeded awkwardly along the winding streets, trying to associate every corner with its daytime activities in order to get my bearings. But the more I walked, the more lost I felt in those intricate streets that defied all laws of reason. With the craftsmen asleep and their shops shut, I couldn't tell whether I was passing through the district of the coppersmiths or the tinsmiths, or whether I was going through the section where by day the thread makers, weavers, and tailors worked. In the area where vendors' stands with honey sweets, round flatbreads, mountains of spices, and bunches of basil might have helped me to orient myself, I found only locked doors and bolted shutters. Time seemed to have stopped, everything seemed like an empty stage set without

171

the voices of the merchants and the buyers, without the trains of donkeys laden with panniers or the women from the Rif sitting on the ground, surrounded by green vegetables and oranges that they might never be able to sell. My anxiety increased: I didn't know what time it was, but I was only too aware that there was less and less time remaining before six o'clock. I picked up the pace; exiting an alleyway, I went into another, and another, and yet another; I retraced my steps, attempting to correct my route again. Nothing. Not a clue, not a sign: everything had suddenly been transformed into an accursed labyrinth with no way out.

My confused steps ended up taking me close to a house with a large lamp hanging over the door. At once I could hear laughing, chatter, immoderate voices singing in chorus the words of "Mi jaca" to the accompaniment of an out-of-tune piano. I decided to approach, anxious to find some reference point that would allow me to recover my sense of direction. I was just a few feet away when a couple came out quickly, speaking Spanish: a man who seemed to be drunk, clinging to an older woman with dyed blond hair who was laughing heartily. I realized then that I was standing outside a brothel, but it was already too late to try to pass myself off as a worn-out old local woman: the couple was just a few steps away from me. *Morita,* come with me, *morita,* my lovely, I've got something to show you, look, look, *morita,* the man said, slobbering, holding an arm out to me while his other hand gripped his crotch obscenely. The woman tried to restrain him as she laughed, while I jumped away from his reach and ran off wildly, clasping the haik around my body with all my strength.

I left the brothel behind me, that place filled with flesh from the barracks playing cards, bellowing out popular songs, and feverishly handling the women; all of them momentarily freed from the certainty that someday soon they'd be crossing the Strait to confront the grim reality of the war. And then, as I sped away in haste, luck finally came to my aid when turning a corner I found myself face to face with the Souq el Foki.

I was filled with relief at having regained my bearings: at last I knew how to escape from the cage that the medina had become. Time was racing, and I would have to do the same. Moving with the longest strides my covering would allow, I reached Puerta de la Luneta in only a few minutes. But a new shock awaited me there: one of the feared military control posts that had prevented the people from Larache from getting into Tetouan. Several soldiers, guard barriers, and a couple of vehicles: enough to intimidate anyone who wanted to get into the city for any reason less than pure. I could feel my throat becoming dry, but I knew I couldn't avoid passing right in front of them, let alone stop to consider what I should do, so with my eyes fixed once again on the ground I decided to continue on my way with the weary walk that Candelaria had advised. I passed the control with my blood pounding in my temples as I held my breath, expecting to be stopped at any moment and asked where I was going, who I was, what I was hiding. To my good fortune, they barely glanced at me. They ignored me, just as I'd been ignored by the officers I'd passed in the narrow alley. What danger could the

173

glorious uprising fear from that plodding old Moroccan woman who made her way through the dawn streets like a shadow?

I came down into the open area of the park and forced myself to recover my composure. With feigned calm I crossed the gardens filled with sleeping shadows, so strange in that stillness, without the noisy children or couples or elderly people who would wander amid the fountains and the palm trees in daytime. As I proceeded I could see the station looming clearer and clearer in sight. Compared to the low houses of the medina, it suddenly looked grand and troubling to me, half Moorish and half Andalusian, with its turrets and green tiles, its huge archways over the entrances. Several dim lamps illuminated the façade, casting its silhouette against the bulk of the Ghorgiz, those imposing mountains from which the men from Larache were supposed to arrive. I'd only been by the station once before, when the commissioner had taken me in his car from the hospital to the boardinghouse. Other times I'd seen it at a distance, from the vista of La Luneta, unable to gauge the scale of the thing. Standing before it in the dimness, I found its size so threatening that I suddenly missed the cozy narrowness of the alleyways in the Moorish quarter.

But there wasn't time to allow fear to bare its teeth at me again, so I recovered my daring and set about crossing the Ceuta road, which at that time of morning had not so much as a speck of dust moving on it. I tried to buoy up my spirits by calculating times, telling myself that in a short while it would all be over, that I'd already gone through most of the ordeal. It comforted me to think that I'd soon be rid of those tight bandages

174

and pistols that were bruising my body and the voluminous clothes that felt so strange. It wouldn't be long now.

I went into the station through the main entrance, which was wide open, and was met by a flood of cold light illuminating the space, a sharp contrast to the darkness of night I'd just left behind. The first thing I noticed was a large clock reading a quarter to six. I sighed in relief under the fabric covering my face: my delay hadn't been too bad. I walked with slow deliberateness across the concourse while my eyes, hidden behind the veil, quickly surveyed the scene. The ticket desks were closed, and there was only an old Muslim man flat out on a bench with a bundle at his feet. At the far end of the room, two big doors opened onto the platform. On the left was another door with a prominent sign marked Café. I found the timetable board to my right, but I didn't stop to study it, just sat down on a bench beneath and settled myself in to wait. No sooner had I done so than a feeling of gratitude ran through my whole body from head to foot. Until that moment I hadn't realized how tired I was after the immense effort of walking nonstop laden with all that sinister weight.

Although no one appeared on the concourse the whole time I remained sitting there immobile, I heard sounds that told me I was not alone. Some of them came from outside, others from the platform. Footsteps and men's voices, sometimes quiet, at other times louder. They were young voices, and I assumed they would have been soldiers in charge of guarding the station. I tried not to think about the fact that they were probably under orders to fire without hesitation at anything suspicious. There were some other sounds, too, coming from the café. It comforted me to hear them, for at least I could tell that the café employee was at work and in place. I let ten minutes pass, which they did with exasperating slowness. There wasn't time for the twenty minutes Candelaria had told me to wait, so when the hands of the clock showed five to six, I gathered up my strength, got heavily to my feet, and walked over to my destination.

The café was large, with at least a dozen tables, all of them unoccupied except for one where a man was dozing with his head hidden by his arm; beside him rested an empty wine bottle. I made my way over to the counter, dragging my slippers, without the slightest idea of what I ought to say or what I was going to hear. Behind the bar, a gaunt, dark-skinned man with a cigarette butt between his lips was busy putting plates and cups in orderly piles, apparently not paying the least attention to that woman with her face covered who was about to place herself right in front of him. As he saw me approach the counter, he simply said loudly and dismissively, without removing his cigarette from his mouth, "Seven thirty, the train doesn't leave till seven thirty." Then, in a low voice, he added a few words in Arabic that I didn't understand. "I'm Spanish, I don't understand you," I mumbled from behind the veil. He opened his mouth, unable to hide his disbelief, and what was left of his cigarette fell unnoticed onto the floor. Then he whispered the message: go to the urinals on the platform and close the door, they're waiting for you there.

I slowly retraced my steps, returning to the concourse, and from there went out into the night.

First, I readjusted the haik and lifted the veil
farther up until it was almost grazing my eyelashes.
The broad platform looked empty, and beyond
there was nothing but the rocky mass of the Ghorgiz, dark and immense. The soldiers, four of them,
were all together, smoking and talking under one
of the arches that opened onto the tracks. They
flinched when they saw a shadow appear; I noticed
how they tensed up, how they brought their boots
together and straightened their postures, how they
adjusted their rifles on their shoulders.

"You there — halt!" shouted one of them as
soon as he saw me. My body stiffened against the
metal weapons stuck to it.

"Leave her, Churruca, can't you see she's a
Moor?" another said immediately.

I remained still, neither advancing nor retreating. They didn't approach but remained where
they were, some fifty feet away, discussing what to
do.

"I don't care one way or another if she's Moorish or Christian. The sergeant said we have to ask
everybody for identification."

"Christ, Churruca, you're so slow. We've told
you ten times already that he meant everybody
Spanish, not the Muslims," the other soldier
explained. "Why can't you learn?"

"You're the ones who don't learn. Come on,
ma'am, let's see your papers."

I thought my legs were going to fold under me,
that I was about to collapse. It seemed the game
was up. I held my breath and felt a cold sweat
soaking my skin.

"You're so dumb, Churruca," said another one
standing behind him. "The natives don't wander
around with their ID documents — when are you

going to learn that this is Africa, not your village square?"

Too late: the scrupulous soldier was already two steps away from me, a hand held out for some document as he searched for my gaze among the folds of fabric covering me. He didn't find it, however — my eyes remained fixed on the ground, focused on his mud-stained boots, on my old slippers, and the little space that separated our two pairs of feet.

"If the sergeant finds out you've been bothering a Moroccan woman who's not under any suspicion, you're going to swallow three long nights of arrest in the Alcazaba, kid."

The grim possibility of that punishment finally made this Churruca see sense. I couldn't see the face of my savior — my gaze was still fixed on the ground. But the threat of arrest had its abrupt effect, and the punctilious pigheaded soldier, after thinking about it for a few nerve-wracking seconds, withdrew his hand, turned, and moved away from me.

I blessed the good sense of his companion who had stopped him, and when the four soldiers were back together under the arch I turned and resumed my course. Making my way slowly along the platform, heading nowhere in particular, I attempted to recover my composure. Once I'd done that, I was finally able to concentrate my efforts on getting to the urinals. I began to pay attention to my surroundings then: a couple of Arabs dozing on the ground, leaning their backs on the walls, and a scrawny dog crossing the tracks. It took me a while to find my goal; to my good fortune it was almost at the other end of the platform, far from where the soldiers were. Holding my breath, I pushed the glass-paneled door and went into a kind of anteroom. There was barely any light, but I didn't want to look for the switch, preferring instead to let my eyes adjust to the darkness. I could make out the sign for men to my left and women to my right. And at the back, against the wall, I could see what seemed like a heap of fabric that was slowly beginning to shift. A head covered by a hood emerged cautiously from the bulk, eyes meeting mine in the gloom.

"Have you brought the merchandise?" asked a low voice quickly in Spanish.

I nodded and the bulk rose up stealthily until it had been transformed into the figure of a man dressed, like me, in the Moorish style.

"Where is it?"

I lowered my veil to be able to speak more easily, opening the haik and showing him my bound-up body.

"Here."

"My God," was all he muttered. There was a world of emotions concentrated in those two words: fear, anxiety, urgency. His tone was serious; he seemed to be a well-educated man.

"Can you take it off yourself?" he asked then.

"I'll need time," I whispered.

He pointed me toward the women's section and we both went in. It was a narrow space, with a small window through which traces of moonlight glimmered, sufficient enough that we didn't need any more.

"Hurry, we can't waste any time. The morning patrol is about to arrive, and they search the station from top to bottom before the first train leaves. I'll have to help you," he said, closing the

179

door behind him.

I let the haik drop to the floor and held my arms out to the sides so that this stranger could start rummaging around every corner of me, untying knots, loosening bandages, and freeing my frame from its sinister covering.

Before starting he lowered the hood of his djellaba, and I found myself looking at a serious, pleasant-faced Spaniard, middle-aged, with several days of stubble. His hair was brown and curly, disheveled by the effects of the big garment under which he'd probably been hidden for quite some time. His fingers began to work, but it wasn't an easy task. Candelaria really had made an effort, and not one of the guns had shifted position, but the knots were so tight and there were so many yards of fabric that undoing them took us longer than we both would have wished. Neither of us spoke, surrounded by white tiles and only accompanied by the squat toilet in the floor, the rhythmic sound of our breathing, and an occasional murmur that punctuated the process: there we go, this way now, move a little, that's it, bring your arm up a little, careful. Despite the pressure, the man from Larache acted with infinite delicacy, almost modesty, avoiding my more intimate areas or grazing past my naked skin an inch beyond what was strictly necessary. As though afraid to stain my integrity with his hands, as though the cargo I had attached to me was an exquisite wrapping of tissue paper and not a black casing of objects destined to kill. At no point did his physical closeness trouble me, neither his involuntary caresses nor the intimacy of our almost-touching bodies. It was without question the most pleasurable moment of the night — not because a man was running his hands across my body after so many months, but because I believed that, with that action, my ordeal was almost over.

Everything proceeded at a good pace. The pistols came out of their hiding places one by one, ending up in a heap on the floor. When there were only a few left, just three or four, I calculated that in five minutes, ten at the most, we'd be done. Then suddenly the calm was broken, making us hold our breaths and freeze in the middle of what we were doing. From outside in the distance came the agitated sounds of the beginning of some new activity.

The man breathed in hard and took a watch out of his pocket.

"They're here already, the relief patrol, they've come early," he said. In his cracked voice I could make out distress and anxiety, and the wish not to convey either of those feelings.

"What do we do now?" I whispered.

"Get out as quickly as possible," he said immediately. "Get dressed, fast."

"And the pistols that are left?"

"Doesn't matter. What you've got to do now is escape: it won't be long before the soldiers come in to check that everything's in order."

As I wrapped myself in the haik, my hands trembling, he unstrapped a filthy canvas sack from his belt and began shoving the pistols inside.

"Which way do we get out?" I whispered.

"That way," he said, raising his head and gesturing at the window with his chin. "You jump first, then I'll throw the pistols and come out myself. But listen carefully: if I'm not able to join you, take the pistols, run with them parallel to the tracks, and leave them next to the first sign you see announcing a stop or a station, and someone will go get them. Don't look back and don't wait for me; just run and escape. All right, let's go — get ready to get up there, put a foot in my hands."

I looked up at the narrow window. It seemed impossible that we'd fit through it, but I didn't say anything. I was so afraid that I just did exactly what I was told, blindly trusting the decisions of this anonymous Mason whose name I'd never learned.

"Wait a moment," he said then, as though he'd forgotten something.

He pulled his shirt open and withdrew a small canvas bag, a sort of pouch.

"First put this away, it's the money agreed. In case things get complicated once we're outside."

"But there are still some guns left . . . ," I stammered as I patted down my body.

"Doesn't matter, you fulfilled your part, so that's what you should be paid," he said as he hung the bag around my neck. I let him do it to me, staying still, as though numbed. "Come on now, we can't waste a second."

Finally I responded. Resting one foot in his linked hands, I pushed myself up until I'd gripped the window frame.

"Open it, fast," he insisted. "Up you go — tell me quickly what you see and hear."

The window opened onto the dark countryside. Sounds were coming from somewhere outside my range of vision: motors, wheels squealing on the gravel, firm footsteps, greetings and orders, imperious voices barking out tasks with sharp determination, as though the world was about to end, even though morning had not yet begun.

"Pizarro and García, to the cafeteria. Ruiz and

Albadalejo, the ticket desks. You to the offices, you two to the urinals. Come on, everyone, quick as a flash," shouted someone with furious authority.

"I can't see anyone, but they're coming this way," I said with my head still outside.

"Jump," he commanded.

I didn't. I was worried about the height, I still had to get my body out, I was unconsciously refusing to get out alone. I wanted the man from Larache to reassure me that he'd be coming with me, that he'd lead me by the hand to wherever I had to go.

The men could be heard coming ever closer. The creak of the boots on the ground, the powerful voices assigning tasks. Quintero, to the women's bathroom; Villarta, to the men's. They certainly weren't the slovenly recruits I'd come across on my arrival, but a patrol of fresh young men eager to fill the beginning of their day with activity.

"Jump and run!" the man repeated urgently, gripping my legs and pushing me upward.

I jumped, and fell, and the sack of pistols fell after me. I'd barely hit the ground before I heard the crash of doors being kicked open. The last sounds I heard were the rough shouts aimed at someone I never saw again.

"What are you doing in the women's bathrooms, *moro?* What were you throwing out the window? Villarta, quick, go outside and see if he's thrown something out there."

I began to run. Blindly, furiously. Sheltered by darkness, and hauling the sack with the guns; deaf, oblivious, not knowing if they were following me or wanting to think about what had become of the man from Larache faced with the soldier's rifle. I lost a slipper, and one of the last pistols finally came detached from my body, but I didn't stop to retrieve either of them, I just kept following the path of the tracks, half barefoot, not stopping, not thinking. I crossed open fields, orchards, fields of sugarcane, and small plantations. I tripped, got up, and kept running without calculating the distance my strides were covering. Not a single living thing greeted me, and nothing got in the way of the deranged rhythm of my feet, until — in the shadows — I was able to make out a sign covered in writing. Malalien Station, it said. That would be my destination.

The station was about a hundred yards from the sign, lit up by a single yellowish lamp. I stopped my wild running at the sign and looked around quickly in every direction to see if there was anyone to whom I could hand over the weapons. My heart was about to burst, and my mouth was dry and filled with grit as I struggled in vain to silence my labored breathing. No one came out to meet me, no one waited for the merchandise. Perhaps they'd arrive later, or perhaps never.

It took me less than a minute to make my decision. I put the sack down on the ground, flattened it as much as possible, and started to pile little rocks on it at a feverish pace, scraping at the ground, yanking up earth, stones, and brush till it was reasonably well covered. When I thought it no longer looked like a suspicious bulge, I left.

With barely enough time to recover my breath, I resumed my running in the direction of what I could make out as the lights of Tetouan. Now that I'd shed the cargo, I decided to shed the rest of my ballast. I opened up the haik without stopping and with some difficulty managed bit by bit to undo the remaining knots. The three pistols that were still tied to me fell out onto the road, first one, then another, and finally the last one. By the time I had almost reached the city, all my body had left was exhaustion, sadness, and pain. And a pouch full of banknotes hanging around my neck. Not a trace of the guns.

I got myself back up onto the curb of the Ceuta road and slowed my pace again. I'd lost the other slipper, too, so I disguised myself again in the figure of a wrapped-up barefoot Moorish woman wearily making her way up to La Luneta gate. I didn't have to make an effort to appear tired, for my legs couldn't manage anything more. My limbs were stiff, I was filthy, and I had blisters and bruises all over. An infinite weakness was invading my bones.

I entered the city as the shadows were beginning to lighten. The muezzin was calling the Muslims to first prayers from a nearby mosque, and the bugle of the Intendencia Barracks was playing reveille. The day's news was appearing hot off the presses of *La Gaceta de África,* and shoeshine boys were beginning to circulate around La Luneta, yawning. Menahen the baker had already fired up his oven, and Don Leandro was piling up his store's groceries with his apron tied firmly around his waist.

All these everyday scenes passed before my eyes as though they were alien, not demanding any of my attention. Although I knew Candelaria would be pleased when I handed over the money and would praise me for carrying out an impressive deed, deep down I didn't feel the least bit of satisfaction, only the black gnawing of a deep anxiety.

While running frantically across the fields, while digging my nails in the earth to cover up the sack, while walking along the road, throughout my last actions of that long night, all I could think about were a thousand different sequences of events with just one protagonist: the man from Larache. In one of these, the soldiers discovered that he hadn't thrown anything out the window, that it had all been a false alarm, that the man was no more than a confused, sleepy Arab, and so they'd let him go; the army was under express orders not to bother the local population unless there seemed to be something particularly disturbing afoot. In another very different scenario, no sooner had they opened the door to the toilets than the soldiers could see it was a Spaniard in disguise; they cornered him in the bathroom, pointing their rifles six inches from his face, and shouted for reinforcements. Once these arrived, they interrogated him, perhaps identifying and detaining him; perhaps they took him back to headquarters and he tried to escape; or perhaps they killed him, a shot in the back as he jumped the tracks. There were a host of other possible scenarios, but I knew I'd never be able to discover which of them turned out to be closest to the truth.

I went in through the front door, exhausted and filled with fears as morning dawned over the map of Morocco.

Chapter Twelve

I found the door of the boardinghouse open and the guests awake, gathered around the dining room table where they daily hurled their insults and oaths. The sisters in their dressing gowns and curlers, sobbing, as the schoolmaster Don Anselmo tried to console them with quiet words I couldn't hear. Paquito and the traveling salesman were retrieving the picture of the Last Supper from the floor, in order to return it to its place on the wall. The telegraph man, in his pajama bottoms and undershirt, smoking nervously in a corner. The fat mother, meanwhile, was trying to cool her linden tea by blowing on it lightly. Everything was topsy-turvy, with bits of broken glass and the curtains torn down from their rods.

No one seemed surprised at the arrival of a Moorish woman at that time of the morning; they must have thought I was Jamila. I stood there contemplating the scene for a few seconds, still trapped in my haik, until a potent hissing from the corridor caught my attention. Turning my head I saw Candelaria waving her arms like a woman possessed while holding a broom in one hand and the dustpan in the other.

"Come inside, honey," she commanded, agitated. "Come in and tell me, I've been sick with worry not knowing what happened."

I'd decided to keep the more shocking details to myself and share with her only the final result. That we no longer had the pistols, and we did have the money: that was what Candelaria wanted to hear, and that's what I was going to tell her. The rest of the story I'd keep to myself.

I talked as she removed the covering from my head.

"It all turned out fine," I whispered.

"Ay, my angel, come here and let me hug you! And isn't my Sira worth more than all the gold in Peru, isn't my girl greater than the Lord's day!" squealed the Matutera. She threw the cleaning things on the floor, captured me in her bosom, and covered my face with big noisy kisses.

"Be quiet, Candelaria, for God's sake; quiet, they'll hear you," I objected, fear still clinging to my skin. With no intention of heeding my warning, she strung her jubilation into a thread of curses directed at the policeman who had turned the house upside down earlier that night.

"What do I care if they hear me now that it's all over? Damn you to hell, Palomares, you and all your kin! Damn you to hell — you couldn't catch me!"

Sensing that this explosion of emotion after a long night of nerves wasn't going to end there, I grabbed Candelaria's arm and dragged her to my room, as she continued raining down curses.

"Screw you, son of a bitch! Screw you, Palomares, you didn't find a thing in my house, even knocking over my furniture and tearing open the mattresses!"

"Quiet now, Candelaria, once and for all be quiet," I insisted. "Forget about Palomares, calm down and let me tell you how it went."

"Yes, child, yes, down to the last detail," she said, finally trying to calm herself. She was still breathing hard, her housecoat was misbuttoned, and locks of tousled hair had escaped from her hairnet. She looked pitiful, and yet she radiated enthusiasm. "Sure enough, the big brute came at five in the morning and chucked us out into the street . . . and also . . . also . . . W ell then, let's forget about him, what's past is past. You talk now, my jewel, tell me everything nice and slow."

I narrated my adventure to her briefly, as I removed the bundle of money that the man from Larache had hung around my neck. I didn't mention escaping out of the window, nor the threatening shouts of the soldier, nor the pistols abandoned under the lone sign for the Malalien stop. I just handed her the contents of the pouch and then started to take off the haik and the nightdress I was wearing underneath.

"You can go rot, Palomares!" she shouted, laughing, throwing the banknotes in the air. "Go rot in hell, you haven't caught me!"

Then her clamor stopped dead, and it wasn't because she had suddenly recovered her good sense, but because what she had before her eyes prevented her from carrying on her excitement.

"But you've been massacred, child! You look just like the Christ of the Five Wounds!" she exclaimed on seeing my naked body. "Does it hurt a lot, my child?"

"A little," I murmured, as I let myself drop like a dead weight onto the bed. I was telling a lie. The truth was that I was hurting right down to my soul.

"And you're filthy as if you'd just been rolling

189

around in a rubbish dump," she said, her good
sense fully recovered. "I'm going to put some pots
of water on the fire to prepare you a nice hot bath.
And then some liniment compresses for you where
you're hurt, and then . . ."

I didn't hear any more. Before the Matutera had
finished her sentence, I'd fallen asleep.

CHAPTER THIRTEEN

As soon as the house had been put back together and we'd returned to our normal routines, Candelaria set about looking for an apartment in the *ensanche* in which she could install my business. Tetouan's *ensanche,* so different from the Moorish medina, had been built according to European standards to meet the needs of the Spanish Protectorate: to house its civil and military installations and to provide lodging and businesses for the families from the Peninsula that were gradually making Morocco their permanent home. The new buildings, with white façades, ornamented balconies, and a look that was somewhere between modern and Moorish, lined the broad streets and spacious squares that made up a harmonious grid. Through them walked well-coiffed women and men in hats, uniformed soldiers, children dressed in the European style, and formal couples arm in arm. There were trolleys and a few automobiles, cake shops, brand-new cafés, and exclusive up-to-date shops. Order and calm permeated this universe, in contrast to the hustle and bustle, the smells and the voices of the souqs in the medina, which seemed to be somewhere out of the past, surrounded by walls and opening out to the world through seven gates. And between the two spaces,

191

the Arab and the European, almost like a border, was La Luneta, the street I was about to leave behind me.

I knew that when Candelaria finally managed to track down a place for me to set up my workshop, my life would take a new turn and I would yet again have to mold myself to it. In anticipation of this, I decided to change: to remake myself altogether, unburdening myself of the old baggage to start from scratch. In the previous few months I'd slammed the door on my entire yesterday; I'd stopped being a humble dressmaker and transformed myself successively into a whole heap of different women. A civil-service candidate, heiress of a major industrialist, globe-trotting lover to a scoundrel, hopeful aspirant to run an Argentine company, frustrated mother of an unborn child, a woman suspected of fraud and theft in debt up to her eyebrows, and a gunrunner camouflaged as an innocent local woman. In even less time now I'd have to forge a new personality for myself, since none of the earlier ones would do. My old world was at war, and my love had evaporated, taking with him my possessions and my illusions. The child who had never been born had dissolved into a puddle of congealed blood as I got off a bus, there was a file with my details circulating through the police forces of two countries and three cities, and the small arsenal of pistols that I'd transported attached to my skin might already have taken a life. Intending to turn my back on such pitiful baggage, I decided to confront the future from behind a mask of security and courage, preventing people from seeing my fear, my miseries, and the dagger that was still piercing my soul.

I decided to begin with the outside, to give

myself the façade of a woman who was worldly and independent, to keep people from seeing my reality as the victim of a bastard and the dark origins of the establishment I was about to open. To do that I'd have to put a layer of makeup over the past, invent a present in great haste, and plan out a future as false as it was magnificent. And I'd have to act quickly; I had to begin right away. Not one more tear shed, not another lament. Not a single submissive look back. Everything should be present, everything should be today. So I chose a new personality that I drew out of my sleeve like a magician might whip out a string of handkerchiefs or the ace of hearts. I decided to transform myself, and my choice was to adopt the appearance of a woman who was solid, solvent, experienced. I'd have to fight hard to get my ignorance mistaken for haughtiness, my uncertainty for sweet apathy, for no one even to suspect my fears, hidden in the firm tread of a pair of high heels and a look of confident determination. For no one to guess at the immense effort I was still making every day to overcome my sadness, one bit at a time.

The first move was to set about changing my style. The uncertainty of recent times, the miscarriage, and convalescence had reduced my body by at least six or seven kilos. The bitterness and the hospital had eliminated the roundness of my hips, some of the volume of my breasts, part of my thighs, and any curviness that had ever existed around my waist. I didn't try too hard to recover any of that but began instead to feel comfortable with my new silhouette: one more step forward. Retrieving from my memory how some of the foreign women in Tangiers dressed, I decided to adapt my scant wardrobe with adjustments and repairs. I'd be less strict than my compatriots, more suggestive without being indecorous or indecent. Brighter, more colorful tones, lighter-weight fabrics. Blouse buttons a little more open at the neck and skirts just a little shorter. At the cracked mirror in Candelaria's room, I reinvented myself, trying out and making my own all those glamorous ways women crossed their legs, which I'd observed every day at aperitif time on the terraces, the elegant way they'd make their way with such poise along the broad sidewalks of the Boulevard Pasteur, and the grace with which their recently manicured fingers would lift up a French fashion magazine, a gin fizz, or a Turkish cigarette in an ivory holder.

For the first time in more than three months I paid attention to how I looked, and I discovered that I needed to quickly revamp myself. A neighbor plucked my eyebrows, another gave me a manicure. I went back to using makeup after months with my face bare: I chose pencils to outline my lips, carmine to fill them out, colors for my eyelids, rouge for my cheeks, liner and mascara for my eyes. One day I had Jamila cut my hair with the sewing scissors, following exactly a photo in the old issue of *Vogue* I'd brought in my suitcase. The thick dark mop that had come halfway down my back fell in worn locks onto the kitchen floor, like the wings of dead crows, till I was left with a smooth straight crop along the line of my jaw, with a part on one side and a tendency to fall untamed over my right eye. To hell with that hot, thick, long hair that had so fascinated Ramiro. I couldn't have said whether the new haircut suited me or not, but it made me feel fresher, freer. Renewed, taken away forever from

194

those afternoons under the fan blades in our room at the Hotel Continental, from those endless hours with no shelter but his body encircling mine and the great thick mane spread like a shawl over the sheets.

Candelaria's plans were realized only a few days later. First she identified three properties in the *ensanche* that were available for immediate rental. She explained the details of each one to me, we weighed up together what was good and bad about each, and finally we made our decision.

The first place Candelaria had told me about seemed to be the perfect site: large and modern, never before lived in, close to the post office and the Teatro Español. "It's even got a movable shower just like a telephone, honey, except that instead of hearing the voice of the person who's talking to you there's a gush of water coming out that you can point wherever you want," explained the Matutera, astounded by the marvel. We ruled it out, however, because it adjoined a still-empty plot littered with stray cats and junk. The *ensanche* was growing, but there were still places, here and there, that hadn't yet been developed. We thought that the setting might perhaps not offer quite the right image to the sophisticated customers we aimed to attract, so the workshop with the telephone shower was ruled out.

The second proposal was positioned on Tetouan's main road, in those days called the Calle República, in a beautiful house with turrets on its corners and close to Plaza de Muley el Mehdi, which would soon become known as Primo de Rivera. This site also seemed at first glance to have everything we needed: it was spacious, with an imposing presence, and it was not located next to a vacant lot, but rather on a corner that opened onto two central, well-used arteries. The building next door, however, was home to one of the finest dressmakers in the city, a seamstress of a certain age with a solid reputation. We weighed up the situation and decided to rule out that place, too: better not to upset the competition.

So we went for the third option. The property that finally would end up being converted into my workplace and my home was a large apartment on the Calle Sidi Mandri, in a building with a tiled façade close to the Casino Español, Benarroch passage, and the Hotel Nacional; not far from the Plaza de España, the High Commission, and the caliph's palace with its imposing sentries guarding the entrance and an exotic array of sumptuous turbans and cloaks swaying in the air.

Candelaria closed the deal with Jacob Benchimol, a Jew who from that moment, and with considerable discretion, became my landlord in exchange for the punctual sum of three hundred and seventy-five pesetas a month. Three days later, I, the new Sira Quiroga, falsely metamorphosed into someone I perhaps wasn't but might end up being one day, took possession of the place and threw open the doors to a new phase in my life.

"On you go, on your own," said Candelaria, handing me the key. "It's best that we're not seen going around together too much from now on. I'll be over in just a little bit."

I made my way through the comings and goings of La Luneta, the subject of constant male glances. I didn't remember ever having received even a quarter as many in the months gone past, when my image was that of an insecure young woman with her hair drawn back into an unattractive bun, walking lethargically and dragging along the clothing and injuries of a past she was trying to forget. Now I moved with feigned confidence, forcing myself to emanate an air of arrogance and savoir faire that no one would have guessed at only a week earlier.

Even though I tried to impose a leisurely rhythm on my steps, it didn't take me more than ten minutes to reach my destination. I'd never noticed the building before, even though it was only a dozen paces from the main road in the Spanish quarter. I was pleased at first sight to note that it combined all the features I'd considered desirable: an excellent location and an imposing front door, a certain air of Arab exoticism from the tiles of the façade, a certain air of European sobriety in the arrangement of the interior. The shared hallways were elegant and well proportioned; the staircase, while not being too broad, had a handsomely forged handrail that curved gracefully as it ascended.

The main door was open, as they all were in those days. I assumed there was a caretaker, though there was none to be seen. I began to climb the stairs nervously, almost tiptoeing, trying to muffle the sound of my tread. While outside I'd increased in confidence and poise, deep down I was still intimidated and preferred to go unnoticed as much as possible. I arrived at the main floor without passing anyone and found myself on a landing with two identical doors. Left and right, both closed. The first belonged to the neighbors I had not yet met. The second was mine. I took the key out of my pocket, inserted it into the lock with nervous fingers, then turned it. I pushed shyly and for several seconds didn't dare to go in;

I just cast my eyes over what the gap in the door allowed me to see. A large reception room with bare walls and a floor of geometric tiles in white and maroon. The start of a corridor at the back. On the right, a large living room.

Over the years there have been many times when my destiny has delivered me unexpected moments, unforeseen twists and turns that I've had to handle on the fly as they appeared. Occasionally I was ready for them; very often I wasn't. Never, however, was I so aware of entering a new stage as I was that afternoon in October when I finally dared to cross the threshold and my steps sounded hollowly in the unfurnished apartment. Behind me was a complicated past, and in front of me, like an omen, I could see a space opening out, a great empty space that time would take care of filling up. But with what? With things, and affections. With moments, sensations, and people: with life.

I walked toward the living room in the half gloom. Three closed balcony doors protected by green wooden shutters kept the daylight out. I opened them one by one, and the Moroccan autumn poured into the room, filling out the shadows with sweet premonitions.

I savored the silence and solitude, waiting a few minutes before undertaking any activity. As those minutes passed I didn't do anything, just remained standing there in the center of that emptiness, getting used to my new place in the world. After a short while, when I thought it was time to break out of that lethargy, I finally summoned a reasonable dose of decisiveness and got going. With Doña Manuela's old workshop as my reference point, I went over the whole apartment and mentally parceled out the different areas. The living room would serve as the main reception area: that's where ideas would be presented, patterns consulted, fabrics and styles chosen, and orders placed. The room closest to the living room, a sort of dining room with a bay window in the corner, would be the fitting room. A curtain halfway down the corridor would separate that outer area from the rest of the apartment. The next stretch of the passageway and its corresponding rooms would be converted into the working area: workshop, storeroom, ironing room, the depository of off-cuts and hopes, whatever would fit. The third part, at the back, the darkest and least elegant part, would be for me. That is where the real me would live, the woman in pain, forcibly expatriated, debt-ridden, burdened with lawsuits and insecurities. The woman who had nothing to her name but a half-empty suitcase and a mother alone in a distant city who was struggling to survive. Who knew that setting up this business had cost the price of a large heap of pistols. That would be my refuge, my private space. From there outward, if luck finally stopped turning her back on me, would be the public domain of the dressmaker lately arrived from Spain to set up the most magnificent fashion house that the Protectorate had ever seen.

I returned to the entrance and heard someone knocking on the door. I opened it at once, knowing who it was. Candelaria slipped in like a particularly solid earthworm.

"How do you find it, girl? Do you like it?" she asked anxiously. She'd tidied herself up for the occasion; she was wearing one of the outfits I'd made for her, a pair of shoes she'd inherited from me and that were two sizes too small for her, and a somewhat unwieldy hairdo that her dear friend Remedios had done for her in great haste. Beyond the clumsy makeup on her eyelids, her dark eyes had a contagious gleam. It was a special day for the Matutera, too, the start of something new and unexpected. With the business almost ready to begin, she had done everything she possibly could do for the first time in her stormy life. Perhaps the new phase would make up for the hunger in her childhood, the beatings she received from her husband, the continual threats she'd been hearing for years from the police. She'd spent three-quarters of her life cheating, constructing cunning wiles, hurtling onward, and arm wrestling with bad luck; maybe it was finally time for her to take a rest.

I didn't reply immediately to her question about what I thought of the place; first I held her gaze a few moments, stopping to weigh up everything that this woman had meant to me ever since the commissioner had deposited me in her house like an unwanted package.

As I regarded her in silence, unexpectedly I saw the shadow of my mother pass in front of her face. Dolores had very little in common with the Matutera. My mother was all rigor and temperance; Candelaria was pure dynamite. Their modes of being, their ethical codes, and the way they faced up to what fate offered them were quite different, but for the first time I saw a certain similarity between the two of them. Each, in her way and in her own world, belonged to a stock of brave women who fight their way through life with the little that luck gives them. For myself and for them, for all of us, I, too, had to fight to make that business stay afloat.

"I like it very much," I replied at last with a smile. "It's perfect, Candelaria; I couldn't have imagined a better place."

She returned my smile and pinched me on the cheek, brimming with affection and a wisdom as old as time. We both sensed that from then on everything would be different. Yes, we'd still see each other, but only from time to time, and discreetly. We'd no longer be sharing a roof, no longer be together to witness the arguments fought across the tablecloth, no longer be clearing the table together after dinner or talking in whispers in the darkness of my wretched room. But we both knew that until the end of time we would be joined by something that no one else would ever hear us speak of.

CHAPTER FOURTEEN

In less than a week I was all set up. Spurred on by Candelaria, I went about organizing the space, asking her for certain pieces of furniture, equipment, and tools. She took it all on, bringing to it her ingenuity as well as the banknotes, ready to sacrifice her very eyelashes to this business whose fortunes remained uncertain.

"Ask me loud and clear, my angel, because I've never seen a fancy dressmaker's workshop in my goddamn life, so I have no idea what equipment a business like this needs. If we didn't have the war on our backs the two of us could just go to Tangiers and get some marvelous French furniture at Le Palais du Mobilier, and while we were there half a dozen pairs of panties in La Sultana, but since we're stuck in Tetouan with broken wings and I don't want people to associate you too much with me, what we'll do is you'll ask me for things and I'll figure out a way to get hold of them through my contacts. So just set me going, child: tell me what I've got to go hunt for and where to start."

"First, the living room. It has to represent the image of the establishment, to give a sense of elegance and good taste," I said, recalling Doña Manuela's workshop and all the residences I'd seen on my deliveries. Although the apartment on Sidi Mandri, built to the proportions of Tetouan, was much smaller in its look and scale than the fine houses of Madrid, my memory of old times could serve as an example of how to arrange the present.

"And what do we put in it?"

"A gorgeous sofa, two pairs of good armchairs, a large table in the center, and two or three smaller ones to serve as side tables. Damask curtains over the balcony doors and a big lamp. That'll be enough for now. Not many things, but very stylish and of the best quality."

"I don't see how I'm going to be able to get hold of all that, girl — Tetouan hasn't got shops with such extravagant stock. Let me think a bit; I have a friend who works with a transport company, I'll see if maybe I can get him to make me a delivery . . . Anyway, don't you worry about it, I'll sort it out somehow, and if any of the things are second- or thirdhand but of good, really good quality, I don't think that matters much, right? That way it'll seem as though the house has more old-fashioned class. Go on."

"Images of designs, foreign fashion magazines. Doña Manuela had them by the dozen; when they got old she'd give them to us and I'd take them home, and I never tired of looking at them."

"That'll be hard to get hold of, too; since the uprising you know the borders have been closed and we aren't receiving very much from outside. But, well, I know someone with a safe-conduct to Tangiers, I'll sound him out to see if he can bring me some as a favor; he'll give me a hefty bill in exchange, but, well, God knows . . ."

"Let's hope he gets lucky, and be sure that

there's a good pile of the best ones." I recalled the names of some of the ones I used to buy myself in Tangiers toward the end, when Ramiro was beginning to drift away from me. I had taken refuge for entire nights in their beautiful drawings and photographs. "The American ones — *Harper's Bazaar, Vogue,* and a couple from France," I added. "As many as he can find."

"Consider it done. What else?"

"For the fitting room, a triple mirror. And another couple of armchairs. And an upholstered bench for putting the clothes down on."

"And?"

"Material. Some swatches of the best fabrics to use as samples, not whole pieces until we've got things under way."

"They have the best ones at La Caraqueña; we're having nothing to do with the *burrakía* that the Moors sell next to the market, which are far less elegant. I'll also go see what the Indians on La Luneta can get me, as they're very smart and always keep something special out back. And they've also got good contacts with the French neighborhood, so let's see if they might not be able to get some interesting little things out of there. Keep talking."

"A sewing machine, a Singer from America if possible. Even though almost all the work is done by hand, it's useful to have one. And also a good iron and ironing board. And a pair of mannequins. As for the rest, it's best if I sort those out quickly myself, just tell me where I'll find the best shop."

And on and on we went, organizing everything. First I would place my order and then Candelaria would scheme tirelessly to get us what we needed. Sometimes things would appear disguised and at

204

strange times, covered in blankets and carried by men with sallow faces. Sometimes the deliveries would happen in daylight, witnessed by whoever was out on the streets. Furniture arrived, and painters, and electricians; I received parcels, tools, and an endless variety of goods. Wrapped in my new image as a woman of the world radiating glamour and ease, I supervised the whole process from beginning to end with an expression of resolve, my eyelashes thick with mascara, my new hairstyle perpetually groomed, my feet shod in stylish high heels. I dealt with any contingencies that presented themselves and allowed myself to come to be known among the neighbors, who would greet me discreetly when they passed me at the front door or on the stairs. Downstairs on the ground floor there was a milliner's and a tobacconist's; on the main floor, opposite me, lived an older lady in mourning and a chubby young man with glasses whom I took to be her son. Upstairs lived families with crowds of children who tried to nose out whatever they could about their newest neighbor.

Everything was ready in a few days; all we still needed were customers. I remember as though it were yesterday the first night I slept there, alone and terrified. I barely managed a moment's sleep. In the small hours I heard the last domestic shufflings in the nearby apartments: some child crying, a radio turned on, the mother and son opposite arguing noisily, the sound of crockery and water coming out of the tap as someone finished washing the last dishes from a late dinner. As the early hours of the morning progressed, the external sounds fell silent and other ones, imaginary ones, took their place: it seemed that the

205

furniture creaked too much, that there were footsteps on the floor tiles in the hallway, that shadows were spying on me from the newly painted walls. Before sensing even the first ray of sunlight, I was already out of bed, unable to contain my anxiety any longer. I made my way to the living room, opened the shutters, and leaned out to wait for morning to come. The minaret of a mosque sounded the call to *fajr,* the first prayers of the day. There still wasn't anyone on the streets, and the mountains of the Ghorgiz, barely perceptible in the gloom, began to appear, majestic, with the arrival of the first light. Bit by bit, sluggishly, the city was being set in motion. The Moorish servant girls began to arrive, wrapped in their haiks and shawls. Some men went out to work headed in the opposite direction, and a number of black-veiled women, in twos and threes, made their way hurriedly to an early Mass. I didn't wait to see the children heading out to school, or the shops and offices opening up for the day, or the maids going out for *churros,* or the mothers heading for the market to choose the things that the young Moorish delivery boys would then carry back to their houses in the big baskets they bore on their backs. Before all that had begun, I'd gone back inside to the living room and sat down on my brand-new maroon-colored taffeta sofa. What for? To wait for my luck to change at last.

Jamila arrived early. We smiled nervously; it was the first day for both of us. Candelaria had given up the girl's services to me, and I appreciated the gesture: we'd become very fond of each other, and she'd be a good ally for me, a younger sister. "It'll take me two minutes to find myself a Moorish maid," Candelaria had said. "You take Jamila, she's a good girl, you'll see how much help she'll be to you." And so sweet Jamila came with me, delighted to be getting out of the heavy burden of boardinghouse chores and beginning a new line of work with her *Siñorita* that would allow her youth to be somewhat less wearisome.

Yes, Jamila arrived, but no one else followed. Not on that first day, or the following one, or the next. Those three mornings I opened my eyes before dawn had broken and I got myself ready with the same scrupulous care. My clothes and my hair impeccable, the house spotless, the glamorous magazines with their elegant smiling women on the covers, the tools in order in the workshop: everything perfect, waiting for someone to require my services. No one, however, seemed to have any intention of doing so.

Sometimes I'd hear noises, footsteps, voices on the stairs. Then I'd run on tiptoes to the door and look anxiously through the peephole, but the sounds never turned out to be for me. My eye fixed to the round opening, I saw figures go past, burdened servant girls, delivery boys, the porter in her apron, the postman coughing, and an endless procession of other figures. But nobody came who was ready to order her wardrobe from my workshop.

I hesitated between telling Candelaria and continuing to wait patiently. I hesitated another day, two days, three, till I had almost lost count. Finally I made my decision: I'd go to La Luneta and ask her to work her contacts, to resort to anything necessary to let potential clients know that the business was now up and running. Unless she could do that, our joint venture would die before it had even begun. But I didn't get the

207

chance to call on the Matutera to act, because that very morning, at last, the doorbell rang.

"*Guten Morgen.* My name is Frau Heinz, I am new in Tetouan and I need some clothes."

I received her dressed in a suit that I'd sewn for myself only a few days earlier. A navy blue tube skirt, narrow like a pencil skirt, with a fitted jacket but no blouse underneath, and with the top button placed just at the point beyond which the décolletage would cease to be decent. And yet tremendously elegant, all the same. As a finishing touch, around my neck hung a long silver chain that ended in an old pair of scissors of the same metal; they were no use for cutting because of their age, but I had found them in an antiquarian's bazaar while I was looking for a lamp and decided immediately that I wanted to make them a part of my new image.

The new arrival had barely looked me in the eye as she introduced herself — her gaze seemed more concerned with gauging the distinction of the establishment in order to be sure that it was of the level she required. It turned out that I found it easy to attend to her — I just had to pretend that I wasn't myself but Doña Manuela reincarnated in the person of an attractive and competent foreigner. We sat down in the living room, each of us in one armchair, her with a determined pose that was a little manly, and me with my very best leg-crossing that I'd practiced a thousand times. With her broken Spanish she told me what she wanted. Two day suits, two outfits for going out at night. And an outfit for playing tennis.

"No problem," I lied.

I didn't have the slightest idea of what the hell an outfit for such an activity might be, but I wasn't prepared to acknowledge my ignorance. I wouldn't have admitted it even if I'd been standing before a firing squad. We consulted the magazines and examined styles. For the evening wear she chose creations from two of the great designers of the time, Marcel Rochas and Nina Ricci, selected from the pages of a French magazine with all the haute couture of the 1936 autumn/winter season. The ideas for the daywear came from the American *Harper's Bazaar:* two outfits from the house of Harry Angelo, a name I'd never heard mentioned before, though I was extremely careful not to admit as much. Delighted at the array of magazines in my possession, the German lady made a great effort to ask me in her rudimentary Spanish where I had obtained them. I pretended not to understand her: if she were to learn of the wiles my business partner the Matutera used in getting hold of them, my first client would have been out the door as fast as her legs could carry her, never to be seen again. After picking the designs, we moved on to the choice of fabrics. With the samples that a variety of shops had supplied me with, I laid out before her a whole catalog whose colors and qualities I described for her, one by one.

It took relatively little time to reach a decision. Chiffon, velvet, and organza for the evening wear; flannel and cashmere for daytime. As for the pattern and fabric for the tennis outfit, we didn't discuss that; I'd work it out when the time came. She stayed a long hour. Halfway through, Jamila, dressed in a turquoise caftan and with her huge dark eyes painted with kohl, made her silent appearance with a burnished tray carrying Moorish pastries and sweet tea with mint. The German

lady accepted, delighted, and with a barely noticeable wink of complicity I conveyed my gratitude
to my new servant. The final task was to take the
measurements. I jotted the information down
quickly in a leather-covered notebook: the cosmopolitan version of Doña Manuela into which I'd
transformed myself was proving extremely useful.
We agreed on a first fitting for five days later and
said our good-byes with exquisite politeness.
Good-bye, Frau Heinz, and thank you for the
visit. Good-bye, Fräulein Quiroga, until next time.
No sooner had I closed the door than I covered
my mouth with my hand to stop myself from
screaming and squeezed my legs together to stop
myself from stamping on the floor like a wild colt.
If I'd given free rein to my impulses, I would have
let loose all the enthusiasm I felt at knowing that
our first client had been snagged and there was
no going back now.

I worked morning, afternoon, and night over
the next few days. It was the first time I'd put
together items of that scope all on my own,
without the supervision or the help of my mother
or Doña Manuela. I worked with all my senses,
and then some, but even so, the fear of failure
didn't leave me for a second. I mentally took apart
the outfits from the magazines, and when I
couldn't get any more out of the pictures I
sharpened my imagination and intuited the things
I wasn't able to see. I marked up the materials
with a bit of soap and cut pieces with as much
fear as precision. I assembled, disassembled, and
reassembled. I tacked, overcast, attached, took
apart, and reconstructed on a mannequin until
the result looked satisfactory. A lot had changed
in fashion since I'd begun to move in that world

of fabrics and threads. When I started at Doña Manuela's workshop in the mid-twenties, loose lines were predominant; low waists and wide cuts for daytime, cleanly cut straight gowns of exquisite simplicity for the night. The thirties brought with them longer garments, fitted waists, bias cuts, prominent shoulders, and voluptuous outlines. Fashions were changing, just as times were changing, and with them the demands of our clientele and the dressmaker's arts. But I knew how to adapt: I would have liked to be able to handle my own life with the same ease that I could accommodate myself to the whims of the fashion trends dictated from Paris.

CHAPTER FIFTEEN

The first few days passed in a whirlwind. I worked without a break and went out little, just to take a quick walk as evening fell. At that hour I would usually run into one of my neighbors: the mother and son arm in arm from the apartment opposite me, two or three of the children from the upper floors racing down the staircase, a woman running home to prepare dinner. Only one shadow disturbed my activities during that first week: the wretched tennis outfit. Until I decided to send Jamila to La Luneta with a note: "I need magazines with pictures of tennis outfits. Doesn't matter if they're old."

"Siñora Candelaria say Jamila come back tomorrow."

So Jamila went back to the boardinghouse the next day and returned with a bundle of magazines she could barely carry.

"Siñora Candelaria say Siñorita Sira look these magazines first," she told me in her sweet voice and awkward Spanish.

She'd arrived flushed with haste, buzzing with energy, brimming with hope. In a way she reminded me of myself in my early years at the workshop on Calle Zurbano, when my role was simply to run back and forth to do errands and make deliveries, moving through the streets agile and unconcerned as a street cat. I'd let myself get distracted by any little amusement that might allow me to steal a few minutes away, putting off my confinement between four walls as long as possible. Nostalgia threatened to bring me down, but in time I was able to withdraw and dodge it breezily: I learned to develop the skill of flight whenever I sensed melancholy approaching.

I threw myself anxiously into the magazines. All of them were out of date, many of them well thumbed, some even missing their covers. Few were fashion magazines, most were general in their subject matter. While some of them were French, by and large they were Spanish or from the Protectorate itself: *La Esfera, Blanco y Negro, Nuevo Mundo, Marruecos Gráfico, Ketama.* Several pages had their corners folded over; perhaps Candelaria had scanned through them already and was flagging pages for me. I opened them, and the first thing I saw wasn't what I'd been expecting. In one photograph, two gentlemen with brilliantine-combed hair and dressed entirely in white shook hands over a net, while their left hands held tennis rackets. In another picture, a group of extremely elegant women were applauding as a trophy was handed over to a male player. I realized at this point that my note to Candelaria hadn't specified that the tennis outfits had to be for women. I was about to call Jamila for her to go back to La Luneta when I let out a cry of delight. In the third magazine I found just what I needed. An extensive feature showed a woman tennis player in a light-colored sweater and a sort of split skirt, halfway between a normal skirt and a pair of broad trousers: something I'd never seen

213

before, and probably neither had any of the magazine's readers, judging by the detailed attention the photographs seemed to be paying to this piece of gear.

The text was in French and I could barely understand it, but a few references immediately stood out: the tennis player Lilí Álvarez, the designer Elsa Schiaparelli, a place called Wimbledon. Despite my satisfaction at having found a reference to the garment I was working on, this feeling was soon clouded over by a sense of unease. I closed the magazine and examined it carefully. It was old, yellowing. I looked for the date: 1931. It was missing its back cover and had stains on its edges, and some of its pages were torn. I was seized with worry. I couldn't show an old relic like this to the German woman to ask her opinion about the outfit; it would overturn my whole false image as a sophisticated dressmaker on the cutting edge of fashion. I paced the house nervously, trying to find a solution, a strategy: anything I could use to resolve this unforeseen problem. After clattering back and forth along the hall tiles several dozen times, the only thing that occurred to me was to copy the design and try to pass it off as an original idea. But I had no idea how to draw, and the result would have been so clumsy that it would have brought me several rungs down the scale of my supposed pedigree. Unable to calm myself, I decided to resort to Candelaria one more time.

Jamila had gone out. The light demands of the new house allowed her endless periods of leisure, something that would have been inconceivable in her days packed with duties at the boardinghouse. Seeking to make up for lost time, the girl was going out constantly, using the excuse of having to do some little errand: "Siñorita want Jamila go buy sunflower seeds, yes?" Before I'd even answered she'd be trotting down the stairs in search of sunflower seeds, or bread, or fruit, or simply fresh air and freedom. I tore the pages out of the magazine and stuck them in my purse, then decided that I would go to La Luneta myself.

When I arrived I didn't find the Matutera. There was no one home but the new servant girl toiling away in the kitchen, and the schoolmaster sitting beside the window, afflicted with a bad cold. He greeted me warmly.

"Well, well, how nicely life seems to be treating us now that we've changed our den," he said, an ironic comment on my new appearance.

I barely paid attention to his remark, having other urgent matters to deal with.

"You don't happen to know where I might find Candelaria, Don Anselmo?"

"Not in the slightest, child; you know she's always here and there, flitting about like a lizard's tail."

I twisted my fingers nervously. I needed to find her, I needed a solution. The schoolmaster sensed my unease.

"Something up with you, girl?"

In desperation I turned to him for help.

"You aren't by any chance good at drawing, are you?"

"Me? Absolutely not. Anything harder than an equilateral triangle and I'm lost."

I didn't have the faintest idea what that was, but all that mattered was that my old boardinghouse ally couldn't help me. I went back to twisting my fingers and leaned out onto the balcony to see if I

215

could see Candelaria returning. I looked at the street filled with people, tapped nervously on the railing. Then I heard Don Anselmo's voice behind me.

"Why don't you tell me what you're after and we'll see if I can help?"

I turned around.

"I need someone who draws well to copy some designs from a magazine."

"Go to Bertuchi's academy."

"Whose?"

"Bertuchi, the painter." The expression on my face gave away my ignorance. "Honestly, girl, you've been in Tetouan for three months and you still don't know who Master Bertuchi is? Mariano Bertuchi, the greatest painter in Morocco?"

I didn't know who this Bertuchi was, nor was I in the least bit interested. All I wanted was an urgent solution to my problem.

"And he'll be able to draw me what I need?" I asked anxiously.

Don Anselmo gave a laugh, followed by a fierce coughing attack. The three packs of Toledo cigarettes a day were costing him dearly.

"The things you think of, Sirita, my child! How is Bertuchi going to draw clothing designs for you? Don Mariano is an artist, a man completely immersed in his painting, in making this country's traditional arts survive and disseminating the image of Morocco beyond its borders — he's not a portrait artist working on a commission! It's just that in his school you'll be able to find a number of people who'll be able to give you a hand: young painters without a lot to do, girls and boys attending painting classes."

"And where is this school?" I asked, putting on

216

my hat and quickly grabbing my bag.

"Next to the Puerta de la Reina."

The confusion on my face must have moved him again, because — after another rough laugh and one more bout of coughing — he got up from his seat with some effort and added, "Come on, then, let's go; I'll come with you."

We left La Luneta and entered the *mellah,* the Jewish quarter. As we walked down its tidy, narrow streets, I silently remembered my aimless wanderings on the night with the guns. Everything seemed different by daylight, however, with the small businesses and the currency exchanges open. We then went into the Moorish alleys of the medina, with its labyrinthine web in which I still found it hard to get my bearings. Despite the height of my heels and the tubular narrowness of my skirt, I tried to walk at a good trot over the cobblestones. Don Anselmo was prevented from keeping pace, due to his age and his cough, not to mention his incessant chatter about the coloring and the luminosity of Bertuchi's paintings; about his oils, his watercolors, and pen-and-ink drawings; about what the painter had done to promote the school of indigenous arts and the fine arts preparatory school.

"Have you sent any letters back to Spain from Tetouan?" he asked. "Well, almost all the stamps of the Protectorate are based on Bertuchi's drawings. Pictures of Alhucemas, Alcazarquivir, Xauen, Larache, Tetouan. Landscapes, people, scenes of everyday life: all come from his brush."

We walked on, he talking, I trying to quicken the pace as I listened.

"And the posters and placards to promote tourism, haven't you seen those either? I don't imagine

217

that in these ill-fated times anyone is planning to come out to Morocco for pleasure, but for years it's been Bertuchi's art that has been responsible for spreading the word about this country's bounties."

I knew which posters he was referring to. They were stuck up in a lot of places; I used to see them every day. Prints of Tetouan, Ketama, Arzila, and other spots of interest. And under them, the line "Spanish Protectorate in Morocco." It would not be long before they changed the name.

We reached our destination after a good walk on which we found ourselves passing men and souqs, goats and children, jackets and djellabas, voices haggling, well-swathed women, dogs and puddles, chickens, the smells of coriander and mint, of baking bread and olive dressings; in short, a torrent of life. The school was on the edge of the city, in a building that belonged to an old fort that loomed over the city wall. There was a certain amount of bustle in its vicinity, with young people coming in and out, some of them carrying large folders under their arms, some of them alone, and some chatting in groups.

"Here we are. I'll leave you and take advantage of this outing to get a little glass of wine with some friends who live in La Suica. I haven't been getting out much lately and I have to make the most of it every time I do."

"And how do I get back?" I asked, doubtful. I hadn't paid the slightest attention to the twists and turns of our route, thinking the schoolmaster would be making the return journey with me.

"Don't worry about that, any of these young men would be delighted to help you. Good luck with the drawings — you'll tell me later how you got on."

I thanked him for coming with me, went up the steps and into the enclosure. I noticed several stares suddenly lighting on me; in those days they can't have been used to the presence of a woman like me in that school. I went halfway into the entrance hall and stopped, uneasy, lost, not knowing what to do or whom to ask for. Before I had time to take my next step, I heard a voice behind me.

"Well, well — my pretty neighbor."

I turned, with no idea who could possibly have uttered those words, and saw the young man who lived opposite me. There he was, this time on his own. Many pounds heavier and with a lot less hair than someone who hadn't yet reached thirty should have. He didn't even let me speak.

"You seem a little adrift. Can I help?"

It was the first time he had ever addressed me. Even though we'd crossed paths several times since my arrival, I'd always seen him accompanied by his mother. On those occasions neither of us had murmured more than a polite good afternoon. I was also familiar with a less pleasant aspect to their voices: the one I heard from my house almost every night, when mother and son became embroiled in the most heated, stormy discussions. I decided to be candid with him: I hadn't prepared any evasions.

"I need someone to do some drawings for me."

"Might I ask what they're of?"

His tone wasn't rude, merely curious. Curious, direct, and slightly affected. He seemed much more confident on his own than in the company of his mother.

219

"I've got some photos from years ago and I want someone to draw me some sketches based on them. As I'm sure you know, I'm a dressmaker. They're for an outfit I need to sew for a client; I have to show it to her first to get her approval."

"Have you got the photographs with you?"

I gave a quick nod.

"Do you want to show them to me? I might be able to help."

I looked around me. There weren't too many people, but enough to make me uncomfortable about showing the clippings publicly. I didn't have to tell him this — he guessed for himself.

"Shall we go outside?"

Once we were out on the street, I took the old pages out of my handbag. Without saying a word, I held them out to him and he looked at them carefully.

"Schiaparelli, the muse of the surrealists — how interesting. I do adore surrealism, don't you?"

I hadn't the slightest idea what he was asking me, and at the same time I was in a terrible rush to solve my problem, so I drew the thread of the conversation back, ignoring his question.

"Do you know who would be able to do them for me?"

He looked at me through his thick glasses and smiled without parting his lips.

"Would you mind if I helped?"

That very night he brought me the sketches; I hadn't expected him to get them done so soon. I was already set for the end of the day, having put on my nightdress and a broad velvet housecoat that I'd sewn for myself to kill time in the empty days I had spent waiting for customers. I'd just had dinner from a tray in the living room, and it still held the leftovers of my frugal sustenance: a bunch of grapes, a piece of cheese, a glass of milk, some crackers. Everything was silent and switched off, except for a standing lamp still on in a corner. I was surprised to hear someone at the door at nearly eleven o'clock. I quickly approached the peephole, curious and alarmed in equal measure. When I saw who it was, I drew the bolt and opened the door.

"Good evening, my dear. I hope I'm not disturbing you."

"Don't worry, I was still up."

"I've got a few little things for you," he said, allowing me to glimpse several pieces of cardboard that he had been hiding behind his back.

He didn't hold them out to me but kept them half concealed as he remained impassive on the threshold, with his work out of my sight and an apparently inoffensive smile on his face. I hesitated a few moments, not wanting to invite him in at that late hour.

I eventually got the message. He didn't mean to show me a single bit until I had let him through.

"Please, do come in," I agreed at last.

"Thank you, thank you," he whispered gently, not hiding his satisfaction at having gotten what he wanted. He was dressed in a shirt and a pair of trousers, but with a felt dressing gown over them. And with his little glasses. And those slightly affected gestures of his.

He studied the entrance hall critically, then went into the living room without waiting for me to invite him all the way in.

"I like your home very much indeed. It's very airy, very chic."

"Thank you, I'm still settling in. Would you be

kind enough to show me what it is you've brought?"

My neighbor didn't need me to say any more to know that if I'd allowed him in at that time of night, it wasn't to hear his comments on decorative matters.

"Here's your little assignment," he said, at last showing me what he had kept hidden.

Three boards sketched in pencil and pastels depicted three angles and poses of a model with such perfect proportions that she no longer appeared realistic, dressed in a unique skirt that wasn't really a skirt. My approval must have shown instantly on my face.

"I take it you think they're good?" he said with a touch of undisguised pride.

"I think they're extremely good."

"You'll keep them, then?"

"Of course. You've gotten me out of a really difficult situation. Please tell me how much I owe you."

"Your thanks, no more than that; it's a welcome present. Mama says we have to be nice to our neighbors, even though she only likes you so-so. I think you seem too confident to her, and just a little bit frivolous," he observed ironically.

I smiled, and the tiniest current of sympathy seemed to join us momentarily; just a whiff that disappeared as quickly as it had come when we heard his progenitor yelling her son's name through the half-open door.

"Féééééé-lix!" She stretched out the *e* like the elastic on a slingshot, and once she'd extended it as far as she could, she fired off the second syllable hard. "Féééééé-lix!" she repeated. He rolled his eyes and made an exaggerated gesture of despair.

"Can't live without me, poor thing. I'm off."

His mother's harsh voice called for him again, a third time with that infinite initial vowel.

"Ask me again whenever you like; I'd be delighted to do more drawings for you, I'm crazy about anything from Paris. Well, I'm going back to the dungeon now. Good night, my dear."

I closed the door and spent a long while examining the drawings. They really were delightful; I couldn't have imagined a better outcome. That night I went to bed with a pleasant feeling.

The next day I was up early; I was expecting my client at eleven for the first fittings, but I wanted to finalize every detail before she arrived. Jamila was not yet back from the market, but she was due at any moment. At twenty to eleven the doorbell rang, and I thought perhaps the German lady had come early. I was again wearing the navy blue outfit: I'd decided to use it as though it were a work uniform, elegance of the most pure and simple kind. That way I'd make the most of my professional attire and conceal the fact that I hardly had any autumn clothes in my wardrobe. My hair was already done, my makeup perfect, and my old silver scissors were hanging around my neck. Just one little touch was missing: the invisible disposition of a woman of the world. I assumed the attitude quickly and opened the door confidently. And then the world crumbled at my feet.

"Good morning, miss," said the visitor, taking off his hat. "May I enter?"

I swallowed.

"Good morning, Commissioner. Of course —

please, do come in."

I led him to the living room and offered him a seat. He approached a chair unhurriedly, distractedly looking about the room as he walked through. His eyes moved slowly over the elaborate plaster moldings on the ceiling, the damask curtains, the large mahogany table covered in foreign magazines. And the old chandelier, beautiful and striking, which Candelaria had gotten hold of God knows where or for how much, and through what dark machinations. I felt my pulse speeding up and my stomach turning over.

At last he sat down and I sat opposite him, in silence, waiting to hear what he had to say, trying to hide my anxiety at his unexpected presence.

"Well, I see that things are progressing full steam ahead."

"I'm doing the best I can. I've started working; I was just waiting for a client."

"And what is the work you're doing exactly?" he asked. He knew the answer all too well, but for some reason he wanted me to tell him.

I tried to speak in a neutral tone of voice. I didn't want him to see me afraid and guilty looking, but on the other hand I didn't mean to come across to him as an overly confident, bold woman either, which he more than anyone knew I wasn't.

"I sew. I'm a dressmaker."

He didn't answer, he just looked at me with his piercing eyes and waited for me to continue my explanations. I gave them to him sitting up straight on the edge of the sofa, without displaying even a trace of the poses from the sophisticated repertoire I'd rehearsed a thousand times for my new persona. No spectacular leg crossing or casual smoothing of my hair. Not even the slightest batting of my eyelashes. Composure and ease, those were the only things I was trying to convey.

"I used to sew before in Madrid; I've spent half my life doing it. I worked in the atelier of a very well regarded dressmaker, where my mother worked as well. I learned a lot there: it was an excellent atelier, and we used to sew for important women."

"I understand. A very respectable occupation. And whom do you work for now, if I might ask?"

I swallowed again.

"Not for anyone. For myself."

He raised his eyebrows in an expression of feigned surprise.

"And may I ask, how was it that you managed to set up this business all on your own?"

Commissioner Vázquez might be inquisitive as the devil and hard as steel, but above all he was a gentleman and as such formulated his questions with immense courtesy. Courtesy seasoned with a touch of skepticism that he didn't try to hide. He seemed much more relaxed than on his visits to the hospital. He wasn't so strained, so tense. It was a shame that I wasn't able to offer him answers that matched the standard of his elegance.

"I had the money lent to me," I said simply.

"My word, how lucky you've been," he said ironically. "And would you be so kind as to tell me who the person was who's done you this extremely generous favor?"

I didn't think I could do it, but the reply came out of my mouth instantly. Instantly, and confidently.

"Candelaria."

"Candelaria the Matutera?" he asked with a half

smile loaded with sarcasm and disbelief in equal measure.

"Yes, that's right, *señor.*"

"Well now, how interesting. I didn't know there was so much to be made from black market dealings these days."

He looked at me again with those eyes like drills, and I knew then that my luck was balanced at exactly the midpoint between survival and being cast into the abyss. Like a coin that's been thrown into the air, with equal odds of landing heads or tails, or a clumsy tightrope walker on the wire, as likely to end up on the floor as to remain suspended. Or a tennis ball served by the model in the picture my neighbor sketched, an unlucky shot propelled by a graceful player dressed in Schiaparelli: a ball that doesn't cross the court but rather stops for the eternity of a few seconds on the edge of the net before tumbling one way or the other, unsure whether to grant the point to the glamorous tennis player sketched in pastels or her anonymous opponent. Salvation on one side, total collapse on the other, and me in the middle. That's how I saw myself in front of Commissioner Vázquez on that autumn morning. I closed my eyes, breathed in through my nose. Then I opened my eyes again and spoke.

"Listen, Don Claudio: you advised me to get some work, and that's what I'm doing. This is a decent business, not a fleeting pastime nor a cover for something unsavory. You have a lot of information about me: you know why I'm here, the reasons for my fall, and the circumstances that prevent me from leaving. But you don't know where I've come from and where I want to go, and now, if you'll allow me, I'm going to tell you.

226

I come from a humble home: my mother was single, raised me on her own. As for my father, the father who gave me the money and jewels that were largely responsible for my misfortune, I didn't learn about him until several months ago. I knew nothing of him until one day he suddenly got the idea into his head that he was going to be murdered for political reasons, and when he stopped to measure up his past, he decided to recognize me as his daughter and bequeath me a part of his inheritance. Until then, however, I hadn't even known his name, nor had I enjoyed a single wretched cent of his fortune. So I started working at a young age. At first my duties were nothing more than making deliveries and sweeping the floor for a pittance, as I was still a child. I was the same age as those girls in their Milagrosa school uniforms who just passed by on the street; maybe one of them was your own daughter on her way to school, that world of nuns, penmanship, and Latin declensions, which I never had the chance to master because in our house I had to learn a trade and earn a living. But I was happy to do it, believe it or not: I loved sewing, and I had a knack for it, so I learned, I tried hard, I persevered and in time became a good seamstress. And if there came a day when I gave it up, it wasn't on a whim, but because things had become difficult in Madrid with the political situation. A lot of our clients went abroad, the workshop shut down, and I was never able to find more employment.

"I've never looked for trouble, Commissioner; everything that's happened to me this past year, all the crimes I'm supposedly implicated in haven't come about of my own will, as you know very well, but because one unfortunate day some swine crossed my path. And you cannot even imagine what I'd give to erase that hour when that bastard entered my life, but there's no going back, and his problems are now my problems, and I know I've got to get myself out of them one way or another: that's my responsibility, and as such I am taking it on. You should know, though, that the only way I can do that is by sewing — I'm not good for anything else. If you shut this door to me, if you cut off these wings, you'll be suffocating me, because I won't be able to devote myself to anything else. I've tried, but I haven't found anyone willing to hire me because I have no other skills. So I'm asking you a favor, just one: let me continue with this workshop and don't investigate any further. Trust in me, don't bring me down. The rent on this apartment and all the furniture has been paid for, down to the last peseta; I haven't cheated anyone for them, and I don't owe anything to anyone. All this business needs is someone to do its work, and that's what I'm for, ready to give it my all, night and day. Just allow me to work in peace, I won't create any trouble for you, I swear to you by my mother, who is all I've got. And when I finally earn the money I owe in Tangiers, when I've settled my debt and the war is over, I'll go back to her and not trouble you any longer. But until then, I'm asking you, Commissioner, don't demand any more explanations of me, and let me keep going. This is all I ask of you: take your foot off my neck and don't suffocate me before I've started, because by doing that you will gain nothing and I, meanwhile, will lose everything."

He didn't reply, nor did I say another word; we just sat looking at each other. Contrary to all my expectations, I'd managed to get to the end of my speech with my voice still firm and my temper serene, without falling apart. At last I had got it all out, stripped myself of all the resentment I'd been feeling for so long. Suddenly I felt immensely tired. I was tired of having been stabbed in the back by an unscrupulous bastard, of the months I'd been living in fear, feeling constantly under threat. Tired of carrying around such heavy guilt, burdened down like those unfortunate Moorish women I used to see walking along together slowly, bent over, wrapped in their haiks and dragging their feet, carrying packages and bundles of firewood on their backs, or bunches of dates, little kids, buckets of clay, and sacks of lime. I was fed up with feeling afraid, humiliated; fed up with living such a sad life in that strange land. Tired, drained, exhausted, and yet ready to fight my way out of my ruin tooth and nail.

It was the commissioner who finally broke the silence. First he stood up; I did the same, carefully smoothing out the wrinkles from my skirt. He picked up his hat and turned it around a few times, looking at it with great concentration. It was no longer the soft summer hat of a few months earlier; now it was a dark winter fedora, a fine hat of chocolate-colored felt that he rotated in his hands as though it hid the key to his thoughts. When he had stopped moving it around, he spoke.

"Very well. I accept. If no one comes to me with any evidence, I won't inquire into how you've fixed things to set this all up. From now on I'm going to allow you to work and move your business forward. I'm going to let you live undisturbed. Let's see if we're lucky and that keeps trouble away from us both."

He didn't say any more, didn't wait for me to reply. No sooner had he finished speaking than he gave a gesture of farewell with a movement of his jaw and went over to the door.

Five minutes later Frau Heinz arrived. What thoughts went through my head during the time that separated the two of them is something I've never been able to remember. The only memory I've retained is that when the German woman rang the doorbell and I went over to open it, I felt like the weight of a whole mountain had been lifted from my soul.

PART TWO

Tangiers in the 1930s

CHAPTER SIXTEEN

Over the course of the autumn there were other clients, moneyed foreigners, for the most part — my business partner the Matutera had been correct in her prediction. Several Germans. The occasional Italian. Several Spanish ladies, too, almost always the wives of businessmen, since the administration and the army were going through some stormy times. The occasional rich Jew, Sephardic, beautiful, with her smooth old Spanish in different cadences, speaking Haketia with its melodious rhythm and strange, archaic words.

Bit by bit the business began to flourish, word began to spread. Money was coming in: in Nationalist pesetas, in French and Moroccan francs, in silver hassani currency. I put it all away in a small strongbox under lock and key in the second drawer of my nightstand. On the last day of every month I'd bring the total over to Candelaria. It took the Matutera less time than an *amen!* to separate a handful of pesetas for day-to-day expenses and roll all the rest of the notes into a tight bundle that she would place deftly down her cleavage. With the monthly earnings in the hot refuge of her opulent breasts, she would rush out to see which of the moneychangers would give her the best deal. Not long afterward she would return to the boardinghouse, out of breath and with a thick roll of sterling pounds protected in the same hiding place. Still catching her breath from all that haste, she would draw the loot out. "Just sticking to what's reliable, honey, because if you ask me the English are the smartest of the lot. Neither you nor I nor anyone else is going to be saving up Franco's pesetas, since if the Nationalists end up losing the war, they won't be any use to us at all, not even to wipe our asses with." She divided it up fairly — half for me, half for her. "And may we never do without again, my angel."

I got used to living alone, calm, unafraid. To being responsible for the workshop and myself. I worked a lot, entertained myself little. The volume of orders didn't require extra hands, so I continued working alone. The activity was incessant nonetheless — threads, scissors, imagination, and an iron. Sometimes I'd go out in search of materials, to stock up on buttons or choose spools of thread and fasteners. I made the most of my Fridays above all: I'd approach the neighboring Plaza de España — the Feddán, the Moors called it — to see the caliph come out of his palace and cross over to the mosque on a white horse, under a green parasol, surrounded by local soldiers in fantastic uniforms, an imposing spectacle. Then I'd usually walk along what was already beginning to be called the Calle del Generalísimo, continuing as far as Plaza de Muley el Mehdi to pass in front of the church of Our Lady of Victories, the Catholic mission, which the war had packed full of prayers and people in mourning.

The war: so far away, and yet so present. From the other side of the Strait we would receive news that came in waves, from the press and by word of mouth. In their homes people would mark out the advances with colored pins on maps fixed to the walls. I learned about what was going on in my country in the solitude of my own home. The only extravagance I allowed myself in those months was to purchase a radio; thanks to this, I learned before the year was out that the government of the Republic had moved to Valencia and left the people to defend Madrid alone. The International Brigades arrived to help the Republicans; Hitler and Mussolini recognized Franco's legitimacy; Primo de Rivera was executed in Alicante prison; my savings reached eighty pounds; Christmas arrived.

I spent that first African Christmas Eve in the boardinghouse. Though I tried to refuse the invitation, its owner persuaded me yet again with her overwhelming insistence.

"You're coming for dinner at La Luneta, and that's all there is to it — as long as Candelaria has room at her table nobody spends the holidays alone."

I couldn't refuse, but it cost me a tremendous effort. As the holiday approached, gusts of sadness began their invasion, through chinks in the windows and spaces under the doors, until the entire workshop was permeated with melancholy. How was my mother, how was she bearing the uncertainty of not hearing any word from me, how was she managing to support herself in these dreadful times? Unanswered questions assailed me at every moment, increasing my sense of uneasiness. My neighborhood did little to cheer me: there was barely a flicker of joy to be felt there despite the shop decorations, the people exchanging greetings, and the children of the neighboring

235

apartments humming carols as they trotted down the stairs. The sure knowledge of what was happening in Spain was so dark and heavy that no one seemed in the mood to celebrate.

I reached the boardinghouse after eight in the evening, after passing hardly anyone on the streets. Candelaria had roasted a couple of turkeys: the first proceeds from the new business had introduced a certain prosperity to her larder. I brought two bottles of sparkling wine and a round Dutch cheese brought over from Tangiers at the price of gold. I found the guests worn down, bitter, so very sad. Candelaria, on the other hand, tried hard to rally everyone's spirits, her sleeves rolled up, singing at the top of her voice as she put the finishing touches on the dinner.

"I'm here, Candelaria," I said, coming into the kitchen.

She stopped singing and stirring the pot.

"And what's the matter with you, if I might know? Coming in with that miserable face like you're being led off to the slaughterhouse."

"Nothing's the matter with me — what could be?" I said, looking for somewhere to put down the bottles while avoiding her gaze.

She wiped her hands on a cloth, grabbed my arm, and forced me to turn toward her.

"You don't fool me, girl. It's about your mother, isn't it?"

I didn't look at her, or answer.

"The first Christmas Eve out of the nest is ever so shitty, but you've got to grin and bear it, honey. I still remember mine, and you know in my house we were poor as mice and hardly did anything the whole night except sing, dance, and clap, with very little there to fill your belly. And yet for all

236

that, blood is thicker than water, even if the only things you've shared with your people have been hardships and miseries."

I still didn't catch her eye, trying to look as though I was concentrating on finding a space to put the bottles down amid the mountain of odds and ends that occupied the table. A mortar, a pot of soup, a large dish of custard. An earthenware bowl filled with olives, three heads of garlic, a sprig of bay leaves. She went on talking, close and sure.

"But bit by bit it all passes, you'll see. I'm sure your mother is fine, that tonight she'll be having dinner with her neighbors, and that even though she's remembering you and missing you, she'll be glad to know that at least you have the luck of being outside Madrid, far away from the war."

Perhaps Candelaria was right and my absence was more of a consolation to my mother than a sorrow. Maybe she thought I was still with Ramiro in Tangiers. She might have imagined us spending the evening having dinner in some stunning hotel, surrounded by unconcerned foreigners who danced between one course and the next, far from the suffering on the other side of the Strait. Although I'd tried to keep her informed by letter, everyone knew that the post from Morocco didn't get to Madrid, so those messages had probably never even left Tetouan.

"You're right," I murmured, barely parting my lips. I was still holding the bottles of wine, looking carefully at the table, unable to find a place to put them. And I wasn't brave enough to look Candelaria in the eye either, afraid that I wouldn't be able to hold back my tears.

"I certainly am, child, don't think about it

anymore. However hard absence may be, knowing your daughter is far from the bombs and machine guns is a good reason to be glad. So come on — be happy, be happy!" she shouted, grabbing one of the bottles from my hand. "You'll see, we'll be livening up very soon, dear heart." She opened it and raised it up. "To your mother, who gave you life," she said. Before I had a chance to reply she had taken a long swallow of sparkling wine. "Now you," she commanded, after wiping her mouth with the back of her hand. I didn't have the least desire to drink, but I obeyed. It was to Dolores's health. Anything for her.

We started dinner, but in spite of Candelaria's efforts to keep spirits merry, the rest of us didn't talk much. No one was even in the mood for an argument. The schoolmaster coughed till he looked like his sternum was going to split, and the shriveled-up sisters, even more shriveled up than usual, shed tears. The fat mother sighed, sniffed. The wine went to her Paquito's head, he started talking nonsense, the telegraph man answered him back, and finally we laughed. Then Candelaria got up and raised her cracked glass to everyone. To those present, those absent, each and every one. We hugged, we cried, and for one night there was only one faction, the one made up of our sorry troupe.

The first months of the new year were calm and filled with nonstop work. During that time my neighbor Félix Aranda became an everyday presence. Besides the proximity of our homes, I was also brought closer to him in another dimension that couldn't be gauged spatially. His somewhat peculiar behavior and my repeated need for assistance helped to establish a friendship between us at late hours of the night that would last for decades, through many phases of our lives. After those first sketches that solved my problem with the tennis player's attire, there would be more occasions when Doña Encarna's son offered a hand to help me leap gracefully over apparently insurmountable obstacles. Unlike the case of the Schiaparelli trouser-skirt, the second stumbling block that led me to seek another favor from him shortly after the first wasn't prompted by artistic necessity, but by my ignorance in matters of money. It had all begun some time earlier with a small inconvenience that wouldn't have posed any problem for anyone with a somewhat privileged education. However, the few years I had attended the modest school in my Madrid neighborhood hadn't amounted to much. Which was why, at eleven o'clock on the night before my workshop's first invoice was due to be delivered to the client, I had found myself hopelessly vexed by my inability to put in writing a description and price that corresponded to the work I had done.

It was in November. Over the course of the afternoon the sky had been turning dark grey, and when night fell it began to rain heavily, the prelude to a storm on its way over from the nearby Mediterranean: one of those storms that uprooted trees, knocked down electric wires, and made people huddle under their covers muttering a feverish torrent of litanies to Saint Barbara. Just a couple of hours before the weather changed, Jamila had taken the first orders, just completed, over to Frau Heinz's house. My first five pieces of work — two for evening, two for daytime, and one for tennis — had been taken down from their hangers in the workshop, where they had been kept awaiting their final ironing. Then they had been packed up in their canvas bags and conveyed in three successive trips to their destination. Jamila's return from the last trip brought with it a request.

"Frau Heinz ask that Jamila bring tomorrow morning bill in German marks."

And in case the message hadn't been absolutely clear, she handed me an envelope bearing a card with the message written on it. I sat down to think about how the hell I was going to make up an invoice, and for the first time my great ally, memory, refused to get me off the hook. Right through the setting up of the business and the creation of the first items of clothing, the designs I still treasured from the world of Doña Manuela had served as a resource I could draw on. The images I had memorized, the skills I'd learned, the mechanical movements and actions so often repeated had up till that moment furnished me with the inspiration to keep going and make a success of it. I knew down to the last detail how a good dressmaker's studio worked, how to take measurements, cut the patterns, pleat skirts, affix sleeves, and attach lapels, but however hard I searched my mental catalog of techniques and observations, I found nothing that would serve as a reference point for how to create an invoice. I had handled so many of them when I worked for Doña Manuela in Madrid, and it had been my job to deliver them to the homes of our clients; in some cases I'd even returned with the payment in my pocket. Yet I had never stopped to open one of those envelopes and examine its contents.

I considered resorting as usual to Candelaria,

but looking out over the balcony I could see how dark it was already, with the imperious wind driving an ever denser rain as relentless flashes of lightning approached from the sea. In consideration of this scenario, the walk over to the boardinghouse seemed to be the sheerest path to hell. So I decided to sort it out on my own: I got hold of a pencil and some paper and sat down at the kitchen table, all ready to begin the task. An hour and a half later and I was still there, with countless scraps of crumpled-up paper surrounding me as I sharpened the pencil with a knife for the fifth time, but still with no idea how many German marks would be equivalent to the two hundred and seventy-five pesetas I had planned on charging her. And right then, in the middle of the night, something suddenly clattered hard against the windowpane. I leapt to my feet so fast that I knocked over the chair. I saw immediately that there was light in the kitchen opposite, and in spite of the rain, and in spite of the time, I could see in it the chubby figure of my neighbor Félix, with his glasses, his sparse, curling hair, and his arm raised, ready to throw a second fistful of almonds. I opened the window to ask him angrily for an explanation for such incomprehensible behavior, but before I'd had the chance to say a word his voice crossed the gap between us, filtered through the thick splattering of the rain on the tiles of the building's central courtyard. The content of his message, however, came over loud and clear.

"I need refuge. I don't like thunderstorms."

I could have asked him if he was crazy. I could have informed him that he'd given me a terrible fright, shouted at him that he was an idiot, and closed the window without another word. But I did none of these things, because at that very moment a little light came on in my brain: perhaps this bizarre request could now be turned to my favor.

"I'll let you come over if you help me out," I said, addressing him informally without even thinking about it.

"Open the door, I'll be right over."

Needless to say, my neighbor knew that the exchange for two hundred and seventy-five pesetas was twelve Reichsmarks fifty. Just as he knew very well that a presentable invoice couldn't be drawn up on a cheap little sheet of paper with a worn old pencil, so he went back over to his house and returned at once with several pieces of marble-colored English paper and a Waterman fountain pen from which purple ink flowed out to create exquisite calligraphy. And he displayed all his ingenuity (which was considerable) and all his artistic talent (likewise considerable) and in just half an hour, between thunderclaps, and in his pajamas, he had not only drawn up the most elegant invoice that any European dressmaker in North Africa could ever have imagined, but he had also given my business a name. Chez Sirah had been born.

Félix Aranda was an unusual man. Amusing, imaginative, and cultured, yes. And also curious, and a busybody. And a bit eccentric and somewhat intrusive, too. The nighttime transit between his apartment and mine became a familiar ritual. Not exactly daily, but frequently. Sometimes we'd go three or four days without seeing each other, sometimes he'd come over five nights in a week. Or six. Or even seven. The regularity of our meetings just depended on something quite apart from us: on how drunk his mother was. What a strange relationship, what a dismal familial existence was being lived out behind the door opposite. Since the death of their father and husband years earlier, Félix and Doña Encarna had traveled through life together, to all appearances utterly harmonious. Every evening between six and seven they would take a walk together; they would attend masses and novenas together, stock up on medicine at the Benatar pharmacy, greet their acquaintances courteously, and have tea and pastries at La Campana. He, always offering her his arm, protecting her affectionately, walking at her pace: careful there, Mama, don't trip, this way, Mama, careful, careful. She — proud of her child — boasting of his talents left and right: my Félix says, my Félix does, my Félix thinks, oh, my Félix, what would I do without him?

The solicitous chick and the clucking hen were transformed, however, into a couple of monsters when they entered their most private territory. No sooner had they crossed the threshold of their home than the old lady wrapped herself in the uniform of a tyrant and took out her invisible whip to inflict the utmost humiliation on her son. Scratch my leg, Félix, my calf itches; not there, higher; you're so useless, child, how could I have given birth to an offspring like you? Put the tablecloth on properly, I can see it's not straight; not like that, that's even worse; put it back the way it was, you ruin everything you touch, little piece of shit, why couldn't I have left you in the foundling hospital when you were born? Look in my mouth and see if my pyorrhea has gotten any worse, get out the Agua de Carmen that relieves

243

my flatulence, rub my back with camphorated alcohol, file down this callus, cut my toenails, be careful, you fat lump of lard, you'll have my toe off; bring over the handkerchief so I can cough up some phlegm, bring me a Sor Virginia patch for my lumbago; wash my hair and put my curlers in, more carefully, idiot, you're going to make me bald . . .

That was how Félix grew up, with a double life whose two sides were as disparate as they were pitiful. No sooner had his father died than the beloved son stopped being that overnight: while he was still growing, and without anyone outside suspecting a thing, he became the focus of affection and treats in public and the object of all his mother's furies and frustrations in private. As though with the slash of a scythe, all his dreams were hacked down to the ground: leaving Tetouan to study fine art in Seville or Madrid, working out his confused sexuality and meeting other people like him, beings with unconventional spirits yearning to fly free. Instead he found himself facing the prospect of living permanently under the black wing of Doña Encarna. He completed his bachelor's with the Marianists at the Colegio del Pilar with brilliant qualifications that were of no use to him because his mother had taken advantage of her position as a suffering widow to get him an administrative position that was colored rat grey. Stamping forms in the General Supplies Office of the Municipal Services Division: the perfect job to beat down the most brilliant kind of creativity and keep it chained like a dog — now I'm offering you a slice of succulent meat, now I'm kicking you hard enough to burst your belly.

He bore the blows with a monklike patience.

244

And so, over the years, they maintained their imbalance unchanged, her tyrannizing him, and him docile, bearing up, tolerating. It was hard to know what it was that Félix's mother was looking for in him, why she treated him like that, what she wanted from her son apart from what he would always have been ready to give. Love, respect, compassion? No, she had these without having to make the least effort. He wasn't stingy with his affections — far from it, dear old Félix. Doña Encarna wanted something more. Devotion, unconditional availability, attention to her most ludicrous whims. Submissiveness, submission. Precisely what her husband had demanded of her in life. I assumed this was why she had gotten rid of him. Félix never told me openly, but like the boy in the fairy tale leaving a trail of breadcrumbs behind him, he left me clues along the way. All I did was follow them to reach my conclusion. The late Don Nicasio had probably been killed by his wife just as one dark night Félix would perhaps end up disposing of his mother.

It would be hard to say how long he would have been able to bear that wretched daily life had a solution not come to him in the most unexpected way. Somebody grateful for a well-done piece of work; a sausage and a couple of bottles of El Mono anisette as a gift; let's try it, Mama, go on, just a little glass, just wet your whistle. But it wasn't only Doña Encarna's lips that enjoyed the sickly sweet taste of the liqueur, but also her tongue, and her palate, and her throat, and her intestinal tract, and from there the fumes went to her head, and that same alcoholic night Félix found himself faced with a way out. From then on, the bottle of anisette was his great ally, his one

245

salvation and escape route out to the third dimension of his life. And never again was he just a model son when out in the public eye and a disgusting little rag in private; from then on he also became an uninhibited night walker, a fugitive in search of the oxygen he was lacking at home.

"A little bit more of the El Mono, Mama?" he would ask after dinner, without fail.

"Oh, go on then, give me just a drop. To clear my throat a bit better, I think I caught a chill in church this afternoon."

The four fingers of thick liquid went down Doña Encarna's gullet at vertiginous speed.

"It's what I've told you before, Mama, you don't wrap yourself up enough," Félix went on affectionately as he refilled the glass to the same level. "Come on, drink it up quickly, you'll see how fast you'll warm up." Ten minutes and three drinks of anisette later, Doña Encarna was snoring, half conscious, and her son was fleeing like a just-freed sparrow on the way to seedy dives, to meet up with people whom in daylight and in the presence of his mother he wouldn't have dared even to greet.

Following my arrival on Sidi Mandri and the night of the storm, my home became a permanent refuge for him. He would come over to leaf through magazines, to bring me ideas, to draw sketches and tell me funny things about the world, about my clients and all those people I used to pass every day with, but whom I didn't know. And so, night by night, I learned about Tetouan and its people: where they had come from and for what reasons. All those families in this alien land; who those ladies were that I sewed for; who had power,

246

who had money; who did what, and why, and when and how.

But Doña Encarna's devotion to the bottle didn't always have soothing effects, and then, regrettably, things would turn upside down. When the anisette wasn't enough to calm her, with the drunkenness would come hell. Those nights were the worst, because the mother didn't get into a state of harmless catatonia, she was transformed into a thundering Zeus capable of demolishing the dignity of the strongest person with her bellowing. And Félix, knowing that the morning hangover would erase any trace of her memory, would match her with other equally indecorous insults with the perfect knack of a knife thrower. Foul witch, evil bitch, crooked whore. God, what a scandal it would have been if their acquaintances from the pastry shop, pharmacy, and church pew had heard them! The following day, however, it seemed that forgetfulness had settled on them and cordiality would reign once more on their evening walk as though there had never been the slightest tension between them. Would you like a sugared bun with your tea today, Mama, or would you rather a meat pie? Whatever you prefer, Félix, you're always so good at choosing for me — go ahead, come on then, let's go now, we've got to pay our condolences to María Angustias, I've heard that her nephew has fallen at the battle of Jarama; oh, such a shame, my angel, just as well that being the son of a widow spared you from being called up; what would I have done — Holy Mother of God — if I'd been left alone here with my son at the front?

Félix was smart enough to know that there was some unhealthy abnormality hanging over that

247

relationship but not brave enough to put a stop to it once and for all. Perhaps that was why he tried to dodge his pitiful reality by turning his mother gradually into a drunk, escaping like a vampire in the small hours or laughing at his own miseries while searching for blame in a thousand ridiculous symptoms and contemplating the most outlandish remedies. One of his diversions was finding odd cures among the advertisements in the newspapers, lying on the sofa in my living room while I finished off a cuff or backstitched the final buttonhole of the day.

And then he'd say things like this to me:

"Do you think my mother's Hydra behavior has something to do with her nerves? Most likely this will take care of it. Listen, listen — 'Nervional. Awakens the appetite, aids digestion, normalizes the stomach. Eliminates changeable moods and dejection. Take Nervional — count on it.' "

Or this:

"If you ask me, the thing with Mama is a hernia. I'd already thought about giving her an orthopedic corset, to see if her bad tempers might pass, but listen to this: 'If you've got a hernia, you can avoid risks and discomforts with the unbeatable, innovative automatic compressor, a mechanical-scientific wonder that — without nuisances, straps, or encumbrances — will completely defeat your affliction.' It might just work — what do you think, girl, should I get her one?"

Or perhaps:

"What if it turns out it's something to do with her blood? Look what it says here. 'Richelet Blood Tonic. Vascular complaints. Varicose veins and ulcers. Remedy for tainted blood. Effective at eliminating uric toxins.' "

Or some other nonsense:

"What if it's piles? Or she has something wrong with her eye? How about if I find a witch doctor in the Moorish quarter to cast a spell on her? Truthfully, I don't think I ought to worry so much, because I trust that her Darwinian tendency will end up eroding her liver and will put an end to her soon enough, now that a bottle doesn't even last the old lady two days and she's burning a hole in my pocket." He stopped his speech, perhaps awaiting a reply, but he received none. Or at least not in words. "I don't know why you're looking at me with that face, girl," he added after a pause.

"Because I don't know what you're talking about, Félix."

"You don't know what I'm referring to when I talk about a Darwinian tendency? Do you not know who I mean by Darwin either? The one with the monkeys, the one with the theory that we humans are all descended from primates. If I say my mother has a Darwinian tendency it's because she's crazy about El Mono anisette, you see? Girl, you have a divine sense of style and you sew like the very angels, but on matters of general culture you really are rather in the dark, aren't you?"

I was, in fact. I knew I had a facility for learning new things and retaining information, but I was also aware of my educational deficiencies. I'd accumulated very little of the kind of knowledge one found in encyclopedias: little more than the names of a handful of kings recited by rote, and that Spain's northern limit is bounded by the Cantabrian Sea and the Pyrenees Mountains separating it from France. I could rattle off my times tables and was quick at using numbers in

249

daily situations, but I'd never read a book in my life, and as far as history, geography, art, or politics was concerned, all I knew was what I'd picked up during my months of living with Ramiro and in the constant free-for-all in Candelaria's boarding-house. I apparently could get away with passing myself off as a young woman with style and an exclusive dressmaker, but I was aware that as soon as anyone scratched beneath my outer shell they would have no trouble finding the fragility on which it was supported. Which was why, that first winter in Tetouan, Félix gave me an odd gift: he began to educate me.

It was worth it. For both of us. On my part, for what I learned and how I refined myself. On his part, because thanks to our meetings he filled his solitary hours with affection and company. In spite of his laudable intentions, however, my neighbor turned out to be a far from conventional teacher. Félix Aranda was a creature with aspirations to a free spirit who spent four-fifths of his time constrained between the despotic outbursts of his mother and the relentless tedium of the most bureaucratic of jobs, which meant that in his free hours the last thing one could expect of him was order, measure, and patience. To find that, I would have had to go back to La Luneta, for Don Anselmo to draw up a didactic plan to suit my ignorance. In any case, while Félix was never a methodical or organized sort of teacher, he did instruct me in many other matters as incoherent as they were disordered, which in the long run, one way or another, would be of quite some use to me in making my way through the world. And so, thanks to him, I became familiar with charac-ters like Modigliani, Scott Fitzgerald, and Josephine Baker, learned to tell cubism from Dadaism, discovered what jazz was, managed to locate the European capitals on a map, memorized the names of their best hotels and cabarets, and got as far as counting to a hundred in English, French, and German.

Also thanks to Félix I learned what my Spanish compatriots were doing in that distant land. I discovered that Spain had been exercising its protectorate over Morocco since 1912, a year after signing the Treaty of Algeciras with France, according to which — as often happens with poor relations — the Spanish nation had been left with the worst part of the country. The less prosperous part, the least desirable. The African cutlet, they called it. There were a number of things Spain was hoping to achieve there: revive the imperial dream; partake in the African colonial banquet being enjoyed by the nations of Europe, albeit dining only on the crumbs that the great powers conceded to them; and aspire to reach the ankle of France and England, now that Cuba and the Philippines had slipped out of our hands and our old Spain was as poor as a cockroach.

It wasn't easy to secure control over Morocco, even though the area allocated by the Treaty of Algeciras was small, the local population scant, and the land harsh and poor. It came at the cost of rebuffs and internal revolts in Spain, and thousands of Spanish and African deaths in the bloody madness of the brutal Rif War. They did manage it, however: they took control and almost twenty-five years after the official establishment of the Protectorate, with any internal resistance now having yielded, there my compatriots still were, with their capital firmly established and continuing to grow. Military men of every rank; civil servants from the postal service, customs, and public works; auditors, bank employees, businessmen and midwives, schoolteachers and nuns, bootblacks, barmen. Whole families who attracted other families in search of good salaries and a future there for the making, living alongside other cultures and religions. And me among them, just one person more. In exchange for its enforced presence over a quarter of a century, Spain had offered Morocco technical advances, developments in sanitation and infrastructure, the first steps toward a moderate improvement in agricultural yields, a school of the arts, and support for traditional crafts. And the native population obtained additional benefits as a result of satisfying the demands of the colonizers: electrification, better drinking water, schools and academies, businesses, public transport, dispensaries, and hospitals; a train linking Tetouan and Ceuta, as well as the one that still took passengers to the Río Martín beach. Spain had in material terms benefited very little from Morocco: there were barely any resources to be exploited. In human terms, however, they had obtained something important for one of the two sides in their civil strife: thousands of soldiers from the local Moroccan forces who were now fighting like wild beasts on the other side of the Strait for the distant cause of the rebel army under Franco.

Apart from learning about these matters and more besides, I enjoyed other things from Félix: company, friendship, and ideas for my business. Some of them turned out to be excellent and others altogether eccentric, but at least they gave us two solitary souls something to laugh about at the

252

end of the day. He never managed to persuade me to transform my workshop into a studio for experimenting in surrealism in which the hats would be shaped like shoes and telephones. Nor did he get me to use sea snails for the beading or bits of esparto grass on the belts, or convince me that I should refuse to take any client lacking in glamour. I did pay attention to him on other matters, however.

Following his recommendation, for example, I changed the way I spoke. I eliminated any slang and all colloquial expressions from my speech and created a new manner to allow me a greater air of sophistication. I started using certain French words and phrases that I'd heard repeatedly in Tangiers and had picked up from nearby conversations in which I'd almost never participated or from unexpected meetings with people with whom I'd never exchanged more than three lines. It was only a handful of expressions, just half a dozen of them, but he helped me to polish up my pronunciation and calculate just the right moments to use them. They were all aimed at my clients, those now and those to come. I'd ask permission to fix pins with a *vous permettez?*, finalize things with *voilà tout,* and praise results with a *très chic.* I'd talk of *maisons de haute couture* whose owners one might have assumed had once been my friends, and of *gens du monde* whom I had perhaps met in my supposed wanderings here and there. Whenever I proposed a style, pattern, or accessory, I'd hang from it the verbal tag *à la française;* all ladies were addressed as *Madame.* To highlight the patriotic dimension of the moment, we decided that whenever I had Spanish clients I would make appropriate reference to people and places I'd known in the old days when I'd been hobnobbing around the best houses in Madrid. I'd drop names and titles as easily as one might drop a handkerchief: lightly, without clamor or ostentation. That such-and-such a suit was inspired by the one I'd made a couple of years before for my friend the Marquise of Puga to debut at the Puerta de Hierro polo festival; how such-and-such a fabric was identical to the one that the eldest daughter of the Count and Countess of Encina used for her coming-out party in their palace on the Calle Velázquez.

It was also at Félix's suggestion that I ordered a box of ivory-white cards from La Papelera Africana bearing the name and address of the business and had a gilt plaque made for the door, inscribed in ornate script: *Chez Sirah — Grand Couturier. Couturier,* he said, was what the best French fashion houses called themselves in those days. That final *h* was his touch, too, to give the workshop a more international flavor, he said. I played along with him — and why not? After all, I wasn't hurting anyone with that little *folie de grandeur.* I heeded his advice on this matter and on a thousand other details, thanks to which I wasn't just able to make my way into the future more securely, but I also managed — drumroll, please — to pull a past out of my top hat, too. I didn't have to try too hard: with three or four poses, a handful of careful brushstrokes, and a few recommendations from my own personal Pygmalion, my small clientele set me up with a whole life in just a couple of months.

To the little colony of exclusive ladies who made up my clientele within that expatriate universe, I became a young haute couture dressmaker, daughter of a ruined millionaire, betrothed to an incredibly handsome aristocrat — both a seducer and an adventurer. It was also supposed that we had lived in several countries and found ourselves obliged by the political instability to shut up our homes and businesses in Madrid. At that moment my betrothed was off managing some prosperous firms in Argentina while I awaited his return in the capital of the Protectorate because I had been advised of the benefits of that climate for my delicate health. As my life had always been so active, so full of bustle, and so worldly, I felt incapable of just sitting around watching the time go by without devoting myself to some activity or other, and so I had decided to open a small atelier in Tetouan. Just for my own amusement, basically. Which explained why I didn't charge astronomical prices, nor turn down any kind of commission.

I never denied a single iota of the image that had been constructed for me thanks to the picturesque suggestions of my friend Félix. Nor did I add to it. I just left it all hanging in the air, feeding the mystique and making myself less defined, more indistinct: a superb hook for bringing out people's baser instincts and catching new clients. If only the other dressmaking girls from Doña Manuela's workshop could have seen me then. Or the women who lived next door to us on the Plaza de la Paja, or my mother. My mother. I tried to think of her as little as possible, but her memory was constantly assailing me. I knew she was strong and determined; I realized that she would know how to get through the hard times. But all the same, how I yearned to hear from her, to learn how she was managing to get on day to day, how she was coping without any company or income. I so wanted to let her know I was well, alone again, and that I'd gone back to sewing. I kept myself informed by listening to the wireless, and every morning Jamila would go to the Alcaraz store to buy *La Gaceta de África*. A Second Triumphant Year under the Aegis of Franco, read the headlines. Even though all the news came to us sifted through the filter of the Nationalist side, I kept more or less up to date with the situation in Madrid and the Resistance. For all that, it was still proving impossible to get any direct word from my mother. How I missed her, how much I would have given to share everything in that strange and luminous city with her, to have set up the workshop together, to go back to eating her stews and hearing her pronouncements, always so sure. But Dolores wasn't there and I was. Surrounded by strangers, unable to go anywhere, struggling to survive as I made up a fraudulent persona that I could step into each morning, I fought to ensure that no one discovered that an unscrupulous con man had battered my soul and a pile of pistols had enabled me to set up my business, thanks to which I had enough to feed myself each day.

I would often remember Ignacio, my first boyfriend, as well. I didn't miss his physical presence, since Ramiro's had been so brutally intense that his — so sweet, so mild — already seemed distant and vague to me, a nearly faded shadow. But I couldn't prevent myself from nostalgically recalling his loyalty, his tenderness, and the certainty that nothing painful could happen to me by his side. And much, much more frequently than it should have, the memory of Ramiro assailed me abruptly, stabbing me sharply in the gut. It hurt, of course it hurt, horribly. Still, I managed to get used to living with it like someone carrying a heavy load: dragging it along though it slows your pace and demands great effort, but not allowing it to prevent you from making your way onward.

All those invisible presences — Ramiro, Ignacio, my mother, things lost, things past — began to transform themselves into companions that were more or less volatile, more or less intense, companions that I'd have to learn to live with. They invaded my mind when I was alone, in the silent evenings toiling away in the workshop between patterns and bastings, when I went to bed or in the gloom of the living room on the nights when Félix wasn't there, when he was off on his clandestine wanderings. The rest of the day they usually left me alone, probably sensing that I was too busy to stop and pay them any attention. I had enough to think about with a business to run and an invented personality to continue fabricating.

CHAPTER SEVENTEEN

With the arrival of spring, the volume of work increased. The weather was changing, and my clients needed lighter outfits for the bright mornings and the imminent Moroccan summer nights. A few new faces appeared, a few more German women, some more Jews. Thanks to Félix I managed to get a more or less precise idea of them all. He used to pass the clients at the main entrance or on the stairs, the landing, or the street when they were entering or leaving the workshop. He amused himself by looking for snippets of information to create their profiles: who they were, their families, where they were going, where they'd come from. Then later, when he'd leave his mother slumped in her armchair, her half-closed eyes rolled up and boozy drool hanging from her mouth, he would reveal to me what he had learned.

That was how, for example, I discovered certain details concerning Frau Langenheim, one of the German ladies who had quickly become regulars. Her father had been the Italian ambassador to Tangiers and her mother was English; her husband, an older mining engineer, was tall, bald, and a respected member of the small but determined German colony in Spanish Morocco. He was one of the Nazis, Félix told me, who almost unexpectedly and to the astonishment of the Republicans had secured directly from Hitler the first outside assistance for Franco's army, just a few days after the uprising. It would be a while before I'd be able to gauge to what extent the activities of my client's stiff husband had proved crucial to the course of the civil war. However, thanks to Langenheim and Bernhardt, another German living in Tetouan — whose half-Argentine wife was an occasional client of mine — Franco's troops, without having planned for it and in a tiny period of time, got hold of a fine arsenal of military assistance, which enabled them to transport their men to the Peninsula. Months later, as a sign of gratitude and recognition for her husband's significant actions, my client would be granted the greatest honor in the Protectorate from the hands of the caliph, and I would dress her in silk and organza for the occasion.

Long before that official event, Frau Langenheim arrived at the atelier one April morning with someone I'd not seen before. She rang the bell, and Jamila opened the door; I was waiting in the living room, meanwhile, pretending to examine the weft of a fabric against the light that was streaming in through the balcony windows. In reality I wasn't examining anything at all; I had simply adopted that pose to receive my clients in order to establish an air of professionalism.

"I've brought an English friend, for her to see the things you make," said the German's wife as she stepped confidently into the room.

A woman appeared beside her, blond and extremely thin. I calculated that she must have been more or less my own age, but because of the ease with which she behaved she could easily have lived a thousand lives by now, each the length of mine. My attention was drawn to the devastating confidence she radiated and the unaffected elegance with which she greeted me, lightly grazing my fingers with hers while with an airy gesture she pushed a wave of hair back from her face. Her name was Rosalinda Fox, and she had skin so light and fine that it seemed to be made of tissue paper, as well as a strange form of speaking in which words from different languages leapt about chaotically in an extravagant and sometimes incomprehensible torrent.

"I need wardrobe immediately; entonces creo que . . . , I believe you and I, vamos . . . er . . . a entendernos. We will understand each other, I mean," she said, polishing off the sentence with a slight laugh.

Frau Langenheim refused the invitation to be seated with an I'm-in-a-rush-dear-I've-really-got-to-go. In spite of her surname and the jumble of her origins, she spoke Spanish fluently.

"Rosalinda, my dear, I'll see you this evening at Consul Leonini's cocktail party," she said, bidding her friend good-bye. "*Adiós, querida* — bye, sweetie, bye."

I sat down with the woman who had just arrived, and I began the routine I'd used on so many first visits. I displayed my catalog of poses and expressions as we leafed through magazines and examined fabrics; I gave her advice and she made choices; then she reconsidered her decisions, corrected herself, and chose again. The elegant naturalness with which she behaved made me feel comfortable with her right from the start. Sometimes I found the artificiality of my behavior tiring, especially when I was facing particularly demanding clients. That wasn't the case here: everything flowed with no tension or unreasonable demands.

We moved into the fitting room and I took measurements, noting the catlike slenderness of her bones, the smallest I'd ever seen. We continued to talk about fabrics and patterns, about sleeves and necklines, then we went back over what she had chosen, confirming the details before I drew up the order. A morning dress in patterned silk, a suit in coral-pink *laine glacée,* and an evening gown inspired by the latest collection from Lanvin. I gave her a fitting date for ten days later and with that I thought we were done. But the new client decided it wasn't yet time to leave, and, still comfortably settled on the sofa, she took out a tortoiseshell cigarette case and offered me one. We smoked awhile, commenting on designs in some of the magazines as she described her tastes to me in her foreigner's half language. Pointing at various photos, she asked me how you said "embroidery" in Spanish, how you said "shoulder straps" and "buckle." I clarified the things she was unsure about, we laughed at the delicate awkwardness of her pronunciation, and we had another cigarette before she decided to leave, calmly, as though she had nothing to do and no one waiting for her anywhere. First she touched up her makeup, looking without much interest at her reflection in the little compact mirror. Then she rearranged her waves of golden hair and retrieved her hat, her bag and gloves, all elegant and of the finest quality, but also brand-new. I said good-bye to her at the door, listened to her heels tapping down the stairs, and heard no word of her until

261

many days later. I never bumped into her on my walks at dusk, never met up with her at any establishment; no one spoke to me of her, nor did I make any attempt to find out who this English-woman was who seemed to have so much time on her hands.

My activity those days didn't stop: the growing number of clients meant that my work hours just kept getting longer, but I managed to arrive at a sensible rhythm, sewing till the early hours without a break and having every garment ready by its allotted time. Ten days after that first meeting, the three items that Rosalinda Fox had ordered were resting on their respective mannequins, ready for the first fitting. But she didn't show up. Nor on the next day, nor the next. Nor did she take the trouble to send me a message explaining her absence, postponing the date, or justifying her lateness. It was the first time this had happened to me with an order. I thought that perhaps she had no intention of coming back, that she'd been a foreigner just passing through, one of those privileged souls able to leave the Protectorate on a whim and move freely beyond its borders: a woman who was truly cosmopolitan, not fake worldly like myself. Unable to find any reasonable explanation for such behavior, I chose to set the matter aside and focus on the rest of my commitments. Five days later than we'd agreed upon, she appeared, as though dropping from the sky, when I was still finishing my lunch. I'd been working in haste all morning and had finally managed to take a break at three in the afternoon. Someone rang the doorbell and Jamila answered it while I was finishing off a plate of plantains in the kitchen. As soon as I heard the Englishwoman's voice at the other end of the corridor, I washed my hands and ran to put on my heels. I rushed out to greet her, cleaning my teeth with my tongue and retouching my hair with one hand while repositioning the seams of my skirt and the lapels of my jacket with the other. Her greeting was as protracted as her delay had been.

"I have to tell you how extremely sorry I am for not coming before and arriving now so unexpectedly. I've been away algunos días — a few days — I had things to sort out in Gibraltar, though I fear I wasn't able to. Anyway, I hope I'm not arriving at a bad time."

"Not at all," I lied. "Please, do come in."

I led her through to the fitting room and showed her the three designs. She praised them as she took off her clothes till she was down to her underwear. She was wearing a satin combination that in its day must have been a delight, but time and wear had partly stripped it of its former splendor. Her silk stockings didn't exactly look like they were fresh from the shop either, but they exuded glamour and exquisitely fine quality. One by one I tried my three creations on her fragile, bony body. Her skin was so transparent that it was possible to see the bluish network of veins underneath. With my mouth filled with pins, I set about making minute corrections and adjusting little pinches of fabric to the delicate contours of her shape. She seemed pleased throughout the process, allowing me to get on with it, agreeing to the suggestions I offered and barely asking for any changes. When we finished the fitting, I assured her that it would all end up being *très chic*. I left her to put her clothes back on and waited in the living room. She only took a couple of minutes to

263

come back in, and I guessed from her attitude that despite her untimely arrival she wasn't particularly anxious to leave that day either. So I offered her some tea.

"I'm dying for a cup of Darjeeling with just a drop of leite — milk, but I'm guessing it will have to be green tea with mint, no?"

I hadn't the least idea what this concoction was that she was talking about, but I hid it.

"Just so, Moorish tea," I said without the slightest concern. I gestured to her to take a seat and called for Jamila.

"Even though I'm English," she explained, "I've lived most of meu vida — my life — in India, and even though I'll probably never go back there are a lot of things I still miss. Like our tea, for example."

"I know what you mean. I also find it hard to get used to some things here and I do miss other things I've left behind."

"Where did you live before here?" she wanted to know.

"In Madrid."

"And before that?"

I was about to laugh at her question, to forget all the impostures I had invented for my supposed past and acknowledge that I'd never set foot outside the city where I was born until a scoundrel decided to drag me along with him only to abandon me like a cigarette butt. But I restrained myself and reverted to my feigned vagueness.

"Oh, different places, here and there, you know how it is, though Madrid is probably the place I've lived longest. And you?"

"A ver — let's see," she said with an amused expression. "I was born in England, but taken out to Calcutta immediately afterward. My parents sent me back to England when I was ten to study, umm . . . then at sixteen I returned to India and at twenty came back again to the West. Once I was here I spent some time in London. Then another long stretch in Switzerland. Then another year in Portugal — that's why I sometimes confuse the two languages, Portuguese and Spanish. And now, at last, I've settled in Africa: first in Tangiers, and then, a short while back, here in Tetouan."

"Sounds like an interesting life," I said, unable to retain the order of that jumble of exotic destinations.

"Bueno, depends how you look at it," she replied, shrugging, as she sipped at the cup of tea Jamila had just served us, careful to not burn her lips. "I wouldn't have minded at all to have stayed in India, but I had some things that happened to me unexpectedly and I had to move. Sometimes luck decides to make our decisions for us, no? Así es la vida. That's life, no?"

Despite the strange way she pronounced her words and the obvious distance that separated our worlds, I knew precisely what she meant. We finished our tea chatting about insignificant things: the little finishing touches I'd have to give the sleeves of the dress in patterned dupioni silk, the date for the next fitting. She looked at the time and immediately remembered something.

"I've got to go," she said, getting up. "I'd forgotten I have to do unas compras, some shopping before I go back to get ready. I've been invited to cocktails at the house of the Belgian consul."

She spoke without looking at me as she adjusted her gloves, her hat. I watched her with curiosity, wondering with whom would this woman be going to all these parties, with whom did she share this freedom to come and go; I wondered about her carefree, privileged background, constantly traversing the world, leaping from one continent to another to speak confusing languages and drink tea that tasted of a thousand different places. Comparing her seemingly leisurely life with my everyday work, I felt the touch of something running down my spine that resembled envy.

"Do you know where I can buy a bathing suit?" she asked suddenly.

"For you?"

"No, for meu filho."

"I beg your pardon?"

"No, sorry — my son?"

"Your son?" I asked in disbelief.

"His name's Johnny, he's five years old and es un amor . . . an absolute darling."

"I haven't been in Tetouan long either, I don't think I can help you," I said, trying not to show my uneasiness. In the idyllic life that only a few seconds earlier I'd been imagining for that flighty, childlike woman, there might have been room for friends and admirers, for glasses of champagne, transcontinental travels, silk lingerie, parties till dawn, haute couture evening wear, and — with a great deal of effort — perhaps a husband as young, frivolous, and attractive as she was. But I never could have guessed that she would have a son, because I had never imagined her to be a woman with a family. And yet it seemed she was.

"Anyway, not to worry, I'll find one somewhere," she said by way of farewell.

"Good luck. And remember, I'll be expecting you in five days."

"I'll be here, I promise."

She left and did not keep her promise. Instead of the fifth day, she turned up on the fourth: without prior notice and in a tearing hurry. Jamila announced her arrival to me at around noon when I was doing a fitting for Elvirita Cohen, the daughter of the owner of the Teatro Nacional on my old street, La Luneta, and one of the most beautiful women I've ever seen in my life.

"Siñora Fox say she need see Siñorita Sira."

"Tell her to wait, I'll be with her in a minute."

One o'clock had gone by, twenty past probably, because I still had to make quite a few adjustments to the dress that the beautiful Jewish girl with the smooth skin was going to show off at some social event. She spoke to me in her musical Haketia: bring it up a bit here, *mi reina,* how lovely it looks, *mi weno,* ah yes."

It was through Félix, as usual, that I had learned what the situation was like for Sephardic Jews in Tetouan. Some of them wealthy, others humble, all of them discreet; good businessmen who had set up shop in North Africa after their expulsion from the Peninsula centuries earlier. At last they were Spaniards with all their rights, ever since the government of the Republic had agreed officially to recognize their origins just a couple of years earlier. The Sephardic community made up more or less one-tenth of Tetouan's population in those days, but it wielded a good part of the city's economic power. They built most of the new buildings in the *ensanche* and set up many of the best shops and businesses in the city: jewelers, shoemakers, fabric and clothing stores. Their financial might was reflected in their educational centers — the Alliance Israélite Universelle — in their own casino and their synagogues, where they gathered for their prayers and festivals. No doubt it would be in one of these that Elvira Cohen would debut the grosgrain dress that she was trying on when I received my third visit from the unpredictable Rosalinda Fox.

She was waiting in the front room, seemingly troubled by something, standing beside one of the balcony doors. The two clients greeted each other from a distance with remote courtesy: the English-woman distracted, the Sephardic girl surprised and curious.

"I've got a problem," she said, approaching me rapidly the moment the click of the door announced that we were alone.

"Tell me. Would you like to sit down?"

"I'd rather have a drink, por favor."

"I'm afraid I can't offer you anything but tea, coffee, or a glass of water."

"Evian?"

I shook my head, thinking I ought to supply myself with a little bar for raising the spirits of my clients at moments of crisis.

"It doesn't matter," she whispered as she sat, languidly. I did the same in the armchair opposite, crossed my legs with careless ease, and waited for her to tell me about the reason for her untimely visit. First she drew out a cigarette from her tortoiseshell case, lit it, and tossed the case carelessly onto the sofa. After the first drag, thick and deep, she realized that she hadn't offered me one and apologized, making a gesture to rectify her behavior. I stopped her — no, thank you. I was expecting another client shortly and didn't want the smell of tobacco on my fingers within the intimate space of the fitting room. She closed the cigarette case, and at last she spoke.

268

"I need an evening gown, a stunning outfit for tonight. An unexpected engagement has come up and I have to go dressed como una princesa."

"Like a princess?"

"Eso — right. Like a princess. In a manner of speaking, of course. I need something very elegant."

"I only have your evening dress ready for the second fitting."

"Could that be ready for tonight?"

"Absolutely impossible."

"And any other designs?"

"I'm afraid I can't help you. I don't have anything I can offer you: I don't work with ready-to-wear clothes, I make everything to order."

She took another long drag on her cigarette, but this time she didn't do it distantly; rather, she watched me fixedly through the smoke. That expression of an unconcerned girl from her previous visits had disappeared from her face, and her gaze was now that of a woman who was anxious but determined not to be defeated.

"I need to find a solution. When I moved from Tangiers to Tetouan, I packed some baúles, some trunks for sending to my mother in England with things I wasn't going to be using. Accidentally the trunk with all my evening wear also ended up there. I'm waiting for them to be sent back. I've just learned that I've been invited tonight to a reception hosted by the German consul. Es la primera ocasión, the first time I'll be seen in public at an event in the company of a, a . . . a person with whom I have a . . . a . . . a very special relationship."

She was speaking quickly but carefully, making an effort for me to understand everything she was saying in that attempted Spanish of hers, which, because of her nerves, sounded more Portuguese influenced and more peppered with words from her own English language than at either of our previous meetings.

"Bueno, it is very important for this person and for me that I make a good impression on the members of the German colony in Tetouan. Hasta ahora, so far, Mrs. Langenheim has helped me to meet some of them because she is half English, but tonight, esta noite, it's the first time I will appear in public with this person openly together and that's why I need to go extremely bien vestida, very, very well dressed, and . . . and —"

I interrupted her; there was no need for her to keep exercising her Spanish so much to no end.

"I'm so sorry, I really am. I'd love to be able to help you, but it really is impossible. As I've just said, I don't have anything ready in my studio and I cannot finish your dress in just a few hours: I'll need at least three or four days for it."

She put out her cigarette stub in silence, lost in thought. She bit her lip and paused for a few seconds before looking up and resuming her assault with a question that was quite clearly uncomfortable.

"Perhaps you might be able to lend me one of your own evening outfits?"

I shook my head while I tried to come up with some plausible excuse to hide the pitiful fact that in reality I didn't have any.

"I don't think so. All my clothes stayed behind in Madrid when the war broke out, and I've been unable to retrieve them. All I have here are a few everyday clothes, nothing for the evenings. I don't have much of a social life, you understand? My fiancé is in Argentina, and I —"

To my great relief she interrupted me at once.

"Ya veo. I see."

We sat in silence for a few endless seconds, each hidden in her discomfort, attention focused on opposite ends of the room. One toward the balcony doors; the other toward the archway separating the living room from the entrance hall. She finally broke the tension.

"Creo que — tengo que irme. I think I must leave now."

"I'm sorry, please believe me. If we'd had just a little more time . . ."

I didn't finish the sentence, realizing at once there was no point in dwelling upon what couldn't be fixed. I tried to change the subject, distract her attention from the sad reality that she was looking forward to a long disastrous night with the man with whom she was no doubt in love. I was still intrigued by the life of this woman who at other times had been so confident and graceful and who, at this moment, was pensively gathering up her things and heading for the door.

"Tomorrow everything will be ready for the second fitting, all right?" I said, as a rather unhelpful solace.

She smiled vaguely and went out without saying another word. I was left alone, standing there immobile, partly annoyed at my inability to help a client in trouble and partly still intrigued by the strange way in which Rosalinda Fox's life was taking shape before my eyes: a globe-trotting young mother who lost trunks filled with eveningwear in the same way that one might forget one's purse hastily on a park bench or café table.

I leaned out onto the balcony half hidden by the

271

shutters and watched as she arrived at the street. She made her way to a bright red automobile parked opposite my front door. I assumed there must have been someone waiting for her, perhaps the man she was so eager to please that night. I couldn't help my curiosity and I tried to make out a face, plotting out imaginary scenarios in my mind. I assumed he was German; perhaps that was why she so longed to create a good impression among his compatriots. I assumed him to be young, attractive, a bon vivant, worldly and confident like her. I barely had time to develop my fantasies because when she reached the car and opened the right-hand door — the one I supposed to be the passenger seat — I saw the steering wheel and realized she would be the one driving. There was no one waiting for her in that English car: she started it up and she left, as alone as she had arrived. Without a man, without a dress for that night, and, most likely, with no hope of finding any solution over the course of the afternoon.

As I tried to get the bad taste from that meeting out of my mouth, I set about reestablishing order among the objects that Rosalinda's presence had altered. I picked up the ashtray, blew off the bits of ash that had fallen onto the table, straightened a corner of the rug with the tip of my shoe, plumped up the cushions on the sofa, and began rearranging the magazines she'd leafed through while I finished attending to Elvirita Cohen. I was about to close the copy of *Harper's Bazaar* that was lying open at an advertisement for Helena Rubenstein lipsticks when I recognized the photograph of a design that looked vaguely familiar. A thousand memories of a different time

272

flocked back to my mind like birds. Without being completely conscious of what I was doing, I shouted Jamila's name as loudly as I could. A mad dash brought her to the living room in a heartbeat.

"Go, quick as you can, to Frau Langenheim's house and ask her to find Señora Fox. She has to come see me immediately; tell her it's a matter of the greatest urgency."

CHAPTER EIGHTEEN

The person who created the design, my dear ignoramus, was Mariano Fortuny y Madrazo, son of the great Mariano Fortuny, who was probably the best painter of the nineteenth century after Goya. He was an incredible artist, closely linked to Morocco, as a matter of fact. He came over during the African war and was stunned by the light and exoticism of this place. He took it upon himself to give it shape in many of his paintings; one of his best known, in fact, is *The Battle of Tetouan*. But if Fortuny *père* was a masterly painter, his son is a true genius. He paints, too, but in his studio in Venice he also designs stage sets, and he's a photographer, an inventor, a scholar of classical techniques, and a designer of fabrics and dresses, like the legendary Delphos that you — you little phony — have just pirated in a domestic reinterpretation, a version I presume to have been highly successful."

Félix was speaking while lying on the sofa and holding the magazine with the photograph that had triggered my memory. As for me, drained by the intensity of the afternoon, I was listening, immobile, with no energy left even to hold a needle between my fingers. I'd just told him everything that had happened in the previous few hours, starting at the moment when my client announced her return to the workshop with a powerful slam of her brakes that brought my neighbors to their balcony windows. She ran up, her haste echoing in the stairwell. I was waiting for her with the door open, and without even stopping to greet her I put forward my idea.

"We're going to try and make an emergency Delphos — do you know what I'm talking about?"

"A Fortuny Delphos?" she asked, incredulous.

"A fake Delphos."

"You think it'll be possible?"

We held each other's gaze a moment. In hers I could see a flash of newly revived hope. I didn't know what she could see in mine. Perhaps determination and fearlessness, a desire to be victorious, to find a way out of her crisis. Deep down my eyes probably also betrayed a certain terror of failure, but I attempted to keep that hidden as much as I could.

"I've tried it before; I think we should be able to do it."

I showed her the fabric that I'd picked out, a big piece of grayish-blue satin that Candelaria had managed to get hold of in one of her latest transactions. Obviously I refrained from mentioning where it had come from.

"What time is your engagement?"

"At eight."

I looked at the time.

"Well then, this is what we're going to do. It's almost one now. As soon as I'm done with my next fitting, which begins in just ten minutes, I'll soak the material and then leave it to dry. I'll need between four and five hours, which takes us to six in the evening. And I'll have to have at least another hour and a half to make it up: it's very simple, just some straight stitches, and besides, I've already got your measurements, you won't need a fitting. Even so, I'll need a bit of time to do it and to do the finishing touches. It'll take us right up to the last minute. Where do you live? I'm sorry to ask, it's not out of curiosity . . ."

"On the Paseo de las Palmeras."

I ought to have guessed; many of the best houses in Tetouan were located there. A remote, discreet neighborhood to the south of the city, close to the park, almost at the foot of the imposing Ghorgiz, with fine residences surrounded by gardens. Beyond them, the orchards and sugarcane plantations.

"In that case it'll be impossible for me to get the dress to your home."

She looked at me inquiringly.

"You'll have to come here to dress," I clarified. "Be here around seven thirty, made up, hair done, ready to go, with the shoes and the jewelry you're planning to wear. I'd advise you not go with too much, or anything too showy: the dress doesn't require it, it'll look more elegant with simple accessories, you understand?"

She understood perfectly. After thanking me for my efforts with great relief, she left again. Half an hour later, and with Jamila's help, I embarked on the most unexpected and reckless piece of work in my brief career as a dressmaker on my own. I knew what I was doing, however, because in my time at Doña Manuela's I'd helped with just that same job on another occasion. We did it for a customer who had as much style as she had irregular economic resources — Elena Barea was her name. When she was going through good

276

economic times, we would sew sumptuous designs for her in the finest materials. Unlike other women of her class, however, who during times of financial duress would invent trips or engagements or illnesses to justify their inability to pay their debts, she never hid herself away. When hard times made an appearance at her husband's unreliable business, Elena Barea never stopped visiting our workshop. She'd come back, laughing, unembarrassed at the volatility of her fortunes, and working right there side by side with the owner, she would contrive to reconstruct old outfits to make them pass for new, changing the cuts, adding trimmings, and reconfiguring the more unexpected parts. Or she would very sensibly choose fabrics that weren't too costly and creations that needed only the simplest kinds of production work: in that way she managed to pare down the total of her bills as far as possible without overly reducing her elegance. Hunger sharpens your ingenuity, she would always conclude with a laugh. Neither my mother nor Doña Manuela nor I could believe our eyes the day she arrived with her strangest order yet.

"I'd like a copy of this," she said, taking something that looked like a rolled tube of blood-colored fabric out of a small box. She laughed at our expressions of astonishment. "This, ladies, is a Delphos, a unique dress. It's a creation of the artist Fortuny: they make them in Venice, and they're only sold in a few extremely select establishments in the great European cities. Look what a wonder of color, look at the pleating. Their creator keeps the techniques used to make them absolutely secret. It fits like a glove. And I, my dear Doña Manuela, want one. Fake, of course."

277

She took one end of the fabric between her fingers and as if by magic a dress appeared, of red satin, sumptuous and stunning, that reached down to the floor, hanging impeccably and ending round and open at the bottom; a bullring end, that's what we used to call that kind of finish. It was a sort of tunic covered with thousands of tiny vertical pleats. Classic, simple, exquisite. Four or five years had passed since that day, but my memory had retained intact the whole process of producing that dress because I had participated in every part of it. From Elena Barea to Rosalinda Fox, the technique would be the same; the only problem, however, was that we barely had any time and I'd have to work at the pace of a demon. Helped throughout by Jamila, I heated pans of water that, once boiled, we tipped into the bathtub. Scalding my hands, I lowered the material into it and left it to soak. The bathroom filled with steam as we nervously watched the experiment, drops of sweat forming on our foreheads and the condensation making our reflections in the mirror disappear. After a while I decided it would be all right to remove the material, which was now dark and unrecognizable. We drained out the water, and each taking an end, we twisted the strip as hard as we could, turning it lengthways in opposite directions as we'd done so many times with the sheets in the boardinghouse on La Luneta to get the last drop of water out of them before stretching them out in the sun. Except that this time we weren't going to stretch the piece of material out to its full extent but rather the exact opposite: the aim was to keep it as tightly squeezed as possible while drying so that once all the humidity had gone, the silk fabric would be

278

transformed into a wrinkled object retaining as many pleats as possible. Then we put the twisted material in a basin and carried it between us up to the roof. We turned the ends of the fabric in opposite directions again until it looked like a thick rope that twisted in on itself in the shape of a big spring. Next we laid out a towel and placed upon it, like a coiled snake, the object that just a few hours later would become the gown in which my English client would make her first public appearance on the arm of the enigmatic man of her life.

After we left the fabric to dry in the sun, we went back down to the apartment and filled the stove with coal until we got it working at full power and the kitchen felt like a boiler room. When we calculated that the afternoon sun was beginning to wane, we went back up to the roof and retrieved the twisted material. We stretched out a new towel on the cast iron of the stove and on top of it placed the still-rolled fabric, circled onto itself. Every ten minutes — without ever stretching it out — we turned it over so that the heat from the coals would dry it evenly. Between trips to the kitchen I constructed a belt consisting of a simple layer of lining with a plain thick band of pressed silk, made from the bit of material that hadn't been used. At five in the afternoon I recovered the twisted fabric from the iron surface and brought it into the workshop. It was like a hot blood sausage: no one could have imagined what I was expecting to do with it in little over an hour.

I stretched it out over the cutting table, and bit by bit, taking the greatest care, I undid the strange creation. And magically — before my very eyes — the silk emerged, pleated and dazzling, beautiful.

We hadn't managed permanent pleats like those on the genuine Fortuny model because we didn't have the means and we did not know the technique for it, but we'd been able to obtain a similar effect that would last the night at least: a special night for a woman in need of something spectacular. I unfolded the fabric to its full size and left it to cool. Then I cut it into four pieces with which I constructed a kind of narrow cylindrical sheath that would adapt itself to the body like a second skin. I fashioned a simple round neckline and worked the openings for the arms. Without the time for any ornamental flourishes, the fake Delphos was finished in the allotted time: a rushed, homemade version of a model that had revolutionized haute couture. It was an imitation but one with the potential to have an effect on anyone feasting his eyes on the body displaying it.

I was trying out the effect of the belt when the doorbell rang. It was only then that I realized how pitiful my appearance had become. The sweat from the boiling water had messed up my makeup and my thick hair; the heat, the strain of twisting the material, going up and down the stairs to the roof, and all the nonstop work of the afternoon had left me looking as though the whole cavalry of the Indigenous Regular Forces had just galloped over me. I ran to my room while Jamila went to open the door; I changed clothes at full speed, combed my hair, got myself together. The result of the work had been satisfactory, and I needed at least to look up to scratch.

I went out to meet Rosalinda, expecting to find her waiting for me in the living room, but when I passed the door to the workshop I saw her standing at the mannequin. She had her back to me; I couldn't make out her face. From the door I asked her simply, "Do you like it?"

She turned at once and didn't reply. She came nimbly to my side, took my hand, and squeezed it hard.

"Thank you, thank you, un millón de thank-yous."

She had her hair back in a chignon, her natural waves a little more noticeable than usual. Her eyes and cheekbones were discreetly made up; the lipstick on her mouth, however, was much more spectacular. Her high-heeled sandals raised her almost three inches above her natural height. A couple of shining white-gold earrings, broad and stunning, were her only embellishment, and she wore a delicious-smelling perfume. As soon as she had removed her street wear, I helped her put on the dress. The irregular pleating of the tunic fell, blue, rhythmic, and sensual, down her body, delineating her exquisite bone structure, the delicacy of her limbs, shaping and showing off the outlines and curves, elegant and sumptuous. I adjusted the wide strip around her waist and knotted it at the back. We contemplated the result in the mirror without exchanging a word.

"Don't move," I said.

I went out into the hall to call Jamila and have her come in. When she saw Rosalinda in her dress she immediately covered her mouth with her hand to stop herself from crying out in astonishment and wonder.

"Turn around so she can see you properly. A lot of the work is hers. I could never have managed it without her."

The Englishwoman smiled at Jamila gratefully and turned around a couple of times, graceful

281

and stylish. The Moorish girl watched her, flustered, shy, and happy.

"And now, hurry. It's already ten to eight."

Jamila and I went out to the balcony to watch her leave, the two of us silent, arm in arm and practically crouching in one corner so as not to be seen from the street. It was almost night. I looked down, expecting to see her little red car again, but in its place was an imposing black automobile with little flags on its hood whose colors — at that distance and with barely any light — I wasn't able to make out. As soon as the silhouette in bluish silk appeared at the front doorway, the headlamps came on and a uniformed man got out of the passenger seat to quickly open the back door. He remained standing in military pose waiting as she emerged, elegant and majestic, taking short light steps onto the street toward the car. With assurance, as though showing herself off, filled with pride and confidence. I couldn't tell whether there was anyone else in the back seat. As she settled herself in, the man in uniform closed the door and returned hastily to his place. Then the vehicle started up, powerfully, and quickly made its way off into the night, carrying within it a woman filled with hope and the most fraudulent dress in the whole history of falsified haute couture.

Chapter Nineteen

Things returned to normal the following day. In the middle of the afternoon someone rang the doorbell; this was strange, as I hadn't arranged any appointments. It was Félix. Without a word he slipped inside and shut the door behind him. His behavior surprised me: he never turned up at my house until well into the night. Once he'd escaped from his mother's indiscreet stares through the spyhole, he spoke quickly, and teasingly.

"Well now, girl, how well we've been doing!"

"Why do you say that?" I asked, surprised.

"Because of the heavenly woman I've just passed in the doorway."

"Rosalinda Fox? She came for a fitting. And this morning she also sent me a bouquet of flowers as a thank-you. She was the one I helped out of that sticky situation yesterday."

"Don't tell me the skinny blonde I've just seen was the one with the Delphos?"

"That was her."

It took him a few seconds to savor what he had just heard. Then he went on with just a hint of mockery in his voice.

"My, how very interesting. You've been able to solve a problem for a woman who is very special,

283

ever so special."

"Special in what way?"

"Special, my dear, in that your client is probably the woman with the greatest power to resolve any matter in the Protectorate. Apart from issues relating to sewing, of course, which is what she has you for, the empress of forgery."

"I don't understand what you're saying, Félix."

"Are you telling me you don't know who Rosalinda Fox is?"

"An Englishwoman who's spent most of her life in India and has a five-year-old son."

"And a lover."

"A German."

"You're cold, cold . . ."

"He's not German?"

"No, my dear. You're very wrong, ever so wrong."

"How do you know?"

He gave an evil smile.

"Because everyone in Tetouan knows it. Her lover is someone else."

"Who?"

"Someone important."

"Who?" I said again, tugging at his sleeve, unable to contain my curiosity.

He gave another mischievous smile and covered his mouth theatrically as though wanting to divulge a great secret. He whispered in my ear, slowly.

"Your friend is the beloved of the high commissioner."

"Commissioner Vázquez?" I asked in disbelief.

He replied to my suggestion first with a laugh and then an explanation.

"No, you lunatic, no — Claudio Vázquez just

deals with the police, keeping the local delinquents in check, not to mention the brainless troop he has in his command. I very much doubt he has free time for extramarital affairs, or at least not to have a regular little friend he puts in a villa with a pool on the Paseo de las Palmeras. Your client, sweetheart, is the lover of Lieutenant Colonel Juan Luis Beigbeder y Atienza, Spain's high commissioner in Morocco and governor general of the Spanish enclaves. The most important military and administrative post in the whole Protectorate, to be quite clear."

"Félix, are you sure?" I murmured.

"Let my mother live to eighty fit as a fiddle if I'm lying to you. No one knows how long they've been together, she's been in Tetouan a little over a month: enough, in any case, for everyone to know who she is and what's going on between them. He's been high commissioner, officially named by the government in Burgos since not that long ago, though he's been acting high commissioner since practically the beginning of the war. They say Franco's delighted with him because he's endlessly recruiting warlike Moorish boys for him, to send to the front."

Not in my most elaborate fantasy could I have imagined Rosalinda Fox as the lover of a lieutenant colonel in the Nationalist faction.

"What's he like?"

The curiosity in my voice made him laugh again delightedly.

"Beigbeder? You don't know him? The truth is, he hasn't been seen as much lately — he must spend most of his time shut away in the High Commission — but in the past when he was undersecretary for Indigenous Affairs you could have

285

seen him out on the street at any time. Back then, of course, he could go about unnoticed: he was just a serious, anonymous officer with barely any social life. He was almost always out on his own and didn't usually attend the soirées at the Hípica Club, the Hotel Nacional, or the Salón Marfil. And he didn't spend his whole life playing cards like the laid-back Colonel Sáenz de Buruaga, who on the day of the uprising even gave the first orders from the casino terrace. A discreet sort, Beigbeder, rather solitary even."

"Attractive?"

"Of course he doesn't do anything for me, but still he does seem to have his appeal to you people — you're ever so strange, you women."

"Describe him to me."

"Tall, thin, stern looking. Dark, his hair combed back. With round glasses, mustache, something intellectual about him. In spite of his post and the way times are right now, he usually goes about dressed in civvies, with exceptionally boring dark suits."

"Married?"

"Probably, though it would seem that while he's been here he's always lived alone. But it's not unusual among soldiers that they don't take their families everywhere they go."

"Age?"

"Old enough to be her father."

"I don't believe it."

"Well, that's your problem. If you worked less and went out more, I'm sure you'd run into him sooner or later and then you'd be able to confirm what I'm telling you with your own eyes. He still goes for a walk from time to time, though now he's always accompanied by a couple of escorts.

They say he's an extremely cultured gentleman who speaks several languages and has lived outside Spain for many years; completely different to begin with from the national heroes we're used to having in these parts, though of course his position indicates that he is on their side. Perhaps he and your client met abroad somewhere; maybe she'll explain it to you sometime and then you will tell me. You know how fascinated I am by these romantic *affaires.* Well, I'll leave you, girl — I'm taking the witch to the cinema. A double bill: *Hermana San Sulpicio* and *Don Quintin the Bitter;* I've really got quite an afternoon of glamour awaiting me. With the chaos of this war, we haven't had a single decent film come over here in nearly a year. How I'd love to see a good American musical. You remember Fred Astaire and Ginger Rogers in *Top Hat?* 'I just got an invitation through the mails: "Your presence requested this evening, it's formal — top hat, white tie, and tails.' "

He went out crooning away to himself, and I shut the door behind him. This time it wasn't his mother watching indiscreetly through the peephole, but me. I observed him, as with that little tune still in his mouth he tinklingly drew his keys from his pocket, found his latchkey, and inserted it into the lock. When he disappeared I went back into the workshop and resumed my work, still struggling to believe what I had just heard. I tried to keep working for a while longer but could feel myself lacking the will. Or the strength. Or both. I remembered the turbulent activity of the previous day and decided to allow myself the rest of the afternoon off. I considered copying Félix and his mother and going to the cinema, since I deserved a bit of distraction. With that in mind I left the house, but inexplicably my steps took me in a different direction, leading me to the Plaza de España instead.

I was met by the beds of flowers and the palm trees, the colored pebbles on the ground and the white buildings surrounding the square. The stone benches, as on any other afternoon, were filled with couples and groups of girls. A pleasant smell of savories was wafting from the little cafés nearby. I crossed the square toward the High Commission, which I'd seen so many times since my arrival and which had aroused so little curiosity in me before now. Very close to the caliph's palace, the large white colonial-style building surrounded by leafy gardens housed the main seat of the Spanish administration. Through the vegetation it was possible to make out the two main stories and a third shorter one, the turrets at the corners, the green shutters and the orange tiles that finished it off. Imposing-looking Arab soldiers, stoic under their turbans and broad cloaks, stood guard at the large iron gate. Imperious high-ranking officers of the Spanish army in Africa wearing chickpea-colored uniforms went in and out of a small side door, looking impeccable in their breeches and well-shined boots. There were also native soldiers swarming around, moving from one side to the other, with European-style military jackets, wide trousers, and some kind of brownish bands around their calves. The bicolor national flag was waving against a blue sky that already seemed to announce the arrival of summer. I stood there watching that incessant movement of men in uniform until I noticed how many stares my immobility was attracting. Flustered and uncomfortable, I turned and went back to the square. What was I looking for outside the High Commission, what was I expecting to find, why had I gone there? No reason, probably; at least, no concrete reason except to get a closer look at the habitat of my client's unexpected lover.

CHAPTER TWENTY

Spring was turning to a gentle summer of luminous nights, and I went on sharing my earnings from the workshop with Candelaria. The bundle of pounds sterling at the bottom of the chest grew till it was almost large enough to pay the amount due; there wasn't long to go before the deadline for me to repay the debt to the Continental. I took comfort in knowing that I'd be able to do it, that I would at last be able to buy my freedom. As ever, news of the war continued to come in on the radio and in the press. General Mola died, the battle of Brunete began. Félix continued his nighttime forays, and Jamila remained always by my side, developing her sweet, strange Spanish, starting to help me out with a few small jobs: a loose piece of tacking, a button, a fastening. There was almost nothing to interrupt the monotony of the days in the workshop, only the sounds of domestic chores and snatches of distant conversations in the neighboring apartments that drifted in through the open windows of the building's central courtyard. That, and the constant commotion of the children upstairs who were already on holiday from school, going out to play on the road, sometimes en masse, sometimes one at a time. None of those noises bothered me. Quite the contrary: they kept me company, they managed to make me feel less alone.

One afternoon in mid-July, however, the noises and voices were louder, the running more hurried.

"They've arrived, they've arrived!" Then more voices, shouts and slamming of doors, names repeated between loud sobs: Concha, Concha! Carmela — my sister! Esperanza, at last, at last!

I heard them moving pieces of furniture around and racing up and down the stairs dozens of times. I heard laughter, crying, orders shouted. Fill the bathtub, get out some more towels, bring the clothes, the mattresses — the girl, the girl, give the girl something to eat. And more crying, more emotional shouting, and more laughter. And the smell of food and the noise of pots and pans in the kitchen at altogether the wrong time of day. And again — Carmela, oh God, Concha, Concha! The bustle didn't calm down until well after midnight. Only then did Félix appear at my house and I was finally able to ask him.

"What's going on in the Herreras' house? Everyone's been behaving so strangely today!"

"Haven't you heard? Josefina's sisters have arrived. They've managed to get them out of the Red Zone."

The following morning I heard the voices and the shuffling around again, though rather calmer now. All the same, there was incessant activity right through the day — people coming and going, the doorbell, the telephone, children running down the corridor. And between-times there was more sobbing, more laughter, more crying, and again more laughter. In the afternoon someone rang my doorbell. I thought that perhaps it was

291

one of them; maybe they needed something, to ask a favor, to borrow something: half a dozen eggs, a quilt, possibly a little jug of oil. But I was wrong. The person at the door was someone altogether unexpected.

"Señora Candelaria says for you to come whenever you can to La Luneta. The schoolmaster Don Anselmo has died."

Paquito, the fat son of the fat mother, had sweatily brought me the message.

"You go on ahead, and tell her I'll be right over."

I told Jamila the news and she cried pitifully. I didn't shed any tears, but I felt them in my soul. Of all the people who made up that restless tribe, he was the one I was closest to, the one who had the most affectionate relationship with me. I put on the darkest suit I had in my closet; I hadn't yet made space in my wardrobe for mourning clothes. Jamila and I made our way hurriedly along the streets and quickly arrived at our destination. After going up the flight of stairs, we couldn't get any farther: a dense group of men stood crammed together, blocking the entrance. We elbowed our way through the teacher's friends and acquaintances who were respectfully waiting their turn to approach and bid their final farewell.

The door to the boardinghouse was open, and before we had even crossed the threshold I could smell burning wax and hear a resonant murmur of female voices praying in unison. Candelaria came out to meet us as we went in. She was in a black suit that was quite clearly too small for her, and on her majestic bosom swung a medallion with the face of the Virgin. In the middle of the dining room, on the table, an open coffin held the ashen body of Don Anselmo in his Sunday best.

A shudder ran down my spine to see him, and I could feel Jamila's nails digging into my arm. I gave Candelaria two kisses and she left the trace of a stream of tears next to my ear.

"There he is — fallen on the battlefield itself."

I recalled those fights between dinner courses that I'd witnessed so many times. The bones of the anchovies and the bits of peel from the African melons, wrinkled and yellow, flying from one side of the table to the other. The poisonous jokes and the indecent ones, the forks poised like spears, the yelling of one faction, then the other. The provocations and the threats of eviction that the Matutera never carried through. The dining table transformed into a virtual battlefield. I tried to hold back a sad laugh. The dried-up sisters, the fat mother, and a few women who lived nearby, sitting at the window and in mourning from head to foot, were still reciting the mysteries of the rosary in monotonous, tearful voices. For a moment I imagined Don Anselmo alive, with a Toledo between his lips, shouting lividly between coughing fits for them to damn well stop praying for him once and for all. But the schoolmaster was no longer among the living, and they were. And sitting by his dead body, however present and warm it might still be, they could now do whatever they saw fit. Candelaria and I sat down beside them, and the Matutera coupled her voice to the rhythm of the prayers while I pretended to do likewise, but my mind was running along other channels.

Lord, have mercy upon us.
Christ, have mercy upon us.

293

I moved my reed chair toward hers till our arms were touching.

Lord, have mercy upon us.

"Candelaria, I have to ask you something," I whispered in her ear.

Christ, listen to us.
Christ, hear us.

"Tell me, my angel," she replied in an equally low voice.

Heavenly God the Father, have mercy upon us.
God the Son, redeemer of the world.

"I've heard they've been getting people out of the Red Zone."

God the Holy Spirit.
Most Holy Trinity, who is One God.

"That's what they're saying . . ."

Holy Mary, pray for us.
Holy Mother of God.
Blessed Virgin of Virgins.

"Can you find out how they're doing it?"

Mother of Christ.
Mother of the Church.

"Why do you want to know?"

Mother of Heavenly Grace.

O purest of Mothers.
Most chaste of Mothers.

"To get my mother out of Madrid and bring her over to me in Tetouan."

Most virginal Mother.
Most immaculate Mother.

"I'd have to ask around . . ."

Kindest of Mothers.
Most admirable of Mothers.

"Tomorrow morning?"

Mother of Good Counsel.
Mother of the Creator.
Mother of the Savior.

"Whenever I can. And now be quiet and keep praying, and let's see whether between us all we can't get Don Anselmo up to heaven."

The wake went on until dawn, and on the following day we buried the schoolteacher at the Catholic mission with solemn prayers for the departed and all the paraphernalia befitting the most fervent of believers. We accompanied the casket to the cemetery. It was very windy, as it so often was in Tetouan: a bothersome wind that ruffled the veils, lifted up skirts, and made the eucalyptus leaves snake along the ground. As the priest pronounced the last verses of the prayer I leaned over to Candelaria and conveyed my curiosity in a whisper.

"If the sisters really thought the schoolmaster

was an atheist son of Lucifer, I don't know how they arranged this burial for him."

"Enough of that, enough of that, his soul is probably wandering in hell and his spirit will soon be coming to drag us off in our sleep . . ."

I had to struggle not to laugh.

"For God's sake, Candelaria, don't be so superstitious."

"Just trust me, all right? I'm an old dog and I know what I'm talking about."

Without another word, she went back to concentrating on the liturgy and didn't so much as look at me again until after the final *requiescat in pace.* Then they lowered the body down into the grave, and when the gravediggers started to throw the first shovelfuls of earth onto him the group began to break up. We were making our way in an orderly manner toward the cemetery gate when Candelaria suddenly crouched down, and, pretending to refasten the buckle on her shoe, she let the sisters go on ahead with the fat woman and the neighbors. We watched them, lagging behind as they went off, their backs to us like a flock of crows, their black veils hanging down to their waists: half cloaks, they called them.

"Come on then, you and I are going off to pay a tribute to the memory of poor old Don Anselmo — all this sadness, my child, it makes me ever so hungry . . ."

We wandered over to El Buen Gusto and chose our pastries, then sat down to eat them on a bench in the church square, between palm trees and flower beds. Finally I asked her the question I'd been keeping on the tip of my tongue since first thing that morning.

"Have you been able to find out anything about

296

what I said?"

She nodded, her mouth full of meringue.

"It's complicated. And costs a great deal."

"Tell me."

"There's someone who deals with arrangements from Tetouan. I haven't been able to find out all the details, but it seems that in Spain things are being done through the International Red Cross. They track people down in the Republican Red Zone, and somehow they're able to bring them to a port on the Mediterranean, don't ask me how because I don't have the damnedest idea. Disguised, in trucks, on foot, God only knows. That's where they board their ships, anyway. The ones who want to go into the Nationalist zone cross the border in the Basque country and go to France. And the ones who want to come to Morocco, they send them to Gibraltar if they can, though often things are difficult and they have to take them to other Mediterranean ports first. Their next destination is usually Tangiers and then, finally, they arrive in Tetouan."

I could feel my pulse racing.

"And do you know who I'd have to talk to?"

She smiled, a little sadly, and gave me an affectionate little slap on the thigh that left my skirt stained with icing.

"Before you talk to anyone, the first thing you need is to have a good pile of banknotes available. And in pounds sterling. Did I or did I not tell you that English money was the best?"

"I have everything I've saved these past months, which I haven't touched," I explained, ignoring her question.

"And you still have the debt outstanding at the Continental."

"Perhaps it'll be enough for both."

"I doubt that very much, my angel. It will cost you two hundred and fifty pounds."

Suddenly my throat was dry and the puff pastry lodged in it like a sticky paste. I started coughing, and the Matutera patted me on the back. When I was finally able to swallow, I blew my nose and asked, "You couldn't lend it to me, Candelaria?"

"I haven't got a cent, child."

"And the money from the workshop that I've been giving you?"

"It's already spent."

"On what?"

She sighed deeply.

"Paying for this funeral, the medicines he's needed lately, and a handful of bills that Don Anselmo left here and there. And it's just as well Doctor Maté was a friend of his and isn't going to charge me for the visits."

I looked at her in disbelief.

"But he must have had some money saved from his pension," I suggested.

"He didn't have a cent left."

"That's impossible: it'd been months since he'd been out, he didn't have any expenses . . ."

She smiled with a mixture of sympathy, sadness, and mockery.

"I don't know how the old devil arranged it, but he managed to get all his savings to the International Red Aid."

Far though I was from having the amount of money I needed to bring my mother to Morocco and also pay off my debt, the idea didn't stop rumbling around in my head. That night I hardly slept, preoccupied with turning the subject around in my mind a thousand times. I fantasized about

298

the craziest possibilities and kept counting and recounting the notes I'd saved, but despite all my efforts, I couldn't get them to multiply. And then, when dawn was almost breaking, another solution occurred to me.

CHAPTER TWENTY-ONE

The conversations, bursts of laughter, and rhythmic clattering of the typewriters all fell silent in unison as the four pairs of eyes turned to look at me. The room was grey, filled with smoke, smelling of tobacco and the rancid stench of concentrated humanity. There was no sound but the buzzing of a thousand flies and the lethargic rhythm of the blades of a wooden fan turning above our heads. And after a few seconds, the admiring whistle of someone passing along the corridor who saw me standing there in my best suit, surrounded by four desks behind which four sweaty bodies in shirtsleeves were trying to work. Or at least, that's how it looked.

"I've come to see Commissioner Vázquez," I announced.

"He's not in," said the fattest one.

"But he won't be long," said the youngest one.

"You can wait for him," said the skinniest one.

"Have a seat if you want," said the oldest one.

I settled in a chair with a gutta-percha seat and waited there, motionless, for more than an hour and a half. Over the course of those endless ninety minutes, the quartet tried to give the impression that they were going back to their activities, but they weren't. They just made a point of pretending to be working, looking at me brazenly and killing flies with a newspaper folded in two, exchanging obscene gestures and passing scrawled notes, no doubt full of references to my breasts, my behind, and my legs, and everything they could do to me if I showed any warmth toward them. Finally Don Claudio arrived, acting like a one-man band — walking fast, simultaneously taking off his hat and jacket, firing off orders while trying to decipher a couple of notes that someone had just handed him.

"Juárez, I want you out on Calle del Comercio, there have been some stabbings. Cortés, if you don't have the thing about the match factory on my desk before I count to ten, I'm sending you to Ifni in the blink of an eye. Bautista, what's happened with the robbery in the Wheat Souq? Cañete . . ."

And there he stopped. He stopped because he'd seen me. And Cañete, who was the skinny one, was left without an assignment.

"Come on through," he said simply, gesturing me toward an office at the back of the room. He put his jacket — which was by now half off — back on. "Cortés, the thing with the match factory can wait. And the rest of you, you have things to do," he warned.

He closed the glass door that separated his little office from the larger one and offered me a seat. Although the room was smaller, it was infinitely more pleasant than the adjacent space. After hanging his hat on a hat stand, he settled in behind a desk covered in papers and folders. Then he turned on a Bakelite fan and the breath of cool air reached my face like a miracle in the middle of the desert.

"Well, tell me." His tone wasn't particularly friendly, nor the contrary. His appearance was somewhere between the nervous, worried air of our first meetings and the calmness of the autumn day when he finally released his grip on my throat. As in the previous summer, his face was once again tanned. Perhaps because like many Tetouanis he often went to the beach nearby at Río Martín. Or perhaps simply because of his nonstop wanderings as he solved problems from one end of the city to the other.

I knew the way he worked, so I made my request and braced myself for his unending battery of questions.

"I need my passport."

"Might I ask why?"

"To go to Tangiers."

"Might I know what for?"

"To renegotiate my debt."

"Renegotiate it in what sense?"

"I need more time."

"I thought your workshop was running without any problems; I'd hoped you would have managed to get together the amount you owe. I know you have good customers, I've been told that, and they speak highly of you."

"Yes, that's right, things are going well. And I've saved."

"How much?"

"Enough to deal with the bill at the Continental."

"So?"

"Certain other matters have come up for which I also need money."

"What sort of matters?"

"Family matters."

He looked at me with feigned disbelief.

"I thought your family was in Madrid."

"Exactly, that's just the point."

"Explain yourself."

"My only family is my mother. And she's in Madrid. I want to get her out of there and bring her to Tetouan."

"And your father?"

"I've already told you, I hardly know him. I'm only interested in tracking down my mother."

"I understand. And how were you planning to do that?"

I told him every little bit of what Candelaria had told me, without mentioning her name. He heard me out as he had always done, his eyes fixed on mine as though concentrating all five of his senses on absorbing my words, although I was sure he already knew all the details of how transfers from one zone to the other were carried out.

"When do you mean to go to Tangiers?"

"As soon as possible, if you'll give me permission."

He sat back in his chair and stared at me hard. With the fingers of his left hand he began a rhythmic tapping on the desk. If I'd been able to see beyond his flesh and bones, I'd have watched his brain getting into gear — weighing up my proposal, discounting possibilities, analyzing and deciding. After what must have been a short while but felt endless to me, his fingers stopped dead and he slapped the surface of the table hard. I knew then that he'd made his decision, but before letting me hear it he went over to the door and stuck his head outside and spoke.

"Cañete, prepare a border pass for El Borch

checkpoint in the name of Miss Sira Quiroga. Immediately."

I breathed in deeply when I knew that at last Cañete had been given something to do, but I said nothing until the commissioner had returned to his place and informed me directly.

"I'm going to give you your passport, a safe-conduct, and twelve hours for you to go to Tangiers and back tomorrow. Talk to the manager of the Continental and see what you can arrange. I don't imagine you'll be able to do much, to be honest with you. But it can't hurt to try. Keep me informed. And remember: I don't want any funny business."

He opened a drawer, rummaged around in it, and when he pulled his hand back out he was holding my passport. Cañete came in, put a piece of paper down on the table, and looked at me with desire. The commissioner signed the document, and without looking up he fired a "Get out of here, Cañete" at his subordinate. Then he folded up the piece of paper, inserted it into my passport, and handed it over to me without a word. Next he got up and held the door open, inviting me to leave. The four pairs of eyes that I had met on my arrival had become seven pairs by the time I left the office. Seven men twiddling their thumbs, awaiting my reappearance like the Second Coming, as though it was the first time in their lives they'd seen a presentable woman in that police station.

"What's going on today, are we all on vacation?" Don Claudio asked no one in particular.

Everyone automatically set to work in a bustle of frantic activity: taking bits of paper out of folders, talking to one another about matters of apparent importance, and sounding typewriter keys that in all likelihood they were hitting randomly.

I left and began to walk along the pavement. As I passed the open window I saw the commissioner come back into the office.

"Fuck, boss, what a nice piece of ass," said a voice I couldn't place.

"Shut your mouth, Palomares, or I'll send you on guard duty to the top of Las Monas Peak."

CHAPTER TWENTY-TWO

I'd been told that before the war started there were several transport services a day covering the forty-five miles separating Tetouan from Tangiers. Nowadays, however, there was less traffic and the timetables varied, so no one was able to give me information with any confidence. Which was why I was anxious as I made my way the following morning to the La Valenciana depot, ready to put up with whatever I needed to in order to get myself taken to my destination by one of the large red buses. If the previous day I'd been able to put up with an hour and a half in the police station surrounded by those lumps of meat with eyes, I imagined that the wait surrounded by unoccupied drivers and grease-covered mechanics would be bearable, too. I put on my best suit again, a silk kerchief protecting my hair, and a pair of large sunglasses behind which I could hide my anxiety. It wasn't yet nine o'clock when I approached the bus company depot on the outskirts of the town. I was walking quickly, focused on my thoughts — previewing the scene when I'd meet the manager of the Continental and going over the arguments I'd considered putting to him. There was something else, though, on top of my concern about paying the debt, another feeling that was equally disagreeable. For the first time since I'd left I would be going back to Tangiers, a city where every corner was infested with memories of Ramiro. I knew it would be painful and that the memory of the times we spent together would become real again. I could tell that it was going to be a difficult day.

I passed few people on the way, and even fewer motorcars — it was still early. Which was why I was so surprised when one of them pulled up right beside me. A luxurious black Dodge, medium sized. I didn't recognize the vehicle at all, but I knew the voice that came out of it.

"Buenos días, Sira — what a surprise to find you here. Can I take you anywhere?"

"I don't think so, thank you. I've already arrived," I said, gesturing to the La Valenciana depot.

As I spoke, I noticed that my English client was wearing one of the suits that had come out of my workshop a few weeks earlier. Like me, she had a light-colored kerchief covering her hair.

"You're planning to take a bus?" she asked, a slight note of disbelief in her voice.

"That's right, Señora Fox, I'm going to Tangiers. But many thanks, all the same, for offering to give me a ride."

As though she'd just heard a particularly funny joke, Rosalinda Fox burst into musical laughter.

"Absolutely not, Sira. Don't even think about taking a bus, sweetie — I'm going to Tangiers, too — hop in. And stop calling me Señora Fox, por favor. We're friends now? Aren't we?"

I quickly weighed up the offer and decided that there was nothing in it that contravened Don Claudio's orders, so I accepted. Thanks to that unexpected invitation I would be able to avoid the

307

uncomfortable journey on a bus that held such bad memories for me, and traveling with her would make it easier for me to forget my own unease.

She drove up the Paseo de las Palmeras, leaving the bus depot behind us and skirting around large, beautiful residences, almost hidden in the leafiness of their gardens. She gestured toward one of them.

"That's my house, though I don't think I'll have it for long. I'll probably be moving again soon."

"Out of Tetouan?"

She laughed.

"No, no, no, not for anything in the world. Only it might be that I'm moving to somewhere more comfortable; this villa is divine, but it's been uninhabited for some time and it needs significant repairs. The pipes are in a horrific state, we almost don't get drinking water, and I don't want to imagine what it would be like spending a winter in conditions like those. I've told Juan Luis and he's looking for another place a bit more comfortable."

She mentioned her lover quite naturally, securely, without the general vaguenesses and approximations of the day of the reception with the Germans. I didn't let her see any reaction, as though I was completely aware of what there was between them, as though referring to the high commissioner by his Christian name was something I was quite used to in my day-to-day life as a dressmaker.

"I do love Tetouan, it's so beautiful. Partly it reminds me of the White Town in Calcutta, with its vegetation and the colonial houses. But that's something I left behind me long ago."

"You don't mean to go back?"

"No, absolutely not. All that is in the past now: things happened that weren't pleasant, and there were people who behaved in a rather ugly way toward me. Besides, I like living in new places: first in Portugal, now in Morocco, tomorrow, quién sabe, who knows? I was in Portugal a little over a year; first in Estoril and later in Cascais. Then the mood changed and I decided to take another route."

She spoke without pause, concentrating on the road ahead. I got the sense that her Spanish had improved since our first meeting; there were almost no traces of Portuguese left in it now, though she was still intermittently dropping in words and phrases from her own language. We had the car roof down, and the noise of the engine was deafening. She almost had to shout to make herself heard.

"Until not that long ago, they had — there, in Estoril and Cascais — a divine colony of British people and other expatriates: diplomats, European aristocrats, Englishmen in the wine business, Americans from the oil companies . . . We had a thousand parties, everything was so very cheap: drinks, rent, domestic staff. But all of a sudden, quite unexpectedly, it all changed. Suddenly half the world wanted to live there. The area filled up with new Brits who having lived in the four corners of the empire absolutely refused to spend their years of retirement being rained on in the old country. And with monarchist Spaniards who were already sensing what was just around the corner. And with German Jews, uncomfortable back home, eager to gauge Portugal's potential as a place to transfer their businesses. And the prices

309

went up immensely." She shrugged, a childlike gesture, and added, "I suppose all that lost its charm, its enchantment."

The monotonous yellowish landscape of our journey was broken up occasionally by clusters of prickly pear cacti and sugarcane plantations. We went through a mountainous spot covered with pines, came back down to the dry area again. The corners of the silk kerchiefs that covered our hair were flying in the wind, bright under the sunlight, while she continued to recount the changes she'd been through upon her arrival in Morocco.

"Back in Portugal people had told me a lot about Morocco, especially about Tetouan. In those days I was very good friends with General Sanjurjo and his delightful wife, Carmen — so sweet — did you know she used to be a dancer? My son Johnny used to play every day with their little son Pepito. I was so sorry to learn of José Sanjurjo's death in that *accidente terrible*, that plane crash. He was an absolutely delightful man; not particularly attractive physically, to tell you the truth, but a very nice person. He always said I was *so beauuuuuutiful.* He was the one who introduced me to Juan Luis in Berlin in February last year. He fascinated me, naturally. I'd gone there from Portugal with my friend Niesha, two women on their own crossing Europe to Berlin in a Mercedes — imagine! We stayed at the Hotel Adlon, I'm sure you know it."

I made a gesture that was neither a yes nor a no; she went on talking without paying me much attention.

"Berlin — my goodness. What a city — the cabarets, the parties, the nightclubs — all of it so vibrant, so full of life; the reverend mother of my

310

Anglican boarding school would have died of shock if she'd seen me there. One night I happened to run into the two of them in the hotel lounge tomando una copa, having a drink. Sanjurjo was in Germany visiting munitions factories; Juan Luis, who had lived there a number of years as military attaché to the Spanish embassy, was accompanying him on his tour. We had a little chitchat. In the beginning Juan Luis wanted to be discreet, not to say anything about their activities in front of me, but José knew I was a good friend. We're on our way to the Winter Games, he said with a laugh, and we're also getting ourselves ready for some war games. My querido José — if it hadn't been for that terrible accident, it might be he and not Franco controlling the Nationalist army now, qué lástima, such a shame. Anyway, when we got back to Portugal, Sanjurjo kept reminding me of that meeting and talking to me about his friend Beigbeder: of the very good impression I'd made on him, of his wonderful life in Spanish Morocco. Did you know José was also high commissioner in Tetouan in the twenties? He was the one who designed the gardens of the High Commission — beautiful! And King Alfonso the thirteenth granted him the title of Marquis of the Rif. Because of that they used to call him the lion of Rif, my poor dear José."

On we went through the dry landscape. Rosalinda, unstoppable, was driving and talking inexhaustibly, jumping from one subject to another, crossing borders and periods of time without even making sure I was keeping up with her. Suddenly we braked in the middle of nowhere, our abrupt stop throwing up a cloud of dust and dry earth. We let a herd of famished-looking goats cross, in the care of a goatherd in a filthy turban and a frayed brown djellaba. When the last animal had crossed he raised the stick that he used as a crook to let us know we could continue on our way and said something we didn't understand, opening a mouth filled with rotting teeth. Then she resumed her driving and her conversation.

"A few months later the events of last July arrived. I'd just left Portugal and was in London, preparing for my move to Morocco. Juan Luis had told me that his work had been difficult at some moments during the uprising; there were a few points of resistance, gunshots and explosions, even blood in the fountains of Sanjurjo's beloved gardens. But the people behind the uprising got what they'd wanted and Juan Luis helped, in his way. He informed Caliph Moulay Hassan, the grand vizier, and the other Muslim dignitaries about what was happening. He speaks Arabic perfectly, you know, he studied in the School of Oriental Languages in Paris and he's lived in Africa for many years. He's a great friend to the Moroccan people and loves their culture; he calls them his brothers and says we Spaniards are all Moors; es tan gracioso, he's so funny."

I didn't interrupt her, but vague images were forming in my mind of hungry Moors fighting in a foreign land, offering up their blood for a cause that wasn't their own in exchange for a wretched wage and the pounds of sugar and flour that the army was said to give to families in the Moroccan villages while their men were fighting at the front. The organization that recruited those poor Arabs, Félix had told me, was run by our good friend Beigbeder.

"Anyway," she went on, "that same night he managed to bring all the Islamic authorities over to the side of the uprising, which was crucial to the success of the military operation. Afterward, in recognition of this, Franco named him high commissioner. They already knew each other from before, they'd been together somewhere or other. But they weren't exactly friends, no, no. Actually, even though he'd accompanied Sanjurjo to Berlin a few months before, to begin with, Juan Luis hadn't been party to the plans for the uprising; the organizers hadn't counted on his involvement, I don't know why. In those days he was in a much more administrative role, as undersecretary for Indigenous Affairs; he lived on the fringes of the military and on the edge of conspiracies, in his own world. He's a very special man, more an intellectual than a military man of action. You know what I mean? He likes to read, talk, discuss, learn new languages . . . my dear, querido Juan Luis, he's so, so romantic . . ."

I was still finding it hard to marry the idea of the charming, romantic man my client was describing with a commanding officer of the rebel army, but I wouldn't have dreamed of letting on. We arrived at a checkpoint manned by local soldiers armed to the teeth.

"Por favor, give me your passport."

I took it out of my handbag together with the border pass that Don Claudio had provided me with on the previous day. I held out both documents of accreditation; she took the first and discarded the second without even looking at it. She put my passport together with hers and a folded piece of paper, which was probably an infinitely powerful safe-conduct that could have

313

allowed her access to the very end of the world, if she were interested in visiting it. She accompanied the whole lot with her best smile and handed it over to one of the Moorish soldiers — *mejanis,* they call them. He took it all away with him into a little whitewashed hut. Immediately a Spanish soldier came out, stood to attention facing us with his most martial salute, and without a word returned our documents and gestured that we could continue on our way. She resumed her monologue, picking it up just where she had left off a few minutes earlier. Meanwhile, I was trying to recover my composure. I knew I had no reason to be nervous, that everything was officially in order, but just the same I couldn't help that a feeling of anxiety had swarmed over my body like a rash.

"In October last year I boarded a coffee ship in Liverpool that was headed for the West Indies with a stop in Tangiers. And there I stayed, just as I'd planned. Disembarking was absolutely crazy! The port at Tangiers is so, so dreadful — you do know it, right?"

This time I nodded, actually knowing what she was talking about. How could I have forgotten my arrival with Ramiro more than a year earlier? The lights, the boats, the beach, the white houses descending from the green hill till they reached the sea. The ships' foghorns and the smell of salt and tar. I turned my attention back to Rosalinda and her adventurous travels: now wasn't the moment to start reopening that sack of melancholy.

"Imagine, I had Johnny with me — my son — and Joker, my cocker spaniel, as well as the car and sixteen trunks of my things: clothes, rugs, porcelain, my books by Kipling and Evelyn

Waugh, photograph albums, golf clubs, and my HMV — you know, the portable gramophone — with all my records: Paul Whiteman and his Orchestra, Bing Crosby, Louis Armstrong . . . And of course I'd brought a good number of letters of introduction with me. That was one of the most important things my father taught me when I was just a girl, apart from horse riding and playing bridge, por supuesto. Never travel without letters of introduction, he always said; poor Daddy, he died a few years ago, of a heart attack," she said.

"I then made English friends right away, thanks to my letters: old civil servants who'd retired from the colonies, army officers, people from the diplomatic corps, the usual people. Quite dull, most of them, to tell you the truth, but it was thanks to them that I met other people who were delightful. I rented a charming little house next to the Dutch legation, found a servant, and settled there for a few months."

A few scattered little white structures had begun to dot our route, in anticipation of our arrival in Tangiers. The number of people walking on the side of the road was increasing, too: groups of Muslim women laden with bundles, children running bare-legged under their short djellabas, men covered in hoods and turbans, animals, yet more animals — donkeys carrying buckets of water, a skinny flock of sheep, occasionally a few chickens running excitedly about. Bit by bit the city began to take shape, and Rosalinda drove skillfully toward the center, turning corners at full speed as she went on describing the house in Tangiers that she'd liked so much and that she hadn't left so very long ago. Meanwhile I was starting to

315

recognize familiar places and trying not to remember the man I'd been there with in a time I'd thought was happy. At last she parked in the Place de France, with a screech of brakes that made dozens of passersby turn to look at us. Oblivious to them all, she removed the kerchief from her head and touched up her rouge in the rearview mirror.

"I'm dying for a morning cocktail at the El Minzah bar. But I've got a little bit of business to sort out first — will you come with me?"

"Where?"

"To the Bank of London and South America. To see if my loathsome husband has sent me my damned allowance once and for all."

I also took off my headscarf, all the while wondering when that woman would stop shattering my assumptions. Not only had she turned out to be a loving mother when I'd supposed her to be a freewheeling young woman; not only had she asked to borrow my clothes to go to a reception of expatriate Nazis when I'd assumed she'd have a luxurious wardrobe sewn by great international designers; not only did she have as her lover a powerful soldier twice her age when I'd expected her to be in love with a handsome, frivolous young foreigner. All that still wasn't enough to put an end to all my suppositions, nothing of the sort. Now it turned out that there was also a husband in her life, absent but living, who didn't seem too eager to support her.

"I don't think I can go with you, I've also got things to do," I said in response to her invitation. "But we can arrange to meet up later."

"Muy bien." She looked at her watch. "One o'clock?"

I accepted. It wasn't yet eleven; I'd have more than enough time for myself. I wouldn't necessarily have any luck, but I would at least have time.

CHAPTER TWENTY-THREE

The bar of the El Minzah Hotel was just as it had been a year earlier. Animated clusters of stylishly dressed European men and women filled the tables and the bar drinking whiskey, sherry, and cocktails, forming groups in which the conversation jumped from language to language as easily as one might shift gears. In the middle of the room a pianist was lightening up the atmosphere with his melodious music. No one seemed to be in a hurry, everything seemed to be just as it had been in the summer of 1936 with the sole exception that there wasn't a man waiting for me at the bar, speaking Spanish to the barman, but an Englishwoman chatting to him in English as she held a glass in one hand.

"Sira, querida!" she said, attracting my attention when she noticed me. "A pink gin?" she asked, holding up her cocktail.

To me, drinking gin with bitters was no different than swigging turpentine, so I accepted with a forced smile.

"Do you know Dean? He's an old friend. Dean, let me introduce you to Sira Quiroga, mi modista, my dressmaker."

I looked at the barman and recognized his lean body and sallow face, in which were set eyes with a dark and enigmatic stare. I remembered how he used to talk to everyone in the days when Ramiro and I would hang around his bar, how everyone seemed to come to him when they needed a contact, a reference, or slippery little bits of information. I saw his eyes running over me, locating me in his past while at the same time weighing up the ways I'd changed and associating me with the vanished presence of Ramiro. He spoke before I did.

"I think you've been here before, some time back, haven't you?"

"A long time ago, yes," I said simply.

"Yes, I think I remember. So many things have happened since then, haven't they? There are a lot more Spaniards around here now; when you were visiting us there weren't so many."

Yes, a lot of things had happened. Thousands of Spaniards had arrived in Tangiers fleeing the war, Ramiro and I had left, each in our own direction. My life had changed, along with my country, my body, and my affections; everything had changed so much that I preferred not to think about it, so I pretended to be concentrating on looking for something at the bottom of my bag and didn't reply. They continued chatting and exchanging confidences, switching between English and Spanish, occasionally trying to include me in gossip that didn't interest me in the slightest. I had enough to think about trying to put my own affairs in order. Some customers left, others arrived: elegant-looking men and women at ease and with no apparent obligations. Rosalinda greeted many of them with a pleasant gesture or a couple of kind words, as though avoiding having to linger over any encounter more than was absolutely necessary. She managed for a while, until the arrival of a couple of women she knew, who no sooner saw her than they decided that a simple hello, dear, how lovely to see you wasn't going to be enough for them. Their appearance was magnificent: blond, slim, and graceful, vague foreigners like those whose gestures and postures I'd so often emulated in front of the cracked mirror in Candelaria's bedroom. They greeted Rosalinda with fleeting kisses, puckering their lips and barely grazing their powdered cheeks. They settled in with us quite naturally, without anyone having invited them. The barman prepared their aperitifs, they took out cigarette cases, ivory cigarette holders, and silver lighters. They referred to names and posts, parties, meetings, and partings from this or that person: do you remember that night in Villa Harris, you're never going to guess what happened to Lucille Dawson with her last boyfriend, oh, by the way, did you know that Bertie Stewart has gone bankrupt? And on and on like that until one of them, the older of the two, the more bejeweled one, quite overtly raised with Rosalinda the subject that they'd doubtless had on their minds from the moment they'd seen her.

"So, my dear, how are things going with you in Tetouan? To tell you the truth, we were all so surprised to hear about your unexpected departure. It was all so, so sudden . . ."

A little laugh filled with cynicism preceded Rosalinda's reply.

"Oh, my life in Tetouan is just marvelous. I've got a dream house and some fantastic friends, like mi querida Sira, who has the best haute couture atelier in all of North Africa."

They looked at me with interest, and I replied

320

with a flick of my hair and a smile falser than Judas.

"Well then, perhaps we'll come one day and pay you a visit. We adore fashion and it's true that we're a little bored of the Tangiers dressmakers, aren't we, Mildred?"

The younger one nodded effusively and took up the baton of the conversation again.

"We'd love to come and see you in Tetouan, Rosalinda dear, but all this business with the border has been such a trial since the beginning of the Spanish war . . ."

"Though maybe you, with your contacts, could get us a safe-conduct; that way we could come and visit you both. And perhaps then we'd also have the chance to meet some more of your new friends."

The blondes made rhythmical progress in their advance toward their goal; Dean, the barman, followed it all impassively from behind the bar, unwilling to miss a single second of the action. Rosalinda, meanwhile, kept a frozen smile fixed on her face. Her two friends went on talking, each of them in turn taking up where the other left off.

"That would be marvelous; my dear, tout le monde in Tangiers is dying to meet your new friends."

"Well, why not say it straight out, since we're among true friends, right? We're dying to meet one of your friends in particular. They say he's someone very, very special."

"Perhaps one evening you could invite us to one of the receptions he hosts; that way you could introduce him to your old friends from Tangiers. We'd love to come, wouldn't we, Olivia?"

"It would be wonderful. We're so bored of

always seeing the same faces — mixing with the representatives of the new Spanish regime would be fascinating for us."

"Yes, it would be fantastic, so fantastic . . . And besides, the company my husband represents has some new products that might be of considerable interest to the Nationalist army. Perhaps with a little push from you we might be able to introduce them into Spanish Morocco."

"And my poor Arnold has got a little tired of his current position in the Bank of British West Africa; perhaps in Tetouan, among your circle, he might be able to find something more on his level . . ."

Bit by bit Rosalinda's smile was fading, and she didn't even try to hold it. And quite simply when she felt she had heard enough nonsense she decided to ignore the blondes and addressed me and the barman in turn.

"Sira, querida, shall we go and have lunch at Roma Park? Dean — por favor — be a love and put our aperitifs on my tab."

He shook his head.

"They're on the house."

"Ours, too?" Olivia asked instantly. Or it might have been Mildred.

Before the barman had a chance to reply, Rosalinda did it for him. "Not yours."

"Why not?" asked Mildred with an expression of astonishment. Or it might have been Olivia.

"Because you're a couple of zorras — how do you say, Sira, querida?"

"A couple of bitches," I said, without a glimmer of doubt.

"Sí — that's it, a couple of bitches."

We left the bar at the El Minzah aware of the many eyes following us: even for a cosmopolitan, tolerant kind of society like Tangiers, the public love affair between a married young English-woman and an older, powerful rebel soldier was a tasty morsel to spice up aperitif time.

Chapter Twenty-Four

"I suppose my relationship with Juan Luis must have come as something of a surprise to a lot of people, but to me it felt as though it were written in the stars from the beginning of time."

Among the many people to whom the couple seemed entirely inconceivable was, of course, myself. I found it enormously difficult to imagine the woman I had in front of me — with her radiant charm, her worldly airs, and her great frivolity — in a solid romantic relationship with a sober, high-ranking officer, let alone one twice her age.

Rosalinda and I were eating fish and drinking white wine on a restaurant terrace while the air from the nearby sea made the blue-and-white striped awnings flutter above our heads, bringing with it the scent of saltpeter and sad associations that I forced myself to drive away, focusing my attention back on Rosalinda's conversation. She seemed to have an enormous desire to talk about her relationship with the high commissioner, to share a completely personal version of the facts, a world away from the distorted whispers that she knew were running from mouth to mouth in Tangiers and Tetouan. But why tell me, someone she barely knew? Despite my disguise as a chic dressmaker, our origins could not have been more different, nor our current lives. She came from a cosmopolitan world, a world of comfort and leisure; I was no more than a worker, the daughter of a humble single mother, raised in a traditional old neighborhood in Madrid. She was living a passionate affair with a distinguished senior officer from the army that had incited the war that was devastating my country; I, meanwhile, worked day and night just to get by. But regardless, she'd decided to confide in me. Perhaps because she thought it might be one way of paying me back for the favor I did her with the Delphos. Perhaps because she thought that, being an independent woman of the same age, I'd be able to understand her better. Or perhaps simply because she felt lonely and had a desperate need to pour her heart out to someone. And that someone, on that summer midday in that city on the African coast, turned out to be me.

"Before his death in that tragic accident, Sanjurjo had insisted that once I was settled in Tangiers I should go and look up his friend Juan Luis Beigbeder in Tetouan; he kept referring to our meeting at the Adlon in Berlin and saying how pleased he'd be to see me de nuevo. And, la verdad, the truth is, I also wanted to meet him again: he'd struck me as a fascinating man, so interesting, so cultured, so, so . . . such a real Spanish gentleman. And so once I'd been settled for a few months I decided the time had come for me to visit the capital of the Protectorate to call on him. By then, claro — obviously — things had changed: he was no longer in his administrative role in Indigenous Affairs, but occupying the senior post in the High Commission. And I turned up there in my Austin 7. Ay, Dios! How will I ever

325

forget that day? I arrived in Tetouan and the first thing I did was to go see the English consul, Monck-Mason — you do know him, don't you? I call him 'Old Monkey' — he's such a dreadfully boring man, pobrecito."

I took advantage of the fact that at that moment I was bringing my wineglass to my mouth and made an imprecise gesture. I didn't know this Monck-Mason, I'd only heard of him occasionally from my clients, but I didn't acknowledge this in front of Rosalinda.

"When I told him I meant to visit Beigbeder, the consul was stunned. As you know, unlike the Germans and the Italians, His Majesty's Government — our government — has almost no contact with the Spanish authorities from Franco's Nationalist side because they still recognize the Republican regime in Madrid as the legitimate one, so Monck-Mason thought my visit to Juan Luis might turn out to be very useful for British interests. Anyway, before noon I headed for the High Commission in my car, accompanied only by Joker, my dog. At the entrance I showed the letter of introduction that Sanjurjo had given me before his death, and someone led me through to Juan Luis's private secretary, along corridors filled with soldiers and spittoons — qué asco! Disgusting. Jiménez Muro, his secretary, took me straight into the office. Bearing in mind the war and his position, I imagined I would find the new high commissioner dressed in an imposing uniform covered with medals and decorations, but no, no, quite the contrary. Just as on that night in Berlin, Juan Luis was wearing a simple dark suit that made him look like anything but a rebel soldier. He was delighted by my visit: he turned out to be

326

enchanting, we chatted, and he invited me to lunch, but I'd already accepted a prior invitation from Monck-Mason, so we arranged to meet the following day."

Bit by bit the tables around us were filling up. Rosalinda would occasionally greet someone with a simple gesture or a quick smile, without showing much interest or interrupting her narrative about those first meetings with Beigbeder. I was also able to recognize the odd familiar face, people I'd met through Ramiro and whom I chose not to acknowledge. So the two of us remained focused on each other: she talking, me listening, both of us eating our fish, drinking cold wine, and ignoring the noise of the world around us.

"The following day I arrived at the High Commission expecting to find some sort of ceremonial meal as befit the setting: a big table, formality, surrounded by waiters . . . But Juan Luis had arranged for them to prepare us a simple table for two beside a window open to the garden. It was an inolvidable lunch, unforgettable, during which he spoke and spoke and spoke nonstop about Morocco, about his beloved Morocco, as he calls it. About its magic, its secrets, its fascinating culture. After lunch he decided to show me some of the area surrounding Tetouan — qué lindo! We went out in his official car — imagine! — followed by a procession of drivers and assistants, all so embarrassing! Pues, anyway, we ended up at the beach, sitting on the shore while the others waited on the road, can you believe it?"

She laughed, and I smiled. The situation she was describing really was peculiar: the most powerful figure in the Protectorate and a recently arrived foreigner who could have been his daughter, flirting openly by the seaside while the motorized retinue watched them shamelessly from a distance.

"And then he picked up two pebbles, one white, the other black. He put his hands behind his back, then brought them back out, fists closed. Choose, he said. Choose what, I asked. Choose a hand. If it has the black pebble in it, you will leave my life today and I will never see you again. If it's the white one, that means destiny wants you to stay with me."

"And it was the white one."

"It was the white one, indeed," she confirmed with a radiant smile. "A couple of days later he sent two cars to Tangiers: a Chrysler Royal to transport my things, and for me the Dodge roadster we traveled in today, a gift from the Hassan Bank of Tetouan that Juan Luis had decided would be for me. We haven't been apart since, except for when his duties require him to travel. At the moment I'm installed with my son Johnny in the house on the Paseo de las Palmeras, in a grand mansion with a bathroom fit for a maharajah, a lavatory like a monarch's throne, but whose walls are crumbling and which doesn't even have running water. Juan Luis is living in the High Commission because that's what his position requires; we didn't even think about living together, but all the same he has decided that he still isn't going to hide his relationship with me, even though it might sometimes put him in a rather compromising position."

"Because he's married . . . ," I offered.

She gave a shrug of unconcern and pushed a lock of hair back from her face.

"Oh no, no, that's not what really matters —

I'm married, too; that's sólo nuestro asunto — it's only our concern, completely private. The problem is of a more public nature — official, you might say; there are people who think that an English-woman could exert influence on him that would be undesirable, and they make their views known to us quite openly."

"Who thinks that?" She had been speaking to me with such familiarity that without even thinking I felt entitled to ask for clarifications.

"The members of the Nazi colony in the Protectorate. Langenheim and Bernhardt especially. They feel the High Commissioner ought to be gloriously pro-German in every facet of his life: one hundred percent faithful to the Germans, the ones supporting his side in your civil war; the ones who right from the start agreed to make the airplanes and munitions available. In fact, Juan Luis was aware of the trip they took from Tetouan to Germany in those first days to have an audience with Hitler in Bayreuth, where — as he did every year — he was attending the Wagner festival. Pues, anyway, Hitler consulted Admiral Canaris, Canaris recommended that he agree to offer the help that was being requested, and on the same day the Führer ordered the dispatch to Spanish Morocco of everything they needed. If he hadn't done that, the troops of the Spanish army in Africa wouldn't have been able to cross the Strait, so the help from Germany really was crucial. Since then the relationship between the two armies has been very close, naturally. But the Nazis in Tetouan feel that my presence and the feelings Juan Luis has for me could lead him to adopt a position that is more pro-British and less faithful to the Germans."

I recalled Félix's comments about Frau Langenheim's husband and his compatriot Bernhardt, his references to that early military help that they had secured in Germany. Apparently it had not only continued but was becoming increasingly well known in the Protectorate. I also remembered Rosalinda's anxiety to create an impeccable impression during her first formal meeting with the German community on her lover's arm. I thought I understood then what it was she was telling me, but I played down its importance and tried to reassure her.

"But all of that shouldn't trouble you too much. He can still be loyal to the Germans while he's with you, they're two different things — one is official, one's personal. I'm sure the people who think that way aren't right."

"They are right, of course they are."

"I don't understand."

Quickly she cast her eyes across the half-empty terrace. The wind had stopped, the awnings barely moved. A number of waiters in white jackets and tarbooshes — the red felt Moorish hat — worked in silence shaking napkins and tablecloths into the air. Rosalinda lowered her voice to something close to a whisper — but a whisper that, though quiet, conveyed an unmistakable determination.

"They're right in their assumptions, because, querida, I have every intention of doing whatever I can to get Juan Luis to establish friendly relations with my compatriots. I can't bear the idea that your war should end in favor of the Nationalist army and that Germany should end up being the great ally of the Spanish people, and Great Britain, meanwhile, an enemy power. And I'm going to do it for two reasons. The first, simple sentimental patriotism: because I want the country of the man I love to be friends with my own. However, the second reason is a much more pragmatic, objective one: we English don't trust the Nazis, and things are turning ugly. Maybe it's a bit risky to talk about another great European war coming, but you never know. And were that to happen, I'd like your country to be on our side."

I was about to say quite openly that our poor country wasn't in a position to get involved in any future war, that it had more than enough misfortune with the one it was living through now. That war of ours seemed quite alien to her, however, despite the fact that her lover was significantly involved in one side of it. Eventually I chose to follow her lead, to focus on a future that might never come and not sink into the tragedy of the present. My day had already had a good dose of bitterness, and I preferred to keep it from getting any sadder.

"And how do you mean to do that?" was all I asked.

"Bueno — well — don't believe for a moment that I've got powerful personal contacts in Whitehall, nothing of the kind," she said with a little laugh. I automatically made a mental note to ask Félix what Whitehall was, but my look of concentration managed to hide my ignorance. She went on. "But you know how these things work: networks of acquaintances, people who can connect you to other people . . . S o I thought I might try things with some friends I have here in Tangiers to begin with, Colonel Hal Durand, General Norman Beynon and his wife, Mary, all of whom have excellent contacts in the Foreign Office. At the moment they're away spending a little time in

London, but I'm planning to meet them later on, introduce them to Juan Luis, try to see if they'll talk and get along."

"And you think he'll agree, he'll let you get involved like that in his official business?"

"Of course, querida," she said without the slightest trace of doubt, as she tossed another lock of hair away from her left eye with an airy shake of her head. "Juan Luis is a terrifically intelligent man. He knows the Germans very well, he's lived with them for many years, and he's afraid that the price that Spain will have to pay for all the help they've been receiving will turn out to be too dear. Besides, he has a high opinion of the English because, after all, we've rarely lost a war. He's a soldier and such things are important to him. And above all, and this is the main reason, because Juan Luis adores me. As he tells me every day, he would go down into the fires of hell for his Rosalinda."

By the time we got up, the tables on the terrace were already set for dinner and the evening shadows were beginning to rise along the adobe walls. Rosalinda insisted on paying for our lunch.

"I've finally managed to get my husband to transfer my allowance; do allow me to treat you."

We strolled to her car and set off back toward Tetouan, barely managing to avoid going over the twelve hours I'd been allowed by Commissioner Vázquez. But the geographical direction wasn't the only thing we reversed on that journey; we also reversed the trajectory of our conversation. If on the way there and for the rest of the day it had been Rosalinda who'd monopolized the talk, on the way back the moment had come for our roles to be reversed.

"You must think I'm dreadfully boring, always going on about myself and my business. Tell me about yourself. Cuéntame — tell me — how did it go this morning with those things you had to sort out?"

"Badly," I said, simply.

"Badly?"

"Yes, very, very badly."

"Lo siento — really, I'm very sorry. Something important?"

I could have answered no. Compared to her own concerns, my problems lacked some of the ingredients necessary to arouse her interest: there were no high-ranking soldiers involved, no consuls or ministers, no political interests, no affairs of state or premonitions of great European wars, nothing remotely related to the sophisticated tempests through which she moved. In the humble territory of my concerns there had been room only for a handful of private miseries that could almost be counted on the fingers of one hand: a love betrayed, a debt to pay and a hotel manager who refused to understand, the daily grind of starting up a business, a homeland drenched in blood to which I couldn't return, and the yearning for an absent mother. I could have answered no, that my little tragedies weren't important. I could have kept quiet about my private business, kept it hidden, shared it only with the darkness of my empty house. Yes, I could have. But I didn't.

"To tell you the truth, it was something very important to me. I want to get my mother out of Madrid and bring her to Morocco, but to do that I need a large sum of money that I don't have because I first have to put my savings toward meeting another urgent payment. This morning I

333

was hoping to postpone that payment, but I wasn't able to, so right now I fear that this thing with my mother will be impossible. And the worst is that, according to what people are saying, it's getting harder and harder to move from one zone to another."

"Is she alone in Madrid?" she asked with what seemed like an expression of concern.

"Yes, alone. Quite alone. She has nobody but me."

"And your father?"

"My father — well, it's a long story, but briefly, they're not together."

"I'm so very sorry, Sira, dear. It must be so hard for you knowing that she's in the Red Zone, exposed to so many things, stuck with all those people . . ."

I looked at her sadly. How could I make her understand what she didn't understand? How could I get into that beautiful blond head the tragic reality of what was happening in my country?

"Those people are her people, Rosalinda. My mother is with her people, in her house, in her neighborhood, with her neighbors. She belongs to that world, to the people of Madrid. If I want to bring her over to me in Tetouan, it's not for fear of what might happen to her there, but because she's all I've got in this life, and with each day that passes I find it harder not hearing anything from her. I haven't heard news in a year; I haven't the slightest idea of how she is, I don't know how she's supporting herself, what she's living on, or how she's getting through the war."

Like a balloon being punctured, the whole sham of my fascinating past disintegrated in a second.

And the strangest thing was, it didn't bother me at all.

"But, but they told me . . . They told me your family was . . ."

I didn't let her finish. She'd been honest with me and had told her story without deceit: it was time for me to do the same. Perhaps she wouldn't like the version of my life that I was going to tell; maybe she would think it wasn't terribly glamorous compared to the adventures she was used to. She might decide that from that moment on she would never again share pink gins with me or offer me rides to Tangiers in her Dodge convertible, but I couldn't stop myself from telling her my truth in detail. After all, it was all I had.

"My family is me and my mother. We're both dressmakers, simple dressmakers with no assets but our own hands. From the time I was born my father never had anything to do with us. He belongs to a different social class, a different world: he has money, companies, contacts, a wife he doesn't love, and two sons he doesn't get along with. That's what he has. Or had, I don't know — the first and last time I saw him was before the war and he already had a feeling they were about to kill him. And my betrothed, the attractive, enterprising fiancé who's in Argentina managing companies and resolving financial matters, he doesn't exist. It's true that there was a man with whom I had a relationship and who may be in that country doing business, but he no longer has anything to do with me. He's nothing more than an undesirable human being who broke my heart and robbed me of everything I had; I'd rather not talk about him. That's my life, Rosalinda, and as you can see, it's very different from yours."

335

In reply to my confession she launched into a paragraph of English in which I was only able to catch the word "Morocco."

"I didn't understand any of that," I said, confused.

She went back into Spanish.

"I said what the hell does it matter where you come from when you're the best dressmaker in all Morocco? And as for your mother, well, as you Spaniards say, God may squeeze us, but He never suffocates us entirely . . . It'll all work itself out, you'll see."

CHAPTER TWENTY-FIVE

Early the next morning I returned to the police station to report to Don Claudio on the failure of my negotiations. Of the four policemen, only two were at their desks: the old one and the skinny one.

"The boss isn't in yet," they announced in unison.

"What time does he usually arrive?" I asked.

"Half past nine," said one.

"Or half past ten," said the other.

"Or tomorrow."

"Or never."

The two of them laughed, with their slobbering mouths, and I found myself without the strength to put up with that pair of creeps a moment longer.

"Please tell him that I came to see him. That I've been to Tangiers and I wasn't able to arrange anything."

"Whatever you say, princess," said the one who wasn't Cañete.

I made for the door without saying good-bye, and I was about to leave when I heard Cañete's voice.

"Whenever you like I can prepare another pass for you, sweetheart."

I didn't stop. I just clenched my fists hard, and almost without realizing it I was revisited by a shadow of my former self. I turned my head a few inches, just enough for my reply to be heard loud and clear.

"Better save that for your whore of a mother."

As luck would have it I ran into the commissioner on the street, far enough away from the police station that he didn't invite me to return with him. It wasn't hard to bump into anyone in Tetouan, where the street grid of the Spanish *ensanche* didn't stretch too far and everyone was constantly coming and going. As usual he was wearing a light-colored linen suit and smelled recently shaved, ready to begin his day.

"You don't look happy," he said the moment he saw me. "I imagine things at the Continental didn't go well." He looked at his watch. "Come, let's get a coffee."

He led me to the Spanish Casino, a beautiful corner building with white stone balconies and big windows open to the main road. An Arab waiter was lowering the awnings with a squeaking iron rod as two or three others were putting out chairs and tables on the sidewalk in the shade. There was no one in the cool interior, just a large marble staircase in the entry and two big rooms, one on each side. He invited me into the one on the left.

"Good morning, Don Claudio."

"Good morning, Abdul. Two coffees with milk, please," he requested, seeking my agreement with his eyes. "Tell me," he then said.

"It didn't work. The manager is new, he wasn't the same one from last year, but he knew all about the matter. He wasn't prepared to negotiate at all.

He just said that their terms had been more than generous and that if I didn't make the payment by the designated date, he would turn me in."

"I understand. And believe me, I am sorry. But I'm afraid I can't help you now."

"Don't worry, you did enough by getting me a year."

"So what are you going to do now?"

"Pay right away."

"And the thing with your mother?"

I shrugged.

"Nothing. I'll keep working and saving, though by the time I've gotten together as much as I need, it might be too late and they will have halted the evacuations. For now, as I said, I'll clear my debt. I have the money, there's no problem there. That's just why I came to see you. I need another pass to cross the border and your permission to keep my passport for a couple of days."

"Keep it, there's no need for you to give it back to me again." Then he brought his hand to the inside pocket of his jacket and took out a small leather case and a fountain pen. "And as for the safe-conduct, this will do," he said as he removed a card and uncapped the pen. He scribbled a few words on the back and signed it. "Here."

I put it away in my handbag without reading it.

"Are you planning to go on the Valenciana?"

"Yes, that's what I'd planned."

"Like you did yesterday?"

I held his inquiring gaze a few seconds before replying.

"I didn't go on La Valenciana yesterday."

"So how did you manage to get to Tangiers?"

I knew that he knew. And I also knew that he wanted me to tell him myself. But first we each took a sip of our coffee.

"A friend gave me a lift in her car."

"Which friend?"

"Rosalinda Fox. An Englishwoman, a client of mine."

Another sip of coffee.

"You do know who she is, don't you?" he said then.

"Yes, I do."

"So just be careful."

"Why?"

"Just because. Be careful."

"Tell me why," I insisted.

"Because there are people who don't like the fact that she's here with the person she's with."

"I know."

"What do you know?"

"That there are certain people who aren't too pleased about her personal life."

"Which people?"

I'd discovered already there was no one like the commissioner for squeezing, crushing, and extracting the very last drop of information.

"Certain people. Don't ask me to tell you what you already know, Don Claudio. Don't ask me to be disloyal to a customer just so you can hear from my mouth the names you already know."

"Fine. Just confirm one thing for me."

"What?"

"The names of these people — are they Spanish?"

"No."

"Perfect," he said simply. He finished his coffee and looked at his watch again. "I have to go, I have work to do."

"So do I."

"Indeed you do, I'd forgotten you were a working woman. You know you've earned an excellent reputation for yourself?"

"You hear about everything, so I'll have to believe you."

He smiled for the first time, and the smile took several years off him.

"I only know the things I need to know. But I'll bet you hear about an awful lot of things, too: women always talk a lot to one another. And you deal with ladies who no doubt have interesting stories to tell."

He was right, my clients did talk. They talked about their husbands, their businesses, their friendships, about the people whose houses they frequented, what various people did, thought, or said. But I didn't answer yes or no to the commissioner; I simply got up, ignoring his observation. He called to the waiter and sketched a flourish in the air. Abdul nodded: no problem, the coffees would go on Don Claudio's tab.

Settling the debt in Tangiers was liberating, like having a rope freed from my neck. It was true that I still had the lawsuits in Madrid to resolve, but from this distance it all seemed terribly far away. Paying the debt at the Continental allowed me to free myself of the burden of my past with Ramiro in Morocco and to breathe differently. More calmly, more freely. The mistress, now, of my own destiny.

Summer progressed, but my clients still seemed lazy about contemplating their autumn wardrobes. Jamila remained with me, looking after the house and doing small jobs in the workshop. Félix came around to visit almost every night, and from time to time I would go over to see Candelaria at La Luneta. Everything at peace, everything quite normal, until an inconveniently timed cold left me without the strength to leave the house or the energy to do any sewing. I spent the first day lying prostrate on the sofa. The second in bed. The third I'd have done the same but for an unexpected appearance. As unexpected as it always was.

"Siñora Rosalinda say Siñorita Sira get up out of bed immediately."

I went out to meet her in my dressing gown; I didn't bother to put on my never-changing suit or hang the silver scissors around my neck, not even to straighten my tousled hair. But if she was surprised at my disheveled state, she didn't let it show: she had come to deal with other more serious matters.

"We're going to Tangiers."

"Who?" I asked, wiping my runny nose.

"You and me."

"What for?"

"To try to resolve this thing with your mother."

I looked at her halfway between disbelief and amazement. I wanted to know more.

"Through your . . ."

A sneeze prevented me from finishing the phrase, which I was grateful for as I wasn't sure how to refer to the high commissioner, whom she always spoke of by his first name.

"No, I'd rather keep Juan Luis out of it: he has a thousand other matters to worry about. This is mine, so his contacts are out. But we have other options."

"Which are?"

"Through our consul in Tangiers I tried to find out whether they're making these sorts of arrangements in our embassy, but without any luck. He told me that our legation in Madrid has always refused to give asylum to refugees, and besides, since the Republican government moved to Valencia that's where the diplomatic officials have been based. All that's left in the capital is an empty building and some minor staff member to look after it."

"So then?"

"I tried with St. Andrew's, the Anglican church in Tangiers, but they weren't able to help me either. Then it occurred to me that some private firm might know something, so I asked around here and there, and I managed to get hold of a tiny bit of information. Not a great deal, but we'll see if we're lucky and we might get a bit more out of it. The director of the Bank of London and South America in Tangiers, Leo Martin, told me that on his last trip to London he heard people in the bank's headquarters talking about someone working in the Madrid branch who had some kind of contact with someone who's helping people get out of the city. I don't know any more than that; all the information he was able to give me was very vague, very imprecise, just a comment that someone made that he overheard. But he's promised to check things out."

"When?"

"Inmediatamente — right now. I was there a couple of days ago, he told me to return today. So you're going to get yourself dressed right away and we're going to Tangiers to see him. I imagine he should have had time to find out a bit more."

I tried to thank her for her efforts, between coughs and sneezes, but she played it all down and just pressed me to get myself ready. The trip

343

was a whirlwind. The road, dry plains, areas covered in pines, goats. Women in big striped skirts with their walking slippers, laden down under their large straw hats. Sheep, prickly pears, more dry plains, barefoot children who smiled at us as we passed and raised their hand to wave good-bye. Dust, more dust, yellow plains to one side, yellow plains to the other, passport control, more road, more prickly pear cacti, more palm trees and sugarcane plantations, and in just an hour we'd arrived. Again we parked in the Place de France, again we were welcomed by the broad avenues and the magnificent buildings of the city's modern quarter. In one of them the Bank of London and South America awaited us — a curious alloy of financial interests, almost as strange as the pair Rosalinda Fox and I made.

"Sira, allow me to introduce you to Leo Martin. Leo, this is my friend Miss Quiroga."

Leo Martin could very easily have been Leoncio Martínez, had he been born just a couple of miles from where he actually was. Short and dark, if he hadn't been shaved and wearing a tie he could have passed for a tough Spanish farmhand. But his face gleamed clean of any shadow of a beard, and a serious-looking striped tie rested on his belly. And he wasn't Spanish, or a peasant, but an authentic subject of Great Britain: a man from Gibraltar capable of expressing himself in English and Andalusian with equal facility. He greeted us with a shake of his hairy hand, offered us a seat, and gave the old crow who served as his secretary an order not to disturb us. Then, as though we were the bank's wealthiest clients, he proceeded to inform us eagerly about what he'd been able to find out. I'd never opened a bank account in my

344

life, and Rosalinda probably didn't have a single pound saved from the allowance that her husband sent her whenever he was in the mood, but the rumors about my friend's amorous pursuits must have reached the ears of this little man with the curious linguistic abilities. And in these turbulent times the director of an international bank couldn't miss an opportunity to do a favor for the lover of the man in charge next door.

"Well, ladies, I think I have some news. I've been able to speak to Eric Gordon, an old acquaintance of mine who was working at our branch in Madrid shortly after the uprising; now he's been reposted to London. He told me he knows someone personally who lives in Madrid and who is involved in these sorts of activities, a British citizen who worked for a Spanish firm. The bad news is that he doesn't know how to contact him; he's lost track of him in the last few months. The good news is that he's supplied me with the details of someone who is familiar with his whereabouts because he was living in the capital until recently. He's a journalist who's gone back to England because there was some problem; I think he was injured, but he didn't give me the details. Well anyway, this person might be prepared to put you in touch with the man who is evacuating the refugees. But he wants something first."

"What?" Rosalinda and I asked in unison.

"To speak to you personally, Mrs. Fox," he said, turning to the Englishwoman. "The sooner the better. I hope you won't consider it too forward, but, given the circumstances, I thought it appropriate to let him know who it was who wanted this information from him."

Rosalinda didn't reply; she just looked at him,

alert, her eyebrows arched, waiting for him to continue talking. He cleared his throat uncomfortably, doubtless having expected a more enthusiastic response to what he had said.

"You know what these journalists are like, don't you? Like carrion birds, always after something."

Rosalinda took a few seconds to reply.

"They aren't the only ones, Leo dear, they aren't the only ones," she said a little sourly. "But anyway, put me in contact with him. Let's see what he wants."

I shifted in my seat, trying to hide my nerves, and blew my nose again. Meanwhile, the British director with the body of an earthenware pot and the accent of a bullfighter gave the telephone operator an order to connect the call. We waited a long while. They brought us coffee; Rosalinda regained her good mood and Martin his composure. At last the moment arrived for the conversation with the journalist. It only lasted three minutes, and Rosalinda spoke so softly I didn't catch a word of it. What I did sense, however, was the serious, sharp tone in my client's voice.

"Done," was all she said when it ended. We bade farewell to the director, thanking him for his help, and went back out past the intense scrutiny of the hawkeyed secretary.

"What did he want?" I asked anxiously as soon as we were out of the office.

"A bit of . . . I don't know how you say it in Spanish. When someone says they'll do something for you only if you do something in exchange."

"Chantaje — blackmail," I said.

"Chantaje," she repeated.

"What form of blackmail?"

"A personal interview with Juan Luis and a few

346

weeks of preferential access to official life in Tetouan. In exchange he would commit to putting us in contact with the person we need in Madrid."

I swallowed before formulating my question. I was afraid she'd say that only over her dead body would anyone impose such extortionate conditions on the highest dignitary in the Spanish Protectorate in Morocco, much less an opportunistic journalist she didn't know. All in exchange for a favor for a simple dressmaker.

"And what did you tell him?" I finally dared ask.

She shrugged, a gesture of resignation.

"To send me a cable with the date of his arrival in Tangiers."

Chapter Twenty-Six

Marcus Logan turned up dragging one leg, almost deaf in one ear and with his arm in a sling. All his injuries were on the same side of his body, the left-hand side, the one that had been closest to the exploding shell that had knocked him over and nearly killed him while he was covering the attacks of the Nationalist artillery on Madrid for his agency. Rosalinda had arranged for an official car to meet him at the port of Tangiers and bring him directly to the Hotel Nacional in Tetouan.

I had waited for them seated on one of the wicker chairs in the hotel's covered courtyard, surrounded by flowerpots and tiles with Arab decorations. The walls were covered in trellises bearing climbing creepers, and large Moorish lanterns hung from the ceiling. The murmur of other people's conversations and the burbling of the water in a little fountain kept me company as I waited.

The last bit of afternoon sun was filtering through the skylight when Rosalinda arrived; the journalist followed ten minutes later. Over the previous days I'd assembled in my mind an image of an impulsive, brusque man, someone sour, with enough nerve to try to intimidate anyone he came across in order to get what he wanted. But I was wrong, just as we are almost always wrong when we construct preconceptions on the fragile basis of a single act or a handful of words. I knew I was wrong the moment the blackmailing journalist came through the archway of the courtyard with his tie loose and his light linen suit full of creases.

He recognized us at once; he only had to sweep the room with his gaze to be sure that we were the only pair of young women sitting alone — a blonde who looked obviously foreign and a dark one with the classic look of a Spaniard. We readied ourselves to receive him without getting up, braced to defend ourselves against this most inconvenient of visitors. But the Marcus Logan who appeared on that early African evening could have awakened any feeling in us but fear. He was tall and seemed to be somewhere between thirty and forty. His brown hair was unkempt, and as he approached limping, supported by a bamboo walking stick, we saw that the left side of his face was covered with the fading marks of cuts and bruises. Even though it was possible to get a sense of the man he must have been before the incident that almost cost him his life, at that moment he was little more than a pained body. No sooner had he greeted us with all the courtesy his pitiful state would allow than he slumped into a chair, trying unsuccessfully to disguise the discomfort and fatigue that were building up in his body, punished by the long journey.

"Mrs. Fox and Miss Quiroga, I suppose," were his first words, which he spoke in English.

"Yes, we are indeed," said Rosalinda. "Nice meeting you, Mr. Logan. And now, if you don't mind, I think we should proceed in Spanish; I'm afraid my friend won't be able to join us otherwise."

"Of course, I'm sorry," he said, addressing me in excellent Spanish.

He didn't look like an unscrupulous extortionist, just a professional who tried to get by as best he could and who grabbed opportunities that presented themselves to him. Like Rosalinda, like me. Like everyone in those days. Before going right into the matter that had brought him to Morocco and seeking confirmation from Rosalinda, he chose to show us his credentials. He worked for a British news agency, he had been accredited to cover the Spanish war on both sides, and although he was based in the capital he'd spent his days constantly on the move. Until the unexpected had happened. They admitted him to a hospital in Madrid, performed emergency surgery, and when they could they evacuated him to London. He'd spent several weeks in the Royal London Hospital, bearing his pain and his treatments — bedbound, immobilized, longing to return to active life.

When news reached him that someone related to the Spanish High Commission in Morocco needed some information he could provide, he saw the clouds part. He knew he wasn't in a physical state to return to his constant comings-and-goings across the Peninsula, but a visit to the Protectorate might allow him to progress with his convalescence while also partially reviving his professional spirit. Before he'd been given permission to travel he'd had to fight with his doctors, his superiors, and everyone else who approached his bed to try to convince him not to move; the frustration combined with his physical state had

350

driven him to the verge of pulling the trigger. So he apologized to Rosalinda for his brusqueness during their telephone call, he crossed and uncrossed his legs painfully several times, and then he finally got down to more pressing concerns.

"I haven't eaten anything since this morning; would it be all right if I invited you for dinner and we talked then?"

We accepted; truth was, I'd have accepted anything to be able to talk to him. I could have eaten in a latrine or rolled in the mud with pigs; I'd have chewed on cockroaches and drunk rat poison to wash them down, anything to get the information I'd spent so many days waiting for. Logan gracefully called over one of the Arab waiters bustling around the courtyard serving drinks and collecting glasses and asked him for a table in the hotel restaurant.

"Just a moment, please, sir." The waiter went off to speak to someone and moments later we were approached by the Spanish maître d', unctuous and reverential. "Right away, sir, right away, do please come with me, ladies, come with me, sir. Not a minute's wait for Mrs. Fox and her friends, naturally."

Logan gestured us ahead of him into the dining room, while the maître d' indicated a showy central table, a conspicuous bullring that would ensure that no one would be left without a prime view of Beigbeder's beloved Englishwoman. The journalist politely turned that table down and pointed toward another more isolated table at the back. All the tables were impeccably set with spotless tablecloths, water and wineglasses, and white napkins folded on the porcelain plates. It was still

351

early, though, and there were only a dozen or so people spread around the room.

We chose from the menu and were served some sherry to occupy us while we waited. It was Rosalinda who took on the role of hostess and got the conversation started. The earlier meeting in the courtyard had been mere formality, but it had helped to ease tension. The journalist had introduced himself and told us how he'd ended up in the condition he was in; we, meanwhile, had relaxed on discovering that he wasn't threatening and had made a few trivial comments about life in Spanish Morocco. All three of us knew, however, that this wasn't just a polite meeting for making new friends, chatting about infirmities, and drawing picturesque images of North Africa. What had brought us together that night was a negotiation, all cut and dried, in which two separate sides were implicated: two sides who had made their demands and their conditions perfectly clear. The time had come to lay everything on the table and find out how far each one could get.

"I want you to know that everything you asked me for on the phone the other day has been arranged," Rosalinda began as the waiter moved off with our order.

"Perfect," replied the journalist.

"You'll have your interview with the high commissioner, in private and as extensively as you find useful. You'll also be given a temporary residence permit for the Spanish Protectorate area," Rosalinda went on, "and invitations will be issued in your name to all the official engagements in the next few weeks. Some of these will be extremely significant."

He raised the eyebrow on the intact side of his

face in a question.

"We're shortly expecting a visit from Ramón Serrano Suñer, Franco's brother-in-law; I imagine you know who I'm talking about."

"Yes, of course," he confirmed.

"He's coming to Morocco to commemorate the anniversary of the uprising; he'll be staying three days. Various activities are being arranged to receive him — the general director of propaganda, Dionisio Ridruejo, arrived yesterday. He's come over to coordinate the preparations with the secretariat of the High Commission. We expect you to attend any official events involving civilians."

"Very many thanks — and do please extend my gratitude to the high commissioner."

"It'll be a pleasure having you here with us," replied Rosalinda with the delicacy of a perfect hostess about to unsheathe a sword. "I hope you understand that we, too, have a number of conditions."

"Of course," said Logan after a sip of sherry.

"Any information you wish to send abroad will first have to be checked by the press office of the High Commission."

"I have no problem with that."

At that moment the waiters approached with our food, and I was overwhelmed by a great sense of relief. In spite of the elegance with which the two of them were managing the negotiations, I hadn't been able to help feeling a little uncomfortable, as though I'd slipped into a party to which I hadn't been invited. They were discussing things that had nothing to do with me, matters that might not have contained any great official secrets but that nonetheless were far from what I imagined a simple dressmaker ought to be hearing. Several times I repeated to myself that I wasn't in the wrong place, that it was my place, too, because it had been my own mother's evacuation that had prompted this dinner. All the same, it wasn't easy convincing myself of that.

The arrival of the food interrupted the exchange of requirements and concessions for a few moments. Sole for the ladies, chicken with trimmings for the gentleman, the waiters announced. We made brief comments about the food, the freshness of the fish on the Mediterranean coast, how divine the vegetables from the Río Martín plain were. The moment the waiters had withdrawn, the conversation picked up exactly where it had left off just a few minutes earlier.

"Any other conditions?" asked the journalist before bringing the fork to his mouth.

"Yes, though I wouldn't exactly call it a condition. Rather it's something that will help you as much as us."

"Then it will be easy for me to accept," he said after swallowing his first mouthful.

"That's what I'm hoping," Rosalinda agreed. "You see, Logan, we move in two quite different worlds, you and I, but we're compatriots and we both know that on the whole the Nationalists tend to be sympathetic to the Germans and the Italians, and haven't the least affection for the English."

"Just so, absolutely," he confirmed.

"Well then, that's why I'd like you to pass yourself off as a friend of mine. Without disguising the fact that you're a journalist, of course, but a journalist associated with me, and by extension the high commissioner. In this way we believe you'll be welcomed with somewhat more moderate feelings of suspicion."

"By whom?"

"By everyone: the Spanish and Muslim local authorities, the foreign consular corps, the press . . . I don't have many fervent admirers in any of those groups, I have to be honest, but at least formally they do maintain a certain respect for my closeness to the high commissioner. If we can introduce you as a friend of mine, perhaps we can get them to extend that respect to you."

"What does Colonel Beigbeder think of that?"

"He agrees entirely."

"Then there's nothing more for us to discuss. It doesn't seem a bad idea to me, and as you say, it could be good for all of us. Any more conditions?"

"None on our side," said Rosalinda, raising her glass as though in a little toast.

"Perfect. That's all clear, then. Well, I think it's time for me to bring you up to date with the matter you've asked me about."

My stomach leapt: the time had come. The food and wine seemed to have brought Marcus Logan a little bit of new vigor; he appeared rather livelier. Although he had maintained a cool serenity during the negotiations, it was possible to make out a positive attitude in him, and an evident desire not to trouble Rosalinda and Beigbeder any more than necessary. I guessed that this might have something to do with his profession, but I had no way of knowing for sure — he was, after all, the first journalist I'd ever met in my life.

"I want you to know first of all that my contact is already on the alert and expects your mother's evacuation when they mobilize the next operation from Madrid to the coast."

I had to grip the edge of the table hard to stop myself from getting up and throwing my arms around him. I did restrain myself, however: the dining room in the Hotel Nacional was now full of people and our table, thanks to Rosalinda, was the main attraction that night. An impulsive reaction like giving that foreigner an ecstatic hug would have focused every gaze and whisper on us instantly. So I contained my enthusiasm and suggested my amazement with just a smile and a quiet thank-you.

"You'll have to supply me with some information, then I'll cable it to my agency in London. From there they'll get in touch with Christopher Lance, who's the person controlling the whole operation."

"Who is he?" Rosalinda wanted to know.

"An English engineer; a veteran of the Great War who's been settled in Madrid for a number of years. Until the uprising he was working for a Spanish firm with British shares, the Ginés Navarro & Sons civil engineering company, with its headquarters in the Paseo del Prado and branches in Valencia and Alicante. His projects with them have included building roads, bridges, a large dam in Soria, a hydroelectric plant near Grenada, and a mooring mast for zeppelins in Seville. When the war broke out, the Navarros disappeared, I don't know whether by choice or by force. The workers set up a committee and took control of the company. Lance could have left then, but he didn't."

"Why not?" we asked in unison.

The journalist shrugged as he took a big swallow of wine.

"It's good for the pain," he said by way of

excuse, raising his glass to us to indicate its medicinal effects. "To tell you the truth," he went on, "I don't know why Lance didn't return to England, I've never been able to get a reason from him that would really justify what he did. Before the war began, the English who were living in Madrid — like almost all the foreigners — weren't involved in Spanish politics and watched the situation with indifference, even with a certain amount of ironic detachment. They were aware, naturally, of the tensions that existed between the conservatives and the parties on the left, but saw them as just something typical of the country, a part of the national character. Bullfighting, siestas, garlic, oil, and fraternal hatred, all very picturesque, very Spanish. Until everything exploded — and then they saw how serious things were and started rushing to get out of Madrid as quickly as possible. With a few exceptions, such as Lance, who chose to send his wife home and remain in Spain."

"Not very sensible," I ventured.

"He's probably a little crazy, yes," he said, half joking. "But he's a good sort and he knows what he's doing; he's no reckless adventurer, or an opportunist like the ones who spring up all over the place at times like these."

"What is it that he does, exactly?" asked Rosalinda.

"He gives help to people who need it. He gets people out of Madrid when he can, takes them to some Mediterranean port and from there puts them on any kind of British boat: a warship is as useful to him as a packet boat or a lemon freighter."

"Does he charge anything?" I wanted to know.

"No, nothing. He doesn't make anything from it. There are people turning a profit from things like this — not him."

He was going to explain more to us, but at that moment a young soldier in breeches, shining boots, and his cap under his arm approached our table. He gave a martial salute with a look of concentration on his face and handed an envelope to Rosalinda. She took out a folded sheet of paper, read it, and smiled.

"I'm truly very sorry, you'll have to excuse me," she said, hurriedly putting her cigarette case, her gloves, and the note in her handbag. "Something has come up, something unexpected," she added, then leaned over toward my ear. "Juan Luis has come back from Seville early," she whispered impulsively.

Despite his burst eardrum, the journalist probably heard it, too.

"You keep talking, you can tell me all about it later," she added loudly. "Sira, querida, I'll see you soon. And you, Logan, be ready tomorrow, a car will be here to fetch you at one. You'll have lunch at my house with the high commissioner and then you'll have the whole afternoon for your interview."

Rosalinda was accompanied to the door by the young soldier and countless brazen pairs of eyes. As soon as she had disappeared from view, I encouraged Logan to resume his explanations.

"If Lance doesn't make any money from it, and he isn't moved by political concerns, why does he do this?"

He shrugged again, a gesture that apologized for his inability to find any reasonable explanation.

"There are people like that. They're called

pimpernels. Lance is a rather singular individual, a sort of crusader for lost causes. According to him, there's nothing political about what he's doing; the concerns that move him are purely humanitarian. Most likely he'd have done the same for Republicans if he'd found himself in the Nationalist zone. Maybe the inclination comes from being the son of a canon of Wells Cathedral — who knows? The fact is, at the moment of the uprising, the ambassador Sir Henry Chilton and most of his staff moved to San Sebastián to spend the summer, and the embassy in Madrid was left in the control of a civil servant who wasn't up to the job. Lance, as a veteran in the British colony, quite spontaneously took the reins. As you Spaniards say, 'Without praying to either God or the Devil,' he opened the embassy as a refuge for British citizens — barely more than three hundred of them at that time, as I've heard. In principle none of them were directly involved in politics, but most were conservatives in sympathy with the right, so they sought out diplomatic protection while they waited to find out how events were unfolding. But what happened was that the situation grew beyond what they'd expected — several hundred other people rushed to the embassy for refuge, too. They claimed to have been born in Gibraltar or on an English ship during a crossing, to have relatives in Great Britain, to have done business with the British Chambers of Commerce; any ruse to get themselves under the protection of the Union Jack, our flag."

"Why your embassy in particular?"

"It wasn't only ours, far from it. Actually, ours was one of the most reluctant to offer refuge. Everyone did almost exactly the same in the early

359

days: they took in their own citizens, and also some Spaniards in need of protection."

"And then?"

"Some legations continued to offer asylum and get involved directly or indirectly in the transfer of refugees. Chile in particular; France, Argentina, and Norway, too. Others, meanwhile, once the first period of uncertainty had ended, refused to carry on. Lance isn't acting as a representative of the British government, however; everything he does, he does on his own account. As I said, our embassy was one of the ones that refused to continue to be involved in offering asylum and evacuating refugees. And it isn't that Lance is dedicated to helping the Nationalist side in the abstract, but people who as individuals need to get out of Madrid. For ideological reasons, for family reasons — whatever the reasons. It's true that he began by installing himself in the embassy and managed somehow to get them to grant him the post of honorary attaché so that he could arrange the evacuation of the British citizens in the early days of the war, but from then on he's acted at his own risk. When it's in his interest — usually to impress the militiamen and sentries at the checkpoints on the roads — he waves about all the diplomatic paraphernalia he can get his hands on: the red, white, and blue armband on his sleeve to identify himself, little flags on the car, and a huge safe-conduct covered in stamps and seals from the embassy, from six or seven trade unions, and the War Office, whatever he can get his hands on. He's a pretty odd sort, this Lance: pleasant, talkative, always showily dressed, with jackets and ties that pain you to look at. Sometimes I think he exaggerates so much just so that no one takes him

360

too seriously and so they don't suspect him of anything."

"How does he transport people to the coast?"

"I don't know exactly; he's reluctant to give away details. At first I think he started off using vehicles from the embassy and vans from his firm, until these were requisitioned. Lately it would seem he's been using a Scottish ambulance that has been made available to the Republic. And he's usually accompanied by Margery Hill, a nurse from the Anglo-American hospital — do you know it?"

"I don't think so."

"It's on Calle Juan Montalvo, near the university, almost right at the front. That's where they first took me when I was injured, then I was moved for the operation to the hospital they set up in the Palace Hotel."

"A hospital at the Palace?" I asked, incredulous.

"Yes, a field hospital — you didn't know?"

"I had no idea. When I left Madrid the Palace was — along with the Ritz — the most luxurious of the hotels in the city."

"Well as you can see, it's now fulfilling other functions. A lot has changed. I was interned there for a few days, till they decided to evacuate me to London. I already knew Lance before I was interned; the British colony in Madrid was already much diminished in those days. Then he came to see me several times at the Palace; part of his self-imposed humanitarian task is also to help his compatriots who're facing difficulties. Which is how I learned a bit about the evacuation process, but I only know the details that he chose to tell me. Normally the refugees arrive in the hospital of their own account; sometimes they're kept

361

awhile so that they can pass for patients, till the next convoy is ready. Usually they both go on all the journeys, Lance and Nurse Hill: apparently she's unique in her ability to handle officials and militiamen at the checkpoints if things go wrong. And they also usually arrange to bring back to Madrid anything they can get off the Royal Navy ships — medicines, medical equipment, soap, canned food . . ."

"How do they actually make the trip?" I was trying to predict my mother's journey, to have some idea of what her adventure would consist of.

"I know they leave early in the morning. Lance is already familiar with all the checkpoints, and there are more than thirty; sometimes it takes them more than twelve hours to make the journey. He has, however, become something of a specialist in the psychology of the militiamen: he gets out of the car, talks to them, calls them his comrades, shows them his impressive safe-conduct, offers them tobacco, shares a joke, and takes his leave with a "Long Live Russia!" or a "Death to the Fascists!": anything that'll allow him to get back on his way. The only thing he never does is bribe them: he set himself that principle and as far as I know he's always kept to it. He's also extremely scrupulous in following the Republic's laws — he never disobeys them. And naturally at all times he avoids provoking any incidents that might harm our embassy. Even though he isn't a diplomat except on an honorary basis, he nonetheless follows the diplomatic code of ethics extremely rigorously."

No sooner had he finished his answer than I was ready to fire off the next question, evidence that

I'd been an apt pupil in acquiring Commissioner Vázquez's interrogation techniques.

"Which port do they take the refugees to?"

"To Valencia, to Alicante, to Denia — it depends. He studies the situation, designs a plan for the route, and finally, one way or other, arranges to dispatch his cargo."

"But have these people got papers? Permits? Safe-conducts?"

"To get themselves around Spain, yes, usually. To go abroad, probably not. That's why the operation to get them embarked is usually the most complicated part: Lance needs to outmaneuver checkpoints, get onto the docks and pass unnoticed among sentries, negotiate with the ships' officers, slip the refugees on board, and hide them in case there's a search. All this has to be done carefully, without arousing any suspicion. It's an extremely delicate business; he's risking ending up in prison. But for now he's always managed to make it work."

We finished our dinner. Logan had struggled to use his cutlery; his left arm wasn't working a hundred percent. Even so, he'd been thorough in his dealings with the chicken, the large dishes of custard, and several glasses of wine. I, meanwhile, absorbed in listening to him, had barely tasted the sole and hadn't ordered any dessert.

"Do you want a coffee?" he asked.

"Yes — thank you."

The truth was that I never drank coffee after dinner except when I needed to stay up working late. But that night I had two good reasons to accept his offer: to prolong the conversation as much as possible, and to stay sharp so as not to miss out on the slightest detail.

"Tell me about Madrid," I asked him then. My voice came out muted; perhaps I was already guessing that I wasn't going to like what I heard.

He looked at me hard before answering.

"You don't know anything about the situation there, do you?"

I dropped my gaze to the tablecloth and shook my head. Learning the details of my mother's forthcoming evacuation had relaxed me: I was no longer nervous. In spite of his crushed body, Marcus Logan had managed to calm me with his solid, reassuring presence. The relaxation didn't bring happiness with it, however, but a heavy sadness about everything I'd heard. For my mother, for Madrid, for my country. Immediately I felt a terrible weakness and tears beginning to spring to my eyes.

"The city's in a very bad way, and there are shortages of basic goods. The situation isn't good, but everyone finds ways to get through it as best they can," he said, summing up his reply with a handful of vague platitudes. "Would you mind if I asked you a question?" he added.

"Ask me anything you want," I replied, my gaze still set on the table. My mother's future was in his hands — how could I refuse?

"Look, the arrangements have been made, and I can assure you that they're going to take care of your mother as they've promised me they would; you needn't worry on that score." He was talking more quietly, more closely. "But to make it work, however, I've had to — let's say — invent a scenario, and I'm not sure how much it corresponds to reality. I've had to say that she's in a high-risk situation and needs evacuating urgently; I didn't need to give any more details than that.

364

But I'd like to know how much I was correct and how much I was lying. So if you wouldn't mind, would you tell me what your mother's situation really is? Do you think she's in real danger in Madrid?"

A waiter arrived with the coffees and we stirred in our sugar, the spoons clinking against the porcelain in a measured rhythm. After a few seconds, I raised my gaze and looked right at him.

"You want to know the truth? The truth is that I don't think her life is in danger, but I'm the only thing my mother has in the world, and she's the only thing I have. We've always lived alone, the two of us together struggling to get by: we're just two working women. But there was a day when I made a mistake, and I let her down. And now the only thing I want is to get her back. You told me before that your friend Lance doesn't do things for political motivations, that he's only moved by humanitarian concerns. You decide whether or not reuniting a mother without means with her only daughter is a humanitarian reason — I don't know."

I couldn't say any more, I knew my tears were about to start pouring out.

"I have to go, tomorrow I've got to be up early, I have a lot of work to do, thank you for the dinner, for everything . . ."

The phrases tumbled out, my voice hoarse, as I stood and picked up my handbag. I tried not to look up, so as not to let him see the damp streaks running down my cheeks.

"I'll go with you," he said, getting up, hiding the pain.

"There's no need, thank you: I live very close, just around the corner."

I turned and began to walk toward the exit. I'd barely gone a few steps when I felt his hand brush against my elbow.

"Lucky that you live nearby, that way I won't have to walk so much. Let's go."

With a gesture he asked the maître d' to charge the bill to his room, and we left. He didn't speak to me or try to calm me; he didn't say a word about what he'd just heard. He simply remained beside me in silence and let me recover my composure. The moment we'd set foot on the street, he stopped dead. Leaning on his walking stick, he looked up at the starry sky and breathed in longingly.

"Morocco smells good."

"There's the mountain nearby, and the sea, too," I replied, already somewhat calmer. "I suppose that must be why."

We walked slowly; he asked me how long I'd been in the Protectorate, what life was like in such a place.

"We'll meet again, I'll keep you informed whenever I get any new information," he said when I indicated that we'd arrived at my door. "And rest assured, you can count on the fact that they'll be doing whatever they can to help her."

"Thank you very much — truly — and sorry about the way I reacted. Sometimes I find it hard to keep myself in check. These aren't easy times," I whispered a bit shyly.

He tried to smile, but only half succeeded.

"I understand perfectly, don't worry."

This time there were no tears; the worst of it had passed. We just held each other's gaze, said good night, and I began my walk up the stairs thinking how little this Marcus Logan resembled

the threatening opportunist Rosalinda and I had
been expecting.

Chapter Twenty-Seven

Beigbeder and Rosalinda were delighted with the following day's interview. She told me later that everything had taken place in a relaxed atmosphere, the two men sitting on one of the terraces of the old villa on Paseo de las Palmeras, drinking brandy and soda opposite the Río Martín plain and the slopes of the imposing Ghorgiz, where the Rif Mountains began. At the start, the three of them were all there together: the critical eye of the Englishwoman needed to gauge her compatriot's level of trustworthiness before leaving him alone with her beloved Juan Luis. Bedouie, the Arab cook, prepared a lamb tajine for them, which was served accompanied by a grand cru burgundy. After the desserts and coffee, Rosalinda retired and the two men settled into wicker chairs to smoke cigars as they immersed themselves in their conversation.

I learned that it was almost eight in the evening when the journalist returned to the hotel following the interview, that he didn't have any dinner that night and only asked that some fruit be brought up to his room. I learned that the following morning he headed over to the High Commission as soon as he was done with his breakfast. I also learned which streets he walked down and what time he returned; about all his comings and goings that day, and the following day, and the next as well. I was given detailed information; I discovered what he'd eaten, what he'd drunk, what newspapers he leafed through, and the color of his ties. Work had kept me busy all day, but I was aware of his every move, thanks to the efficient work of a couple of collaborators. Jamila took charge of trailing him the whole day; for a small tip, a young bellhop at the hotel informed me with equal precision what time Logan retired at night; for a little bit extra he even recalled what the journalist had eaten for his dinners, what clothes he had sent to be laundered, and what time he turned out his lights.

I managed to bear the wait for three days, receiving the minutest details about all his movements and awaiting the arrival of any news regarding the progress of his arrangements. On the fourth, having not heard anything from him, I began to think ill of him, so much so that in my mind I constructed an elaborate story according to which Marcus Logan, having attained his aim of interviewing Beigbeder and gathering the information about the Protectorate that he needed for his work, had planned to leave, quite forgetting that he still had something to settle with me. And to prevent reality from bearing out my perverse assumptions, I decided that it might be best for me to take some steps myself. Which was why, the following morning, I had no sooner sensed the approaching dawn and heard the muezzin's call to the first prayers of the day than I was out of the house. Smartly dressed in a new wine-colored suit, carrying one of my fashion magazines under my arm, I proceeded to the courtyard of the Hotel

Nacional and installed myself in a corner, my back straight, legs crossed. On guard duty, just in case.

I knew that what I was doing was utter silliness. Rosalinda had talked about granting Logan a temporary residency permit for the Protectorate; he'd given me his word, promising to help me; these arrangements just took time. If I analyzed the situation coolly, I knew I had nothing to be afraid of: all my fears were groundless, and my sitting there waiting was no more than an absurd manifestation of my insecurities. Yes, I knew that, but all the same, I decided to stay put.

He came down at nine fifteen, when the morning sun was already blazing through the crystal ceiling. The courtyard had livened up with the presence of guests who had just woken up, the bustle of the waiters, and the incessant movement of young Moroccan bellhops carrying packages and suitcases. He was still limping slightly, and his arm was in a blue cloth sling, but the bruising on his face had improved. His overall appearance, reflected in his clean clothes, the hours of sleep he'd had, and his damp, just-combed hair, was significantly better than the way he'd looked the day of his arrival. I felt a flicker of anxiety on seeing him, but I hid it with a toss of my hair and another elegant crossing of my legs. He also saw me at once and came over to greet me.

"My word, I had no idea the women here were such early risers."

"You know the saying — God helps the early risers."

"And what is it you want God's help for, if you don't mind my asking?" he said, taking a seat beside me.

"To make sure you don't leave Tetouan without

370

telling me how everything is going, whether the business with my mother is under way."

"I haven't told you anything because I don't know anything yet," he said. Then he leaned forward, coming closer. "You still don't completely trust me, do you?"

His voice was certain, and close. Almost complicit. It took me a few seconds to answer as I tried to make up some lie. But I couldn't come up with any, so I opted for being frank.

"I'm sorry, lately I don't trust anyone."

"I understand, don't worry about it," he said, smiling, still with some effort. "These aren't good times for loyalty and trust."

I gave a shrug that spoke volumes.

"Have you had breakfast?" he asked.

"Yes, thank you," I lied. I hadn't had breakfast, nor did I feel like having any. All I needed was to be sure that he wasn't going to abandon me without keeping his word.

"Well, then perhaps we could . . ."

A whirlwind wrapped in a haik appeared between us, interrupting our conversation: Jamila, breathless.

"Frau Langenheim is waiting at home. She's going to Tangiers, to buy materials. She needs Señorita Sira say how many yards to buy."

"Tell her to wait a couple of minutes; I'll be with her right away. Tell her to have a seat and have a look at the new pictures Candelaria brought over the other day."

Jamila ran off again and I apologized to Logan.

"My maid; I have a client waiting for me, I'll have to go."

"In that case I shan't keep you any longer. And don't worry: everything's already in progress and

371

we'll get confirmation sooner or later. But bear in mind that it might be a matter of days or weeks, it could take more than a month; it's not possible to rush anything," he said, getting up. He seemed more agile than he had been previously, and in much less pain.

"Really, I don't know how to thank you," I replied. "And now, if you'll excuse me, I've got to go: I have a lot of work waiting for me, I barely have a moment free. There are going to be a number of social functions in the next few days and my clients need new outfits."

"And you?"

"What about me?" I asked, confused, not understanding the question.

"Are you planning to attend any of these functions? Serrano Suñer's reception, perhaps?"

"Me?" I said with a little laugh, pushing my hair back from my face. "No, I don't go to those things."

"Why not?"

My first impulse was to laugh again, but I restrained myself when I realized he was being serious, that his curiosity was genuine. We were both standing now, side by side, close. I could see all the detail in the texture of the light-colored linen of his jacket and the stripes of his tie; he smelled good, the smell of good soap, of a clean man. I still had my magazine in my arms, he was resting a hand on his walking stick. I looked at him and half opened my mouth to answer. I had any number of replies to justify my absence from those alien celebrations: because no one had invited me, because it wasn't my world, because I had nothing to do with all those people . . . A t last, however, I decided not to give him any reply;

I just shrugged and said again, "I've got to go."

"Wait," he said, gently taking hold of my arm. "Come with me to Serrano Suñer's reception, be my date for the night."

The invitation echoed like a whip crack and left me so overwhelmed that when I tried to find reasons to turn him down, none came to my mouth.

"You've just said you don't know how to thank me for what I've done. Well, now there's a way for you to do that: come to this event with me. You could help me to learn who's who in this city, it would do me a lot of good in my work."

"I . . . I hardly know anyone either, I haven't really been here for long."

"And besides, it'll be an interesting night; we might enjoy ourselves," he insisted.

That was a preposterous idea, absurd. What was I going to do at a party in honor of Franco's brother-in-law, surrounded by the military top brass and the local powers that be, by people of means and representatives of foreign countries. The proposal was altogether ludicrous, and yet there was a man standing before me waiting for an answer. A man who was arranging the evacuation of the person who mattered most to me in the whole world, a foreigner I didn't know who'd asked me to trust him. Quick bursts of conflicting thoughts rushed through my mind: some of them advised me to refuse, insisting that this was a pointless extravagance; others reminded me of the old saying I'd so often heard from my mother's lips, about how being well bred is about knowing how to be thankful.

"Very well," I said, swallowing hard. "I'll go with you."

The figure of Jamila reappeared in the hallway, waving her arms exaggeratedly, trying to move me along, not to keep the demanding Frau Langenheim waiting too long.

"Perfect. I'll let you know the day and exact time as soon as I get my invitation."

I shook his hand and walked back across the courtyard, my heels tapping along in haste. It wasn't until I reached the door that I turned around and saw Marcus Logan still standing at the far end, watching me, leaning on his cane. He hadn't moved from the spot where I'd left him, and his presence had been transformed into a silhouette set against the light. His voice, however, could be heard loud and clear.

"I'm glad you're coming. And don't worry, I'm in no hurry to leave Morocco."

Chapter Twenty-Eight

Doubt assailed me the moment I set foot in the street. I realized that perhaps I'd been too hasty in accepting the journalist's proposal without first consulting Rosalinda, who might have had quite different plans for her enforced guest. My second thoughts didn't take long to disappear, however: as soon as she arrived that afternoon for a fitting, she was in a flurry of haste.

"I've only got half an hour," she said, unbuttoning her silk blouse with nimble fingers. "Juan Luis is waiting for me, there are still a thousand details that need preparing for Serrano Suñer's visit."

I'd planned to put my question to her tactfully, choosing my words with care, but I decided to take advantage of the moment and broach the subject right away.

"Marcus Logan has asked me to go to the reception with him."

I didn't look at her as I spoke, pretending to concentrate on removing her outfit from the mannequin.

"You don't say!"

I gathered from her tone that the news had come as a pleasant surprise to her.

"You think it's all right for me to go with him?" I asked, still uncertain.

"Of course! It would be wonderful having you around. Juan Luis will have a very official role to play, so I expect to be able to spend a bit of time with the two of you. What are you going to wear?"

"I don't know yet, I'll have to think about it. I think I'll make myself something with this material," I said, pointing to a roll of raw silk leaning against the wall.

"Dios mío, you're going to be stunning."

"If I survive," I muttered, my mouth full of pins.

After several weeks without too much work, the headaches and obligations were thronging around me all of a sudden, threatening to bury me at any moment. I had so many commissions to finish that I was up every day at dawn like a rooster, and it was rare for me to make it to bed before three in the morning. The doorbell didn't stop ringing, and clients were endlessly coming in and out of the workshop. I wasn't bothered about feeling so overwhelmed, however — I was almost grateful for it. This way I had less time to think about what the hell I was going to do at that reception, which was now just over a week away.

Having got past the obstacle of Rosalinda, the second person to hear about the unexpected invitation, inevitably, was Félix.

"My, my, you sneaky little thing, you're so lucky! You're making me green with envy!"

"I'd gladly swap places with you," I said, quite truthfully. "The party doesn't thrill me in the slightest; I know I'll feel out of place, there with a man I barely know and surrounded by strangers, by soldiers and politicians whose fault it is that my city is under siege and I can't go back home."

"Come on, girl, don't be silly. You're going to be part of a spectacular event that'll go down in the history of this little corner of the African map. And besides, you'll be there with a man who's not bad at all, really not bad at all."

"How do you know, if you don't know him?"

"What do you mean I don't know him? Where do you think I took the old she-wolf for afternoon tea today?"

"The Nacional?" I asked, incredulous.

"Exactly. It came out three times as expensive as the buns at La Campana, because the old tart filled herself up to the eyeballs with tea and scones, but it was worth it."

"So you got to see him then?"

"And to talk to him. He even gave me a light."

"You're shameless!" I said, unable to hold back a smile. "And what did you make of him?"

"Pleasingly attractive when his wounds heal. In spite of the limp and the half of his face that's massacred, he's not bad looking and seems every inch the gentleman."

"Do you think he'll be trustworthy, Félix?" I asked with a trace of concern. Even though Logan had asked me to trust him, I still wasn't sure I could. My neighbor responded to my question with a laugh.

"I wouldn't have thought so, but you needn't worry about that. Your new friend is just a simple journalist passing through, who's involved in some deal with the woman who has mesmerized the high commissioner. So for his own sake, if he doesn't want to leave this country in an even worse state than when he arrived, he'd be wise to behave himself with you."

Félix's perspective made me see things differently. The disastrous way my interlude with Ramiro had ended had made me distrustful and suspicious, but what was at stake with Marcus Logan wasn't a question of personal loyalty but a straightforward exchange of interests. You give me, then I'll give you; otherwise, no deal. Those were the rules; there was no need for me to go on obsessing about how trustworthy he was. He was the person with the greatest interest in maintaining good relations with the high commissioner, so he had no reason to let me down.

That same night Félix also told me who exactly Serrano Suñer was. I'd often heard him spoken about on the radio and I'd read his name in the newspapers, but I knew hardly anything about the person hidden behind those two names. Félix, as he so often did, supplied me with the most comprehensive information.

"As I imagine you already know, querida, Serrano is Franco's brother-in-law, married to Zita, the younger sister of Franco's wife, Carmen Polo. This woman is quite a bit younger, more beautiful, and less conceited than Franco's wife, as far as I've been able to make out from a few photographs. They say he's an extraordinarily brilliant guy, with an intellectual capacity a thousand times greater than the Generalísimo's, something it would seem that Franco himself doesn't appreciate all that much. Before the war he was a state attorney and member of parliament for Zaragoza."

"From the right."

"Naturally. The insurgency, however, trapped him in Madrid. He was detained because of his political affiliations, he was locked up in the Modelo Prison and finally managed to get himself transferred to a hospital. He has an ulcer or something like that. They say that then, thanks to the help of Dr. Marañón, he escaped from there dressed as a woman, with a wig, a hat, and his trousers rolled up under his coat: what a picture."

We laughed as we imagined the scene.

"He then managed to get out of Madrid and reached Alicante. From there, disguised as an Argentine sailor, he left the Peninsula on a torpedo boat."

"He left Spain for good?" I asked.

"No, he disembarked in France and came back into the Nationalist zone by land, with his wife and his string of little kids, I think he's got four or five. From Irún they arranged to get themselves to Salamanca, which is where the Nationalist faction originally had their headquarters."

"That would be easy, as a relative of Franco's."

He gave an evil smile.

"Oh, nothing of the sort, my dear. They say General Franco — El Caudillo, as they call him — didn't lift a finger for them. He could have offered his brother-in-law in a trade, something that happened on both sides of the conflict, but he never did. And when they did manage to get to Salamanca, apparently the reception they received wasn't terribly enthusiastic. Franco and his family were settled in the Episcopal Palace and they say that all of the Serrano Polo troops were lodged in an attic on rickety cots while Franco's little girl had an enormous bedroom with a bathroom to herself. The truth is, apart from all these slanders that are being passed from mouth to mouth at the moment, I haven't been able to learn much about Serrano Suñer's private life; I'm sorry, love. What I do know is that in Madrid two of his brothers were killed who had nothing to do with his own political causes. This seems to have traumatized him and motivated him to get actively involved in the construction of what they're calling the New Spain. And the thing is now he's managed to transform himself into the general's right-hand man. Which is why they've taken to calling him the In-law-ísimo — a joke on his brother, the Generalísimo. They also say that much of his current power is thanks to the influence of the powerful Doña Carmen, who was already fed up that her fly-by-night other brother-in-law, Nicolás Franco, had so much influence on her husband. So the moment Serrano appeared, she made herself absolutely clear: 'From now on, Paco, more Ramón and less Nicolás.' "

His impression of the voice of Franco's wife made us both laugh.

"Serrano's a really smart guy, they say," Félix went on. "Very wise, much more experienced than Franco on political, intellectual, and human matters. Besides that, he's hugely ambitious and works tirelessly; they say he spends his days trying to construct a judicial basis for legitimizing the Nationalist faction and his relative's ultimate power. That is to say, he's working to provide a civil institutional order for a structure that is purely military, you see?"

"In case they win the war," I said.

"In case they win the war, who knows?"

"And what do people think of Serrano? Do they like him?"

"So-so. The old *arrastrasables* — the high-ranking officers, that is — don't like him all that much. They consider him an inconvenient intruder; they speak different languages, they don't understand each other. They'd be happiest with an entirely military state, but Serrano, who's smarter than all of them, is trying to make them

380

see that this would be a crazy idea, that they'd never be able to get legitimacy or international recognition that way. And Franco, even though he hasn't a clue about politics, does trust him in this. So even if they don't like it, the others just have to swallow it. Nor has he quite managed to persuade all the long-standing Falangists. It seems he used to be close friends with José Antonio Primo de Rivera, with whom he studied at the university, but he never belonged to the Falange before the war. Now he does: he had no choice, he's currently Falangist to the bone, but the people who were Falangists before, the old guard, see him as an arriviste, an opportunist who's only just adopted their creed."

"So who supports him? Just Franco?"

"And his blessed wife, which is no small matter. Though we'll see how long the affection lasts."

Félix was a lifesaver in the lead-up to the event. From the moment I told him the news, and with a theatrical gesture he pretended to gnaw on the five fingers on his hand to demonstrate his envy, there wasn't a night when he didn't come by my house to bring me some interesting piece of information about the party, stray bits that he'd picked up here and there in his constant explor-atory zeal. We didn't spend those evenings in the living room as we used to do: I had so much work that our nighttime meetings had been transferred temporarily to the workroom. This small move didn't seem to matter to him, however: he loved observing the threads, the fabrics, and all that was hidden behind the stitching. And he always had some idea to bring to the design I was working on. Sometimes he was right; many other times, however, he suggested the most outrageous nonsense.

"This velvet marvel of a gown you said you're making for the wife of the president of the High Court? Make a hole in the ass, see if anyone is actually looking at her. What a waste of material, look how ugly the old whore is," he said, running his fingers along the pieces of fabric assembled on a mannequin.

"Don't touch," I warned him severely, concentrated on my backstitching without even looking at him.

"Sorry, it's just that the fabric's got such a beautiful sheen."

"That's exactly why: be careful or you'll leave fingerprints all over it. Come on, let's get down to business, Félix — tell me, what have you learned today?"

In those days Serrano Suñer's visit was the talk of Tetouan. In the shops, at the tobacconist's and the hairdresser's, in any doctor's office, in cafés and in groups gathered on the sidewalks, at market stalls and on the way out of Mass, no one talked of anything else. I, however, had so much work that I barely had a minute free to step out onto the street — that was what my good neighbor was for.

"No one is going to miss out on him, the best people in local society are going to gather there for their rendezvous with the In-law-ísimo: the caliph and his great retinue, the grand vizier and the Makhzen, his entire government. All the senior authorities from the Spanish administration, soldiers laden with decorations, attorneys and magistrates, representatives from Morocco's political parties and the Jewish community, the whole diplomatic corps, the directors of the banks, posh civil servants, powerful businessmen, doctors, every Spaniard, Arab, and Jew of high social standing, and — naturally — the odd parvenu like you, you shameless little thing, slipping in through the back door with your limping reporter on your arm."

Rosalinda had warned me, though, that the sophistication and glamour of the event would be kept to a minimum: Beigbeder meant to welcome his guest with every honor, but he hadn't forgotten that we were in a time of war. So there wouldn't be showy displays, or dancing, or any music other than the caliph's band. All the same, in spite of the austerity, it was going to be the most dazzling reception the High Commission had organized in a long while, which was why the capital of the Protectorate was in agitated preparation.

Félix also instructed me on some matters of protocol. I never found out where he'd learned them, since his social background was nil and his circle of friends almost as paltry as my own. His life was bounded by his routine work at the General Supplies Office, his mother and her wretchedness, his sporadic nighttime excursions to squalid dives, and the recollection of occasional trips to Tangiers before the war — that was all. He hadn't so much as set foot in Spain his whole life. But he loved cinema and knew all the American movies shot by shot, in addition to being a voracious reader of foreign magazines, a shameless observer, and the most incorrigible busybody. And cunning as a fox, so that when he went to one source or other it was easy for him to furnish himself with the tools he needed to train me and transform me into an elegant guest with no trace whatsoever of my lack of pedigree.

Some of his pieces of advice were so obvious they were unnecessary. In the time I'd spent with the undesirable Ramiro, I'd known and observed people from the most varied social strata and origins. Together we'd been to a thousand parties and dozens of assorted establishments and good restaurants, in Tangiers as well as Madrid; as a result I had assimilated a host of little routines to get by confidently at social gatherings. Just the same, Félix decided to begin my instruction with the most basic information.

"Don't speak with your mouth full, don't make noise while you're eating, and don't wipe your mouth on your sleeve, or put your fork all the way into your mouth, or gulp down all your wine at once, or hold up your glass whimpering to the waiter to fill it back up for you. Use 'please' and 'thank you very much' where appropriate, but only murmured, not overly effusively. And as you know, say a simple 'pleased to meet you' each time you're introduced to someone, none of that 'the pleasure is all mine' or vulgarities of that sort. If people talk to you about things you don't know about or don't understand, give them one of your dazzling smiles and keep nice and quiet, just nodding from time to time. And when you have no choice but to speak, remember to keep your lies to an absolute minimum, or you'll find yourself caught in them: it's one thing having told just a few teeny little fibs to promote yourself as a *haut couturier,* but quite another putting yourself in the lion's mouth strutting around in front of people with enough insight or enough class to spot your lies the moment they're out of your mouth. If anything astonishes you or delights you, just say 'that's good' or 'most impressive' or a similar adjective; at no point should you demonstrate your enthusiasm with excessive arm waving, slapping your thigh, or using phrases such as 'well I never!' or 'you don't say!' If someone makes a comment you find funny, don't laugh wildly, showing your wisdom teeth, or double over holding your belly. Just smile, blink, and avoid making any comment at all. And don't give your opinion when you aren't asked for it or say indiscreet things like 'And who might you be, my good man?' or 'Don't tell me that fat lady is your wife?' "

"But I know all this, Félix dear," I said, laughing. "I may be only a simple dressmaker, but I wasn't brought up in a cave. Tell me some things that are a little more interesting, please."

"Very well, then, darling, as you wish; I was only trying to be useful, in case any little detail eluded you. Down to the serious stuff, then."

And so over the course of several nights, Félix sketched out for me the profiles of the most distinguished, and one by one I went about memorizing their names, positions, and responsibilities, and on several occasions their faces, too, thanks to the array of newspapers, magazines, photographs, and catalogs that he brought over. In this way I learned where they lived, what they did with their time, how wealthy they were, and where they were ranked in the local hierarchy. To tell the truth, these things really didn't interest me all that much, but Marcus Logan was counting on my being able to identify the relevant people, and to do that I needed to prepare myself.

"I would imagine that given where your compan-

385

ion is from, the two of you will probably be mostly with the foreigners," he said. "And I suppose, apart from the locals, there will be a few others coming over from Tangiers; the In-law-ísimo has no plans to go there on his tour, so, as you know, if Mohammed won't go to the mountain . . ."

That gave me some comfort: mixed up with a group of expatriates I'd never seen before and whom I'd probably never see again in my life, I'd feel much safer than surrounded by locals I might run into daily on a street corner. Félix informed me, too, of the order of protocol, how the guests would be greeted and the sequence of events, one step at a time. I listened to him, memorizing the details while sewing more intensely than I'd ever sewed before.

Until at last the big day arrived. Over the course of the morning the final orders left the workshop in Jamila's arms; at noon all the work had been delivered and there was calm at last. I imagined that the other guests would already be finishing their lunches now, getting ready to take a rest in the dark of their bedrooms with their shutters closed or waiting their turn at Justo and Miguel's *haute coiffure* salon. I envied them: with barely a moment to get a bite to eat, I still had to devote my siesta time to sewing my outfit. When I set to work, it was a quarter to three. The reception was due to start at eight, and Marcus Logan had sent me a message notifying me that he would be coming to collect me at half past seven. I still had a world of things to do and less than five hours ahead to do them all.

CHAPTER TWENTY-NINE

When I'd finished the ironing I looked at my watch. Six twenty. The garment was ready; all I needed to do now was make myself presentable.

I sank into the bath and let my mind go blank. The nerves would be there when the event drew closer, but for now I deserved a rest: a rest in hot water and soap bubbles. I felt my tired body relax, felt my fingers, weary of sewing, loosen up from their stiffness and my neck muscles unclench. I started to doze off; the world seemed to be melting into the porcelain of the bathtub. I couldn't remember such a pleasurable moment in months, but the lovely feeling didn't last long: it was interrupted by the bathroom door being thrown wide open without so much as a knock.

"But what are you thinking of, girl?" yelled Candelaria. "It's after six thirty and you're still soaking like a chickpea; honey, you won't have enough time! When were you thinking about getting yourself together?"

The Matutera had brought along what she considered to be her vital emergency kit: her dear friend Remedios the hairdresser and Angelita, a woman who lived next door to the boardinghouse and had a gift for manicure. A short while before I'd sent Jamila to La Luneta to buy some hairpins;

387

she'd run into Candelaria on the way, which was how the Matutera learned that I was much more concerned about my clients' clothes than my own and barely had a minute free to get myself ready.

"Hurry up, then, girl; get yourself out of the tub, we've got a lot of work ahead of us and we're desperately short on time."

I allowed myself to be taken over; it would have been impossible to fight against that whirlwind. And of course I was deeply grateful for her help: there was only three-quarters of an hour left before Marcus Logan would arrive and I still looked (as the Matutera put it) like a scrub brush. The moment I managed to get a towel wrapped around my body, the work began.

Angelita the neighbor focused on my hands, rubbing them with oil, removing rough areas, and filing my nails. Candelaria's dear Remedios, meanwhile, took charge of my hair. Knowing I wouldn't have much time in the evening, I'd washed it that morning; what I needed now was a decent hairdo. Candelaria served as assistant to them both, holding out tweezers and scissors, curlers and pieces of cotton, while — never once stopping talking — she filled us in on the latest information about Serrano Suñer that was circulating around Tetouan. He'd arrived two days earlier and had been escorted by Beigbeder around all the relevant places and met all the relevant personalities in North Africa: from Ksar el Kabir to Chefchaouen and then to Dar Riffien, from the caliph to the grand vizier. I hadn't seen Rosalinda since the previous week; yet the news had been circulating from mouth to mouth.

"They say they had a Moorish meal yesterday in Ketama, surrounded by pine trees, sitting on rugs on the ground. They say the In-law-ísimo almost had conniptions when he saw everyone eating with their fingers; the man had no idea how to bring couscous to his mouth without dropping half of it along the way . . ."

"And the high commissioner was utterly thrilled, playing the great host and smoking one cigar after another," added a voice from the doorway. It was Félix, naturally.

"What are you doing here at this hour?" I asked, surprised. His afternoon walk with his mother was sacred, even more so on a day like today when the whole city was out on the street. Tipping his thumb against his mouth, he indicated that Doña Encarna was at home, obligingly drunk earlier than usual.

"And since you're going to be abandoning me tonight for some upstart journalist, at least I didn't want to miss out on the preparations. Anything I can help with, ladies?"

"Aren't you the one who paints divinely?" Candelaria asked him suddenly. Each knew about the other, but this was the first time they'd met.

"Like Murillo himself."

"Then how about seeing if you can do this girl's eyes?" she said, holding out a makeup case that she'd got hold of from heaven knows where.

Félix had never made anyone up in his life, but he didn't flinch from the task. Quite the contrary: he accepted the Matutera's order as though it were a gift, and having consulted the photographs in a couple of issues of *Vanity Fair* in search of inspiration, he became engrossed in my face as though it were a canvas.

At seven fifteen I was still wrapped in my towel with my arms stretched out, while Candelaria and her neighbor blew the nail polish dry. At seven twenty Félix finished going over my eyebrows with his thumbs. At twenty-five past, Remedios put the final pin in my hair, and just a few seconds later Jamila ran like a maniac in from the balcony, announcing at the top of her lungs that my date had just appeared at the end of the street.

"And now, just a couple of little things left," my business partner announced.

"It's all perfect, Candelaria: there's no time for anything else," I said, going off half naked to fetch my outfit.

"Don't even think about it," I heard her warning behind me.

"I really can't stop, Candelaria, honestly . . . ," I insisted anxiously.

"Shut up and look, I said," she commanded, grabbing me by the arm halfway down the corridor. Then she held out a small flat packet wrapped in crinkled paper.

I tore off the wrapping, realizing I couldn't refuse any longer; I knew there was no way I was going to win this one.

"Candelaria, I don't believe it!" I said, unfolding a pair of silk stockings. "How did you get hold of these? You told me there weren't any to be had for months."

"Just stop talking once and for all and open this one now," she said, stopping my flow of gratitude and handing me another packet.

In the coarse wrapping paper I found a beautiful object, shell shaped and golden edged.

"It's a compact," she explained proudly. "For you to powder your nose all up, to show you're no less than any of the grand important ladies you're going to be rubbing shoulders with."

"It's lovely," I whispered, stroking the surface. Then I opened it: inside there was a tablet of compacted powder, a small mirror, and a white cotton powder puff. "Thank you very much, Candelaria. You needn't have bothered, you've already done so much for me . . ."

I couldn't say any more for two reasons: I was about to cry, and at just that moment the doorbell sounded. The noise of the bell made me react, there was no time to get sentimental.

"Jamila, open it — quick!" I commanded. "Félix, bring me the slip that's on the bed; Candelaria, help me with the stockings, if I rush I'll end up making a run in them. Remedios, you get the shoes; Angelita, draw the curtain in the hallway. Let's go, everyone into the workroom so he won't hear us."

I'd finally used the raw silk to sew myself a two-piece outfit with broad lapels, a fitted waist, and *évasée* skirt. Since I didn't have any jewels, the only accessory I wore was a tobacco-colored cloth flower at my shoulder, which matched the vertiginously heeled shoes that a cobbler in the Moorish quarter had fashioned for me. Remedios had succeeded in transforming my hair into an elegant loose bun that gracefully emphasized Félix's improvised makeup job. Despite my friend's inexperience, the result was superb: he'd filled my eyes with joy, and lips with voluptuousness, and found a glow in my tired face.

Between all of them, they managed to dress me, put my shoes on, and retouch my hair and my rouge. I didn't even have time to look at myself in the mirror; as soon as I knew that I was ready I went out into the hallway and rushed along it on the tips of my shoes. Arriving at the foyer I stopped and, feigning an easy pace, walked into the living room. Marcus Logan had his back to me, watching the street through one of the balcony windows. He turned when he heard my footsteps on the floor tiles.

Nine days had passed since our previous meeting, and over that time the traces of the aches and pains with which the journalist had arrived seemed to have diminished. He was waiting for me with his left hand in the pocket of a dark suit, and he no longer wore a sling. On his face there were now barely more than a few traces of what used to be bloody wounds, and his skin had absorbed the Moroccan sun until it was a tanned color that contrasted starkly with the spotless white of his shirt. He stood without any apparent effort, his shoulders firm, his back straight. He smiled on seeing me, and this time it didn't seem hard for him to stretch his lips in both directions.

"The In-law-ísimo isn't going to want to go back to Burgos after seeing you tonight," was how he greeted me.

I tried to give a reply that was equally clever but was distracted by a voice behind me.

"Very nice, girl," pronounced Félix in a hoarse whisper from his hiding place in the foyer.

I stifled a smile and just said, "Shall we go?"

He didn't get a chance to reply, for just as he was about to do so an overwhelming presence invaded the room.

"Hang on just a sec, Don Marcus," the Matutera insisted, raising her hand as though seeking an audience. "Just one little piece of advice I'd like to give you before the two of you are off, if I may."

Logan looked at me, rather disconcerted.

"She's a friend," I explained.

"In that case you can say whatever you want to me."

Candelaria walked over to him and started talking to him while pretending to remove some non-existent lint from the front of his jacket.

"You just watch yourself, scribbler, this girl's already got a lot of misfortunes on her back. So if you make a move on her with your moneyed outsider's ways, I'm just going to have to come down on you like a ton of bricks, because if you start getting too cocky and harm a single hair of her head, my cousin and I will get someone to do a little number on you before you know what's what, and one of these fine nights you'll find yourself taking a blade in one of the streets in the Morería and getting the good side of your face slashed till it's left like the hide of a piglet, all marked up for the rest of your days, you get me, sweetheart?"

The journalist was unable to reply; fortunately, in spite of his impeccable Spanish, he'd barely been able to understand a word of my business partner's threatening speech.

"What did she say?" he asked, turning to me with a confused expression.

"Nothing important. Come on, it's getting late."

I was struggling to hide my pride as we left. Not at how I looked, or at the attractive man I had beside me, or the celebrated event that was awaiting us that night, but for the unshakable affection of the friends I was leaving behind.

The streets were adorned with red and gold flags, with garlands and posters greeting the distinguished visitor and exalting his brother-in-law. Hundreds of people, Arab and Spanish, were milling about, toward no apparent destination. The balconies, adorned with the Nationalist colors, were full of people, the roof terraces, too. There were young men perched in the most implausible places — on poles, railings, lampposts — trying to find the best spot to witness the action; girls walking arm in arm, their lips newly painted. Children ran around in packs, zigzagging in every direction. The Spanish kids were all combed and smelling of cologne, the boys with their little ties and the girls with satin bows at the end of their plaits; the Moorish children were in their djellabas and tarbooshes, many of them barefoot.

As we made our way toward the Plaza de España, the mass of bodies became denser, the voices louder. It was hot and the light was still intense; we could hear a band tuning up. Temporary wooden bleachers had been set out; the whole space was already occupied to the last inch. Marcus Logan needed to show his invitation several times for them to let us past the security barriers that separated the mob from the areas through which the dignitaries were to pass. We barely spoke as we walked: the hubbub and the constant interruptions to get past some obstacle or other made conversation difficult. Sometimes I had to grab hard on to his arm to prevent us from being separated by the crowd; other times it was he who had to hold firmly on to my shoulders to stop me from being swallowed up by the hungry chaos. It took us a while to get there, but we made it. As we went in through the gate to the High Commission, I felt a jolt of anxiety, then tried to suppress it.

There were several Arab soldiers guarding the

entrance, imposing in their dress uniforms, with big turbans and capes flapping in the wind. We crossed the garden, which was adorned with flags and banners, and an adjutant directed us to a large group of guests who were waiting for things to begin, gathered under the white awnings that had been erected for the occasion. Waiting in its shade were peaked caps, gloves and pearls, ties, fans, blue shirts under white jackets with the Falange crest embroidered at the breast, and a decent number of dresses sewn — stitch by stitch — by my own hands. I discreetly gestured a greeting to several clients, pretending not to notice the few stares and hidden whispers that we received from various places — Who is she, Who is he, I could read in the movement of some of their lips. I recognized certain faces, many of which I'd only seen in the photographs Félix had shown me in the preceding days; with others, meanwhile, I had a more personal connection. With Commissioner Vázquez, for example, who masterfully hid his disbelief at seeing me in that setting.

"Well, what a pleasant surprise," he said, moving away from a group and approaching us.

"Good evening, Don Claudio." I tried hard to sound natural; I don't know whether I succeeded. "Good to see you."

"Sure about that?" he asked with an ironic smile.

I couldn't reply because — to my astonishment — he'd gone straight on to greet my companion.

"Good evening, Mr. Logan. I see you've gotten yourself well accustomed to local life."

"The commissioner called me into his office as soon as I arrived in Tetouan," the journalist explained as they shook hands. "Formalities for visiting foreigners."

"Right now he's not under suspicion for anything, but let me know if you see him acting strangely," joked the commissioner. "And you, Logan, you take care of Miss Quiroga for me — she's had a tough year, working nonstop."

We left the commissioner and continued on our way. At all times the journalist was relaxed and attentive, and I did what I could to avoid feeling like a fish out of water. He hardly knew anyone either, but this didn't seem to trouble him in the least: he got by with great composure, with an enviable confidence that was probably a result of his occupation. Remembering what Félix had taught me, I discreetly pointed out to him who some of the guests were: that man in a dark suit is José Ignacio Toledano, a rich Jew, the director of the Hassan Bank; that elegant woman with the feathered headdress who's smoking with a cigarette holder is the Duchess of Guise, a French noblewoman who lives in Larache; the large man whose glass is being refilled is Mariano Bertuchi, the painter. Everything went according to protocol. More guests arrived, then the Spanish civil authorities, and then the soldiers; the Moroccans next, in their exotic outfits. From the coolness of the garden we could hear the clamor from the streets — the shouts, the cheering and applause. He's arrived, he's here, we heard again and again. But the guest of honor still took a while to come into view: first he stopped in the crowds, to be acclaimed like a bullfighter or one of those American movie stars who so fascinated my neighbor.

And finally he arrived, the man so long awaited, so desired, El Caudillo's brother-in-law, and long live Spain. He wore a black suit and looked serious, stiff, extremely thin, and tremendously handsome with his almost white hair combed back. His expression was resolute, as the Falange anthem said, with those intelligent cat's eyes and his thirty-seven somewhat ill-worn years.

I must have been one of the few people without the slightest curiosity to see him up close or to shake his hand, but all the same I didn't look away. It wasn't Serrano who interested me, but someone who was very close to him and whom I hadn't yet seen in person: Juan Luis Beigbeder. My client and friend's lover turned out to be a tall man, thin but not too thin, somewhere around fifty. He wore a dress uniform with a broad sash tied around his waist and a peaked cap and carried a light cane, a sort of riding crop. His nose was thin and prominent: beneath it, a dark mustache; above it, round-framed glasses, two perfect circles through which it was possible to make out a pair of intelligent eyes that followed everything that was happening around him. He seemed an odd man, perhaps a little quaint. In spite of his attire, he didn't have a martial bearing at all: far from it. There was something in the way he moved that was a little theatrical, which nonetheless didn't seem to be a pretense: his gestures were refined and opulent at the same time, his laugh expansive, his voice quick and resonant. He moved around among the guests nonstop, greeting people effusively, distributing hugs, pats on the back, and prolonged handshakes; he smiled as he talked to people, to Moors, Christians, Jews, and then back to the beginning again. Perhaps in his free time he let out the intellectual romantic that according to Rosalinda he had inside him, but at that moment the only thing he displayed to his audience was an extraordinary gift for public relations.

He seemed to have tied Serrano Suñer to him with an invisible rope; sometimes he allowed him to move away just a little, gave him some freedom of movement to greet people and have little chats with them himself, to allow him to be adored. And yet he would then immediately reel him back to his vicinity: he'd explain something to him, introduce him to someone, put his arm around his shoulders, say a few words into his ear, give a laugh, and then let him go again.

I tried repeatedly to find Rosalinda, but I couldn't. Not at the side of her dear Juan Luis, nor far from him.

"Have you seen Señora Fox anywhere?" I asked Logan when he finished exchanging a few words in English with someone from Tangiers to whom he introduced me and whose name and position I forgot instantly.

"No, I haven't seen her," he replied simply, focusing his attention on the group that was forming around Serrano. "Do you know who they are?" he said, gesturing toward them with a discreet movement of his chin.

"The Germans," I replied.

There was the demanding Frau Langenheim, in the magnificent outfit of violet shantung that I'd sewn for her; Frau Heinz, who'd been my first client, dressed in black and white like a harlequin; Bernhardt's wife, who had an Argentine accent and this time was not premiering an outfit; and one other I didn't know. All of them accompanied by their husbands, all of them fêting the In-lawísimo while he dispensed smiles in the midst of the tight group of Germans. This time, however, Beigbeder didn't interrupt their conversation and allowed him to stay where he was, unaccompanied, for a long time.

CHAPTER THIRTY

As night began to fall, they lit lamps as though it were an open-air dance. The atmosphere was lively without being loud, the music soothing, and Rosalinda was still absent. The group of Germans remained firmly surrounding the guest of honor, but at a certain moment the women had disengaged themselves from their partners' sides, leaving just five foreign men and the Spanish dignitary. They seemed engrossed in conversation and passed something from hand to hand, bringing their heads closer, pointing, making comments. I noticed that my companion hadn't stopped covertly watching them.

"You seem to find the Germans interesting."

"Fascinating," he said, ironically, "but I have my hands tied."

I replied with a questioning raise of my eyebrows, not understanding what he meant. He didn't clarify it for me, but changed the course of the conversation to territory that seemed completely unrelated.

"Would it be very cheeky of me if I were to ask you a favor?"

He tossed the question out casually, just as a few minutes earlier he'd asked me if I wanted a cigarette or a fruit cup.

"That depends," I replied, likewise feigning nonchalance. Although the evening was turning out to be reasonably relaxed, I still wasn't at ease, unable to enjoy this party that had absolutely nothing to do with my world. Besides, I was worried about Rosalinda's absence; it was very strange that she hadn't been seen once. The last thing I needed now was for Marcus Logan to ask me for another awkward favor: I'd already done enough by agreeing to attend the event with him.

"It's something very simple," he explained. "I'm curious to know what it is that the Germans are showing Serrano that they're all looking at so attentively."

"And is this personal or professional curiosity?"

"Both. But I can't approach him: you know how little they think of us English."

"You're suggesting I go over and take a look?" I asked in disbelief.

"Without it being too obvious, if possible."

I was ready to laugh.

"You're not serious, are you?"

"Entirely. That's what my job is: I try to find information, and the means of getting hold of it."

"And now that you can't get hold of this information for yourself, you want me to be the means?"

"But I don't wish to take advantage of you, I promise you that. It's a simple proposition, you have no obligation to accept it. Just think about it."

I looked at him, wordless. He seemed sincere and trustworthy, but as Félix had predicted, he probably wasn't. At the end of the day it was all a question of personal interests.

"Very well, I'll do it."

He tried to say something, perhaps to thank me in advance. I didn't let him.

"But I want something in exchange," I added.

"What?" he asked, surprised. He didn't expect my action to come at a price.

"Find out where Señora Fox is."

"How?"

"You'll know how to do it, that's why you're a journalist."

I didn't wait for his reply; I turned on my heel immediately and walked away, asking myself how the hell I could approach the German group without being too brazen.

The solution presented itself to me in the form of the compact that Candelaria had given me a few minutes before I left home. I took it out of my handbag and opened it. As I walked, I pretended to look at a tiny part of my face in it, anticipating a visit to the *toilettes*. Except that while I was concentrating on the mirror I veered slightly off my path and instead of making my way through the clear gaps, instead — what bad luck! — I bumped into the back of the German consul.

My collision stopped the group's conversation abruptly and knocked the compact to the ground.

"I'm so very sorry, forgive me, I just wasn't paying attention . . . ," I said, my voice loaded with fake embarrassment.

Four of the men immediately made as if to bend down and retrieve my compact, but one was faster than the rest. The thinnest of them all, the one with the near-white hair combed back. The only Spaniard. The one with the cat's eyes.

"I think the mirror's broken," he said as he straightened up. "Look."

I looked. But before fixing my eyes on the cracked mirror I tried quickly to make out what else he was holding in his so-slender fingers.

"Yes, seems to be broken," I murmured, delicately running my index finger over the splintered surface that he still held in his hands. My just-painted nails were reflected in it a hundred times.

We were shoulder to shoulder, our heads close together, both of us bending over the little object. I could see the fair skin on his face from just inches away, his delicate features and the white at his temples, the dark eyebrows, the fine mustache.

"Careful, you'll cut yourself," he said softly.

I lingered a few seconds longer, checking that the tablet of powder was in one piece, that the powder puff was still in place. And in the process I took another look at what he was still holding between his fingers, what just a few minutes earlier had passed from hand to hand between them. Photographs. It was a few photographs. I could only see the first one: people I didn't recognize, making up a tight little group of anonymous faces and bodies.

"Yes, probably better to close it," I said at last.

"Here you are, then."

I brought the two parts together with a loud click.

"It's a shame; it's a very beautiful compact. Almost as beautiful as its owner," he added.

I accepted the compliment with a flirtatious expression and my most dazzling smile.

"Oh, it's nothing, don't worry about it, really."

"It's been a pleasure, señorita," he said, holding out his hand. I noticed it weighed almost nothing.

"Likewise, Señor Serrano," I replied with a blink. "My apologies again for the interruption.

Good evening, gentlemen," I added, sweeping my gaze over the rest of the group. Each one had a swastika on his lapel.

"Good evening," the Germans repeated in chorus.

I resumed my path, making my walk as graceful as I possibly could. When I sensed they could no longer see me, I took a glass of wine from a waiter's tray, downed it in one gulp, and tossed it empty into the rosebushes.

I cursed Marcus Logan for having set me onto that idiotic adventure, and I cursed myself for having accepted. I'd got much closer to Serrano Suñer than any of the other guests — his face had been practically touching mine, our fingers had brushed against each other's, I'd heard his voice in my ear with a closeness almost bordering on intimacy. I'd shown myself to him as a frivolous, scatterbrained woman, glad to be the object of the attention of this distinguished personage for a few moments, while the truth was that I hadn't been the least bit interested in meeting him. And it had all been for nothing; just to discover that the group had been looking at a handful of photographs in which I wasn't able to make out a single person I recognized.

I dragged my irritation all the way across the garden till I reached the door to the main building of the High Commission. I needed to find a bathroom — use the lavatory, wash my hands, get away from it all for a few minutes and calm myself down before meeting up with Marcus Logan again. I followed the directions that someone gave me: I went down an entrance hall decorated with metopes and portraits of officers in uniform, turned right and went along a broad corridor.

Third door on the left, they'd told me. Before I reached it, some voices alerted me to what was going on at my destination; just a few seconds later I saw it with my own eyes. The floor was soaked, water seemed to be gushing from somewhere inside, probably from a burst tank. Two ladies were angrily complaining about the damage it was doing to their shoes, and three soldiers were dragging themselves across the floor on their knees, working away with rags and towels, trying to stem the flow of the water, which was already beginning to invade the tiled corridor. I remained still, watching the scene as reinforcements arrived with arms full of rags — it looked like they'd even brought some bedsheets. The lady guests moved away, complaining and grumbling, then someone offered to escort me to the other bathroom.

I followed a soldier along the corridor in the opposite direction. We crossed the main hallway again and went into a new corridor, this one silent and dimly lit. We turned several times, first left, then right, then left again. More or less.

"Would madam like me to wait?" he asked when we'd arrived.

"Thank you, there's no need, I'll find my own way."

I wasn't too sure of that, but the idea of having a sentry waiting for me made me feel extremely uncomfortable, so once I'd dispatched my escort I did what I needed to do, smoothed out my dress, retouched my hair, and readied myself to go back out. But I didn't have the heart, and faced with returning to reality my strength failed me. So I decided to treat myself to a few moments of solitude. I opened the window, and through it came the African night with its jasmine scent. I sat down on the windowsill and contemplated the shadow of the palms and heard the distant sound of the conversations in the front garden. I distracted myself without actually doing anything, savoring the tranquillity and allowing my worries to dissipate. After a time, however, in some remote corner of my brain, I heard a call. Tick tock, time to go back. I sighed, got up, and closed the window. I had to return to the world. To mix with those souls with whom I had so little in common, return to the side of that foreigner who had dragged me to this ridiculous party and asked me the most extravagant of favors. For the last time I looked at myself in the mirror, switched off the light, and went out.

I made my way along the dark corridor, turning a corner, then another. I thought I knew where I was going, then found myself confronting a double door I didn't think I'd seen before. Opening it, I found a dark, empty room. I'd gone wrong somewhere, no doubt, so I changed my route. Another corridor, now turning left, I seemed to recall — but I was wrong again and had gone into a less regal area of the house, without the gleaming wood paneling or oil-painted generals on the walls; probably I was going into some service area. Just relax, I told myself not very convincingly. A vision of the night with the guns, with me in a haik and lost in the alleys of the medina, suddenly fluttered over me. I shook it off, focused, and immediately changed direction again. And straightaway found myself where I'd started, next to the bathroom. So, a false alarm — I wasn't lost anymore. I thought back to the moment I'd arrived with the soldier and got my bearings. All perfectly clear, problem solved, I thought, making my way toward the exit. And everything did indeed start looking familiar again. A display of antique firearms, framed photographs, hanging flags. I'd seen it all minutes earlier and recognized it all. Even the voices I heard just around the corner that I was about to turn — the same ones I'd heard in the garden in the ridiculous scene with the powder compact.

"We'll be more comfortable here, my dear Serrano; we'll be able to talk more calmly here. It's the room where Colonel Beigbeder usually receives us," said a man with a thick German accent.

"Perfect," was his interlocutor's only reply.

I stopped still, not breathing. Serrano Suñer and at least one German were just a few feet away, approaching along a stretch of corridor at right angles with the one I was walking along. When they or I came around the corner, we'd be face-to-face. My legs trembled at the very thought. In fact, I had nothing to hide; I had no reason to be afraid of the meeting. Except that I didn't have the strength to strike yet another pretend pose, to allow me to pass once again for an airheaded fool and give some pathetic explanation about a broken tank and puddles of water in order to justify my solitary wanderings through the corridors of the High Commission in the middle of the night. It took me less than a second to weigh my options. I didn't have time to retrace my steps, and I wanted at all costs to avoid meeting them face-to-face, which meant I couldn't go backward or forward. That being the case, my only option was sideways, through a closed door. Without giving it a second thought, I opened it and went in.

The room was unlit, but traces of moonlight

were coming in through the windows. I leaned my shoulder on the door, waiting for Serrano and his companions to pass by the room and disappear so that I could go out and continue on my way. The garden with its festival lights, the hum of the conversations, and the imperturbable solidity of Marcus Logan suddenly seemed like a paradise to me, but I was afraid this wasn't the moment for me to reach it. I breathed heavily, with each gulp of air trying to expel a bit of the anxiety from my body. I focused my eyes on my sanctuary, and among the shadows I could make out chairs, armchairs and a glass-fronted bookcase against the wall. There were other pieces of furniture, too, but I didn't stop to identify them because at that moment something else caught my attention. Close by, behind the door.

"Here we are," announced the German voice, accompanied by the sound of the door handle releasing the latch.

I moved away with rapid strides and reached a side wall of the room as the door began to open.

"Where might the switch be?" I heard someone say as I slipped behind a sofa. The moment my body touched the floor, the light came on.

"Well then, here we are. Do sit down, my friend, please."

I was lying facedown, my left cheek on the cold of the floor tiles, controlling my breathing and with my eyes opened wide, filled with terror. At first not daring to breathe in, to swallow, or to move so much as an eyelash. Like a marble statue, like someone shot but not yet dead.

The German seemed to be acting as the host and to be addressing just one interlocutor — I knew this because I only heard two voices, and because under the sofa, from my unexpected hiding place and looking between the legs of the furniture, I could only make out two pairs of feet.

"Is the high commissioner aware that we're here?" asked Serrano.

"He's busy looking after the guests; we can talk to him later if you wish," replied the German vaguely.

I heard them sit: their bodies settled, the springs creaked. The Spaniard sat in an armchair; I saw the cuffs of his dark trousers, their creases well ironed, his black socks around his thin ankles lost in a pair of conscientiously shined shoes. The German positioned himself opposite him, on the right-hand end of the sofa behind which I was hiding. His legs were thicker and his footwear less refined. If I'd reached out I could almost have tickled him.

They talked for a long while: I couldn't have said how long exactly, but it was enough that my neck was aching horribly, enough that I was desperate to scratch an itch, struggling to stop myself from shouting, crying, running out of the room. I heard the sound of a lighter and the room filled with cigarette smoke. From floor level I saw Serrano's legs cross and uncross countless times; the German, meanwhile, barely moved. I tried to tame my fear, find the least uncomfortable position, and beg heaven that none of my limbs would demand any unexpected movement.

My field of vision was very small, and my capacity for movement nil. I had access to nothing but what was floating in the air and coming in my ear: to what they were talking about. So I concentrated on the thread of conversation; since I'd been unable to obtain any interesting information during the powder-compact encounter, I thought that this might be of interest to Marcus Logan. Or at least that it would keep me distracted and prevent my mind from becoming so unsettled that I'd end up losing my grip on reality.

I heard them talk about installations and transmissions, about ships and aircraft, quantities of gold, German marks, pesetas, bank accounts. Signatures and terms of payment, supplies; balances of power, numbers of companies, ports and loyalties. I learned that the German was Johannes Bernhardt, that Serrano was using Franco as an excuse to put more pressure on him and avoid acceding to certain conditions. And even though I was missing information that would have allowed me to understand the whole situation, I could tell that the two men were both concerned that the matter they were discussing should turn out well.

And it did. At last they reached an agreement, then they got up and sealed their agreement with a handshake that I heard but couldn't see. But I could see their feet moving toward the door, the German allowing the guest to walk ahead of him, acting the host again. Before leaving, Bernhardt threw out one last question.

"Will you talk to Colonel Beigbeder about this, or would you rather I told him about it myself?"

Serrano didn't reply right away. First I heard him light a cigarette. His umpteenth one.

"Do you really think it's absolutely essential to do that?" he asked after breathing out his first drag of smoke.

"The installations will be located in the Spanish Protectorate, so I suppose he ought to know something about it."

"Leave it to me, then. El Caudillo will inform

him directly. And as to the terms of the agreement, best not to let any details out. That can be kept between us," he added as the German turned out the lights.

I let a few minutes go by, until I calculated that they were out of the building. Then I got up cautiously. All that remained of their presence was the thick smell of tobacco and an ashtray full of cigarette butts. And yet I was incapable of lowering my guard. I straightened my skirt and jacket and approached the door stealthily on tiptoes. I brought my hand slowly to the doorknob, as though afraid that touching it would give me a whip-sharp pain, afraid to go out into the corridor. I didn't get as far as moving the latch, however; my fingers were just about to touch the handle when I noticed that someone else was moving it from the other side. Automatically I threw myself back and pressed myself against the wall as though trying to sink into it. The door burst open almost hitting me in the face, and a second later the light came on. I couldn't see who'd come in, but I could hear his voice cursing through his teeth.

"So where the hell has the bastard left the damned cigarette case then . . ."

Even without being able to see him I could tell it was just a simple soldier reluctantly carrying out an order, retrieving an object left behind by Serrano or Bernhardt. I didn't know at which of them the soldier was aiming his epithet. Darkness and silence returned in seconds, but I wasn't able to recover enough courage to venture out into the corridor. For the second time in my life, my salvation came by jumping out of a window.

I returned to the garden and to my surprise

found Marcus Logan in animated conversation with Beigbeder. I tried to retreat, but I was too late: he'd already seen me and called me over to join them. I approached, trying not to let them see how nervous I was: after what had just happened, a private audience with the high commissioner was the last thing I needed.

"So you're my Rosalinda's pretty dressmaker friend, then," he said, greeting me with a smile.

He had a cigar in his hand and put the other arm over my shoulders familiarly.

"I'm so pleased to meet you at last, my dear. It's such a shame our Rosalinda is indisposed and hasn't been able to join us."

"What's the matter with her?"

With the hand that was holding the cigar he traced circles over his belly.

"Intestinal troubles. She gets them when she's anxious, and these past days we've been so busy attending to our guest that my poor little thing has barely had a moment's peace."

He gestured for me and Marcus to bring our heads closer and dropped the tone of his voice with apparent complicity.

"Thank God the brother-in-law's going tomorrow; I don't think I could bear him a day longer."

He finished off this confidence with a booming laugh and we imitated him.

"Well, friends, I really ought to go," he said, looking at his watch. "Much as I love your company, duty calls: now it's time for the anthems, the speeches, and all that paraphernalia, undoubtedly the most boring part. Go see Rosalinda whenever you can, Sira — she'd appreciate the visit. And you, too, Logan, stop by her house; the company of a compatriot would be good for her.

412

And let's see if we can't all arrange to have dinner one night, the four of us, to relax a little. 'God save the king!' " he added in English by way of farewell, raising his hand theatrically. And without a further word he turned and left.

We remained in silence a few moments, watching him walk away, unable to find an adjective to assign to the uniqueness of the man who'd just left us.

"I've been looking for you for an hour, where were you?" Marcus asked finally, his eyes still fixed on the high commissioner's back.

"I've been solving your problems, just like you asked me to do."

"You mean you managed to see what it was that the group was passing around?"

"Nothing important. Family photographs."

"God, what bad luck."

We talked without looking at each other, both with our eyes on Beigbeder.

"But I've learned other things that might be of interest to you," I announced.

"Such as?"

"Agreements. Negotiations. Deals."

"About what?"

"Antennas," I explained. "Large antennas. Three of them. About three hundred feet high, a console system, the Electro-Sonner brand. The Germans want to install them to intercept radio signals from air and maritime traffic in the Strait, to make up for the presence of the English in Gibraltar. They're negotiating to have them installed next to the Tamuda ruins, a few miles from here. In exchange for express permission being granted by Franco, the Nationalist army will receive a substantial sum from the German government. It will

413

all be run by HIS MA, a firm whose senior partner is Johannes Bernhardt, who's the one Serrano closed the deal with. They intend to marginalize Beigbeder, to hide it from him."

"My goodness," he muttered. Then in Spanish: "How did you find out?"

We went on without exchanging a glance, both of us apparently still looking attentively at the high commissioner, who made his way, greeting people as he went, toward a decorated platform on which someone was setting up a microphone.

"Because I happened to be in the same room where they were closing the deal."

"And they closed the deal right in front of you?" he asked, incredulous.

"No, don't worry; they didn't see me. It's a rather long story, I'll tell you about it another time."

"Very well. Tell me something else, did they talk about dates?"

The microphone squeaked with an unpleasantly shrill sound. Testing, testing, said a voice.

"The parts are ready, and they're docked at Hamburg. As soon as they have El Caudillo's signature they'll be unloaded at Ceuta and the assembly will begin."

In the distance we saw the colonel energetically step up onto the dais, calling Serrano over to join him with an expansive gesture. He was still smiling, still greeting people confidently. I asked Marcus a couple of questions.

"Do you think Beigbeder should know that they're leaving him out? Do you think I should tell Rosalinda?"

He thought about it before answering, his eyes still on the two men, who were now receiving the

414

feverish applause of the audience.

"I suppose so; it would be worthwhile for him to know that. But I think it's best for the information not to get to him through you and Mrs. Fox, it could compromise her. Leave it to me, I'll work out the best way of passing it on to him. Don't say anything to your friend; I'll find an opportunity."

A few more seconds of silence went by, as though he were still considering everything he'd just heard.

"You know something, Sira?" he asked, turning to face me at last. "Even though I don't know how you did it, you've managed to get hold of an amazing piece of information, much more interesting than I originally thought it would be possible to get during a reception like this. I don't know how to thank you."

"There's a very simple way," I interrupted him.

"Which is?"

At that moment, the caliph's orchestra launched enthusiastically into "Cara al sol" and dozens of arms were immediately raised as though propelled by a spring. I stood on tiptoes and brought my mouth close to his ear.

"Get me out of here."

Without another word, he held his hand out to me. I gripped it hard and we slipped away toward the end of the garden. As soon as we could tell that no one could see us, we broke into a run, into the shadows.

CHAPTER THIRTY-ONE

The following morning the world started up again at a different pace. For the first time in several weeks, I didn't wake up early, didn't drink a hurried cup of coffee or install myself immediately in the workshop pressured by things to do. Rather than returning to the frantic activity of the previous week, I began my day by resuming the long bath that had been interrupted the previous evening. And then took a walk, to Rosalinda's house.

I'd gathered from Beigbeder's words that her illness was just something mild and passing, no more than an unfortunate upset. Which was why I was expecting to find my friend just the same as ever, ready for me to tell her every detail of the event she'd missed and keen to enjoy my comments on the outfits that the guests were wearing, which of them was the most elegant, which the least.

A maid led me to her bedroom, where I found her still in bed, surrounded by bolster cushions, with the shutters closed and a thick stale smell of tobacco and medication, and a lack of air. The house was spacious and beautiful: Moorish architecture, English furnishings, and an exotic kind of chaos in which the rugs and the upholstery of the sofas were covered with old records out of their sleeves, letters marked "air mail," forgotten silk scarves, and Staffordshire porcelain cups with unfinished tea, now cold.

That morning, however, Rosalinda had an air of anything but glamour.

"How are you?" I tried not to let my voice come out sounding too concerned. I had good reason to be, however, because of the way she looked: pale, haggard, her hair dirty, slumped in a dead weight on a disheveled bed with the sheets dangling onto the floor.

"Terminal," she replied with the blackest humor. "I'm not well at all, but come sit here close to me," she commanded, patting the bed. "It's not contagious."

"Juan Luis told me last night that it was intestinal trouble," I said, doing as I'd been told. First I had to move off a few crumpled handkerchiefs, an ashtray filled with half-smoked cigarettes, the remnants of a package of butter cookies, and a decent-sized pile of crumbs.

"That's right, but that's not the worst of it. Juan Luis doesn't know the whole story. I'll tell him tonight; I didn't want to trouble him on the last day of Serrano's visit.

"So what's the worst of it?"

"This," she said, furious, taking up what looked like a telegram and holding it in her fingers as though with pincers. "This is what has made me ill, not the preparations for the visit. This is the worst part of all."

I looked at her, confused, and then she summarized its contents.

"I received it yesterday. Peter arrives in six weeks."

"Who's Peter?" I didn't remember anyone by that name among her friends.

She looked at me as though she'd just heard the most preposterous of questions.

"Who else would it be, Sira, for God's sake? Peter is my husband."

Peter Fox was scheduled to arrive in Tangiers on a P&O ship, keen to spend a long period with his wife and son after nearly five years of barely hearing anything from them. He was still living in Calcutta but had decided to make a temporary visit to the West, perhaps weighing his options for leaving imperial India once and for all, since the place was becoming more unsettled with the locals' movements toward independence, according to what Rosalinda had told me. And what better perspective for considering the possibilities for a potential move than a family reunion in his wife's new world?

"And will he be staying here in your house?" I asked in disbelief.

She lit a cigarette, and as she sucked the smoke in she nodded emphatically.

"Claro que si — he's my husband, he has every right."

"But I thought you were separated . . ."

"In practice, yes, but not legally."

"And you've never planned to get a divorce?"

She gave the cigarette another deep drag.

"A million times. But he refuses."

Then she told me all the twists and turns of that troubled relationship, and through it I discovered a Rosalinda who was more vulnerable, more fragile. Less unreal and closer to the earthly troubles of the residents of the human world.

"I married at sixteen; he was thirty-four at the

time. I'd spent five years in a boarding school in England; I left India when I was still a girl and returned a young woman almost of marrying age, absolutely determined not to miss out on a single one of the parties in colonial Calcutta. At the first one, I was introduced to Peter, who was a friend of my father's. I thought him the most attractive man I'd ever met in my life; I hadn't met all that many — almost none, in fact. He was fun, capable of undertaking the most unimaginable adventures, and the life and soul of any meeting. At the same time he was mature, experienced, a member of an aristocratic English family that had settled in India three generations earlier. I fell in love like a fool, or at least that's what I thought then. Five months later we were married. We set ourselves up in a magnificent house with stables, tennis courts, and fourteen rooms for the servants; we even had four Indian boys permanently in uniform to be ball boys in case one day we happened to decide to play a game — just imagine! Our life was filled with activity: I loved dancing and horse riding, and I was as skilled with a rifle as I was with my golf clubs. Our life was an unstoppable merry-go-round of parties and receptions. And what was more, we then had Johnny. We built an idyllic world within another world that was equally lavish, but I realized too late how fragile were the foundations upon which it was all supported."

She stopped talking, and her eyes were fixed on emptiness, as though taking a few moments for reflection. Then she put her cigarette out in the ashtray and went on.

"A few months after giving birth, I started noticing something wrong with my stomach. I was examined, and to begin with they told me there

419

was nothing for me to worry about, that my troubles were merely related to the natural health problems that we nonnatives were exposed to in that tropical climate. But I got worse and worse. The pain increased, my fever began to rise daily. They decided to operate and they didn't find anything unusual, but I didn't get any better. Four months later, faced with my relentlessly worsening condition, they gave me another close examination and were finally able to put a name to my illness: aggressive bovine tuberculosis, contracted from the milk of an infected cow that we'd bought after Johnny was born so I'd have fresh milk for my recovery. The animal had fallen sick and died long ago, but the vet hadn't found anything abnormal when he examined it, just as the doctors had been unable to find anything in me; bovine tuberculosis is extremely difficult to diagnose. But what happens is that you start developing tubercles, sort of nodules, like lumps in the intestine that keep constricting it."

"And then?"

"And then you end up chronically ill."

"And then?"

"And then each morning when you open your eyes you thank heaven for allowing you another day to live."

I tried to hide my unease with another question.

"How did your husband react?"

"Ah, marvelously!" she said sarcastically. "The doctors who saw me advised me to return to England; they thought — albeit not all that optimistically — that perhaps an English hospital would be able to do something for me. And Peter could not have agreed more."

"Thinking of what was best for you, no

doubt . . ."

A bitter laugh prevented me from finishing my sentence.

"Peter never thinks about what's best for anyone, querida, but himself. Sending me far away was the best possible solution, but rather than it being for my own health it was for his own well-being. He had lost all interest in me, Sira. He stopped finding me fun, I was no longer a precious trophy to take around with him to clubs, to parties, and on hunts; the pretty, fun young wife had transformed into a burdensome invalid whom he had to get rid of as quickly as possible. So the moment I was able to stand on my own two feet again, he arranged tickets for me and Johnny for England. He didn't even deign to come with us. With the excuse that he wanted his wife to receive the best medical treatment possible, he dispatched a grievously sick woman who hadn't yet turned twenty and a little boy barely old enough to walk. As though we were just another couple of pieces of luggage. Adiós, and good riddance, my dears."

A couple of thick tears rolled down her cheeks. She brushed them away with the back of her hand.

"He pushed us away from him, Sira. He spurned me. He sent me to England, purely and simply to be rid of me."

A sad silence settled between us, until she recovered her strength and went on.

"During the journey, Johnny began to have high fevers and convulsions. It turned out to be a virulent form of malaria; he would need to spend two months in the hospital to recover. My family took me in, in the meantime; my parents had also lived in India for a long time but had returned the previous year. I spent the first few months relatively peacefully, and the change of climate seemed to do me good. But then I got worse, so much so that the medical tests showed that my intestine had shrunk till it was almost totally constricted. They ruled out surgery and decided that only with absolute rest might I manage to get even a tiny bit better. That way, they thought, the organisms that were invading me wouldn't continue advancing through the rest of my body. Do you know what that first period of rest was like?"

I didn't know, and I couldn't guess.

"Six months tied to a board, with leather straps holding me still, over my shoulders and my thighs. Six whole months, with its days, its nights."

"And did you get better?"

"Very little. Then my doctors decided to send me to Leysin, in Switzerland, to a sanatorium for tuberculosis. Like Hans Castorp in Thomas Mann's *Magic Mountain.*"

I guessed that she was talking about some book, so before she could ask me if I'd read it I encouraged her to continue with her story.

"And Peter, meanwhile?"

"He paid the hospital bills and established a routine of sending us thirty pounds a month to support us. No more than that. Absolutely nothing else. Not a letter, not a telegram, not a message via some acquaintance, or, needless to say, any intention of visiting us. Nothing, Sira, nothing at all. I never heard anything personally from him again. Until yesterday."

"And what did you do with Johnny during that time? It must have been hard on him."

"He was with me in the sanatorium the whole time. My parents insisted that he should stay with them, but I didn't accept. I hired a German nanny to entertain him and take him out, but every day he ate and slept in my room. It was a rather sad experience for such a small boy, but I didn't want him away from me for anything in the world. He'd already lost his father, in a way; it would have been too cruel to punish him further with the absence of his mother."

"And did the treatment work?"

A little laugh lit up her face for a moment.

"They advised me to spend eight years in the sanatorium, but I was only able to bear eight months. Then I asked to be voluntarily discharged. They told me it was foolish, that it would kill me; I had to sign a million pieces of paper releasing the sanatorium from any responsibility. My mother offered to come to collect me in Paris for us to make the journey home together. And then, on that return journey, I made two decisions. The first, I wouldn't speak of my illness anymore. The truth is, in recent years only you and Juan Luis have heard about it from me. I decided that perhaps tuberculosis might grind down my body, but it wouldn't crush my spirit, so I chose to keep the idea that I was an invalid out of my thoughts."

"And the second?"

"To begin a new life as though I were a hundred percent healthy. A life outside of England, away from my family and the friends and acquaintances who automatically associated me with Peter and with my chronic illness. A different life that to begin with would include only me and my son."

"And it was then that you decided to go to Portugal . . ."

"The doctors recommended that I settle somewhere temperate — the south of France, Spain, Portugal, perhaps northern Morocco; somewhere between the excessive tropical heat of India and the miserable English climate. They designed a diet for me, recommended that I eat a lot of fish and little meat, relax in the sun as much as possible, not do physical exercise, and avoid emotional upsets. Then someone told me about the British colony in Estoril, and I decided that that might be as good as anywhere else. And that's where I went."

Now everything fitted much better into the mental map that I'd built up to understand Rosalinda. The pieces began to link to one another; they were no longer fragments of a life that were independent and hard to connect. Everything now began to make sense. I wished with all my strength that things would turn out well for her: now that I finally knew her life hadn't all been a bed of roses, I thought her more deserving of a happy fate.

Chapter Thirty-Two

The following day I accompanied Marcus Logan to visit Rosalinda. As on the night of the Serrano reception, he came to fetch me at my house, and together we walked the streets. Something had changed between us, however. The hasty flight from the reception at the High Commission, that impulsive run through the gardens, and the leisurely walk through the shadows of the city in the small hours had somehow managed to break through my feelings of reticence toward him. Perhaps he was trustworthy, perhaps not; maybe I'd never know. But in a way, that didn't matter to me. I knew he was making an effort to evacuate my mother; I also knew he was attentive and polite toward me, that he felt at ease in Tetouan. And that was more than enough: I didn't need to know any more about him or try to go in any different direction, because the day of his departure wouldn't be long in arriving.

We found her still in bed, but with a bit more color in her cheeks. She'd had the room tidied, she'd bathed, the shutters were open, and the light was gushing in from the garden. On the day after our visit she moved from the bed to a sofa. On the next she changed her silk nightgown for a flowery dress, went to the hairdresser's, and took up the reins of her life again.

Although her health was still unsettled, she decided to make as much as she possibly could of the time she had left before her husband arrived, as though those weeks were the last she had left to live. She resumed the role of the great hostess, creating the perfect setting so that Beigbeder could devote himself to public relations in an atmosphere that was relaxed and discreet, trusting implicitly in his beloved's efficiency. However, I never learned what many of their guests made of the fact that those gatherings were hosted by the young English lover, and that the high commissioner of the pro-German faction felt so at home at them. But Rosalinda was still active in her plans to bring Beigbeder closer to the British, and many of those less formal receptions were planned with that end in mind.

Over the course of that month, as she had done before and would do again, she invited her compatriots from Tangiers on several occasions, members of the diplomatic corps, military attachés well outside the Italo-German orbit, and representatives of important and wealthy multinational institutions. She also organized a party for the Gibraltarian authorities and for the officers of a British warship docked on "the Rock," as they called it. And among all those guests Juan Luis Beigbeder and Rosalinda Fox circulated, a cocktail in one hand and a cigarette in the other, comfortable, relaxed, hospitable, and affectionate. As though there were nothing going on — as though in Spain brothers weren't killing one another and Europe wasn't heating up for the worst possible nightmare.

I got to be close to Beigbeder again several

426

times, and again was able to witness his very unusual manner. He frequently put on Moorish dress, sometimes the slippers, sometimes a djellaba. He was friendly, uninhibited, a touch eccentric; above all he utterly adored Rosalinda and said as much to anyone without the slightest blush. Meanwhile, Marcus Logan and I continued to see each other regularly, increasing in friendship and building an affectionate closeness that I struggled daily to contain. If I hadn't, that initial friendship probably wouldn't have taken long to develop into something much more passionate and profound. But I fought not to let that happen and to remain firm, so that the thing that was beginning to draw us together wouldn't go any further. The hurt I'd suffered from Ramiro still hadn't completely healed, and I knew it wouldn't be long before Marcus would leave, and I didn't want to suffer again. All the same, the two of us became regular presences at the parties in the villa on the Paseo de las Palmeras, sometimes even joined by Félix, who was delighted to enter into that alien world that so fascinated him. From time to time we would go out of Tetouan as a little gang: Beigbeder invited us to Tangiers for the launch of the *España de Tánger* newspaper, created on his own initiative to tell the world what those from his cause wanted to say. Another time we went off, the four of us — Marcus, Félix, Rosalinda, and I — in my friend's Dodge, for the sheer *plaisir* of doing so: to go to Saccone & Speed in search of provisions of Irish beef, bacon, and gin; to dance at Villa Harris; to watch an American movie at the Capitol or order the most stunning hats from the studio of Mariquita the milliner.

During that time we also wandered Tetouan's

white medina, ate couscous, *jarira,* and *chuparquías,* climbed the Dersa and the Ghorgiz, and visited Río Martín beach and the Ketama inn, surrounded by pines. Until time ran out, and the unwelcome visitor appeared. It was only then that we discovered that reality can exceed even the bleakest expectations. That was what I heard from Rosalinda just a week after her husband's arrival.

"It's much worse than I'd imagined," she said, collapsing into an armchair the moment she arrived at my atelier.

This time, however, she didn't seem bewildered. She wasn't angry in the way she had been when she first heard the news. This time she simply radiated sadness, exhaustion, profound disappointment: at Peter, at the situation they found themselves trapped in, at herself. After half a dozen years of roaming the world alone, she thought she'd be ready for anything; she thought that the experience she'd accumulated would have brought her the resources to face any kind of adversity. But Peter was much tougher than she'd anticipated. He once again took on the simultaneous role of father and husband, as though they hadn't spent all those years living apart, as though nothing had happened in Rosalinda's life since she married him when she was still a girl. He reproached her for the casual manner in which she was educating Johnny; it appalled him that his son wasn't attending a good school, that he would go out to play with the neighborhood children without a nanny close by, that his entire sporting prowess consisted of his ability to throw stones with the same excellent aim as all the Moorish boys in Tetouan. He complained, too, about the lack of radio programs to his taste, the absence of a club where he could meet up with his fellow countrymen, the fact that no one around him spoke English, and how hard it was to get a British paper in this city that was so cut off from the world.

Not everything appalled the demanding Peter, however. He turned out to be absolutely satisfied with the Tanqueray gin and the Johnnie Walker Black Label that in those days you could get hold of in Tangiers at ludicrous prices. He used to drink at least a bottle of whiskey a day, nicely punctuated by a couple of gin cocktails before every meal. His tolerance for alcohol was astonishing, almost as astonishing as the degree of cruelty he meted out to the domestic staff. He spoke to them reluctantly, in English, without bothering to take account of the fact that they didn't understand a word of his language, and when it finally became clear that they didn't understand what he was saying he shouted at them in Hindustani, the language of his former Indian servants, as though the condition of serving a master had a universal language. To his great surprise, one by one they stopped showing up at the house. And all of us, from his wife's friends to the most humble of their servants, took no more than a few days to work out what sort of creature Peter Fox was. Egotistical, irrational, capricious, alcoholic, arrogant, and tyrannical: it was impossible to find fewer positive attributes in a single person.

Beigbeder naturally stopped spending so much time at Rosalinda's house, but they still saw each other daily in other places: at the High Commission, on jaunts to the outskirts of town. To many people's surprise — including my own — Beigbeder consistently treated his lover's husband impec-

429

cably. He organized a day's fishing for him at the mouth of the Smir River, and a wild boar hunt in Jemis de Anyera. He helped to arrange his travel to Gibraltar for him to drink English beer and talk polo and cricket with his countrymen. He did everything he could, in short, to behave toward him as his position demanded when dealing with such a peculiar foreign guest. The two men's characters could not have been more different, however; it was curious to witness the contrast between these two men who were both so important in the life of the same woman. Perhaps that was exactly why they never clashed.

"Peter considers Juan Luis a proud, backward Spaniard, like an old-fashioned Spanish caballero out of a Golden Age portrait," Rosalinda explained to me. "And Juan Luis thinks Peter is a snob, a ridiculous, incomprehensible snob. So they are like two parallel lines: they can never come into conflict because they'll never find a point where they meet. The only difference being — for me — that as a man Peter doesn't even come up to Juan Luis's heel."

"And no one has told your husband about the two of you?"

"About our relationship?" she asked, lighting a cigarette and brushing her hair back from her eyes. "I imagine they have, some viper tongue must have come to his ear to spit poison, but he's utterly indifferent."

"I don't understand how he could be."

She shrugged.

"Nor do I, but as long as he doesn't have to pay for a house and he's surrounded by servants, copious amounts of alcohol, hot food, and blood sports, I don't think anything else matters to him.

It would be different if we lived in Calcutta; there I suppose he would probably make an effort to keep up appearances at the very least. But here no one knows him; this isn't his world, so he isn't the slightest bit bothered by anything people tell him about me."

"I still don't understand."

"The one thing we know for sure, querida, is that he has no interest in me whatsoever," she said with a mix of sarcasm and sadness. "Anything at all is worth more to him than I am: a morning's fishing, a bottle of gin, or a hand of cards. I've never mattered to him. What would have been strange is if I'd started mattering now."

And while Rosalinda was in hell battling with a monster, I also — at last — found my life overturned. It was a windy Tuesday and Marcus Logan showed up at my house before noon.

Our friendship had been getting stronger — a good friendship, no more than that. We were both aware that one day when we least expected it he would have to leave, that his presence in my world was transitory. Marcus and I were of course very much attracted to each other, and we weren't short on opportunities for that to transform itself into something more. There was a complicity, there were glances, and glancing touches, veiled comments, admiration, and desire. There was closeness, there was tenderness. But I forced myself to hold back my feelings; I refused to go any further, and he accepted it. Restraining myself took a huge effort on my part: doubt, uncertainty, nights lying awake. But rather than having to face the pain of being left by him, I preferred to remain with the recollection of those memorable moments we'd spent together in those agitated, intense times. Nights of laughter and drinking, of kif pipes and noisy rounds of cards. Trips to Tangiers, outings, chats; moments that I would never get back and that I treasured in my store of memories.

Marcus's unexpected arrival at my Sidi Mandri house that morning brought with it the end of one time and the start of another. One door was closing, and another was beginning to open. And me, right there in the middle, unable to hold on to what was ending, longing to embrace what was to come.

"Your mother is on her way. Last night she boarded a British merchant vessel at Alicante headed for Oran. She arrives in Gibraltar in three days. Rosalinda will make sure she can come across the Strait without any trouble; she'll tell you herself how the crossing will happen."

I wanted to give him my deepest thank-you but was suddenly overtaken by a torrent of tears. So all I was able to do was hug him as hard as I could and soak the lapels of his jacket.

"I've also reached the moment when it's time for me to be on my way," he added a few moments later.

I looked at him, sniffing. He reached for his white handkerchief and held it out to me.

"My agency is recalling me. My job in Morocco is over, I've got to go back."

"To Madrid?"

"To London, for now. Then to wherever they send me."

I hugged him again, and I cried again. And when I was finally capable of containing the turmoil of emotions and starting to control that unruly assault of sentiments that mixed the greatest of joys with a terrible sadness, my broken voice finally came out.

"Don't go, Marcus."

"If only it were up to me. But I can't stay, Sira, they need me somewhere else."

I looked at his beloved face again. It still bore the leftovers of scars, but very little remained of the battered man who'd arrived at the Nacional one summer night. That day I was meeting a stranger and was filled with anxieties and fears; now I was facing the painful task of saying good-bye to someone very close to me, closer perhaps than I wanted to admit.

I sniffed again.

"Whenever you want to give an outfit to one of your girlfriends, you'll know where to find me."

"When I want a girlfriend, I'll come and get you," he said, holding his hand out to my face. He tried to dry my tears with his fingers, and I shivered at his caress, wishing violently that this day had never arrived.

"Liar," I murmured.

"Lovely."

His fingers ran over my face to the roots of my hair and through it down to the back of my neck. Our faces came closer, slowly, as though afraid to act on something that had been hovering in the air for so long.

The unexpected click of a key made us pull apart. Jamila came in, panting, bringing an urgent message.

"Siñora Fox say Siñorita Sira run to las Palmeras."

Things were up and running, and we were approaching the end. Marcus took his hat, and I couldn't resist hugging him one more time. There

433

were no words, there was nothing more to say. A few seconds later, all that remained of his solid, close presence was the trace of a light kiss on my hair, the image of his back, and the painful noise of the door closing behind him.

PART THREE

El Casino de Madrid

Chapter Thirty-Three

From the moment of Marcus's departure and my mother's arrival, my life turned upside down. She arrived one cloudy afternoon looking emaciated, her hands empty and her soul battered. She had no luggage, just her old handbag, the dress she had on, and a fake passport attached by a safety pin to the strap of her brassiere. Her body looked like it had borne the passing of twenty years; her thinness made her eye sockets and collarbones stand out, and the first few greying hairs I remembered were now entire locks. She came into my house like a child dragged awake in the middle of the night: disoriented, confused, disconnected. As though she hadn't fully understood that her daughter lived there, and that from that moment on, she would, too.

I'd imagined that reunion, which I'd so wished for, as a moment of unbounded joy. That's not how it was. If I had to choose one word to describe the picture, it would be sadness. She barely spoke and didn't display any enthusiasm for anything. She just hugged me hard and then kept hold of my hand, clinging to it as though afraid that I was about to run off somewhere. Not a laugh, not a tear, and very few words — that was all. She hardly wanted to taste the meal that

Candelaria, Jamila, and I had prepared for her: chicken, omelet, tomato salad, anchovies, Moorish bread, all the things we imagined she'd gone without in Madrid for such a long time. She didn't have anything to say about the workshop, nor about the room where I'd put her, with a big oak bed and a cretonne quilt that I'd sewn. She didn't ask me what had become of Ramiro, or show any curiosity about what it was that had led me to settle in Tetouan. Needless to say, she didn't speak a word about the grim journey that had brought her to Africa, or even once mention the horrors she had left behind.

It took her some time to adjust — I never thought I'd see my mother like that. The ever-determined Dolores, who was always in control, with just the right thing to say at the right moment, had been transformed into a furtive, inhibited woman I found hard to recognize. I devoted myself to her, body and soul. I practically stopped working; there weren't any major events coming up, and my clients wouldn't mind waiting. Day after day I brought her breakfast in bed: buns, *churros,* toast with olive oil and sugar, anything that would help her put some weight back on. I helped her bathe and I cut her hair; I sewed her new clothes. It was hard getting her out of the house, but bit by bit our morning walk became compulsory. We went arm in arm along the Calle del Generalísimo, reached the square with the church; sometimes, if the timing worked out, I would accompany her to Mass. I took her to see picturesque corners, little nooks and crannies, made her help me choose fabrics, listen to popular songs on the radio, and decide what we were going to eat. Till slowly, step by little step, she began to return to the person she used to be.

I never asked her what went on in her head over the course of this transition, which seemed to last an eternity: I hoped she'd tell me sometime, but she never did, and I didn't insist. Nor was I particularly curious: I guessed that her behavior was no more than an unconscious way of dealing with the uncertainty produced by relief mixed with pain and sorrow. Which was why I simply allowed her to adapt, just remaining by her side, ready to help her if she needed support, with a handkerchief in my hand to dry the tears she would never shed.

I noticed that she was getting better when she began to make little decisions for herself: today I think I'll go to the ten o'clock Mass; I thought I might go with Jamila to the market to buy ingredients to make a paella, what do you think? Bit by bit she stopped cowering each time she heard the crash of something falling on the floor, or the engine of a plane flying over the city. Going to Mass and the market soon became a routine, and other activities were then added to these. The most important of all was returning to her sewing. In spite of my efforts, ever since she'd arrived she hadn't shown the slightest interest in dressmaking, as if that hadn't been the framework of her existence for more than thirty years. I showed her the foreign fashion illustrations that I had purchased in Tangiers, I talked to her about my clients and their foibles, tried to animate her by reminding her about different outfits we'd once sewn together. Nothing. I got nowhere, as though I were speaking a language she didn't understand. Until one morning she poked her head through the doorway into the workroom and asked, Can I

439

give you a hand? I knew then that my mother had come back to life.

Three or four months after her arrival we managed to attain a state of peace. Now that she was back on her feet, the days became less full of frantic activity. The business was going well and allowed us to give Candelaria some money each month with enough left to keep us comfortably, so there was no longer any need to work relentlessly. We started getting along well again, even though neither of us was the woman she had once been, and we were a bit like strangers. Strong Dolores had become vulnerable, and little Sira was now an independent woman. But we accepted each other, appreciated each other, and with our roles clearly defined there was never any more tension between us.

The bustle of the first phase of my life in Tetouan seemed so distant, as though it were centuries ago. The adventures and anxieties were in the past. Staying out till the early hours and living without having to explain myself; all that had been left behind, giving way to ease. And sometimes the palest normality, too. My memories of the past, however, lived on with me still. Although the pain of Marcus's absence began to lessen bit by bit, memories of him still clung to me, like an invisible companion whose outline only I could make out. How often I regretted not having ventured further in my relationship with him, how often I cursed myself for having remained so strict, how much I missed him. All the same, I was glad that I hadn't let myself get carried away by my feelings; if I had, the fact that he was far away from me would have been much more painful.

I didn't lose touch with Félix, but with my mother's arrival came an end to his nighttime visits and the traffic between our front doors, the outlandish lectures on culture, and his exuberant, delightful company.

My relationship with Rosalinda changed, too: the presence of her husband was much more protracted than we'd anticipated, sucking up her time and health like a leech. Fortunately, after almost seven months, Peter Fox decided to return to India. No one ever knew how the alcohol fumes had permitted a shard of lucidity to enter his thoughts, but he did make the decision of his own accord, one morning, when his wife was about ready to fall apart. All the same, his departure didn't bring about much good, apart from providing a sense of immense relief. Naturally he was never convinced that the sensible thing to do would be to carry through the divorce and put an end to that sham of a marriage. On the contrary, he thought he would go to Calcutta to sell off his business interests and then return to settle down once and for all with his wife and son, to enjoy an early retirement with them in the peaceful, cheap Spanish Protectorate. And just so they didn't start getting used to the good life too early, he also decided that their allowance, unchanged for years, wasn't going to be raised by a single pound.

"In an emergency you can get your friend Beigbeder to help," he suggested by way of farewell.

To everybody's good fortune, he never returned to Morocco. The stress of that unwelcome cohabitation did, however, cost Rosalinda nearly half a year of convalescence. In the months that followed Peter's departure, she remained in bed, leaving the house no more than three or four times. The high commissioner practically relocated his work to her bedroom, and the two of them used to spend long hours there, she surrounded by pillows, reading, and he doing his paperwork at a small table by the window.

The doctor's orders to remain in bed until she returned to normal didn't prevent her social bustle, but it did reduce it considerably. All the same, no sooner had her body begun to show signs of recovery than she made an effort to open her house up to her friends, giving little parties without leaving her bed. I was at almost all of them, and my friendship with Rosalinda remained absolutely firm. But nothing was ever the same again.

CHAPTER THIRTY-FOUR

On April 1, 1939, the end of the civil war was declared; from then on there were no more factions or currencies or uniforms dividing the country. Or at least that was what they told us. My mother and I received the news with mixed feelings, unable to predict what that peace would bring with it.

"And what's going to happen in Madrid now, Mother? What are we going to do?"

We spoke almost in whispers, unsettled, standing on a balcony watching the bustling crowds teeming on the street. There were shouts nearby, an explosion of euphoria and unleashed nerves.

"How I wish I knew," was her dark reply.

The news flew back and forth riotously. They said that passenger boats would be resuming their crossings of the Strait, that trains would soon be ready to reenter Madrid. The pathway toward our past was beginning to clear, and there was no longer any reason for us to remain in Africa.

"Do you want to go back?" she asked me at last.

"I don't know."

I really didn't know. I was filled with nostalgia for Madrid: images of childhood and youth, tastes, smells, the names of streets, and recollections of people. But deep down I wasn't sure that this was weighty enough to demand a return that would mean dismantling everything I'd worked so hard to build in Tetouan, the white city that was home to my mother, my new friends, and the atelier that supported us.

"Perhaps, for the time being at least, it would be best if we stayed," I suggested.

She didn't reply; she just nodded, left the balcony, and returned to work, to take refuge among the threads so as not to have to think about the implications of that decision.

A new state was born; a New Spain, they called it. For some people, what arrived were peace and victory; others, however, saw the blackest of chasms opening up before them. Most foreign governments gave legitimacy to the triumph of the Nationalists, recognizing their regime without a moment's hesitation. The structures that had been set up during the conflict began to be dismantled, and the institutions of power began to take their leave of Burgos and prepare for a return to the capital. A new administrative tapestry began to be woven, and work had begun on reconstructing everything that had been destroyed. They accelerated the process of purging undesirables, while those who'd contributed to the victory lined up to receive their piece of the pie. The wartime government continued finalizing decrees, measures, and laws for a few months: its restructuring had to wait until well into the summer. I didn't learn of all this myself, however, until July, when word reached Morocco. Even before it had escaped the walls of the High Commission and spread into the Tetouan streets; long before the name and photograph appeared in the newspapers and everyone in Spain started wondering who that dark-haired man was, with the dark mustache and the round glasses; even before all that, I already knew whom El Caudillo had designated to sit at his right hand in the sessions of his first peacetime Council of Ministers: Don Juan Luis Beigbeder y Atienza. The new minister for foreign affairs, the only military member of the cabinet ranking lower than general.

Rosalinda received the unexpected news with conflicting emotions. Gratitude at what the role meant to him; sadness anticipating his final departure from Morocco. Her feelings were in turmoil during those frantic days that the high commissioner spent between the Peninsula and the Protectorate, starting new dealings there, finishing off old ones here, giving a definitive farewell to the state of temporariness that had been generated by the three years of conflict, and beginning to set up the structures for the country's new network of foreign relations.

The official announcement came on August 10, and on the following day the press revealed to the public the formation of the cabinet that was meant to fulfill the nation's historic destiny under General Franco's triumphant banner. To this day I still have — yellowing and practically disintegrating in my fingers — a couple of pages torn out of the newspaper *ABC* from that time, with the photographs and biographical profiles of the ministers. In the middle of the first page, like the sun in the universe, is Franco, self-satisfied in a circular portrait. To his left and right, occupying preferential positions in the two upper corners, Beigbeder and Serrano Suñer, heading respectively Foreign Affairs and Governance, the most powerful ministries. On the second page they set

445

out the details of their accomplishments and praised the attributes of those recently appointed with the overblown rhetoric of the times. Beigbeder was described as a distinguished Africanist and an expert in Islam; they praised his mastery of Arabic, his solid training, his lengthy periods domiciled in Muslim cities, and his magnificent work as military attaché in Berlin. "The war has brought the name of Colonel Beigbeder to the attention of the general public," said *ABC*. "He managed the Protectorate, and in Franco's name, and always according to the wishes of El Caudillo, he secured the valuable participation of Morocco, which has been so very significant." As for Serrano Suñer, they praised his prudence and his energy, his vast capacity for work, and his well-earned prestige. In recognition of his achievements, he was offered the Ministry of Governance, entrusted with handling all the country's domestic matters as it entered into its new era.

The champion for the anonymous Beigbeder's surprising entry into that government was, as we later learned, Serrano himself. On his visit to Morocco he had been impressed by the high commissioner's rapport with the Muslim population: his warm approach, his mastery of the language and enthusiastic appreciation of their culture, his effective recruitment campaigns, and even, paradoxically, his sympathy for the population's eagerness for independence. A hardworking, enthusiastic man this Beigbeder, a polyglot with a knack for dealing with foreigners and faithful to the cause, Franco's brother-in-law must have thought; one who definitely won't give us any trouble. When I first learned of his appointment, my mind flared back to the night of the reception and the

446

end of the conversation I'd overheard from behind the sofa. I never asked Marcus whether he'd passed on what I'd told him to the high commissioner, but for Rosalinda's sake and that of the man she loved I hoped that Serrano's trust in him had strengthened with the passing of time.

The day after his name appeared in black and white in the papers and on the radio waves, Beigbeder moved to Burgos, bringing an end to his formal connection to his beloved Morocco forever. All Tetouan came together to bid him farewell: Moors, Christians, and Jews, indiscriminately. Representing Morocco's political parties, Sidi Abdeljalak Torres made a heartfelt speech and presented the new minister with a document inscribed in silver naming him favorite brother of the Muslims. Visibly moved, Beigbeder responded with words filled with affection and gratitude. Rosalinda shed a few tears, but those didn't last much longer than it took for the twin-engined airplane to take off from the Sania Ramel Aerodrome, to fly low over Tetouan by way of goodbye and disappear into the distance on its way across the Strait. She felt Juan Luis's departure very deeply, but her haste to be reunited with him required her to get things moving as soon as possible.

In the days that followed, Beigbeder accepted the ministerial portfolio in Burgos from the hands of the deposed Count of Jordana, entered the new government, and began to receive a flood of protocol visits. Rosalinda, meanwhile, traveled to Madrid in search of a house for the new phase she was entering. And that was how the August of victory year passed, with him accepting the congratulations of ambassadors, archbishops, military attachés, mayors, and generals, while she was negotiating a new rental agreement, dismantling her lovely home in Tetouan, and organizing the transportation of her countless pieces of furniture, five Moorish servants, a dozen laying hens, and all the bags of rice, sugar, tea, and coffee that she was able to gather up in the souqs.

The house she chose was on Calle Casado del Alisal, between the Retiro park and the Prado Museum, just a step away from the church of Los Jerónimos. It was a large residence that was certainly of a standard befitting the beloved of the most unexpected of the new ministers. It was a building within the reach of anyone prepared to pay slightly under a thousand pesetas a month, a price Rosalinda considered ludicrous and for which most of Madrid's starving citizens in the first postwar days wouldn't have minded giving three fingers of one of their hands.

They'd planned their living arrangements as they had done in Tetouan. Each would keep his or her own residence — he, his dilapidated palace adjacent to the ministry, and she, her new mansion — though they would be together whenever they could. Before her final departure from Tetouan, in a house that was already empty, Rosalinda threw her last party: there she mixed us all up together, a few Spaniards, quite a number of Europeans, and a good handful of distinguished Arabs, for us all to say good-bye to that woman who, fragile as she was, had entered each of our lives with the strength of a gale. In spite of the uncertainty of the time, and trying hard not to let her mind dwell on the unsettling news that was arriving about the situation in Europe, my friend didn't want to be parted sorrowfully from the

Morocco in which she'd been so happy. Which was why she made us promise, between toasts, that we would come visit her in Madrid as soon as she was settled and assured us that in exchange she would return frequently to Tetouan.

I was the last person to leave that night; I didn't want to go without saying good-bye alone to the woman who had played such a big part in that phase of my life.

"Before I go I want to give you something," I said. I'd prepared a little Moorish silver case for her, which I'd transformed into a sewing box. "For you to remember me whenever you need to change a button and don't have me there with you."

She opened it, excited, delighted by the gifts, insignificant as they were. Little spools of various-colored threads, a tiny needle case and a little tube of needles, a pair of scissors that almost looked like a toy, and a small supply of mother-of-pearl, bone, and glass buttons.

"I'd rather have you there with me to keep solving these problems for me, but I love the gift," she said, embracing me. "Like the genie in Aladdin's lamp, every time I open the box you will come out of it."

We laughed — we chose to face the farewell with good spirits masking our sadness; our friendship didn't deserve a bitter ending. And with her spirits raised, forcing herself not to lose the smile on her face, she left the following day, headed for the capital by plane, while the servants and belongings clattered their way across the countryside of southern Spain under the olive-green canvas of a military vehicle. Our optimism didn't last long, however. The day after her departure, September

3, 1939, following the German refusal to withdraw from Poland, Great Britain declared war on Germany, and Rosalinda Fox's country entered what would come to be the Second World War, the bloodiest conflict in history.

The Spanish government was finally installed in Madrid, as were the diplomatic legations, having first cleaned up their premises, which till then had been covered in a dirty patina the color of war and neglect. And so, as Beigbeder familiarized himself with the obscure offices of the seat of his ministry — the old Santa Cruz Palace — Rosalinda didn't waste a second, launching herself with equivalent enthusiasm into the double task of settling into her new home and throwing herself headfirst into the pool of social relations, the most elegant and cosmopolitan that Madrid had to offer. It was an unexpected oasis of abundance and sophistication, an island the size of a fingernail floating in the middle of a capital that had been destroyed.

Perhaps another woman would have chosen to wait until her influential partner had established his bonds with the powerful people around him. But Rosalinda was not of that ilk, and much as she adored her Juan Luis, she hadn't the slightest intention of being transformed into a meek mistress trailing behind after his prestigious job. She'd muddled her way around the world on her own since before she'd turned twenty, and in these circumstances — albeit now with a lover whose contacts would open a thousand doors for her — she decided once again to make it happen for herself. To this end she used the strategies of approach for which she had such a gift — she made contact with old acquaintances from other times and places, and through them, and their friends, and friends of their friends, came new faces, new jobs and titles with foreign names or, if Spanish, names that were impeccably aristocratic. It wasn't long before the first invitations arrived in her mailbox, invitations to receptions and balls, to lunches, cocktails, and hunts. Before Beigbeder was even able to raise his head from the mountains of papers accumulating in his dismal office, Rosalinda had already begun to find her way into a network of social relations whose purpose was to keep her entertained in the new setting to which her turbulent life had brought her.

Not everything was a hundred percent successful in those first months in Madrid, however. Ironically, in spite of her remarkable gift for social relations, she was unable to establish the faintest bonds of affection with her compatriots. The British ambassador, Sir Maurice Peterson, was the first to deny her a seat at his table. At his own urging, this lack of acceptance quickly extended to practically all the members of the British diplomatic corps posted in the capital. They were unable or unwilling to see Rosalinda Fox as a potential firsthand source of information coming from a member of the government, or even as a compatriot whom they ought as a matter of protocol to invite to their events and celebrations. They saw only an awkward presence who boasted the unworthy honor of sharing her life with a minister of the new pro-German regime, toward which the government of His Gracious Majesty didn't show the slightest friendliness.

Those days weren't all that rosy for Beigbeder either. The fact of having spent the whole war on the margins of the political intrigues meant that, as minister, he was often passed over in favor of other dignitaries of more illustrious form and weightier connections, such as Serrano Suñer, for example: the already powerful Serrano of whom everyone was so suspicious and for whom so few people seemed to feel the least bit of affection. *There's three things here for which you'll find my patience has worn thin: / That's subsidies, Falangists, and His Excellency's kin!* joked an old rhyme among the Madrileños. *Here he comes, along the road, the Lord o'er all the others — That used to be Lord Jesus, now it's one of Franco's brothers,* they sang mockingly in Seville.

When Serrano ended his visit to Morocco he held the high commissioner in elevated respect. But he began to be transformed into his bitterest opponent, as Spain's relations with Germany grew closer and Hitler's expansionist forces crept across Europe with terrifying speed. It wasn't long before the In-law-ísimo began to play dirty, and as soon as Great Britain declared war on Germany, he knew he'd been wrong to suggest to Franco that he appoint Beigbeder to the Foreign Ministry. That ministry, he thought, should have been for himself from the very beginning, not for that nobody from Africa, however pertinent his cross-cultural gifts and however many languages he spoke. Beigbeder was not, to him, the right man for this job. He wasn't sufficiently committed to the German cause, he defended Spain's neutrality in the European war, and he showed no intention of submitting blindly to the pressures and demands coming out of the Ministry of Governance. And what was more, he had an English lover, that attractive young blonde he'd met in Tetouan. In three words: he wouldn't do. Which was why, only a month after the formation of the new Council of Ministers, the owner of the most talented head and the most impressive ego in the government began spreading his tentacles over his rival's territory like a voracious octopus, enveloping it all and appropriating at will those areas that were properly within the purview of the Ministry for Foreign Affairs, without consulting its leader and without missing the smallest opportunity, on the way, to chuck in his face the fact that his personal love affair could end up costing Spain her relations with friendly countries.

Amid that tangle of politics, it wasn't possible for anyone to be completely certain of what was really on Beigbeder's mind. Having been persuaded by Serrano's machinations, the Spaniards and Germans saw him as pro-British, because he seemed tepid in his affection for the Nazis and because his heart was set on a frivolous, manipulative Englishwoman. To the British, who snubbed him, he was pro-German because he belonged to a government that enthusiastically supported the Third Reich. Rosalinda, ever the idealist, thought of him as a potential catalyst for political change: a magician capable of rerouting the channel down which his government was traveling if he put his mind to it. He, meanwhile, with admirable good humor given the pitiful circumstances, saw himself as a simple shopkeeper and tried to make her see him in that way, too.

"What power do you think I have to get this government to favor an increased closeness to your country? Very little, my love, very little indeed. I'm just one more person within a cabinet in which almost everyone is in favor of Germany and of possible Spanish intervention in the

European war on their side. We owe them money and favors; the thrust of our foreign policy was set before the war ended, before I was chosen for this job. Do you think I have any way of changing the course of our actions? No, dear Rosalinda, none at all. My role as a minister in this New Spain isn't to be a strategist or a diplomatic negotiator; I'm just a grocery vendor or a merchant from the Bread Souq. My job is focused on getting loans; haggling over commercial agreements; offering olive oil, oranges, and grapes to foreign countries in exchange for wheat and gasoline. Even so, just to get that done I have to wage daily battles within the cabinet, fighting with the Falangists for them to let me work on the fringes of their autocratic ravings. I might just be able to manage to get us enough so that our people don't die of cold and hunger this winter, but there's nothing, nothing I can do to change the government's stance on this war."

That was how the months passed for Beigbeder, buried under his responsibilities, wrestling with opponents within and without, kept apart from the maneuverings of the real powers in charge, more isolated with each passing day. In order not to succumb to total frustration during those dark days, he would seek refuge in nostalgia about the Morocco he had left behind. He missed that other world so much that he always kept an open copy of the Koran on his desk at the ministry and would recite its Arabic verses aloud from time to time, to the astonishment of anyone who happened to be nearby. He so yearned for that country that he kept his official residence in the Viana Palace filled with Moroccan clothing, and as soon as he was back home in the evenings he would remove his dull grey suit and dress in a velvet djellaba. He would eat directly from the serving dishes with three fingers, in the Moorish fashion, and wouldn't stop repeating to anyone who'd listen that we were all brothers, the Moroccans and the Spaniards. Sometimes, when he was finally alone after fighting his way through a thousand and one battles over the course of his day, listening to the squeaking of the trams that made their way down dirty streets crammed full of people, he thought he could hear the rhythm of the Moorish reed pipes, flutes, and tambourines. On the greyest mornings he even thought that mingled with the foul vapors emanating from the sewers his nose could detect the scent of orange blossoms, jasmine, and mint. Then he could see himself once again walking between the white-washed walls of the Tetouani medina, under the light filtering through the shadow of the creepers, amid the sound of the water spouting from the fountains and the wind stirring the cane fields.

He clung to nostalgia as a shipwrecked man clings to a piece of timber in the middle of a stormy ocean, but like the shadow of a scythe the acid tongue of Serrano was never far away, ready to rip him out of his dream.

"For God's sake, Beigbeder, stop with this business of us Spaniards all being Moors, once and for all. Do I happen to look like a Moor? Does El Caudillo look like a Moor? So stop repeating this shit, I've had it up to here, the same damn song all day long."

Those were difficult days for both of them. In spite of Rosalinda's tenacious efforts to ingratiate herself with British ambassador Peterson, things didn't right themselves in the months that followed. The only gesture she received from her compatriots toward the end of that victory year was an invitation to join the other mothers in singing carols with their children around the embassy piano. She would have to wait till May 1940 for things to turn around, when Churchill was named prime minister and decided abruptly to replace his diplomatic representative in Spain. And from then on, the situation changed radically, for everyone.

CHAPTER THIRTY-FIVE

Sir Samuel Hoare arrived in Madrid at the end of May 1940, boasting the pompous title of Extraordinary Ambassador on Special Mission. He'd never before set foot on Spanish soil and didn't speak a word of our language. Nor did he show the slightest sympathy for Franco or his regime, but Churchill placed every confidence in him and had urged him to accept the posting since Spain was a key player in the future of the European war and he wanted a strong man as his standard-bearer. It was fundamental to British interests that the Spanish government should maintain a neutral position, respecting a Gibraltar free from invasion and preventing the Atlantic ports from falling into German hands. In order to secure a minimum of cooperation, they'd used foreign trade to put pressure on a hungry Spain, restricting the supply of oil and squeezing them till they choked. As the German troops advanced across Europe, however, that ceased to be enough: the British needed to become involved in Madrid in a more active, more operational way. And with that goal in mind this small, rather worn-out-looking man, seemingly so unimpressive, landed in the capital: Sir Sam to his close colleagues, Don Samuel to the few friends he would end up making in Spain.

Hoare didn't take up the post with much optimism: he didn't like the place he'd been sent, had no sympathy for the quirks of Spanish life, and knew absolutely nobody in that devastated, dusty foreign town. He realized he wouldn't be well received and that the Franco government was openly anti-British. Just so that this would be absolutely clear to him from the outset, on the very morning of his arrival the Falangists gathered in front of his embassy with a noisy protest, welcoming him with shouts of "Gibraltar for the Spanish!"

Having presented his credentials to the Generalísimo, he began the tortuous ordeal that was to become his life during the four years of his posting. Countless times he regretted having accepted the position: he felt tremendously uncomfortable in such a hostile atmosphere, to a degree that he'd never experienced in any of his previous assignments. The mood was tense, the heat unbearable. The Falangists demonstrated outside his embassy daily; they threw stones at his windows, tore the flags and crests off his official cars, and insulted the British staff without the authorities batting an eyelid. The press began an aggressive campaign accusing Great Britain of responsibility for the famine that was ravaging Spain. The only people with any sympathy for him were a small number of conservative monarchists, just a few people nostalgic for Queen Victoria Eugenie with little room to maneuver in the government and clinging to the idea of a past to which they would never be able to return.

He felt alone, groping his way through the darkness. Madrid overwhelmed him. He found it absolutely impossible to breathe in that atmosphere: the terribly slow way the administrative machinery worked oppressed him; he stared with bewilderment at the streets filled with police and Falangists armed to the teeth; he watched how the Germans behaved, emboldened and threatening. Plucking up his courage, and fulfilling the obligations of his position, as soon as he was settled he set about establishing relations with the Spanish government, and in particular with its three key figures: General Franco and ministers Serrano Suñer and Beigbeder. In his meetings with each of them, he sounded them out, and from each received quite a different response.

He was granted an audience with the Generalísimo in El Pardo Palace one sunny summer's day. In spite of the weather, Franco received him with the curtains closed and the electric light on, sitting behind a desk over which large signed photographs of Hitler and Mussolini glared arrogantly. During this awkward encounter, in which they spoke through an interpreter and without the possibility of any proper dialogue, Hoare was struck by just how disconcertingly self-confident the head of state was — he possessed the smugness of a man who believed himself to have been chosen by Providence to rescue his country and create a new world.

Everything that went badly with Franco went worse with Serrano Suñer. The In-law-ísimo's power was at its most dazzling peak. The whole country was in his hands — the Falange, the press, the police — and he enjoyed unlimited personal access to El Caudillo, for whom many people suspected he felt a certain contempt as his intellectual inferior. While Franco, hidden away in El Pardo, was barely seen, Serrano seemed to be

459

everywhere, with a finger in every pie, so different from that discreet man who'd come out to the Protectorate in the middle of wartime, the one who bent down to retrieve my powder compact and whose ankles I stared at for so long under that sofa. As though he had been reborn with the regime, a new Ramón Serrano Suñer appeared: impatient, arrogant, always tense, quick as a flash in both word and deed, his catlike eyes ever alert, his Falangist uniform well starched, and his nearly white hair combed back like a movie star's. He was exquisitely disparaging toward any representative of what he called the "plutodemocracies." Neither on that first meeting nor on the many more they were required to have during Hoare's posting did the two men ever come close to anything resembling a mutual understanding.

The only one of the three dignitaries with whom the ambassador was able to get along was Beigbeder. From his very first visit to the Santa Cruz Palace, the communication between the two men was very fluid. The minister listened, acted, tried to fix things, to resolve problems. In Hoare's presence he declared himself to be a keen supporter of nonintervention in the war. He openly recognized the great needs of the hungry population and struggled to come to agreements and negotiate pacts to fill those needs. It's true that at first the ambassador did think him a little quaint in appearance, at times even eccentric: his sensibility, culture, manners, and ironic tone utterly incongruous in a Madrid with its arm raised in a military salute, the city of "order and command," as the military saying would have it. To Hoare's eyes, Beigbeder seemed obviously uncomfortable amid the Germans' aggressiveness, the Falangists' arrogance, and his own government's despotic attitudes, as well as the daily miseries of the capital. Perhaps for this reason, because of Beigbeder's own abnormality in that world of madmen, Hoare found him a pleasant sort, a singular minister with a Moorish temperament, a balm that soothed the lashings Hoare received from the rest of the government. They had their disagreements, naturally: points of view that conflicted and diplomatic positions openly argued; objections, complaints, and dozens of crises that they attempted to resolve together. Such as when Spanish troops entered Tangiers in June, finally putting an end to its status as an international city. Or when the government was about to authorize parades of German troops through the streets of San Sebastián. Or so many other incidents in those days of disorder and haste. Despite everything, the relationship between Beigbeder and Hoare became closer and more comfortable by the day, and the urbane Spaniard became the ambassador's only place of refuge in that stormy land where problems sprung up like weeds.

As he slowly adapted to the country, Hoare became aware of just how extensive the Germans' influence in Spanish affairs was, their considerable reach into almost every aspect of public life. Businessmen, executives, salesmen, movie producers — people involved in a range of activities with excellent contacts in the administration and power structures — were working as agents in the service of the Nazis. He soon learned, too, of the iron grip the Germans exerted on the communications media. The press office of the German embassy, with the full approval of Serrano Suñer, made a daily decision about what information about the

461

Third Reich would be published in Spain, how and in what words, inserting all the Nazi propaganda they wanted into the Spanish papers, and in the most brazen, offensive way into *Arriba,* the organ of the Falange, which monopolized most of the paper that was available for newspapers in those penurious times. The campaigns against the British were unrelenting and bloody, marked by lies, insults, and perverse distortions. Churchill was the subject of the most malicious caricatures and the British Empire the object of constant mockery. The simplest accident in a factory or on a mail train in any Spanish province was, without the slightest qualm, attributed to sabotage by the perfidious English. The ambassador's complaints about these falsehoods would always — inexcusably — fall on deaf ears.

And as Sir Samuel Hoare settled somehow or other into his new post, the antagonism between the ministers of Governance and Foreign Affairs became ever more apparent. From his all-powerful position, Serrano Suñer arranged a strategic campaign in his own style: he put out poisonous rumors about Beigbeder, supplementing them by spreading the notion that things could only be resolved if they were given into his own hands. And as the former high commissioner's star plummeted like a stone in water, Franco and Serrano, Serrano and Franco, two men with absolutely no knowledge of international politics, neither of whom had barely seen anything of the world, sat down to drink hot chocolate with fried bread in El Pardo and sketched out a new global order on the teatime tablecloth with the shocking audacity that can only come from ignorance and overweening pride.

Until Beigbeder snapped. They were going to throw him out, and he knew it. They were going to wash their hands of him, give him a kick in the rear, and send him packing: he was no longer useful in their glorious crusade. They had torn him away from his beloved Morocco and appointed him to a highly desirable position, only to bind his hands and feet and stuff a gag into his mouth. They'd never valued his opinions: in fact, they'd probably never even asked for them. He'd never been able to take the initiative or express his views; all they wanted was to have his name on the cabinet list while he acted as a servile functionary, timid and mute. All the same, even though he didn't like the situation one bit, he complied with the restrictions and worked tirelessly in everything they asked of him, putting up for months with the systematic mistreatment meted out by Serrano. First it was the treading on toes, the shoving around, the *that's-not-for-you-that-one's-for-me.* It wasn't long before those shoves had been transformed into humiliating cuffs to the neck. And those rabbit punches soon turned into kidney punches, which ended up becoming knives in the jugular. And at the point when Beigbeder could tell that the next move would be stamping on his head, he finally snapped.

He was tired, fed up with the In-law-ísimo's rudeness and haughtiness, with Franco's obscurantism in his decision making; fed up with swimming against the current and being isolated from everything, in command of a ship that from the moment it set off had been headed in the wrong direction. Which was why he decided simply to throw himself into a decision, boldly. The time had come for the discreet friendship he'd main-

463

tained with Hoare to come out into the daylight and be made public, to transcend the boundaries of private sanctuaries, offices, and halls where it had remained till now. And with this as his banner, he threw himself out into the street in broad daylight, with no protection. Into the fresh air, under the ruthless summer sun. They took to having lunch together almost every day, at the most visible tables in the best-known restaurants. And then, like two Arabs walking the narrow alleyways of the Moorish quarter of Tetouan, Beigbeder would take the ambassador's arm, calling him "brother Samuel," and with ostentatious ease they would wander the sidewalks of Madrid. Beigbeder was issuing a challenge, provoking, almost quixotic. On one day, and the next, and the next, chatting familiarly with the man sent as an envoy by the enemy, arrogantly demonstrating his contempt for the Germans and the Germanophiles. In that way they wandered past the General Secretariat of the Movement on Calle Alcalá, past the headquarters of the *Arriba* newspaper and the German embassy on the Paseo de la Castellana, past the very doors of the Palace or the Ritz, veritable beehives of Nazis, so that everyone could plainly see how well Franco's minister and the ambassador of the undesirables got along. And all the while Serrano — on the verge of a nervous breakdown and with his ulcer troubling him — paced back and forth across his office, ruffling his hair and asking himself at the top of his lungs where this lunatic Beigbeder's mad behavior would lead.

Although Rosalinda's efforts had managed to awake in him a certain amount of sympathy for Great Britain, Beigbeder was not so incautious that he would throw himself into the arms of a foreign country — just as nightly he threw himself into the arms of his beloved — for no other reason than pure romanticism. Yes, he had developed a certain amount of sympathy for that country thanks to her. But if he threw himself at Hoare so completely that by doing so he burned all his bridges, it was for other reasons. Perhaps because he was a utopian and he believed that in the New Spain things weren't working as he felt they ought to. Maybe it was because this was the only way he had of openly showing his opposition to entering the war on the side of the Axis powers. He might have done it as a rejection of the man who had humiliated him utterly, someone with whom he had expected to be working shoulder to shoulder to lift the country up out of the ruins, the country whose demolition they had participated in with such eagerness. And possibly he moved closer to Hoare because he felt alone, terribly alone in a hostile and bitter environment.

I didn't learn about this firsthand, but rather because during those months Rosalinda kept me up to date with a string of long letters that I received in Tetouan like a godsend. In spite of her lively social life, illness still forced her to spend many hours in bed, hours she dedicated to writing letters and reading what her friends sent her. And in that way we established a habit that kept us connected to each other, an invisible thread binding us across space and time. In her most recent piece of news from late August 1940 she told me that the Madrid newspapers were already discussing the imminent departure of the minister of foreign affairs from the government. But for that we had to wait a few weeks yet, six or seven.

And over that time, things happened that — yet again — transformed the course of my life forever.

CHAPTER THIRTY-SIX

One of the activities with which I'd passed my time since my mother's arrival in Tetouan was reading. She usually went to bed early, Félix no longer came across the landing, and I began to have a lot of free hours, until yet again he came up with an idea for filling up that tedium. It had the name of two women and arrived between a pair of covers: *Fortunata and Jacinta*. From then on, I devoted my leisure time to reading the massive novels in my neighbor's house. As the months passed, I was able to finish them all and moved on to the shelves in the Protectorate library. When the summer of 1940 came to a close, I'd already polished off the two or three dozen novels in the little library and wondered what I'd be able to find to keep me entertained from then on. And then, quite unexpectedly, a new text arrived at my door. Not in the form of a novel, but a telegram on blue paper. And not for me to take pleasure in reading, but for me to act on the instructions it contained. "Personal invitation. Private party in Tangiers. Madrid friendships waiting. September 1. 7 p.m. Dean's Bar."

My stomach clenched, but despite that I couldn't help giving a little laugh. I knew who had sent the message; there was no need for a

467

signature. Dozens of recollections swarmed back into my memory: music, laughter, cocktails, unexpected emergencies and foreign words, little adventures, excursions with the car roof down, a joy for living. I compared those days in the past with my current calm present in which the weeks went monotonously by with sewing and fittings, radio serials and walks with my mother at dusk. My only moderately exciting experience was the occasional film Félix would drag me along to see, and the misfortunes and love affairs of the characters in the books that I devoured nightly to overcome my boredom. Knowing that Rosalinda was waiting for me in Tangiers gave me a little shudder of happiness. Although they wouldn't last long, my feelings of hopefulness were reemerging.

At the appointed day and time, however, I didn't find any sort of party at the El Minzah where Dean worked, just four or five little isolated groups of people I didn't know and a couple of solitary drinkers at the bar. Dean wasn't behind the bar, either, and it was perhaps too early for the pianist. The atmosphere was flat, unlike so many nights in the past. I sat down to wait at a discreet table and shooed away the waiter who approached. Ten past seven, a quarter past, twenty past, and still no sign of a party. At seven thirty I went up to the bar and asked after Dean. He no longer worked there, they told me. He'd opened his own business, Dean's Bar. Where? In the Rue Amérique du Sud. I was there in two minutes, as the places were only a few hundred feet apart. Dean, gaunt and dark as ever, spotted me from behind the bar the moment my silhouette appeared at the entrance. His bar was livelier than the one at the hotel: there weren't more patrons, but the conversations were louder, more relaxed, and you could hear people laughing. The owner didn't greet me, but with a quick glance as black as coal he gestured me toward a curtain at the back. I went over. I drew the heavy green velvet aside and went in.

"You're late for my party."

Neither the dirty walls, nor the dim light of the one sad bulb, not even the crates of liquor and sacks of coffee piled all around could take away a speck of my friend's glamour. She, or perhaps Dean, or maybe the two of them before opening the bar that evening, had temporarily transformed the small storeroom into an exclusive little shelter for a private meeting. So private that there were just two chairs, separated by a barrel covered in a white tablecloth. On top of that were a couple of glasses, a cocktail shaker, a pack of Turkish cigarettes, and an ashtray. In one corner, balancing on a big stack of wooden crates, a portable gramophone played Billie Holiday singing "Summertime."

We hadn't seen each other for a whole year, since her departure for Madrid. She was still extremely thin, her skin transparent, and that wave of blond hair was constantly about to tumble into her eyes. But her expression wasn't the same one I knew from her untroubled days in the past, not even from the most difficult periods of living with her husband or her subsequent convalescence. I couldn't tell where exactly the change was to be found, but everything about her had altered a little. She seemed rather older, more mature. A little tired, perhaps. Through her letters I'd learned about the difficulties that Beigbeder and she faced in the capital. She hadn't told me,

469

however, that she'd planned a trip to Morocco.

We hugged, laughed like schoolgirls, complimented each other on our outfits, and began laughing again. I'd missed her so much. I had my mother, of course. And Félix. And Candelaria. And my atelier and my new passion for reading. But I'd felt her absence keenly — those unexpected arrivals, her way of seeing things from a completely different perspective from the rest of the world. Her witty remarks, her little eccentricities, her riotous chatter. I wanted to know everything about her new life and unleashed a torrent of questions: how was Madrid, how was Johnny, how was Beigbeder getting along, what was it that had brought her back to Africa? She gave me vague replies, avoiding any reference to the difficulties they'd been facing. Only when I stopped tormenting her with my curiosity, and only then, as she filled the glasses, did she finally state clearly what was on her mind.

"I've come to offer you a job."

I laughed.

"I've got a job already."

"I'm going to propose another one."

I laughed again and drank. Pink gin, as on so many other occasions.

"Doing what?" I said.

"The same as you're doing now, but in Madrid."

When I realized she was being quite serious, my laughter dried up, and I, too, changed my tone of voice.

"I'm comfortable in Tetouan. Things are going well here, better every day. My mother likes living here, too. Our atelier is going wonderfully well; actually, we're thinking about taking on an apprentice to help us. We haven't made plans to go back to Madrid."

"I'm not talking about your mother, Sira, only about you. And there won't be any need to close the workshop in Tetouan; I'm sure this will only be a temporary thing. Or at least I hope it will. When it's all over, you can come back."

"When what's all over?"

"The war."

"The war ended more than a year ago."

"Yes, yours did. But now there's another one."

She got up, changed the record, and raised the volume. More jazz, just instrumental this time. She was trying to prevent our conversation from being heard on the other side of the curtain.

"There's another war, a terrible one. My country is in it and yours might enter at any moment. Juan Luis has done everything he can to keep Spain on the sidelines, but the course of events seems to indicate that it'll be very hard. Which is why we want any help we can get to minimize the pressure that Germany is putting on Spain. If our plan works, your nation will stay out of the war, and mine will have a better chance of winning it."

I still didn't understand what my job had to do with all that, but I didn't interrupt her.

"Juan Luis and I," she went on, "are trying to make a few of our friends aware so that they'll contribute in any way that they can. He hasn't been able to put any pressure on the government from the ministry, but it's possible to do things from outside, too."

"What sorts of things?" I asked in a whisper. I didn't have the slightest idea what was going through her head. My expression must have been amusing, because she finally laughed.

"Don't panic, querida. We're not talking about

471

planting bombs in the German embassy or sabotaging major military operations. I'm referring to discreet campaigns of resistance. Observing. Infiltrating. Obtaining information through little gaps here and there. Juan Luis and I are not alone in this. We're not just a couple of idealists looking for foolhardy friends to get involved in some implausible plot."

She refilled the glasses and turned up the volume on the gramophone again. We each lit another cigarette. She sat down again and her blue eyes fixed themselves on mine. Around them were dark circles I'd never seen before.

"We're trying to set up a network of underground collaborators in Madrid linked to the British secret services. Collaborators with no connection to political life, to the diplomatic service or the military. People who aren't known, who under the appearance of a normal life can find out about things and then pass them on to the SOE."

"What's the SOE?" I murmured.

"The Special Operations Executive. A new organization within the secret services that has just been created by Churchill, for matters relating to the war, and on the fringes of what the regular agents are doing. They're signing people up all over Europe. It's like an espionage service, but not a very orthodox one. Not a very conventional one."

"I don't understand." I was still whispering.

I really didn't understand. Secret services. Underground collaborators. Agents. Espionage. Infiltrating. This was the first time I'd heard about any of this in my life.

"Well, you shouldn't imagine I'm so used to all this terminology myself. It's practically new to me, too; I've had to learn an awful lot terribly fast. As I told you in one of my letters, Juan Luis has become close to British ambassador Hoare lately. And now that his days at the ministry are numbered, the two of them have decided to work together. Hoare doesn't directly control the secret services in Madrid himself, however. Let's say he oversees it, he's ultimately responsible for it, but he doesn't coordinate it personally."

"So who does, then?"

I was waiting for her to tell me she did it herself and reveal that it had all been no more than a joke. And we'd both laugh wildly about it and then finally go out for dinner and dancing at Villa Harris as we'd done so many times before. But she didn't.

"Alan Hillgarth, our embassy's naval attaché; he's the person in charge of the whole thing. He's a very special fellow, a marine from a family with a long navy tradition, married to a lady from the high aristocracy who is also involved in his activities. He arrived in Madrid at the same time as Hoare, under the cover of his official position, to take covert charge of the activities of the SOE and the SIS, the Secret Intelligence Service."

SOE: Special Operations Executive. SIS: Secret Intelligence Service. The whole thing sounded completely strange to me. I pressed her to clarify.

"The SIS is the Secret Intelligence Service, also known as MI6, the Directorate of Military Intelligence Section 6; the sixth section of Military Intelligence, an agency dedicated to the secret services' operations outside Great Britain. Espionage activities in non-British territories, to be quite clear. It's been in operation since before the Great War, and its staff, usually under some diplomatic or military cover, are involved in covert actions normally through existing power structures, through influential people or authorities in the countries in which they are operating. The SOE, in contrast, is new. It's riskier, because they don't depend just on professionals, but for the same reason it's also much more flexible. It's an emergency operation for the new wartime, if I can put it like that. They're prepared to collaborate with anyone who might be of use to them. The organization has only just been established, and Hillgarth, the coordinator for Spain, needs to recruit agents. Urgently. And for this he's sounding out people he trusts who can put him in contact with other people who in turn can be directly helpful. So you might say that Juan Luis and I are that kind of intermediary. Hoare hasn't been around for long at all, he hardly knows anyone. Hillgarth spent the whole civil war as vice consul in Majorca, but he's also new in Madrid and not yet in absolute control of his territory. We haven't been asked, Juan Luis and I — he as an openly Anglophile minister and I as a British citizen — to be directly involved: they know that we're too well known and we'll always be suspected. But they have approached us to supply them with contacts. So we've thought about a few of our friends. You, among others. And that's why I've come to see you."

I preferred not to ask what exactly it was that she wanted from me. Whether or not I did, she was going to tell me anyway, and it would provoke just the same panic in me, so I decided to focus my attention on filling the glasses again; all this was far too heavy to deal with without a drink. But the cocktail shaker was empty. So I got up

474

and rummaged among the boxes stacked against the wall. I took out a bottle of something that turned out to be whiskey, removed the cap, and took a long swig. I passed it to Rosalinda. She did the same and handed it back, then continued talking. Meanwhile, I went back to my drinking.

"We thought that you could set up an atelier in Madrid and sew for the wives of the high-ranking Nazis."

My throat closed up, and the shot of whiskey I had almost swallowed shot back out of my mouth in a loud spray. I wiped my face with the back of my hand. When I was finally able to speak, only four words came out.

"You're both raving mad."

She didn't even seem to acknowledge that I was referring to her and went on.

"They all used to get their clothes in Paris, but since the German army invaded France in May most of the haute couture houses have shut down; not many people want to keep working in occupied Paris. La Maison Vionnet, La Maison Chanel on the Rue Cambon, the Schiaparelli shop on the Place Vendôme: almost all the major ones have gone."

Rosalinda's references to Parisian haute couture, perhaps coupled with my nerves, the cocktails, and the shots of whiskey, made me give a hoarse laugh.

"And you want me to replace all these designers in Madrid?"

I couldn't get her to share my laughter, and she went on talking seriously.

"You could try it out in your own way, on a small scale. This is the perfect moment, because there aren't that many choices. Paris is now out of the question, and Berlin is too far. Either they get their wardrobes in Madrid or they don't get to show off new designs for the season that's just about to begin, which would be a tragedy for them because the essence of their lives these days is centered exclusively on an intense social life. I've been learning about it: a lot of Madrid's ateliers are back in operation now, getting ready for the autumn. There was a rumor that Balenciaga was going to reopen his workshop this year, but he ended up not doing it. I've got the names here of the ones that are planning to open," she said, removing a folded piece of paper from her jacket pocket. "Flora Villareal; Brígida at number thirty-seven, Carrera de San Jerónimo; Natalio at number eighteen Lagasca; Madame Raguette at number two, Bárbara de Braganza; Pedro Rodríguez at number sixty-two Alcalá; Cottret at number eight, Fernando Sixth."

Some of them were familiar to me, others weren't. Doña Manuela could have been among them, but Rosalinda didn't mention her: perhaps she hadn't reopened her workshop. When she had finished reading the list she tore the bit of paper into a thousand little pieces and left them in the ashtray filled with cigarette butts.

"In spite of the efforts to show new collections and offer customers the best designs, they all, however, share the same problem, they all have the same limitation. So it won't be easy for any of them to make a success of it."

"What's the problem?"

"The scarcity of fabric, the severe scarcity of fabric. Neither Spain nor France is producing materials for this sort of sewing; those factories that haven't closed down are focusing on fulfilling

476

the basic needs of the population or developing materials destined for the war. They use the cotton to make uniforms; the linen, bandages; any sort of fabric has a function that's a higher priority than fashion. You'll be able to overcome this problem by bringing fabrics from Tangiers. There's still trade here, there's no problem with imports like there is on the Peninsula. You get products coming here from America and Argentina, there's still a good stock of French fabrics and English wools, Indian and Chinese silks from previous years: you can take it all with you. And if you end up needing more supplies, we'll find some way for you to get hold of them. If you arrive in Madrid with material and ideas, and if I can spread the word among my contacts, you could be the dressmaker of the season. You won't have any competition, Sira: you'll be the only person who can give them what they want: ostentation, luxury, utter frivolity, as though the world were a grand ballroom rather than the bloody battlefield they've made it. And the German women, all of them, will be over you like vultures."

"But they'll connect me to you," I said, trying to cling to anything that might prevent me from being swept away by this lunatic plan.

"Not at all. No one has any reason to. The Germans in Madrid have mostly just arrived and they have no contact with the ones in Morocco; no one has to suspect that you and I know each other. Though naturally your experience of sewing for their compatriots in Tetouan will be a great help to you: you know their tastes, you know how to handle them and how to behave with them."

As she was speaking, I closed my eyes and just shook my head from side to side. For a few

477

seconds my mind went back to my early months in Tetouan, to the night Candelaria showed me the pistols and proposed that we sell them to open the atelier. The feeling of panic was just the same, and the scenario was similar: two women hidden away in a dark little room, one laying out a dangerous, fully thought out plan, and the other, terrified, refusing to accept it. But there were certain differences — big differences. The plan Rosalinda was proposing to me was on quite another scale.

Her voice brought me back from the past, made me abandon the wretched bedroom in the La Luneta boardinghouse and reposition myself in the reality of the little storeroom at the back of Dean's Bar.

"We'll give you a reputation, we have ways of doing that. I'm well connected in the circles that are of interest to us in Madrid; we'll get word of mouth going so that people hear about you without ever connecting you to me. The SOE will cover all the initial costs: they'll pay for the rental of the place, the setup of the workshop, and the initial investment in fabric and equipment. Juan Luis will take care of the paperwork for customs and get you the permits you need to move the merchandise from Tangiers to Spain; it'll have to be a considerable supply, because once he's out of the ministry these things will be much harder to arrange. You'll take all the profit from the business. All you have to do is what you're doing in Morocco, but paying greater attention to what you hear from your German clients, as well as any Spanish women connected to the structures of power and to the Nazis. The German women are utterly idle and they have more money than they need. Your atelier could become a place for them to meet. You'll hear about where their husbands are going, the people they meet, the plans they have, and the visitors they're receiving from Germany."

"I barely speak any German."

"You can communicate well enough to make them feel comfortable with you."

"I don't know much more than numbers, greetings, colors, the days of the week, and a handful of random phrases," I insisted.

"It doesn't matter; we've already thought about that. We've got someone who can help you. All you'll have to do is assemble the bits of information and then get them to their destination."

"How?"

She shrugged.

"That's something Hillgarth will have to tell you if you accept. I don't know how these operations work; I imagine they'll design something especially for you."

I shook my head again, this time more emphatically.

"I'm not going to accept, Rosalinda."

She lit another cigarette and inhaled deeply.

"Why not?" she asked through the smoke.

"Because I won't," I said bluntly. I had a thousand reasons not to embark on that nonsense, but I preferred to pile them all up into a single refusal. No. No, I wouldn't do it. Decisively no. I took another slug of whiskey from the bottle; it tasted horrible.

"Why not, querida? Because you're afraid, no?" She was speaking quietly now, confidently. The music had come to an end; the only sound was the needle scratching over the surface of the record and a few voices and some laughter coming from the other side of the curtain. "We're all afraid, we're all utterly terrified," she murmured. "But that's not a good enough reason. We have to get involved, Sira. We have to help. You, me, all of us, each in whatever way we can. We have to contribute our grain of sand to make sure this madness doesn't go any further."

"Besides, I can't go to Madrid. I have unfinished business to deal with. You know what I'm referring to."

The matter of the fraud charges from Ramiro's time still hadn't been resolved. Since the end of the civil war I'd talked to Commissioner Vázquez about it a couple of times. He'd tried to find out what the situation was in Madrid, but he hadn't gotten anywhere. Everything's still very chaotic, we'll let some time go by, wait for things to calm down, he'd say to me. And having no intention of going back, I'd waited. Rosalinda knew the situation; I'd told her about it myself.

"We've thought about that, too. About that, and about the fact that you have to be covered, you have to be protected from any eventuality. Our embassy couldn't be responsible for you if there were to be any problem, and the way things are it's risky for a Spanish citizen. But Juan Luis has had an idea."

I wanted to ask her what it was, but I couldn't find my voice. Nor did I need to say anything; she set it all out for me right away.

"He can get you a Moroccan passport."

"A fake passport," I countered.

"No, querida, a real one. He's still got very good friends in Morocco. You could be a Moroccan citizen within a few hours. With of course a differ-

480

ent name."

I got up and noticed I was finding it hard to keep my balance. In my brain — amid the pool of whiskey and gin — all those alien words were splashing messily around. Secret service, agents, operatives. False names, Moroccan passports. I leaned against the wall and tried to recover my composure.

"Rosalinda — no. Please, don't go on. I can't agree."

"You don't have to make a decision right now. Think about it."

"There's nothing to think about. What time is it?"

She looked at her watch; I tried to do the same with mine but the numbers seemed to dissolve before my eyes.

"A quarter to ten."

"I have to get back to Tetouan."

"I've arranged for a car to come and collect you at ten, but I don't think you're in any state to go anywhere. Stay the night in Tangiers. I'll get them to give you a room in the El Minzah and to let your mother know."

A bed to sleep in and forget that whole dark conversation seemed the most tempting of offers. A big bed with white sheets, in a beautiful room in which I'd wake up the following day to find that this meeting with Rosalinda had just been a nightmare. A wild nightmare out of nowhere. Suddenly some lucidity sparked up from a distant corner of my brain.

"They can't let my mother know. We don't have a telephone, you know that."

"I'll get someone to call Félix Aranda and he'll tell her. I'll also arrange for someone to pick you

481

up and take you to Tetouan tomorrow morning."

"And where are you staying?"

"At the home of some English friends on the Rue de Hollande. I don't want anyone to know I'm in Tangiers. A car brought me straight here from their house; I haven't even set foot on the street."

She fell silent for a few seconds and then started speaking again, her voice lower. Lower and more ominous.

"Things are looking really bad for Juan Luis and me, Sira. We're being permanently watched."

"Who?" I asked, hoarse.

She gave a sad half smile.

"Everyone. The police. The Gestapo. The Falange."

My fear burst out of me in a question, my voice a thick whisper. "And what about me? Will they be watching me, too?"

"I don't know, querida, I don't know."

She smiled again but this time didn't manage to conceal the trace of anxiety that lingered on her lips.

Chapter Thirty-Seven

There was a knock at the door, and someone came in without waiting for permission. With my eyes still half closed, through the gloom I could make out a uniformed maid carrying a tray. She put it down somewhere outside my field of vision and drew the curtains. The room immediately filled with light, and I covered my head with the pillow. Although this muffled the noise, my ears filled with little signals that allowed me to follow what the recent arrival was doing. The porcelain of the cup coming into contact with the saucer, the bubbling of the hot coffee coming out of the pot, the scraping of a knife against a piece of toast as it spread the butter. When everything was ready, she approached the bed.

"Good morning, señorita. Your breakfast is ready. You'll have to get up now, there will be a car at the door for you in an hour."

I replied with a grunt. I wanted to say thank you, I get it, leave me alone. The girl hadn't understood that I meant to keep sleeping.

"They've asked me not to leave till you're up."

She spoke Spanish with a Spanish accent. Tangiers had filled up with Republicans since the war had ended, and she was probably a daughter of one of those families. I grunted again and rolled over.

"Please, señorita, get up. Your coffee and toast will get cold."

"Who sent you?" I asked without removing my head from its refuge. My voice sounded like it was coming from inside a cave, perhaps because of the barrier of feathers and material that separated me from the outside world, perhaps an effect of the catastrophic night before. Even as I finished formulating it, I realized how ridiculous the question was. How could this girl know who it was who'd sent her to me? I, on the other hand, had no doubt whatsoever.

"I got the order from the kitchen, señorita. I'm the maid for this floor."

"Well, you can go now."

"Not until you're up."

The young maid was obstinate, with the persistence of someone who has been well drilled. Finally I withdrew my head and pushed the hair away from my face. When I moved the sheets aside I realized that I was wearing an apricot-colored nightgown that didn't belong to me. The girl was waiting for me, holding a matching dressing gown; I decided not to ask her where it had come from — how would she know? I guessed that somehow or other Rosalinda had arranged for both things to be brought to the room. There weren't any slippers, however, so I walked barefoot over to the little round table that had been set with my breakfast. My stomach was growling.

"Can I give you any milk, señorita?" she asked as I sat down.

I nodded, unable to say anything: my mouth was already full of toast. I was ravenous as a wolf;

484

I remembered I hadn't had dinner the previous night.

"If it's all right, I'll draw your bath for you."

I nodded again while I chewed, and within a few seconds I heard the water gushing hard out of the taps. The girl returned to the room.

"You can go now — thank you. Tell whoever sent you that I'm up."

"They've told me to take your clothes to be ironed while you're having your breakfast."

I took another bite of toast and nodded wordlessly again. Then she took up my clothes, which had been tossed in a jumble on a little armchair.

"Does señorita require anything else?" she asked before leaving.

With my mouth still full, I brought a finger to my temple, as though simulating a gunshot, though unintentionally. She looked at me in alarm and I noticed then that she was only a child.

"Something for my headache?" I explained when I was finally able to swallow.

She showed that she'd understood with an emphatic nod and slipped away without another word, keen to escape as soon as possible from the bedroom of the madwoman she must have thought me.

I polished off the toast, an orange juice, a couple of croissants, and a bun. Then I poured myself a second cup of coffee, and when I picked up the milk jug the back of my hand brushed past the envelope that was leaning against a little vase that held a couple of white roses. I felt something like an electric shock, but I didn't pick it up. There wasn't anything written on it, not a single letter, but I knew it was for me and I knew who'd sent it. I finished my coffee and went into the steam-filled bathroom. I closed the taps and tried to make out my reflection in the mirror, which was so misted up that I had to wipe it with a towel. Pitiful, that was the only word that occurred to me as I looked at my reflection. I undressed and got into the water.

When I came out of the bathroom the remains of the breakfast had been taken away and the balcony doors were wide open. The palm trees in the garden, the sea, and the intense blue sky over the Strait seemed to fill the room, but I barely paid them any attention — I was in a hurry. I found my clothes, ironed, at the foot of my bed: the suit, slip, and silk stockings, all ready to put back onto my body. And on the nightstand, on a little silver tray, a bottle of water, a glass, and a bottle of aspirin. I gulped down two tablets; I reconsidered and took another. Then I returned to the bathroom and drew my damp hair back into a low bun. I put on just a little bit of makeup — all I had with me was powder and lipstick. Then I got dressed. All set, I muttered to the air. I corrected myself at once. All *nearly* set. Just one little detail missing. The one that had been waiting for me on the table where I'd had breakfast half an hour earlier: the cream-colored envelope with no apparent addressee. I sighed, and picking it up with just two fingers put it away in my bag without giving it another look.

I went out, leaving behind someone else's nightdress and the dent of my body in the sheets. My fear didn't want to be left behind, so it came with me.

"Mademoiselle's bill has already been settled, and there's a car waiting for you," the concierge said discreetly. I didn't recognize the vehicle or the driver, but I didn't ask whom the former belonged to and whom the latter worked for. I just settled into the back seat and without saying a word let them take me home.

My mother didn't ask me how the party had gone or where I'd spent the night. I assumed that whoever had brought her the message the previous night had been so convincing that he or she barely left space for any concern. If she noticed how out of sorts I was looking, she didn't give any indication that she was at all curious about it. She just looked up from the piece of clothing she was working on and said good morning. Not effusive, not annoyed. Neutral.

"We're out of silk braid," she announced. "Aracama's wife wants us to move the fitting from Thursday to Friday, and Frau Langenheim wants us to change the way the shantung dress hangs."

She went on with her sewing, making comments on the latest news, while I drew up a chair opposite her and sat down, so close that my knees were almost touching hers. Then she started telling me something about the delivery of some pieces of satin that we'd ordered the previous week. I didn't let her finish.

"They want me to go back to Madrid and work for the English, to pass them information about the Germans. They want me to spy on their wives."

Her right hand stopped in midair, holding the threaded needle between stitches. She was halfway through a sentence, her mouth open. Her posture immobile, she looked over the little spectacles she used for sewing and fixed on me a look that was filled with unease.

I didn't go on talking right away. First I took a breath in, and out, a couple of times — deeply, big gulps, as though finding it hard to breathe.

"They're saying Spain's full of Nazis," I went on. "The English need people to inform them about what the Germans are doing: who they're meeting, where, when, how. They thought about setting me up in a workshop to sew for their wives, and then afterward to tell them what I see and hear."

"And what answer did you give them?"

Her voice, like mine, was barely a whisper.

"I told them no. That I couldn't, that I didn't want to. That I'm doing well here, with you. That I have no interest in going back to Madrid. But they're asking me to think about it."

The silence stretched out across the whole room, between the fabric and the mannequins, surrounding the spools of thread, coming to rest on the sewing boards.

"And would it help stop Spain from getting into another war?" she asked finally.

I shrugged. "In theory anything might help, or at least that's what they think," I said, not too convinced. "They're trying to set up a network of secret informers. The English want us Spaniards to remain on the sidelines of what's happening in Europe, not to ally ourselves with the Germans and not to intervene; they say that'd be best for everyone."

She lowered her head and focused her attention on the piece of fabric she was working on. She didn't say anything for a few seconds: she just thought, contemplated unhurriedly as she caressed the material with the tip of her thumb. Finally she looked up and slowly removed her glasses.

"Do you want my advice, my child?" she asked.

I nodded emphatically. Yes, of course I wanted

her advice: I needed her to confirm that my turning them down was reasonable, I longed to hear from her mouth that the plan was utter madness. I wanted her to go back to being my old mother and ask who on earth did I think I was, going around playing at being a secret agent? I wanted to be reunited with the strong Dolores of my childhood: the prudent, decisive one, the one who always knew what was right and what was wrong. The one who brought me up, showing me the straightest path, from which one unfortunate day I had diverged. But the world hadn't changed only for me: my mother's foundations were different now, too.

"Join them, child. Help them, collaborate. Our poor Spain can't get into another war, it hasn't the strength left."

"But, Mother . . ."

She didn't let me go on.

"You don't know what it's like to live through a war, Sira. You haven't woken up day in and day out to the noise of machine-gun fire and mortars exploding. You haven't eaten worm-infested lentils month after month, you haven't lived through a winter without bread, without coal, without glass in the windows. You haven't existed alongside broken families and starving children. You haven't seen eyes that were filled with hate, with fear, or both at once. The whole of Spain has been devastated, no one has the strength anymore to go through that same nightmare again. The only thing the country can do now is weep over its dead and move forward with what little it has left."

"But . . . ," I insisted.

She interrupted me again. Without raising her voice, but firm.

"If I were you, I'd help the English, I'd do what they ask. They're working in their own interests, don't kid yourself about that; everything they're doing they're doing for their own country, not for ours. But if what's good for them benefits us all, thank God for it. I imagine the request came to you from your friend Rosalinda?"

"We talked for hours yesterday; she left a letter for me this morning, though I haven't read it yet. I presume it's instructions."

"Everywhere people are saying that Beigbeder only has a matter of days left as a minister. It looks like they're going to kick him out for exactly this reason, for becoming friendly with the English. I imagine he's mixed up in this somewhere, too."

"Both of them had the idea," I confirmed.

"Well, he should have put the same effort into getting us out of the other war that they got us into in the first place, but that's in the past and there's nothing to be done about it now. What we have to do is look to the future. You'll decide, child. You've asked my advice and I've told you what I think: with a great deal of pain in my heart, but understanding that it's the most responsible thing to do. It will be hard for me, too: if you leave, I'll go back to being alone, and I'll have to live again with the uncertainty of not hearing from you. But yes, I think you should go to Madrid. I'll stay here and keep the workshop going. I'll find someone to help me, you needn't worry about that. And God knows when it'll all be over."

I couldn't reply. I no longer had any excuses. I decided to go outside onto the street, to get some air. I had to think.

CHAPTER THIRTY-EIGHT

I walked into the Palace Hotel at noon one day in the middle of September, with the confident stride of someone who had spent half her life strutting along the hallways of the best hotels on the planet. I was in a suit of *laine glacée* the color of thick blood, and my hair had been recently cut to just above the shoulder. On my head was a sophisticated felt hat with feathers on it, from the studio of Madame Boissenet in Tangiers: a real pièce de résistance, which (according to her) was how the elegant women in occupied France referred to such hats. The outfit was complemented by a pair of crocodile shoes with ultra high heels, which I'd obtained from the best shoemaker on the Boulevard Pasteur. In my hands a matching handbag and a pair of calfskin gloves dyed pearl grey. Two or three heads turned as I passed. I didn't react.

Behind me a bellhop was carrying a *nécessaire de voyage,* two Goyard suitcases, and a few more hatboxes. The rest of the baggage, the furniture, and the shipment of fabrics would be arriving by truck the following day, having made it across the Strait without any trouble — as they were bound to do, given that the customs transit papers were stamped and restamped till they appeared to be the most official documents in the universe, courtesy of the Spanish Ministry of Foreign Affairs. I, meanwhile, had arrived by plane; it was the first time I had flown in my life. From the Sania Ramel Aerodrome to Tablada in Seville; from Tablada to Barajas. I left Tetouan with my Spanish papers in the name of Sira Quiroga, but someone altered the passenger list so that I wouldn't appear on it under that name. During the course of the flight I used my little emergency sewing scissors to cut my old passport into a thousand shreds, which I hid in a knotted handkerchief; after all, it was a document from the Republic, which wouldn't be of any use to me in the New Spain. I landed in Madrid with a brand-new Moroccan passport. Alongside the photograph an address in Tangiers and my newly acquired identity: Arish Agoriuq. Strange? Not particularly. It was just my name and surname written back to front, with the *h* that my neighbor Félix had added in the early days of the business left just where it was. It wasn't really a proper Arab name, but it sounded foreign, and it wouldn't arouse suspicion in Madrid, where no one had a clue what people were called down there in the land of the Moors, down there in the land of Africa, in the words of the old paso doble.

In the days leading up to my departure I followed all the instructions in Rosalinda's long letter, word for word. I made contact with the people I was supposed to in order to get hold of my new identity. I chose the best materials from the shops she recommended and ordered them to be sent with the bills to a local address, of whom I never discovered. I went back to Dean's Bar and ordered a Bloody Mary. If my decision had been no, I would have had to settle for a modest lemonade.

492

The barman served me, impassive. He made comments — as though reluctantly — on what might have seemed just banalities: that the previous night's storm had wrecked one of the awnings; a boat named *Jason* sailing under an American flag was due to dock the following Friday at ten in the morning with a cargo of English merchandise. From that innocuous comment I was able to extract the information I needed. On that Friday at the specified hour I headed for the American embassy in Tangiers, a beautiful Moorish mansion stuck right in the medina. I informed the soldier who was controlling access to the building that I was there to see Mr. Jason. He lifted a heavy internal telephone and announced in English that his visitor had arrived. After receiving instructions, he hung up and invited me into an Arab courtyard surrounded by whitewashed arches. There I was met by an official who almost without a word led me swiftly through a labyrinth of corridors, stairways, and galleries to a white terrace in the highest part of the building.

"Mr. Jason," he said simply, gesturing toward a man at the far side of the roof terrace, then vanished, trotting back down the stairs.

This man had extremely thick eyebrows, and his name wasn't Jason, but Hillgarth. Alan Hillgarth, naval attaché of the British embassy in Madrid and coordinator of the activities of the Secret Intelligence Service in Spain. A wide face, ample brow, and dark hair perfectly parted and combed back with brilliantine. He approached me, dressed in a grey alpaca suit whose quality I was able to recognize even at a distance. He walked confidently, holding a black leather briefcase in his left hand, and then introduced himself, shaking my hand and inviting me to take a few moments to enjoy the view. It was indeed impressive. The port, the bay, the whole strait, and a strip of land beyond.

"Spain," he said, pointing to the horizon. "So near, and yet so far away. Shall we sit?"

He gestured toward a wrought iron bench and we sat down. He drew a small metal box of Craven A cigarettes from his jacket pocket. I accepted one and together we smoked, looking out to sea. We could barely hear any sounds from nearby, just a few voices in Arabic wafting up from the nearby streets, and from time to time the shrill sounds of the gulls that were flying over the beach.

"Everything is almost ready in Madrid and awaiting your arrival," he announced at last.

His Spanish was excellent. I didn't reply, I had nothing to say — all I wanted was to hear his instructions.

"We've rented an apartment on Calle Núñez de Balboa — do you know where that is?"

"Yes, I worked near there for a bit."

"Mrs. Fox is taking charge of furnishing it and getting it ready. Via intermediaries, naturally."

"I understand."

"I know she's already got you up to speed, but I think it would be best for me to remind you. Colonel Beigbeder and Mrs. Fox are in an extremely delicate position right now. We're all expecting the colonel's dismissal from the ministry; it would appear that it won't be long in coming, and it'll be a dreadful loss to our government. Right now Mr. Serrano Suñer, the minister of governance, has just left for Berlin: they've arranged for him to meet von Ribbentrop, Beigbeder's counterpart, and then Hitler. The fact that

Spain's own minister of foreign affairs isn't involved in this trip but staying behind in Madrid is an indication of how fragile his position is. In the meantime, the colonel and Mrs. Fox are collaborating with us, bringing us some very interesting contacts. Everything, naturally, is happening in a clandestine fashion. Both are closely followed by agents of certain bodies that are rather unfriendly, if you'll allow the euphemism."

"The Gestapo and the Falange," I noted, recalling Rosalinda's words.

"I see you're already well informed. Yes, in fact. We don't want the same to happen to you, though I can't guarantee that we'll be able to avoid it. But don't get too worried. Everyone in Madrid watches everyone else: everyone is under suspicion for something and nobody trusts anybody, but fortunately for us there isn't a lot of patience around: everyone seems to be in a tearing hurry, so if they don't manage to find anything interesting, in a few days they forget about the target and move on to the next one. That notwithstanding, if you do think you're being watched, let us know and we'll try to find out who's doing it. And above all, keep calm. Move about quite naturally, don't try to throw them off, and don't get nervous, you understand me?"

"I think so," I said, without sounding very convinced.

"Mrs. Fox," he said, changing the subject, "is getting the ball rolling in anticipation of your arrival; I think she's already secured you a handful of potential clients. Which is why — and now that autumn is already almost upon us — it would be good for you to get yourself installed in Madrid as soon as possible. When do you think you could do it?"

"Whenever you say."

"Thank you for being so obliging. We've taken the liberty of arranging a flight for you for next Tuesday — does that suit you?"

I discreetly rested my hands on my knees — I was afraid they'd start to shake.

"I'll be ready."

"Excellent. As I understand it, Mrs. Fox has already told you a bit about the aims of your mission."

"More or less."

"Well, I'm going to give you some further details now. What we need from you, to begin with, is to send us periodic reports about certain German women, and other Spanish women, who we expect will shortly become your clients. As Mrs. Fox has told you, the shortage of fabrics has been turning into a serious problem for Spanish dressmakers, and we know firsthand that there are a number of women living in Madrid who are eager to find someone who can offer them dressmaking skills as well as materials. That's where you'll come in. If our predictions are correct, your collaboration will be extremely valuable to us, since right now our contacts with the German authorities in Madrid are nil, and contacts with the Spanish authorities almost nonexistent, with the exception of Colonel Beigbeder, and him not for too much longer, I fear. The information we want to get hold of through you will be largely on the movements of the Nazi colony living in Madrid and of a few Spaniards connected to them. Following each one of them individually is quite beyond our capacities, which is why we thought that through their wives and girlfriends we might get some idea of their contacts, their relationships and activities. All clear so far?"

"Yes, all clear."

"Our primary interest is to learn in advance of the social plans of the German community in Madrid: the events they're organizing, which Spaniards they're in contact with, where they meet and how often. A great deal of their strategic activity is carried out more in social events than through office work, so to speak, and we'd like to get people we trust infiltrating them. When they go to these functions the Nazi representatives are usually accompanied by their wives, and we assume that they have to go appropriately dressed. We hope, therefore, that you'll be able to get advance information about where your clothes are going to be worn. Do you think that would be possible?"

"Yes, it's quite usual for clients to talk about all that. The problem is that my German is very limited."

"We've already thought about that. We've arranged a little help for you. As I'm sure you know, Colonel Beigbeder spent several years as military attaché in Berlin. Working in the embassy kitchens at the time was a Spanish couple with two daughters; apparently the colonel was very good to them, helped them out with some problems, took an interest in the girls' education, and in short they had a good relationship, which was interrupted when he was posted to Morocco. Well, when they heard that the former attaché had been named the new minister, the family — who had been back in Spain for a few years — got in touch with him, asking his help again. The mother died before the war and the father suffers from chronic asthma and can barely leave the house; he doesn't have any formal political affiliation either, which suits us very well. The father asked Beigbeder to find work for his daughters, and now we're going to offer them some, if you'll agree. They're two young women, aged seventeen and nineteen, who understand and speak German absolutely fluently. I don't know them personally, but Mrs. Fox interviewed them both a few days ago and was quite satisfied. She's asked me to say that you won't miss Jamila with them in the house. I don't know who Jamila is, but I hope you understand the message."

I smiled for the first time since the conversation had begun.

"Very well. If Mrs. Fox thinks they are acceptable, I will, too. Can they sew?"

"I don't think so, but they can help you to take care of the house and maybe you can teach them some of the basics of sewing. In any case, you have to be clear that these girls shouldn't know what you're secretly involved in, so you'll have to come up with some way for them to help you but without ever letting them see why you're interested in the things you ask them to translate when you don't understand. Another cigarette?"

He took the Craven A box out again, and once again I accepted.

"I'll deal with them, don't worry about that," I said after slowly exhaling the smoke.

"Well then, let's move on. As I've said, our main interest is to keep up to date with the social lives of the Nazis in Madrid. But we're also keen to know about their movements and the contact they have with Germany: if they travel to their country and what for; if they receive visitors, who these visitors are, how they mean to receive them . . . I n short, any sort of extra information that might be of interest to us."

"And what will I do with this information if I'm able to get hold of it?"

"As to how you are to transmit the information you can get your hands on, we've been considering the matter at some length, and we think we've come up with a way to start. Perhaps this won't be the definitive method of communication, but we think it's worth putting to the test. The SOE uses a number of codes with differing levels of security. Sooner or later, however, the Germans always end up breaking them. It's very common to use codes based on literary works — poems, especially. Yeats, Milton, Byron, Tennyson. Well, we're planning to try something different. Something much simpler, and at the same time more befitting the circumstances. Do you know what Morse code is?"

"The one from the telegraphs?"

"Precisely. It's a code where letters and numbers are represented through intermittent signals — audio signals on the whole. These audio signals also have a very simple graphic representation, however, by means of a system of dots and short horizontal dashes. Look."

He drew a medium-sized envelope from his briefcase and out of it took a sort of chart on a piece of card. The letters of the alphabet and numbers from zero to nine were listed in two columns. Beside each of them was the corresponding combination of dots and dashes to identify them.

"Now imagine you want to transcribe some

word — Tangiers, say. Do it out loud."

"Dash. Dot dash. Dash dot. Dash dash dot. Dot dot. Dot. Dot dash dot. Dot dot dot."

"Perfect. Try to visualize what it would look like now. No, better still, write it down on a piece of paper. Here, use this," he said, taking a silver retractable pencil from the inside pocket of his jacket. "Right here, on this envelope."

Again following the table, I transcribed the seven letters: — .——. ——. .. . .——. ...

"Excellent. Now look at it closely. Does it remind you of anything? Does it look at all familiar?"

I looked at what I'd written. I smiled. Of course it looked familiar. How was I not going to recognize something I'd spent my whole life doing?

"It's like stitches," I said quietly.

"Exactly," he confirmed. "That's the point I'm getting at. You see, what we're planning is for any information you get your hands on to be passed on to us using this system. Obviously you'll have to refine your skills of summarizing so as to express what you want to say using as few words as possible, otherwise each sequence will go on forever. And I want you to hide it in such a way that it looks like a pattern, a sketch or something along those lines, anything you might associate with a dressmaker without arousing any suspicion. Do you understand?"

"I think so."

"Well then, let's try it out. Imagine that the message is 'Dinner at the home of the Baroness de Petrino on the fifth of February at eight. The Countess de Ciano will be going with her husband.' I'll explain who these people are later, don't worry about that. First thing you have to do is get rid of any superfluous words — articles, prepositions, et cetera. That way we can shorten the message considerably. Look: 'Dinner home Baroness Petrino five February eight p.m. Countess Ciano going with husband.' And now, after stripping away the extra words, we're going to invert the order. Instead of transcribing the code from left to right as usual, we're going to do it from right to left. And you'll always start in the bottom right-hand corner of the surface you're working on, going upward. Imagine a clock face showing four twenty, now imagine the minute hand starts going backward, do you follow me?"

"Yes — please, let me try."

He handed me the folder and I put it down on my lap. I took his pencil and drew an apparently amorphous shape that covered most of the sheet. Rounded on one side, sharp at the corners. Impossible to interpret for an inexpert eye.

"What's that?"

"Wait," I said, without looking up.

I finished outlining the figure and positioned the pencil at the bottom right-hand corner of the figure, and running parallel to the edge I transcribed the letters in Morse code. Replacing the dots with shorter dashes. Long dash; short dash, long dash; another long dash, then a short dash . . . When I'd finished, the whole internal perimeter of the outlined shape was edged with what looked like an innocent bit of stitching.

"Ready?" he asked.

"Not yet." Out of the little sewing case that I always carried in my handbag I took a pair of scissors and with them cut out the shape, leaving a border of just a quarter inch around it.

"You said you wanted something associated with

a dressmaker, didn't you?" I said, handing it over to him. "Well, there you are: the pattern for a puff sleeve. With the message in it."

The straight line of his pursed lips curved slowly into the faintest of smiles.

"Brilliant," he murmured.

"I can prepare the patterns for various parts each time I have to communicate with you. Sleeves, fronts, collars, waists, cuffs, sides, depending on how long the message needs to be. I can do as many shapes as I have messages I need to get to you."

"Brilliant, brilliant," he repeated in the same tone, still holding the cut-out shape between his fingers.

"And now you have to tell me how I'm to get them to you."

He spent a few more seconds looking at my handiwork with a slight expression of surprise; finally he put it away inside his briefcase.

"Very well, then, let's go on. Unless there's any order to the contrary, we'd like you to send us information twice a week. To begin with, it'll be Wednesdays in the early afternoon and Saturday mornings. We thought the hand-overs should happen in two different places, both of them public. And in neither case should there be the least possible contact between you and the person collecting."

"Won't it be you doing it?"

"No, not whenever I can help it. And especially never in the place we've assigned for the Wednesday drop-offs. I'd find it difficult: I'm talking about Rosa Zavala's beauty salon, next to the Palace Hotel. It's currently the best establishment of its kind in Madrid, or at least the one most highly thought of among foreigners and the more refined Spanish women. You should become a regular customer and start frequenting the place. In fact, it's best that you should fill your life with routines so that your movements become highly predictable and seem altogether natural. In this salon there's a room the moment you go in on the right-hand side, which is where the customers leave their handbags, hats, and outdoor coats. One of the walls is completely covered in little individual lockers where ladies can leave their belongings. You'll always use the last one of these lockers, the one in the corner at the back of the room. At the entrance there's usually a young girl, not particularly bright: her job is to help the customers with their things, but a lot of them refuse her help and do it for themselves, so it won't seem strange that you do the same; just leave her a good tip and she'll be happy. When you open the door to your locker and are about to leave your things inside, it'll almost completely obscure your body, so it'll be possible for people to guess at your movements but no one will ever be able to see what you're up to. That's when you'll take out the thing you need to get to us, rolled into a tube; you should leave it on the top shelf of the locker. Be sure to push it to the back so it's not visible from the outside."

"And who'll collect it?"

"Someone we trust, you needn't concern yourself with that. Someone who that same afternoon, very shortly after you leave, will go into the salon to get her hair done just as you did earlier, and will use the same locker."

"And if it's taken?"

"That doesn't usually happen because it's the

503

last one. If that happens, however, use the one before it. And if that one is, too, then the next. And so on. Is that clear? Now repeat it all back to me, please."

"Hairdresser's on Wednesday early afternoon. I'll use the last locker, I'll open the door, and as I'm putting my things inside I'll take out of my bag, or wherever I've been keeping it, a tube in which I've placed all the patterns I have to get to you."

"Tie them with a ribbon or a rubber band. Sorry to interrupt — go on."

"Then I'll leave the tube on the top shelf, pushed all the way back. Then I'll close the locker and go get my hair done."

"Very good. Now for the Saturday delivery. For those days we've planned to work at the Prado Museum. We have a contact who has infiltrated the cloakroom staff — for these days it would be best for you to arrive at the museum with one of those folders that artists use, do you know the ones I mean?"

I remembered the portfolio that Félix used for his painting classes in Bertuchi's school.

"Yes, I won't have any trouble getting hold of one of those."

"Perfect. Take that with you, and inside it you should have basic drawing equipment — a notebook, some pencils — in short, the usual sort of thing, which you can get your hands on anywhere. You should also add whatever you have to get to me, this time in a large open envelope. For identification you should attach a cutting of fabric in some bright color to it, fixed with a pin. You'll go to the museum every Saturday around ten in the morning; it's a very common activity among the foreigners living in the capital. Arrive with your portfolio filled with things that mark you out as a dressmaker, in case you're being watched at all: older drawings, sketches of outfits — again, things related to your usual work."

"Very well. What do I do with the portfolio when I arrive?"

"You hand it over at the cloakroom. You ought always to leave it with some other item — an overcoat, a raincoat, some small purchase, so it isn't too conspicuous on its own. Then head for one of the rooms and wander around at a leisurely pace, enjoy the paintings. After half an hour, return to the cloakroom and ask them to give the portfolio back to you. Then take it to one of the rooms and sit and draw for at least another half hour. Look at the clothes that appear in the paintings, pretend that they're inspiring you for your future creations; behave, in short, in whatever way you think most convincing, but first check that the envelope has been removed from inside. If it hasn't, you'll need to return on the Sunday and repeat the operation, though I don't think that should be necessary: using the hairdresser's salon as cover is new, but we've used the Prado before and it's always been satisfactory."

"And I won't know who's picking up the patterns there either?"

"Again, someone trustworthy. Our contact in the cloakroom will take charge of passing the envelope from your portfolio to another belonging left there by another contact the same morning — that's something they can do very easily. Are you hungry?"

I looked at the time. It was past one. I didn't know whether I was hungry or not: I'd been so busy absorbing each syllable that I'd barely noticed the time passing. I looked out to sea again; it seemed to be a different color now. Everything else was just the same: the light on the white walls, the gulls, the voices in Arabic from the street. Hillgarth didn't wait for my reply.

"I'm sure you must be. Please, come with me."

CHAPTER THIRTY-NINE

We ate alone in a wing of the American embassy that we reached by going down still more corridors and staircases. On the way Hillgarth explained to me that the building was the result of a number of extensions to an old main house; that explained why it lacked uniformity. The room we arrived in wasn't exactly a dining room; it was more like a little drawing room with few furnishings and lots of paintings of old battles in golden frames. The windows, firmly closed despite the beautiful day, looked out over a courtyard. In the middle of the room someone had set out a platter of veal for two. A waiter with a military crew cut served us some rare-cooked meat accompanied by roast potatoes and salad. On a side table he left two plates of cut-up fruit and a coffee service. As soon as he'd finished filling our glasses with wine and water, he disappeared, closing the door behind him without a sound. The conversation resumed its former course.

"When you arrive in Madrid you'll be staying at the Palace for a week; we've made a reservation in your name — I mean, in your new name. Once you're there, you're to go in and out all the time, get yourself seen. Go to shops, walk over to your new residence to familiarize yourself with it. Go for walks, go to the cinema; in short, move about as you like. With just two restrictions."

"Which are?"

"The first is that you stay within the bounds of the smarter parts of Madrid. Don't make any contact with people from outside that world."

"You're telling me not to set foot in my old neighborhood or see my old friends or acquaintances, right?"

"Precisely. No one should be able to link you to your past. You're a new arrival in the capital: you don't know anybody, and no one knows you. In the event that you run into anyone who happens to recognize you, do whatever you can to deny it. Be rude if you have to, do anything you need to, just don't let anyone discover that you aren't who you claim to be."

"I'll bear that in mind, don't worry. And the second restriction?"

"Absolutely no contact with anyone of British nationality."

"You mean I can't see Rosalinda Fox?" I said, unable to hide my disappointment. Even though I knew our relationship couldn't be public, I'd been counting on being able to have her support in private; being able to rely on her experience and her instincts whenever I found myself in trouble.

Hillgarth wiped his mouth with his napkin and took a sip of water before replying.

"I'm afraid that's the way it has to be. I'm sorry. Not her, nor anyone else who's English, except for me and then only in absolutely unavoidable situations. Mrs. Fox knows all about this: if by any chance you find yourselves in the same place, she knows she's not to approach you. And as much as possible avoid contact with North

Americans as well. They're our friends — you can see how well they treat us," he said, opening his hands as though taking in the whole room with them. "Regrettably they are not equally good friends of Spain and the Axis countries, so try to keep your distance from them, too."

"Very well," I agreed. I didn't like the restriction that prevented me from seeing Rosalinda, but I knew I had no choice but to observe the rule.

"And talking about public places, there are a few where I'd advise you to allow yourself to be seen," he continued.

"Go on."

"Your hotel, the Palace. It's full of Germans, so keep going there regularly with any excuse even when you're no longer staying there. Eating at the grill there, that's very fashionable right now. Go for a drink, or to meet up with a client. Of course, in the New Spain it doesn't look good for women to go out on their own, smoke or drink or dress showily. But remember that you're not a Spaniard anymore, but a foreigner from a country that's a bit exotic, newly arrived in the capital, so you can behave accordingly. Go by the Ritz often, too, that's another nest of Nazis. And especially to Embassy, the tearoom on the Paseo de la Castellana — do you know it?"

"Of course," I said. I refrained from telling him about the times in my childhood when I'd pressed my nose against the glass, my mouth watering at the sweets on display. Cream tarts garnished with strawberries, butter pastries, charlotte russes. In those days I never even dreamed that crossing that threshold would one day be within my reach, let alone the range of my pocketbook. In one of life's little ironies, I was now, years later, being

509

asked to go there as often as possible.

"The owner, Margaret Taylor, is Irish, and she's a great friend of ours. Right now it's perfectly possible that Embassy is the most strategically interesting spot in Madrid, because there — a small shop not much larger than seven hundred and fifty square feet — you find us all, members of the Axis and Allies alike, meeting in one place, without any apparent friction. Separately, of course, each with his own. But you'll often find Baron von Stohrer, the German ambassador, there at the same time as the top brass of the British diplomatic corps as he drinks his lemon tea, or I'll find myself at the bar shoulder to shoulder with my German counterpart. The German embassy is almost exactly across the street and ours is very close by, too, on the corner of Fernando el Santo and Monte Esquinza. As well as hosting a large number of foreigners, Embassy is the main meeting point for a lot of Spaniards from the noblest families: it would be hard to find more aristocratic titles all together anywhere in Spain than you'll meet there at aperitif time. Most of these aristocrats are monarchists, and Anglophiles, meaning that on the whole they tend to be on our side, so that in terms of gathering information they're not very valuable to us. But it would be interesting if you could get some clients from that milieu, because they are the class of women whom the Germans admire and respect. The wives of the high command in the new regime tend to be a different matter entirely: they know little of the world, they're much more demure, they don't wear haute couture, they enjoy themselves much less, and they naturally don't frequent Embassy for champagne cocktails before lunch; you understand what I mean?"

"I'm getting the picture."

"If we're unlucky enough that you end up in any serious trouble, or you think you have any information you need to get to me urgently, Embassy at one p.m. is the place you can contact me any day of the week. Let's say it's my undercover meeting place for a number of our agents: it's a place that's so brazenly exposed that it's extremely unlikely to arouse the least suspicion. To communicate we'll use a very simple code: if you need to meet me, come in with your bag on your left arm; if you've just come for a drink and to be seen, carry it on your right. Remember: left, problem; right, normal. And if the situation is an absolute emergency, drop the bag as soon as you've come in, as though it's just carelessness or an accident."

"What would you consider an absolute emergency?" I asked. I sensed that his words, which I didn't completely understand, hid something extremely unappealing.

"Direct threats. Severe coercion. Physical aggression. Breaking into your home."

"And what will you do with me then?" I asked, once I'd swallowed the knot that had formed in my throat.

"That depends. We'll analyze the situation and act, depending on the risk. In the most severe case we would abort the operation, try to put you somewhere safe, and evacuate you as soon as possible. In an intermediate situation, we'd study a variety of ways we could protect you. In any case, rest assured that you can count on us, that we'll never leave you out on your own."

"Thank you."

"You needn't thank us — that's our job," he said as he cut one of the last pieces of meat on his plate. "We're confident that everything will work out well — the plan we've designed is very safe, and the information you're going to be passing us isn't high risk, for the moment. Would you like some dessert?"

This time once again he didn't wait for me to accept his offer or refuse it; he just got up, gathered up the plates, took them over to the side table, and returned with others filled with cut-up fruit. I watched his quick, precise movements, perfect for someone whose absolute priority was efficiency, someone unused to wasting a second of his time or allowing himself to be distracted by trivialities and vagueness. He sat back down, stabbed at a piece of pineapple, and continued with his instructions as though there had been no interruption.

"In case we're the ones who need to make contact with you, we'll use two channels. One will be the Bourguignon florist on the Calle Almagro. The owner — a Dutchman — is another good friend of ours. We'll send you flowers. White, maybe yellow; in any case, they'll be light colored. The red ones we'll leave to your admirers."

"Very thoughtful," I remarked ironically.

"Look at the bunch of flowers very carefully," he went on without acknowledging the comment. "There will be a message inside. If it's something innocent, it'll be in a simple handwritten card. You should always read it a number of times, try to figure out whether the apparently trivial words might have a double meaning. When it's something more complex, we'll use the same code as you, inverted Morse code transcribed on the rib-

512

bon tied around the flowers: undo the bow and decode the message in just the way you'd write it yourself — right to left, in other words."

"Very well. And the second channel?"

"Embassy again — not the place itself, though, but the candies. If you receive a box unexpectedly, you'll know it's come from us. We'll arrange for it to leave the shop with the message inside it, which will also be in code. Take a good look at the cardboard box and the wrapping paper."

"Such gallantry," I said with a touch of sarcasm. He didn't seem to notice it, or if he did he didn't show it.

"It's simply how we deal with it: using unlikely mechanisms to transmit confidential information. Coffee?"

I hadn't yet finished my fruit but I accepted. He filled the cups, having first unscrewed the top part of a metallic receptacle. Miraculously the liquid came out hot. I had no idea what it was, this machine that could pour out the coffee that had been there for at least an hour as though it had just been prepared.

"A thermos, a great invention," he said, noticing my curiosity. He took out several pale slim folders from his briefcase and placed them in a pile in front of him. "Next I'm going to show you the characters we're most interested in having you watch for us. Our interest in these women might increase or decrease with time. Or indeed disappear entirely, though I doubt that. Most likely we'll be adding new names; we'll be asking you to concentrate your attentions on one of them in particular or to try to track down certain specific pieces of information. For now, though, these are the people whose agendas we want to learn about right away."

He opened the first folder and took out a few typewritten sheets. In the top corner there was a photograph affixed with a metal clip.

"Baroness de Petrino — of Romanian origins. Maiden name, Elena Borkowska. Married to Josef Hans Lazar, head of press and propaganda for the German embassy. Her husband is one of our top targets for acquiring information: he's an influential man with immense power. He's very capable and extremely well connected in the Spanish regime, in particular with the most powerful of the Falangists. On top of that he's extremely gifted in public relations: he organizes wonderful parties at his Castellana mansion and invites dozens of journalists and businessmen whose support he buys by regaling them with food and drink that he brings over directly from Germany. His lifestyle is scandalous in a Spain that's suffering so much right now; he's a sybarite and a lover of antiques — he's probably been able to get hold of the most valued pieces, paid for by other people's hunger. Ironically it would appear that he's Jewish and of Turkish origin, something he's careful to hide. His wife is completely a part of his hectic social life and is just as showy as he is in her incessant public appearances, so we have no doubt that she'll be one of your first clients. We're hoping that she's one of the ones who'll bring you the most work, both in sewing and when it comes to passing us information about her activities."

He didn't give me time to see the photograph, because he immediately closed the folder and pushed it across the tablecloth toward me. I was about to open it but he stopped me.

"Leave that for later. You can take all these files

away with you today. You'll have to memorize the information and destroy the papers and photographs as soon as you're able to retain them in your head. Burn everything. It's absolutely critical that these dossiers do not travel to Madrid and that nobody but you should know what's in them, is that clear?"

Before I'd had the chance to say yes, he'd opened the next folder and continued.

"Gloria von Fürstenberg. Of Mexican origin in spite of her name. Be very careful what you say in front of her because she'll be able to understand everything. She's an incredible beauty, really elegant, the widow of a German aristocrat. She has two children and somewhat catastrophic economic circumstances, which is why she's constantly on the hunt for a new rich husband or, in the absence of one of them, any gullible man with a fortune who might offer her enough support to maintain her grand lifestyle. Which is why she's always attached to powerful men; she's linked to various lovers, including the Egyptian ambassador and Juan March, the millionaire. Her social activity never stops, always within the Nazi community. She'll give you a lot of work, too, you can count on that, though she might also take some time to pay her bills."

He closed the folder back up and passed it to me; I put it on top of the previous one without opening it. He went on to the third.

"Elsa Bruckmann, born the Princess of Cantacuzène. A millionaire, passionate admirer of Hitler though much older than him. They say she was the person who introduced him to Berlin's lavish social scene. She's given an absolute fortune to the Nazi cause. Lately she's been living in

Madrid, in the ambassador's residence, we don't know why. That notwithstanding, she seems to be very comfortable here, and she's another who never misses a social event. She's known to be a bit eccentric and quite indiscreet, so she may be an open book when it comes to divulging relevant information. Another cup of coffee?"

"Yes, but I can serve myself. Please go on, I'm listening."

"Very well — thank you. The last of the German ladies: the Countess Mechthild Podewils, tall, beautiful, about thirty, separated, a good friend of Arnold, one of the top spies active in Madrid and high up in the SS; his surname is Wolf — she calls him *Wölfchen,* the diminutive, Little Wolf. She is extremely well connected with both Germans and Spaniards, the latter belonging to the aristocratic and governmental circles, including Miguel Primo de Rivera y Sáenz de Heredia, brother to José Antonio, who founded the Falange. She's a fully fledged Nazi agent, though she may not know it herself; they say she doesn't understand a word of politics or espionage, but they pay her fifteen thousand pesetas a month to tell them everything she sees and hears, and in Spain today that's an absolute fortune."

"I'm sure it is."

"Now we're onto the Spaniards. Piedad Iturbe von Scholtz, Piedita to her friends. The Marchioness of Belvís de las Navas, married to Prince Max of Hohenlohe-Langenburg, a rich Austrian landowner, a legitimate member of European royalty, though he's spent half his life in Spain. In principle he does support the German cause because that's his country, but he's in regular contact with us and with the Americans because we're important

516

to his business interests. Both are extremely cosmopolitan and they don't seem to like the Führer's ravings one bit. The truth is, they're a charming couple and very well regarded in Spain, but they're still on the fence, if I might put it like that. We want to keep an eye on them to learn whether they're leaning more toward the German side than to ours, you understand?" he said, closing the relevant file.

"I understand."

"And the last of the highest-valued targets, Sonsoles de Icaza, Marchioness of Llanzol. She's the only one we're not interested in for her consort, who's a soldier and aristocrat thirty years older than her. Our target here is her lover: Ramón Serrano Suñer, minister of governance and secretary-general of the movement. The minister of the Axis, we call him."

"Franco's brother-in-law?" I asked, surprised.

"The very same. Their relationship is quite brazen, on her part especially — she boasts publicly and without the slightest hesitation about her affair with the second most powerful man in Spain. This woman is as elegant as she's arrogant, and very tough, so be careful. She'll be of very considerable value to us, however, for all the information we'll be able to get from her about those movements and contacts of Serrano Suñer's that aren't public knowledge."

I hid my surprise at this comment. I knew that Serrano was a gallant man — he'd shown me that himself when he retrieved the powder compact that I'd dropped on the floor at his feet — but at the time he'd also seemed to me to be a discreet, restrained man; it was hard to imagine him participating in a scandalous extramarital affair

517

with a stunning lady of the noblest birth.

"We have one more folder left, with information about a number of people," Hillgarth went on. "According to the data we have, the wives of those mentioned here are less likely to have an urgent need to visit an elegant fashion house the moment it opens, but just in case they do it wouldn't do you any harm to memorize their names. And in particular you should learn their husbands' names well, as they're our real targets. It's also quite possible that they'll be mentioned in your other clients' conversations, so you should keep alert. Let me make a start; I'll go through these ones quickly, and you'll have plenty of time to go over them yourself more calmly. Paul Winzer, the Gestapo's strongman in Madrid. Very dangerous; he's feared and hated even by many of his compatriots. He's Himmler's henchman in Spain — Himmler's the head of the German secret services. He's barely forty, but already he's an old dog — round glasses, a distracted gaze. He has dozens of collaborators right across Madrid, so beware. Next: Walter Junghanns, one of our most particular nightmares. He's the main saboteur of cargoes of Spanish fruit headed for Great Britain: he plants bombs that have already killed a number of workers. Next: Karl Ernst von Merck, a distinguished member of the Gestapo, highly influential within the Nazi party. Next: Johannes Franz Bernhardt, businessman . . ."

"I know him."

"Excuse me?"

"I know him from Tetouan."

"How well do you know him?" he asked slowly.

"Little. Very little. I've never spoken to him, but we were at the same reception from time to time

518

when Beigbeder was commissioner there."

"And does he know you? Would he be able to recognize you in a public place?"

"I doubt it. We've never exchanged a single word, and I don't imagine he'd remember those meetings."

"Why do you think that?"

"Women can tell perfectly when a man looks at us with interest, or when he looks at us as you might examine a piece of furniture."

He remained silent a few moments, as though considering what he'd heard.

"I suppose that's feminine psychology," he said at last, skeptical.

"Exactly."

"And his wife?"

"I made her a jacket once. You're right, she'd never be one of the especially sophisticated ones. She's not the kind of woman who'd mind at all about wearing last season's wardrobe."

"Do you think she'd remember you, that she'd recognize you if you ran into each other somewhere?"

"I don't know. I don't think so, but I can't guarantee it. In any case, if she did, I don't think it'd be too problematic. My life in Tetouan isn't in contradiction with anything I'm going to be doing from now on."

"Don't be so sure. Out there you were a friend of Mrs. Fox, and by extension eventually of Colonel Beigbeder, too. In Madrid nobody can know anything about that."

"But I was barely with them at public events, and as for our private meetings Bernhardt and his wife have no way of knowing anything about them. Don't worry, I don't think there should be any problems."

"I hope you're right. In any case, Bernhardt is more or less on the fringes of intelligence matters: his world is that of business. He's the front man of the Nazi government in a hugely complex web of German corporations operating in Spain: transport, banking, insurance . . ."

"Does he have anything to do with HISMA?"

"HISMA, the Spanish-Moroccan Transportation Corporation, became a small business when they made the move back to the Peninsula. Now they operate under the auspices of another more powerful firm, SOFINDUS. But tell me, how come you've heard about HISMA?"

"I heard it mentioned in Tetouan during the war," I replied vaguely. This wasn't the moment to go into detail about the negotiation between Bernhardt and Serrano Suñer; that was something we'd left far behind.

"Bernhardt," he went on, "has a bunch of political informers on his payroll, but what he's really always after is information of commercial value. We're assuming you're never going to meet him — in fact he doesn't even live in Madrid but on the eastern coast. They say that Serrano Suñer himself paid for the house by way of thanks for services rendered; we don't know if the truth is quite that extreme or not. One more very important thing about him, though."

"Tell me."

"Wolfram."

"What?"

"Wolfram," he repeated. "A mineral of vital importance for the manufacturing of components for artillery projectiles for the war. We think Bernhardt's in negotiations with the Spanish government to sell him mining concessions in Galicia and Extremadura in order to get hold of small sites so that he can buy directly from their owners. I don't imagine people will be talking about these things in your workshop, but if you happen to hear anything about this, you're to let us know at once. Remember: *wol-fram.* Sometimes they call it tungsten. It's written down here, in the section on Bernhardt," he said, pointing at the document.

"I'll bear it in mind."

We each lit another cigarette.

"Well then, let's go on to some things you should avoid. Are you tired?"

"Not in the least. Please, go on."

"As to clients, there's one small group you should avoid at all costs: the employees of the Nazi administration. It's easy to recognize these women: they're extremely showy and arrogant, they go around with a lot of makeup on, heavily perfumed and showily dressed. The truth is that they have no social pedigree at all and relatively modest professional qualifications, but their salaries are astronomical by current Spanish standards and they spend them ostentatiously. The wives of the powerful Nazis despise them, and they themselves — in spite of their apparent conceit — hardly dare to cough in front of their superiors. If they show up at your workshop, get rid of them without a second thought: you don't want them there, they'll drive away the more desirable clientele."

"I'll do as you say, don't worry about it."

"As for public establishments, we advise against your presence at places like Chicote, Riscal, Casablanca, or Pasapoga. They're full of nouveaux riches, black marketeers, parvenus from the regime, and theater people. Company that isn't to be recommended in your circumstances. As far as possible, restrict yourself to the hotels I've already mentioned to you, to Embassy, to other safe places like the Puerta de Hierro club or the casino. And needless to say, if you manage to get invited to dinners or parties with the German women in private homes, you're to accept at once."

"I will," I said, not adding how much I doubted that I'd ever be invited to any such thing.

He looked at his watch and I did the same. There wasn't much light left in the room; we were already surrounded by a premonition of nightfall. Around us there wasn't a sound, just a thick smell from the lack of ventilation. It was past seven in the evening; we'd been together since ten in the morning, Hillgarth spewing information like a hose, and me absorbing it through all my senses to take in the tiniest details, digesting facts, trying to allow every last fiber of my being to become imbued with his words. The coffee had been finished some time ago, and the cigarette butts were overflowing the ashtray.

"Well, we're almost done now," he announced. "All I have left are a few recommendations. The first of these is a message from Mrs. Fox. She's asked me to tell you that — both in terms of your own appearance and your sewing work — you should try to be either bold and daring or pure elegance in its utmost simplicity. Either way, she advises you to avoid the conventional, and especially not to be mainstream, because if you do, she thinks there's a risk that the workshop will fill up with the wives of big shots from the regime looking for modest jacket suits to go to Mass on Sundays with their husbands and children."

I smiled. Rosalinda, incorrigible and unmistakable, even in messages delivered by someone else.

"Coming from that person, I'll follow the advice without a second thought," I said.

"And now, finally, our own suggestions. First: read the papers, keep up to date with the political situation, in Spain and also abroad, though bear in mind that all the information will always be slanted toward the German side. Second: always keep calm. Get yourself into character and convince yourself you are who you are, no one else. Act fearlessly, confidently: we can't offer you diplomatic immunity, but I guarantee you that whatever happens you'll always be protected. And our third and final piece of advice: be extremely wary in your personal life. A beautiful, single foreign woman will always attract all manner of playboys and opportunists. You can't imagine how much confidential information has been revealed irresponsibly by careless agents in moments of passion. Be alert, and please do not share anything with anyone, anything at all of what you've heard here today."

"I won't, you can count on it."

"Perfect. We trust you and hope that your mission will be successful."

He began to gather up his papers and organize his briefcase. The moment had arrived that I'd been fearing all day: he was getting ready to leave and I had to stop myself from asking him to stay, to keep talking and giving me more instructions, not to let me fly free just yet. But he was no longer looking at me, so he probably hadn't noticed my reaction. He moved at the same pace with which he'd delivered his sentences, one by one, over the course of the previous hours: quick, direct, methodical, reaching the end of every subject without wasting a single second on banalities. While he put away his belongings, he passed on his final recommendations.

"Remember what I've told you about the files: study them and then make them disappear immediately. Someone's going to accompany you now to a side door; there's a car waiting close by to take you home. Here is the airline ticket and money for your initial expenses."

He handed me two envelopes. The first, slimmer, contained my documentation to cross the skies to Madrid. The second, thicker, was filled with a big wad of banknotes. He kept talking as he deftly fastened the clasps of the briefcase.

"The money should cover your preliminary expenses. The stay at the Palace and your rent for the new atelier are being taken care of by us; that's all been arranged already, as has the salary for the girls who'll be working for you. Income for the work will be all yours. Just the same, if you do need any more cash, let us know right away: we have an open budget line for these operations, so there are no problems as far as financing is concerned."

I was all ready now, too. I was holding the folders against my chest, sheltered in my arms as though they were the child I'd lost years earlier rather than an assortment of information about a swarm of undesirables. My heart was still in its place, obeying my internal orders not to rise up to my throat and choke me. Finally we got up from that table on which nothing was left but what looked like the innocent remains of a lengthy lunch: plates, empty coffee cups, a full ashtray, and two displaced chairs. As though nothing had happened there but a pleasant conversation between a couple of friends who — chatting away, relaxed, between one cigarette and the next — had been catching up on each other's lives. Except that Captain Hillgarth and I weren't friends. And neither of us was remotely interested in the other's past, or our presents. All we were concerned about, the two of us, was the future.

"One last detail," he warned.

We were about to leave; he already had his hand on the doorknob. He drew it back and looked at me fixedly from under his thick eyebrows. In spite of the long session we'd had together, he still looked exactly as he had in the morning: not a hair out of place, his tie still impeccably knotted, his shirt cuffs spotless. His face remained impassive, not particularly tense, nor particularly relaxed. The perfect image of a man capable of handling himself with perfect self-control in any situation. He lowered his voice till it was little more than a hoarse murmur.

"You don't know me, and I don't know you. We've never met before. And as for your enrollment into the British Secret Intelligence Service, from this moment you're no longer the Spanish citizen Sira Quiroga to us, nor the Moroccan Arish Agoriuq. You're just the SOE special agent code-named Sidi, with a base of operations in Spain. The least conventional of the recent conscripts, but just the same, one of our own."

He held out his hand. Firm, cold, self-confident. The firmest, coldest, most self-confident hand I'd ever shaken in my life.

"Good luck, Agent Sidi. We'll be in touch."

CHAPTER FORTY

No one but my mother knew the real reasons for my unexpected departure. Not my clients, not even Félix and Candelaria: I deceived everyone with the excuse that I was going to Madrid to empty out our old house and settle a few matters. My mother would have to invent little lies to justify the length of my absence: business, some indisposition, perhaps a new boyfriend. We weren't worried that anyone would suspect any intrigue or connect the dots: even though the channels of transport and communication were fully functional by now, contact between the Spanish capital and North Africa remained very limited.

I did, however, want to say good-bye to my friends and to ask them wordlessly to wish me luck, so we organized a lunch for my last Sunday. Candelaria came dressed like a fine lady in her own right, with her bun thick with hairspray, a necklace of fake pearls, and the new outfit we'd sewn for her a few weeks earlier. Félix came over with his mother, whom he hadn't been able to get rid of. Jamila was with us, too — I was going to miss her like a little sister. We toasted with wine and soda water and said good-bye with noisy kisses and earnest wishes for a good journey. It wasn't until I closed the door when they left that I

526

realized how much I was going to feel their absence.

With Commissioner Vázquez I used the same strategy, but I immediately realized that the lie would never stick. How would I be able to pull the wool over his eyes? He knew all about the outstanding debts in Madrid and the panic I felt at having to face up to them. He was the only person who sensed that there was something more complex behind my innocent departure, something I couldn't talk about. Not to him, not to anybody. Perhaps that was why he preferred not to inquire. In fact he barely said a word: he just did what he always did, he looked at me with his explosive gaze and advised me to take care. Then he accompanied me to the exit to shield me from the dirty slobberings of his subordinates. At the police station door we said good-bye. Until when? Neither of us knew. Perhaps soon, or perhaps never.

Apart from the fabrics and sewing tools I carried to Spain, I also bought a decent number of magazines and a few pieces of Moroccan craftwork in the hope of giving my Madrid workshop an exotic air suited to my new name and my supposed past as a prestigious dressmaker in Tangiers. Embossed copper trays, lamps with pieces of glass in a thousand colors, silver jugs, a few ceramic pieces, and three large Berber rugs. A little bit of Africa right in the center of our exhausted Spain.

When I went into the grand apartment on Núñez de Balboa for the first time, everything was ready, waiting for me. The walls painted in glossy white, the oak floor recently polished. The layout, organization, and order were a replica on a larger scale of my Sidi Mandri house. The first section was a series of three adjoining rooms, three times the size of their equivalent in my old place. The ceilings infinitely higher, the balcony doors more stately. I opened one, but when I looked out I didn't find Dersa Mountain, or the Ghorgiz, or the air fragrant with traces of orange blossom and jasmine, or lime wash on the neighboring walls, or the voice of the muezzin calling to prayer from the mosque. I closed it quickly, cutting off my melancholy. Then I walked on. In the last of the three main rooms were the rolls of material that had come over from Tangiers, a paradise of dupioni silk, guipure lace, muslin, and chiffon. Their shades ranged from the palest memory of sand on the beach to fire red, pink, coral, and every possible blue between the sky of a summer morning and a turbulent sea on a stormy night. The fitting rooms — two of them — felt double their size thanks to the imposing three-way mirrors framed in gilt marquetry. The large cutting table, ironing boards, naked mannequins, tools, and threads, just the usual. Beyond that, my own space: immense, disproportionate, ten times more than I needed. I immediately sensed Rosalinda's hand in the whole setup. Only she knew how I worked, how I'd organized my house, my things, my life.

In the silence of my new home I was visited once again by the question that had been drumming in my head for a couple of weeks. Why, why, why? Why had I agreed to this, why was I embarking on this uncertain, lonely adventure, why? I still had no answer. Or at least, no definitive answer. Perhaps I'd accepted out of loyalty to Rosalinda. Perhaps because I thought I owed it to my mother and my country. Perhaps I hadn't done it for anyone else, but just for myself. What's certain is that I'd said yes, let's do it: fully aware of what I was doing, with a promise to myself that I'd take on the job with determination and without hesitation, fears, or insecurities. There I was, squeezed into the character of the nonexistent Arish Agoriuq, walking through her new habitat, heels clicking down the stairs, dressed with all the style in the world and ready to transform herself into the falsest dressmaker in Madrid. Was I afraid? Yes, intense fear was clinging to the pit of my stomach. But in check. Tamed. Under my control.

My first message reached me via the building's porter: the girls who would be working for me would be turning up the following morning. They arrived together, Dora and Martina, with an age difference of two years. They looked alike, and yet different at the same time, as though complementing each other. Dora seemed to be in better shape, Martina won out on features. Dora seemed smarter, Martina sweeter. I liked them both. What I didn't like, however, were the wretched clothes they were wearing, their faces of chronic hunger, and their shyness. Fortunately these things were quickly resolved. I took their measurements and soon I had a couple of uniforms ready for each of them: the first people to make use of my arsenal of fabrics. With a few of the banknotes from Hillgarth's envelope I sent them to the La Paz market in search of provisions.

"And what are we to buy, señorita?" Dora asked, eyes like saucers.

"Whatever you can find. They're saying there isn't much of anything right now. Whatever you see — didn't you tell me you can cook? Well then, get to it."

The timidity took some time to disappear, though it did dissolve bit by bit. What were they afraid of, what was it that made them so introverted? Everything. Working for the strange African lady they believed me to be, the imposing building that housed my new home, the fear of not knowing how to get by in a sophisticated dressmaker's atelier. As the days went by, however, they adapted themselves to their new lives: to the house, to the daily routines, to me. Dora — the elder — turned out to have a knack for sewing and was soon able to start helping me. Martina, meanwhile, was more like Jamila, more like I'd been in my youth — she liked being out on the street, the errands, the constant coming and going. Between them they managed the household; they were efficient and discreet, good girls, as they said in those days. They mentioned Beigbeder once; I never told them that I knew him. Don Juan, they called him. They remembered him fondly: they associated him with Berlin, with a time in the past from which they still retained vague memories and the residuals of the language.

Everything progressed according to Hillgarth's expectations. More or less. The first clients appeared; some of them were the ones he'd predicted, others weren't. The season opened with Gloria von Fürstenberg, beautiful, majestic, her ebony-black hair combed into thick plaits that gathered at the back of her neck like the black crown of an Aztec goddess. Sparks flew from her large eyes when she saw the fabrics I had. She examined them, felt them, determined their caliber, asked about prices, discarded some of them immediately, tested the effect of others against her body. With her expert hand she chose the ones that best suited her out of the ones that weren't excessively overpriced. She also ran her expert eye over the magazines, pausing on the designs that complemented her body and style. That Mexican woman with the German name knew exactly what she wanted, so she didn't ask me for any advice, nor did I bother to give her any. Finally she opted for a gown in chocolate-colored silk gazar and an Ottoman evening coat. The first time she came alone and we spoke Spanish. For the first fitting she brought a friend, Anka von Fries, who ordered a wide dress in georgette and a ruby-colored velvet cloak decorated with ostrich feathers. As I listened to them talking to each other in German, I asked Dora to come in and join us. Well dressed, well fed, well groomed, the girl retained no trace of the terrified little sparrow who'd arrived with her sister just a few weeks earlier: she'd been transformed into a slender, silent assistant who kept mental notes of everything she heard and discreetly left the room every few minutes to jot the details down in a notebook.

"I always like to keep exhaustive records of all my clients," I'd warned Dora. "I want to understand what they say so I know where they're going, who they're going around with, and what plans they have. That way I may be able to get hold of new clients. I'll be in charge of whatever they say in Spanish, but when they're speaking German you're responsible for that."

If Dora thought there was anything strange about the close attention paid to our clients, she didn't show it. She probably thought it was quite reasonable, that this was normal behavior in this business that was so new to her. But of course it wasn't. Noting down every syllable of names, positions, places, and dates that came out of the mouths of one's clients isn't normal in the least, but we did it every day, devoted and methodical, like good students. Then at night I'd go through my notes and Dora's, extract any information I thought might be of interest, synthesize it into brief phrases, and finally transcribe it into inverted Morse code, adapting the long and short dashes to the straight and curving lines of the patterns that would never be part of a complete piece of work. The bits of paper with the handwritten notes were transformed to ashes in the small hours of each morning with a simple match. By the following dawn not a word of what had been written down remained, only a handful of messages hidden in the outlines of a lapel, a waistband, or a camisole.

I acquired Baroness de Petrino as a client, too; wife to the powerful press officer Lazar, she was less spectacular than the Mexican woman but had far more money to spend. She chose the most expensive fabrics and didn't skimp on indulging her whims. She brought me more clients — two German women, as well as a Hungarian. Over the course of many mornings my atelier was transformed into their main social meeting place, buzzing with a jumble of languages. I taught Martina to prepare tea the Moorish way, with the mint we planted in clay pots on the kitchen windowsill. I instructed her how to handle the teapots, how to casually pour the boiling water into the little glasses with silver filigree; I even taught her to paint her eyes with kohl and sewed her a silky gardenia-patterned caftan to give her an exotic air. A stand-in for my Jamila, so that I would have her with me always.

Everything was going well, surprisingly well. I was moving ahead in my new life with complete confidence, entering the finest places with a sure step. When I was with my clients I acted with aplomb and decisiveness, protected by the armor of my fake exoticism. I brazenly muddled words from French and Arabic into my conversations; I might have been saying all kinds of nonsense in these languages, bearing in mind that I was only repeating simple expressions I'd heard on the streets of Tangiers and Tetouan whose precise meaning and usage I didn't know. I made sure that in my polyglotism — as false as it was chaotic — I didn't allow any bursts of the broken English I'd learned from Rosalinda to slip out. My position as a newly arrived foreigner allowed me a useful refuge for covering up my weak points and avoiding treacherous territory. No one seemed at all interested in my origins, however: they were more interested in my materials and what I was able to make from them. My clients would talk freely in the atelier; they seemed to feel comfortable there. They'd chat to one another and to me about what they'd done, what they were going to do, their common friends, their husbands and their lovers. And meanwhile Dora and I worked tirelessly — with materials, designs, and measurements out in the open; with secret notes in the back room. I didn't know whether all those pieces of information I recorded every day had any value at all to Hillgarth and his people, but just in case, I tried to be minutely rigorous. On Wednesday afternoon, before my session at the hairdresser's, I'd leave the tube of patterns in the predetermined locker. On Saturdays I'd visit the Prado, marveling so much at the artwork that I'd sometimes

533

forget that I had something important to do there besides being enraptured by the paintings. Nor did I have the slightest problem with the transfer of envelopes filled with coded patterns: everything progressed so smoothly that my nerves didn't even get a chance to gnaw at my innards. My portfolio was always received by the same person, a thin, bald employee who was probably also the one responsible for extracting my messages, although he never gave me the slightest sign of complicity.

I went out from time to time, not too often. I went to Embassy on a few occasions at aperitif time. On my first visit I spotted Captain Hillgarth far off drinking whiskey on the rocks as he sat amid a group of compatriots. He noticed me right away, too — he couldn't not have. But I was the only person who knew it — he didn't make the slightest move at my arrival. I held my bag firmly in my right hand and we pretended not to have seen each other. I greeted a couple of clients who publicly praised my workshop to some other ladies; I drank a cocktail with them, received appreciative glances from several young men, and from the fake vantage point of my cosmopolitanism I discreetly watched the people around me. Class, frivolity, and money in their purest form spread across the counter and around the tables of a small corner bar decorated without the least bit of showiness. There were women in outfits made of the finest wools, alpacas, and tweeds, soldiers with swastikas on their armbands, and others in foreign uniforms I didn't recognize, all of them with cuffs adorned with military stripes and many-pointed stars. There were incredibly elegant ladies dressed in two-piece suits, with three strands of hazelnut-sized pearls around their necks, with impeccable lipstick on their lips and divine hats, caps, and turbans on their perfectly coiffed heads. There were conversations in several languages, discreet laughter, and the sound of glass against glass. And floating in the air, subtle traces of perfumes from Patou and Guerlain, the feeling of cosmopolitan savoir faire and the smoke of a thousand Virginia cigarettes. The Spanish war that had just come to an end and the brutal conflict that was devastating Europe seemed to be tales from another galaxy in that environment of pure, simple sophistication.

At one corner of the counter, standing erect and proud, solicitously greeting her customers while simultaneously controlling the incessant movement of the waiters, I saw the woman I assumed to be the proprietress of the establishment, Margaret Taylor. Hillgarth hadn't told me in what kind of way he collaborated with her, but I had no doubt that it was more than a simple exchange of favors between the owner of a watering hole and one of her regular customers. I watched her as she handed a bill to a Nazi officer in a black uniform, with a swastika armband and high boots that shone like mirrors. That foreign woman, who looked both austere and distinguished, who had to have been some years past forty already, was surely another piece in the secret mechanism that the British naval attaché had activated in Spain. I couldn't tell whether she and Captain Hillgarth exchanged glances at any point, whether any kind of silent message passed between them. I looked at them again out of the corner of my eye before I left. She was in discreet conversation with a young white-jacketed waiter, to whom she seemed to be giving instructions. Captain Hillgarth was still at his table, listening with interest to what one of his friends was saying. The whole group around him seemed to be just as alert to the words of the young man, who looked more carefree than the rest. From my vantage point on the other side of the shop I could see his theatrical gesticulations, perhaps imitating somebody. When he'd finished they all burst into laughter, and I heard the naval attaché crowing delightedly. Maybe it was only my imagination teasing me, but for a fraction of a second I thought he'd focused his gaze on me and winked.

Madrid was entering autumn, while the number of my clients increased. I hadn't yet received any flowers or candies, from Hillgarth or anyone else. Nor did I want any; I didn't have time. Because if there was one thing that I was beginning to lack in those days, it was just that: time. The popularity of my new atelier spread quickly; word was getting around about the stunning fabrics to be found there. The number of orders increased daily, and I began to struggle to get them all done; I found myself having to deliver orders late and to postpone fittings. I was working hard, harder than ever before in my life. I went to bed very late, toiling through the small hours, and barely had any time to rest. There were days when the tape measure remained hanging around my neck from morning until the moment I got into bed. Money flowed constantly into my little safe box, but I was so uninterested that I didn't even bother to stop and count it. Sometimes my memory — with a twinge of nostalgia — would return to those early days in Tetouan. The nights counting the banknotes one by one in my Sidi Mandri room, calculating anxiously how long it would be before

I could clear my debt. Candelaria rushing back from the Jewish exchange houses with a roll of pounds sterling secreted in her cleavage. The almost childish delight the two of us took in dividing up the total: half for you, half for me, the Matutera would say, month after month, and may we never go without again, my precious. It felt as though there were centuries separating me from that other world, and yet only four years had passed. Four years like four eternities. Where was she now, that Sira who had had her hair cut by a little Moorish girl with the sewing scissors in the kitchen of the La Luneta boardinghouse? Where had they gone, the poses I'd practiced so many times in my friend's cracked mirror? They'd been lost between the folds of time. Now I had my hair done in the best salon in Madrid, and those self-assured gestures were more mine than my own teeth.

My hard work earned me more money than I'd ever dreamed of; I charged high prices and was constantly receiving hundred-peseta bills bearing the face of Christopher Columbus, five hundreds with the face of Don John of Austria. Yes, I was earning a lot, but a moment came when I couldn't give any more of myself, and I had to notify Hillgarth through the pattern for a shoulder. It was raining that Saturday over the Prado Museum. As I gazed in delight at the paintings of Velázquez and Zurbarán, the inoffensive cloakroom man received my portfolio and, within it, an envelope with eleven messages that — as ever — would reach the naval attaché without delay. Ten of them contained conventional information abbreviated in the agreed manner. "Dinner 14th, home Walter Bastian, Calle Serrano, Lazars attending. Bode-

537

muellers travel San Sebastián next week. Lazar wife making negative comments about Arthur Dietrich, her husband's adjutant. Gloria von Fürstenberg and Anka Frier visit German consul end October. Various young men arrived last week from Berlin, staying Ritz, Friedrich Knappe receives, trains them. Husband Frau Hahn dislikes Kutschmann. Himmler arrives Spain 21 October, government and Germans preparing large reception. Clara Stauffer gathering material for German soldiers, her house Calle de Galileo. Dinner Puerta de Hierro club, date not sure, Count and Countess Argillo to attend. Heberlein organizing lunch his house, Toledo, Serrano Suñer, and Marchioness Llanzol invited." The final message was different, and transmitted something more personal. "Too much work. Not time for everything. Fewer clients or seek help. Please inform."

The next day a beautiful bunch of white gladioli arrived at my door. They were delivered by a young man in a grey uniform whose cap bore the embroidered name of the florist: Bourguignon. I read the card first. "Always ready to fulfill your desires." And a scribble by way of a signature. I laughed: I could never have imagined the cold-blooded Hillgarth writing that ridiculously soppy phrase. I moved the bouquet to the kitchen and undid the ribbon that was tying the flowers together; after asking Martina to get them into some water, I shut myself up in my room. The message leapt out of an interrupted line of short and long dashes: "Hire someone utterly trustworthy, no Red past or political affiliation."

Order received. And uncertainty had come with it.

CHAPTER FORTY-ONE

When she opened the door I didn't say a word; I just looked at her, containing my desire to throw my arms around her. She looked at me confused, running her eyes over me. Then she tried to meet my eyes, but perhaps the *voilette* of my hat prevented her from seeing them.

"What can I do for you, señora?" she finally said.

She was thinner. The passage of the years was visible on her. As petite as ever, but thinner and older. I smiled. She still didn't recognize me.

"I bring you greetings from my mother, Doña Manuela. She's in Morocco, she's gone back to sewing."

She looked at me, surprised, not understanding. She was turned out with her usual care, but her hair hadn't been dyed for a couple of months and the dark suit she was wearing had accumulated the shine of many winters.

"I'm Sira, Doña Manuela. Sirita, the daughter of Dolores, your employee."

She looked at me again, up and down. I bent down to bring myself to her level and lifted the little piece of netting on my hat so she could see my face.

"It's me, Doña Manuela, it's Sira. Don't you remember me?" I whispered.

"Holy Mother of God, Sira! My child, I'm so delighted to see you!" she said at last.

She hugged me and began to cry as I struggled not to let myself be set off, too.

"Come in, my child, come in, don't just stand there in the doorway," she said when she was finally able to get her emotions under control. "But how incredibly elegant you are, child, I wouldn't have recognized you. Come in, come into the living room. Tell me, what are you doing in Madrid, how are things, how is your mother?"

She led me through to the main room and once again homesickness engulfed me. How many Feasts of the Magi had I, as a young girl, visited that room, holding my mother's hand, how excited I'd become as I tried to guess what gift would be waiting for me there. I remembered Doña Manuela's home on the Calle Santa Engracia as a large, opulent apartment; not as fancy as the one on Zurbano where she'd set up her workshop, but infinitely less humble than ours on the Calle de la Redondilla. On this visit, though, I discovered that my childhood recollections had infected my memory with a perception that distorted reality. The house that Doña Manuela had lived in for her whole life as a single woman was neither large nor opulent. It was just a mediocre home, poorly laid out, cold, dark, and full of somber furnishings with worn, heavy velvet curtains that barely allowed any light in; an apartment covered with water stains, in which all the pictures were faded engravings and yellowed crochet doilies filled every corner.

"Sit, child, sit. Would you like a drink? Can I make you a little coffee? It's not really coffee, it's roasted chicory, you know how hard it is to get hold of provisions these days, but a little bit of milk will hide the taste, though even that gets more watery every day, what can we do? I have no sugar as I've given my ration card to a neighbor for her children; at my age it hardly matters —"

I interrupted her, taking her hand.

"I don't want anything, Doña Manuela, don't worry about it. I've just come to see you to ask you something."

"Tell me."

"Are you still sewing?"

"No, child, no. Ever since we closed the workshop in thirty-five I've not gone back to it. I've done the odd little thing for a friend or out of a sense of duty, but no more than that. If my memory serves, your wedding dress was the last big thing I did, and, well, since after all . . ."

I preferred to dodge the subject she was referring to, so I didn't let her finish.

"Would you like to come and sew with me?"

It took her a few seconds to reply, perplexed.

"Go back to work, you say? Go back to the old job, just like we used to do?"

I nodded, smiling, trying to inject a trace of optimism into her bewilderment. But she didn't answer me right away; first she changed the direction of the conversation.

"And your mother? Why have you come to ask me instead of sewing with her?"

"I've told you, she's still in Morocco. She went there during the war, I don't know if you knew."

"I knew, I knew," she said softly, as though fearing that the walls would hear her and pass on the secret. "She showed up here one afternoon, just all of a sudden, unexpectedly, like you've done now. She told me everything was arranged for her to go to Africa, that you were there, and that somehow you'd managed to arrange for someone to get her out of Madrid. She didn't know what to do; she was frightened. She came to ask my advice, to see what I thought of it all."

My impeccable makeup didn't allow her to see the distress that her words were causing: I'd never imagined that my mother would have had any hesitation between staying and going.

"I told her to go, to leave as soon as possible," she went on. "Madrid was a hell. We all suffered so much, child, all of us. Those on the left, fighting day and night to stop the Nationalists getting in; those on the right, longing for just that, in hiding so as not to be found and taken in by the secret police. And those — like your mother and me — who weren't of either faction, waiting for the horror to be over so that we could get on with our lives in peace. All this without a government in charge, without anyone imposing a bit of order in that chaos. So I advised her that yes, she should go, she should get out of this agony and not pass up the opportunity to be reunited with you."

Despite feeling overwhelmed by emotion, I decided not to ask anything about that meeting, which was now so long ago. I'd gone to see my old boss with a plan for the immediate future, so I chose to steer the conversation in that direction.

"You were right to encourage her, you don't know how grateful I am to you for that, Doña Manuela," I said. "She's doing terrifically well now, she's happy and working again. I set up a workshop in Tetouan in thirty-six, just a few months after the war started. Things were calm there, and even though the Spanish women weren't in the mood for parties and dresses, there were some foreigners for whom the war hardly mattered. So they became my clients. When my mother arrived, we went on sewing together. And now I've decided to come back to Madrid and start again with a new workshop."

"And you've returned alone?"

"I've been alone a long time, Doña Manuela. If you're asking me about Ramiro, that didn't last long."

"So Dolores has stayed behind there without you?" she asked, surprised. "But she left specifically to be with you . . ."

"She likes Morocco: the climate, the atmosphere, the quiet life. We had very good clients and she's made friends, too. She preferred to stay. But I missed Madrid too much," I lied. "So we decided that I'd come back, I'd start to work here, and once the second atelier was up and running then we'd decide what to do."

She looked at me for a few endless seconds. Her eyelids were drooping, her face covered in wrinkles. She must have been sixty-something now, perhaps already approaching seventy. Her curved back and the calluses on her fingers showed traces of each and every one of those tough years she had spent slaving away with needles and scissors. First as a simple seamstress, then later as an employee in a workshop, then as the owner of a business, and finally as a sailor without a ship, inactive. But in no way was she done yet. Her eyes, full of life, small and dark like little black olives, reflected the sharpness of someone who still had a good head on her shoulders.

"You're not telling me everything, child, right?" she said at last.

The sly fox, I thought admiringly. I'd forgotten how smart she was.

"No, Doña Manuela, I'm not telling you everything," I acknowledged. "I'm not telling you everything because I can't. But I can tell you a part of it. The thing is, in Tetouan I got to know some important people, people who are still very influential nowadays. They persuaded me to come to Madrid, to set up a studio and sew for certain high-class clients. Not for women close to the regime, but mainly for foreign ladies and for monarchist Spanish aristocrats, the ones who think Franco is usurping the king's place."

"But why?"

"Why what?"

"Why do your friends want you to sew for these ladies?"

"I can't tell you. But I need you to help me. I've brought some magnificent materials over from Morocco, and there's a terrible shortage of fabrics here. The word has got around and my reputation has spread, but I have more clients than I'd expected and I can't handle them all on my own."

"But why, Sira?" she repeated slowly. "Why are you sewing for these women, what do you and your friends want from them?"

I pursed my lips resolutely shut, determined not to say a word. I couldn't. I shouldn't. But an alien force seemed to be dragging the words up from the pit of my stomach. As though Doña Manuela were back in charge and I was no more than an adolescent apprentice, when she had every right to demand explanations from me because I'd skipped a whole morning's work going to buy three dozen mother-of-pearl buttons in the Plaza de Pontejos. The words were spoken by my entrails, and by yesterday, not by me myself.

"I'm sewing for them in order to get information about what the Germans in Spain are doing. Then I pass the information on to the English."

I bit my bottom lip the moment I'd spoken the final syllable, aware of how careless I'd been. I regretted having broken my promise to Hillgarth not to reveal my mission to anyone, but it had already been said and there was no going back. I thought about clarifying the situation — adding that it was the best thing for Spain to remain neutral, that we were in no state to face another war, all those things they'd been so insistent about to me. But there was no need, because before I had the chance to add anything I could see a strange gleam in Doña Manuela's eyes and the trace of a smile on one side of her mouth.

"With the compatriots of the queen Doña Victoria Eugenie, child, whatever you need me to do. Just tell me when you want me to start."

We went on talking all afternoon, planning out how we'd divide up the work, and at nine o'clock the next morning she was at my house. She was all too happy to take on a secondary role in the workshop. Not having to deal with the clients was almost a relief to her. We complemented each other perfectly: just as she and my mother had done for all those years, but the other way around. She took to her new position with total humility, accommodating herself to my life and rhythm, getting along with Dora and Martina, bringing to us her experience and an energy that would have been the envy of many women thirty years younger. She adapted easily to my being the one in charge, to my less conventional lines and ideas, and to taking on a thousand little tasks that so often before she would delegate to the simple sewing girls. Returning to the breach after long years of inactivity was a gift to her, and like a patch of poppies in the April rains she emerged from her dark days and was revived.

With Doña Manuela in charge of the back room, my working days became calmer. We both toiled long hours, but I was finally able to move without too much rush and enjoy a few spells of free time. I began to have more of a social life: my clients encouraged me to attend a thousand events, keen to show me off as their great discovery of the season. I accepted an invitation to a concert of German military bands at El Retiro park, a cocktail party at the Turkish embassy, a dinner at the Italian embassy, and the occasional lunch in fashionable places. Pests began to buzz around me: passing bachelors, potbellied married men with the means to keep a handful of sweethearts, attractive diplomats from the most exotic places. After a couple of drinks and a dance I was fighting them off. The last thing I needed at that moment was a man in my life.

But it wasn't all parties and recreation, far from it. Although Doña Manuela made my day-to-day life less harried, absolute peace and quiet didn't follow. Not long after I'd unloaded the heavy burden of working alone, a new storm cloud appeared on the horizon. The simple fact that I was walking the streets with less haste, being able to pause at a shop window and slacken the rhythm of my comings and goings, made me notice something that I hadn't seen till then, something that Hillgarth had warned me about during that long dessert in Tangiers. I realized I was being followed. Perhaps they'd been doing it for a while and my constant rush had stopped me from taking any notice. Or maybe it was something new, which happened by chance to coincide with Doña Manuela's entry into Chez Arish. But the fact was, a new shadow seemed to have settled over my life. A shadow that was not even constant, not even total; perhaps this was why it wasn't easy for me to become fully aware of its proximity. I thought at first that the things I was seeing were just my imagination playing tricks on me. In autumn, Madrid was full of men with hats and raincoats with the collars up; that look was actually very common in those postwar times, and thousands of replicas filled the streets, offices, and cafés. The figure who had stopped, turning away from me, as soon as I'd stopped to cross Castellana wasn't necessarily the same one who a couple of days later pretended to stop to give alms to a ragged blind man while I was looking at some shoes in a store. Nor was there any good reason why his raincoat should be the same one that followed me that Saturday to the entrance of the Prado Museum. Or for it to be the same as the back that I saw hiding discreetly behind a column at the Ritz grill while I was having my lunch with my client Agatha Ratinborg, a supposed European princess with highly dubious roots. It was true, there was no definitive way of confirming that all those raincoats scattered along streets and days converged in a single individual, and yet somehow my gut told me that the owner of them all was one and the same man.

The tube of patterns that I prepared that evening to leave in the hairdresser's salon contained seven conventional messages of average length and a personal one with just two words:

"Being followed." I finished them late — it had been a long day of fittings and sewing. Doña Manuela hadn't gone home till after eight; following her departure I'd finished up a couple of invoices that needed to be ready first thing in the morning, I'd taken a bath, and then, still wrapped in my crimson velvet dressing gown, I had a couple of apples and a glass of milk for my dinner, standing up, leaning against the kitchen sink. I was so tired that I was barely hungry; no sooner had I finished than I sat down to encode the messages, and once these were done and the day's notes sensibly burned I began turning out the lights to go to bed. Halfway down the corridor I stopped dead. I thought at first that I'd heard a single isolated knock, then it was two, three, four. Then silence. Till they started up again. It was clear where they were coming from — someone was at the door. He or she was knocking, knuckles against the wood, rather than ringing the bell. Dry knocks, getting less and less far apart, till they'd become a nonstop pounding. I stood stock still, gripped by fear, unable to go forward or back.

But the knocking didn't stop, and its insistence forced me to react: whoever it was had no intention of going away without seeing me. I pulled the belt of my dressing gown tight, swallowed, and made my way slowly toward the door. Very slowly, without making the slightest sound, and still terrified, I lifted the cover of the peephole.

"Come in, for God's sake, come in, come in," was all I was able to whisper after opening the door.

He came in quickly, nervous. Unsettled.

"That's it, that's it, I'm out, it's all over."

He didn't even look at me; he talked like a madman, as though speaking to himself, to the air, or to nothing. I led him quickly to the living room, almost pushing him, made fearful by the idea that someone in the building might have seen him. The apartment was dark, but before I'd even turned on a light I tried to get him to sit down, to relax a little. He refused. He kept walking from one end of the room to the other, looking around wildly and repeating the same thing over and over again.

"That's it, that's it, everything's finished, it's all over."

I turned on a small corner lamp, and without asking I poured him a generous glass of cognac.

"Here," I said, forcing him to take the glass in his right hand. "Drink," I commanded. He obeyed, shaking. "And now sit down, relax, and tell me what's going on."

I hadn't the faintest idea why he should have shown up at my house after midnight, and even though I was sure he would have been discreet in his movements his attitude was so changed that he might no longer have cared about such things. It had been more than a year and a half since I'd seen him, since the day of his official farewell from Tetouan. I preferred not to ask him anything, not to pressure him. Quite clearly this visit wasn't a mere courtesy, but I decided it would be best to wait for him to calm down: perhaps then he'd tell me himself what it was he wanted from me. He sat down with the glass held in his fingers; he took another drink. He was dressed in civilian clothes, in a dark suit with a white shirt and striped tie; without his peaked cap, his stripes, and the sash across his chest that I'd seen him wear on so many formal occasions and that he wouldn't remove until the event was over. He seemed to calm down a bit and lit a cigarette. He puffed on it, staring out into the void, surrounded by the smoke and his own thoughts. I didn't say a word; I just sat down on a nearby chair, crossed my legs, and waited. When the cigarette came to an end he leaned forward slightly to put it out in the ashtray. And from that position he raised his eyes at last and spoke.

"They've dismissed me. It's going public tomorrow. The press release has already been sent to the *Official State Bulletin* and the press; in seven or eight hours the news will be out there on the streets. Do you know how many words they're going to eliminate me with? Eighteen. I've counted them. Look."

He drew a handwritten note out of his jacket pocket and showed it to me. It bore just a couple of lines that he recited from memory.

" 'Don Juan Beigbeder y Atienza leaves his role as minister for foreign affairs, with my gratitude for his services rendered.' Eighteen if you don't count the 'Don' before my name, which will probably be abbreviated. If not, it'll be nineteen. It'll be followed by the statement from El Caudillo, in which he thanks me for the services I've performed. That one's a real joke."

He drained the glass in a gulp and I poured him another.

"I knew I'd been walking a tightrope for months, but I didn't expect the blow to be so sudden. Or so degrading."

He lit another cigarette and went on talking through puffs of smoke.

"Yesterday afternoon I was with Franco in El Pardo; it was a long, relaxed meeting. At no point

550

was he critical, nor did he make any speculations about my possible replacement. You know things have been tense lately, ever since I've been allowing myself to be seen openly with Ambassador Hoare. Actually I left the meeting quite satisfied, thinking that Franco was considering my ideas, that perhaps he'd finally decided to give some weight to my opinions. How could I have imagined that what he was about to do the moment I was out the door was sharpen the knife to plunge it into my back the following day. I had sought an audience with him to discuss some matters concerning his forthcoming interview with Hitler in Hendaya, knowing what a humiliation it was for me that he'd not planned for me to go with him. All the same, I wanted to talk to him, to pass on certain pieces of important information that I'd obtained through Admiral Canaris, the head of the Abwehr, the German military intelligence organization — do you know who I'm talking about?"

"I've heard the name before, yes."

"Although the position he occupies might appear rather unappealing, Canaris is a pleasant, charismatic man, and I have an extremely good relationship with him. We're both part of a strange class of rather sentimental soldiers who don't have much affection for uniforms, decorations, and barracks. In theory he's under Hitler's command, but he doesn't bow to his plans and acts quite autonomously. So much so that they say he has the sword of Damocles hanging over his head, too, just as I had these past months."

He got up from his place, took a few steps, and approached one of the balcony doors. The curtains were open.

"Best not to get too close," I warned him firmly. "You could be seen from the street."

He turned abruptly and crossed the room several times from end to end as he continued talking.

"I call him my friend Guillermo, like that, in Spanish; he speaks our language very well, he lived in Chile for a bit. A few days ago we met for lunch at the Casa Botín — he loves roast pork. I noted that he was more alienated than ever from the influence of Hitler, so much so that I wouldn't have been surprised if he'd been plotting against the Führer with the English. We talked about the absolute advisability of Spain not getting involved in the war on the side of the Axis powers, and to that end we spent the meal working on a list of provisions that Franco should ask Hitler for in exchange for agreeing to join the conflict. I'm perfectly familiar with our strategic requirements, and Canaris knows all about Germany's weaknesses, so between the two of us we compiled a roster of demands that Spain should make as nonnegotiable conditions of its participation and that Germany would be in no position to agree to, even in the medium term. The proposal included a long list of impossible requests, from territorial possessions in French Morocco and Oran to exorbitant quantities of grains and arms, and Gibraltar being taken over exclusively by Spanish soldiers; all of it, as I say, quite impossible. Canaris also advised me that he would not recommend that we begin the reconstruction of everything that had been destroyed by the war in Spain, that it would be better to leave the railways destroyed and the highways broken up so that the Germans were aware of the pitiful state of the country and how difficult it would be for their troops to get across it."

He sat back down and took another sip of cognac. Fortunately the alcohol was relaxing him. I, meanwhile, remained utterly unsettled, unable to understand why Beigbeder had come to seek me out at this time of night and in such a state to talk about his meetings with Franco and his contact with German soldiers, which had so little to do with me.

"I arrived at El Pardo with all this information and conveyed it to El Caudillo in detail," he went on. "He listened very intently, held on to the document, and thanked me for my work. He was so cordial with me that he even made a personal reference to the old times we'd shared in Africa. The Generalísimo and I have known each other for many years, did you know that? Actually apart from his ineffable brother-in-law, I think I am — sorry, I was — the only member of his government not to address him as 'sir.' Our little Franquito in charge of the Glorious National Movement — we never would have imagined such a thing. We were never great friends, in truth; actually, I don't think he's ever thought very highly of me at all — he didn't understand my lack of military enthusiasm and my desire for postings that were urban, administrative, and, if at all possible, foreign. He didn't fascinate me particularly either, I have to be honest with you; he was always so serious, so upright and dull, so competitive and obsessed with promotions and the career ladder, a real pain in the ass of a man. We were together in Tetouan; he was already a commandant, I was still a captain. Do you want me to tell you a story? When night fell all the officers used to get together in a seedy little café on the Plaza de España to have a few glasses of tea — do you remember those little cafés?"

"I remember them perfectly," I said. How could I erase from my memory the wrought iron chairs under the palm trees, the smell of kebabs and tea with mint, the subdued movement of djellabas and European suits around the central pavilion with its clay tiles, and the whitewashed Moorish arches.

Nostalgia caused him to smile briefly for the first time. He lit another cigarette and leaned back in the sofa. We were talking in near darkness, with the small lamp in the corner of the room providing the only light. I was still in my dressing gown: I hadn't found a moment to excuse myself to run and change. I didn't want to leave him alone for a single second until he was quite calm.

"One evening he didn't show up, and we all began to speculate about his absence. We came to the conclusion that he must have a girl and decided to seek out some confirmation; you know, basically just the nonsense that young officers get up to when they have too much time on their hands and not much to do. We drew lots and it fell to me to be the one to spy on him. The next day I clarified the mystery. On leaving the citadel I followed him as far as the medina and saw him go into a house, a typical Arab home. Although I found it hard to believe, I first imagined that he was having an affair with some little Muslim girl. I made some excuse to get myself into the house — I can't even remember what it was. And what do you think I found? Our man getting Arabic lessons, that's what he was up to. Because the great Africanist general, Spain's notable and unvanquished Caudillo, the savior of the nation, doesn't speak Arabic, however much he may have tried to learn. Nor does he understand the Moroccan people, nor does he care about them in the least. But I do. I care about them a great deal. And I get along with them because they're my brothers. I can understand them in the most elevated Arabic, in Cherja, the dialect of the Rif villages, in whatever dialect they speak. And that was extremely troublesome to Spain's youngest commandant, the pride of the troops in Africa. And the fact that it was I who discovered him trying to amend his fault annoyed him even more. But anyway, all youthful foolishness."

He said some words in Arabic that I didn't understand, as though to demonstrate his mastery of the language. As though I wasn't already aware of it. He drank again, and I filled the glass for the third time.

"Do you know what Franco said when Serrano put me forward for the ministry? 'You're telling me you want me to put little Juan Beigbeder in Foreign Affairs? But he's an utter lunatic!' I don't know why he's branded me a madman; perhaps because his soul is cold as ice and anyone who's a little bit more passionate than he is seems to him utterly insane. Me crazy — I hardly think so!"

He drank again. As he talked he barely looked at me, spewing out his bitterness in a ceaseless monologue. He talked and drank, talked and smoked. With rage, and without pause, while I listened in silence, unable to understand why he was telling me all this. We'd hardly ever been alone together before; he'd never addressed more than a handful of phrases to me without Rosalinda present; almost everything he knew about me came from her mouth. And yet at this moment, a moment so important in his life and his career, at this instant that marked the end of an era, for some unknown reason he had decided to confide in me.

"Franco and Serrano say I've gone crazy, that I'm the victim of the pernicious influence of a woman. The goddamned nonsense I've had to listen to lately. And the In-law-ísimo wants to lecture me on morality; he of all people, who has six or seven legitimate kids at home while he spends his days bedding a marchioness who he then takes out to the bullfights in his convertible! And on top of that they're considering including the crime of adultery in the penal code; the whole thing's a joke. Of course I like women, how could I not? I haven't shared a conjugal life with my wife for years, and I don't have to answer to anyone for the way I feel or whom I go to bed with or whom I get up in the morning with, that's all there is to it. I've had my escapades, as many as I could, to be absolutely honest with you. So? Does that make me unusual in the army or the government? No. I'm just like all the rest, but they've decided to pin a label on me, a frivolous playboy bewitched by an Englishwoman. That's just how stupid they are. They wanted my head to demonstrate their loyalty to the Germans, like Herod and the Baptist. And now they've got it, may it do them some good. But they didn't need to trample all over me to get it."

"What have they done to you?" I asked.

"Spread all kinds of calumnies about me: they've fabricated an intolerably bad reputation for me, as a depraved womanizer capable of selling out his country for a good screw, if you'll pardon the language. They've spread the story that Rosalinda has kidnapped me and forced me to betray my country, that Hoare has been bribing me, that I receive money from the Jews in Tetouan in exchange for maintaining an anti-German position. They've had me watched night and day — I've even begun to fear for my physical safety — and don't believe for a moment that I'm imagining these things. And all this because as a minister I've tried to act sensibly and put forward my ideas accordingly. I've told them that we can't just drop our relations with the British and the North Americans because our supplies of wheat and oil, which we need to stop this country from starving to death, depend on them; I've insisted that we shouldn't let Germany interfere in our domestic matters, that we should oppose their interventionist plans, that it's not in our interest to get embroiled in their war, not even for the colonial empire they think we might be able to gain by it. Do you think they've given my opinions the slightest consideration? Not a bit: not only have they not paid me the least attention, but they've also accused me of lunacy for thinking that we shouldn't bow down to an army that is passing through all Europe in triumph. Do you know what one of the divine Serrano's latest brilliant notions is, what phrase he's been repeating lately? 'War, with bread, or war without it!' What do you think of that? And now it turns out that I'm the crazy one — imagine that! My resistance has cost me the position; who knows if it might end up costing me my life, too. I've been left with nothing, Sira. My ministerial post, my military career, and my personal relations: everything, absolutely everything, dragged through the mud. And now they're

557

sending me to Ronda under house arrest, and who's to know if they haven't planned to set up a court-martial and get rid of me one fine morning with a firing squad?"

He took off his glasses and rubbed his eyes. He seemed weary. Exhausted. Old.

"I'm confused, I'm drained," he said quietly. Then he sighed deeply. "What I wouldn't give to go back, not to have ever abandoned my beloved Morocco. What I wouldn't give for this whole nightmare never to have started. Rosalinda is the only person who could console me, and she's gone. Which is why I've come to see you: to ask you to help me get my news to her."

"Where is she now?"

I'd been wondering about that question for weeks, not knowing where to go to find an answer.

"Lisbon. She had to leave at short notice."

"Why?" I asked in alarm.

"We learned that the Gestapo was after her; she had to get out of Spain."

"And as minister you weren't able to do anything?"

"Me do something about the Gestapo? Not me, not anyone, my dear. My relations with all the German representatives have been very tense lately: some members of our own government have taken it upon themselves to leak my thoughts against our possible intervention in the war and excessive Hispano-German friendship to the ambassador and his people. Though I probably wouldn't have managed anything even if I'd been on good terms with them, because the Gestapo operates quite autonomously, on the fringes of the official institutions. We learned through a leak that Rosalinda was on one of their lists. Overnight she prepared her things and flew to Portugal; we sent everything else on after her. Ben Wyatt, the North American naval attaché, was the only person who came with us to the airport; he's a great friend. No one else knows where she is. Or at least, no one should know. Now, however, I wanted to share the information with you. I'm sorry to have invaded your home at this time of night and in this state, but tomorrow they take me to Ronda and I don't know how long I'll have to go without being able to contact her."

"What do you want me to do?" I asked, finally sensing the purpose of his strange visit.

"Find some way to arrange for these letters to get to Lisbon through the diplomatic bag of the British embassy. Get them to Alan Hillgarth, I know you're in contact with him," he said as he took three thick envelopes out of his inside jacket pocket. "I've written them over the last few weeks, but I've been so closely watched that I haven't dared dispatch them via normal channels; as you'll understand, I don't even trust my own shadow right now. Today, with this business of their having formalized the dismissal, they seem to have let up a little and lowered their guard. Which is why I've been able to get here without being followed."

"Are you sure?"

"Absolutely, don't worry," he said, calming my fears. "I took a taxi — I didn't want to use the official car. There weren't any cars following us the whole way, I checked. And following me on foot would have been impossible. I stayed in the taxi till I saw the doorman bring the rubbish out; only then did I come into the house. No one saw me, you can be sure of that."

"How did you know where I lived?"

"How could I not have known? It was Rosalinda who chose this house and kept me abreast of the developments in its preparation. She was very excited about your arrival and your agreement to join with her country's cause." He smiled again with his lips closed, just tensing one side of his mouth. "I really love her, Sira, you know that? I've really loved her so much. I don't know if I'll see her again, but if I don't, tell her I'd have given my life to have had her with me on this desperately sad night. Would you mind if I poured myself another drink?"

"Of course not, no need to ask."

I'd lost count of what number he was on, probably five or six. With the next gulp, the moment of melancholy passed. He'd relaxed and didn't seem to have any intention of leaving.

"Rosalinda is happy in Lisbon, she's building a life for herself there. You know what she's like, able to adapt to anything with impressive ease."

Rosalinda Fox — there was no one like my friend for reinventing herself and starting from scratch as many times as she needed to. What an odd couple she and Beigbeder made. How different they were, and yet how well they complemented each other.

"Go see her in Lisbon when you can, she'd so enjoy spending a few days with you. Her address is on the letters I've given you: don't pass them on till you've copied it down."

"I'll try, I promise. Are you considering going to Portugal, too? What do you mean to do when all this is over?"

"When my arrest is over? How should I know, it could last years — I might never get out of it alive. The situation is very uncertain; I don't even know

560

what charges they're going to bring against me. Revolt, espionage, treason against the fatherland: any outrageous thing. But if Fortune takes my part and it's all over soon, then yes, I think I will go abroad. God knows I'm no liberal, but I'm absolutely repelled by the megalomaniac totalitarianism with which Franco has emerged from his victory, the monster that it's engendered, and that many of us have conspired to feed. You can't imagine how much I regret having played a part in enhancing his reputation in Morocco during the war. I don't like this regime, not one bit. I don't think I even like Spain; at least, I don't like this monstrosity of *Una, Grande y Libre* that they're trying to sell us. United, great and free! I've spent more years of my life outside this country than in it; I feel like a foreigner here, there are so many things that are strange to me."

"You could always go back to Morocco," I suggested. "With Rosalinda."

"No, no," he replied forcefully. "Morocco is over now. There's no future for me there; after having been high commissioner I couldn't take on a more modest post. Though it pains my heart to say it, I fear Africa is a closed chapter in my life now. Professionally, I mean, because in my heart I'll be connected to it for as long as I live. *Inshallah.* May it be so."

"And next?"

"Everything will depend on my military position; I'm in the hands of El Caudillo, Generalísimo of all the armies by the grace of God; there's nothing to be done. As though God had anything to do with these devious matters. He might lift my arrest in a month or decide simply to execute me and put out a press release. Who'd have thought it twenty years ago — my whole life in the hands of little Franquito."

He took his glasses off once again to rub his eyes, then refilled his glass and lit another cigarette.

"You're very tired," I said. "Why don't you go to sleep?"

He looked at me with the face of a little lost boy. A little lost boy who was carrying the weight of more than fifty years of existence on his back, along with the highest posting in the Spanish colonial administration and a ministerial role with a precipitous ending. He replied with crushing honesty.

"I don't want to leave because I can't bear the idea of going back to being alone in that big gloomy house that up till now has been my official residence."

"Stay and sleep here if you prefer," I offered. I knew it was reckless on my part to invite him to spend the night, but I could sense that given the state he was in, he might do something crazy if I shut the doors of my house and drove him out to wander the streets of Madrid alone.

"I fear I won't be able to sleep a wink," he acknowledged, with a half smile heavy with sadness, "but I would be grateful if you'd allow me to rest here awhile; I won't be any trouble, I promise. It will be like a refuge in the midst of the storm: you can't imagine how bitter the solitude of the banished man can be."

"Consider yourself at home. I'll bring you a blanket in case you want to lie down. Take off your jacket and tie — make yourself comfortable."

He followed my instructions while I went off in search of a blanket. When I returned he was in his shirtsleeves, refilling the glass with cognac once again.

"Last one," I said authoritatively, taking the bottle away.

I put a clean ashtray on the table and the blanket on the back of the sofa. Then I sat down next to him and gently took his arm.

"It'll all pass, Juan Luis, give it time. Sooner or later, eventually, it'll all pass."

I rested my head on his shoulder and he put his hand in mine.

"From your mouth to God's ears, Sira," he whispered.

I left him alone with his demons and retired to bed. As I made my way back through the hallway to my bedroom I heard him talking to himself in Arabic; I didn't understand what he was saying. It took me some time to fall asleep; it was probably past four when I managed to reconcile myself to a strange, troubling slumber. I woke to the sound of the front door closing at the other end of the hallway. I looked at the time on my alarm clock. Twenty to eight. I would never see him again.

CHAPTER FORTY-TWO

My fears about being followed suddenly lost all urgency. Before troubling Hillgarth with suppositions that might be unfounded, I had to make immediate contact with him to get Beigbeder's information and letters to him. His situation was much more important than my fears: not only for himself, but for my friend, and everyone. Which was why that morning I tore to shreds the pattern I'd planned to use to convey my suspicions about being followed and replaced it with a new one: "Beigbeder visited me last night. Out of ministry, state of extreme nervousness. Being sent under arrest to Ronda. Fears for his life. Gave me letters to send to Mrs. Fox to Lisbon by embassy diplomatic bag. Awaiting instructions. Urgent."

I considered going to Embassy at noon to attract Hillgarth's attention. Although the news of the ministerial dismissal would undoubtedly have reached him first thing in the morning, I knew that all the details the colonel had told me would be of considerable interest. And besides, I sensed that I should get rid of the letters addressed to Rosalinda as quickly as possible: knowing the sender's position, I was sure those pages went beyond mere intimate personal correspondence and constituted an arsenal of political fury that I really never ought to have in my possession. But it was Wednesday, and like every Wednesday I had my trip to the beauty salon planned, so I preferred to use the regular channels of transmission before raising the alarm with an emergency action that would allow me to hand over the information only a couple of hours earlier. I forced myself to work through the morning, I was visited by two clients, I picked unenthusiastically at some food, and at a quarter to four I left home for the hairdresser's, with the tube of patterns firmly wrapped in a silk handkerchief in my handbag. It looked like there was rain on the way, but I decided against taking a taxi: I needed to get some fresh air on my face to dispel the fog that was destroying me. As I walked, I recalled the details of Beigbeder's unsettling visit the previous night and tried to predict the plan that Hillgarth and his people would come up with for getting hold of the letters. Lost in these thoughts, I wasn't aware of anyone following me; perhaps my own concerns kept me so engrossed that if there was someone there, I simply didn't notice.

The messages were hidden in the locker without the curly-haired girl who looked after that sort of cloakroom showing the slightest sign of complicity when she caught my eye. Either she was a superb collaborator or she hadn't the faintest idea what was happening right under her nose. The hairdressers dealt with me as skillfully as they did every week, and while they put a wave in my hair — which had now grown down past my shoulders — I pretended to be absorbed in the current issue of a magazine. Though I had little interest in that women's magazine full of pharmaceutical remedies, sickly sweet stories full of morals, and a long article on Gothic cathedrals, I read it from cover to cover without taking my eyes off it, so as to avoid contact with the rest of the clientele sitting nearby, whose conversations didn't engross me in the slightest. Unless my visit coincided with that of a client of mine — which happened not infrequently — I had no desire to have even the most cursory chat with anybody.

I left the hairdresser's salon without the patterns, my hair perfect and my soul still troubled. The afternoon weather remained disagreeable, but I decided to take a walk instead of returning directly home. I preferred to keep myself distracted, distanced from Beigbeder's letters, while I waited for news from Hillgarth about what to do with them. I wandered aimlessly up the Calle Alcalá as far as the Gran Vía; the stroll was calm and safe at first, but as I went on walking I noticed how the density of people on the pavements increased, well-turned-out passersby mixing with bootblacks, street sweepers, and crippled tramps showing their scars shamelessly in the hope of some charity. It was then that I realized I'd ventured beyond the perimeter that Hillgarth had marked out: I was entering a rather dangerous zone where I might perhaps run into someone who had once known me. They probably wouldn't ever suspect that this woman walking in an elegant grey wool coat had supplanted the sewing girl I was years ago, but just in case I decided to go into a cinema to kill time for the rest of the afternoon, while also avoiding being any more exposed than I needed to be.

The Palacio de la Musica movie theater was playing *Rebecca*. The showing had already started, but I didn't care; I wasn't there for the plot, I just wanted a little privacy while enough time went by for someone to get instructions to my home about what to do. The usher accompanied me to one of the last rows on one side, while Laurence Olivier and Joan Fontaine hurtled down a twisting highway in a car with the roof down. As soon as my eyes had become used to the dark, I realized that the main seating area was almost full; my row and the ones around it, however, being farther back, had only a few people scattered here and there. To my left were several couples; to my right, no one. But not for long: just a couple of minutes after I arrived, I noticed someone taking a seat at the far end of the row, no more than ten or twelve places away. A man. Alone. A man alone whose face I couldn't make out in the shadows. Some man or other, whom I wouldn't have paid any attention to but for the fact that he was wearing a light-colored raincoat with the collar up, identical to that of the person who'd been following me for more than a week. A man who seemed — judging by the direction of his gaze — to be less interested in the plot of the movie than in me.

A cold sweat trickled down my back. Suddenly I knew that all my suspicions hadn't been imaginary: that man was there because of me, he'd most probably followed me from the hairdresser's, perhaps followed me even since I'd left home; he'd been following me the whole time; he'd watched as I paid for my ticket at the box office and as I went through the foyer into the hall and found my seat. Watching me without my noticing him hadn't been enough for him, however: once he'd tracked me down, he'd installed himself a few feet away, blocking my exit. And I — careless and overwhelmed by the news of Beigbeder's

567

dismissal — had decided at the last minute not to share my suspicions with Hillgarth, even though they'd been growing with each day that passed. My first thought was to escape, but I realized at once that I was cornered. I couldn't get to the right-hand aisle without him letting me by; if I decided to go to the left I'd have to bother a whole mass of patrons who'd grumble at the interruption and would have to get up or move their legs aside to let me pass, which would give the stranger more than enough time to leave his seat and follow me. Then I remembered Hillgarth's advice during our lunch at the American legation: faced with any suspicion that I was being followed, maintain calm, self-control, and an appearance of normality.

The brazenness of the stranger in the raincoat didn't presage anything good, however; what till now had been a hidden, subtle pursuit had given way abruptly to an ostentatious declaration of intent. I'm here so that you can see me, he seemed to be saying wordlessly. So that you know I'm watching you, and that I know where you go; so that you're aware that I can step into your life anytime I want to: look, today I've decided to follow you to the cinema and block your exit; tomorrow I can do with you whatever I feel like.

I pretended to ignore him and tried hard to focus on the movie, unsuccessfully. The scenes passed before my eyes without any meaning or coherence: a gloomy, majestic mansion, an evil-looking housekeeper, a heroine who always does the wrong thing, the ghost of a fascinating woman floating in the air. The whole audience seemed captivated; my concerns, however, were on another matter closer at hand. As the minutes ticked by

568

and the screen was filled with a succession of images in white, black, and grey, I let my hair fall over the right side of my face several times and so tried covertly to scrutinize the stranger. I wasn't able to make out his features: the distance and the darkness prevented me. But a sort of silent, tense relationship was established between us, as though we were united by a common lack of interest in the movie. Neither of us held our breath when the nameless heroine broke that porcelain figurine, nor were we overcome with a sense of panic when the housekeeper tried to persuade her to hurl herself out of the window. We didn't even feel our hearts freeze when we suspected that Maxim de Winter himself might have murdered his depraved wife.

The words "The End" appeared after the fire at Manderley, and the cinema began to be flooded with light. My immediate reaction was to hide my face; for some ridiculous reason I felt that the light would make me seem more vulnerable to my pursuer. I tilted my head, allowed my hair to obscure my face again, and pretended to be engrossed in looking for something in my handbag. When I finally raised my eyes slightly and looked over to my right, the man had disappeared. I remained in my seat until the screen had gone blank, fear clutching the pit of my stomach. Once they had turned on all the lights and the final dawdling spectators left the hall, the ushers came in to collect bits of trash and items accidentally dropped between the seats. It was only then — still afraid — that I steeled myself and got up.

The main lobby was still crammed full and noisy; a downpour was falling on the street and the spectators waiting to leave were mingling with those waiting for the next showing to begin. I took refuge, half hidden behind a column off to one corner, and amid the crowds, the voices, and the thick smoke of a thousand cigarettes, I felt anonymous and momentarily safe. But the fragile feeling of security only lasted a few minutes, which was how long it took for the mass to start to dissolve. The new arrivals were now ready to enter the main hall to lose themselves in the adventures of the de Winters and their ghosts. The remainder of us — the better prepared under the protection of umbrellas and hats, the more reckless under jackets with hoods or collars up and newspapers held open over their heads, the bravest simply filled with daring — began gradually to quit the lavish world of the cinema and go out into the street to confront everyday reality, a reality that on that autumn night showed itself through a thick curtain of inclement falling water.

Finding a taxi was a lost cause, so just like the hundreds of other people who preceded me I braced myself, and with nothing but a silk scarf to cover my hair and the collar of my coat up, I set off back home in the rain. I kept up a fast pace, wanting to get to shelter as soon as possible, to escape from the downpour and from the dozens of suspicions that assailed me as I walked. I turned my head constantly: now I thought he was following me, now I thought he'd stopped. Anyone in a raincoat made me quicken my pace, even if his silhouette wasn't that of the man I feared. Someone ran past me, and when I felt him brush my arm I ducked for cover by the window of a closed pharmacy; a tramp tugged at my sleeve begging for charity and all he received was a startled cry. I tried to adjust my pace to match that of various respectable-looking couples, until my closeness made them suspicious and they moved away from me. The puddles were covering my stockings with spatterings of mud; my left heel got trapped in a drain. I crossed the streets quickly and anxiously, barely looking at the traffic. The headlights of a car dazzled me at a crossing; a little farther on I was honked at by another car and almost run over by a tram; just a few yards beyond that I managed to leap out of the way of a dark car that probably hadn't seen me in the rain. Or maybe it had.

I arrived drenched and breathless; the doorman, the night watchman, a handful of neighbors, and five or six nosy passersby were milling about just inside the entrance, assessing the damage done by the water that had seeped into the building's basement. I went up the stairs two at a time without anyone noticing me, pulling off the drenched scarf as I looked for my keys, relieved at having managed to make it back without running into my pursuer and longing to sink into a hot bath to tear the cold and panic from my skin. But my relief was short-lived. As brief as the seconds it took me to reach the door, enter the apartment, and see what was going on.

That there was a lamp lit in the living room when the house should have been dark was unusual, but there could have been an explanation for it: although Doña Manuela and the girls usually turned everything off before leaving, it's possible that that night they'd forgotten to do one final check. Which was why it wasn't the light that struck me as out of place, but what I found at the entrance. A raincoat. A man's, light colored. Hanging on the coatrack and dripping water with sinister calm.

CHAPTER FORTY-THREE

Its owner was waiting for me, sitting in the living room. No words came to my mouth for a stretch of time that seemed to last till the end of the world. The unexpected visitor didn't speak right away either. We just both stared at each other, in a flustered jumble of memories and feelings.

"So," he asked at last, "did you enjoy the film?"

I didn't answer. Sitting in front of me was the man who had been following me for days. The same man who five years ago had left my life dressed in a similar coat; the same man who had disappeared into the mist dragging a typewriter when he learned that I was going to leave him because I had fallen in love with a man who wasn't him. Ignacio Montes, my first boyfriend, had come back into my life.

"How far we've come, eh, Sirita?" he said then, getting up and walking over toward me.

"What are you doing here, Ignacio?" I managed to whisper finally.

I hadn't yet taken off my coat; I noticed water was dripping onto my feet and forming little puddles on the floor. But I didn't move.

"I've come to see you," he replied. "Dry yourself off and change your clothes; we've got to talk."

He was smiling, and his smile said *Damn my*

desire to smile. I realized then that I was only a few feet from the door I'd just come in; perhaps I could try to run away, to tear down the stairs three at a time, reach the front door, go out into the street, run. I discarded the idea. I suspected it wouldn't be in my interest to react impulsively without first learning what it was that I was being confronted by, so I simply walked toward him and looked him in the eye.

"What do you want, Ignacio? How did you get in, what have you come for, why have you been watching me?"

"Slowly, Sira, slowly. Ask me one question at a time, don't get all worked up. But first, if you don't mind, I'd rather the two of us could make ourselves comfortable. I'm a bit tired, you know — you had me up later than usual last night. Would you mind if I poured myself a drink?"

"You didn't used to drink," I said, trying to keep calm.

A laugh as cold as the blade of my scissors tore the room from end to end.

"What a good memory you have. With all the interesting things that must have happened to you in your life over all these years, it's amazing that you still remember something that simple."

It was amazing, yes, but I did remember. That, and a whole lot more. Our long evenings of aimless wandering, the dances amid the Chinese lanterns at the fair. His optimism and his tenderness in those days; myself when I was no more than a humble seamstress whose horizon stretched no farther than marriage with a man whose presence filled me now with fear and doubt.

"What'll you have?" I asked, finally, trying to sound calm, not to show how unsettled I was.

"Whiskey. Cognac. I don't mind: whatever you offer your other guests."

I served him a glass, draining the bottle Beigbeder had been drinking from the previous night; there were just a couple of fingers left. When I turned back toward him I could see that he was wearing a regular grey suit — a better cloth and cut than he'd have worn when we were together, lower quality work than the ones worn by the men I'd been surrounded by lately. I put the glass down on the table beside him, and it was only then that I noticed that on the table there was also a box of Embassy candies, wrapped in silver paper and finished off with a pink ribbon tied in a bow.

"Some admirer's sent you a gift," he said, stroking the box with his fingertips.

I didn't reply. I couldn't, I was suddenly breathless. I knew that somewhere in the wrapping of that unexpected gift was a coded message from Hillgarth, a message intended to pass unnoticed by anyone but me.

I sat far from him, at one end of the sofa, tense and still soaked. I pretended to ignore the box of candies and contemplated Ignacio in silence, drawing the wet hair back off my face. He was as thin as ever, but his face was no longer the same. The first white hairs were appearing at his temples even though he was barely more than thirty. He had bags under his eyes, lines at the edges of his mouth, and the weary air of not having led a peaceful life.

"Well, well, Sira, how long it's been."

"Five years," I specified firmly. "Now tell me please what you've come for."

"Several things," he said. "But first I'd rather you put on some dry clothes. And when you come back, be so kind as to bring me your papers. Asking you for them while on the way out of the cinema seemed rather vulgar under the circumstances."

"And why should I show you my papers?"

"Because from what I hear you're a Moroccan citizen now."

"And what's that to you? You have no right to meddle in my life."

"Who said I don't?"

"You and I have nothing in common. I'm a different person, Ignacio, I have nothing to do with you or with anyone from the time we were together. A lot has happened in my life over these years; I'm no longer who I used to be."

"None of us are who we used to be, Sira. No one ever is as they were after a war like ours."

Silence spread out between us. My mind was filled with a thousand images from the past that flocked in like maddened seagulls, a thousand feelings that crashed into one another without my being able to control them. Sitting opposite me was the man who might have ended up being the father of my children, a good man who did nothing but adore me and into whose heart I'd plunged a knife. Sitting opposite me, too, was the man who could become my worst nightmare, who might have spent five years gnawing on his rancor and might be able to do anything to make me pay for my betrayal. Turn me in, for example, accuse me of not being who I said I was, and bring the debts from my past back out into the light.

"Where did you spend the war?" I asked, almost afraid.

"In Salamanca. I went for a few days to see my mother and that's where the uprising found me. I joined the Nationalists, I had no choice. What about you?"

"In Tetouan," I said without thinking. Perhaps I shouldn't have been so specific, but it was too late to turn back now. Strangely, my reply seemed to please him. A faint smile appeared on his lips.

"Of course," he said softly. "Of course, now it all makes sense."

"What makes sense?"

"Something I needed to find out from you."

"There is nothing you need to find out from me, Ignacio. The only thing you need to do is forget me and leave me in peace."

"I can't," he said forcefully.

I didn't ask why. I was afraid he'd ask me to explain myself, that he'd reproach me for leaving him and throw back in my face all the pain I'd caused him. Or even worse: I was afraid that he'd tell me he still loved me and beg me to come back to him.

"You've got to leave, Ignacio, you've got to get me out of your head."

"I can't, sweetheart," he repeated, this time with a note of bitter irony. "I'd like nothing more than never to remember the woman who destroyed me, but I can't. I work for the General Directorate of Security of the Governance Ministry; I'm charged with watching and following foreigners who cross our borders, especially those who settle in Madrid with a suggestion that they mean to remain permanently. And you're one of them. At the top of the list."

I didn't know whether to laugh or cry.

"And what do you want from me?" I asked, when I was again able to summon words to my mouth.

576

"Papers," he insisted. "Passport, and customs papers for everything in this apartment that's come from abroad. But first of all, change your clothes."

He talked coldly, sure of himself. Professional, completely different from that other Ignacio, tender and almost childlike, whom I had stored in my memory.

"Can you show me some sort of credentials?" I said quietly. I guessed that he wasn't lying, but I wanted to buy time to take it all in.

He drew a wallet from his inside jacket pocket. He opened it with the same hand that held it, with the facility of someone accustomed to proving his identity over and over again. And there indeed was his face and his name alongside the job and the ministry he had just mentioned.

"Just a moment," I mumbled.

I went to my room; I quickly unhooked a white blouse and blue skirt from my closet, then opened the underwear drawer, about to take out something clean to put on, when my fingers brushed against Beigbeder's letters, hidden under the folded slips. I hesitated a few seconds, unsure what to do about them, whether to leave them where they were or quickly find someplace safer. I ran my eyes hungrily across the room: maybe on top of the closet, maybe under the mattress. Perhaps between the sheets. Or behind the dressing-table mirror. Or in a shoe box.

"Be quick, please," Ignacio shouted from far away.

I pushed the letters to the back, covered them completely with half a dozen bits of underwear, and closed the drawer with a dry thud. Anywhere else might be as good a place or as bad, but it wasn't worth tempting fate.

I dried off, changed, took my passport from the nightstand, and returned to the living room.

"Arish Agoriuq," he read slowly after I'd handed it over. "Born in Tangiers, resident in Tangiers. Shares your birthday — what a coincidence."

I didn't reply. I was suddenly overtaken by a terrible desire to throw up and had to struggle to stop myself.

"Might I know what this change in nationality was in aid of?"

My mind fabricated a lie, fast as the blinking of an eye. I'd never envisaged finding myself in a situation like this, nor had Hillgarth.

"I had my passport stolen and wasn't able to request my papers from Madrid because it was the middle of the war. A friend fixed it for me to be given Moroccan citizenship so that I could travel without any trouble. It's not a fake passport, you can check."

"I already have done. And the name?"

"They thought it was better to change it, to make it more like an Arab name."

"Arish Agoriuq? Is that Arab?"

"It's Cherja," I lied. "The dialect of the Rif villages," I added, remembering Beigbeder's linguistic skills.

He remained silent a few seconds, not taking his eyes off me. I could still feel my stomach turning over, but I fought to keep it under control to avoid having to run to the bathroom.

"I also need to know the objective of your stay in Madrid," he insisted finally.

"To work. Sewing, as usual," I replied. "This is a dressmaker's studio."

"Show me."

I took him through to the back room and wordlessly showed him the rolls of material, the pictures of designs, and the magazines. Then I led him along the hallway and opened the doors to all the rooms. The spotless fitting rooms. The clients' bathroom. The sewing room filled with fabric, patterns, and mannequins with half-assembled bits of clothing. The ironing room with various items awaiting their turn. And finally the storeroom. We walked together, side by side, as we'd walked so many times all those years before. I recalled that then he was almost a head taller than I — the difference didn't seem so great now. It wasn't that memory was playing tricks on me, however; when I was just a seamstress's apprentice and he a would-be civil servant I wore shoes with barely any heel on them; five years on, my heels raised my height to halfway up his face.

"What's in the back?" he asked.

"My bedroom, a couple of bathrooms, and four other rooms, two of them for guests and the other two empty. And also a lunch room, kitchen, and service quarters," I reeled off.

"I want to see them."

"What for?"

"I don't have to give you an explanation."

"Very well."

I showed him the rooms one by one, my stomach tight, feigning a coolness that was a world away from my genuine state and trying not to let him see how my hand shook as it switched on the lights and opened the doors. I'd left Beigbeder's letters to Rosalinda in the closet in my bedroom beneath my underwear; my legs trembled at the idea that it might occur to him to open the drawer and that he might find them. As he stepped into

579

the room I watched him with my heart clenched. He went through it slowly and deliberately. He leafed through the novel I had on my nightstand with feigned interest, then put it back in its place; then he ran his fingers along the foot of the bed, picked up a brush from the dressing table, and looked out through the balcony doors a few seconds. I was praying that that would bring his visit to a close, but it didn't. The part I most feared was still to come. He opened one side of the closet, the one containing my outer clothes. He touched the sleeve of a long jacket and the belt of another, then closed it. He opened the next door and I held my breath. He was face to face with a stack of drawers. He pulled out the first: scarves. He lifted the corner of one of them, then another, and another; and closed it back up again. He pulled out the next and I gulped: stockings. He closed it. When his fingers touched the third I felt the floor turn to liquid under my feet. There, covered by the silk slips, were the handwritten documents that revealed in detail and in the first person the circumstances of the scandalous ministerial dismissal that was being passed by word of mouth across all of Spain.

"I think you're going too far, Ignacio," I managed to whisper.

He kept his fingers on the handle of the drawer a few seconds more, as though considering what to do. I felt hot, I felt cold, anxious, thirsty. I felt as though it was about to be over. Until I noticed his lips parting for him to speak. "Let's go on," was all he said. He closed the closet door while I held back a sigh of relief and a desperate desire to burst into tears. I masked my emotions as best I could and resumed my role as a guide under duress. He saw the bathroom where I bathed and the table where I ate, the larder where I kept my food, the sink where the girls washed the clothes. Perhaps he didn't go any further out of respect for me, maybe out of simple modesty, or because the protocols of his job set out certain restrictions he didn't dare transgress; I never found out. We returned to the living room without a word while I thanked heaven that his search hadn't been more exhaustive.

He sat back down in the same place and I sat opposite him.

"So, everything in order?"

"No," he said emphatically. "Nothing's in order — nothing at all."

I shut my eyes, squeezed them tightly, and opened them again.

"And what is wrong?"

"Everything is wrong, nothing's as it should be."

Suddenly I thought I could see a chink of light.

"What did you expect to find, Ignacio? What did you hope to find that you didn't find?"

He didn't answer.

"You thought the whole thing was just a front, didn't you?"

Again he didn't answer, but he did veer the conversation back onto his turf and resumed his grip on the reins.

"I'm perfectly well aware of who it was that set up this show."

"What show do you mean?" I asked.

"This joke of a workshop."

"It's no joke. We work hard here. I do more than ten hours a day, seven days a week."

"I doubt it," he said sourly.

I got up and walked over to his chair. I sat on

one of the arms and took his right hand. He didn't resist, nor did he look at me. I let his fingers touch my palms, my own fingers, slowly, for him to feel every inch of my skin. I just wanted to show him the evidence of my work, the calluses and rough patches that the scissors, needles, and thimbles had given me over the years. I noticed the way my touch made him shudder.

"These are the hands of a working woman, Ignacio. I can guess what it is you think I am, and what you think I do, but I want you to be absolutely clear that these aren't the hands of a woman who's being kept by anybody. I'm deeply sorry to have hurt you, you can't imagine how sorry. I didn't behave well with you. But that's all in the past now and there's no going back; you won't make anything better by meddling in my life in search of ghosts that don't exist."

I stopped running my fingers over his but kept hold of his hand. It was icy. Bit by bit it began to warm up.

"Do you want to know what became of me after I left you?" I asked quietly.

He nodded without a word. He still wasn't looking at me.

"We went to Tangiers. I fell pregnant and Ramiro abandoned me. I lost the child. I found myself suddenly in a strange country, sick, without any money, burdened with the debts that he'd left in my name and without so much as a place to drop dead. I had the police on my case, I found myself embroiled in certain activities on the very edge of the law. Then I set up a workshop thanks to the help of a friend and I started sewing again. I worked night and day, and I made friends, too, very distinguished people. I got used to spending

582

time with them and became part of a world that was new to me, but I never stopped working. I also met a man I was able to fall in love with, and with whom I might perhaps have been happy again, a foreign reporter, but I knew that sooner or later he'd have to leave, and I fought against getting into another relationship for fear of making myself suffer again, of re-experiencing that atrocious feeling of being ripped apart that I'd had when Ramiro went off without me. Now I've come back to Madrid, alone, and I'm still working; you've seen all there is in this house. And as for what happened between you and me, I did penance for my sins, you needn't have any doubt about that. I don't know whether or not that's good enough for you, but you can be sure I've paid a high price for all the pain I caused you. If there's such a thing as divine retribution, I know in my conscience that between what I did to you and what was later done to me, the scales are more than balanced."

I couldn't tell whether what I'd said affected him, calmed him down, or confused him still further. We remained in silence a few minutes, his hand in my hands, our bodies close, each aware of the other's presence. After a while I separated myself from him and moved back to my place.

"What have you got to do with Minister Beigbeder?" he demanded to know then. He spoke without bitterness. Without bitterness but without weakness either, halfway between the intimacy we'd shared moments earlier and the infinite distance of the time before. I could tell that he was making an effort to return to a professional attitude and that, unfortunately, it didn't take him too much effort to achieve it.

583

"Juan Luis Beigbeder is a friend of mine from my Tetouan days."

"What sort of friend?"

"He's not my lover, if that's what you're wondering."

"He spent the night with you yesterday."

"He spent it in my house, not with me. I don't have any reason to explain my private life to you, but I'd rather clarify things so that you're in no doubt: Beigbeder and I don't have any kind of romantic attachment. Last night we didn't go to bed together. Not last night, not ever. I'm not being kept by any minister."

"Why then?"

"Why didn't we go to bed together, or why don't I have a minister keeping me?"

"Why did he come here and stay till eight in the morning?"

"Because he'd just learned that they'd sacked him and he didn't want to be alone."

He got up and walked over to one of the balcony doors. He started talking again as he looked out, his hands in his trouser pockets.

"Beigbeder is a cretin. He's a traitor who's sold himself to the British, a madman in thrall to an English slut."

I laughed despite myself. I got up and walked over behind his back.

"You have no idea, Ignacio. You work for whomever it is you work for in the Governance Ministry and they've told you to terrorize all the foreigners who come through Madrid, but you don't have the vaguest idea of who Colonel Beigbeder is or why he's behaved the way he has."

"I know what I need to know."

"And what's that?"

584

"That he's been plotting, and that he's disloyal to his country. And incompetent as a minister. That's what everyone says about him, beginning with the press."

"As if anyone could believe what this press says," I remarked ironically.

"And who else should we believe? Your new foreign friends?"

"Perhaps. They know a lot more than you do."

He turned and took a few decisive steps until he was just inches from my face.

"What do they know?" he asked hoarsely.

I realized it would be best if I said nothing, so I let him go on.

"Do they know I can get you deported by tomorrow? Do they know I can have you detained, that I can get this exotic Moroccan passport of yours turned into scrap paper and throw you blindfolded out of the country without anyone being any the wiser? Your friend Beigbeder is out of the government now; you don't have a god-father anymore."

He was so close to me that I could see just how much his beard had grown since he'd shaved that morning. I could see how his Adam's apple rose and fell as he spoke; I could make out every move-ment of those lips that had once kissed me so often and were now spitting out rough threats.

With my reply I gambled everything on a single card. A card as false as I was myself.

"I no longer have Beigbeder, but I've still got other resources that you can't even imagine. The clients I sew for have powerful husbands and lov-ers, and I'm good friends with many of them. They could give me diplomatic asylum in any one of half a dozen embassies if I asked for it, beginning with the German embassy — and I'm pretty sure they're the ones who have a tight grip over your minister. I can save my skin with a simple phone call. The person who might not be able to save his skin is you if you keep sticking your nose where you aren't wanted."

I'd never lied so brazenly to anyone; it was probably the immensity of the fabrication that gave me my arrogant tone. I couldn't tell whether or not he believed me. Perhaps he did — the story was only as unlikely as the course of my own life and yet there I was, his ex-fiancée, transformed into a Moroccan subject, as evidence that the most unlikely things can at any moment be transformed into pure reality.

"We'll see about that," he spat between his teeth.

He moved away from me and sat back down.

"I don't like the person you've become, Ignacio," I whispered behind him.

He gave a bitter laugh.

"And who are you to judge me? Maybe you think you're superior because you spent the war in Africa and now you've come back with all the airs of a fine lady? You think you're a better person than me because you take rogue ministers into your house and allow yourself to be fawned upon with candies while everyone else has even their black bread and lentils rationed?"

"I'm judging you because you matter to me, and because I want the best for you," I said. My voice barely came out.

He replied with another laugh. Even more bitter than the one that had come before. More sincere, too.

"You don't care about anyone but yourself, Sira. It's all about me, myself, I. *I've* worked, *I've* suffered, *I've* paid for my guilt: just me me me. You're not interested in anyone else — anyone. Have you even bothered to find out what became of your people after the war? Did it ever occur to you to go back to your neighborhood, in one of those elegant suits of yours, to ask after them all, to see if anyone could use a little help? Do you know what became of your neighbors and your friends during all these years?"

His questions echoed like heavy blows to my conscience, like a fistful of salt thrown deliberately into my open eyes. I had no answer to that: I didn't know anything because I'd chosen not to know. I'd respected my orders, I'd been disciplined. They told me not to leave a certain area and I hadn't. I'd made an effort not to see the other Madrid, the authentic one, the real one. I focused my movements within the limits of an idyllic city and forced myself not to look at its other face: the one whose streets were filled with holes, craters in the buildings, windows without glass, and empty fountains. I preferred not to let my gaze light on whole families who rummaged through the trash in the hope of finding some potato peelings; not to look at the women in mourning who wandered the pavements with babies hanging from their shriveled breasts; I didn't even spare a glance for the hordes of dirty, barefoot children who swarmed around there, and who, with their faces covered in dry snot and their little shaved heads covered in scabs, tugged at the sleeves of pedestrians and asked for some charity, please, señor, alms, I beg of you, señorita, some charity, señorita, God will repay your kindness. I'd been an excellent and obedient agent in the service of British intelligence. Scrupulously obedi-

587

ent. Disgustingly obedient. I'd followed the instructions they'd given me to the letter: I hadn't returned to my neighborhood or set foot on the paving stones of my past. I'd avoided finding out what had become of my people, of the girlfriends from my childhood. I didn't go to seek out my square, didn't step into my narrow little street or go up my staircase. I didn't knock at my neighbors' doors, I didn't want to know how they were doing, what had become of their families during the war or since. I didn't try to discover how many of them had died, how many were in prison, how the ones who were still alive had managed to make it through. I wasn't interested in hearing what rotten scraps they'd filled their cooking pots with, or whether their children were consumptive, malnourished, or barefoot. I didn't worry about their wretched lives, filled with lice and chilblains. I belonged to another world now, a world of international conspiracies, lavish hotels, luxury hairdressers, and cocktails at aperitif time. That other wretched universe, rat grey, smelling of urine and boiled chard, had nothing to do with me. Or at least, that's what I thought.

"You don't know anything about them, do you?" Ignacio went on slowly. "Well then, you pay attention now, because I'm going to tell you. Your neighbor Norberto fell at Brunete; his elder son was shot the moment the Nationalist troops entered Madrid, although if you believe what people were saying he had also been involved in political repression on the other side. The middle one is breaking rocks in Cuelgamuros and the youngest is in the El Dueso prison: he joined the Communist Party, so he probably won't be getting out any time soon, that is if they don't just execute him one of these days. Their mother, Señora Engracia, the one who used to look after you and treated you like her daughter when your mother went to work when you were just a kid, she's on her own now: she's gone half blind and wanders the streets as though deranged, turning over whatever she finds with a stick. There are no longer any pigeons or cats left in your neighborhood, they've eaten them all. And you want to know what happened to the girlfriends you used to play with on the Plaza de la Paja? I can tell you about them, too: Andreíta was blown up by a shell one evening as she was crossing Calle Fuencarral on her way to the workshop where she had a job —"

"I don't want to know any more, Ignacio, I get the idea," I said, trying to hide my agitation. He didn't seem to hear me; he just went on enumerating these horrors.

"As for Sole, the one from the dairy, she became pregnant with twins by a militiaman who disappeared without leaving them so much as his surname; since she couldn't look after the children because she didn't have enough to support them, the people from the foundling hospital took them away and she never heard about them again. They say that she goes around offering herself up to the men who do the unloading in the Cebada market, asking one peseta for each act that she does right there up against the tiles of the wall; they say she goes over there without any panties, lifting up her skirt as the trucks start arriving in the early morning."

Tears were beginning to stream down my cheeks.

"Shut up, Ignacio, shut up now, for God's sake," I whispered. He ignored me.

"Agustina and Nati, the poulterer's daughters, they joined a group of nurses and spent the war working in the San Carlos hospital. When it all came to an end they were picked up at their house, put into a van, and from there taken to Las Ventas prison; they were tried in Las Salesas and sentenced to thirty years and a day. As for Trini, the baker —"

"Shut up, Ignacio, let it go," I begged.

At last he yielded.

"I could tell you a lot more stories, I've heard almost all of them. People come daily to see me, people who knew us back then. All of them show up with the same refrain: I talked to you once, Don Ignacio, back when you were engaged to Sirita, the daughter of Señora Dolores, the seamstress who lived on the Calle de la Redondilla . . ."

"What do they come to you for?" I managed to ask through my tears.

"They all want the same things: to ask me to get some relative of theirs out of prison, to see if I can use my contacts to spare someone the death penalty, to help them find a job, no matter how mean . . . You can't imagine what day-to-day life is like in the General Directorate — in the lobbies, along the corridors, on the staircases, a fearful crowd pile-up waiting to be seen, ready to bear anything for a crumb of what they've come for: for someone to listen to them, for someone to attend to them, to give them some clue about somebody close to them who's missing, to tell them whom they should beg for a relative's freedom . . . A lot of women come, especially — an awful lot of them. They have nothing to live for, they've been left alone with their children and can't find any way to get ahead."

"And is there anything you can do for them?" I asked, trying to overcome my distress.

"Very little. Almost nothing. The military tribunals handle the crimes relating to the war. These people come to me out of desperation, just like they approach anyone they know who works for the administration."

"But you're part of the regime —"

"I'm just a simple functionary without any power at all, just another rung in the whole big hierarchy," he interrupted me. "I don't have any way of doing anything more than hear their troubles, give them some indication of where they should go if I happen to know, and give them ten pesetas when they seem to be on the verge of despair. I'm not even a member of the Falange: I just fought on the side that I happened to find myself on and fate decided that ultimately I should end up winning. That was why I entered the ministry and took on the task they gave me. But I'm not on anyone's side: I saw too many horrors and ended up losing respect for all of them. That's why I just obey the orders I'm given, because it puts food on the table. So I keep my mouth shut, keep my head down, and work my ass off so that I can help my family get ahead, that's all."

"I didn't know you had a family," I said as I wiped my eyes with the handkerchief he held out to me.

"I got married in Salamanca, and when the war ended we came to Madrid. I have a wife, two little children, and a home where at least there's always someone waiting for me at the end of the day, however tough and sickening that day has been.

591

Our house isn't anything like this one, but it's always got the hearth lit and the children's laughter in the hallway. My sons are named Ignacio and Miguel, my wife Amalia. I've never loved her like I loved you, and her ass doesn't sway like yours as she walks down the street, and I've never desired her half as much as I desired you tonight when you held my hand. But she always puts on a brave face when there are troubles, she sings in the kitchen while she's making a stew out of what little there is, and she puts her arms around me in the middle of the night when I'm assailed by nightmares and shout and cry because I'm dreaming that I'm back at the front and going to be killed."

"I'm sorry, Ignacio," I said in a whisper. My own tears barely allowed me to speak.

"I may be just a conformist, nothing special, a puppy-dog servant of a revanchist state," he went on, looking me straight in the eye, "but you're no one to tell me whether or not you like the man I've become. You can't give me moral lectures, Sira, because if I'm bad, you're even worse. At least I still have a drop of compassion left in my soul; I don't think you have even that. You're nothing but an egotist who lives in a massive house where all you can see is loneliness wherever you look; a woman without any roots, who denies her origins and is incapable of thinking of anyone but herself."

I wanted to shout at him to shut up, to leave me in peace, to get out of my life forever, but before I was able to utter the first syllable my guts were transformed into a wellspring of uncontainable sobs, as though something had sprung loose inside. I cried. With my face covered, inconsolably, unstoppably. When I was able to stop and return to the immediate reality, it was past midnight and Ignacio was no longer there. He had left without making a sound, with the same delicacy with which he used to treat me. The fear and distress caused by his presence still clung to my skin, however. I didn't know what the consequences of this visit would be; I didn't know what would become of Arish Agoriuq after that night. Maybe the Ignacio of a few years ago would have taken pity on a woman he'd loved so much and would have decided to let her go on her way in peace. Or maybe as a devoted functionary of the New State he would choose to pass on to his superiors the suspicions he had about my fake identity. Perhaps — just as he himself had threatened — I'd end up being detained. Or deported. Or dead.

On the table there sat a box of candies that was much less innocent than it seemed. I opened it with one hand, while the other dried the last of my tears. All I found inside were two dozen milk chocolates. Then I looked over the wrapping until I found a light, almost imperceptible stitching on the pink ribbon tied around the packet. It took me just three minutes to decipher it. "Urgent meeting. Consult Doctor Rico. Caracas, 29. 11 a.m. Extreme caution."

Alongside the box of candies was a glass I'd poured some hours earlier. Untouched. As Ignacio himself had said, none of us were the people we used to be. But even though life had turned us all around, he still didn't drink.

■ ■ ■ ■

PART FOUR

■ ■ ■ ■

Palacio des Galveias in Lisbon

CHAPTER FORTY-FOUR

Several hundred people, all of them well fed and even better dressed, saw in the New Year of 1941 in the Madrid Casino's Royal Hall to the sound of a Cuban band. And among them, one more in the crowd, was me.

My original plan had been to spend that night alone, perhaps to invite Doña Manuela and the girls to share a capon and a bottle of cider, but the tenacious insistence of two of my clients, the Álvarez-Vicuña sisters, forced me to change my plans. I took great care in getting ready for the night, albeit reluctantly: I got my hair done in a low bun and made myself up, emphasizing my eyes with Moroccan kohl to give myself the appearance of the strange displaced creature that I was supposed to be. I designed a kind of tunic, silver grey, with full sleeves and a broad belt wrapped around it to complete the silhouette, something halfway between an exotic Moorish caftan and an elegant European evening dress. The sisters' unmarried brother collected me at home, a man by the name of Ernesto whom I never got to know beyond his birdlike face and his oily deference toward me. On arriving at the casino I made my way confidently up the large marble staircase and once in the main hall pretended not to notice the splendor of the room, or the various pairs of eyes that undisguisedly bored into me. I even pretended to ignore the gigantic chandeliers from the La Granja glass factory that hung from the ceiling and the elaborate moldings on the walls that provided a backdrop for the grandiose paintings. Confidence, mastery over myself: that's what my image emanated, as though I were a fish, and that opulence, water; as though that sumptuous place were my natural milieu.

But of course it wasn't. In spite of living surrounded by fabrics as dazzling as the ones being worn that night by the women around me, the pace of the previous months hadn't exactly been a leisurely ride, but instead a succession of days and nights in which my two occupations sucked away like leeches the integrity of a time that was ever more rarefied.

The meeting I'd had with Hillgarth two months earlier, immediately following the encounters with Beigbeder and Ignacio, had marked a before-and-after point in my way of behaving. I gave him detailed information about the former; the latter, meanwhile, I didn't even mention. Perhaps I should have, but something stopped me: modesty, insecurity, perhaps fear. I was aware that Ignacio's presence was the result of my carelessness: I should have informed the naval attaché the moment I suspected I was being followed. Perhaps if I had, I would have avoided having a representative of the Governance Ministry break into my house with no trouble at all, to sit and wait for me in my living room. But that meeting had been too personal, too emotional and painful to fit into the cold patterns of the Secret Intelligence Service. Keeping quiet about it went against the protocols

I had been given. I'd ridden roughshod over the most fundamental rules of my mission, that was for sure. All the same, I risked it. Besides, it wasn't the first time I'd hidden something from Hillgarth; I also hadn't told him that Doña Manuela was a part of the past he'd forbidden me from revisiting. Fortunately neither the hiring of my old mistress nor the visit from Ignacio had any immediate consequences: no deportation order had appeared on the atelier door, no one had called me in for questioning in some sinister office, and the trench-coat ghosts had finally stopped their assault. Whether it was over for good, or just a temporary reprieve, I had yet to find out.

At the urgent meeting to which Hillgarth summoned me after Beigbeder's removal from office, he appeared as neutral as on the day I met him, but his interest in absorbing every last detail about the colonel's visit made me suspect that his embassy was unsettled and confused at the news of the dismissal.

I didn't have any trouble finding the address he'd given me, a first floor in a distinguished old building: nothing that looked at all suspicious. Once I'd rung the bell I only had to wait a few seconds for the door to open, and an old nurse invited me in.

"Dr. Rico is expecting me," I announced, following the instructions on the ribbon of the box of candies.

"Follow me, please."

As I'd expected, when I entered the large room to which she led me I didn't find any doctor, but an Englishman with luxuriant eyebrows who had an altogether different profession. Although on a number of previous occasions I'd seen him at

Embassy in his blue navy uniform, on that day he was in civilian clothes: a light-colored shirt, dotted tie, and an elegant grey flannel suit. Quite apart from the apparel, his presence was altogether incongruous in that consulting room fitted out with all the equipment of a profession that wasn't his: a metal screen with cotton curtain, glass cabinets full of jars and equipment, a stretcher over to one side, certificates and diplomas covering the walls. He shook my hand energetically, but didn't waste any more time on unnecessary formalities.

No sooner had we sat down than I started talking. I recalled the night with Beigbeder second by second, trying hard not to forget the slightest details. I related everything I'd heard from him, described his condition with minute precision, answered dozens of questions, and finally handed over his letters to Rosalinda intact. My explanation took more than a hour, during which time he listened as he sat with a focused expression while — cigarette by cigarette — he made his way methodically through an entire box of Craven A.

"We still don't know the impact this ministerial change will have on us, but the situation looks far from positive," he declared at last, putting out his final cigarette. "We've just notified London and haven't yet had a reply; in the meantime we're all just waiting. Which is why I ask you to be extremely cautious and not to make any mistakes now. Receiving Beigbeder in your house was a real act of rashness; I understand that you couldn't have denied him access, and you did well to calm him down and prevent his condition from degenerating, but the risk you ran was extremely high. From now on, do please be as cautious as you possibly can, and in the future try not to get yourself into similar situations. And take care with any suspicious presences around you, especially close to your home: don't rule out the possibility that you may be being watched."

"I won't, don't worry." I guessed that he might have suspected something about Ignacio following me, but I preferred not to ask.

"Everything's going to get even more complicated, that's the only thing we know for sure," he added as he held his hand out to me again, this time in farewell. "Once they're rid of the inconvenient minister, we can assume that Germany's pressure on Spain will increase, so remain vigilant and ready for any eventuality."

Over the months that followed I worked accordingly: I minimized the risks I took, tried to appear in public as little as possible, and focused on my work with all my energy. We went on sewing, more and more. The relative calm I'd gained by adding Doña Manuela to the workshop lasted barely a few weeks: the growing clientele and the approaching Christmas season obliged me to go back to devoting myself one hundred percent to my sewing. Between fittings, however, I remained engrossed in my other responsibility — the clandestine one. And so, as I was adjusting the sides of a cocktail dress, I'd also be obtaining information about what guests would attend the reception being held at the German embassy to honor Himmler, head of the Gestapo, and while I took measurements for a new suit for a baroness, I'd learn how enthusiastically Madrid's German colony was awaiting the arrival of Otto Horcher's new restaurant, modeled after the favorite restaurant of the Nazi high command back in their own capital. I told Hillgarth about all this and much more: dissecting the material minutely, choosing the most exact words, camouflaging my messages in supposed stitches, and dispatching them punctually. Following his warnings, I remained constantly alert and focused, bearing in mind everything that was happening around me. And as a result I did notice some things change in those days, little details that might have been a result of the new situation, or that were perhaps just mere chance. One Saturday at the Prado Museum I didn't see the silent bald man who usually received my portfolio filled with coded patterns; I never saw him again. A few weeks later the girl from the hairdresser's cloakroom was replaced by another woman: older, heavier, and equally inscrutable. I also noticed more vigilance on the streets and in the shops, and I learned to recognize who the people were who were watching: Germans the size of closets, silent and threatening with their overcoats down almost to their feet; skinny Spaniards who smoked nervously outside a front door, next to a business, behind a sign. Even though I wasn't really the target of their efforts, I did my best to ignore them, changing my route or crossing over to the opposite sidewalk when I spotted them. Sometimes, in order to avoid having to walk past or approach them directly, I would take refuge in some shop or other or pause at a roasted chestnut seller's stall or a window display. Other times they were impossible to avoid because I ran into them unexpectedly and with no opportunity to change direction. Then I'd steel myself with courage and formulate a silent Here Goes . . . picking up my pace firmly, looking straight ahead. Sure of myself, distant, almost haughty, as though what I was carrying were something purchased on a whim, or a little case full of makeup, rather than a shipment of coded information on the private agendas of the Third Reich's most powerful figures in Spain.

I also kept abreast of the political changes that surrounded me. As I used to do with Jamila in Tetouan, every morning I'd send Martina to buy the papers: *ABC, Arriba, El Alcázar.* Over breakfast, between sips of coffee, I'd devour the tales of what was happening in Spain and Europe. That was how I learned that Serrano Suñer had taken over as the new minister of foreign affairs. I scrutinized every word of the related news concerning the trip he and Franco made to meet Hitler in Hendaya. I read as well about the tripartite pact between Germany, Italy, and Japan; about the invasion of Greece; about the thousand movements occurring at vertiginous speed during those tempestuous times.

I read, I sewed, I passed on information. Passed on information, sewed, and read: that had been my day-to-day life during the final phase of that year that was drawing to a close. Perhaps that was why I agreed to celebrate its ending at the casino: some kind of entertainment would be good for me, to soothe all that tension.

Marita and Teté Álvarez-Vicuña approached their brother and me the moment they saw us enter the hall. We praised one another's dresses and hairdos, we remarked on frivolous, silly matters, and as usual I dropped in a few words of Arabic and the occasional phony expression in French. Meanwhile I was casting sidelong glances at the room and saw a number of familiar faces, several uniforms, and a few swastikas. I wondered how many of the people walking about so apparently relaxed were in fact, like me, informers and stool pigeons. Several, I guessed, and decided to trust no one and keep my eyes peeled; perhaps I could pick up some information that would be of interest to Hillgarth and his people. While my mind was musing on these plans and I pretended to be listening to the conversation, my hostess Marita moved away from me and disappeared for a few moments. When she returned she had someone on her arm, and I knew at once that the course of the night had changed.

CHAPTER FORTY-FIVE

"Arish, my dear, let me introduce you to my father-in-law-to-be, Gonzalo Alvarado. He's very keen to talk to you about his travels to Tangiers and the friends he left there; you probably know some of them."

And there indeed he was, Gonzalo Alvarado, my father. Dressed in tails and holding a crystal glass of whiskey that he had half drunk. The very first moment our eyes met I knew he was well aware of who I was. The second moment, I guessed that my invitation to that party had been his idea. But when he took my hand and brought it to his mouth to greet me with just the lightest trace of a kiss, no one in that hall could ever have imagined that the five fingers he was holding belonged to his own daughter. We'd only seen each other for a couple of hours in our lives, but they say that the call of blood is so powerful that sometimes recognitions like this are possible. Though, upon consideration, I wondered if perhaps it was his perceptiveness and good memory that outweighed any paternal instinct.

He was thinner and his hair whiter, but he still looked very fine. The orchestra struck up with "Aquellos ojos verdes," and he asked me to dance.

"You can't imagine how pleased I am to see you

605

again," he said. I could make out something like sincerity in his tone of voice.

"Me, too," I lied. The truth was, I wasn't sure if I was pleased or not; I was still too overwhelmed by the surprise to be able to formulate a reasonable judgment about it.

"So you've got a new name now, a new surname, and they say you're Moroccan. I don't suppose you're going to tell me what's behind all those changes."

"No, I don't think I will. Besides, Señor Alvarado, I don't think it would be of much interest to you; it's my own affair."

"Please, don't call me Señor Alvarado."

"As you wish. And would you like me to call you *papá,* then?" I asked with a trace of sarcasm.

"No, thank you. Gonzalo is fine."

"Very well. How are you, Gonzalo? I thought they'd killed you in the war."

"I survived, as you can see. It's a long story, too grim for a New Year's Eve. How's your mother?"

"Well. She's living in Morocco now, we have an atelier in Tetouan."

"So you listened to my advice after all and left Spain at the right moment?"

"More or less. Ours is a long story, too."

"Perhaps you'd like to tell it to me one day. We could meet for a chat; let me invite you to lunch," he suggested.

"I don't think I can. I don't have much of a social life, I have a lot of work. I came today at the behest of some clients. Naïve of me; at first I thought their insistence was completely disinterested. Turns out that behind an innocent, friendly invitation extended to the dressmaker of the moment there was something else. Because the idea

606

came from you, didn't it?"

He didn't say yes or no, but the affirmative hovered in the air, hanging between the chords of the bolero.

"Marita, my son's fiancée, is a good girl: affectionate and lively, more than most, though none too smart. In any case, I'm very grateful to have her: she's the only girl who's been able to tame your fly-by-night brother Carlos, and she'll be walking him down the aisle within a couple of months."

We both looked over toward my client. At just that moment she was whispering to her sister Teté, both of them keeping their eyes fixed on us, both of them in dresses from Chez Arish. With a false smile tightly on my lips, I solemnly promised myself never again to trust clients who with their siren songs lured solitary souls into danger on sad nights like this, marking the end of a year.

Gonzalo, my father, went on.

"I've seen you three times over the autumn. One time you were getting out of a taxi and going into Embassy; I was walking my dog just one hundred feet from the door, but you didn't notice."

"No, I didn't notice, you're right. I'm almost always in a hurry."

"It looked like you, but I was only able to see you for a few seconds, and I thought it might have been no more than an illusion. The second time was a Saturday morning at the Prado Museum. I like to go from time to time, and I followed you from a distance as you walked through a number of rooms. I still wasn't sure that you were who I thought you were. Then you headed for the cloakroom to pick up your portfolio and you sat down to draw opposite the portrait of Isabella of

Portugal, the one by Titian. I positioned myself in the opposite corner of the same room and stayed there watching, till you started gathering up your things. I left convinced that I hadn't made a mistake. It was you with a new style: more mature, more confident and elegant, but without a doubt the same daughter I met when she was scared as a mouse just before the war broke out."

I didn't want to allow the tiniest chink of melancholy in, so I interrupted at once.

"And the third?"

"Just a couple of weeks ago. You were walking along Velázquez, I was in the car with Marita; I was taking her home after a lunch at her friends' house, Carlos had things to do. The two of us saw you at the same time, and she — to my great surprise — pointed to you and told me you were her new designer, that you were from Morocco, and that you were called Arish something-or-other."

"Agoriuq. Actually it's my usual surname, turned back to front. Quiroga, Agoriuq."

"It sounds good. Shall we get a drink, Señorita Agoriuq?" he asked, with a teasing smile.

We made our way through, took two glasses of champagne from the silver tray that a waiter held out to us, and moved over to one side of the hall as the orchestra began playing a rumba and the dance floor filled up again with couples.

"I presume you'd rather I didn't reveal your real name to Marita, or my relationship to you," he said once we'd managed to withdraw from the hubbub. "As I've said, she's a good girl, but she loves gossip, and discretion isn't exactly her strong suit."

"I'd be grateful if you wouldn't say anything to

anyone. I do want you to understand, in any case, that my new name is official and my Moroccan passport is real."

"I imagine you have some serious reason for making the change."

"Naturally. I gain an air of exoticism in the eyes of my clientele, and at the same time I avoid the pursuit of the police over the charges your son is pressing against me."

"Carlos is pressing charges against you?" The hand holding his glass had stopped halfway to his mouth — his surprise seemed altogether genuine.

"Not Carlos; your other son, Enrique. Just before the war started. He accused me of having stolen the money and jewels that you gave me."

He smiled with his lips closed, bitterly.

"Enrique was killed three days after the uprising. A week earlier we'd had a terrible argument. He was deeply involved in politics; he sensed that something serious was about to happen and was very keen that we should get all the money we had in cash out of Spain, as well as the jewels and other valuables. I had to tell him that I'd given you a part of my estate: truth is, I could have remained silent, but I chose not to. Which was why I told him about Dolores, and I talked about you . . ."

". . . and he took it badly," I finished the sentence for him.

"He became like a man possessed and said all sorts of atrocious things. Then he called Servanda, the old servant — I imagine you remember her. He questioned her about you. She told him that you'd rushed out carrying a package and then he must have come up with this ridiculous story about the theft. After the argument he left, giving the door a slam that shook the walls of the building. The next time I saw him was eleven days later, in the morgue at the Metropolitan Stadium with a bullet in his head."

"I'm sorry."

He shrugged, a gesture of resignation. I could see a great sorrow in his eyes.

"He was foolish and wild, but he was my son. Our relationship toward the end was unpleasant and stormy; he was a member of the Falange, and I didn't like it. Looking back now, however, that Falange seems almost a blessing. At least they shared some romantic ideals and some principles that were rather utopian but still moderately reasonable. Its members were a gang of spoiled brats, dreamers, mostly quite idle, but mercifully they didn't have much to do with today's opportunists, who chant out the 'Cara al sol' anthem with their arms raised in salute and the veins in their neck throbbing, invoking the name of Primo de Rivera as though he were the Sacred Host, when before the war began they'd never even heard of him. They're no better than a gang of arrogant, grotesque good-for-nothings . . ."

Suddenly he returned to the blaze of the chandeliers, the sound of the maracas and the trumpets, the measured movement of the bodies to the time of "El manisero." He was back to reality, and back with me; he touched my arm, caressed it gently.

"I'm sorry, sometimes I get more worked up than I realize. I'm boring you, this isn't the time to be talking about such things. Do you want to dance?"

"No, I don't, thank you. I'd rather keep talking to you."

A waiter approached. We deposited our empty glasses on the tray and took full ones.

"We were talking about Enrique pressing charges against you," he said.

I didn't let him go on; first I wanted to clarify something that had been turning over in my mind since the beginning of our meeting.

"Before I tell you about that, tell me one thing — where's your wife?"

"I'm a widower. Before the war, not long after seeing you and your mother, in the spring of thirty-six. María Luisa was in the south of France with her sisters. One of them had a Hispano-Suiza and a driver who was too fond of nighttime parties. One morning he picked them up to take them to Mass; he probably hadn't gotten any sleep the night before and in a moment of extreme recklessness he went off the road. Two of the sisters were killed, María Luisa and Concepción. The driver lost a leg, and the third of the sisters, Soledad, ended up escaping injury. One of life's ironies, she was the eldest of the three."

"I'm so sorry."

"Sometimes I think it was best for her. She was very fearful, by nature she was extremely easily alarmed. The tiniest domestic occurrence upset her terribly. I don't think she could have borne the war, whether in Spain or outside it. And of course she never would have gotten over Enrique's death. So perhaps it was divine Providence doing her a favor by taking her before her time. And now, tell me more: we were talking about Enrique's accusation — do you know anything further, do you have any idea how the matter stands now?"

"No. In September, before I came over, the

police commissioner in Tetouan tried to investigate."

"To incriminate you?"

"No, to help me. Commissioner Vázquez isn't exactly a friend, but he's always been good to me. You have a daughter who's been in some trouble, do you realize that?"

It must have been clear from my tone that I wasn't joking.

"Will you tell me about it? I'd like to be able to help you."

"I don't think I need any help just now; at the moment everything's more or less under control, but thank you for the offer. In any case, you might be right: we should see each other again and talk at more leisure. These problems of mine partly affect you, too."

"Give me some idea first."

"I no longer have your mother's jewels."

He seemed not to be too perturbed.

"You had to sell them?"

"They were stolen."

"And the money?"

"That, too."

"All of it?"

"Everything."

"Where?"

"In a hotel in Tangiers."

"Who?"

"Someone extremely undesirable."

"Did you know him?"

"Yes. And now, if you don't mind, let's change the subject. Some other time I'll tell you the details more calmly."

It wasn't long till midnight now, and all around the room there were more and more bodies in

612

tails, dress uniforms, and evening gowns, and décolletages covered in jewels. There were Spaniards mostly, but also a good number of foreigners. German, English, American, Italian, Japanese — a whole potpourri of countries at war, in between a tangle of respectable, wealthy local citizens, all of them, for just a few hours, far away from the savage shredding of Europe and the squalor of a devastated people about to say good riddance to one of the most savage years in their history. Everywhere there was laughter and couples still sliding about to the infectious rhythm of the congas and *guaracha* folk songs that the orchestra of black musicians played without a break. The liveried lackeys who had received us, flanking the staircase, began to distribute small baskets of grapes and urged the guests to move out to the terrace to follow tradition and eat them in time with the chiming of the Puerta del Sol clock next door. My father offered me his arm and I took it; although we'd each arrived separately, we'd somehow silently agreed to see in the new year together. On the terrace we met up with a few friends, his son and my scheming clients. He introduced me to Carlos, my half brother, who looked like him and not in the least like me. How could he have guessed that the woman standing in front of him was a parvenue dressmaker of his own blood, whom his brother had accused of having done both of them out of a good slice of their inheritance?

No one seemed to mind the intense cold on the terrace: the number of guests had multiplied, and the waiters circulated tirelessly between them, emptying bottles of champagne wrapped in large white napkins. The animated conversations, the

613

laughs and clinking of glasses seemed suspended in the air, about to touch the dark winter sky. From the street, meanwhile, like a hoarse roaring, rose the sound of the voices of the unfortunate masses, those whom bad luck had doomed to remain out on the streets, sharing some cheap wine or a bottle of harsh liquor.

The chimes began, first the quarters, then the hour chimes. I began to eat my grapes, concentrating hard. Dong — one — dong — two — dong — three — dong — four. On the fifth I noticed that Gonzalo had brought his arm down to rest on my shoulders and was pulling me toward him; on the sixth my eyes filled with tears. The seventh, eighth, and ninth I swallowed blindly, struggling to stop myself from crying. On the tenth I succeeded, with the eleventh I gathered myself together, and as the last one chimed I turned to embrace my father for the second time in my life.

Chapter Forty-Six

In mid-January I met up with him again, to explain the details of the theft of my inheritance. I presumed that he believed the story; if he didn't, he hid it well. We had lunch at Lhardy and he suggested that we go on seeing each other. I said no, without having any very solid reason. Perhaps I thought it was too late for us to try to recover all those things we'd never shared. He kept insisting and seemed unprepared to accept my refusal easily. And he succeeded in part: bit by bit the wall of my resistance began to give way. We had lunch again, we went to the theater, to a concert at El Real; we even spent a Sunday morning together walking through El Retiro just as thirty years earlier he had done with my mother. He had a lot of time on his hands, since he was no longer working; when the war came to an end he'd had the opportunity to recover his foundry but chose not to reopen it. Then he sold the land where it stood and began to live off the income from the sale. Why didn't he want to go on, why didn't he start his business back up after the conflict? Out of sheer disappointment, I think. He never told me in any detail about the vicissitudes of those years, but comments dropped in other conversations we shared in those days allowed me more or less to reconstruct his painful journey. He didn't seem to be a resentful man, though: he was too rational to allow his emotions to take charge of his life. Although he belonged to the winning side, he was also extremely critical of the new regime. He was witty and a fine conversationalist, and between the two of us there grew a special relationship that we didn't intend as a compensation for his absence over all those years of my childhood and youth, but as a starting from scratch by way of a friendship between adults. There were mutterings about us in his circle, people speculated about the nature of the connection that held us together, a thousand wild assumptions reached his ears, which he shared with me, amused, never bothering to put anyone right.

My meetings with my father opened my eyes to a side of reality that I hitherto hadn't known. It was thanks to him that I learned that even though the newspapers never reported it, the country was going through a constant governmental crisis, in which rumors of dismissals and resignations, ministerial changeovers, rivalries, and conspiracies multiplied like the loaves and fishes. Beigbeder's fall, fourteen months after being sworn in in Burgos, had certainly been the most dramatic, but it was by no means the only one.

As Spain set slowly about its reconstruction, the various families that had contributed to winning the war, far from living together in harmony, began to squabble like cats and dogs. The army in confrontation with the Falange, the Falange at daggers with the monarchists, the monarchists furious because Franco wouldn't commit to restoration, and he himself, in El Pardo, never expressing his position clearly, remaining distant, signing sentences with a firm hand and never coming down in anyone's favor; Serrano Suñer above everyone, and everyone in turn against Serrano; some plotting on the side of the Axis, others for the Allies, each placing their bets blindly with no idea which side would eventually, as Candelaria had put it, driving the herd home.

In those days the British and the Germans were keeping up their constant tug-of-war both across the world and in the streets of the Spanish capital. Unfortunately for the cause in which fortune had positioned me, the Germans seemed to have a much more powerful and effective propaganda machine. As Hillgarth had told me in Tangiers, these efforts were managed from the embassy itself, with more than generous economic resources and a formidable team led by the famous Lazar, who was also able to count on the indulgence of the regime. I knew firsthand that his social activities never stopped: his dinners and parties were mentioned constantly in my workshop by the Germans and certain of the Spaniards, and every night one of my creations would make an appearance in his drawing rooms. Campaigns to promote Germany's reputation appeared with increasing frequency in the press, too. They used showy advertisements that displayed gas engines and fabric dyes with equal enthusiasm. The propaganda was incessant, merging ideas and products, persuading readers that the German ideology was capable of making advances that were unattainable to the world's other countries. The apparently commercial pretext of the advertisements didn't hide the real message: Germany was ready to dominate the planet, and they wanted to make this known to their good friends in Spain. And just so that there should be no doubt, they would often include in their propaganda some visually striking drawings, large lettering, and attractive maps of Europe in which Germany and the Iberian Peninsula were connected by means of bold arrows, while Great Britain appeared to have been swallowed up into the center of the earth.

In the pharmacies, cafés, and barbershops people passed around satirical magazines and books of crosswords that were gifts from the Germans; the jokes and stories were mixed up with accounts of victorious military operations, and the correct solution to all the puzzles was always politically inclined, and in favor of the Nazi cause. And there were also informational leaflets for professionals, adventure stories for young people and children, and even the parish newsletters of hundreds of churches. People also said that the streets were full of Spanish moles who'd been brought in by the Germans to disseminate propaganda directly to the people at tram stops and on lines in shops and cinemas. The messages were sometimes reasonably believable, at other times utter nonsense. There were malicious rumors flying back and forth that always spoke unfavorably of the British and those who supported them. That they were stealing the Spaniards' olive oil and taking it in diplomatic cars to Gibraltar. That the flour donated by the American Red Cross was so bad that it was making the Spanish people sick. That there was no fish to be had in the markets because our fishermen had been detained by ships from the British navy. That the quality of the bread was so terrible because His Majesty's subjects were sinking the Argentine ships that were carrying the wheat. That the Americans, in collaboration with the Russians, were putting finishing touches on their plans for an imminent invasion of the Peninsula.

The British, meanwhile, didn't fail to respond. Their reaction consisted mainly of finding every possible way to blame the Spanish regime for all the people's calamities, in particular striking them where it hurt most: the scarcity of food; the ravenous hunger that led people to make themselves sick eating filth from the trash; whole families running along desperately behind charity trucks; mothers having to manage, God only knows how, to make fritters without oil, omelets without eggs, sweets without sugar, and a strange sausage without a shred of pork and tasting suspiciously of cod. In order to strengthen the Spaniards' sympathy for the Allies' cause, the English sharpened their wits, too. The embassy's press office in Madrid drafted a homemade publication that the civil servants themselves worked diligently to hand out on the streets close to the legation, with the young press officer, Tom Burns, leading the way. The British Institute had been started up not long before, headed by one Walter Starkie, an Irish Catholic whom some people nicknamed Don Gitano. It had been opened, apparently, without any authorization from the Spanish authorities but with the genuine — albeit already weakened — support of Beigbeder, in the final throes of his time as a minister. It gave every appearance of being a cultural center that taught English and organized conferences, salons, and various other events, some of them more social than purely intellectual. But apparently it was at its core an undercover British propaganda operation that was much more sophisticated than the German one.

And so winter passed in this way, tense and full of hard work for almost everyone, countries and people alike. Then suddenly, without my even being aware of it, spring was upon us. With it came a new invitation from my father: the Zarzuela Hippodrome, the racecourse, was opening its doors — why didn't I go along with him?

When I was just a young apprentice at Doña Manuela's, we used to hear constant references to the Hippodrome, which our clients frequented. I don't suppose many of the ladies were interested in the racing itself, but just like the horses, they too were in competition. If not for speed, for elegance. In those days the old Hippodrome had been located at the end of the Paseo de la Castellana, and it was a social meeting place for the *haute bourgeoisie,* the aristocracy, and even royalty, with Alfonso XIII often to be seen in the royal box. Shortly before the war, work began on a new, more modern facility, but the conflict brought the project to an abrupt stop. After two years of peace, it was now — albeit still only half finished — opening its doors on the El Pardo hill.

For weeks, the opening was announced in the headlines and spread by word of mouth. My father came to fetch me in his car; he enjoyed driving. On the journey he explained to me just how the Hippodrome had been built with its innovative wavy roof and spoke about the enthusiasm of thousands of Madrileños to get back to the old races. I in turn described my recollections of the riding club in Tetouan, the imposing bearing of the caliph crossing the Plaza de España on horseback on Fridays, going from his palace to the mosque. We went on talking at such length

620

that he didn't have time to warn me that we would be meeting anyone else that afternoon. It wasn't till we arrived at our seats that I realized that by attending that apparently innocent event, I'd just stepped of my own free will directly into the very jaws of the wolf.

CHAPTER FORTY-SEVEN

The crowd attending the races was immense: a mass of people thronging around the ticket desks and in long lines to place their bets. The stands and the area closest to the track were filled to bursting with nervous, noisy groups of spectators. The privileged few who occupied the reserved boxes floated about in an altogether different dimension: untroubled, removed from the shouting, sitting in proper chairs rather than on cement steps, and being attended to by waiters in spotless jackets ready to provide diligent service.

As we entered the box, I could feel, deep down, something like the bite of an iron jaw. It only took me a couple of seconds to recognize the absurdity of my situation there, with only a handful of Spaniards mixed in with a large number of English men and women, glasses in hand and armed with binoculars, smoking, drinking, and chatting in their language while they waited for the galloping to begin. And lest there was any doubt about their cause or their origins, a large British flag had been draped over the handrail.

I wanted the earth to swallow me up, but my time hadn't come quite yet: my capacity for astonishment had not yet peaked. For that to happen, all I needed to do was take a few steps back and look over to my left. In the neighboring box, still nearly empty, three vertical banners fluttered in the wind: on the red background of each one was a white circle with a black swastika in the middle. The Germans' box, separated from ours by a low fence barely more than three feet high, awaited the arrival of its occupants. For now the only people in it were a couple of soldiers guarding the entrance and a handful of waiters setting up, but given the time and the haste with which they were making their preparations, I had no doubt at all that the Germans wouldn't be long in arriving.

Before I was able to calm myself down sufficiently to decide the quickest way to escape from this nightmare, Gonzalo explained to me in a whisper who all those subjects of His Gracious Majesty were.

"I forgot to tell you we'd be meeting some old friends I've not seen in a while, English engineers from the Río Tinto mines. They've come over with some of their compatriots from Gibraltar, and I imagine there will be some embassy people coming, too. They're all very excited about the reopening of the Hippodrome; you know they're crazy about horses."

I didn't know, nor did I care: at that moment I had other urgent matters to deal with besides these people's hobbies. How to fly from them like the plague, for example. Hillgarth's words in the American legation in Tangiers were still echoing in my ears — absolutely no contact with the English. And still less, he should have said, right under the noses of the Germans. When my father's friends became aware of our arrival, they started up with their greetings for "Gonzalo, old boy" and for his unexpected young companion. I returned the greetings with very few words, trying to mask my nerves behind a smile as weak as it was false, while at the same time secretly weighing up just how risky my situation was. As I clasped the hands that the anonymous faces held out to me, my eyes scanned my surroundings, looking for somewhere I might disappear without showing my father up. But it wasn't going to be easy. Not at all. To the left was the Germans' stand with its ostentatious banners; the right-hand side was occupied by a handful of individuals with generous bellies and thick gold rings, smoking cigars the size of torpedoes in the company of women with bleach-blond hair and lips as red as poppies, for whom I would never have sewn so much as a handkerchief in my workshop. I looked away from them all: the black marketeers and their gorgeous darlings didn't interest me in the least.

As I was blocked to my left and right, and with a handrail in front suspended over the void, the only solution was to escape the way we'd come, though I knew that would be extremely rash. There was only one means of access to those boxes, I'd learned on my arrival: a sort of brick-paved passageway only nine feet wide. If I decided to return that way, I ran a good risk of running straight into the Germans. And among them no doubt I'd bump into the thing that scared me the most: German clients whose careless mouths had often dropped tasty pieces of information that I'd gathered, with my most false of smiles, and passed on to the Secret Intelligence Service of their enemy country; ladies I'd have to stop to say hello to, and who without any doubt would wonder suspiciously what their Moroccan *couturière* was doing running from a box filled with Englishmen like a soul with the devil in pursuit.

Not knowing what to do, I left Gonzalo still greeting his friends and sat down in the corner best protected from the stand, with my shoulders hunched, the lapels of my jacket raised, and my head slightly bowed, trying — or so I was fooling myself — to pass unnoticed in an open space where I knew all too well it was impossible to hide.

"Are you feeling all right? You look pale," said my father, holding out a fruit cup.

"I think I'm just a bit queasy, it'll pass soon enough," I lied.

If there was anything darker than black on the spectrum of colors, my soul would have been about to turn that shade the moment the German box began to buzz with movement. Out of the corner of my eye I saw more soldiers coming in; behind them their solid-looking superior, giving orders, pointing this way and that, throwing glances filled with contempt toward the English box. They were followed by various officers in shiny boots, peaked caps, and the inevitable swastika on their arms. They didn't even deign to look over toward us: they just remained haughty and distant, their ramrod posture demonstrating an obvious contempt for the occupants of the neighboring box. A few other men in civilian clothes followed, and I noticed with a shudder that some of the faces were familiar to me. They had probably all — soldiers and civilians — dovetailed that event with a preceding one, which was why they'd arrived practically all together, already in their little clusters, and just in time to see the first race. At the moment there were only men; unless I was very much mistaken their wives wouldn't be far behind.

With each passing second the atmosphere became livelier, and my anxiety along with it. The British group had fed themselves, the field glasses were being passed from hand to hand, and the conversation flowed just as easily on the subjects of turf, paddock, and jockeys as it did on the invasion of Yugoslavia, the dreadful bombings of London, or Churchill's latest radio broadcast. And it was then that I saw him. I saw him and he saw me. And I caught my breath. Captain Alan Hillgarth had just entered the box with an elegant blond woman on his arm: his wife, most probably. His eyes lighted on me for just a fraction of a second and then, hiding a minute expression of alarm and distress that no one noticed but I, he looked swiftly over to the German box, where an endless trickle of people were still arriving.

I avoided him, getting up so as not to have to face him, convinced that I'd come to the end, that there was no earthly way of getting out of that mousetrap. I couldn't have foreseen a more pathetic denouement to my brief career as a collaborator with British intelligence: I was about to be unmasked in public, in front of my clients, my boss, and my own father. I grabbed hold of the handrail, squeezing tight, and wished with all my heart that this day had never come: that I'd never left Morocco, absolutely never accepted the ludicrous proposal that I'd received from an unwise, ridiculously clumsy conspirator. The gun went off for the first race, the horses began their feverish gallop, and the enthusiastic cries of the crowds tore through the air. My gaze seemed to be fixed on the track, but my thoughts were trotting along far from the horses' hooves. I sensed that the Germans must have been filling up their box and guessed at Hillgarth's unease as he tried to find some way to handle the setback that we were just about to face. And then, like a flash, the solution appeared before my eyes when I noticed a couple of Red Cross stretcher bearers leaning lazily against a wall in anticipation of a mishap. If I couldn't leave that poisoned box myself, someone would have to remove me.

The justification might have been the excitement of the moment, or tiredness that had been building up for months, perhaps nerves or stress. None of these was the real reason, however. The only thing that brought me to that unexpected reaction was my survival instinct. I chose the most suitable place, the right-hand side of the stand, the side farthest from the Germans. And I calculated the perfect moment: a few seconds after the first race had come to an end, when hubbub filled the stands and shouts of enthusiasm mingled with noisy expressions of disappointment. At that exact moment, I collapsed. With a premeditated movement I turned my head and made sure my hair would cover my face once I was on the ground, in case any curious glances from the adjacent box might make it through the pairs of legs that surrounded me. I remained still, my eyes closed and my body limp; my hearing was still alert, however, taking in each and every one of the voices around me. *Faint, air, Gonzalo, quick, pulse, water, more air, quick, quick, they're coming, first-aid box,* and various other words in English that I didn't understand. The stretcher bearers only took a couple of minutes to arrive. They lifted me from the ground onto the canvas and covered me with a blanket right up to my neck. One, two, three, up, and I felt myself being lifted.

"I'll go with you," I heard Hillgarth say. "If we need to, we can call the doctor from the embassy."

"Thank you, Alan," replied my father. "I don't think it'll be anything serious, she's just fainted. Let's take her to the infirmary, then we'll see."

The stretcher bearers made their way quickly down the access tunnel, carrying me between them; behind, rushing to keep the pace, followed my father, Alan Hillgarth, and a couple of other Englishmen I wasn't able to identify, colleagues or deputies of the naval attaché's. I had tried to get my hair at least partly covering my face again once I was on the stretcher, but I needn't have bothered; before they carried me out of the box I recognized Hillgarth's firm hand pulling the blanket up to my forehead. I couldn't see anymore, but I could hear everything that happened next quite clearly.

Over the first few yards of the exit corridor we didn't meet anyone, but about halfway down the situation changed. And with it, my grimmest premonitions were confirmed. First I heard more footsteps and men's voices speaking quickly in German. *Schnell, schnell, sie haben bereits begonnen.* They were approaching us from the opposite direction, almost running. I could tell by the firmness of their step that they were soldiers; the certainty and forcefulness of their tone led me to conclude that they were officers. I imagine that the sight of the enemy naval attaché escorting a stretcher with a body covered by a blanket must have caused them a certain alarm, but they didn't stop; they just exchanged a few brusque greetings and continued vigorously along their way to the box adjacent to the one we'd just left. The tapping of heels and the women's voices reached my ears just a few seconds later. I heard them approach — also with firm steps — solid and dominating. Inhibited by such a display of determination, the stretcher bearers moved over to one side, pausing a moment to let them by; they almost touched us as they passed. I held my breath and noticed that my heart was pounding hard; then I heard them move away. I didn't recognize any of the voices in particular, nor could I have said how many of them there were, but I calculated at least half a dozen. Six German women, perhaps seven, perhaps more; maybe several of them were clients of mine, the ones who selected the most elegant fabrics and who paid me both in banknotes and in freshly baked news.

I pretended to regain consciousness a few minutes later, when the noises and the voices had died down and I guessed that we were on safe ground at last. I said a few words, calmed them down. We reached the infirmary; Hillgarth and my father sent away the stretcher bearers and the Englishmen who'd been accompanying us; the latter were dismissed by the naval attaché with a few brief orders in their language, the former Gonzalo released with a generous tip and a packet of cigarettes.

"I'll take care of it, Alan, thank you," said my father at last, when the three of us were alone. He took my pulse and made sure that I was reasonably all right. "I don't think there's any need to call a doctor. I'll try to bring the car around here: I'll get her home."

I noticed that Hillgarth hesitated a few seconds.

"Very well," he said. "I'll stay with her till you get back."

I didn't move until I had calculated that my father was far enough away. Only then did I summon up my courage, standing up to face him.

"You're fine, aren't you?" Hillgarth asked, eyeing me severely.

I could have said no, that I was still feeling weak and disoriented, I could have pretended that I still hadn't recovered from the effects of the apparent faint. But I knew he wouldn't believe me. And rightly so.

"Perfectly," I replied.

"Does he know anything?" he asked, referring to my father's awareness of my collaboration with the English.

"Not a thing."

"Keep it that way. And don't even think of allowing yourself to be seen with your face uncovered on the way out," he commanded. "Lie down on the back seat of the car and remain covered up the whole time. When you get home, make sure that no one has followed you."

"That's fine. Anything else?"

"Come and see me tomorrow. Same time, same place."

Chapter Forty-Eight

"A magnificent performance at the Hippodrome," was his greeting to me. In spite of the apparent compliment, his face didn't show the slightest trace of satisfaction. He was waiting for me at Dr. Rico's office again, in the same place where we'd met months earlier to talk about my encounter with Beigbeder following his dismissal.

"I had no other choice, believe me when I say how sorry I am," I said as I sat down. "I had no idea we were going to be watching the races from the English box. Nor that the Germans would be occupying the one right alongside us."

"I understand. And you responded well, coolly and quickly. But you ran an extremely high risk and almost set off a completely unnecessary crisis. We can't permit ourselves such carelessness, especially with the situation so complicated right now."

"Are you referring to the situation in general, or to mine in particular?" I asked with an arrogant tone that I hadn't intended.

"Both," he declared firmly. "Look, it's not our intention to meddle in your private life, but given what's happened, I feel we have to bring something to your attention."

"Gonzalo Alvarado," I suggested.

631

He didn't reply right away; first he took a few moments to light a cigarette.

"Gonzalo Alvarado, indeed," he said after blowing out the smoke from his first drag. "What happened yesterday wasn't an isolated incident: we know that you've been seen together in public places relatively often."

"If you're interested, let me say quite clearly before we go on that I'm not having any kind of romantic relationship with him. And as I told you yesterday, he knows nothing about my activities."

"The precise nature of your relationship with him is an entirely private matter and in no way our concern," he explained.

"So then?"

"I'm asking that you don't consider this a thoughtless invasion of your private life, but you must understand that the situation right now is extremely tense and we have no choice but to warn you." He got up and took a few steps with his hands in his pockets and his eyes fixed on the floor tiles as he went on talking, without looking at me. "Last week we learned that there is an active group of Spanish informers cooperating with the Germans to develop files on local Germanophiles and supporters of the Allies. They're including information on all those Spaniards with a significant attachment to one cause or the other, as well as their degree of affiliation to them."

"And you think I'm in one of those files."

"We don't think it, we know it with absolute certainty," he said, fixing his eyes on mine. "We have collaborators who have infiltrated them and they've told us that you're there among the Germanophiles. Right now you're still uncompromised, as we might have suspected: you have copious clients related to the Nazi high command, they visit you in your workshop, you sew beautiful clothes for them, and in exchange they don't just pay you, they also confide in you, so much so that when they're in your house they speak absolutely freely about things they shouldn't speak about and that you pass straight on to us."

"And Alvarado, what does he have to do with all this?"

"He's also in their files. But he's on the opposite side, on the roster of citizens supportive of the British. And we've received news that there's been a German order for maximum surveillance of Spanish people from certain sectors who are connected to us: bankers, businessmen, liberal professionals — citizens with means and influence who would be prepared to help our cause."

"I imagine you know he's no longer working, that he didn't reopen his firm after the war," I pointed out.

"Doesn't matter. He has excellent relationships with members of the embassy staff and the British colony in Madrid and allows himself to be seen with them frequently. Sometimes even with me, as you will have learned yesterday. He's very familiar with Spanish industry, which is why he advises us disinterestedly on a number of related matters. But unlike you, he isn't an undercover agent, merely a good friend to the English people who doesn't disguise his sympathies toward us. Which is why if you allow yourself to be seen with him too much, it might look suspicious, given that you appear in opposing files. There's actually already been a rumor about it."

"About what?" I asked, a little rudely.

"About what the devil someone so close to the

wives of the German high command is doing letting herself be seen in public with a loyal friend to the British," he replied with a thump on the table. Then his tone became gentler, as he immediately regretted his reaction. "Forgive me, please; we've all been very nervous lately, and besides, we knew you weren't informed of the situation and couldn't possibly have predicted the risks in advance. But trust me when I tell you that the Germans are planning a very powerful campaign to put pressure on British influence in Spain. This country is still crucial to Europe and could join the war at any moment. Actually the government is continuing to help the Axis shamelessly: they allow them to use the Spanish ports freely, they authorize mining operations wherever they please, and they're even using Republican prisoners to work on military construction that could help with a possible German attack on Gibraltar."

He stubbed out his cigarette and was silent for a few moments, concentrating on what he was doing. Then he went on.

"In the current circumstances we are at a clear disadvantage, and the last thing we want is to complicate matters even further," he said slowly. "Months ago the Gestapo launched a series of threatening actions that have already borne fruit: your friend Mrs. Fox, for example, had to leave Spain because of them. And regrettably there have been several other such cases: to take one close-to-home example, the old embassy doctor, who was a very good friend of mine. From now on, things are looking worse still. More direct and aggressive. More dangerous."

I didn't interrupt, I just watched, waiting for him to end his explanations.

"I don't know if you understand the extent to which you're compromised and exposed," he added, lowering his voice. "Arish Agoriuq has become a very well-known figure among the German women living in Madrid, but if they start to see some wavering in your position as was almost the case yesterday, you could find yourself implicated in highly undesirable situations. And that's no good. Neither for you, nor for us."

I got up from my seat and walked over toward a window but didn't dare approach it all the way. With my back to Hillgarth, I looked through the glass into the distance. The branches of the trees, filled with leaves, reached the height of the second story. It was still light — the evenings were already getting long. I tried to consider the implications of what I'd just heard. Despite the grim outlook, I wasn't afraid.

"I think it would be best for me to stop collaborating with you," I said at last without looking at him. "We'd avoid problems and live more peacefully. You, me, everybody."

"Not at all," he protested firmly behind me. "All I've just said was merely by way of prevention and as a warning for the future. We have no doubt of your ability to adapt when the time comes. But under no circumstances do we want to lose you, especially not now when we need you somewhere new."

"I beg your pardon?" I asked, astonished, turning around.

"We have another mission. We've received a request to collaborate, coming directly from London. Although in the beginning we were considering other options, in view of what happened this weekend we've decided to assign it to

635

you. Do you think your assistant could take care of your workshop for a couple of weeks?"

"Well . . . I don't know . . . perhaps . . . ," I stammered.

"I'm sure she can. Put the word out among your clients that you're going to be away for a while."

"Where do I tell them I'm going to be?"

"There's no need to lie, just tell them the truth: that you have some business to attend to in Lisbon."

CHAPTER FORTY-NINE

The Lusitania Express left me at the Santa Apolónia Station one morning in mid-May. I was carrying two huge suitcases with my best clothes, a handful of detailed instructions, and an invisible supply of aplomb; I was trusting that this would be enough for me to make it through this tricky situation without too much trouble.

I'd hesitated for a while before I was able to convince myself to go ahead with this assignment. I'd reflected, weighed my options, and evaluated alternatives. I knew that the ball was in my court — only I could choose between continuing with that murky life or leaving it all behind and returning to normality.

The latter would probably have been the more sensible of the two options. I was fed up with deceiving everybody, with not being able to be straight with anyone, with complying with inconvenient orders and living in a constant state of alert. I was about to turn thirty. I'd become an unscrupulous liar and my personal history was no more than a pile of deceits, inconsistencies, and falsehoods. In spite of the apparent sophistication with which I lived, at the end of the day — as Ignacio had insisted on reminding me some months earlier — all that remained of me was a

637

lonely ghost living in a house filled with shadows. And when I'd left the meeting with Hillgarth I felt a burst of hostility toward him and his people. They'd entangled me in a strange, sinister adventure that was supposedly in my country's interests, but as the months passed nothing appeared to straighten itself out, and the fear that Spain would enter the war continued to hang in the air on every street corner. All the same, I kept to his conditions without venturing from the rules — they'd forced me to become selfish and insensitive, to stick to an unreal side of Madrid and be disloyal to my people and my past. They'd made me fearful and unsettled; I'd spent nights lying wide awake, through hours of infinite anxiety. And now they wanted me to leave my father, too, the only presence who brought a speck of light into the dark passage of my days.

There was still time for me to say no, to dig my heels in and shout, "That's it, enough is enough." To hell with the British Secret Intelligence Service and all its stupid demands. To hell with the eavesdropping in the fitting rooms, the ridiculous lives of the Nazi wives and messages sewn into patterns. I didn't care who would win that conflict that was so far away; it was entirely their problem if the Germans invaded Britain and ate their children raw or if the British bombed Berlin till it was left flat as an ironing board. That wasn't my world: to hell with them all, forever.

To leave it all, and go back to normality: yes, that was undoubtedly the better option. The problem was, I didn't know where to find it. Was it on the Calle de la Redondilla of my youth, among the girls I grew up with and who after the war were still struggling to keep their heads above water? Did Ignacio Montes take it away on the day he walked out of my square dragging a typewriter along with him, his heart broken into pieces? Or perhaps it was stolen from me by Ramiro Arribas when he left me, alone and pregnant and ruined, inside the walls of the Continental? Would I find normality in the Tetouan of my first few months, surrounded by the sad inhabitants of Candelaria's boardinghouse, or did it dissolve into the sordid intrigues that had allowed the two of us to get ahead? Did I leave it behind in the house on Sidi Mandri, hanging from the threads in the workshop that I struggled so hard to set up? Maybe Félix Aranda took it one rainy night, or Rosalinda Fox when she left the storeroom at Dean's Bar to disappear like a secret shadow into the Tangiers streets? Would normality be with my mother, working wordlessly in the African afternoons? Was it eliminated by a deposed, arrested minister, or perhaps it was torn away by a journalist whom I never dared to love out of sheer cowardice? Where was it, when had I lost it, what had become of it? I searched for it everywhere: in my pocket, in the closets and drawers, between folds and stitches. That night I fell asleep without having found it.

The following day I awoke with a strange feeling of lucidity, and no sooner had I opened my eyes than I saw it: close by, just there with me, clinging to my skin. Normality wasn't in the days I'd left behind me: it was only to be found in whatever fortune placed in my path each morning. In Morocco, in Spain, or in Portugal, running a dressmaker's studio or in the service of British intelligence: wherever I chose to direct my course or lay down the foundations of my life, there it would be, my normality. Amid the shadows, under the palm trees on a square that smelled of mint, in the dazzle of grand halls lit by chandeliers or the stormy waters of war. Normality was simply whatever my own will, my commitment, and my word accepted as such, which was why it would always be with me. To look for it somewhere else or to try to retrieve it from yesterday made no sense at all.

I went to Embassy at midday with my thoughts in order and my mind clear. I checked that Hillgarth was finishing off his aperitif, leaning on the bar as he chatted to a couple of uniformed soldiers, before I dropped my handbag on the floor with brazen carelessness. Four hours later I received my first orders about the new mission: they summoned me for a facial the following morning at the beauty salon where I had my hair done every week. Five days later, I arrived in Lisbon. I stepped down onto the platform in a patterned gauze dress, white spring gloves, and an enormous sun hat: a froth of glamour amid the coal smoke from the locomotives and the grey hurry of the travelers. An anonymous motorcar was awaiting me, ready to transport me to my destination: Estoril.

We made our way through a Lisbon that was filled with wind and light, without rationing or electricity blackouts, with flowers, tiles, and street stalls of fresh fruits and vegetables. Without plots of land filled with rubbish or ragged tramps, without shell craters, without arms raised in salute or the yoke and arrows of the Falange emblem painted in thick brushstrokes on the walls. We went through the posher neighborhoods, elegant with wide stone sidewalks and grand buildings

640

guarded by statues of kings and explorers; we also crossed working-class neighborhoods with winding roads full of bustle and geraniums, and smelling of sardines. I was surprised by the majesty of the Tagus, the wailing of the foghorns at the port, and the squealing of the trams. Lisbon fascinated me — it was a city neither at peace nor at war. Nervous, agitated, throbbing.

We left Alcántara behind us, and Belém and its monuments. The waters beat hard as we made our way along the coast road. To our right were old villas protected by wrought iron railings that supported creeping vines heavy with flowers. Everything seemed different and noteworthy, but perhaps in another way than its mere appearance. I'd been warned to expect it — the picturesque Lisbon that I'd just been looking at out of my car window and the Estoril where I'd be arriving in a few minutes were full of spies. The slightest rumor came at a cost, and anyone with two ears was a potential informer, from the highest-ranking members of an embassy staff to waiters, shopkeepers, maids, and taxi drivers. The message I received once again was "Extreme caution."

I had a room reserved at the Hotel do Parque, a magnificent residence for a largely international clientele, which tended to house more German guests than English. Nearby, at the Hotel Palacio, the opposite was the case. And then, at nighttime at the casino, everyone would come together under the same roof: in this theoretically neutral country, gaming and luck took no interest in war. The moment my car stopped a liveried bellhop opened the door while another took charge of my luggage. I entered the lobby as though stepping onto a carpet of safety and unconcern, and I

641

removed the dark glasses that had been protecting me since I'd disembarked from the train. My eyes swept across the grand reception hall with a gaze of studied disdain. The sheen of the marble didn't impress me, nor the rugs and velvet upholstery, nor the columns rising up to the ceiling, vast as those of a cathedral. Nor did I pause to examine the elegant guests who individually or in groups sat reading the papers, chatting, drinking a cocktail, or watching life pass by. My potential to react to all that glamour was more than under control by now: I didn't pay them the least attention, merely made my way decisively over to the desk to check myself in.

I ate alone at the hotel restaurant, then spent a couple of hours in my bedroom lying on my back staring at the ceiling. At a quarter to six the phone yanked me out of my self-absorption. I let it ring three times, swallowed, raised the receiver, and answered. And then the wheels began to turn.

CHAPTER FIFTY

I'd received my instructions days earlier in Madrid via a most unconventional channel. For the first time it hadn't been Hillgarth who'd been responsible for giving them to me, but someone under his command. The woman who worked at the beauty salon who was there every week led me dutifully to one of the inner rooms where they did their beauty treatments. Of the three reclining chairs they used for these functions, the one on the right, almost horizontal, was already occupied by a client whose features I wasn't able to make out. She had a towel wrapped around her hair like a turban, another round her whole body from her neckline to her knees. She had a kind of white mask covering her whole face apart from her mouth and eyes, which were closed.

I changed behind a screen and sat down in the adjacent seat in identical apparel. After the employee had reclined my backrest with a pedal and put the same mask on me, she left silently, shutting the door behind her. Only then did I hear the voice next to me.

"We're glad that you will be undertaking the mission after all. We trust you, we think you'll do a good job."

She spoke without moving, her voice low and

with a heavy English accent. Like Hillgarth she used the plural "we." She didn't identify herself.

"I'll do my best," I replied, looking at her out of the corner of my eye.

I heard the click of a lighter and a familiar smell filled the air.

"We've had a request directly from London to provide reinforcements," she went on. "There are suspicions that a supposed Portuguese collaborator might be playing a double game. He isn't an agent, but he has an excellent relationship with our diplomatic staff in Lisbon and he's involved in various deals with British firms. There are indications, however, that he's beginning to establish parallel relationships with the Germans."

"What kind of relationships?"

"Commercial relationships — very powerful ones, probably aimed not only at benefiting the Germans but also at boycotting us. It isn't entirely clear. Food, minerals, perhaps arms: products for the war. As I say, everything is still only within the realm of suspicion."

"And what would I have to do?"

"We need a foreigner who won't be suspected of having any relationship with the British. Someone coming from a more or less neutral territory, completely unconnected with our country, who might need to go to Lisbon to acquire stock of something concrete. And you fit that profile."

"So the idea is that I'm going to Lisbon to buy fabrics, or something like that?" I asked, as I cast another glance over at her that she did not return.

"Precisely. Fabrics and merchandise related to your work," she confirmed without moving a muscle. She was still in the same position in which I'd found her, with her eyes closed and almost exactly horizontal. "You'll go under the cover of a dressmaker wanting to obtain materials that are still not possible to get hold of in this ruined Spain."

"I could have had them sent to me from Tangiers," I interrupted.

"That, too," she said after exhaling the smoke from another drag on her cigarette. "But for different reasons you're going to have to rule out all the other alternatives. Silk from Macao, the Portuguese colony in Asia, for example. One of the sectors in which our suspect has thriving commercial interests is in textile import and export. Normally he works on a large scale, only dealing with wholesalers and not with private buyers, but we've managed to arrange for him to meet you personally."

"How?"

"Thanks to a chain of varied undercover connections: quite common in the world we move in. It's not the time to go into details now. That way, not only will you arrive in Lisbon free of any suspicion of affinity to the British, but you'll also be backed up with contacts with direct connections to the Germans."

That whole widespread network of relationships was quite beyond me, so I chose to ask as little as possible and wait for this stranger to go on dispensing information and instructions.

"The suspect's name is Manuel Da Silva. He's a businessman, a good one and very well connected, who seems ready to multiply his fortune in this war even though to do it he'd have to betray the people who have been his friends. He'll get in touch with you and secure you access to the best fabrics available in Portugal today."

"Does he speak Spanish?"

"Perfectly. And English. And possibly also German. He speaks all the languages he requires to do his business."

"And what am I expected to do?"

"Infiltrate his life. Be charming, win his affection, work hard to make him ask you to go out with him, and above all get yourself invited to a meeting with Germans. If you're finally able to get close to them, what we need is for you to sharpen your senses and register any relevant information that reaches your eyes and ears. Get hold of as complete an account as possible: names, businesses, firms, and products they mention; plans, activities, and any additional pieces of information you consider interesting."

"You're telling me that you're sending me over to seduce a suspect?" I asked in disbelief, sitting up in my chair.

"Use whatever resources you think most appropriate," she replied, fully justifying my assumption. "It would appear that Da Silva is a confirmed bachelor who likes to wine and dine beautiful women without involving himself in any kind of relationship. He enjoys being seen with elegant, attractive ladies, and if they're foreign, so much the better. But according to our sources, in his dealings with the female gender he's also the perfect old-style Portuguese gentleman, so you needn't worry because he won't try to go any farther than you're prepared to go."

I didn't know whether to be offended or to burst out laughing. I was being sent over to seduce a seducer, that's what my thrilling Portuguese mission was going to be. For the first time in the whole conversation, however, the unknown woman in the neighboring chair seemed to read my mind.

"Please don't believe that your assignment is something frivolous that any beautiful woman could take on in exchange for a few banknotes. It's a delicate operation, and you're the person to do it because we have confidence in your abilities. It's true that your physical appearance, your apparent origins, and the fact that you're a single woman could help, but your responsibility will go far beyond mere flirtation. You'll have to win Da Silva's trust, weighing each step you take with great care; you'll have to calculate your moves and balance them precisely. You'll be gauging the scope of situations yourself, controlling the timing, evaluating the risks, and deciding to proceed as each situation demands. We place great value on your experience in the systematic obtaining of information and your capacity to improvise in unexpected situations: you haven't been selected for this mission at random, but because you've demonstrated that you have the resources to get by effectively in difficult circumstances. And on personal matters, as I've already said, you needn't go beyond whatever limits you yourself choose to impose. But please, stick it out for as long as possible until you get the information you need. It's basically not all that different from your work in Madrid."

"Except that here I don't need to flirt with anyone or sneak into private meetings," I pointed out.

"That's true, my dear. But it won't require much time, and with a gentleman who it would appear is far from unattractive." Her tone of voice surprised me: she wasn't trying to minimize the matter, but merely making a cool statement of what to her was objective fact. "Just one more thing, something important," she added. "You won't have any local contact support, because London doesn't want any suspicion about your assignment to be aroused in Lisbon. Remember there aren't any guarantees about Da Silva's dealings with the Germans, which is why his supposed disloyalty to the British is yet to be proved: as I've said, everything is currently in the realm of mere speculation and we don't want him to suspect anything of our compatriots in Portugal. So no English agent based there is going to know who you are or what your relationship to us is: your mission will be brief, quick, and clean, and we'll inform London about its conclusions directly from Madrid. Get in, gather the information you need, and come back home. Then we'll see how things progress from here. No more than that."

It wasn't easy for me to reply; the mask had solidified on the skin of my face. I managed at last, barely parting my lips.

"And no less."

At that moment the door opened. The employee came back in and set to work on the Englishwoman's face. She worked for more than twenty minutes, during which time we didn't exchange another word. When she finished, the girl went out again and my unknown instructor proceeded to get dressed behind the screen.

"We know that you have a good friend in Lisbon, but we don't think it wise that you see each other," she said from the other side of the room. "Mrs. Fox has accordingly been advised to act as though you don't know each other if you happen to run into her at any point. We'd ask you to do the same."

"Very well," I muttered through stiff lips. I didn't like that instruction one bit. I'd have loved to have seen Rosalinda again. But I understood why it was inconvenient and I obeyed: there was no other way.

"Tomorrow you'll receive details about the journey, with perhaps some additional information as well. The time we're predicting for your mission is no more than two weeks: if for some extremely urgent reason you need to stay a little longer, send a cable to the Bourguignon florists and ask them to send a bouquet of flowers to a nonexistent friend for her birthday. Invent the name and address; the flowers will never leave the shop, but if they receive an order from Lisbon they'll pass the message on to us. Then we'll get in touch with you somehow, you can count on that."

The door opened again, and the employee came back in, laden with towels. This time I would be the object of her ministrations. With apparent docility I let her do her work, while I tried to see the just-dressed person who was about to emerge from behind the screen. She didn't take long, but when she finally came out she was very careful not to turn her face toward me. I saw that her hair was fair and wavy, and she was wearing a tweed jacket, a typical outfit for the English. She reached out her arm to pick up a leather handbag that was resting on a little stool against the wall, a bag that looked vaguely familiar: I'd seen someone carrying it recently and it wasn't the sort of accessory one could buy in Spanish shops in those days. Then she reached out a hand to a little red pack of cigarettes that had been left carelessly on a bench. And then I knew — the lady who smoked Craven A and who at that moment was leaving the room with no more than a muttered "Goodbye" was Captain Alan Hillgarth's wife. The same one I'd seen just a few days earlier, on the arm of her husband, when he, the steely head of the Secret Intelligence Service in Spain, saw me at the Hippodrome and received one of the greatest shocks of his career.

Chapter Fifty-One

Manuel Da Silva was waiting for me at the hotel bar. The place was busy: groups, couples, men on their own. No sooner had I gone in through the double doors than I knew which one was him. And he knew me.

Thin and elegant, dark, with his temples beginning to go silver and wearing a light dinner jacket. Carefully tended hands, dark eyes, elegant gestures. He did indeed have the bearing and the manners of a Don Juan. But there was something more to him than that: something I could tell the moment we exchanged our first greeting and he ushered me onto the terrace overlooking the garden. Something that put me instantly on my guard. Intelligence. Wisdom. Determination. Worldliness. To deceive a man like that I'd need a whole lot more than a few charming smiles and an arsenal of flirtatious gestures.

"I can't tell you how sorry I am not to be able to have dinner with you, but as I said on the phone I have a prior engagement that was arranged weeks ago," he said as he gallantly held the back of my chair.

"Don't worry in the slightest," I replied, settling myself with feigned languor. The saffron-colored gauze of my dress almost brushed against the floor; with a studied gesture I flicked my hair back over my bare shoulders and crossed my legs to reveal an ankle, the arch of a foot, and the pointed tip of a shoe. I noticed how Da Silva didn't take his eyes off me for a second. "Besides," I added, "I'm a little tired after the journey; it'd do me good to get an early night."

A waiter positioned the champagne bucket beside us and placed two glasses on the table. The terrace looked out over a luxuriant garden filled with trees and plants; it was getting dark, but it was still possible to make out the last glimmers from the sun. A light breeze reminded us that the sea was very close. It smelled of flowers, of French perfume, of salt and greenery. There was a piano playing inside, and from the nearby tables came relaxed conversations in a variety of languages. The dry, dusty Madrid that I'd left behind me less than twenty-four hours earlier suddenly seemed like a dark nightmare from another world.

"I have a confession to make," said my host once the glasses had been filled.

"As you wish," I replied, bringing mine to my lips.

"You're the first Moroccan woman I've met in my whole life. This area is full of foreigners at the moment, of a thousand different nationalities, but they all come from Europe."

"You've never been in Morocco?"

"No. And I wish I had; especially if all the Moroccan women are like you."

"It's a fascinating country with marvelous people, but I'm afraid you'd find it hard to find many women like me there. I'm an atypical Moroccan, because my mother is Spanish. I'm not Muslim, and my mother tongue isn't Arabic

652

but Spanish. But I adore Morocco: that's where my family lives, too, and that's where I have my house and my friends. Though I'm living in Madrid at the moment."

I drank again, satisfied at not having had to lie any more than necessary. Brazen falsehoods had become a constant in my life, but I felt safer when I didn't need to have excessive recourse to them.

"Your Spanish is excellent, too," I noted.

"I've worked a lot with Spaniards; actually, my father had a Spanish business partner for many years. Before the war — the Spanish war, that is — I used to go to Madrid on business often; lately I've been concentrating more on other dealings and I travel less to Spain."

"It's probably not the best time."

"That depends," he said with a touch of irony. "It would seem that things are going very well for you."

I smiled again, wondering what the hell they'd been telling him about me.

"I see you're well informed."

"I do my best."

"Well, yes, I must admit, my little business hasn't been doing badly at all. Actually that's why I'm here, as you know."

"To take the best materials back to Spain for the new season."

"Indeed, that's my plan. I've heard that you have some wonderful Chinese silks."

"Do you want to know the truth?" he asked with a wink of pretend complicity.

"Yes, please," I said, lowering my voice and playing along.

"Well, the truth is, I have no idea," he explained with a laugh. "I don't have the slightest idea of

653

what the silks we're importing from Macao are like; I don't deal with them directly. The textile sector . . ."

A slender young man with a thin mustache, perhaps his secretary, approached discreetly, excusing himself in Portuguese, and came up to his left ear, whispering a few words I wasn't able to hear. I pretended to be looking out into the night that was falling over the garden. The white spheres of the street lamps had just been lit, the animated conversations and the piano chords still floated through the air. But my mind, far from relaxing in that paradise, remained alert to what was happening between the two men. I guessed that this interruption was something they had planned in advance: that way if he wasn't enjoying my presence, Da Silva would have an excuse to make an immediate disappearance, justifying himself with some unexpected matter that needed taking care of. If, however, he decided I was worth spending his time with, he could acknowledge the fact and dismiss the new arrival without any further fuss.

To my good fortune, he chose the latter.

"As I was saying," he went on once his assistant had left, "I don't deal directly with the fabrics we import; that is, I keep myself informed about the facts and figures, but I don't know about the aesthetic matters that I presume will be of interest to you."

"Perhaps you have an employee who might be able to help me," I suggested.

"Yes, of course; my staff is extremely efficient. But I'd like to look after you myself."

"I wouldn't want to cause you any —" I interrupted.

He didn't let me finish.

"It would be a pleasure to be able to assist you," he said, gesturing to the waiter to refill our glasses. "How long did you mean to stay with us?"

"A couple of weeks. Apart from the materials, I'd like to make the most of my trip to visit some other suppliers, perhaps some designers' studios. And shops, too: for shoes, hats, lingerie, notions . . . I n Spain, as I'm sure you know, it's barely possible to find anything decent these days."

"I'll give you all the contacts you need, you can count on that. Let me think: tomorrow morning I'm going on a short trip, I'm sure it'll be a matter of a couple of days, no more than that. Would meeting on Thursday morning suit you?"

"Of course, but I must insist, I really don't want to trouble you . . ."

He sat forward in his chair and leaned over, looking me straight in the eye.

"You could never be any trouble."

That's what you think, I thought, quick as a flash. My mouth, however, was fixed in a smile.

We went on chatting about trivialities; ten minutes, maybe fifteen. When I calculated that it was time to bring the meeting to an end I faked a yawn and immediately mumbled an embarrassed apology. "I'm so sorry. The overnight train was exhausting."

"I'll let you get some rest then," he said, getting up.

"And besides, you have a dinner."

"Ah yes, the dinner, that's right." He didn't even bother to look at his watch. "I suppose they'll be waiting for me," he added reluctantly. I could tell he was lying. Or perhaps not.

As we walked over to the entrance lobby, he

greeted various people we passed, switching languages with incredible ease. A handshake here, a pat on the shoulder there; an affectionate kiss on the cheek of a frail old lady who looked like an Egyptian mummy, and a mischievous wink at two showy women overloaded with jewels from head to toe.

"Estoril is full of old cockatoos who used to be rich and aren't any longer," he whispered in my ear, "but they cling to yesterday tooth and nail, preferring to live on bread and sardines rather than sell what little they have left of their faded glory. You can see them with all their pearls and diamonds, wrapped in minks and ermines even in the height of summer, but they're carrying handbags filled with cobwebs that haven't seen a single escudo for months."

The simple elegance of my dress fitted perfectly with our surroundings, and he made sure that everyone around us noticed it. He didn't introduce me to anyone, nor did he tell me who anyone was: he just walked beside me, keeping to my pace, as though he were my escort: ever attentive, showing me off.

As we headed toward the exit I quickly weighed the result of the meeting. Manuel Da Silva had come to greet me, to invite me to a glass of champagne, and above all to measure me up: to evaluate with his own eyes just how far it was worth making the effort to take personal charge of the request that had come from Madrid. Someone via someone at the request of someone else had asked him as a favor to look after me, but there were two possible ways of doing that. One was by delegating: getting me looked after by some competent employee while he spared himself the obligation. The other required his own involvement. His time was worth gold dust, and he undoubtedly had countless commitments. The fact that he had offered to look after my insignificant needs himself suggested that my assignment was progressing along the right lines.

"I'll get in touch as soon as I can."

He held out his hand in farewell.

"A thousand thanks, Senhor Da Silva," I said, offering mine. Not one hand, both of them.

"Please call me Manuel," he said. I noticed that he held my hands a few seconds longer than was necessary.

"In that case, I'll have to be Arish."

"Good night, Arish. It's been a real pleasure meeting you. Till we meet again, then, have some rest and enjoy our country."

I went into the elevator and held his gaze until the two golden doors began to close, progressively narrowing my view of the lobby. Manuel Da Silva remained in front of them until he — first his shoulders, then his ears and neck, and finally his nose — disappeared as well.

When I was sure that I was beyond the reach of his gaze and we were beginning our ascent, I sighed so deeply that the young elevator attendant seemed about to ask if I was all right. The first step of my mission had just been completed: I'd passed the test.

Chapter Fifty-Two

I came down to breakfast early. Orange juice, the trilling of birds, white bread with butter, the cool shade of an awning, ladyfingers, and superb coffee. I stayed in the garden as long as I possibly could: compared to the bustle with which I began my days in Madrid, this felt like heaven itself. When I returned to my room I found an arrangement of exotic flowers on the desk. Out of pure thoughtless habit, the first thing I did was quickly untie the ribbon that adorned them in search of a coded message. But instead of finding any dots or dashes on the ribbon, what I found was a handwritten card.

My dear Arish,
Do make use of my driver João at your convenience, so that your stay is more comfortable.
Till Thursday,

Manuel Da Silva

His penmanship was elegant and vigorous, and in spite of the good impression that I'd apparently made the previous night, his message wasn't the least bit fawning, not even deferential. Courteous, but restrained and firm. Better that way. For now.

João turned out to be a grey-haired man in a

grey uniform, with an impressive mustache, and at least a decade over sixty. He was waiting for me at the entrance to the hotel, chatting with other drivers who were much younger than he, smoking compulsively. Senhor Da Silva had sent him to take the young lady anywhere she wanted to go, he announced, looking me up and down, and making no attempt to hide it. I presumed this wasn't the first time he'd been given a job of this kind.

"Shopping in Lisbon, please." The truth, though, was that rather than seeing the streets and the shops, what really interested me was killing time while I waited for Manuel Da Silva to show his face again.

I learned at once that João was far from your typical discreet chauffeur focused on his work. No sooner had he started up the Bentley than he made some comment about the weather; a couple of minutes later he complained about the state of the roads; later I think I understood him to be ranting about prices. Faced with this clear eagerness to speak, I could assume one of two possible roles: that of a distant lady who considered employees inferior beings whom one needn't even deign to look at, or an elegantly friendly foreigner who — while still maintaining her distance — was able to share her delight, even with the staff. It would have been more comfortable for me to take on the former personality and spend the day isolated in my own world, free from the interference of that old chatterbox, but I knew I shouldn't when he mentioned, a couple of miles later, the fifty-three years he'd been working for the Da Silvas. The role of a haughty lady would have suited me extremely comfortably, certainly, but the

659

alternative would prove much more useful. I needed to keep João talking, however exhausting it might become: if I could learn about Da Silva's past, then perhaps I might find out something about his present.

We made our way along the coast road, with the sea roaring to our right, and by the time we began to spot the Lisbon docks I already had a clear idea of the Da Silva clan's business empire. Manuel Da Silva was the son of Manuel Da Silva and the grandson of Manuel Da Silva: three men from three generations whose fortune had begun with a simple harborside tavern. From serving wine behind a counter the grandfather went on to sell it by the barrel; then the business moved to a warehouse — dilapidated and no longer in use — that João pointed out to me as we passed. The son took up the inheritance and expanded the business, selling not only wine but other merchandise wholesale, soon making the first attempts at colonial trading. When the reins passed to the third Manuel, the business was already prosperous, but he achieved the greatest success of all. Cotton from the Cape Verde Islands, wood from Mozambique, Chinese silks from Macao. Lately he'd gone back to focusing on domestic operations, too: from time to time he'd travel to the interior of the country, although João wasn't able to tell me what he dealt in there.

Old João was practically retired: a few years earlier a nephew of his had taken his place as personal chauffeur to the third Manuel Da Silva. But he remained active, carrying out a few minor tasks that the boss occasionally put his way: short trips, messages, errands of little significance. Such as — for example — taking a dressmaker at leisure around Lisbon one May morning.

At a shop in Chiado I bought several pairs of gloves, which were so hard to find in Madrid. At another, a dozen pairs of silk stockings, an impossible dream for Spanish women in the tough postwar years. A bit farther on, a springtime hat, perfumed soaps, and two pairs of sandals, then American cosmetics: mascara, lipstick, and heavenly scented night creams. What bliss in comparison with the sparseness of my poor Spain: everything available, opulent and varied, within immediate reach; you only had to take your purse out of your bag. João diligently took me from one place to the next, carried my shopping bags, opened and closed the back door of the car countless times for me to get in and out comfortably, recommended that I eat in a charming restaurant, and showed me streets, squares, and monuments. And along the way he furnished me with the thing I most desired: an incessant pattern of brushstrokes about Da Silva and his family. Some of them weren't especially interesting: that his grandmother was the real driving force behind the original business, that his mother died young, that his elder sister was married to an ophthalmologist and the younger entered a convent of barefoot nuns. Other little tidbits excited me more. The old chauffeur reeled them off with a free and easy naïveté: Don Manuel had a lot of friends, both Portuguese and foreign, some English, and yes, of course, the odd German lately, too; yes, he frequently had guests at his house; indeed, he liked everything always to be ready in case he decided to show up with guests for lunch or dinner, sometimes at his Lisbon residence in Lapa, sometimes in the Quinta da Fonte, his country house.

Over the course of the day I also had the chance to take a good look at the human fauna inhabiting the city. Lisboans of every kind, men in dark suits and elegant ladies, *nouveaux riches* lately arrived from the country into the capital to buy gold watches and fit false teeth, crowlike women in mourning, intimidating-looking Germans, Jewish refugees walking with heads bowed or queuing for a ticket to salvation, foreigners with a thousand different accents fleeing the war and its devastating effects. Among them, I suppose, would be Rosalinda. At my request, as though it had been a simple whim, João showed me the beautiful Avenida da Liberdade, with its black and white paving stones and trees that were almost as tall as the buildings that flanked its width. That was where she lived, at number 114; that was the address on the letters that Beigbeder had brought to my house on what was probably the bitterest night of his life. I looked for the number and found it above the large wooden door in the middle of an impressive tiled façade. Well, of course it would be this impressive, I thought, with a touch of melancholy.

Over the course of the afternoon we continued to make our way through the little crannies of the city, but at about five I felt myself beginning to wilt. The day had been devastatingly hot, and João's relentless conversation had left my head fit to explode.

"Just one last stop, right here," he suggested when I told him it was time to go back. He stopped the car in front of a café with a modern-looking entrance on the Rua Garrett. The

Brasileira.

"No one can leave Lisbon without having a good cup of coffee," he said.

"But João, it's terribly late . . . ," I protested, a plaintive tone in my voice.

"Five minutes, no more than that. Go in and ask for a shot, you won't regret it."

I agreed reluctantly: I didn't want to be rude to my unexpected confidant, who might at any moment prove useful to me again. In spite of the overloaded decoration and the excessive number of locals, the place was cool and pleasant. The counter to the right, the tables to the left, a clock in front, golden moldings on the ceiling, and large paintings on the walls. They served me a small white porcelain cup and I took a cautious sip. Black coffee — strong and wonderful. João was right: a real pick-me-up. As I waited for it to cool, I reviewed the day's events in my mind. I went back over a few little details about Da Silva, weighed them, and mentally organized them. When there was nothing left in the cup but the dregs, I put a banknote down beside it and stood up.

The meeting was so unexpected, so sudden and powerful, that there was no way I could react. There were three men walking in, chatting to one another at just the moment I was about to leave: three hats, three ties, three foreign faces speaking English. Two of them were unknown, the third wasn't. And it had been more than three years since we'd said good-bye. In that time, Marcus Logan had barely changed.

I saw him before he saw me, so that by the time he noticed me I — in distress — had already turned away toward the door.

"Sira . . . ," he murmured.

No one had called me that in a long time. My stomach tensed and I felt as if I was about to vomit my coffee onto the marble floor. Right there in front of me, little more than six feet away, with the last letter of my name still hanging from his lips and surprise fixed on his face, was the man with whom I'd shared such fears and joy; the man with whom I'd laughed and talked, wandered, danced, and cried; who had managed to give me back my mother and whom I resisted falling in love with even though for a few intense weeks there was something much stronger than a simple friendship that held us together. Instantly the past unfolded as if on a screen: Tetouan, Rosalinda, Beigbeder, the Hotel Nacional, my old workshop, the agitated days and endless nights. What could have been and yet was not, in a time that would never return. I wanted to throw my arms around him, say yes, Marcus, it's me. I wanted to ask him to take me away from here, to run hand in hand with him as we'd once done through the shadows of an African garden, to go back to Morocco, forget that there was such a thing as the Secret Intelligence Service, ignore the fact that I had a dark job to do and a sad, grey Madrid to return to. But I did none of those things, because clarity — with a cry of alarm stronger even than my own will — warned me that I had no choice but to pretend not to know him. And I obeyed.

I didn't respond to my name or even deign to look at him. As though I were deaf and blind, as though that man had never been anything in my life and I hadn't soaked his lapels with tears as I begged him not to leave me. As though the profound affection we'd formed between us had dissolved in my memory. I simply ignored him, fixed my gaze on the exit, and headed toward it with cold determination.

João was waiting for me with the back door open. Fortunately his attention was on a small mishap on the opposite pavement, a roadside commotion that included a dog, a bicycle, and various arguing pedestrians. He only became aware of my arrival when I made my presence quite clear.

"Let's go, quickly, João: I'm exhausted," I whispered as I settled inside.

He closed the door when I was in, then immediately positioned himself behind the wheel and started up the car, asking me what I'd thought of his last recommendation. I didn't answer. All my energy was focused on keeping my eyes fixed forward and not turning my head. And I almost succeeded. But as the Bentley began to slip across the paving stones something irrational inside me overcame my resistance and commanded me to do something I should not have done: to look at him again.

Marcus had come out of the door and was standing there immobile, upright, his hat still on, staring hard, watching my departure with his hands plunged into his trouser pockets. Perhaps he was wondering whether he'd just seen the woman he might have fallen in love with once, or only her ghost.

CHAPTER FIFTY-THREE

When we arrived back at the hotel I asked the chauffeur not to return for me the following day; although Lisbon was a reasonably large city I couldn't run the risk of bumping into Marcus Logan again. I claimed to be tired and predicted a pretend migraine; I assumed that the news of my intention not to go out again would quickly reach Da Silva, and I didn't want him to think I was turning down his friendly offer without a very good reason. I spent the rest of the evening soaking in the bathtub and a large part of the night sitting on my balcony, distractedly watching the lights over the sea. During those long hours I couldn't stop thinking about Marcus for a minute: about him as a man, about everything our time together had meant to me, and about the consequences I might face if I were to run into him again at some inconvenient moment. It was getting light by the time I went to bed. My stomach was empty, my mouth dry, and my soul all shriveled up.

The garden and the breakfast were the same as on the previous morning, but although I tried hard to behave just as naturally, I didn't enjoy it as much. I forced myself to eat a hearty breakfast in spite of not being hungry, and I spent as much time as I could leafing through a number of magazines written in languages I didn't understand. I got up from the table only when there were no more than a handful of straggling guests left scattered around the tables. It was not yet eleven in the morning: I had a whole day ahead of me and nothing but my own thoughts to fill it with.

I went back to my room; it had already been tidied. I lay down on the bed and shut my eyes. Ten minutes. Twenty. Thirty. I didn't get to forty: I couldn't bear my brain going around and around the same thing a second longer. I changed my clothes: I put on a light skirt, a white cotton blouse, and a pair of low sandals. I covered my hair with a patterned scarf, hid myself behind a pair of large sunglasses, and left the room, avoiding looking at my reflection in the mirror: I didn't want to see the glum expression that had fixed itself to my face.

There was hardly anyone on the beach. The waves, broad and flat, followed one another, monotonous. Not far away, what looked like a castle and a promontory with grand villas; ahead, an ocean almost as large as my unease. I sat down on the sand to look at it, and with my gaze fixed on the advancing and retreating of the foam, I lost all sense of time and let myself get swept away. Each wave carried a memory with it, an image of the past: memories of the young woman I once was, of my accomplishments and my fears, of the friends I'd left behind, scenes from other lands, with other voices. And above all that morning, the sea brought me feelings that had been forgotten between the folds of memory: the caress of a dear hand, the strength of a friendly arm, the joy of what was shared, and a longing for what was desired.

It was almost three in the afternoon when I shook the sand off my skirt. Time to go back, as good a time as any. I crossed the road to the hotel; there were barely any cars passing. One was disappearing into the distance, another was approaching slowly. That one seemed familiar, vaguely familiar. A needling curiosity made me slow my pace until the car passed me. And I knew then what car it was and who was driving. Da Silva's Bentley, with João behind the wheel. What a coincidence, what a very fortuitous meeting! Or not, I suddenly thought with a shudder. There were probably a thousand reasons why the old chauffeur should have been driving calmly through the streets of Estoril, but my instinct told me that he had just come for me. Candelaria and my mother would have said, *Snap out of it, girl, snap out of it!* But since they weren't around, I said it to myself. Yes, I had to snap out of it; I'd lowered my guard. Meeting Marcus had made a violent impression on me and had unearthed so many recollections and feelings, but now was not the time to allow myself to be taken over by nostalgia. I had an assignment, an obligation: a role to play, an image to project, and a task to take care of. Sitting looking at the waves wasn't going to achieve anything except waste time and plunge me into melancholy. The moment to return to reality had arrived.

I picked up the pace and did my best to look sprightly and lively. Although João had disappeared, there could have been other eyes watching me from any little corner on Da Silva's orders. It was quite impossible that he should have suspected me, but perhaps his nature — as a powerful, controlling man — insisted on his knowing what exactly his Moroccan visitor was doing instead of taking advantage of his car. And I would have to be sure to show him.

I went up to my room by a side staircase; I changed my clothes and reappeared. Whereas a half hour earlier I'd been in a light skirt and a cotton blouse, I was now in an elegant mandarin-colored suit, and my flat sandals had been replaced by a pair of snakeskin high heels. My sunglasses had disappeared and I'd made myself up with the cosmetics I'd bought the previous day. My hair, no longer covered in a scarf, fell loosely over my shoulders. I went down the main staircase with a rhythmic step and wandered in leisurely style along the landing of the upper floor that looked down over the main entrance hall. I descended one more flight to the lobby floor, not forgetting to smile at everyone I passed on the way. I greeted the ladies with an elegant tilt of my head — regardless of how old they were, their language, or whether they even bothered to return the attention. With the gentlemen, a few of them local, many of them foreign, I accelerated my blinking; I even made a flirtatious gesture to a particularly decrepit one. I asked one of the receptionists to send a cable to Doña Manuela and asked for it to be transmitted to my own address. "Portugal wonderful, excellent shopping. Headache today and resting. Tomorrow visiting a helpful supplier. Best wishes, Arish Agoriuq." Then I chose one of the armchairs that were scattered around the spacious lobby in clusters of four; I wanted to be somewhere people had to walk past, and very conspicuous. And then I crossed my legs, asked for two aspirins and a cup of tea, and devoted the rest of the afternoon to being seen.

I managed to put up with pretending to be bored for almost three hours, until my stomach began to growl. Mission concluded — I'd earned the right to go back to my room and order some dinner from room service. I was about to get up when a bellhop approached carrying a little silver tray. And on it, an envelope. And inside, a card.

Dear Arish:
I hope the sea has dispelled your discomfort. João will come to fetch you tomorrow morning at ten to bring you to my office. I hope you have a good rest.

Manuel Da Silva

News really did get around. I was tempted to have a little wander about in search of the driver or Da Silva himself, but I stopped myself. Although one of them was probably somewhere nearby, I feigned a cool lack of interest and pretended to be concentrating on one of the American magazines I'd used to while away part of the afternoon. Half an hour later, when the lobby was half empty and most of the guests had already headed off for the bar, the terrace, and the dining room, I returned to my room, ready to get Marcus out of my head altogether and concentrate on the complicated day that lay ahead of me once this night was done.

CHAPTER FIFTY-FOUR

João threw his cigarette on the ground, greeting me with a *bom dia,* and stamped out the butt with his shoe as he held open the door to the Bentley. Again he looked me up and down, but this time he wouldn't have the opportunity to inform his boss of anything about me, as I'd be seeing him myself in just half an hour.

Da Silva's offices were on the centrally located Rua do Ouro, the street of gold that connected Rossio with the Praça do Comércio in Baixa. The building was elegant in an unshowy way, with everything around it exuding a powerful aura of money, negotiations, and successful business: there were banks, pawnshops, offices, men in suits, employees scurrying, and hotel bellhops dashing about.

As I got out of the Bentley I was received by the same thin man who had interrupted our conversation the night Da Silva came to meet me. Alert and discreet, this time he shook my hand and introduced himself as Joaquim Gamboa, then he led me deferentially to the elevator. At first I thought that the company's offices were on one of the floors of the building, but it didn't take me long to realize that in fact the whole building was the company's headquarters. Gamboa led me directly to the second story.

"Don Manuel will be with you right away," he announced before disappearing.

The waiting room where I settled had walls paneled with gleaming wood that looked as though it had recently been waxed. Six leather chairs marked out the waiting area; a bit farther in, closer to the double door that led to Da Silva's office, there were two desks: one of them occupied, the other empty. At the first there was a secretary working, fiftyish, who — judging by the formal greeting with which she received me and the exquisite care she took to make a note of something in a thick notebook — must have been an efficient, discreet worker, any boss's dream. Her companion, who was quite a bit younger, appeared within just a couple of minutes, opening one of the doors from Da Silva's office and emerging with a dull-looking man. A client, probably a business contact.

"Senhor Da Silva is ready for you, senhorita," she said with a bland expression. I pretended not to pay much attention to her, but a single look was enough to size her up. My age, give or take a year. With glasses for her nearsightedness, light hair and skin, painstaking in her attire, though with clothes of rather modest quality. I couldn't observe her any further because at that moment Manuel Da Silva came out to meet me in the waiting room.

"A pleasure to have you here, Arish," he said in his excellent Spanish.

In exchange I held out my hand slowly to give him time to look at me and decide if I was still worthy of his attention. To judge by his reaction, I gathered that I was. I'd put in a great effort to make a good impression, choosing for this business meeting a silver-colored suit with a pencil skirt and fitted jacket, and placing on the lapel a white flower to minimize the sobriety of the suit's color. The result was recompensed with a veiled look of appreciation and a gentlemanly smile.

"Please, come in. They've already been by this morning to bring all the things I want to show you."

In one corner of the spacious office, under a large map of the world, stood various rolls of fabric. Silks. Natural silks, smooth and radiant, and magnificent dyed silks in lustrous colors. Just by touching them I could anticipate the beautiful drape of the gowns I could sew from them.

"Are they of the quality you'd been expecting?"

I heard Manuel Da Silva's voice behind me. For a few seconds, perhaps a few minutes, I'd forgotten all about him and his world. The pleasure of examining the exquisite fabrics, of feeling their softness and imagining how the end products might look, had distanced me from reality for a moment. Fortunately I didn't have to make any effort to compliment the merchandise that he had brought me.

"Better. They're marvelous."

"In that case I'd advise you to take as many yards as you can, because I don't think we'll be having these on hand for very long."

"There's that much demand?"

"We expect so. Although not for them to be used for fashion exactly."

"What for, if not fashion?" I asked, surprised.

"For other requirements that are more pressing nowadays: for the war."

"For the war?" I repeated, feigning disbelief. I knew that material was being used in other countries; Hillgarth had told me about it in Tangiers.

"They use the silk to make parachutes, to protect gunpowder, and even for bicycle tires."

I gave a pretend little laugh.

"What a ridiculous waste! With the silk they need for one parachute we could make at least ten evening gowns."

"Yes, but times are hard. And the countries that are at war will pay anything they need to for it."

"And what about you, Manuel, who will you be selling these treasures to, the Germans or the English?" I asked in a teasing tone, as though I hadn't been taking what he said altogether seriously. I even surprised myself with my boldness, but he played along with my joke.

"We Portuguese have long-standing commercial links to the English, though in these turbulent days you never know . . ." He finished off his worrying response with a laugh, but before I had the time to work out what it meant he changed the subject to more practical, immediate questions. "Here you'll find a folder with detailed information about the materials: reference numbers, qualities, prices — in short, all the usual," he said as he made his way over to his desk. "Take it with you to the hotel, take your time, and when you've decided what you'd be interested in having, fill out an order form and I'll arrange for it all to be sent direct to Madrid; you'll have it in less than a week. You can make the payment from there when you receive the merchandise, you needn't worry about that. And don't forget to include a twenty percent discount on each price, on the house."

"But —"

"And here," he said, not letting me finish, "you'll

674

find another folder with the details of local suppliers of materials and merchandise that might be of interest to you: thread, braiding, buttons, tanned leather . . . I've taken the liberty of setting up some appointments with them, and this is the schedule, in this section here. Look: this afternoon the Soares brothers will be expecting you, they have the finest thread in the whole of Portugal; tomorrow, Friday, in the morning, Casa Barbosa will see you, that's where they make buttons from African ivory. Saturday morning you have a visit set up with the Almeida furriers, and then there's nothing else arranged till Monday. But you should be prepared, because the week will start packed with engagements again."

I studied the piece of paper filled with little boxes and hid my admiration at how well it had been arranged.

"As well as Sunday, I see I'll have tomorrow afternoon and evening to rest," I said without looking up from the document.

"I'm afraid you're wrong."

"I don't think I am. It's blank on your plan — look."

"Yes, it is indeed blank, because I asked my secretary to leave it that way because I've planned something to fill it up. Would you have dinner with me tomorrow night?"

I took the second folder that he was still holding and didn't answer. First I paused to examine its contents: several pages with names, information, and numbers that I pretended to study with interest, although in reality I just cast my eyes across them without stopping to look at any of them.

"Very well, I accept," I said, after leaving him a few long seconds waiting for my reply. "But only if you promise me something first."

"Very well, anything within my power."

"Well then, this is my condition: I'll have dinner with you if you'll assure me that you're not going to let any soldiers jump out of their planes with these precious fabrics strapped to their backs."

He laughed delightedly and once again I noticed what a lovely laugh he had. Masculine, powerful, elegant, all at the same time. I remembered the words of Hillgarth's wife: Manuel Da Silva really was an attractive man. And then, fleeting as a comet, the shadow of Marcus Logan passed in front of me once more.

"I'll do what I can, don't worry about that, but you know how it is with business," he said, shrugging, a trace of irony at the corner of his lips.

An unexpected ringing prevented him from continuing. The sound came from his desk, from a grey machine with a blinking green light.

"Please excuse me a moment." He seemed to have gone back to being serious in an instant. He pressed a button and the distorted voice of his young secretary came out of the machine.

"Herr Weiss is waiting for you. He says it's urgent."

"Take him through to the meeting room," he said roughly. His body language had changed utterly: the cold businessman had swallowed up the charmer. Or perhaps he was simply reverting back to character. I didn't yet know him well enough to know which was the real Manuel Da Silva.

He turned to me and tried to resume his affable manner, but he didn't entirely succeed.

"Excuse me, sometimes my work just piles up."

"Please forgive me for having taken up so much of your time —"

He didn't let me finish. Though he tried to hide it, he exuded a certain sense of impatience. He held out his hand.

"I'll come and get you tomorrow at eight, if that suits you?"

"Perfectly."

Our good-bye was quick; it wasn't the time for flirtation. The witty comments and frivolities had been left behind — we'd resume them another time. He escorted me to the door, and as I went out into the waiting room I looked for this Herr Weiss but found only the two secretaries. One of them was typing conscientiously and the other was putting a pile of letters into their envelopes. They said good-bye with varying degrees of friendliness: they had other, much more pressing things on their minds.

CHAPTER FIFTY-FIVE

I'd brought a sketchbook with me from Madrid, aiming to make a note in it of anything I thought might be interesting, and that night I began to lay out on paper what I'd seen and heard up till that moment. I arranged the information in the most ordered way I could and then compressed it as much as possible. "Da Silva joking about business relationship with Germans, impossible to know degree of truth. Expects demand for silk for military purposes. Personality changes with situation. Confirmed link to German Herr Weiss. German appears unannounced and demands immediate meeting. Da Silva tense, no doubt that Herr Weiss will be seen."

Then I drew a few sketches of dresses that would never materialize and pretended to edge them with penciled stitches. I tried to make the difference between the short and long dashes minimal, so that only I'd be able to distinguish them. I had no problem doing that; I was more than practiced at it. I distributed the information among the sketches, and when I'd finished I burned the pieces of handwritten paper in the bathroom, threw them in the toilet, and pulled the chain. I left the sketchbook in the closet: not particularly hidden, not ostentatiously visible. If anyone decided to rummage through my things, they'd never suspect that I'd meant to hide it.

Time flew by now that I had things to distract me. I traveled the coast road between Estoril and Lisbon several more times with João at the wheel. I chose dozens of spools of the best thread and exquisite buttons in countless shapes and sizes; I felt as though I was being treated like the most exclusive of clients. Thanks to Da Silva's recommendations, the suppliers were all attentive, offering easy terms of payment, discounts, and little gifts. And I barely noticed that we'd reached the moment when I was to have dinner with him.

The meeting was like our previous meetings — prolonged glances, bewitching smiles, and shameless flirtation. Although I had mastered the basic rules of performance and was by now a consummate actress, I had no doubt that Manuel Da Silva himself was making things easier for me with his attitude. Again he made me feel like I was the only woman in the world capable of attracting his attention, and again I acted as though being the object of the affections of a rich, attractive man was something that happened to me every day. But it wasn't, which was why I had to redouble my caution — under no circumstances could I allow my emotions to run away with me: it was all work, just duty. It would have been very easy to relax, to enjoy the man and the moment, but I knew that I needed to keep my mind cool and my feelings far away.

"I've booked a table for dinner at the Wonderbar, the casino club: they have a marvelous band and the casino is right next door."

We walked under the canopy of palm trees; it wasn't yet completely dark, and the lights from the street lamps gleamed like dots of silver on the violet sky. Da Silva went back to being the man he was at his better moments: pleasant and charming, with no sign of the tension that had appeared when the German was in his office.

There, too, everyone seemed to know him, from the waiters and car valets to the most distinguished patrons. He distributed greetings as he'd done on the first night: friendly slaps on the back, handshakes, and half hugs for the men, pretend hand kissing, smiles, and immoderate compliments for the women. He introduced me to some of them, and I made a mental note of the names to transfer them to the outlines of my sketches.

The atmosphere in the Wonderbar was like that in the Hotel do Parque: ninety percent cosmopolitan. The only difference, I noted with a trace of concern, was that here the Germans weren't in the majority: English was spoken everywhere, too. I tried to separate myself from these concerns and concentrate on the part I had to play. My head clear, my eyes and ears wide open: that was the only thing I had to concern myself with. And with deploying all my charm, naturally.

The maître d' led us to a small reserved table in the best corner of the room: a strategically chosen place for seeing and being seen. The band was playing "In the Mood" and there were already countless couples filling the dance floor. Others were having dinner, and I could hear conversations, greetings, laughter; I could inhale the relaxation and the glamour. Manuel waved away the menu and without hesitation ordered for us both. And then — as though he'd been waiting for that moment all day — he settled himself in his chair, ready to turn all his attention on me.

"So, Arish — tell me. How have my friends treated you?"

I told him all about my transactions, spicing up the stories a bit. I exaggerated the situations, I made humorous observations, I imitated voices in Portuguese, I made him laugh out loud and scored some points for myself.

Finally it was my turn to listen and take things in. And if luck was on my side, perhaps to draw a few things out of him, too. "So, tell me, Manuel, how have things been since we were together yesterday morning?"

He couldn't tell me right away, because we were interrupted. More greetings, more amiability. If it wasn't genuine, it certainly seemed so.

"Baron von Kempel, an extraordinary man," he noted when the elderly aristocrat with the leonine mane of hair had stepped haltingly away from the table. "Well, we left off talking about how my recent days had been. I need only two words to describe them: excruciatingly boring."

I knew he was lying, of course, but I adopted a sympathetic tone.

"At least you have pleasant offices in which to bear your tedium, and efficient secretaries to help you."

"You're right, I can't complain. It would be harder if I was working as a stevedore at the port, or if I didn't have anyone helping me out."

"Have they been with you long?"

"You mean the secretaries? Elisa Somoza, the older of the two, more than three decades: she joined the company in my father's day, before even I joined. Beatriz Oliveira, the younger, I hired her only three years ago, when I saw that the company was growing and Elisa wasn't capable of dealing

681

with everything. Congeniality isn't her strong suit, but she's organized, responsible, and good with languages. I suppose the new working classes don't enjoy being too friendly with the boss," he said, raising his glass as for a toast.

I didn't find his sarcasm amusing, but I disguised it, joining him in a sip of white wine. Then a couple approached the table: a stunning older lady in purple shantung down to her feet, with a companion who barely came up to her shoulder. We paused our conversation again; they switched into French; he introduced me and I greeted them with a gracious gesture and a brief *enchantée.*

"The Mannheims — Hungarian," he explained when they'd retreated.

"Are they all Jews?" I asked.

"Rich Jews waiting for the war to end or to be granted a visa to travel to America. Shall we dance?"

Da Silva turned out to be a wonderful dancer. Rumbas, habaneras, jazz, and paso dobles: there was nothing he couldn't do. I let myself get carried away: it had been a long day, and the two glasses of Douro wine I'd had with my lobster must have gone to my head. The couples on the dance floor were reflected a thousand times in the mirrors on the columns and the walls. It was hot. I closed my eyes a few moments — two seconds, three, maybe four. The moment I opened them, my worst fears had been incarnated in human form.

In an impeccable tuxedo, hair combed back, his legs slightly apart, hands in his pockets again, and a newly lit cigarette in his mouth — there sat Marcus Logan, watching us dance.

Get far away, I had to get far away from him —

that was the first thing that came to my mind.

"Shall we sit down? I'm a little tired."

Although I tried to leave the dance floor via the opposite side from Marcus, it didn't do me any good, because I could tell with furtive glances that he was moving in the same direction. We dodged around dancing couples, and he did the same with tables of diners, but we were heading in parallel toward the same place. I noticed my legs shaking, and the heat of the May night suddenly began to feel unbearable. When we were just a few feet from the table, he stopped to greet someone, and I thought that might perhaps be where he'd been heading, but he said good-bye and kept approaching, decisive and determined. We all three reached our table at the same time, Manuel and I from the right, he from the left. And then I thought the end had come.

"Logan, you old fox, where have you been keeping yourself? It's been a century since I've seen you!" exclaimed Da Silva the moment he spotted him. To my astonishment, they patted each other affectionately on the back.

"I've called you a thousand times, but I can never get hold of you," said Marcus.

"Let me introduce you to Arish Agoriuq, a Moroccan friend who arrived a few days ago from Madrid."

I held out my hand, trying not to tremble, not daring to look him in the eye. He shook it firmly, as if to say *It's me, here I am — react.*

"Delighted to meet you." My voice was hoarse and dry, almost cracked.

"Take a seat, have a drink with us," Manuel offered.

"No, thanks. I'm with some friends, I just came

over to say hello and remind you that we must meet up."

"Sometime very soon, I promise."

"Be sure — we have things to talk about." And then he turned his attention to me.

"Delighted to meet you, Miss . . ." he said with a little bow. This time I had no choice but to look right at him. There was no longer any trace on his face of the injuries he had when I met him, but he had the same expression: the sharp features and the complicit eyes that asked me, wordlessly, *What the hell are you doing here with this man?*

"Agoriuq," I managed to say as though trying to expel a rock from my mouth.

"Miss Agoriuq, that's it, I'm sorry. It's been a pleasure meeting you. I hope to see you again."

We watched him as he moved away.

"A good guy, that Marcus Logan."

I took a long drink of water. I needed to refresh my parched throat.

"English?"

"Yes, English; we've done some business together."

I drank again to dispel the unsettled feeling that had overcome me. So he's no longer a journalist. Manuel's words pulled me out of my reverie.

"It's too hot here. Shall we try our luck on the roulette wheel?"

Again I pretended to be unimpressed by the opulence of the hall. Magnificent chandeliers hung from golden chains over the tables, around which swirled hundreds of players speaking as many languages as there used to be nations on the map of the old Europe. The carpeted floor muffled the sounds of people's movements, which emphasized the other sounds that best befitted this paradise of chance: the clicking of the chips against one another, the buzz of the roulette wheels, the clattering of the ivory balls in their wild dances, and the cries of the croupiers closing play with a *Rien ne va plus!* There were a lot of people throwing away their money sitting around the green baize tables, and even more standing around them watching the games. Aristocrats who in another time had been regular losers and modest winners in the casinos at Baden-Baden, Monte Carlo, and Deauville, Da Silva explained. Impoverished bourgeois, paupers who had become rich, respectable beings who'd been transformed into riffraff, and true riffraff disguised as gentlemen. They'd all dressed up in their finery, triumphant and sure of themselves, the men stiff-collared and with their shirt fronts starched, the women arrogantly displaying their dazzling jewelry collections. There were also some decadent-looking individuals, fearful or furtive in their search for some acquaintance to touch for a bit of cash, perhaps clinging to the more than improbable hope of a glorious night; others prepared to gamble the last of their family jewels or the following morning's breakfast on the baccarat table. The former were moved by the sheer emotion of the game, by the desire to enjoy themselves, by dizziness, or covetousness; for the latter it was, simply, the barest desperation.

For a few minutes we wandered around, watching the various tables; he continued to dispense greetings and exchange friendly words. I barely spoke: all I wanted was to get out of there, to shut myself in my room and forget about the world. I just wished that this accursed day would come to an end once and for all.

"You don't look like you fancy becoming a millionairess tonight."

I smiled weakly.

"I'm exhausted," I said. I tried to put a bit of sweetness into my voice; I didn't want him to sense my concerns.

"Would you like me to take you to the hotel?"

"I'd be grateful."

"Just give me a moment." He took a few steps away from me to hold out his hand to an acquaintance he'd just seen.

I remained still, absent, not even bothering to distract myself with the fascinating bustle of the hall. And then, almost like a shadow, I realized that he was approaching. He passed behind me, stealthy, almost touching me. Surreptitiously, without even stopping, he took my right hand, opened my fingers, and put something inside. And I let him do it. And then, without a word, he left. As I kept my attention apparently fixed on one of the tables, I nervously felt the thing he'd left me: a bit of paper, folded several times over. I hid it under the wide belt of my dress just as Manuel stepped away from his acquaintance and walked back toward me.

"Shall we go?"

"I've just got to go to the powder room a moment first."

"Very well, I'll wait for you here."

I tried to spot some trace of him as I walked, but he was nowhere to be seen. There was no one in the powder room, just a sleepy-looking old black woman at the door. I took the piece of paper from out of its hiding place and unfolded it with nimble fingers.

"Whatever happened to the S. I left in T.?"

S. was of course Sira, and T., Tetouan. Where was the old me of the African days, Marcus was asking. My eyes filled with tears. I opened my handbag in search of a handkerchief and an answer. I found the first, but not the second.

CHAPTER FIFTY-SIX

On Monday I resumed my outings in search of merchandise for the atelier. They'd arranged a visit for me to a milliner's on the Rua da Prata, just around the corner from Da Silva's offices: the perfect excuse for me to drop by, for no reason other than to say hello. And in doing so, to have a look around and see who was in his territory.

I only found the young, unfriendly secretary; Beatriz Oliveira, he had said was her name.

"Senhor Da Silva is traveling. Work," she said, without any further explanation.

Just as on my previous visit, she made it clear she had no interest in being friendly, but just the same, it occurred to me that this might be the only time I'd be alone with her, so I didn't want to waste it. Judging by her somber expression and her terseness, I expected it to be extremely difficult to extract even a tiny crumb of anything worthwhile from her, but I had nothing better to do, so I decided to give it a try.

"Oh my, what rotten luck. I wanted to consult him on a matter concerning the fabrics he showed me the other day. Are they still in his office?" I asked. My heart began to beat hard at the possibility that I might be able to get in without Manuel being around, but she cut short my false hope before it had even taken shape.

"No. They've been taken back to the ware-house."

I thought fast. My first attempt had failed; well then, I'd just have to keep trying.

"Would you mind if I sat down for a minute? I've been on my feet all morning looking at caps, turbans, and picture hats; I think I need a bit of a rest."

I didn't give her time to reply: before she had the chance to open her mouth, I dropped into one of the leather armchairs, feigning an exaggerated weariness. We remained in silence for a long while, as she continued to go over a several-page document, from time to time making a little mark or a comment in pencil.

"Cigarette?" I asked after two or three minutes. Although I wasn't much of a smoker, I usually had a cigarette case in my handbag. To use at just such moments.

"No, thank you," she said without looking at me. She went on working while I lit one. I let her continue for another couple of minutes.

"It was you who found all the suppliers and arranged the appointments and prepared the folder with all the information, wasn't it?"

Finally she looked up for a moment.

"Yes, it was me."

"A great piece of work; you can't imagine how useful it's been for me."

She muttered a quick thank-you and went back to focusing on her task.

"Of course, Senhor Da Silva isn't short of contacts," I went on. "It must be amazing having business dealings with so many different companies. And so many foreign ones, especially. In

689

Spain everything's much less interesting."

"I'm not surprised," she murmured.

"I beg your pardon?"

"I said I'm not surprised it's not very interesting, bearing in mind who you've got in charge," she muttered between her teeth with her attention apparently still on her assignment.

A quick shock of delight ran down my spine: the devoted secretary is interested in politics. All right, I'd try a different approach.

"Yes, of course," I replied, slowly stubbing out my cigarette. "What do you expect from someone who thinks we women should stay home making dinner and bringing children into the world?"

"And who has filled up the prisons and denies his defeated opponents the slightest shred of compassion," she added firmly.

"It certainly looks that way." This was going in an unexpected direction; I'd have to act with extreme caution to win her trust and get her on my side. "Do you know Spain at all, Beatriz?"

I noticed she was surprised that I knew her name. Finally she deigned to put down her pencil and look at me.

"I've never been, but I know what's going on there. I have friends who tell me. Though you probably don't have any idea what I'm talking about; you belong to a different world."

I got up, approached her desk, and sat down boldly on the edge. I looked at her close up, to check out what there was beneath that outfit made from cheap material, which had undoubtedly been sewn for her years ago by some neighbor for a handful of escudos. Behind her glasses I saw intelligent eyes, and hidden amid the furious devotion with which she approached her work, I could

690

sense a fighting spirit that seemed somehow familiar. Beatriz Oliveira and I weren't so different. Two hardworking girls from similar backgrounds, backgrounds that were modest and filled with struggle. Two journeys that began from points close to each other and at some point the paths diverged. Time had made her into a meticulously dedicated employee; me, an entirely fake façade. Most likely, though, what we had in common was much more real than our differences. I was staying in a luxury hotel and she would be living in some leaky house in a humble neighborhood, but we both knew what it meant to struggle our whole lives to prevent ill luck from nipping at our heels.

"I know a lot of people, Beatriz; very different people," I said in a low voice. "Right now I'm dealing with powerful people because that's what my job demands of me and because certain unexpected circumstances have introduced me to them, but I know what it's like to feel the cold in winter, to eat beans day after day and struggle out into the street before the sun has risen to earn a miserable day's wage. And in case it's of any interest to you, I don't like this Spain that's being built any more than you do. Now will you accept a cigarette?"

She held out her hand without replying and took one. I held out the lighter, then took another myself.

"How are things in Portugal?" I asked.

"Bad," she said, after exhaling the smoke. "Perhaps Salazar's Estado Novo isn't as repressive as Franco's Spain, but the authoritarianism and the lack of freedom aren't all that different."

"At least here it looks like you're going to

remain neutral in the European war," I said, trying to move in closer to my target. "In Spain things aren't so clear."

"Salazar has agreements with the English and the Germans, an uncommon balancing act. The British have always been friends to the Portuguese people, which is why it's so surprising how generous he's being with the Germans, granting them export licenses and other privileges."

"Well, that's not unusual nowadays, is it? These are delicate matters in turbulent times. I don't understand much about international politics, to tell you the truth, but I imagine it's all a question of self-interest." I tried to keep my tone trivial, as though the subject barely troubled me: the moment had come to cross the line between the public and the close to home. "The same must happen in the business world, I guess," I added. "Without going too far afield, just the other day, when I was in the office with Senhor Da Silva, you yourself announced a visit by a German."

"Well yes, that's a different matter." The expression on her face was one of disgust, and she didn't seem keen to say any more.

"The other night Senhor Da Silva invited me to join him for dinner at the casino in Estoril and I was amazed by how many people he knew. He was greeting English people and Americans as well as Germans and a fair number of Europeans from other countries; I've never seen anyone with such a facility for getting along with everybody."

A twisted grimace displayed her annoyance once again. Still she said nothing, however, so I had no choice but to try to keep talking to prevent the conversation from petering out.

"I felt sorry for the Jews there, the ones who

had to abandon their homes and their businesses to escape from the war."

"You felt sorry for the Jews at the Estoril casino?" she asked with a cynical smile. "I don't feel in the least bit sorry for them: they live like they are permanently on a luxury vacation. The ones I feel sorry for are the poor wretches who have arrived with a pathetic cardboard suitcase and spend their days standing in line outside consulates and shipping offices hoping to get hold of a visa or a passage to America that they might never receive; I feel sorry for the families who sleep all piled up in filthy boardinghouses and go to the soup kitchens for their food, the poor girls offering themselves up on street corners in exchange for a handful of escudos, the old men who kill time in the cafés, sitting in front of dirty cups that have been empty for hours, until the waiter throws them out onto the street to make room for someone else. Those are the ones I feel sorry for. But the ones who gamble away a part of their fortune every night at the casino — I don't have any pity for them at all."

What she was describing to me was moving, but I couldn't allow myself to be distracted: we were on the right track, we had to keep going whatever it took. Even if it meant tugging at her conscience.

"You're right; the situation is much more extreme for those poor people. Besides, it must be painful for them to see so many Germans moving so freely all over the place."

"I imagine so . . ."

"And it must be especially hard for them knowing that the government of the country they've come to is so keen to oblige the Third Reich."

"I suppose so . . ."

"And that there are even some Portuguese businessmen who are expanding their businesses at the cost of a few juicy contracts with the Nazis . . ."

I spoke those words in a thick, dark tone, moving closer to her and lowering my voice. We held each other's gaze, both unable to look away.

"Who are you?" she asked finally, her voice barely audible. She'd leaned back, moving her body away from the desk and against the back of her chair, as though trying to get away from me. Her unsettled tone was full of fear; her eyes, however, didn't look away from mine for a second.

"I'm just a dressmaker," I whispered. "A simple working woman like you, who doesn't like what's happening around her any more than you do."

I noticed how her neck tensed up as she swallowed, and then I formulated two questions. Slowly. Very slowly.

"What does Da Silva have to do with the Germans, Beatriz? What's he involved in?"

She swallowed again and her throat moved as though she were trying to get an elephant down it.

"I don't know anything about it," she managed to murmur at last.

An annoyed voice came from the door.

"Remind me never to go back to the restaurant on the Rua de São Julião. It took us more than an hour to get served, and me with all the things I have to get ready before Don Manuel comes back. Oh! I'm sorry, Senhorita Agoriuq, I didn't know you were here . . ."

"I was just going," I said with feigned self-assurance, picking up my bag. "I came by to pay a surprise visit to Senhor Da Silva, but Senhorita

Oliveira has told me he's traveling. Anyway, I'll come back some other day."

"You've left your cigarettes," I heard a voice say behind me.

Beatriz Oliveira was still talking in a dull tone. When she held her arm out to pass me the cigarette case, I held on to her hand and squeezed it.

"Think about it."

I didn't take the elevator but went down the stairs instead, going back over the scene in my mind. Perhaps it was rash on my part to expose myself like that so quickly, but the secretary's attitude led me to suspect that she knew something: something she didn't tell me more out of uncertainty about me than loyalty to her employer. Da Silva and his secretary somehow didn't quite fit together, and I was sure she'd never tell him what happened during that strange visit. While he'd been busy playing both sides, not only had a fake Moroccan woman been poking around in his business, but a subversive leftist had already infiltrated his staff. I'd have to arrange things somehow so that I could see her alone again. As to how, when, and where, I hadn't the faintest idea.

Chapter Fifty-Seven

Tuesday dawned rainy, and I repeated my routine from the previous days, playing the role of buyer and allowing João to take me to my destination, this time a textile mill on the outskirts of Lisbon. The chauffeur came to pick me up again three hours later.

"Let's go to Baixa, please, João."

"If you were expecting to see Don Manuel, he's not back yet."

Perfect, I thought. I wasn't planning to see Da Silva, but to find some way of approaching Beatriz Oliveira again.

"That doesn't matter, the secretaries can help me. I just have a question on my order."

I was counting on the older assistant having gone out to lunch again and her frugal companion remaining chained to her desk, but as though someone had gone to great efforts to thwart my desires, what I found was exactly the opposite. The veteran was at her post, going over documents with her glasses down on the tip of her nose. And no sign of the younger one at all.

"Good afternoon, Senhora Somoza. So I see they've left you all alone."

"Don Manuel is still traveling, and Senhorita Oliveira hasn't come in to work today. How can I help you, Senhorita Agoriuq?"

I felt a taste of annoyance mixed with alarm, but I swallowed it as best I could.

"I hope she's not unwell," I said, not answering her question.

"No, I'm sure it's nothing serious. Her brother came by this morning to let me know that she was indisposed and had a bit of a fever, but I'm sure she'll be back tomorrow."

I wavered for a few seconds. Fast, Sira, think fast: act, ask where she lives, try to track her down, I commanded myself.

"Perhaps, if you could give me her address, I might send her some flowers. She's been very kind to me arranging all my visits to suppliers."

Despite her natural discretion, the secretary couldn't help a condescending smile.

"Don't worry about that, miss. I don't think that's necessary — really. We're not accustomed to receiving flowers when we're off work for a day. It's probably just a cold or some other insignificant ailment. If there's anything I might do to help you myself?"

"I've lost a pair of gloves," I improvised. "I thought that maybe I'd forgotten them here yesterday."

"I haven't seen them anywhere here this morning, but they might have been picked up by the women who come in early to clean. Leave it to me, I'll ask them."

The absence of Beatriz Oliveira had left my spirit just like the Lisbon noon I found when I stepped back out onto the Rua do Ouro: cloudy, blustery, stormy. And it had taken my appetite away, too, so I just had a cup of tea and a cake at the nearby Café Nicola and went on with my business. For that afternoon the efficient secretary had scheduled a meeting with importers of exotic goods from Brazil: she thought, cleverly, that the feathers of some rare birds might perhaps be of some use to me in my creations. And she was right. If only she'd go to as much trouble to help me with other things I needed.

The weather didn't improve as the hours went by, nor did my mood. On the way back to Estoril I added up the successes I'd achieved since my arrival, and the total was disastrous. The initial comments I'd had from João had proved to be hardly useful — just the same few brushstrokes repeated again and again with the tiresome verbosity of an old codger who has spent too long on the fringes of his boss's real day-to-day concerns. On the subject of private meetings with Germans that Hillgarth's wife had mentioned, I'd not yet heard a word. And the one person I thought of as a potential informer had slipped like water through my fingers, claiming some made-up illness. If I added to that the painful encounter with Marcus, the trip was an utter failure on all fronts. Except for my clients, naturally, who on my return would find a veritable arsenal of wonders impossible to imagine in the squalor of ration-book Spain. With this grim attitude, I had a light dinner in the hotel restaurant and decided to retire early.

As usual, the chambermaid had prepared the room with great care and left everything ready for a good night's sleep. The curtains drawn, the dim light on the bedside table switched on, the bed turned down with the corner folded with military precision. Perhaps those newly ironed Swiss batiste sheets would help me to escape from consciousness and forget my feelings of frustration, at least for a few hours.

I was about to lie down when I noticed a draft of cold air. I approached the balcony barefoot, drew apart the curtains, and saw that the balcony doors were open. A moment of forgetfulness on the part of the staff, I thought as I closed them. I sat down on the bed and turned out the light: I didn't feel like reading a single line. And then, as I stretched my legs out under the sheets, my left foot became entangled in something. I stifled a scream, tried to turn on the bedside light, but accidentally knocked it to the floor; I retrieved it with clumsy hands, tried again to switch it on with the lampshade askew. I finally managed to get it on and yanked off the bedclothes. What the hell was this tangle of black cloth that I'd touched with my foot? I didn't dare to touch it till I'd examined it carefully by sight. It looked like a veil: a black veil, a veil for Mass. I held it with two fingers and lifted it up: the fabric bundle came undone, and something that looked like a picture fell out from inside. I picked it up gingerly by a corner, as though I were afraid it would come apart if I handled it too firmly. Bringing it up to the light, I could make out the façade of a church. And the image of the Virgin. And two printed lines in Portuguese. "The Church of São Domingos. Novena in worship of Our Lady of Fátima." On the reverse was a penciled note in handwriting I didn't recognize. "Wednesday, 6 p.m. Left side, tenth row from the back." There was no signature; there was no need for one.

The whole of the following day I kept away from Da Silva's offices, in spite of the fact that the meetings I had scheduled for that day were in the center of town.

"Come fetch me this evening, João. At seven thirty outside Rossio station. Before that I want to attend a Mass, it's the anniversary of my father's death."

The driver accepted my orders, lowering his gaze with an expression of condolence, and I felt a stab of remorse at having eliminated Gonzalo Alvarado so blithely. But I had no time for such regrets, I thought, covering my head with the black veil: it was a quarter to six and the novena would be starting shortly. The church of São Domingos was next to Praça do Rossio, facing the square. When I arrived at the broad façade of white lime wash and stone, I ran into a memory of my mother that was fluttering around the doorway. The last time I'd been to a religious service had been with her in Tetouan, accompanying her to the little church on the square. São Domingos, in contrast, was magnificent, with its huge grey stone columns rising up to a sepia-colored ceiling. And there were people, lots of people, a few men and hordes of women, all of them faithful parishioners who had come to fulfill the mandate of the Virgin by praying a holy rosary.

I went down the left-side aisle, walking slowly, with my hands clasped together and my head bowed, simulating devotion while I counted the rows out of the corner of my eye. When I reached the tenth, I could see through my veil a figure dressed in mourning sitting at the end. With a black skirt and shawl and coarse woolen stockings: the attire of so many humble women in Lisbon. She wasn't wearing a veil but a scarf tied under her chin, which hung so low it was impossible to see her face. Beside her there was an empty place, but for a few moments I didn't know what I was expected to do. Until I saw a pale, careful hand emerge from the skirts. A hand that settled on the empty space next to its owner. Sit here, she seemed to be telling me. I obeyed her at once.

We sat in silence as the members of the congregation continued to fill the empty places. The altar boys shuffled around the altar, and in the background we could hear the purr of a sea of quiet murmurings. Although I looked at the woman several times out of the corner of my eye, her headscarf prevented me from seeing her features. In any case, I had no need: I had no doubt whatsoever who she was. I decided to break the ice with a whisper.

"Thank you for asking me here, Beatriz. Please, there's no need to be afraid: no one in Lisbon will ever know about this conversation."

It was a few seconds before she replied. When she did it was with her eyes still fixed on her lap and her voice barely audible.

"You work for the English, don't you?"

I lowered my head slightly in assent.

"I'm not really sure that this will be of any use to you, it's not a lot. I only know that Da Silva is in negotiations with the Germans over something related to the mines in Beira, a region in the interior of the country. He's never had any dealings in that area before. It's all recent, just over the last few months. Now he goes almost every week."

"What's it about?"

"Something they call 'the spit of the wolf.' The Germans are insisting on exclusivity, for him to cut off his dealings with the British altogether. And on top of that he is to get the owners of the adjacent mines to join him and stop selling to the English, too."

The priest came up to the altar from a side door, a tiny figure in the distance. The entire congregation rose to its feet, including the two of us.

"Who are these Germans?" I whispered from under my veil.

"Weiss is the only one who's come to the office — three times. He never speaks to them on the telephone; he thinks the line might be being tapped. I know that outside the office he's also met up with another one, Wolters. This week they're expecting a third one to come from Spain. They're all going to be having dinner at his estate tomorrow — Thursday night: Don Manuel, the Germans, and the Portuguese owners of the neighboring mines in Beira. That's where they're expecting to close the deal: he's been in discussions with the mine owners for weeks to get them to supply only to the Germans, nobody else. They'll all be there with their wives and he's anxious to treat them well: I know that because he made me order flowers and chocolates to welcome them."

The priest finished, and the whole church sat back down amid the sounds of rustling, sighs, and the creaking of old wood.

"He's alerted us" — she went on, her head bent down again — "not to put through any calls from certain Englishmen he used to be on good terms with. And this morning he had a meeting in the basement with two men, two ex-convicts he sometimes uses for protection; from time to time he's found himself in trouble. I was only able to

702

overhear the end of the conversation. He ordered them to deal with these Englishmen, and, if necessary, to neutralize them."

"What did he mean, 'neutralize them'?"

"Get them out of the way, I guess."

"How?"

"Use your imagination."

The congregation stood up again, and again we joined them. They began to chant with fervent voices, and I felt my blood thundering in my temples.

"Do you know what the names of these Englishmen are?"

"I've written them down."

Stealthily she pressed a folded piece of paper into my hand.

"I promise I don't know anything else."

"Send someone again if you hear anything new," I said, thinking of my open balcony doors.

"I will. And please, don't use my name. And don't come by the office anymore."

I couldn't promise her that I'd do as she said because like a black crow she immediately took flight. I remained a short while longer, sheltered between the stone columns, the off-key chants, and the murmur of the litany. When I had finally managed to get over the impact of what I'd heard, I unfolded the piece of paper and confirmed that my worst fears were not unfounded. Beatriz Oliveira had given me a list of five names. The fourth was Marcus Logan.

Chapter Fifty-Eight

Like every afternoon at that hour, the hotel lobby was lively and crowded. Filled with foreigners, ladies with pearls and men in linen suits or in uniform; filled with conversation, with the smell of expensive tobacco and the movement of bustling bellhops. And most likely filled with some undesirable types, too. One of them was there to meet me. Although I faked a reaction of surprised delight, I felt my skin crawl when I saw him. To look at him, he was just the same Manuel Da Silva of the previous days: sure of himself in his perfect suit, his first white hairs giving a sign of his forthcoming maturity, alert and smiling. Just seeing him provoked such revulsion in me that I had to curb my impulse to turn around and run. Out onto the street, to the beach, to the end of the world. Anywhere far from him. Before, everything had been mere suspicion; there had still been room to hope that beneath that attractive appearance was a decent human being. I knew now that that wasn't the case, that regrettably the worst predictions had been correct. The Hillgarths' assumptions had been confirmed in the church meeting: integrity and loyalty don't go well with business during wartime, and Da Silva had sold himself to the Germans. And as if that wasn't

704

enough, he'd made a sinister addition to the deal: if his old friends bothered him, he'd have to get rid of them. Remembering that Marcus was among them gave me a jolt in the gut all over again.

My body was begging to run away from him but I couldn't do it: not only because a heavy load of trunks and suitcases was momentarily blocking the hotel's large revolving door, but for other much more forceful reasons. I'd just learned that twenty-four hours from now Da Silva was planning to wine and dine his German contacts. No doubt that was the meeting that Hillgarth's wife had predicted, and it would probably be there that all the detailed information that the English were so keen to learn would be circulating. My next aim would be to try by any means to get myself invited to attend, but time wasn't on my side. I had no choice but to rush ahead.

"My condolences, my dear Arish."

It took me a couple of seconds to figure out what he was referring to. He probably attributed my silence to the fact that I was moved.

"Thank you," I murmured when the penny dropped. "My father wasn't a Christian, but I like to honor his memory with a few minutes of religious devotion."

"Do you feel like a drink? Maybe it's not a good time, but I heard you've been by my office a couple of times and I've just come to return the visit. Please excuse my repeated absence: I've been traveling much more than I'd like lately."

"I think a drink would do me good, thank you, it's been a long day. And yes, I did stop by your office, but just to say hello; everything else has been going perfectly." Plucking up all my courage,

705

I managed to polish off the sentence with a smile.

We made our way out to the terrace where we'd sat on that first night and everything returned to how it had been. Or almost. All the props were the same; the palm trees moved by the breeze, the ocean in the background, the silver moon, and the champagne at just the right temperature. And yet there was something not quite right with the scene. Something that had nothing to do with me, or the setting. I watched Manuel as he greeted the patrons around us again, and then I realized that it was he who was jarring in the middle of the harmony: he wasn't behaving naturally. He was trying hard to be charming, and as usual deploying the whole catalog of friendly phrases and amiable expressions, but no sooner had the person he was addressing turned away than his mouth adopted a serious, determined grimace that automatically disappeared again the moment he turned his focus back on me.

"So you've bought more material . . ."

"And also thread, accessories, ornaments, and a million notions."

"Your clients are going to be delighted."

"The Germans especially."

Now I'd thrown a stone into a pool of still water — it had to draw a response from him: this was my last chance to get myself invited to his house; if I couldn't do it, the mission would be over. He raised an eyebrow inquiringly.

"The German ladies are my most demanding clients, the ones who really appreciate quality," I explained. "The Spaniards are concerned with the final look of the piece, but the Germans concentrate on the perfection of every little detail; they're much more exacting. Fortunately I've been able to conform to their wishes and we get along without any problem. I think I've actually got a gift for keeping them happy," I said, finishing off my sentence with a mischievous wink.

I brought the glass to my lips and had to force myself not to drain the whole thing in one go. Come on, Manuel, come on, I thought. React — invite me. I could be useful to you, I could entertain your guests' companions while you negotiate over the spit of the wolf and find out how to get the English off your back.

"There are a lot of Germans in Madrid, too, aren't there?" he asked.

It wasn't an innocent question about the social environment of a neighboring country: it was a genuine interest in who my acquaintances were and what sort of relationship I had with them. He was coming closer. I knew what I had to say, which words to use: certain key names, weighty posts, and a feigned air of detachment.

"Oh, so many," I went on dully. I sat back in my chair, dropping my hand with an apparent lack of interest; I crossed my legs again, had another sip. "It was Baroness von Stohrer, the ambassador's wife, who made that comment last time she was in my studio, that Madrid had become the perfect German colony. And the truth is, some of them bring us a huge amount of work; Elsa Bruckmann, for example, who they say is a personal friend of Hitler's, she's in two or three times a week. And at the most recent party at Hans Lazar's house — he's the attaché for press and propaganda . . ."

I alluded to a couple of trivial anecdotes and dropped a few more names. With apparent uncon- cern, as though not finding them particularly important. And the more I spoke with feigned uninterest, the more I noticed Da Silva hanging on my words as though the whole world around him had stopped. He barely noticed the greetings that came at him from both sides, didn't pick up his glass from the table, and allowed his cigarette to burn away between his fingers, the ash forming a fat grey worm at the tip. Until I decided to stop increasing the pressure.

"I'm sorry, Manuel; I'm sure this is all terribly boring for you: the parties, clothing, and frivolity of women with nothing to do. Tell me, how was your trip?"

Our conversation went on for another half hour, during which time neither he nor I mentioned the Germans again. Their scent, however, seemed still to be lingering in the air.

"I think it's approaching dinnertime," he said, looking at his watch. "Would you like . . . ?"

"I'm worn out. Would you mind if we left it for tomorrow?"

"Tomorrow won't be possible." I noticed him hesitating a moment and held my breath; then he went on. "I have an engagement."

Go on, go on, go on. All it needed was a little push.

"What a shame, it will be our last night." My disappointment seemed genuine, almost as genuine as my desire to hear him say what I'd been waiting for over so many days. "I've arranged to go back to Madrid on Friday; there's an awful lot of work waiting for me next week. Baroness de Petrino, Lazar's wife, is hosting a reception next Thursday and I've got half a dozen German clients who want me to —"

"Perhaps you'd like to join us?"

I thought my heart had stopped beating.

"It's just a little get-together of a few friends. Germans and Portuguese. At my house."

Chapter Fifty-Nine

"How much would it be for you to take me to Lisbon?"

The man looked one way then the other to make sure that there wasn't anyone watching us. Then he took off his cap and scratched his head furiously.

"Ten escudos," he said, without taking the cigarette out of his mouth.

I held out a twenty.

"Let's go."

I had tried unsuccessfully to sleep: emotions and sensations raced across my mind all jumbled together, bumping against the walls of my brain. Satisfaction that the mission had finally begun to make progress, anxiety about what was awaiting me, unease at the terrible certainty of what I had learned. And on top of all that, the fear of knowing that Marcus Logan was on a grim list, which he probably had no idea existed, and frustration at having no way of alerting him about it. I had no clue where to find him, I'd only run into him in two places that were as different from each other as they were far apart. Perhaps the only place where they could give me any information would have been Da Silva's own offices, but I didn't dare approach Beatriz Oliveira again,

710

especially now that her boss was back.

One in the morning, half past, a quarter to two. Sometimes I was hot, sometimes cold. Two, two ten. I got up several times, opened and closed the balcony doors, drank a glass of water, turned on the light, turned it off. Twenty to three, three, three fifteen. And then, suddenly, I thought I'd found the solution. Or at least something approaching it.

I put on the darkest clothes I could find in my closet: a black mohair suit, a lead-grey jacket, and a wide-brimmed hat pulled down to my eyebrows. The last things I took were the key to my room and a handful of banknotes. I didn't need anything else, apart from luck. I tiptoed down the back stairs; everything was calm and there was practically no light. I continued on with no clear idea of where I was, letting my instinct guide me. The kitchens, the storerooms, the washrooms, the boiler rooms. I reached the street through a back door out of the basement. It definitely wasn't a good omen; I'd just realized that it was the way they took out the trash, albeit rich people's trash.

It was a dark night, with the lights of the casino glimmering a few hundred yards away, and from time to time I could hear one of the last late-night partygoers: a good-bye, a muffled laugh, the engine of a car. Then silence. I settled down to wait, my lapels raised and my hands in my pockets, sitting on a curb and protected by a pile of soda-siphon crates. I was from a working neighborhood myself, and I knew it wouldn't be long before the bustle would start: there were a lot of people who woke at the crack of dawn in order to make life more pleasant for those who could allow themselves the luxury of sleeping well into the morning. The first lights in the lower service floors of the hotel were on by four, and soon after that a couple of employees came out. They stopped to light a cigarette in the doorway, cupping the flame with their hands, and then wandered off in no apparent hurry. The first vehicle was a sort of van; without pulling in too close it disgorged more than a dozen young women and then was off again. They went in grumbling tiredly: the waitresses on the next shift, I guessed. The second motor was that of a three-wheeler. A skinny, badly shaved man got out and began to rummage in the back for something or other. Then I saw him go into the kitchen carrying a large wicker basket that didn't seem to weigh much, and whose contents, with the darkness and the distance, I wasn't able to identify. When he had finished, he headed back to the little vehicle, and it was then that I approached him.

Using a handkerchief, I tried to clean off the straw that covered the seat, but I couldn't do it. The interior smelled of chicken droppings, and there were feathers, broken shells, and old bits of excrement everywhere. The breakfast eggs were presented to the guests exquisitely fried or scrambled on gold-edged porcelain plates. The vehicle that transported them from the laying coops to the hotel kitchens was a whole lot less elegant. I tried not to think about the soft leather of the seats in João's Bentley as we made our way, swaying to the rhythm of the three-wheeler's clattering. I was sitting on the egg-deliveryman's right, the two of us squeezed into a narrow front seat less than three feet wide. Despite the tight quarters, we didn't exchange a word, except when

I needed to give him the address where he was to take me.

"Here it is," I said when we arrived.

I recognized the façade.

"Another fifty escudos if you come and collect me in two hours."

A gesture touching the brim of his cap meant that we had a deal.

The main door was shut; I sat on a stone bench to wait for the night watchman. With my hat pulled down and the lapels of my jacket still up, I got rid of my doubts by concentrating on trying to remove one by one the pieces of straw and feathers that had stuck to my clothes. Fortunately I didn't have to wait long: within a quarter of an hour the man I was waiting for arrived, brandishing a large set of keys. He swallowed the tale I spun for him, in fits and starts, about having forgotten a handbag and let me in. I looked for the name on the mailboxes, ran up two flights of stairs, and rapped on the door with a bronze knocker that was bigger than my own hand.

It didn't take them long to wake. First I heard somebody moving, with the weary tread of someone dragging along a pair of old slippers. The peephole was opened and on the other side I could see a dark eye full of sleep and surprise. Then I heard the sound of quick, more energetic footsteps. And voices — low, urgent voices. Though they were muffled by the thickness of the solid wooden door, I recognized one of them. The one I was here for. It was confirmed when another eye, lively and blue, appeared at the little hole.

"Rosalinda, it's me, Sira. Please, open up."

A bolt — *thunk.* Another.

Our greeting was hasty, full of restrained joy

713

and excited whispers.

"What a marvelous surprise! But what are you doing here in the middle of the night, querida? They told me you were coming to Lisbon but I wouldn't be able to see you — how is everything in Madrid? How's —"

My joy was great, too, but fear made me revert to a state of caution.

"Shhhhhhh . . . ," I said, trying to contain her. She ignored me and continued with her enthusiastic welcome. Even having been dragged out of bed in the early hours of the morning didn't diminish her usual glamour. Her delicate bone structure and transparent skin were covered by an ivory silk dressing gown that came down to her feet, her wavy hair was perhaps a little shorter, but her mouth was still running on in a jumble of English, Spanish, and Portuguese, just as it used to.

Having her so close to me unleashed a million questions that had long been coiled and ready to spring. What had become of her in the long months since she'd left Spain, what cunning wiles had allowed her to get ahead, how had she taken Beigbeder's fall? Her house emanated an aura of luxury and well-being, but I knew that the fragility of her financial resources prevented her from affording a place like this on her own. I preferred not to ask. However heavy the pressures may have been, and however dark the circumstances, Rosalinda Fox continued to radiate the same positive vitality she always had, an optimism that could topple any wall, get around any obstacle, or raise the dead if she so willed it.

We walked down the long hallway arm in arm, talking amid whispers and shadows. Upon reaching her bedroom, she closed the door behind us and a memory of Tetouan immediately assailed me like a gust of African air. The Berber rug, a Moorish lamp, the pictures on the walls. I recognized a Bertuchi watercolor: the whitewashed walls of the Moorish quarter, the Riffian women selling oranges, an overloaded mule, haiks and djellabas, and — way out in the background — the minaret of a mosque cut out against the Moroccan sky. I looked away; this wasn't the time for nostalgia.

"I need to find Marcus Logan."

"My, what a coincidence. He came to see me just a few days ago: he wanted to know about you."

"What did you tell him?" I asked in alarm.

"Only the truth," she said, raising her right hand as though about to swear an oath. "That the last time I'd seen you was last year in Tangiers."

"Do you know how to find him?"

"No. We left it that he'd come by El Galgo again sometime, that's all."

"What's El Galgo?"

"My club," she said with a wink, lying back onto the bed. "A brilliant business I've opened, going halves with a friend of mine. We're making a mint," she finished with a laugh. "But I'll tell you all that some other time; let's concentrate on urgent matters for now. I don't know where to find Marcus, querida. I don't know where he lives, nor do I have his telephone number. But come now, sit down next to me and tell me the story, and let's see if something occurs to us."

It was such a consolation to be reunited with the same old Rosalinda. Extravagant and unpredictable, but also efficient, quick, and decisive even at the break of dawn. Once she'd gotten over

715

the initial surprise and understood that my visit had a concrete objective, she didn't waste any time asking about matters that weren't any use, nor did she want to know about my life in Madrid or my assignments for the Secret Intelligence Service, into whose arms she'd thrown me. She simply understood that there was something that needed resolving urgently and she set about helping me.

I summarized the Da Silva story and the part Marcus played in it. We were lit only by the dim light that filtered through a pleated silk lampshade, both of us on her large bed. Although I knew I was going against the express orders I'd received from Hillgarth not to contact Rosalinda under any circumstances, I didn't worry about letting her in on the details of my mission: I trusted her implicitly, and she was the only person I could run to. Besides, in a way it was their fault that I'd ended up seeking her out: they'd sent me to Portugal so unprotected, so unsupported, that I had no choice.

"I see Marcus very occasionally: sometimes he comes by the club, from time to time we run into each other at the restaurant at the Hotel Aviz, and there have been a couple of nights when like you we've crossed paths in the Estoril casino. Always charming, but somewhat evasive about the work he's involved in: he's never explained to me what it is he's up to at the moment, but at any rate I very much doubt it's journalism. Every time we meet we chat for a couple of minutes and say an affectionate farewell, promising to meet up more often, but we never do. I have no idea what he's got himself into, querida. I don't know if his business dealings are clean or whether they're in need of a little laundering. I don't even know if he lives in Lisbon permanently or comes and goes from London or somewhere else. But if you give me a couple of days, I can make some inquiries."

"I don't think there's time. Da Silva has already given orders for him to be removed to leave the way free for the Germans. I have to warn him as soon as possible."

"Be careful, Sira. You might be involved in something shady that you're not aware of. You haven't been told what sort of dealings linked him to Da Silva, and a lot of time has gone by since we were with him in Morocco; we don't know what's become of his life from the day he left up till now. And to tell the truth, we didn't know all that much back then, either."

"But he managed to bring my mother . . ."

"He was simply a mediator, and what's more, he did it in exchange for something. It wasn't a disinterested favor, don't forget that."

"And we knew he was a journalist."

"That's what we believed, but we never saw a published copy of the famous interview with Juan Luis, which was apparently his motive for coming to Tetouan."

"Maybe —"

"Or the report on Spanish Morocco that kept him there for all those weeks."

There were a thousand reasons we might not have seen his published pieces, and no doubt it would be easy to think of them, but I couldn't waste any time. Africa was yesterday — Portugal was the present. And the pressure was in the here and now.

"You have to help me find him," I insisted, leaping over all my fears. "Da Silva already has his people on the alert. Marcus at least needs to be

717

warned; he'll know what to do after that."

"Of course I'm going to try to track him down, querida, rest easy, but I just want to ask you to be cautious and to bear in mind that we've all changed tremendously, that none of us are who we used to be. In the Tetouan of a few years ago, you were a young dressmaker and I was the happy lover of a powerful man; look what we've become now, look where the two of us are and how we've had to meet. Most probably Marcus and his circumstances have changed, too: those are the facts of life, especially in times like these. And if we knew little about him then, we know even less now."

"He's in business, that's what Da Silva told me."

She took my explanation with a wry laugh.

"Don't be naïve, Sira. Nowadays the word 'business' is like a huge black umbrella that can cover a multitude of sins."

"So are you telling me I shouldn't help him?" I said, trying not to sound confused.

"No. What I'm trying to do is advise you to be very careful and not to take any more risks than you have to, because you don't even know who this man is you're trying to protect or what he's involved in. It's strange the turns life takes, isn't it?" she went on with a half smile, pushing that eternal blond lock of hair back from her face. "He was crazy about you in Tetouan, and you refused to get involved with him at all despite the attraction between you. And now after such a long time, in order to protect him you'd risk being unmasked, throwing away the mission, and God knows what else, and all this in a country where you're on your own and barely know anybody. I still don't understand why you were so reluctant

718

to start something serious with Marcus, but whatever impression he made on you must have been extremely deep for you to be exposing yourself like this for him."

"I've told you a hundred times. I didn't want a new relationship because my betrayal by Ramiro was still fresh, because I still had wounds that hadn't healed."

"But some time had passed . . ."

"Not enough. I was panicking at the idea of suffering again, Rosalinda, I was so afraid. The thing with Ramiro was so painful, so brutal, so, so overwhelming . . . I knew that sooner or later Marcus would end up leaving, too, and I didn't want to go through that again."

"But he never would have left you like that. Sooner or later he would have come back, perhaps you could have left with him."

"No. Tetouan wasn't his home, and it was mine, with my mother just about to arrive, two charges against me in Madrid, and Spain still at war. I was confused, I was bruised, still distressed by what had happened to me before, anxious for news of my mother, and constructing a fake personality to win clients in a foreign land. Yes, I built a wall to avoid falling desperately in love with Marcus, you're right. And just the same he managed to get past it. He slipped through the net and reached me. I haven't loved anyone else since, nor have I been attracted to any man, not really. His memory has been what's kept me strong, allowed me to face my solitude, and believe me, Rosalinda, when I tell you I've been very much alone this whole time. And when I thought I was never going to see him again, life put him in my path at the worst possible moment.

I don't mean to rescue him, or build a bridge back to the past in order to recover what's lost; I know that'd be impossible in this lunatic world we're living in. But if I can at least help him avoid being wiped out on some street corner, I've got to try to do it."

She must have noticed that my voice was shaky, because she took my hand and squeezed it hard.

"Well then, let's focus on the present," she said firmly. "As soon as the morning gets going I'll start to mobilize my contacts. If he's still in Lisbon, I'll be able to find him."

"I can't see him, and I don't want you to talk to him either. Use some intermediary, someone who can get the information to him without him knowing it's coming from you. All he needs to know is that Da Silva not only doesn't want anything to do with him but he's given orders for him to be removed if he becomes a bother. I'll notify Hillgarth about the other names when I get to Madrid. Or rather, no," I corrected myself. "Better to give Marcus all the names; write them down, I know them by heart. Let him deal with getting the word around; he probably knows them all."

I felt a huge tiredness, almost as great as the distress I'd been carrying around inside me ever since Beatriz Oliveira had passed me that sinister list in the church of São Domingos. It had been a horrible day: the novena and what had come with it, the subsequent meeting with Da Silva, and the exhausting struggle to get him to invite me to his house; the sleepless hours, the wait in the dark beside the hotel trash cans, the tortuous journey to Lisbon stuck to the body of that foul-smelling egg man. I looked at my watch. There was still a half hour before he was to fetch me in his three-wheeler. Just to shut my eyes now and curl up on Rosalinda's unmade bed seemed like the greediest of temptations, but now wasn't the moment to think about sleep. First I had to catch up with my friend about her life, if only briefly: who knew if we would meet again?

"Tell me, quickly — I don't want to go without hearing a bit about you. How have you worked things out since leaving Spain, what's become of your life?"

"At first it was hard, I was alone, with no money and plagued by the uncertainty surrounding Juan Luis's situation in Madrid. But I couldn't just sit down and cry over what I'd lost: I had to make a living. At times it was even fun. I lived through a few scenes worthy of the finest comedy: there were a couple of decrepit old millionaires who offered to marry me, and I even managed to dazzle a senior Nazi officer who swore that if I'd agree, he was prepared to run off to Rio de Janeiro with me. Sometimes it was enjoyable; other times, to tell the truth, it was no fun whatsoever. I found ex-admirers who pretended not to recognize me, and old friends who turned away from me, people I'd helped once upon a time and who now seemed to be afflicted with amnesia, and liars who pretended to be very badly off to avoid my asking to borrow anything from them. That wasn't the worst of it, however; the hardest thing in all that time was having to break off all contact with Juan Luis. First we gave up the telephone calls after he learned that they were being tapped, then we stopped using the post. And then came the dismissal and the arrest. The last letters for a long while were the ones he gave you and that you

721

passed on to Hillgarth. And then, the end."

"Have you been able to secure any information about how he is doing now?"

She sighed deeply before answering and pushed her hair back from her face one more time.

"Reasonably well. They sent him to Ronda, which was almost a relief because he'd thought they were going to destroy him completely, with accusations of high treason against the fatherland. But they ended up not establishing a court martial against him, more out of their own self-interest than out of compassion — getting rid of a minister like that, a minister who'd only been appointed a little more than a year earlier, would have had a serious negative impact on the Spanish population and on world opinion."

"Is he still in Ronda?"

"Yes, but now just under house arrest. He lives in a hotel, and it seems they're beginning to give him some freedom of movement. He's started getting excited about some plans again, you know how restless he is, always needing to be active, involved in something interesting, coming up with ideas and making things happen. I'm confident that he'll be able to come over to Lisbon before too long, and then we'll see," she concluded, her smile heavy with melancholy.

I didn't dare to ask her what they were, these new plans that followed his being hurled into the pit with those who'd been stripped of glory. The ex-minister who was so friendly toward the English had very little clout in the New Spain that was so cozy with the Axis; a lot would have to change before he'd be in any position to show up back there.

I looked at my watch again; I only had ten

minutes left.

"Keep telling me about yourself, how you managed to get by."

"I met Dimitri, a White Russian who'd fled to Paris after the Bolshevik Revolution. We became friends, and I convinced him to make me his partner in the club he was planning to open. He'd provide the money, I'd be responsible for the décor and for providing contacts. El Galgo was a success right from the start, which meant that not long after the business started operating, I threw myself into the search for a house to allow me finally to get out of the little room where some Polish friends had been hiding me. And then I found this apartment. If you can call something with twenty-four bedrooms an apartment."

"Twenty-four bedrooms — that's madness!"

"Don't you believe it; I did it in order to make something from it. Lisbon is full of expatriates without much cash who can't manage a long stay in a fine hotel."

"Don't tell me you're running a guest house here."

"Something like that. For elegant guests, worldly people whose sophistication can't save them from being at the edge of an abyss. I share my home with them, they share their capital with me as far as their means allow. There's no price: there are some who've enjoyed a room for two months without paying me a single escudo, and others who in exchange for having stayed a week made me a present of a diamond rivière bracelet or a Lalique brooch. I don't give anyone a bill: each contributes whatever he or she can. These are tough times, querida: everyone just needs to survive."

Indeed, to survive. And for me, the most immediate survival meant getting back into a three-wheeler smelling of chickens and making it back to my room in the Hotel do Parque before the morning began. I would have loved to keep chatting with Rosalinda until the end of time, lying on her big bed with no greater concerns than ringing a little bell to get someone to bring us our breakfast. But the time had come for me to go back, to resume reality, however dark it might appear. She accompanied me to the door; before opening it, she hugged me with her light body and breathed a piece of advice in my ear.

"I barely know Manuel Da Silva, but everyone in Lisbon has heard of his reputation: a great businessman, seductive and charming, and also hard as ice, merciless with his opponents, and ready to sell his soul for a good deal. Be very careful — you're playing with fire in the company of a dangerous man."

Chapter Sixty

"Clean towels," announced the voice on the other side of the bathroom door.

"Leave them on the bed — thank you," I shouted.

I hadn't asked for towels, and it was odd that they should come and replace them at that time of the afternoon, but I assumed it was just a simple service mix-up.

I was standing in front of the mirror in my bathrobe and had just finished putting on my mascara. That completed my makeup: all I had left to do was get dressed. There was still nearly an hour before João was due to collect me. I'd started getting ready early to occupy my mind with some activity to stop it from imagining a disastrous ending to my brief career. But I still had plenty of time. I left the bathroom knotting the belt of my bathrobe and then hesitated, deciding what to do. I'd wait a while before getting dressed. Or maybe not, maybe I should at least start putting my stockings on. Or no, perhaps I should . . . And then I saw him, and instantly everything else in the world ceased to exist.

"Marcus, what are you doing here?" I stammered in disbelief. Someone had let him in when they were bringing the towels. Or perhaps not — I scanned the room and there wasn't a towel to be seen.

He didn't answer my question. Nor did he greet me, or even bother to justify boldly invading my room.

"Stop seeing Manuel Da Silva, Sira. Keep away from him, that's all I've come to tell you."

He spoke firmly. He was standing, his left arm resting on the back of an armchair in one corner of the room. In a white shirt and grey suit, neither tense nor relaxed: just restrained. As though he had an obligation to fulfill and no intention of failing to fulfill it.

I couldn't reply: no words came to my mouth.

"I don't know what kind of relationship you have with him," he went on, "but there's still time to stop yourself from getting too involved. Get away from here, go back to Morocco . . ."

"I live in Madrid now," I managed to say at last. I was standing on the rug, still, barefoot, not knowing what to do. I remembered Rosalinda's words that very same morning: I ought to be careful with Marcus, I didn't know what world he was a part of now, or what business he was mixed up in. I shuddered. I didn't know now, and maybe I never would. I waited for him to go on talking, to be able to gauge how honest I could be or how cautious; how much I should let out the Sira he knew, and how much I should keep playing the distant part of Arish Agoriuq.

He moved away from the armchair and took a few steps toward me. His face was still the same, his eyes, too. The limber body, the hairline, the color of his skin, the line of his jaw; the shoulders, the arms that had so often linked with mine as we walked, the hands that had held my fingers, the voice. Everything was suddenly so near to me, so close, and so distant at the same time.

"Leave as soon as you can, don't see him again," he insisted. "You don't deserve to be with a fellow like that. I haven't the slightest idea why you've changed your name, or why you've come to Lisbon, or what it was that brought you into contact with him. Nor do I know whether your relationship is something genuine or whether someone else has got you involved in this whole business, but I can assure you —"

"There's nothing serious between us. I've come to Lisbon to buy some materials for my workshop; someone I know in Madrid put me in touch with him and we've met a few times. He's just a friend."

"No, Sira, don't kid yourself," he interrupted me sharply. "Manuel Da Silva doesn't have friends. He has conquests, he has acquaintances and flatterers, and he has interested professional contacts, that's all. And lately those contacts haven't been quite to his taste. You're getting involved in a murky business; we learn something new about him every day, and you should keep away from all that. He's not the man for you."

"Then he isn't for you, either. But you seemed good friends that night at the casino . . ."

"We're of interest to each other for purely commercial purposes — or rather, we used to be. Last I heard he doesn't want to hear from me anymore. Not from me or anyone else English."

I sighed with relief; his words suggested that Rosalinda had managed to track him down and have someone pass on the message. We remained standing, facing each other, but the distance between us had become smaller without either of us even noticing. A step forward from him, one from me. Another from him, another from me. When we'd started talking we'd occupied opposite ends of the room, like boxers, suspicious and on our guard, each fearful of what the other might do. As the minutes had passed we'd been getting closer, perhaps unconsciously, until we were in the middle of the room, between the desk and the foot of the bed. Within reach of each other if we just made one more move.

"I know how to look after myself, don't worry. In the note you gave me at the casino you asked what had become of the Sira of Tetouan. Well, now you can see her — she's become stronger. And also more skeptical, more disillusioned. Now I ask you the same question, Marcus Logan: what became of the battered journalist who arrived in Africa to conduct a long interview with the high commissioner that was never —"

A knock at the door interrupted my question; there was someone outside. At an entirely unexpected time. Instinctively I grabbed hold of Marcus's arm.

"Ask who it is," he whispered.

"Who's there?" I called.

"It's Gamboa, Senhor Da Silva's assistant. I've got something for you from him," said the voice from the hall.

With three stealthy strides, Marcus disappeared into the bathroom. I approached the door slowly, put my hand on the door handle, and took several breaths. Then I opened it, feigning casualness, to find Gamboa holding something light and colorful wrapped in tissue paper. I held out my hand to receive this thing I still hadn't identified, but he didn't give it to me.

"It would be best if I were to put them down on

728

a flat surface myself, they're very delicate. Orchids," he explained.

I hesitated a few seconds. Although Marcus was hidden in the bathroom, it was rash to allow that man into the bedroom, but at the same time if I didn't let him through it would look as though I were hiding something. And at that moment the last thing I wanted was to arouse suspicions.

"Come in," I accepted at last. "Please, put them down on the desk."

And then I realized. And wished the ground would open up under my feet and swallow me. That I'd be ingested in one gulp, sucked in, vanished forever. That way I wouldn't have to face the consequences of what I'd just seen. There in the center of the table, between the telephone and a golden lamp, was something inconvenient. Something immensely inconvenient that nobody ought to see there. Still less the trusty manservant of Manuel Da Silva.

I corrected myself as quickly as I spotted it.

"Oh, no, it'd be better to put them here, on the stool at the foot of the bed."

He obeyed without comment, but I also knew that he'd noticed. How could he not have? The thing that was on that polished wooden desk surface was something that was so unconnected to me and so incongruous in a bedroom occupied by an unaccompanied woman that it had to stand out: Marcus's hat.

He came out of his hiding place when he heard the door close.

"Go, Marcus. Get out of here — please," I insisted, trying to guess how long it would take Gamboa to tell his boss what he'd just seen. If Marcus had realized the scale of the disaster that his hat could unleash, he gave no sign of it. "Stop worrying about me: tomorrow night I'm going back to Madrid. Today will be my last day, as of —"

"You're really leaving tomorrow?" he asked, taking hold of my shoulders. Despite my anxiety and fear, a feeling ran down my spine that I hadn't felt in a long time.

"Tomorrow night, yes. On the Lusitania Express."

"And you're not coming back to Portugal?"

"No, right now I'm not planning to."

"And to Morocco?"

"Not there either. I'll stay in Madrid; that's where I have my workshop and my life."

We were silent for a few seconds. We were probably both thinking the same thing: how unlucky that once again our destinies had crossed paths at such a stormy time, how sad to have to lie to each other like this.

"Take good care of yourself."

I nodded, without a word. He brought his hand to my face and slowly ran a finger down my cheek.

"It was a pity we never got closer in Tetouan, wasn't it?"

I went up onto my tiptoes and brought my mouth toward his face to kiss him good-bye. When I smelled his scent and he smelled mine, when my skin brushed his and my breath spilled into his ear, I whispered my answer.

"Yes it was, such a pity."

He left without a sound and I remained behind, in the company of the most beautiful orchids I would ever see in my life, struggling against my desperate desire to run after him and hold him, as

I tried to measure the consequences of that mistake.

CHAPTER SIXTY-ONE

As we approached I saw several cars parked in a
row on one side of the road. Big cars, dazzling,
dark and imposing.

Da Silva's estate was in the countryside, not too
far from Estoril, but far enough that I'd never be
able to get back on my own. I made a mental note
of a few signs: Malveira, Sintra, Colares, Guincho.
All the same, I didn't have the faintest idea where
we were.

João braked gently and the tires crunched on
the gravel. I waited for someone to open the door
for me. I put one foot out first, gradually, then the
other. Then I saw his hand held out to me.

"Welcome to the Quinta da Fonte, Arish."

I got out of the car slowly. The gold lamé clung
to my body, accentuating its contours, while in
my hair I was wearing one of the three orchids
that he'd sent me. I glanced quickly about, looking for the assistant, but he wasn't there.

The night smelled of orange trees and cooling
cypresses, and the lamps on the façade gave off a
light that seemed to melt on the stones of the
grand house. As I climbed the front steps on his
arm, I noticed that above the main entrance there
hung a massive coat of arms.

"The Da Silva family crest, I presume."

I was well aware that his tavern-owning grand-father could hardly have had an ancestral crest even in his wildest dreams, but I didn't think he'd notice the irony.

The guests were waiting in a grand hall full of heavy furnishings, with a large unlit fireplace at one end. The floral arrangements throughout the room weren't enough to mitigate the chilly atmosphere. Nor did the uncomfortable silence of all those present help to warm it up. I counted them quickly. Two, four, six, eight, ten. Ten people, five couples. And Da Silva. And me. Twelve altogether.

As though he'd been reading my thoughts, Manuel announced: "There's still one more to come, another German guest who won't be long. Come, Arish, let me introduce you."

At that point the ratio was almost balanced: three Portuguese couples, two German couples, plus the one still to come. But that was where the symmetry ended, because everything else was curiously dissonant. The German men were dressed in dark clothes — reserved, discreet, in keeping with the place and the occasion. Their wives, though not displaying a dazzling elegance, wore their dresses with sophistication and poise. The Portuguese, on the other hand, were a different kettle of fish altogether. The men, the women — all of them. Although the men's suits were cut from good cloth, their quality was marred by the scant elegance of the peasant bodies wearing them: short legged, thick necked, with broad hands full of calluses and broken nails. In the breast pocket of their jackets they each ostentatiously displayed a pair of gleaming fountain pens, and whenever they smiled their mouths revealed several shiny gold teeth. Their wives, likewise vulgar in style, were trying hard to keep their balance in their shiny high-heeled shoes into which their swollen feet could barely fit. One of them was wearing her hat askew; another had a huge fur stole dangling over one shoulder, which kept slipping down onto the floor; the third wiped her mouth with the back of her hand each time she ate a canapé.

Before arriving I'd thought that Manuel had invited me in order to show me off in front of his guests — an exotic decorative object that reinforced his position as a powerful male, someone who might be useful to entertain the ladies with talk about fashion, anecdotes about high-ranking Germans in Spain, and other trivialities of the kind. No sooner had I gotten a sense of the atmosphere, however, than I knew I'd been wrong. Although I'd been welcomed as just another guest, Da Silva hadn't invited me there to fill out the numbers, but to share the role of host with him and to help him to tend to this curious fauna with finesse. My role would be to act as liaison, to provide a bridge between the German women and the Portuguese women; otherwise, the two groups wouldn't have been able to do more than look at each other all night long. If he had important matters to resolve, the last thing he wanted was a lot of bored, ill-tempered women desperate for their husbands to get them out of there. That's what he wanted me there for, to give him a hand. I'd thrown down the gauntlet the previous day, and he'd taken it up: we both stood to gain something by it.

Well then, Manuel, I'm going to give you what you want, I thought. I hope you do the same for me later. And in order for everything to work just as he'd planned it, I squeezed all my fears into a tight little ball, swallowed them down, and brought out the most entrancing side of my false personality. With that façade as my banner, I stretched my apparent charm to its limit and radiated warmth, spreading it equally between the two nationalities. I praised in turn the hat and the stole of the women from Beira, I made a couple of jokes that everybody laughed at, I allowed one of the Portuguese men's hands to graze my backside, and I extolled the virtues of the German people. Shamelessly.

Until a black cloud appeared in the doorway.

"Excuse me, my friends," Da Silva announced. "I'd like to introduce you to Johannes Bernhardt."

He was older, had put on some weight and lost some hair, but without a doubt he was the same Bernhardt from Tetouan. The one who so often used to stroll along the Calle del Generalísimo, on the arm of a lady who wasn't with him at the moment. The one who negotiated with Serrano Suñer to install German antennas on Moroccan territory and agreed to keeping these matters from Beigbeder. The one who never knew that I'd been listening to them, lying on the floor, hidden behind a sofa.

"Sorry I'm late. Our car broke down and we had to make a long stop in Elvas."

I tried to hide my unease, accepting a glass from a waiter while I did some quick calculations: when the last time was that we'd been in the same place, how many times we'd passed each other on the street, how long I'd spent with him that night at the High Commission. When Hillgarth had informed me that Bernhardt had settled on the

735

Peninsula and was in charge of the large corporation that managed the Nazis' economic interests in Spain, I told him that he probably wouldn't recognize me if he ever met me again. Now, however, I wasn't so sure.

As Bernhardt's introductions began, I kept my back turned to the group of men chatting and devoted myself to the task of being charming to the ladies. The new topic of conversation was the orchid in my hair, and as I bent slightly and turned my head so that everyone could admire it, I was trying to catch snippets of information. I registered the names again, so that my memory of them would be more secure: Weiss and Wolters were the Germans whom Bernhardt, who'd only just got in from Spain, didn't know. Almeida, Rodrigues, and Ribeiro were the Portuguese from Beira, men from mountain country. Mine owners — or rather, to be more accurate, owners of shabby little pieces of land where divine Providence had happened to place some valuable minerals. What kind of minerals? That was still a mystery to me: at this point I still didn't know what the "spit of the wolf" was that Beatriz Oliveira had mentioned in the church. And then at last I heard the word I'd been waiting for: "tungsten."

From somewhere deep in my memory I retrieved the information Hillgarth had furnished me with in Tangiers: it was a mineral crucial to the production of projectiles for the war. And as I held on to that memory, I recovered another: one of the people involved in buying it on a massive scale was Johannes Bernhardt. Except that Hillgarth had talked to me about his interest in deposits in Galicia and Extremadura; at the time he probably couldn't have predicted that Bernhardt's tentacles would end up crossing the border into Portugal and entering negotiations with a treacherous businessman who'd decided to stop supplying the English in order to fulfill the demands of their enemies. I felt my legs tremble and sought refuge in a sip of champagne. Manuel Da Silva wasn't busy buying and selling silk, wood, or any other equally innocuous products from the colonies, but something much more dangerous, more sinister: his new business concerned a metal that the Germans would use to reinforce their weaponry and enhance their capacity to kill.

The guests demanded my attention, pulling me out of my reverie. They wanted to know where I'd obtained that wonderful flower resting behind my left ear, to get confirmation that it was in fact real, to know how they were grown: a thousand questions I took absolutely no interest in, but that I couldn't refuse to answer. It was a tropical flower; yes, absolutely natural, of course; no, I had no idea of whether Beira would be a suitable place for cultivating orchids.

"Ladies, allow me to introduce you to our last guest," Manuel interrupted us again.

I held my breath until it was my turn. The last one.

"And this is my dear friend, Senhorita Arish Agoriuq."

He looked at me without blinking for a second. Two. Three.

"Have we met?"

Smile, Sira, smile, I commanded myself.

"No, I don't think so," I said, holding out my right hand languidly.

"Unless you crossed paths somewhere in

737

Madrid," Manuel added. Fortunately he didn't seem to know Bernhardt well enough to be aware that at some point in his past he'd lived in Morocco.

"At Embassy, perhaps?" I suggested.

"No, no; I've been in Madrid very little lately. I travel a lot and my wife likes the sea, so we've settled in Denia, close to Valencia. No, your face is very familiar from somewhere else, but . . ."

I was saved by the butler. Ladies, gentlemen, dinner is served.

In the absence of a consort to play hostess, Da Silva ignored protocol and placed me at one end of the table. He took the other. I tried to hide my nerves, turning my attention to the guests, but I was so anxious I could barely eat. The shock caused by Gamboa's visit to my room had now been elevated by the unexpected arrival of Bernhardt and the confirmation of the dirty business Da Silva was implicated in. As if that wasn't enough, I also had to maintain my composure and play the role of lady of the house.

The soup arrived in a silver tureen, the wine in crystal decanters, and the seafood on huge trays overflowing with crustaceans. I went out of my way to seem attentive to all the guests. I discreetly indicated to the Portuguese women which cutlery they should use at any given moment and exchanged phrases with the Germans: yes, of course I knew Baroness von Stohrer; yes, Gloria von Fürstenberg, too; of course, yes, of course I'd heard that Horcher would soon be opening its doors in Madrid. The dinner proceeded without incident, and to my good fortune Bernhardt paid me no more attention.

"Well, ladies, now — if you don't mind — we

738

gentlemen will retire to chat," Manuel announced when we'd finished dessert.

I forced myself not to react, twisting the end of the tablecloth between my fingers. It wasn't possible, he couldn't do this to me. I'd done my part; now it was my turn to get something back. I'd satisfied everyone, I'd behaved like an exemplary hostess even though I wasn't, and I needed my recompense. At the very moment that they were going to talk about just the thing I was interested in, I couldn't let them escape. Fortunately, our dinner had been accompanied by a substantial quantity of wine, and moods seemed to have relaxed. Those of the Portuguese, particularly.

"Oh no, Da Silva, for God's sake!" shouted one of them, slapping the table loudly. "Don't be so old-fashioned, my friend! In the modern world men and women go everywhere together!"

Manuel wavered a second; no doubt he would have preferred to keep the rest of the conversation private, but the Beira crowd gave him no choice: they got up noisily and headed back to the living room all excited. One of them draped his arm over Da Silva's shoulders, another offered his to me. Once they'd gotten over their initial reticence at being received in a rich man's grand home, they seemed utterly delighted. That night they were going to close a deal that would allow them to slam the door on poverty for themselves, their children, and their children's children; there was no reason whatsoever why they should do it behind their own wives' backs.

They served coffee, liqueurs, and candies; I remembered that Beatriz Oliveira had been responsible for buying these as well as the floral displays, which were elegant without being too showy. I guessed it had been she, too, who had ordered the orchids I'd received that same afternoon, and I felt another shudder as I recalled the unexpected visit from Marcus.

A double shudder. Of affection and gratitude toward him for having been worried about me like that; of fear, again, at the memory of the incident of the hat right under the assistant's nose. There was still no sign of Gamboa; perhaps with a little bit of luck he'd be dining on a homemade stew with his family somewhere, listening to his wife complaining about the price of meat and forgetting that he'd suspected the presence of another man in the bedroom of the foreign woman who was being courted by his boss.

Although he hadn't been able to put us in different rooms, Manuel did at least manage to keep us in separate areas. The men were at one end of the large hall, on leather armchairs facing the unlit fireplace, the women beside a large window that opened out onto the garden.

They started talking business while we praised the quality of the chocolates. The Germans opened the conversation, asking their questions in a restrained tone, while I did my best to sharpen my hearing and make a mental note of everything I was able to catch at that distance. Wells, concessions, licenses, tons. The Portuguese men pointed out difficulties and brought up objections, raising the volume, talking fast. Perhaps the Germans wanted to steal their very innards from inside them, while the men from Beira — coarse mountain dwellers who weren't in the habit of trusting even their own fathers — weren't ready to let themselves be bought at any price. The mood, to my good fortune, began to heat up. The voices were entirely audible now, sometimes even explosive. And my head, like a machine, recorded everything they said. Even though I didn't yet have a complete picture of what it was they were negotiating, I was able to take in a large amount of loose information. Galleries, baskets, and trucks; boreholes and skips. Free tungsten and controlled tungsten. High-quality tungsten, without any quartz or pyrite. Export taxes. Six hundred thousand escudos per ton. Bonds, gold ingots, and bank accounts in Zurich. And I was also able to get a few tasty morsels, complete portions of information. About how Da Silva had spent weeks cleverly pulling strings to get the main owners of the deposits to join forces to start dealing exclusively with the Germans. How if everything went according to plan, within two weeks they'd collectively put an abrupt stop to any sales to the English.

The quantities of money being discussed made clear to me the reasons for the nouveau riche behavior of these tungsten mine owners and their wives. Humble peasants were being transformed overnight into prosperous owners who no longer even needed to work: the fountain pens, the gold teeth, and the fur stoles were only a small clue to the millions of escudos they stood to make if they allowed the Germans exclusive rights to drill on their land.

The night went on, and as my mind continued to get a sense of the true magnitude of the deal, my fears increased. What I was hearing was so confidential, so appalling, so compromising that I preferred not to consider the consequences I'd have to face if Manuel Da Silva found out who I was and whom I worked for. The men's conversation went on for almost two hours, but the livelier it got, the more the women's gathering deflated. Each time I got the sense that the negotiations were getting bogged down by a particular point that didn't add anything new, I concentrated my attention on the wives. But the Portuguese women had long ago given up on me and my attempts to keep them entertained, and they were already beginning to nod off, unable to fight their sleepiness. In their rough, rural day-to-day life, they probably went to bed at sunset and rose at dawn to feed the animals and see to the chores of countryside and kitchen; that late night, with all its wine, candy, and opulence, had far exceeded what they were able to handle. So I focused on the German women instead, but they weren't particularly communicative either: once we'd been over our shared ground, we didn't have enough in common or sufficient linguistic ability to keep our chat going.

I was running out of an audience and also rather short of resources: my effectiveness as hostess was fading away, and I had to think of some way of stopping it from dying once and for all. At the same time I had to remain alert and keep taking in information. Suddenly, from the men's side of the room, came a big collective laugh. Then handshakes, hugs, and congratulations. The deal was done.

Chapter Sixty-Two

"The first-class carriage, cabin number eight," I said.

"Are you sure?" asked Manuel.

I showed him the ticket.

"Perfect. I'll go with you."

"There's really no need."

He ignored me.

The suitcases I'd arrived in Lisbon with were now joined by several hatboxes and two large traveling bags full of whimsical purchases; everything had left the hotel that afternoon, earlier than planned. The rest of the purchases for the atelier would be arriving in Madrid over the course of the coming days, sent directly by the suppliers. As hand baggage I had just a small bag with the things I would need for the night. And one more thing — a sketchbook filled with information.

As soon as we'd left the car, Manuel insisted on carrying the overnight bag.

"It hardly weighs anything, there's no need," I said, trying not to let go of it.

The battle was lost even before I'd begun, and I knew that I couldn't insist. We went into the main hall of the train station, the most elegant couple of the evening — I wrapped in all my glamour, and he unwittingly carrying the evidence of his betrayal. Santa Apolónia Station, looking like a huge mansion, was receiving the trickle of night-time travelers bound for Madrid. Couples, families, friends, men traveling alone. Some of them seemed ready to set off with cool indifference, as though leaving something that hadn't affected them at all; others shed tears, hugged, sighed, made promises for the future that they might never keep. I didn't fit into either one of those categories: I wasn't one of the detached, nor one of the sentimental. I was quite different — one of those running away, trying to put some distance between themselves and this place, to dust themselves off and forget what they'd left behind forever.

I'd spent most of the day in my room preparing for my return journey. Supposedly. Yes, I took the clothes down from their hangers, emptied the drawers, and put everything in the suitcases. But that didn't take me long. I spent the rest of the time dedicated to something more important: transferring all the information I'd gathered at Da Silva's party into thousands of little pencil-sketched stitches. The task took me many hours. I started on it as soon as I'd arrived back at the hotel in the small hours of the morning, when everything I'd heard was still fresh in my mind; there were so many dozens of details that a lot of it ran the risk of dissolving into oblivion if I didn't make note immediately. I slept no more than three or four hours; when I woke up, I set about finishing the job. Over the course of the morning and the early afternoon, one piece of information at a time, stitch by stitch, I emptied my head out onto the paper until it made up an arsenal of terse messages. The result comprised more than forty sup-

744

posed patterns covered in names, numbers, dates, places, and operations, all gathered in the pages of my innocent sketchbook. Patterns for sleeves, cuffs, and backs; for waistbands, body lengths, and fronts; outlines for parts and segments of clothing I would never sew, within whose edges were hidden the details of a grim business transaction intended to facilitate the devastating progress of the German troops.

In the midmorning the telephone rang. The call made me jump, so much so that one of the telegraphic dashes I'd been marking down at that moment was transformed into a harsh twisted stroke that I had to erase.

"Arish? Good morning, it's Manuel. I hope I didn't wake you."

Though I was wide awake — showered and alert, having been working for several hours — I contorted my voice to sound sleepy. Under no circumstances could I let him know that what I'd seen and heard the previous night had sent me off into a torrent of nonstop activity.

"Don't worry, it must be terribly late already . . . ," I lied.

"Nearly noon. I was just calling to thank you for attending my gathering last night and for behaving the way you did with my friends' wives."

"No need to thank me, I had a very pleasant evening, too."

"Are you sure? You didn't get bored? Now I feel bad for not having paid you a bit more attention."

Careful, Sira — be careful. He's just testing you, I thought. Gamboa, Marcus, the forgotten hat, Bernhardt, the tungsten, Beira, everything was coming together in my head with the coolness of frozen glass, while I kept on faking an untroubled,

745

sleepy voice.

"No, Manuel, really, don't worry about it. The conversations with your friends' wives kept me very well entertained."

"And so what do you have planned for your last day in Portugal?"

"Nothing at all. Taking a long bath and preparing my luggage. I don't mean to leave the hotel all day."

I hoped the reply would satisfy him. If Gamboa had informed on me, and he thought I was going around with some man, perhaps a prolonged stay within the hotel walls would dispel his suspicions. Of course, my word wouldn't be strong enough — he would already be getting someone to watch my room, and perhaps also monitor my telephone conversations, but with the exception of him I had no intention of speaking to anyone today. I'd be a good girl — I wouldn't move from the hotel, I wouldn't use the telephone and wouldn't entertain any visitors. I'd let myself be seen, bored and alone, in the restaurant, at reception, and in the sitting rooms, and when the time came for me to leave I'd do it in full view of all the hotel's other guests and employees, with only my luggage for company. Or at least that's what I thought until he made me another proposition.

"Yes, of course, you deserve a rest. But I don't want you to go without my getting the chance to say good-bye to you first. Let me take you to the station. What time does your train leave?"

"At ten," I replied. Damn me for wanting to see him again.

"I'll come by your hotel at nine, then, all right? I'd like to be able to come earlier, but my whole day is going to be busy."

"Don't worry, Manuel, I'll need time to arrange my things, too. I'll send my luggage on to the station in the early evening, then I'll be waiting for you."

"Till nine o'clock, then."

"Nine o'clock — I'll be ready."

Instead of João's Bentley, I found a dazzling new Aston Martin sports car. I felt a knot of nerves when I realized that the old chauffeur wasn't anywhere to be seen: the idea that we were alone made me feel unsettled and vulnerable. Manuel didn't feel the same way, apparently.

I couldn't see any change in his attitude toward me. He didn't show the least sign of suspicion; he was just as he'd always been — attentive, pleasant, and seductive, as though his whole world revolved around those rolls of beautiful Macao silk that he'd shown me in his office and had nothing to do with the foul darkness of the tungsten mines. We made our final journey down the coast road, then raced along the streets of Lisbon, making the pedestrians' heads turn. We were on the platform twenty minutes before the train's scheduled departure time, and Manuel insisted on boarding the train with me and accompanying me to my cabin. We made our way down the side corridor, me ahead and him behind me, just a step behind, still carrying my little overnight bag in which the proof of his foul enterprise was muddled up with innocent toiletries, cosmetics, and lingerie.

"Number eight, I think this is it," I announced.

The door opened into an elegant, clean cabin. Wood-paneled walls, curtains open, a chair in place, and the bed not yet made up.

"Well then, my dear Arish, the time has come to

say good-bye," he said, putting my overnight bag down on the floor. "It's been a real pleasure getting to know you. It's not going to be at all easy for me to get used to not having you around."

His feelings seemed genuine; perhaps my speculations about Gamboa's accusation were unfounded after all. Perhaps I'd been more alarmed than I needed to be. Perhaps he'd never even thought of saying anything to his boss, whose esteem for me remained perfectly intact.

"It's been an unforgettable visit, Manuel," I said holding my hands out to him. "It couldn't have been more satisfactory — my clients are going to be most impressed. And you've done so much to make it easy and enjoyable — I don't know how to thank you."

He took my hands and held them protected in his. And in exchange received my most dazzling of smiles, a smile that hid a huge desire for the final curtain to fall on that whole farce once and for all. In just a few minutes the stationmaster would blow his whistle and lower his little flag, and the Lusitania Express would begin to roll along the tracks, getting farther and farther from the Atlantic toward the center of the Peninsula. And I would be leaving Manuel Da Silva and his dark dealings, vibrant Lisbon, and that whole universe of strangers behind me forever.

The final travelers were hurrying onto the train; every few seconds we had to step aside to let someone past, leaning back against the carriage walls.

"Best for you to go, Manuel."

"I think so, yes I ought to go now."

The moment to bring that pantomime farewell to an end had arrived, time to enter my cabin and

748

resume my privacy. All I needed was for him to vanish, and everything else was all set. And then suddenly, unexpectedly, I felt his left hand on the back of my neck, his right arm around my shoulders and the hot, strange taste of his mouth on mine and a shudder running right down my body from my head to my toes. It was an intense kiss; a long, powerful kiss that left me confused, disarmed, and unable to react.

"Bon voyage, Arish."

I wasn't able to respond; he didn't give me enough time. Before I was able to find the right words, he was gone.

CHAPTER SIXTY-THREE

I fell back into my seat, my head filling with the scenes of the previous days as if on a cinema screen. As I recalled the events and settings, I wondered how many of the characters from that strange film would make another appearance in my life, and which ones I would never see again. I reminded myself how each of the strands of the drama had ended: a few of them happily; most, inconclusively. And when the reel was about to end, everything filled with that final scene: the kiss from Manuel Da Silva. I could still taste it in my mouth, but I felt unable to find an adjective to describe it. Spontaneous, passionate, cynical, sensual. Perhaps all of them. Perhaps none.

I sat up in my seat and looked through the window, already being rocked by the gentle clatter of the train. The last lights of Lisbon sped past my eyes, becoming less and less dense, more diffuse, thinning out further and further until the landscape was filled with darkness. I got up; I needed some air. It was time for dinner.

I went into the restaurant car, which was already almost filled with people, as well as the smell of food, the noise of cutlery and conversations. It only took the staff a few minutes to seat me; I chose from the menu and ordered some wine to celebrate my freedom. Killing time while I waited to be served, I thought ahead to my arrival in Madrid and pictured Hillgarth's reaction when he learned the results of my mission. He probably never imagined that it would end up being so productive.

The food and wine arrived quickly, but by the time they did I already knew for certain that the dinner wasn't going to be a particularly pleasant one. Luck had decided to position me close to a couple of coarse-looking individuals who didn't stop staring at me quite brazenly from the moment I'd sat down. Two rough guys who didn't fit the tranquil setting that surrounded us. They had a couple of bottles of wine on their table and a crowd of dishes that they were devouring as though the world were set to end that very night. I barely enjoyed my *bacalhau à brás;* the linen tablecloth, the engraved glass, and the formal attentiveness of the waiters were all quickly relegated to secondary importance. My priority had become gulping down my food as quickly as possible in order to get back to my cabin and escape from that unwelcome company.

I found the curtains drawn and the bed made, everything ready for the night. Bit by bit the train was calming down and falling silent; almost without noticing it we would be leaving Portugal and crossing the border. I realized how little I'd been sleeping. I'd spent the early hours of the day transcribing messages, and the previous morning I'd been visiting Rosalinda. My poor body needed a break, so I decided to go to bed right away.

I opened my hand luggage, but I didn't have time to take anything out of it because a call from the door made me stop.

"Tickets," I heard. I opened the door cautiously and checked that it was indeed the ticket collector. But I also realized that, though he probably didn't even know it himself, he wasn't alone in the corridor. Behind the conscientious railway worker, just a few feet away, I could make out two shadows swaying to the rhythm of the train. Two shadows that were unmistakable: the two men who'd unsettled me during dinner.

The moment the ticket collector had finished his task I bolted the door shut, planning not to open it again until we arrived in Madrid. The last thing I wanted after the tough times I'd had in Lisbon was a couple of uncouth travelers with nothing more to do than spend the night bothering me. So at last I readied myself for bed; I was exhausted, both physically and mentally; I needed to forget everything, even if it was only for a couple of hours.

I began to take everything I needed out of my hand luggage: the toothbrush, a soap dish, my night cream. A few minutes later I noticed that the train was slowing down: we were approaching a station, the first on the journey. I drew open the little curtain that covered the window. *"Entroncamento,"* I read.

Just a few seconds later, there was another knock at my door. Hard, insistent. It didn't sound like the ticket collector. I stayed quite still, my back to the door, with no intention of answering. I guessed that it was the men from the restaurant car, and there was no way I was going to open up for them.

But they knocked again. Harder than before. And then I heard my name on the other side. And I recognized the voice.

I drew back the bolt.

"You've got to get off the train. Da Silva has two men on board. They've come for you."

"The hat?"

"The hat."

Chapter Sixty-Four

Panic mixed with a desire to burst out laughing. A laughter that was bitter, and dark. How strange our emotions are, how easily they can deceive us. One simple kiss from Manuel Da Silva had toppled all my convictions about his shady morals, and just an hour later I'd learned that he'd given the order to have me eliminated, my body tossed out through a train window into the night. The Judas kiss.

"You don't need to take anything, just your papers," Marcus warned me. "You'll get everything back in Madrid."

"There's one thing I can't leave behind."

"You can't take anything, Sira. There isn't time, the train's about to leave again; if we don't hurry, we'll have to jump while it's on the move."

"Just a second . . ." I went over to the overnight bag and grabbed its contents out with both hands. The silk nightgown, a slipper, the hairbrush, a bottle of eau de cologne: everything was spread out on the bed, as though hurled around by the fury of a madman or the strength of a tornado. Finally I found what I'd been looking for right at the bottom: the notebook with the fake patterns, the minutely stitched statement of Manuel Da Silva's betrayal of the British. I squeezed it hard

754

to my chest.

"Let's go," I said, grabbing my handbag with my other hand. I couldn't leave that behind either; it contained my passport.

We raced out into the corridor just as the whistle sounded; when we reached the door, the locomotive had already replied with its own, and the train was beginning to pull away from the station. Marcus got off first as I threw the notebook, handbag, and shoes onto the platform — it would have been impossible to jump with the shoes on: I'd sprain an ankle the moment I hit the ground. Then he reached his hand out to me; I took it and jumped.

The furious shouts of the stationmaster weren't long in coming; we saw him running toward us, flapping his arms. Two railway workers came out from inside the station, alerted by the voices; meanwhile the train, oblivious to what it was leaving behind, continued on its way, picking up speed.

"Come, Sira, come on, we've got to get out of here," Marcus said tensely.

He picked up one of my shoes and handed it to me, then the other. I held them in my hands but didn't put them on: my attention was on something else. The three railway employees had gathered around us, while the stationmaster reprimanded us for our behavior with angry shouts and gestures. A couple of tramps wandered toward us, curious, and a few moments later the man from the station canteen and a young waiter joined the group, wondering what had happened.

And then, in the middle of that chaos of urgent movement and clamorous voices, we heard the sharp squeal of the train braking.

Everyone on the platform suddenly fell silent

and still, blanketed in silence, while the wheels crunched over the tracks, emitting a long, high-pitched sound.

Marcus was the first to speak.

"They've set off the alarm." His voice turned more serious, more commanding. "They've realized that we jumped. Come on, Sira, we've got to get out of here right away."

The whole group automatically sprang into action again. We were back to the bellowing, the orders, the steps in no particular direction, and the irate gestures.

"We can't go," I replied, turning around and around, scanning the ground. "I can't find my notebook."

"Forget the damned notebook, for God's sake!" he shouted, furious. "They're coming for you, Sira, they're under orders to kill you!"

He grasped my arm and pulled, as though ready to drag me bodily after him.

"You don't understand, Marcus, I've got to find it, whatever happens, we can't leave it behind," I insisted as I kept looking. Then I spotted something. "There it is! There!" I shouted, trying to wriggle free while gesturing at something in the middle of the darkness. "There, on the tracks!"

The screeching sound of the brakes was lessening and finally the train drew to a halt, the windows filled with heads leaning out, trying to see what was going on. The voices and shouts of the passengers added to the incessant scolding of the railway workers. And then we saw them. Two shadows, dropping down from one of the coaches and running toward us.

I calculated the distance and time. I could still climb down and get the notebook, but climbing back up onto the platform would take much longer; it was a considerable height and my legs probably weren't up to it. But in any case I had to try to recover those patterns, whatever it took. I couldn't go back to Madrid without all the information I'd recorded in them. Then I felt Marcus's arms grabbing me hard from behind. He moved me away from the edge, almost knocking me off my feet, and jumped down onto the tracks.

From the exact moment I took the notebook, everything was a mad dash. A dash across the platform, a dash echoing on the flagstones of the empty station hall, a dash across the dark forecourt outside the station entrance. Hand in hand, tearing through the night, as we'd done once before. Until we reached the car.

"What the hell have you got in this notebook that you'd risk our lives for it?" he asked, trying to recover his breath as he started up the car and left the station with a powerful burst of acceleration.

My breathing labored, I kneeled on the seat to look behind us. In the dust thrown up by our back wheels I could make out the men from the train running toward us as hard as they could. At first there were only a couple of meters between us, but bit by bit the distance grew, until I saw them giving up. One of them first, slowing down until he came to a stop, spent, with his legs apart and his hands on his head as though he couldn't believe what had just happened. The other held out for a few feet more and then lost energy, too. The last thing I saw was him doubling over, clutching his stomach, and throwing up what he'd so eagerly eaten not long before.

When I was sure that they were no longer following us, I sat back down and — still having trouble breathing — answered Marcus's question. "The best patterns I've ever done in my life."

Chapter Sixty-Five

"Yes, Gamboa did indeed suspect something when he brought you the orchids. So he hid and waited to see who the owner of the hat was. And then he saw me coming out of your room. He knows me very well, I've been in the company's offices several times. Armed with this information, he went in search of Da Silva, but his boss didn't want to see him — he told him he was busy with some important business and that they'd talk the following morning. And they did talk today. When Da Silva found out what it was about, he flew into a rage, fired him, and began to take measures."

"And how do you know all this?"

"Because Gamboa came looking for me this afternoon. His nerves are in shreds, he's terribly afraid and looking for someone to protect him, which is why he thought he might feel safer approaching the English, with whom he used to have excellent relations. Even he doesn't know what Da Silva is up to, because he hides things from everyone, including the people he trusts, but his current state made me fear for your safety. As soon as I'd spoken to Gamboa I went to your hotel, but you'd already left. I reached the station as the train was just pulling away, and when I saw Da

Silva alone on the platform I thought everything was all right. Until the very last moment, when I saw him gesturing to two men leaning out of one of the windows."

"What kind of gesture?"

"An eight — five fingers of one hand and three of the other."

"My cabin number . . ."

"It was the only detail they were still missing. Everything else had already been arranged."

I was assailed by a strange feeling — terror mixed with relief, weakness, and rage all at once. The taste of betrayal, perhaps. But I knew I had no reason to feel betrayed. I'd deceived Manuel, hidden behind an inoffensive, seductive front, and he'd tried to repay me in kind, without getting his hands dirty or compromising a speck of his elegance. Disloyalty in exchange for disloyalty — that's the way things worked.

We continued along dusty roads, over potholes and craters, passing through sleeping towns, desolate villages, and patches of wasteland. The only light we saw in all that time was from the headlamps of our car opening a path for us through the thick darkness — there wasn't even a moon. Marcus realized that Da Silva's men would not remain at the station — they'd probably find some way of following us — so he kept driving fast, never letting up, as though we still had those two undesirables clinging to our tail.

"I'm almost sure they won't dare cross into Spain; they'd be getting themselves into unknown territory where they don't control the rules of the game. Of their own private game, that is. So we shouldn't lower our guard till we're over the border."

It would have been natural for Marcus to question me further about why Da Silva was trying to get rid of me after treating me so deferentially only days earlier. He'd seen us with his own eyes, dining and dancing at the casino; he knew that I'd been going around in his car every day, receiving gifts from him at my hotel. Perhaps he was waiting for some explanation of the nature of our relationship, maybe some clarification of what had gone on between us, something that could throw a little light on the reasons for his brutal order when I was just about to walk out of his country and his life. But I didn't utter a word.

He kept talking, without taking his attention from the road, making observations and proposing interpretations in the hope that at some point I might decide to contribute something. "Da Silva," he went on, "opened the doors to his house wide for you, allowing you to witness everything that happened there last night, though I don't know what that is."

I didn't reply.

"And you don't seem to have any intention of telling me."

It was true, I didn't.

"Now he's convinced that you got close to him because you were under orders from someone else, and he suspects that you're not just a simple foreign dressmaker who showed up in his life by chance. He thinks you became friends with him because you meant to investigate his affairs, but he's wrong in his assumptions about who it is you're working for, because according to our tip-off from Gamboa, he incorrectly believes you to be working for me. In any case, he wants you to

761

keep your mouth shut. Forever, if that can be arranged."

Still I didn't say anything; I preferred to keep my feelings hidden behind a front of feigned obliviousness. Until my silence had become intolerable for both of us.

"Thank you for protecting me, Marcus," I murmured.

I didn't fool him. I didn't fool him, or soften him up, or move him with my false helplessness.

"Who is it you're mixed up with, Sira?" he asked slowly, never taking his eyes off the road.

I turned and looked at his profile in the gloom. The refined nose, the strong jaw, the determination, the certainty. He seemed like the same man from our days in Tetouan. Seemed.

"Who are you with, Marcus?"

On the back seat, invisible but so close, we were joined by a third passenger in the car: suspicion.

When we crossed the border it was past midnight. Marcus showed his British passport, and I showed my Moroccan one. I noticed him looking at it, but he didn't ask any questions. We didn't see any sign of Da Silva's men, just a couple of sleepy policemen who weren't particularly keen to waste their time on us.

"Perhaps we should find somewhere to get some sleep, now that we're in Spain and we know they haven't followed us, and they can't have overtaken us. Tomorrow I can take a train and you can go back to Lisbon," I suggested.

"I'd rather go on to Madrid," he muttered.

We continued driving, passing not a single other vehicle on the road, each of us absorbed in our own thoughts. Suspicion had brought doubt, and the doubt had led to silence: a silence that was thick and uncomfortable, pregnant with mistrust. An unfair silence. Marcus had just yanked me out of the worst fix I'd been in in my life and was going to drive through the night just to make sure I arrived safely at my destination, and I was repaying him by refusing to give him any information that might ease his mind. But I couldn't speak, I couldn't say any more to him. First I had to be sure about what I'd suspected ever since Rosalinda opened my eyes during our early morning conversation. Or perhaps I could say something. A fragment from the previous night, a snippet, a clue. Something that would be useful to us both — to him by satisfying his curiosity at least in part, and to me as a way of preparing the ground while I waited to confirm what I suspected.

We'd gone past Badajoz and Mérida. We'd been silent since the frontier post, dragging our mutual distrust along worn-out old roads and Roman bridges.

"Do you remember Bernhardt, Marcus?"

The muscles of his arms seemed to tense up, his fingers clinging more tightly to the steering wheel.

"Yes, of course I remember him."

Suddenly the dark interior of the car was flooded with images and smells of that day we'd shared, after which nothing had ever been the same between us. A summer evening in Morocco, my house on Sidi Mandri, a supposed journalist standing by the balcony doors waiting for me. Tetouan's packed streets, the gardens of the High Commission, the caliph's band enthusiastically singing anthems, jasmine and orange trees, military stripes and uniforms. Rosalinda absent, and an enthusiastic Beigbeder playing the great

763

host, still unaware that the time would come when the man to whom he was paying tribute would end up striking off his head and sending it spinning in the dirt. A group of German backs forming a ring around the special guest with the cat's eyes, and my companion asking my help to get hold of secret information. Another time, another country, and yet, deep down, everything almost exactly the same. Almost.

"I was at dinner with him yesterday at Da Silva's estate. Afterward they talked into the early hours."

I knew that he was holding back, that he wanted to know more — that he needed information, details, but he didn't dare to ask because he didn't completely trust me yet either. His sweet Sira — I really wasn't the person I used to be either.

Finally he couldn't stop himself.

"Did you hear anything of what they said?"

"Nothing at all. Do you have any idea what they might have to do with each other?"

"None whatsoever."

I was lying and he knew it. He was lying and I knew it. And neither of us was prepared to show his or her hand, but thinking about the past did loosen the tension between us. Maybe because it brought with it recollections of a past in which we hadn't yet lost all our innocence. Perhaps because that memory made us recover a tiny bit of our complicity and forced us to remember that there was still something that bound us besides lies and suspicion.

I tried to keep my attention on the road and to remain fully alert, but the tension of the recent days, the lack of sleep, and the nervous exhaustion caused by everything I'd been through that night had debilitated me to the point of collapse.

764

Too long spent walking a tightrope.

"Are you sleepy?" he asked. "Go on, rest your head on my shoulder."

He put his right arm around me and I huddled closer to receive some of his warmth.

"Sleep. It won't take long now," he whispered.

I began to fall into a dark, troubled well in which I relived recently experienced scenes through a distorted filter. Men pursuing me brandishing knives, the long, moist kiss of a serpent, the wives of the tungsten mine owners dancing on a table, Da Silva counting on his fingers, Gamboa crying, Marcus and I running through the dark alleys of the Tetouan medina.

I didn't know how much time had passed before Marcus woke me.

"We're here, Sira. We're arriving in Madrid. You have to tell me where you live."

His voice pulled me out of my sleep. As I began to emerge slowly from my torpor, I realized that I was still stuck to him, clinging to his arm. Straightening up my stiff body and parting myself from his side was going to take an infinite amount of effort. I did so slowly: my neck was stiff, my joints numb. His shoulder must have been hurting, too, but he didn't show it. Without saying a word, I looked through the side window while trying to comb my hair with my fingers. Dawn was breaking over Madrid. There were still some lights on. Just a few discrete, sad lights. I remembered Lisbon and its impressive display of nighttime brightness. In a Spain ruled by restrictions and wretchedness, people still lived in near darkness.

"What time is it?" I asked finally.

"Almost seven. You've had a good long nap."

"And you must be aching all over," I said, still sleepy.

I gave him my address and asked him to park on the far side of the street, a few yards away. It was almost day now, and the first few souls were beginning to come out onto the street. The deliverymen, a couple of servant girls, the odd shop assistant and waiter.

"What are you planning to do?" I asked, studying the activity through the glass.

"Get myself a room at the Palace for now. And when I wake up, first thing I do will be to send this suit to be cleaned and buy myself a shirt. I'm completely filthy from the cinders on the tracks."

"But you managed to get my notebook . . ."

"I don't know if it was worth it: you still haven't told me what's in it."

I ignored his words.

"And after you've put on some clean clothes, what are you going to do?" I spoke without looking at him, still concentrating on what was happening outside the car, waiting for just the right moment to take the next step.

"Go to my company's headquarters," he answered. "We have offices here in Madrid."

"And do you mean to escape as quickly as you did from Morocco?" I asked, my eyes sweeping over the street's morning comings and goings.

He replied with a half smile.

"I don't know yet."

At that moment my doorman left the building, heading out to the dairy. The coast was clear.

"Just in case you do end up escaping again, I'd like to invite you up for breakfast first," I said, quickly opening the car door.

He grabbed my arm, trying to hold me back.

"Only if you tell me what you're up to."

"Not until I know who you are."

We went up the staircase together hand in hand, ready to call a truce. Dirty and exhausted, but alive.

Chapter Sixty-Six

Without even opening my eyes I already knew that Marcus was no longer next to me. There was no visible trace of his visit to my home and my bed. Not a single forgotten item of clothing, not a good-bye note: just his scent clinging to my skin. But I knew that he would come back. Sooner or later, when I least expected it, he would show up again.

I would have liked to delay the moment of getting up. Just another hour, maybe even half an hour would have been enough — enough time to recall calmly everything that had happened in the preceding days, and especially in that last night: what I'd experienced, what I'd seen, what I'd felt. I wanted to stay there between the sheets, recreating each moment of the hours that had passed, but that wasn't possible. I had to get moving: a hundred obligations were awaiting me; I had to start functioning again. So I took a shower and got going. It was Saturday, and although neither the girls nor Doña Manuela had come into the workshop, everything was ready and in full view so that I might be able to get up to date with the hectic work that they'd been dealing with in my absence. Things seemed to have proceeded at a good pace — there were samples on the man-

768

nequins, measurements jotted down in the note-
books, remnants and cuttings that I hadn't left,
and records kept in sharp pencil of who had been
in, who had called, and what needed to be
resolved. I didn't have time to deal with all that,
however: by noon I still had much left to work
out, but I had no choice but to postpone it all.

Embassy was absolutely heaving with people,
but I was counting on Hillgarth being able to see
me drop my handbag as I came in. I did it
deliberately, almost cheekily. Three gentlemanly
backs immediately bent down to retrieve it. Only
one of them was successful, a tall German officer
in uniform who at just that moment had been
pushing the door to step out onto the street. I
thanked him with my very best smile, while out of
the corner of my eye I tried to see whether Hillgarth had noticed my arrival. He was at a table at
the back, in the usual company. I saw that he had
spotted me and registered the message. I need to
see you urgently, it meant. Then I looked at my
watch and faked an expression of surprise, as
though I'd only just remembered that at that very
moment I had an important appointment somewhere else. By two o'clock I was back home. At
three fifteen the box of candies arrived. Hillgarth
had summoned me for four thirty, back at Dr.
Rico's office.

It was the usual routine. I arrived alone and
didn't pass anyone on the staircase. The same
nurse opened the door for me and led me through
to the consulting room.

"Good afternoon, Sidi. It's good to have you
back. Have you had a good trip? I've heard great
things about the Lusitania Express."

He was standing by the window, dressed in one

of his impeccable suits. He walked over to shake my hand.

"Good afternoon, Captain. An excellent trip, thank you; the first-class cabins are an absolute delight. I wanted to see you as soon as possible to update you on my stay there."

"I'm grateful for that. Please, do sit down. Cigarette?"

He was relaxed and seemed in no particular hurry to learn the results of my work. The urgency of the previous weeks seemed to have disappeared as if by magic.

"Everything went well and I think I've managed to get hold of some very interesting information. Your suspicions were correct: Da Silva has been negotiating with the Germans to supply them with tungsten. The final deal was closed on Thursday night at his house, with the help of Johannes Bernhardt."

"Good work, Sidi. That information is going to be very useful to us."

He didn't seem surprised. Or impressed. Or grateful. Neutral and impassive, as though this didn't come as news to him.

"It doesn't seem to come as any surprise to you," I said. "Did you know about this already?"

He lit a Craven A and gave his reply through the first puff of smoke.

"We were informed about Da Silva's meeting with Bernhardt this very morning. Since he's involved, the only thing it could relate to right now would be the supply of tungsten, which confirms what we'd suspected: Da Silva's disloyalty. We've already sent a memo to London informing them."

Although I gave a slight start at this, I tried to

sound natural. My suspicions were being confirmed, but I had to keep going.

"Well, that's quite a coincidence that someone informed you just this morning. I thought I was the only person handling this mission."

"This morning we received a surprise visit from an agent based in Portugal. It was entirely unexpected — he came in from Lisbon by car overnight."

"And did this agent see Bernhardt and meet Da Silva?" I asked with feigned surprise.

"Not him personally, no, but someone he completely trusts did witness the meeting."

I was about to burst out laughing. So his agent had been informed about Bernhardt by someone he trusted completely. Well, after all, that was a compliment.

"We're extremely interested in Bernhardt," Hillgarth went on, oblivious to what was going on in my head. "As I told you in Tangiers, he's the brain behind SOFINDUS, the corporation through which the Third Reich is conducting its business in Spain. Knowing that he's having dealings with Da Silva in Portugal is going to be enormously significant for us, because —"

"Excuse me, Captain," I interrupted him. "Can I ask you another question? This agent who notified you that Bernhardt had done a deal with Da Silva, is this also someone with the SOE, one of your recent recruits like me?"

He stubbed out his cigarette thoroughly before replying. Then he looked up.

"Why do you ask?"

I smiled with all the candor that I was able to fake.

"No particular reason," I said, shrugging. "It's

771

just such a coincidence that we've both turned up with the same information on exactly the same day — it's almost amusing."

"Well, I'm sorry to disillusion you, but no, I'm afraid he isn't a new SOE agent just recruited for this war. The information has come to us through one of our men in the SIS, our — as it were — 'conventional' intelligence service. And we haven't the slightest doubt about its veracity: this is an absolutely reliable agent with years of experience. An 'old hand,' as you Spaniards would say."

Click. A shiver ran down my spine. All the pieces had fallen into place. What I'd heard vindicated perfectly what I'd already suspected, but to have it confirmed absolutely was like a breath of cold air against my soul. This wasn't the moment to lose myself in sentiment, however, but to keep moving forward. To show Hillgarth that we new recruits were also capable of working ourselves to the bone for the missions we were entrusted with.

"And your SIS man, did he give you any more information?" I asked, looking him straight in the eye.

"Regrettably not, he wasn't able to give us any precise details, but —"

I didn't let him go on. "He didn't tell you how and where the meeting took place and didn't give you the names and surnames of everyone who attended? He didn't inform you about the terms that they agreed upon, the quantities of tungsten they expected to extract, the price per ton, the method of payment, and the procedure for evading export taxes? He didn't tell you that they're going to stop supplying the English abruptly within two weeks? He didn't say that Da Silva was not only betraying you, but had also brought the major mine owners in Beira along with him in order to be able to negotiate collectively and secure better terms for the Germans?"

Beneath his bushy eyebrows, the naval attaché's gaze had turned to steel. His voice was hoarse.

"How have you learned all this, Sidi?"

I held his gaze proudly. They'd forced me onto the very brink of a precipice for more than ten days, and I'd managed to reach the end without toppling over the edge: it was time for him to learn what I'd found there.

"Because when a seamstress does her job well, she pays attention to every little detail."

During our whole conversation I had kept my notebook of patterns discreetly on my lap. The cover was slightly torn, some of the pages folded over, and a large number of stains and bits of dirt bore witness to the tempestuous vicissitudes it had been through since it had left my hotel closet in Estoril. I put it down on the table and rested my open hands on it.

"All the details are in here: every last syllable of what was agreed that night. Your SIS agent didn't tell you anything about a notebook either, then?"

The man who had just reentered my life in such an overwhelming way was undoubtedly an experienced spy for His Majesty's intelligence services, but on this shady matter of tungsten, on this particular round, I had just beaten him.

CHAPTER SIXTY-SEVEN

I left the building where we'd had our secret meeting with something strange clinging to my skin. Something without a name, something new. I walked slowly through the streets, trying to find a label for that feeling, not worrying about whether there was anyone following me and indifferent to the chance of bumping into someone undesirable whenever I went around a corner. There were no external signs to suggest that I wasn't the same woman who'd walked this pavement in the opposite direction just a few hours earlier, in just the same clothes, her feet in the same shoes. No one who had seen me going then and returning now would have been able to make out any change, except that I was no longer carrying a notebook with me. But I knew what had happened. And Hillgarth knew, too. We were both aware that on that late May afternoon the order of things had altered irreversibly.

Although he was sparing with his words, his manner made it quite clear that the information I'd just supplied him was an enormously valuable contribution that needed to be analyzed in great detail by his people in London, without a moment to lose. This information was going to set alarm bells ringing, it was going to shatter alliances and reconfigure the direction of hundreds of operations. And with it, I got the sense that the naval attaché's attitude had been radically altered, too. He'd seen a new image of me: his most reckless recruit, the inexperienced seamstress, who showed some promise but who was still untested, had been transformed overnight into someone capable of resolving delicate matters with the boldness and execution of a professional. Perhaps my methods were unorthodox, and I didn't have much technical expertise; my world, my country, and my language weren't the same as his. But I'd responded to the challenge with much more skill than he'd expected, and that put me on a new rung in the hierarchy.

But what I felt in my bones, as the final rays of sunlight accompanied my return home, wasn't exactly happiness, either. Or emotion, or excitement. Perhaps the word that best fit the feeling that overwhelmed me was pride. For the first time in a long while, perhaps for the first time in my life, I felt proud of myself. Proud of what I was capable of, what I had been able to get through, proud of having acquitted myself better than had been expected of me. Proud to know that I was capable of making this world full of madmen a safer place. Proud of the woman I had become.

Yes, it was true that Hillgarth had spurred me on to do it, placing me teetering at the very edge of a chasm. Just as it was true that Marcus had saved my life by getting me off a moving train, and that without his timely help I wouldn't have lived to tell the tale. Yes, all that was true. But it was also true that I'd made my own contribution, with my courage and my determination, to bring the mission I'd been assigned to a successful conclusion. All my fears, all the sleepless nights and the leaps without a safety net had been worth something after all: not only to get hold of information that would come in handy for the dirty art of war, but also, and especially, to show myself and those around me what I was capable of.

And then, as I became aware of my possible scope, I knew the time had come for me to stop going blindly down the paths that other people had set for me. It had been Hillgarth's idea to send me to Lisbon, Manuel Da Silva had decided to get rid of me, Marcus Logan had chosen to come to my rescue. I'd passed between them from hand to hand, like a puppet: for good or ill, for the glory of heaven or the fires of hell, they had all made decisions for me, manipulated me like someone moving a pawn on a chessboard. No one had been open with me, no one had been honest with me about his intentions: it was time now to demand some enlightenment. Time for me to take up the reins of my own existence, to choose my own path, to decide how and with whom I was to follow it. I'd stumble along the way, make missteps, encounter broken glass, accidents, and pools of dark mud. I wasn't facing an easy future, I was quite sure about that. But the time had come to stop moving forward without any awareness of the terrain I was on and the risks I'd be taking when I got up each morning. In short, it was time to be the mistress of my own life.

Those three men, Marcus Logan, Manuel Da Silva, and Alan Hillgarth, each of them in his own way — and probably without any of them being aware of it — had helped me to grow in just a few short days. Or perhaps I'd been growing slowly for a long time and it wasn't until now that I'd become aware of my new stature. I probably wouldn't see Da Silva again; as for Hillgarth and Marcus, however, I was sure I'd be staying close to them for quite some time. One of them in particular I was eager to keep exactly as close as he'd been in the early hours of that morning: a closeness of affections and bodies — the recollection still made me shiver. But first of all I had to mark out the limits of the new terrain. Clearly. Visibly. Like someone drawing a line on the ground with a piece of chalk.

When I arrived home I found an envelope that somebody had slipped under the door. It bore the logo of the Palace Hotel and a handwritten card inside.

"Going back to Lisbon. I'll be back the day after tomorrow. Wait for me."

Of course I'd wait for him. Figuring out how and where took me just a couple of hours.

That night I once again bypassed the rules about chain of command without the slightest flicker of remorse. After more than three uninterrupted hours that afternoon, when Hillgarth and I had finished going through all the details of the meeting at the estate, I asked him about the lists he'd brought up when we met the day after the events at the Hippodrome.

"It's all still the same; for now there's no news, as far as we know."

That meant that my father was still on the side of the friends of the English, and I was with the Germans. A great pity, because the moment had come for our paths to cross once more.

I turned up without giving him any warning.

Ghosts from another age fluttered furiously when they saw me walk through the front door, bringing with them memories of the day my mother and I had climbed that same staircase, filled with worry. They quickly vanished, fortunately, and took with them some bitter recollections I preferred not to face.

The door was opened by a servant who bore no resemblance to old Servanda.

"I need to see Señor Alvarado immediately. It's urgent. Is he home?"

She nodded, confused at my haste.

"In the library?"

"Yes, but . . ."

Before she was able to finish her sentence, I was already inside.

"No need to announce me, thank you."

He was glad to see me, much more so than I'd expected. Before leaving for Portugal I'd sent him a brief note informing him about my trip, but something must have seemed strange to him. All too hasty, he must have thought; too close to that unsettling scene at the races. He was reassured to know I was back.

The library was just as I'd remembered it. Perhaps more books and papers had accumulated: newspapers, letters, piles of magazines. Everything else was just as it had been when we'd met there, my father, my mother, and me, years earlier: the first time the three of us had been together, and also the last. That distant autumn afternoon I'd arrived burdened down with nerves and innocence, inhibited and oppressed by the unknown. Almost six years later, my feeling of self-confidence was quite different. I'd won it with blows, with work, through missteps and longings, and it clung to my skin like a scar; nothing could free me from it. However strongly the winds blew, however tough the times to come might be, I knew I'd have the strength to face them and make it through.

"I need to ask you a favor, Gonzalo."

"Anything you want."

"A meeting for five people. A little private party. Here at your house, on Tuesday night. You and me and three other guests. You'll have to invite two of them directly, without letting them find out that I'm involved. There won't be any problem, as you know them both."

"And the third?"

"I'll take care of the third myself."

He accepted without any further questions or any reservations. In spite of my unnerving behavior, my unexpected disappearances, and my fake identity, he seemed to trust me blindly.

"What time?" he asked simply.

"I'll be here in the midafternoon. And the guest you don't yet know will arrive at six; I'll have to talk to him before the others arrive. Can I meet him here in the library?"

"It's all yours."

"Perfect. Invite the other couple for eight, please. And one more thing — do you mind them knowing that I'm your daughter? It'll stay between the five of us."

It took a few seconds for him to reply, during which I thought I saw a new sparkle come to his eyes.

"It would be a matter of honor and pride."

We chatted a little while longer: about Lisbon and Madrid; about this, that, and the other, always remaining on safe ground. When I was just about to leave, however, his usual discretion failed him.

"I know it's not my place to meddle in your life at this stage, Sira, but . . ."

I turned and hugged him.

"Thank you for everything. You'll find out all about it on Tuesday."

CHAPTER SIXTY-EIGHT

Marcus appeared at the appointed time. I'd left a message for him at his hotel, and as I'd expected it reached him easily. He had no idea whose address that was: he just knew that I'd be waiting for him there. And there I was indeed, in a red silk crêpe suit, dazzling right down to my toes. Made up to perfection, with my long neck uncovered and dark hair gathered in a high bun. Waiting.

He arrived, looking impeccable in his dinner jacket, his shirt front starched and his body hardened by a thousand unmentionable adventures. Or at least, unmentionable until now. I went to open the door for him myself the moment I heard the bell. We greeted each other, struggling to hide our affection, standing so close, almost intimate at last.

"I'd like to introduce you to someone."

Taking his arm, I led him to the living room.

"Marcus, this is Gonzalo Alvarado. I've brought you to his house because I want you to know who he is. And I also want him to know who you are. For him to be quite clear who we both are."

They greeted each other politely, Gonzalo poured us a drink, and the three of us chatted about banalities for a few minutes, until the maid

— in a very timely fashion — came to the door to summon the host to take a telephone call.

We were left alone, looking like the perfect couple. To see something that was closer to the truth, however, you just needed to hear the hoarse words that Marcus murmured in my ears, barely moving his lips.

"Can we speak in private a moment?"

"Of course. Come with me."

I led him to the library. The grand portrait of Doña Carlota still presided from the wall behind the desk, with her diamond tiara that once was mine, and later no longer mine.

"Who's the man you just introduced me to, why do you want him to know about me? What is this ambush all about, Sira?" he asked roughly when we were separated from the rest of the house.

"It's one I've prepared specially for you," I said, sitting down in one of the chairs. I crossed my legs and stretched my right arm out over the backrest. Comfortable, mistress of the situation, as though I'd spent my whole life setting up traps like this. "I need to know whether it is convenient for me that you should remain in my life, or if it's better that we don't see each other again."

He didn't find my words the least bit funny.

"This doesn't make any sense; maybe it would be best for me to go . . ."

"You're giving up so easily? Only three days ago it seemed as though you were prepared to fight for me. You promised you would at any cost: you told me you'd lost me once and you weren't going to let it happen again. Have your feelings cooled that quickly? Or were you lying to me, perhaps?"

He looked at me without saying a word, still standing, tense and cold, distant.

"What do you want from me, Sira?" he said at last.

"I want you to be honest with me about your past. In exchange you'll know everything you need to know about my present. And on top of that you'll get a reward, too."

"What is it about my past that you want to know?"

"I want you to tell me what you went to Morocco for. Do you want to know what your reward will be?"

He didn't reply.

"Your reward will be me. If I'm satisfied with your answer, you get to keep me. If I'm not convinced, you lose me forever. You choose."

He was silent again. Then he walked slowly toward me.

"Why on earth should you care now why I went to Morocco?"

"Once, years ago, I opened my heart to a man who didn't show me his true face, and it took infinite efforts on my part to close up the wounds he made in my soul. I don't want the same thing to happen with you. I don't want any more lies, any more shadows. I don't want men simply availing themselves of me to suit their whims, coming closer and moving away again without any warning, even though it might be to save my life. That's why I need to see your whole hand now, Marcus. I've seen some of your cards already: I know who you work for and I know that you aren't really in the business world, I know you weren't really in journalism back then, either. But there are other gaps in your story that I still need to fill."

Finally he settled on the arm of a sofa. He kept one foot on the floor and crossed the other over it. His back straight, his glass still in his hand, his face set in determination.

"Very well," he agreed after a few seconds. "I'm prepared to talk. In exchange for your being honest with me. About everything."

"Afterward, I promise."

"Tell me what you know about me, then."

"That you're a member of the British military secret service. The SIS, MI6, whatever you prefer to call it."

The surprise didn't show on his face: he'd probably been trained not to reveal his emotions. Not like me. I hadn't been trained to do anything, I hadn't been prepared, I hadn't been protected: I'd just been thrown naked out into a world of ravenous wolves. But I'd learned, on my own, struggling, stumbling, falling, and getting back up; setting off again — one foot, then the other. My head held high, eyes fixed straight ahead of me.

"I don't know how you got hold of that information," was his only reply. "In any case, it doesn't matter: I suppose your sources are reliable and there wouldn't be any point in my denying what's obvious."

"But there are a few other things I still don't know."

"Where do you want me to start?"

"You could start from the moment we met, for example. Start with the real reason you came to Morocco."

"Very well. The main reason was that in London they knew very little about what was going on within the Protectorate, and they were hearing from a number of sources that the Germans were infiltrating it freely with the acquiescence of the

Spanish authorities. Our intelligence service hardly had any information on High Commissioner Beigbeder: he wasn't one of the better-known military men, we didn't know how he behaved, or what plans or opinions he had, and above all we didn't know what his position was on the Germans, who were apparently so free to do whatever they wanted in the territory he controlled."

"And what did you learn?"

"That as expected the Germans were operating in whatever way took their fancy, sometimes with his consent and sometimes without it. You helped me get part of that information yourself."

I ignored that comment.

"And about Beigbeder?"

"I found out the same things about him that you know, too. That he was — and I imagine still is — an intelligent man, distinguished and rather unusual."

"And why did they send you to Morocco, given the dreadful state you were in?"

"We got word of the existence of Rosalinda Fox, a compatriot of ours who was in a relationship with the high commissioner: a precious jewel to us, the best possible opportunity. But approaching her directly was too risky: she was so valuable to us that we couldn't risk losing her with an operation that had been clumsily planned. We had to wait for just the right moment. So when we learned that she was looking for someone to help evacuate the mother of a friend of hers, the machinery was set in motion. And it was decided that I was just the right person because while I was in Madrid I'd had contact with someone who handled those evacuations to the Mediterranean.

I'd kept London informed about Lance's movements myself, so they thought I'd have the perfect alibi to show up in Tetouan and approach Beigbeder with the excuse that I was carrying out a service for his lover. There was a small problem, however: at the time I was half dead in the Royal London Hospital, flat on my back in bed with my body all bashed up, semiconscious and pumped full of morphine."

"But you risked it, you fooled us all and got what you wanted . . ."

"Much more than we'd ever expected," he said. I could see the trace of a smile on his lips, the first I'd seen since we'd shut ourselves in the library. I felt the pinch of a confused emotion: the Marcus I'd so yearned for, the Marcus I wanted to keep by my side, had finally returned. "They were very special times," he went on. "After more than a year living in the turmoil of war-stricken Spain, Morocco was the best thing that could have happened to me. I recovered, and I carried out my mission with exceptional results. And I met you. I couldn't have asked for more than that."

"How did you do it?"

"Almost every night I sent messages from my room at the Hotel Nacional. I had a small radio transmitter with me, hidden at the bottom of my suitcase. And I wrote an encrypted message daily about what I'd seen, what I'd heard. Then, whenever I could, I passed it on to a contact in Tangiers, a shop assistant at Saccone & Speed."

"And no one ever suspected you?"

"Of course they did. Beigbeder was no fool, you know that as well as I do. My room was searched several times, but they probably sent someone who just wasn't all that skillful: they never found anything. The Germans were suspicious, too, but they weren't able to get hold of any information either. For my part, I did my best never to make a single false move. I didn't contact anyone outside official circles and didn't venture onto any hazardous terrain. Quite the reverse — my behavior remained irreproachable. I allowed myself to be seen with all the right people and always went around in the plain light of day. All apparently entirely clean. Any more questions?"

He already seemed less tense, closer. More the Marcus he used to be.

"Why did you leave so suddenly? You didn't warn me: you just showed up one morning at my house, gave me the news that my mother was on her way, and I never saw you again."

"Because I received urgent orders to get out of the Protectorate immediately. There were more and more Germans arriving every day, and word got out that someone suspected me. I still managed to delay my departure a few days, even though I was risking being uncovered."

"Why?"

"I didn't want to leave without confirming that your mother's evacuation had gone ahead as we'd hoped. I'd promised you that. There was nothing I would have wanted more than to have been able to stay with you, but it wasn't possible: that wasn't my world, and my time had come. And besides, it wasn't the best time for you, either. You were still recovering from a betrayal and you weren't ready to put your trust entirely in another man, least of all someone who would have to abandon you suddenly without being able to be absolutely honest about why. That's it, my dear Sira. The end. Is that the story you wanted to hear? Will this version do?"

"It will," I said, getting up and walking toward him.

"So, have I earned my reward?"

I didn't say anything. I just approached him, lowered myself onto his lap, and brought my mouth to his ear. My made-up face brushed against his freshly shaved skin; my lips, bright with lipstick, spilled out a whisper just half an inch from his earlobe. I noticed how he tensed when he felt my closeness.

"Yes, you've earned your reward. But you might find that this gift is poisoned."

"Perhaps. If I'm to know that, I need to find out about you now. When I left you in Tetouan you were a young dressmaker filled with tenderness and innocence, and when I found you in Lisbon you'd been transformed into a grown woman who had become close to someone entirely inappropriate. I want to know what happened in between."

"You'll find out very soon. And so that you absolutely trust my story, you're going to hear it from someone else, someone I believe you already know. Come with me."

We walked arm in arm down the corridor. I heard my father's powerful voice in the distance and once again couldn't help remembering the day I'd met him. How many turns had my life taken since then? How many times had I been nearly drowned, unable to come up for air, and how many times had I managed to get my head back above the surface? But that was all in the past now, and the days for looking back were past. It was time to concentrate on the present alone, to face it head-on in order to attend to the future.

I guessed that the other two guests were already

there and that everything had gone according to plan. When we arrived at our destination we unlocked our arms, though our fingers were still entwined. Until we both saw who was waiting for us. And then I smiled. Marcus did not.

"Good evening, Mrs. Hillgarth; good evening, Captain. I'm glad to see you," I said, interrupting their conversation.

The room filled with a dense silence. A dense, anxious silence — electrifying.

"Good evening, miss," replied Hillgarth after a few everlasting seconds. His voice sounded as though it were coming out of a cave. A dark, cold cave, because the head of the British secret service in Spain, the man who knew everything or ought to know everything, was feeling his way blind. "Good evening, Logan," he added after a pause. His wife, this time without the makeup from the beauty salon, was so stunned to see us together that she was unable to respond. "I thought you'd gone back to Lisbon," continued the naval attaché, addressing Marcus. "And I wasn't aware that you two knew each other."

I noticed Marcus was on the verge of saying something, but I didn't let him. His hand was still in mine and I gave it a hard squeeze and he understood. I didn't look at him, either: I didn't want to see whether he was as confused as the Hillgarths were, and I didn't want to see his reaction to them sitting there in that unfamiliar living room. We'd talk about it later, when everything had calmed down. I was sure that we would have plenty of time for that.

Looking into the wife's big, light-colored eyes, I saw only confusion. It was she who had given me the guidelines for my Portuguese mission; she was completely involved with her husband's activities. They were probably both struggling to connect the same dots I'd finished connecting the last time the captain and I had met. Da Silva and Lisbon, Marcus's untimely arrival in Madrid, the same information delivered by the two of us just a few hours apart. All that, quite clearly, wasn't merely the product of chance. How could they have missed it?

"Agent Logan and I have known each other for years, Captain, but we hadn't seen each other for a long time, and we're just finishing catching up on what we've each been doing," I explained. "I know all about his situation and his responsibilities now, and since you were extremely helpful to me not so long ago, I thought you might be so kind as to assist me again by informing him about mine. And that way my father can hear about it at the same time. Oh — sorry! I'd forgotten to tell you: Gonzalo Alvarado is my father. And don't worry: we'll try to be seen in public together as little as we can, but you can understand that breaking off my relations with him completely won't be possible."

Hillgarth didn't reply: he looked at us both again with a granite stare from under his bushy eyebrows.

Imagine Gonzalo's bewilderment: it was probably as extreme as Marcus's, but neither of them spoke so much as a syllable. They just waited — as did I — for Hillgarth to digest my boldness. His wife, uneasy, resorted to a cigarette, opening the case with nervous fingers. A few uncomfortable seconds passed in which the only sound was the repeated click of her lighter. Until at last the naval attaché spoke.

"If I don't reveal it, I presume you'd do it yourself anyway . . ."

"I fear you wouldn't leave me any other choice," I said, giving him my best smile. A new smile — full, confident, and slightly challenging.

The silence was only broken by the clink of the ice cubes against the glass as he brought the whiskey to his mouth. His wife hid her confusion behind a thick drag on her Craven A.

"I suppose this is the price we have to pay for what you brought us from Lisbon," he said at last.

"For that, and for all the missions to come in which I'll work myself to the bone, I give you my word on that. My word as a dressmaker, and my word as a spy."

CHAPTER SIXTY-NINE

What I received this time wasn't the straight-forward bunch of roses tied with a ribbon covered in coded dashes that Hillgarth used to send when he needed to get a message to me. Nor were they exotic flowers like the ones Manuel Da Silva had sent to me before deciding that having me killed would be better. What Marcus brought to my house that night was just a small, almost insignificant single bud that had been pulled off some rosebush that had grown up miraculously against an adobe wall that spring after a terrible winter. A tiny flower, almost scrawny. Dignified in its simplicity, without any subterfuge.

I wasn't expecting him, and at the same time I was. He'd left my father's house a few hours earlier, with Hillgarth; the naval attaché had invited him to accompany him, no doubt wanting to talk to him without me present. I returned home alone, not knowing when he would reappear. Or if he was going to come back at all.

"For you," was his greeting.

I took the little rose and let him in. His tie was undone, as though he'd actively made the decision that he was going to relax. He walked slowly into the middle of the living room; it was as though with each step he was calculating the words he had to say to string together a thought. Finally he turned and waited for me to approach.

"You know what we've got ahead of us, don't you?"

I did know. Of course I knew. Our lives moved in swamps of murky waters, in a jungle of lies and furtive creatures with teeth that could cut like glass. An undercover love in a time of hatred, privations, and betrayal, that's what we were facing.

"Yes, I do know what we have ahead of us."

"It won't be easy," he added.

"Nothing's ever easy," I added.

"It could be very hard."

"Perhaps."

"And dangerous."

"That, too."

Outwitting traps, overcoming risks and setbacks. Without any plans, in the shadows; that was how we'd have to live. Combining willingness and daring. With integrity, courage, and the realization that we were fighting for a common cause.

We looked hard at each other and my memory of the African land where it had all begun flooded back to me. His world and my world — so far away then, and now so close — had locked together at last. Then he embraced me, and in the tenderness and heat of our closeness I felt with absolute certainty that this was another mission at which we would not fail.

And that is my story, or at least that's how I remember it, perhaps varnished over with the sheen that decades and nostalgia give to things. What happened in Spain after the European war, as well as the traces of many people who have passed through this account — Beigbeder, Rosa-linda Fox, Serrano Suñer, and others — can be found in history books and archives, and in the memories of older generations. Their comings and goings, their glories and miseries were objective facts that in their day filled newspapers and fed the salons and the clusters of people gossiping on street corners.

What happened after the war to Marcus and me and to those in our immediate circle, however, was never recorded. Our destinies might have gone in any direction, as we succeeded in remaining unnoticed, forever on the reverse side of history, crisscrossed by stitches, invisible lives from the time in between.

AUTHOR'S NOTE

The conventions of the academic life to which I have been bound for more than twenty years demand that writers recognize their sources in an ordered, rigorous way; this is why I've decided to include a list of the more significant bibliographic references I consulted. A large proportion of the resources I've depended on when re-creating settings, describing certain historical figures, and bringing some coherence to the plot, however, go beyond the margins of the printed page, so I want to mention them here.

In order to reconstruct the details of colonial Tetouan, I've made use of countless testimonials that have been gathered in the bulletins of the La Medina Association of Former Residents of the Spanish Protectorate in Morocco, and for these I would like to acknowledge the collaboration of its nostalgic members and the kindness of its directors Francisco Trujillo and Adolfo de Pablos. Equally useful and touching were the Moroccan recollections unearthed by my mother and my aunts Estrella Vinuesa and Paquita Moreno, as well as the countless documents provided by Luis Álvarez, who was almost as excited by this project as I was. The bibliographical reference supplied

795

by translator Miguel Sáenz, about a curious book partly set in Tetouan, was also extremely useful; it provided the inspiration for two of the supporting characters in this story.

In my reconstruction of the complicated life journey of Juan Luis Beigbeder, I was greatly interested in the information supplied by the Moroccan historian Mohamed Ibn Azzuz, zealous custodian of his legacy. For my introduction to him, and for welcoming me into the headquarters of the Tetouan-Asmir Association — the beautiful old Indigenous Affairs Bureau — I'd like to thank Ahmed Mgara, Abdeslam Chaachoo, and Ricardo Barceló. I would like to extend my thanks, too, to José Carlos Canalda for biographical details about Beigbeder; to José María Martínez-Val for dealing with my queries about his novel *Llegará tarde a Hendaya,* in which the then-minister appears as a character; to Domingo del Pino, who through his article opened the door for me to the memoirs of Rosalinda Powell Fox, vital to the plotline of the novel; and to Michael Brufal de Melgarejo for offering to help me follow her unclear trail in Gibraltar.

For providing me with firsthand information about Alan Hillgarth, the British Secret Services in Spain, and the Embassy cover, I'd like to acknowledge the personal kindness of Patricia Martínez de Vicente, author of *Embassy, or the Mambrú Intelligence,* and the daughter of an active participant in those clandestine operations. I'd like to extend my thanks to Professor David A. Messenger of the University of Wyoming for his article on the SOE's activities in Spain.

Finally, I'd like to express my gratitude to all those who one way or another were close to me during the process of creating this story, reading the whole or parts, encouraging, correcting, supplying wolf whistles and applause, or simply stepping from one day to the next by my side. To my parents for their unconditional support. To Manolo Castellanos, my husband, and my children Bárbara and Jaime, whose unceasing vitality has been a daily reminder of what it is that really matters. To my many siblings and their many circumstances, to my extended family, to my *in vino amicitia* friends and my dear colleagues from the Anglophile *crème.*

To Lola Gulias, from the Antonia Kerrigan Literary Agency, for having been the first person to take a chance on my writing.

And very especially to my editor Raquel Gisbert, for her redoubtable professionalism, her positivity, and her energy, and for having put up with my arm-wrestling with indefatigable steadfastness and good humor.

BIBLIOGRAPHY

Alcaraz, Ignacio. *Entre España y Marruecos. Testimonio de una época: 1923–75.* Madrid: Catriel, 1999.

———. *Retratos en la memoria.* Madrid: Catriel, 2002.

Alpert, Michael. "Operaciones secretas inglesas en España durante la segunda guerra mundial." *Espacio, tiempo y forma,* series V, *Historia Contemporánea* no. 15, (2002).

Armero, José Mario. *La política exterior de Franco.* Barcelona: Planeta, 1978.

Barfour, Sebastián, and Paul Preston. *España y las grandes potencias en el siglo XX.* Barcelona: Crítica, 1999.

Berdah, Jean-François. "La propaganda cultural británica en España durante la segunda guerra mundial a través de la acción del British Council: Un aspecto de las relaciones hispano-británicas 1939–46." In *El régimen de Franco: Política y relaciones exteriores,* edited by J. Tusell. Madrid: UNED, 1993.

Cardona, Gabriel. *Franco y sus generales: La manicura del tigre.* Madrid: Temas de Hoy, 2001.

Caruana, Leonardo. "A wolfram in sheep's clothing: Economic warfare in Spain, 1940–44." *Journal of Economic History* 16, no. 1 (2003).

Collado, Carlos. *España refugio nazi*. Madrid: Temas de Hoy, 2005.

Eccles, David. *By Safe Hand: The Letters of Sybil & David Eccles, 1939–42*. London: The Bodley Head, 1983.

Fox, Rosalinda Powell. *The Grass and the Asphalt*. Puerto de Sotogrande: Harter & Associates, 1997.

Franco Salgado-Araujo, Francisco. *Mis conversaciones privadas con Franco*. Barcelona: Planeta, 1976.

Halstead, Charles R. "Un africain méconnu: le colonel Juan Beigbeder." *Revue d'Histoire de la Deuxième Guerre Mondiale* 21 (1971).

———. "A 'Somewhat Machiavellian' Face: Colonel Juan Beigbeder as High Commissioner in Spanish Morocco, 1937–1939." *The Historian* 37, no. 1 (1974).

Hoare, Samuel. *Ambassador on Special Mission*. London: Collins, 1946.

Ibn Azzuz, Mohamed. "Una visión realista del protectorado ejercido por España en Marruecos." *Actas del encuentro España-Marruecos*. Tetouan: Asociación Tetouan-Asmir, 1998.

Iglesias-Sarria, Manuel. *Mi suerte dijo sí*. Madrid: San Martín, 1987.

Irujo, José María. *La lista negra. Los espías nazis protegidos por Franco y la Iglesia*. Madrid: Aguilar, 2003.

Madariaga, María Rosa de. *Los moros que trajo Franco*. Madrid: Martínez Roca, 2002.

Martínez de Vicente, Patricia. *Embassy o la inteligencia de Mambrú*. Madrid: Velecío, 2003.

Merino, Ignacio. *Serrano Suñer. Historia de una conducta.* Barcelona: Planeta, 1996.

Messenger, David. "Against the Grain: Special Operations Executive in Spain 1941–45." In *Special Issue on Special Operations Executive: New Approaches and Perspectives,* edited by N. Wylic. *Intelligence and National Security* 20, no. 1 (2005).

Moradiellos, Enrique. *Franco frente a Churchill.* Barcelona: Península, 2005.

Morales, Víctor. *España y el norte de África: El Protectorado español en Marruecos.* Madrid: UNED, 1986.

Moreno, Xavier. *Hitler y Franco: Diplomacia en tiempos de guerra.* Barcelona: Planeta, 2007.

Nerín, Gustau. *La guerra que vino de África.* Barcelona: Crítica, 2005.

Nerín, Gustau, and Alfred Bosch. *El imperio que nunca existió: La aventura colonial discutida en Hendaya.* Barcelona: Plaza y Janés, 2001.

Palacios, Jesús. *Los papeles secretos de Franco.* Madrid: Temas de Hoy, 1996.

———. *Las cartas de Franco.* Madrid: La Esfera de los Libros, 2005.

Phillips, Lucas. *El pimpinela de la guerra española 1936–39.* Barcelona: Juventud, 1965.

Pino, Domingo del. "Rosalinda Powell Fox: ¿Espía, amante, aventurera aristocrática?" *AFKAR Ideas* 6 (2005).

Platón, Miguel. *Los militares hablan.* Barcelona: Planeta, 2001.

Ridruejo, Dionisio. *Casi unas memorias.* Barcelona: Península, 2007.

Rojas, Carlos. *Diez crisis del franquismo.* Madrid: La Esfera de los Libros, 2003.

Romero, Ana. *Historia de Carmen: Memorias de Carmen Díez de Rivera.* Barcelona: Planeta, 2002.

Ros Agudo, Manuel. *La guerra secreta de Franco.* Barcelona: Crítica, 2002.

————. *La gran tentación: Franco, el imperio colonial y los planes de intervención española en la segunda guerra mundial.* Barcelona: Styria, 2008.

Rubio, Javier. *Asilos y canjes durante la guerra civil española.* Barcelona: Planeta, 1979.

Salas Larrazábal, Ramón. *El Protectorado español en Marruecos.* Madrid: MAPFRE, 1992.

Saña, Heleno. *El franquismo sin mitos: Conversaciones con Serrano Suñer.* Barcelona: Grijalbo, 1982.

Sánchez Ruano, Francisco. *Islam y guerra civil española.* Madrid: La Esfera de los Libros, 2004.

Schulze, Ingrid. "La propaganda alemana en España 1942–44." *Espacio, tiempo y forma,* series V, *Historia Contemporánea* 7 (1994).

Serrano Suñer, Ramón. *Entre Hendaya y Gibraltar.* Madrid: Ediciones y Publicaciones Españolas, 1947.

————. *Entre el silencio y la propaganda, la historia como fue. Memorias.* Barcelona: Planeta, 1977.

Smyth, Denis. *Diplomacy and Strategy of Survival: British Policy and Franco's Spain.* Cambridge: Cambridge University Press, 1986.

Stafford, David. *Churchill and Secret Service.* London: John Murray, 1997.

Suárez, Luis. *España, Franco y la segunda guerra mundial.* Madrid: Actas Editorial, 1997.

Tussell, Javier, ed. *El régimen de Franco: Política y*

relaciones exteriores. Madrid: UNED, 1993.

————. "Los cuatro ministros de asuntos exteriores de Franco durante la segunda guerra mundial." *Espacio, tiempo y forma,* series V, *Historia Contemporánea* 7 (1994).

Velasco, Carlos. "Propaganda y publicidad nazis en España durante la segunda guerra mundial: Algunas características." *Espacio, tiempo y forma,* series V, *Historia Contemporánea* 7 (1994).

Viñas, Ángel. *La Alemania nazi y el 18 de julio.* Madrid: Alianza, 1974.

————. *Franco, Hitler y el estallido de la guerra civil.* Madrid: Alianza, 2001.